In the past decade, Sheri S. Tepper has moved to the forefront of the speculative fiction ranks, achieving a hard-fought, much-deserved success shared by precious few. An award-winner and national bestseller, her fiction has found widespread acclaim and acceptance that transcends the boundaries of science fiction and fantasy. Now, read the masterful trilogy that launched her career. For the first time in one volume comes . . .

# THE TRUE GAME

Let the Players beware.
The son of Mavin Manyshaped has returned.

## KING'S BLOOD FOUR

In the lands of the True Game, your lifelong identity will emerge as you play. Prince or Sorcerer, Armiger or Tragamor, Demon or Doyen . . . Which will it be?

## NECROMANCER NINE

He wears the guise of a Necromancer, the black cloak, the broadrimmed hat, the gauze mask painted with a death's head. But raising the dead is the least of his Talents. He is a wild card that threatens the True Game itself . . .

## WIZARD'S ELEVEN

A giant stalks the mountains. The Shadowpeople gather by the light of the moon. The Bonedancers raise up armies of the dead. And the Wizard's Eleven sleep, trapped in their dreams . . .

Players, take your places. The final Game begins . . .

# THE TRUE GAME

*Sheri S. Tepper*

ACE BOOKS, NEW YORK

THE TRUE GAME

An Ace Book / published by arrangement with
the author

PRINTING HISTORY
Ace edition / June 1996

The Putnam Berkley World Wide Web site address is http://www.berkley.com

ISBN: 0-441-00331-1

ACE®
Ace Books are published by The Berkley Publishing Group,
200 Madison Avenue, New York, NY 10016.
ACE and the "A" design are trademarks
belonging to Charter Communications, Inc.

PRINTED IN THE UNITED STATES OF AMERICA

10  9  8  7  6  5  4  3  2

# THE ORDER OF DESCENT BY LINEAGE

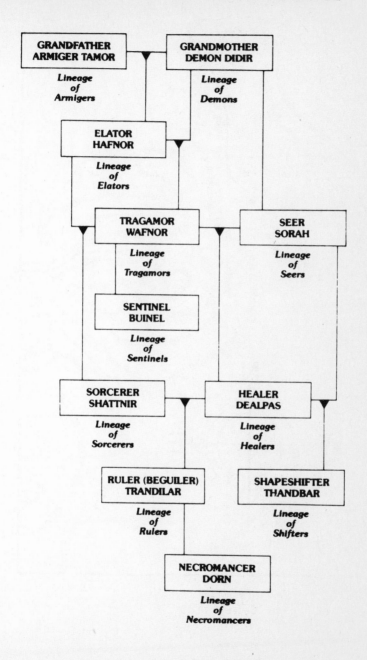

**GRANDFATHER ARMIGER TAMOR**

*Lineage of Armigers*

**GRANDMOTHER DEMON DIDIR**

*Lineage of Demons*

**ELATOR HAFNOR**

*Lineage of Elators*

**TRAGAMOR WAFNOR**

*Lineage of Tragamors*

**SEER SORAH**

*Lineage of Seers*

**SENTINEL BUINEL**

*Lineage of Sentinels*

**SORCERER SHATTNIR**

*Lineage of Sorcerers*

**HEALER DEALPAS**

*Lineage of Healers*

**RULER (BEGUILER) TRANDILAR**

*Lineage of Rulers*

**SHAPESHIFTER THANDBAR**

*Lineage of Shifters*

**NECROMANCER DORN**

*Lineage of Necromancers*

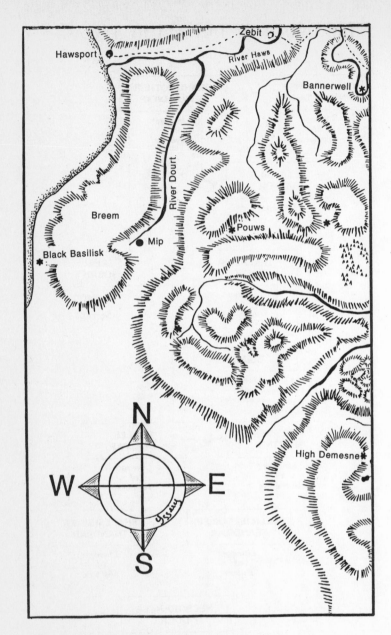

Lands of the True Game

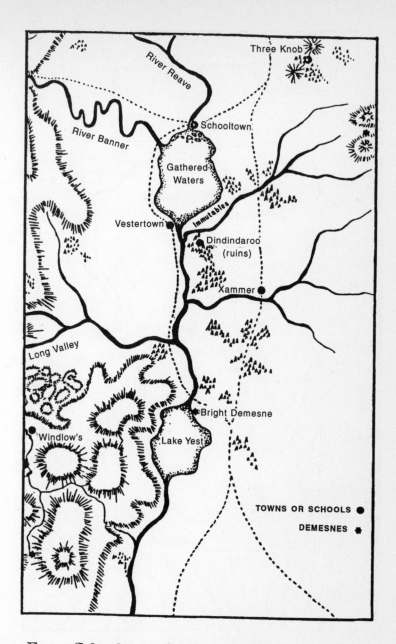

# From Schooltown South & West

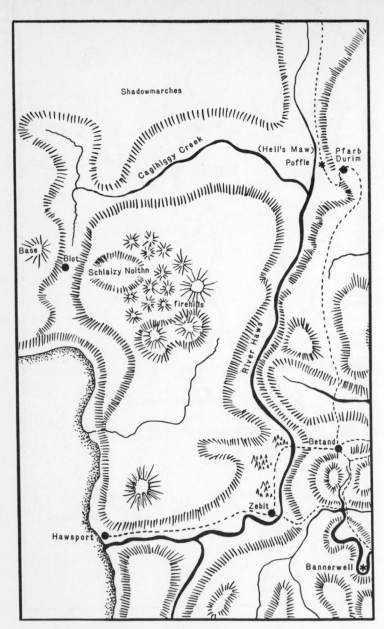

Lands of the True Game

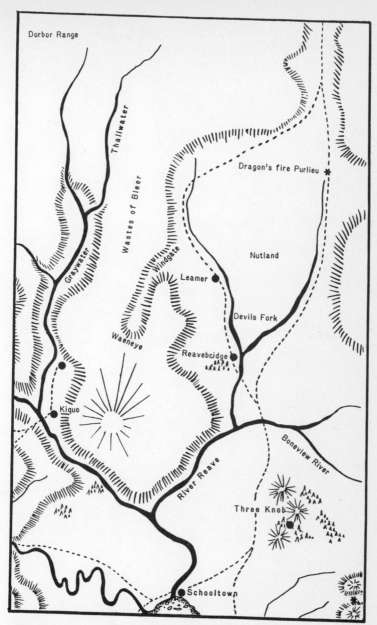

From Schooltown North & West

# King's Blood Four

# 1

# King's Blood Four

"TOTEM TO KING'S BLOOD FOUR." The moment I said it, I knew it was wrong. I said, "No!"

Gamesmaster Gervaise tapped the stone floor with his iron-tipped staff, impatiently searching our faces for a lifted eye or for a raised hand. "No?" he echoed me. Of the three Gamesmasters of Mertyn's House, I liked Gervaise the best.

"When I said 'no,' I meant the answer wasn't quite right." Behind me Karl Pig-face gave a sneaky gasp as he always does when he is about to put me down, but Gamesmaster Gervaise didn't give him a chance.

"That's correct," he agreed. "Correct that it isn't quite right and might be very wrong. The move is one we haven't come across before, however, so take your time. Before you decide upon the move, always remember who you are." He turned away from us, staff tap-tapping across the tower room to the high window which gaped across the dark bulk of Havad's House down to River Reave where it wound like a tarnished ribbon among all the other School Houses—each as full of students as a dog is of fleas, as Brother Chance, the cook, would say. All the sloped land between the Houses was crowded full of dwellings and shops, all humping their way up the hills to the shuttered Festival Halls, then scattering out among the School Farms which extended to the vacant land of the Edge. I searched over the Gamesmaster's shoulder for that far, thin line of blue which marked the boundaries of the True Game. Karl cleared his throat again, and I knew his mockery was only deferred, unless I could find an answer quickly. I wouldn't find it by staring out at Schooltown.

I turned back to the game model which hung in the air before us, swimming in icy haze. Somewhere within the model, among the game pieces which glowed in their own light or disappeared in their own shadow—somewhere in the model was the Demesne, the focal area, the place of power where a move could be of significance. On our side, the students' side, Demon loomed on a third level square casting a long, wing-shaped shadow. Two fanged Tragamors boxed the area to either side. Before them stood Gamesmaster Gervaise's only visible piece, the King, casting ruddy light before him. It was King's Blood Four, an Imperative—which meant I had to move something. None of the battle pieces were right; it had to be something similar to Totem. Almost anything could be hiding behind the King, and Gamesmasters don't give hints. Something similar, of like value, something . . . then I had it.

"Talisman," I blurted. "Talisman to King's Blood Four."

"Good." Gervaise actually smiled. "Now, tell me why!"

"Because our side can't see what pieces may be hiding behind the King. Because Talisman is an absorptive piece, that is, it will soak up the King's play. Totem is reflective. Totem would splash it around, we'd maybe lose some pieces . . ."

"Exactly. Now, students, visualize if you please. We have King, most durable of the adamants, whose 'blood,' that is, essence, is red light. Demon, most powerful of the ephemera, whose essence is shadow. Tragamors making barriers at the sides of the Demesne. The player is a student, without power, so he plays Talisman, an absorptive piece of the lesser ephemera. Talisman is lost in play, 'sacrificed' as we say. The player gains nothing by this, but neither does he lose much, for with this play the Demesne is changed, and the game moves elsewhere in the purlieu."

"But, Master," Karl's voice oozed from the corner. "A strong player could have played Totem. A powerful player."

I flushed. Of course. Everyone in the room knew that, but students were not strong, not powerful, even though Karl liked to pretend he was. It was just one more of his little pricks and nibbles, like living with a hedgehog. Gamesmaster tilted his head, signifying he had heard, but he didn't reply. Instead, he peered at the chronometer on the wall, then out the window to check where the mountain shadow fell upon the harbor, finally back to our heavily bundled little group. "So. Enough for today. Go to the fires and your supper. Some of you are half frozen."

We were all half frozen. The models could only be controlled if they were kept ice cold, so we spent half our lives shivering in frigid aeries. I was as cold as any of them, but I wanted to let Karl get out of the way, so I went to the high window and leaned out to peer away south. There was a line of warty little islands there separating the placid harbor with its wheeling gulls from the wide, stormy lake and the interesting lands of the True Game beyond. I mumbled something. Gervaise demanded I repeat it.

"It's boring here in Schooltown," I repeated, shamefaced.

He didn't answer at once but looked through me in that very discomforting way the Masters sometimes have. Finally he asked me if I had not had Gamesmaster Charnot for Cartography. I said I had.

"Then you know something of the lands of the True Game. You know of the Dragon's Fire purlieu to the North? Yes. Well, there are a King and Queen there who decided to rear their children Outside. They wanted to be near their babies, not send them off to a distant Schooltown to be bored by old Gamesmasters. They thought to let the children learn the rules of play by observation. Of the eight sons born to that Queen, seven have been lost in play. The eighth child sleeps this night in Havad's House nursery, sent to Schooltown at last.

"It is true that it is somewhat boring in Schooltown, and for no one more so than the Masters! But, it is also safe here, Peter. There is time to grow, and learn. If you desire no more than to be a carter or laborer or some other pawn, you may go Outside now and be one. However, after fifteen years in Mertyn's House, you know too much to be contented as a pawn, but you won't know enough for another ten years to be safe as anything else."

I remarked in my most adult voice that safety wasn't everything.

"That being the case," he said, "you'll be glad to help me dismantle the model."

I bit my tongue. It would have been unthinkable to refuse, though taking the models apart is far more dangerous than putting them together. Most of us have burn scars from doing one or the other. I sighed, concentrated, picked a minor piece out of the game box at random and named it, "Talisman!" as I moved it into the Demesne. It vanished in a flash of white fire. Gervaise moved a piece I couldn't see, then the King, which released the Demon. I got one Tragamor out, then got stuck. I could not remember the sequence of moves necessary to get the other Tragamor loose.

One thing about Gervaise. He doesn't rub it in. He just looked at me

*5*

again, his expression saying that he knew what I knew. If I couldn't get a stupid Tragamor out of the model, I wouldn't survive very long in the True Game. Patiently, he showed me the order of moves and then swatted me, not too gently.

"It's only a few days until Festival, Peter. Now that you're fifteen, you'll find that Festivals do much to dispel boredom for boys. So might a little more study. Go to your supper."

I galloped down the clattering stairs, past the nurseries, hearing babies crying and the unending chatter of the baby-tenders; down past the dormitories, smelling wet wool and steam from the showers; into the fire-warm commons hall, thinking of what the Gamesmaster had said. It was true. Brother Chance said that only the powerful and the utterly unimportant lived long in the True Game. If you weren't the one and didn't want to be the other, it made sense to be a student. But it was still very dull.

At the junior tables the littlest boys were scaring each other with fairy tales about the lands of the Immutables where there was no True Game. Silly. If there weren't any True Game, what would people do? At the high table the senior students, those about to graduate into the Game, showed more decorum, eating quietly under the watchful eyes of Gamesmaster Mertyn, King Mertyn, and Gamesmaster Armiger Charnot. Most of those over twenty had already been named: Sentinel, Herald, Dragon, Tragamor, Pursuivant, Elator. The complete list of Gamesmen was said to be thousands of titles long, but we would not study Properties and Powers in depth until we were older.

At the visitor's table against the far wall a Sorcerer was leafing through a book as he dawdled over his food, the spiked band of his headdress glittering in the firelight. He was all alone, the only visitor, though I searched carefully for one other. My friend Yarrel was crowded in at the far end of a long table with no space near, so I took an open bench place near the door. Across from me was Karl, his red, wet face shining slickly in the steam of the food bowls.

"Y'most got boggled up there, Peter-priss. Better stick to paper games with the littly boys."

"Oh, shut up, sweat-face," I told him. It didn't do any good to be nice to Karl, or to be mean. It just didn't matter. He was always nasty, regardless. "You wouldn't have known either."

"Would so. Grandsire and Dadden both told me that 'un.'' His face split into his perpetual mocking grin, his point made. Karl was son of a Doyen, grandson of a Doyen, third generation in the School. I was a Festival Baby, born nine months after Festival, left on the doorsteps of Mertyn's House to be taken in and educated. I might as well have been hatched by a toad. Well, I had something Karl didn't. He could have his family name. I had something else.

Not that the Masters cared whether a student was first generation or tenth. There were more foundlings in the room than there were family boys. "Sentlings," those sent in from outside by their parents, had no more status than foundlings, but the family boys did tend to stick together. It took only a little whipping-on from someone like Karl to turn them into a hunting pack. Well, I refused to make a chase for them. Instead, I stared away down the long line of champing jaws and lax bodies. They all looked as I felt—hungry, exhausted from the day's cold, luxuriating in warmth, and grateful night had come. I thought of the promised Festival.

I would sew bells onto my trouser hems, stitch ribbons into the shoulder seams of my jacket, make a mask out of leather and gilt, and so clad run through the streets of Schooltown with hundreds of others dressed just as I, jingling and laughing, dancing to drum and trumpet, eating whatever we wanted. During Festival, nothing would be forbidden, nothing required, no dull studies, the Festival Halls would be opened, people would come from Outside, from the School Houses, from everywhere. Bells would ring . . . and ring . . .

The ringing was the clangor of my bowl and spoon upon the stones where I had thrust them in my sleep. The room was empty except for one lean figure between me and the fire: Mandor, Gamesmaster of Havad's House, teeth gleaming in the fireglow.

"Well, Peter. Too tired to finish your supper?"

"I . . . I thought you weren't coming."

"Oh, I drift here and there. I've been watching you sleep for half an hour after bidding some beefy boy to leave you alone. What have you done to attract his enmity?"

I think I blushed. It wasn't anything I wanted to talk about. "Just . . . oh, nothing. He's one who always picks on someone. Usually someone smaller than he is, usually a foundling."

"Ah." He understood. "A Flugleman. You think?"

I grinned weakly. It would be a marvelous vengeance if Karl were named Flugleman, petty tyrant, minor piece, barely higher than a pawn. "Master Mandor, no one has yet named him that."

"You needn't call me Master, Peter."

"I know." Again, I was embarrassed. He should know some things, after all. "It's just easier than explaining."

"You feel you have to explain?"

"If someone heard me."

"No one will hear you. We are alone. Still, if this place is too public, we'll go to my room." And he was sweeping out the door toward the tunnel which led to Havad's House before I could say anything. I followed him, of course, even though I had sworn over and over I would not, not again.

The next morning I received a summons to see King Mertyn. It didn't exactly surprise me, but it did shock me a little. I'd known someone was going to see me or overhear us, but each day that went by let me think maybe it wouldn't happen after all. I hadn't been doing anything different from what many of the boys do in the dormitories, nothing different from what I'd refused to do with Karl. Oh, true, it's forbidden, but lots of things are forbidden, and people do them all the time, almost casually.

So, I didn't know quite what to expect when I stood before the Gamesmaster in his cold aerie, hands in my sleeves, waiting for him to speak. I was shocked at how gentle he was.

"It is said you are spending much time with Gamesmaster Mandor of Havad's House. That you go to his room, spend your sleep time there. Is this true?" He was tactful, but still I blushed.

"Yes, Gamesmaster."

"You know this is forbidden."

"Gamesmaster, he bade me . . ."

"You know he is titled Prince and may bid as he chooses. But, it is still forbidden."

I got angry then, because it wasn't fair. "Yes. He may bid as he chooses. And I am expected to twist and tarry and try to escape him, like a pigeon flying from a hawk. I am expected to bear his displeasure, and he may bid as he chooses . . ."

"Ah. And have you indeed twisted and tarried and tried? Hidden among the books of the library, perhaps? Pled sanctuary from the head of your own House? Taken minor game vows before witnesses? Have you done these things?"

I hadn't. Of course I hadn't. How could I. Prince Mandor was my friend, but more than a friend. He cared about me. He talked to me about everything, things he said he couldn't tell anyone else. I knew everything about him; that he had not wanted to leave the True Game and teach in a Schooltown; that he hated Havad's House, that he wanted a House of his own; that he picked me as a friend because there was no one, no one in Havad's House he cared for. The silence between the Gamesmaster and me was becoming hostile, but I couldn't break it. At last he said, "I must be sure you understand, Peter. You must be aware of what you do, each choice you make which aids or prevents your mastery of the Game. You cannot stand remote from this task. You are in it. Do you know that?"

I nodded, said, "We all know that, Gamesmaster."

"But do you perceive the reality of it? How your identity will emerge as you play, as your style becomes unique, as your method becomes clear. Gradually it will become known to the Masters—and to you—what you are: Prince or Sorcerer, Armiger or Tragamor, Demon or Doyen, which of the endless list you are. You must be one of them, or else go down into Schooltown and apprentice yourself to a shopkeeper as some failed students do."

"It is said we are born to it," I objected, wanting to stop his talk which was making me feel guilty. "Karl says he will be Doyen because father and grandfather were Doyens before him. Born to it."

"What Karl may say or do or think is not important to you. What you are or may become should be important." He seized me by the shoulders and turned me to stare out the tall window. "Look there. In ten years you must go out there, ready or not, willing or not. In ten years you must leave this protected town, this Schooling place. In ten years you will join the True Game.

"You do not know this, but it was I who found you, years ago, outside Mertyn's House, a Festival Baby, a soggy lump in your bright blankets, chewing your fist. If you have anyone to stand Father to you, it is I. It may be unimportant, but there is at least this tenuous connection between us which leads me to be concerned about you.'' He leaned forward to lay his face against mine, a shocking thing to do, as forbidden as anything I had ever done.

''Think, Peter. I cannot force you to be wise. Perhaps I will only frighten you, or offend you, but think. Do not put yourself in another's hands.'' Abruptly he left me there in the high room, still angry, confused, wordless.

''Do not put yourself in another's hands.'' The first rule of the game. Make alliances, yes, they told us, but do not give yourself away to become merely a pawn. This is why they forbid us so many things, deny us so much while we are young and defenseless. I leaned on the sill of the high window where golden sunlight lay in a puddle. A line of similar color reflected from a high House across the river, Dorcan's House, a woman's house. I wondered if they gamed there as we did; learning, waiting for their Mistresses and peers to name them, being bored. I knew little about women. We would not study the female pieces for some years yet, but the sight of that remote house made me wonder what names they had, what name I would have.

It was said among the boys that one could sometimes tell what name one would bear by the sound of it in one's own ears. I tried that, speaking into the silent air. ''Armiger. Tragamor. Elator. Sentinel.'' Nothing. ''Flugleman,'' I whispered, fearfully, but there was no interior response to that, either. I had not mentioned the name I dreamed of, the one I most desired to have, for I felt that to do so would breed ill luck. Instead, I called, ''Who am I?'' into the morning silence. The only reply came in a spate of gull-scream from the harbor, like impersonal laughter. I told myself it didn't matter who I was so long as I had more than a friend in Mandor. A bell tolled briefly from the town, and I knew I had missed breakfast and would be late for class.

In the room below, the windows were shut for once to let the fire sizzling upon the hearth warm the room. That meant no models that day, only lectures; dull, warm words instead of icy, exciting movement. Gamesmaster Gervaise was already stalking to and fro, mumble-murmuring toward the cluster of student heads, half of them already nodding in the unaccustomed heat.

''Yesterday we evolved a King's game,'' he was saying. ''Those of you who were paying attention would have noticed the sudden emergence of the Demesne from the purlieu. This sudden emergence is a frequent mark of King's games. Kings do not signal their intentions. There is no advance 'leakage' of purpose. There may be a number of provocations or incursions without any response, and then, suddenly, there will be an area of significant force and intent—a Measurable Demesne. Think how this differs from a battle game between Armigers, for instance, where the Demesne grows very gradually from the first move of a Herald or Sentinel. Just as the Demesne may emerge rapidly in a King's game, so it may close as rapidly. Mark this rule, boys. The greater the power of the piece, the more rapid the consequence.'' He rattled his staff to wake the ones dozing. ''Note this, boys, please. If a powerful player were playing against the King's side, the piece played might have been one of the reflective durables such as Totem, or even Herald. In that case . . .''

He began to drone again. He was talking about measuring, and it bored everyone to death. We'd had measuring since we came into class from the nurseries, and if any of us didn't know how to measure a Demesne by now, it was hopeless. I looked for Yarrel. He wasn't there, but I did see the visiting Sorcerer leaning against the back wall, his lips curved in an enigmatic smile. ''Sorcerer,'' I defined to myself, automatically. ''Quiet glass, evoking but unchanged by the evocation, a conduit through which power may be channeled, a vessel into which one may pour acid, wine, or fire and from which one may pour acid, wine, or fire.'' I shivered. Sorcerers were very major pieces indeed, holders of the power of others, and I'd never seen or heard of one going about alone. It was very strange to have one leaning against the classroom wall, all by himself, and it gave me an itchy, curious feeling. I decided to sneak down to the kitchen and ask Brother Chance about it. He had been my best source of certain kinds of information ever since I was four and found out where he hid the cookies.

''Oh, my, yes,'' he agreed, sweating in the heat of the cookfire as he gave bits of meat to the spit dog. He poked away at the Masters' roast with a long fork. The odors were tantalizing. My mouth dropped open like a baby bird's, and he popped a piece of the roast into it as though I had been another spit dog. ''Yes, odd to have a Sorcerer wandering about loose, as one might say. Still, since King Mertyn returned from Outside to become Gamesmaster here, he has built a great reputation for Mertyn's

House. A Sorcerer might be drawn here, seeking to attach himself. Or, there are always those who seek to challenge a great reputation. It probably means no more than the fact that Festival is nigh-by, only days away, and the town is full of visitors. Even Sorcerers go about for amusement, I suppose. What is it to you, after all?''

"No one ever tells us anything," I complained. "We never know what's going on."

"And why should you? Arrogant boy! What is it to you what Sorcerers do and don't do?" Ask too many questions and be played for a pawn, I always say. Keep yourself to yourself until you know what you are, that's my advice to you, Peter. But then, you were always into things you shouldn't have bothered with. Before you could talk, you could ask questions.

"Well, ask no more now. You'll get yourself into real trouble. Here. Take this nice bit of roast and some hot bread to sop up the juices and go hide in the garden while you eat it. It's forbidden, you know."

Of course I knew.

Everything was forbidden.

Roast was forbidden to boys. As was sneaking down to the kitchens.

As was challenging True Game in a Schooltown. Or during Festival.

As was this, and that, and the other thing. Then, come Festival, nothing would be forbidden. In Festival, Kings could be Jongleurs, Sentinels could be Fools, men could be women and women men for all that. And Sorcerers could be . . . whatever they liked. It was still confusing and unsettling, but the lovely meat juices running down my throat did much to assuage the itchy feeling of curiosity, guilt, and anger.

Late at night I lay in the moonlight with my hand curled on Mandor's chest. It threw a leaflike shadow there which breathed as he breathed, slowly elongating as the moon fell. "There is a Sorcerer wandering about," I murmured. "No one knows why." Under my hand his body stiffened.

"With someone? Talking with anyone?"

I murmured sleepily, no, all alone.

"Eating with anyone? At table with anyone?"

I said, no, reading, eating by himself, just wandering about. Mandor's graceful body relaxed.

"Probably here for the Festival," he said. "The town is filling up, with more swarming in every day . . ."

"But, I thought Sorcerers were always with someone."

He laughed, lips tickling my ear. "In theory, lovely boy, in theory. Actually, Sorcerers are much like me and you and the kitchen churl. They eat and drink and delight in fireworks and travel about to meet friends. He may be meeting old friends here."

"Maybe." My thought trailed off into sleepy drifting. There had been something a little feverish about Mandor's questions, but it did not seem to matter. I could see the moonlight reflected from his silver, serpent's eyes, alert and questing in the dark. In the morning I remembered that alertness with some conjecture, but lessons drove it out of my head. A day or two later he sought me out to give me a gift.

"I've been looking for you, boy, to give you something." He laughed at my expression, teasingly. "Go on. Open it. I may give you a gift for your first Festival. It isn't forbidden! It isn't even discouraged. Open it."

The box was full of ribbons, ribbons like evening sky licked with sunset, violet and scarlet, as brilliant and out of place in the gray corridor as a lily blooming in a crypt. I mumbled something about already having bought my ribbons.

"Poof," he said. "I know what ribbons boys buy. Strips of old gowns, bought off rag pickers. No. Take these and wear them for me. I remember my first Festival, when I turned fifteen. It pleases me to give them to you, my friend . . ."

His voice was a caress, his hands gentle on my face, and his eyes spoke only affectionate joy. I leaned my head forward into those hands. Of course I would wear them. What else could I do? That afternoon I went to beg needle and thread from Brother Chance. Gamesmaster Mertyn was in the kitchen, leaning against a cupboard, licking batter like a boy. I turned to go, but he beckoned me in and made me explain my business there, insisting upon seeing the ribbons when I had mumbled some explanation.

"Fabulous," he said in a tight voice. "I have not seen their like. Well, they do you credit, Peter, and you should wear them in joy. Let me make you a small gift as well. Strip out of your jacket, and I'll have my servant, Nitch, sew them into the seams for you." So I was left shivering in the kitchen, clad from the waist up only in my linen. I would rather have sewn them myself, even if King Mertyn's manservant would make a better job of it, and I said as much to Chance.

"Well, lad. The high and powerful do not always ask us what we would prefer. Isn't that so? Follow my rule and be in-conspic-u-ous. That's best. Least noticed is least bothered, or so I've always thought. Best race up to the dormitory and get into your tunic, boy, before you freeze."

Which I did, and met Yarrel there, and we two went onto the parapet to watch the Festival crowds flowing into town. The great shutters had been taken from the Festival Halls; pennants were beginning to flicker in the wind; the wooden bridge rolled like a great drum under the horses' hooves. We saw one trio go by with much bravura, a tall man in the center in Demon's helm with two fanged Tragamors at his sides. Yarrel said, "See there. Those three come from Bannerwell where your particular friend, Mandor, comes from. I can tell by the horses." Yarrel was a sentling, a farrier's son who cared more for horses than he ever would for the Game. He cared a good deal for me, too, but was not above teasing me about my particular friend. Well, I thought Yarrel would not stay in the School for ten years more. He would go seek his family and the countryside, all for the sake of horses.

I asked him how he knew that Mandor had come from Bannerwell, but he could not remember. He had heard it somewhere, he supposed.

Nitch brought the jacket that evening, sniffing a little to show his disapproval of boys in general. It felt oddly stiff when I took it, and my inquiring look made Nitch sniff the louder. "There was nothing left of the lining, student. It was all fallen away to lint and shreds, so while I had the seams open, I put in a bit of new wadding. Don't thank me. My own sense of the honor of Mertyn's House would have allowed no less." And he sniffed himself away, having spoken directly to me for the first and last time.

I was glad of the new lining come morning, for we put on our Festival garb and masks while it was still cold. Yarrel smoothed the ribbons for me, saying they made a lovely fall of color. We had sewn on our bells and made our masks, and as soon as it was full light we were away, our feet pounding new thunder out of the old bridge. Yarrel's ribbons were all green, so I could pick him from the crowd. All the tower boys wore ribbons and bells which said, "Student here, student here, hold him harmless for he is yet young . . ." Thus we could thieve and trick during the time of Festival without hindrance, though it were best, said the Masters, to do it in moderation.

And we did. We were immoderately moderate. We ate pork pies stolen from stalls and drank beer pilfered from booths until we were silly with it. Long chains of revelers wound through the streets like dragon tails, losing bits and adding bits as they danced to the music blaring at every street corner, drums and horns and lutes and jangles, up the hill and down again. There were Town girls and School girls and Outside girls to tease and follow and try to snuggle in corners, and in the late, late afternoon Yarrel and one of the girls went into a stable to look at the horses and were gone rather longer than necessary for any purpose I could think of. I sprawled on a pile of clean straw, grinning widely at nothing, sipping at my beer, and watching as the sun dropped behind the town and the first rockets spangled the dark.

The figure which came out of the dark was wholly strange, but the voice was perturbingly familiar. "Peter. Here you are, discovered in the midst of the multitude. Come with me and learn what Festival food should be!"

For a moment I wanted to say that I would rather wait for Yarrel, rather just lie on the straw and look at the sky, but the habit of obeying that voice was too much for me. I staggered to my feet, feeling shoddy and clumsy beside that glittering figure with its princely helm masked in sequins and gems. We went up the hill to a lanterned terrace set with tables where stepped gardens glimmering with fountains sloped down into green shade. There was wine which turned into dizzy laughter and food to make the pork pies die of shame and many sparkling gamesmen gathering out of the darkness to the table where my friend held court, the tall Demon and the Tragamors, from Bannerwell, as Yarrel had said, all drinking together until the night swirled around us in a maelstrom of light and sound.

Except that in the midst of it all, something inside me got up and walked away. It was as though Peter left Peter's body lolling at the table while Peter's mind went elsewhere to look down upon them all from some high, clean place. It saw the Demon standing at the top of one flight of marble stairs, one Tragamor halfway down another flight, and the other brooding on the lower terrace beside a weeping tree. Torches burning behind the Demon threw a long, wing-shaped shadow onto the walkway below where red light washed like a shallows of blood. Into that space came a lonely figure, masked but unmistakable. King Mertyn. The warm, night air turned chill as deep winter, and the sounds of Festival faded. Mertyn looked up to see Mandor rise, to hear him call, "I challenge, King!"

The King did not raise his voice, yet I heard him as clearly as though he spoke at my ear. "So, Prince Mandor. Your message inviting me to join you did not speak of challenge."

The Peter-who-watched stared down, impotent to move or call. Couldn't the King see those who stood there? Demon and Tragamor, substance and shade, True Game challenged upon him here, and the very air alive with cold. King's Blood Four, here, now, in this place and no other, a Measurable Demesne. But Mandor surely would not be so discourteous. Not now. It was *Festival.*

Drunken-Peter reached a hand, fumbled at the Prince's sleeve. "No. No, Mandor. It's not . . . not courteous . . ." The hand, my hand, was slapped away by an armored glove, struck so violently that it lay bleeding upon the table before drunken-Peter while the other me watched, watched.

The King called again. "Is it not forbidden to call challenge during Festival or in a Schooltown, Mandor? Have you not learned it so?"

Answered by crowing laughter. "Many things are forbidden, Mertyn. Many things. Still, we do them."

"True. Well, if you would have it so, Prince—then have it so. I move."

And from behind one of the crystal fountains which had hidden him from us came that lonely Sorcerer I had wondered at, striding into the light until he stood just behind the King, full of silent waiting, clear as glass, holding whatever terrible thing he had been given to hold.

Drunken-Peter felt Mandor stiffen, saw the armored hand clench with an audible clang. Drunken-Peter looked up to see sweat bead the Prince's forehead, to see a vein beating beside a glaring eye. From the Sorcerer below light began to well upward, a force as impersonal as water building behind a dam. Peter-who-watched knew the force would be unleashed at the next move. Drunken-Peter knew nothing, only sat dizzy and half sick before the puddled wine and remnants of the feast as Prince Mandor stooped above him to say, "Peter . . . I do not wish to be . . . discourteous . . .'' The voice hummed with tension, cracked with strain. With what enormous effort did he then make it light and caressing? "Go down and tell Gamesmaster Mertyn I did but . . . jest. Invite him to have wine with us . . .''

Peter-who-watched screamed silently above. Drunken-Peter staggered to his feet, struggled into a jog past the tall Demon, imagining as he went an expression of—was it scorn? on that face below the half helm, then down the long flight of stairs toward the garden, lurching, mouth open, eyes fixed upon Gamesmaster Mertyn, onto the red-washed pave, hearing from above the cry of frustrated fury, "Talisman . . . to King's Blood Four."

Peter-above saw the power strike. Drunken-Peter cried as he fell, "No. No, Mandor. You would not be so false to me . . . to me . . .'' before the darkness fell.

I woke in a tower room, a strange room, narrow windows showing me clouds driven across a gray sky. It hurt to move my head. At the bedside Chance sat, dozing, and my movement wakened him. He hrummed and hruphed himself into consciousness.

"Feel better? Well then, you wouldn't know whether you do or not, would you? You wouldn't even know how lucky you are."

"I'm not . . . dead. I should be dead."

"Indeed you should. Sacrificed in the play, like a pawn, dead as a pantry mouse under the claws of the cat. You would be, too, except for this." He picked my ragged jacket from the floor, holding it so that I could see what the rents revealed, a tracery of golden thread and silver wire, winking red eyes of tiny gems set into the circuits of stitchery in the lining. "He bade Nitch sew this into your jacket. Just in case."

"How did he know? I don't understand . . .''

"It would be hard to understand," said Chance, "except by one long mired in treachery. Ah. But Mertyn is not young, lad. He has seen much and studied more. He saw those ribbons, and he knew. Oh, if they'd been a few colorful things such as any friend might give, he'd have understood. A love gift, after all. But those you had? Nothing else like them in the town? What purpose a gift like that?"

"I thought he gave them to me so that he would know me among all the other maskers . . .''

"Then you saw deep, lad, and didn't know it."

"Did he mean to play me, even then?" I cried in my belly, a hard knot of pain there which hurt more than the fire beneath the bandages on my face and arms.

Chance shrugged, leaned to smooth my pillow. "Do you students know what you will play before the game begins? You set your pieces out in the game box, all shining, the ones you think you'll play and the ones you hold in reserve. Maybe he brought you along to see him win. But, he wasn't strong enough to win against the King, and he wasn't brave enough to stand against the move and bear the play as it came, so he threw you into the game like a bone to a Fustigar."

I think I cried then, for he said nothing more. Then I slept. Then I woke again, and it was morning, with Mertyn in the chair beside my bed.

"I am sorry you were hurt, Peter," he said. "Perhaps you would rather be dead, but I gambled you would not feel so a year from now. Had I the skill with shields and deflectors I do with other strategy, I would have saved you these wounds."

For a long time I simply looked at him, at the gray hair falling in a tumbled lock across his forehead, at the line of his cheeks and the curve of his lips, so much like my own. There was nothing there unkindly, and yet I was angry with him. He had saved my life, and I hated him. The anger and hatred made no sense, were foolish. I would not repay him with foolishness, therefore I could not repay him.

He stared at his boots. "When you were put into play, Sorcerer struck. An Imperative. Nothing I could do. The screen in your jacket was not perfect. There was considerable splash, and you caught a little of it. Mandor caught most."

I had to ask. "The Prince? Gamesmaster Mandor?"

"I do not know. His players carried him away. They do not know at Havad's House. Likely he is lost in play. He had provoked me more than once, Peter, but even then I did not call for that Game."

"I know."

He sighed, very deeply. "I am sending you away from Mertyn's House. Shielding you was forbidden. When we do things that are forbidden, there is always a price. For me, the price will be to lose you, for I have been fond of you, Peter." He leaned forward and kissed me, forbidden, forbidden, forbidden. Then he went away. I did not see him again.

For me, the price was to be sent away from everything I had ever known. It was hard, though not as hard as they could have made it, for they let Yarrel and Chance go with me. We were to become an Ordo Vagorum, so Chance said. I had put myself in another's hands, truly and completely. I had learned why that is foolish. Never mind that it is forbidden. It is foolish.

They did not forbid me to play the Game—someday. I was no nearer to being named. There were wounds on my face which would make scars I would always carry. They said something about sending us to another House, one far away, one requiring a very long journey.

I got over being angry at King Mertyn. Each morning when I woke I had tears on my face left over from brightly colored dreams, but I could not really remember what they were.

# 2

# Journeying

I REMEMBER ONLY ODDS AND ENDS about the time that followed, pictures, fragments as of dreams or stories of things that happened to someone else. I remember sitting in a window at harborside, water clucking against the wall beneath me, the blue-bordered curtain flapping in the wind, flap, flap, striking the bandage on my head. The border was woven with a pattern of swans, and I bore the pain of it rather than move away. Chance and Yarrel seem to have ignored me then as they went about the business of readying us for travel. The piles of supplies in the room behind me grew larger, but I had no idea what was in them.

I remember Chance reading the let-pass which had been issued by Mertyn's House and countersigned by the Council of Schooltown, a pass begging the indulgence of Gamesmen everywhere in letting us go by without involving us in whatever might be going on. It was only as good as the good nature of those who might read it, but Chance seemed to take some comfort from it, nonetheless. Chance spoke of Schooltown as built remote from the lands of the True Game and warded about with protections in order to "keep our study academic and didactic rather than dangerously experiential." Yarrel mocked him for sounding pompous, and he replied that he merely quoted Gamesmaster Mertyn. That sticks in my head, oddly.

I remember Chance buying charts from a map-man, the map-man waxing poetic about the accuracy with which the Demesnes were shown and the delicacy with which the cartouches were drawn—these being the symbols mapmakers use to show which Gamesmen may dwell in a given place.

I remember boarding the Lakely Lass, a fat-bellied little ship which was to take us from the mouth of the River Reave along the north and western shores of the Gathered Waters until we came at last to Vestertown and the highroad leading south. There was a Seer standing at the rail as we came aboard, his gauze-covered face turned toward me so that I could see the glitter of his eyes beneath the painted pattern of moth wings. Then I remember huddling with Chance and Yarrel over a chart spread on the rough table, shadows scurrying across it from the hanging lantern each time the ship rolled, Chance pointing and peering and mumbling . . .

"Over there, east, is the Great Dragon Demesne. See the cartouche, dragon head, staff—that's for a warlock, a slather of spears showing he's got Armigers. Well, we'll miss that by a good bit."

"How will we know the highroad is safe?" asked Yarrel in his usual practical tone.

"We'll go mousey and shy, my boys, mousey and shy. Quiet, like so many owl shadows under the trees, making no hijus cries or bringing on us the attentions of the powerful. Well, hope has it there are many alive in the world of the Game who have never seen the edge of it played."

I said, "I don't understand that." They both stared at me in astonishment.

"Well, well, with us again are you? We'd about given you up, we had, and resolved to carry your senseless carcass the whole way to its new House without your tenancy. You don't understand it? Why, boy, it's 'most the first lesson you learned."

"I can't remember," I mumbled. It was true. I couldn't.

"Why," he said, "when you were no more than four or five, we used to play our little two-space games in the kitchen before the fire, you and me. You with your little-bit queen and king on each side, the white and the black, and your wee armigers and priests and the tiny sentinels at each end, standing high on their parapets, and me the same. All set out on the board in such array, like the greatest army of ever was in a small boy's head. You remember that?"

I nodded that I did, wondering how it connected.

"Well, then. We'd play a bit, you and me, move by move, and maybe I'd win, or maybe by some strange cleverness," he winked and nodded at Yarrel, "some most exceptional cleverness, you'd win. And there on the board would be the lonely pawn, perhaps, or the sentinel on his castle walk, never moved once since the game began. True?"

Again, I nodded, beginning to understand.

"So. That piece was not touched by the edge of the game. It stood there and wasn't bothered by the armigers jumping here and there or churchmen rushing up and down. It's the same in the True Game, lad. Of course, in House they don't talk much about the times that Gamesmen *don't* play, but truth to tell much of life is spent just standing about or traveling here and there, like the little pawn at the side of the board.''

He was right. We didn't spend any time in House learning a thing about not playing. All our time was spent in learning to play, learning what moves could be made by which Gamesmen, what powers each had, what conditions influenced the move, how to determine where the edge of a Demesne would lie.

"But even if they're not involved in the play," I protested, "surely they *feel* the power . . .''

" 'Tis said not,'' he said. "No more than in the lands of the Immutables who stand outside the Game altogether.''

"Nothing is outside the Game," I protested once more, with rather less certainty.

"Nothing but the Immutables, Lad, and they most unquestionably are.''

"I thought them mythical. Like Ghost Pieces.'' Even saying it, I made the diagonal slash of the hand which warded evil. Chance cocked his head, his cheeks bulging in two little, hard lumps as he considered this, eyes squeezed almost shut with thought under the fluffy feathers of his gray hair. "No, not myth. And, it may be that ghost pieces are not mythical either. In the Schooltowns many things are thought to be myths, as they may be—in Schooltowns. Out in the purlieus, though, many things happen which we do not hear of in the towns. Who knows what may be, where we are going.''

I remarked wonderingly that I did not know where we were going, and they laughed at me. Not as though they were amused, but more as if they would as soon have tied me up and used me for fish bait but allowed laughter as a more or less innocent substitute for that. I knew from their laughter they must have told me before, more than once. There was even slight annoyance in Yarrel's voice as he said, "We're sent to the School at Evenor, near the High Lakes of Tarnoch." When he saw no comprehension, he went on, "Where the High King's sons are schooled, ninny." I wanted very much to inquire why we went there but was hurt enough by the laughter to give them no room for more of the same. Where had

I been those last days? Well, I knew where I had been, and there was no good sense in it.

Chance patted my shoulder kindly. "That's a'right, lad. King Mertyn said you'd suffer some from shock and from the painkillers they gave you for the burns. We'll welcome you back whenever you arrive. Now, try a little sleep to hurry things along."

The next thing I remember after that is the sun, broken into glittering shards by the waves, and shouts of men on the fantail where they trolled for lake sturgeon. Two enormous fish were already flopping on the deck surrounded by determined fish hackers. I knew they were after caviar, the black pearls of the Gathered Waters, famous all over the purlieus of the South, so they say. Later that day we came to a little lakeport, and there was much heaving of sacks and cartons, much jocularity and beer. We ate in a guest house, grilled fish with sour herbs, lettuces, sweet butter, and new bread. Chance and the kitchen wife became quite friendly; I had wine; the moon broke the night into pieces through the diamond panes of the window of our cabin. And the next morning I was myself.

The world had hard edges once more; there were no odd-shaped holes between one moment and the next; I began to think about where we were going and the process of getting there; I saw the lake, amazed at the extent of it. From Schooltown it had seemed small enough, limited to the south by the line of little islands which made a falsely close and comforting shore. Out here, it had no edge but the horizon, a sparkling line which moved to stay always the same distance from us. This world edge was furred with cloud, red in the rising sun. Our Captain stared into that haze, his face tilted to one wrinkled side as he considered. "I smell wind," he announced. "Tyeber Town is but two hours down coast. We'll go no farther than that today."

He was wrong. The wind came up strongly to push us farther and farther into the lake, wallowing and heaving. Then, toward evening, when the wind began to abate, there was a singing twang and a shout from the helmsman. It seemed something essential had broken and our little ship could no longer steer itself. While Chance and Yarrel slept, and I tried to, there was a clamor of feet and tools around and above us as the sailors tried to fix it. I went on to the deck to stare at the scudding clouds and saw there the bundled figure of the Seer. He turned his featureless face to me and asked, through the gauze, if I were Peter, son of Mavin. I said no, I was Peter of Mertyn's House, without family. He stared at me long enough to make me uncomfortable, so I went back to the narrow bunk and eventual sleep.

By morning the repair effort had succeeded, and we went wallowing away in a wind more violent than before, only to sight a black sail on the quivering horizon. There were general cries of dismay.

"Pawners," Chance cried out with the others. "Would you believe it? Coastal boats don't get taken by pawners."

"We're not coastal at the moment," I pointed out. This did not seem to comfort him. As the hours wore on the pawners drew closer across the wind-whipped waters, making our Captain give up his attempt to return to the western shore and turn instead to flee eastward before the black-sailed boat. Thus we sped away, like a fat wife running from a tiger, the slender black sail gaining upon us until the ship was within hailing distance.

"...oh," the voice came. "...oy...ai...ame...eeter." Chance and Yarrel looked at me in astonishment, and the Seer drew close enough to lay hand upon my arm.

"'Ware, lad," he said. "I see evil and agony in this. 'Ware, Captain. Do not believe what these men say." Around us the air grew chill, and we knew the Seer had drawn power making a little Demesne where we stood. I shivered, not entirely from the cold.

"They say they want only the boy named Peter," said the Captain. "That if we give him up, they'll go away and leave us alone. I have little need of your warning, Gamesman. Pawners are not to be believed." I looked at the man with respect. He did not cringe or beg. He simply told us what the circumstances were and left it for us to respond. On impulse I took the spyglass from his hand to set it upon our pursuer. High upon her foredeck a cadaverous man leaned against the rail, another glass fixed upon us so that we looked, he and I, eye to eye. I could see the curve of his lip and the slant of black brow, altogether villainous, as why should he not be, being what he was. I whispered to the Captain, "What may we do?"

"There's a small fog coming up, lad. We can run on before him, for he closes slowly, waiting for it to get a bit dimmer, meantime calling back and forth with much misunderstanding. If the fates are willing, we may lose ourselves and run into the harbor of the Muties."

"I might have known," breathed Chance.

"Muties?" I asked.

"The Immutables, young sir. The one place that pawners might not follow. If they follow and catch us up, we are lost for we are outmanned." Indeed, it was so. The black-sailed ship had twice our crew, young and strong. I nodded at the Captain, telling him by this to do as he thought best. You are thinking that I was quite mad? That would be a reasonable thought. At that moment none of us asked why such a ship should come out of the wind in search of me, an unnamed foundling boy, half-schooled and wholly unsatisfactory in his own House. I did not say, "why me?" nor did Yarrel, nor Chance. It was only when the little wraiths of fog had grown into curtains and we had sneaked away among the velvet folds of mist, only when we heard a yell of fury from the other ship, bodiless and directionless in the half light, only then did I turn to Chance to say for the first time, "Why me? The Captain must have misunderstood. No one would come after *me* . . ."

To which the Seer, who had stood by us throughout the long flight, murmured, "You, none other, Lad. And the time will come when you will know why too well . . ." to drift away then, as I understand Seers often do, into a silent musing from which he would not be aroused.

I did not know why then. Moreover, I could not imagine why. There was an exercise frequently called for by Gamesmasters when student attention flagged in the mid afternoon. They called it simply "imagining," and the task was to imagine a series of moves at the end of which some extremely unlikely configuration of pieces might occur. I had never been good at it. Yarrel had been better. It was not surprising then, that by the time our pathetic fat ship waddled into the harbor of the Immutables, Yarrel had thought up at least three reasons why.

"Mandor may have sent them. If he is not dead, he may be remorseful and desirous of making it up to you." I thought this most unlikely. I had seen Mandor's face when Mertyn moved against him. "Mertyn may have sent them," he went on. "He has decided he made a mistake to send you away and . . ." Chance hushed him, as did I. In our opinion, mine for what small count it has, Mertyn makes very few mistakes of any kind. "Or, someone may have seen the play," Yarrel continued, "when the power flew at Mandor, and may have thought it came from you . . ."

I said nonsense.

"Truly, Peter. Some kin of Mandor may have thought so and desires to take you for vengeance."

"Me! I did nothing to him. It was he who tried to kill me."

"But, they may not know that. Someone watching from a bad vantage point, they might think it was you."

"Or someone from afar," agreed Chance. "Someone who saw or heard about it but did not know the truth. Perhaps they think you a Wizard Emergent, and the pawners are recruiting for a True Game somewhere."

"Where?"

"Who knows where. Somewhere. Some petty King of a small purlieu may have offered high for a Wizard. No tested Gamesman would go to a small purlieu, so a pawner would be paid to look for a student, or a boy with talent just emerging."

"But, it was Mertyn's Sorcerer, not me. Mertyn's power, not mine. Power bled into that Sorcerer for days, perhaps, little by little, so that we'd not feel it going, so that he'd be ready when the moment came. It was Mertyn! Not me."

Chance agreed, pursing his lips and cocking his head like a bird listening to bugs in the wood. "You know it, lad. I know it, and so does Yarrel, here. Someone else may not."

I exploded. "What do I look like? Some Wizard Child?" There was a moment's terrified silence. One does not shout about Wizards or their children if one cares about surviving, but no lightning struck at me out of the fog. "I look like what I am. A student. No sign of talent yet. No sign of a name. No nothing. Oh, I know what they said at the house, what that fat-faced Karl always claimed, that I was Mertyn's Festival get. Well. So much for that and that. I'm gone from Mertyn's House with no sign of Kinging about me to rely on. Now, this is nonsense and makes me sick inside."

Yarrel had the grace to put his arms around my shoulders and hug me, after which Chance did the same, and we stood thus for a long moment while the ship wallowed and splashed itself toward the jetty. Around us masts of little boats sketched tall brush strokes of stone gray against cloud gray, tangles of rigging creaked and jingled while a circle of wan light hung far above us like a dead lantern. It was mid-day masked as evening with dusk bells tolling somewhere in the fog, remote and high, as though from hills, and such a feeling of sadness as I had not felt before. Long minutes told me it came from the pungent soup of salt and smoke, as of grasses burning on the water meadows, a smell as sad and wonderful as youth in speaking of endings and beginnings. Came a hail out of the shadow, and we grated against the stones. The Captain was over the rail in a moment, talking earnestly to those he met there. The plank clattered down to let us off the unquiet deck, our legs buckling and weaving like dough from the long time on the water. Howsoever, we stiffened them fast enough to gather up our gear and follow Chance up through the lanes, twisting and dodging back upon our trail until we came to a tavern. That is, I suppose they would have called it a tavern, though most they served there was tea and things made of greenery.

There was one there to meet us, their "governor," so they said, a brown, lean man with a little silver beard like the chin hairs of a goat. He said his name was Riddle.

"Riddle. A question with a strange answer, or an answer with strange sense, or so my daughter says. She'll be along by and by to guide you south overland. We want no part of you, nor of those pawners who came after you."

"They actually came into harbor after us?" Chance's question was more curious than fearful. Well, it wasn't him the pawners were after.

"They did so. The Demon with them is already complaining that he is blind and deaf here in our land. So, we say, let him get out of it." He smiled sarcastically. "And let you get out as well. You Gamesmen have no Game here. Your Demons cannot read any thought but their own; your Seers cannot see further than their eyes will reach. Your Sentinels can make no fire but with steel and spark, as any child can."

"Your land truly is outside the Game? Almost I thought Chance was jesting with us when he said it . . ."

"No jest. Here, no Game of any kind. Howsoever, we bear no malice, either, and will send you away as you would. South, I think you said."

"I thank you for helping us," I mumbled, only to be stopped by his harsh laughter.

"No help, lad. No. We want none of the nonsense of the Game, none of its blood and fire here. If you are gone, so will the pawners go. It is for our own peace, not yours."

So I learned that people may be kind enough while not caring a rather. He sent his girl child to us after a bit, she with long, coltish legs, scarred from going bare among the brush, and hair which fell to her waist in a golden curtain. Tossa, her name was. Riddle held her by the shoulder, her eyes level with mine, unsmiling, as he spoke to Chance.

"We have none of the Festival brutishness here, sir. These your boys need be made 'ware of that. See to it you make it clear to them, or you'll not walk whole out of our land." Chance said he would make it clear, indeed, and Yarrel was already blushing that he understood. I was such an innocent then that I didn't know what they were talking about. It made no difference to me to be guided by a girl or a lad or a crone, for that. Tossa threw her head up, like a little horse, and I thought almost to hear her whinny, but instead she told us to come after her quick as we might and made off into the true night which was gathering.

Oh, Tossa. How can I tell you of Tossa? Truly, she was only a girl, of no great mind or skill. In the world of the Game she would have been a pawn, valued perhaps for her youth or her virginity, for some of the powerful value these ephemera because they are ephemera, and perhaps she would have had no value at all to spend her life among the corn. But to me—to me she became more than the world allows in value. Her arms reaching to feel the sun, her long-fingered hands which floated in gestures like the blossoms of trees upon least winds, her hair glinting in the sun or netting shadow at dusk, her laugh when she spoke to me, her touch upon the bandage at my head as she said, "Poor lad, so burned by the silliness abroad in the land . . ."

She was only teasing me, so Yarrel said, as girls tease boys, but I had no experience of that. Seven days we had, and seven nights. She became my breath, my sight, my song. I only looked at her, heard her, filled myself with the smell of her, warm, beastly, like an oven of bread. She was only a girl. I cannot make more of her than that. Yet she became the sun and the grass and the wind and my own blood running in me. I do not think she knew. If she knew, she did not care greatly. Seven days. I would not have touched her except to offer my hand in a climb. I would not have said her name but prayerfully . . .

Except that on the seventh dusk we came to the end of the lands which the Immutables call their own. We stood upon a tall hogback of stone, twisty trees bristling about us, looking down the long slope to a river which meandered its way through sand banks, red in the tilting sun, wide as a half-day's march and no deeper than my toes. A tumbled ruin threw long shadows on the far side, some old town or fortification, and Chance got out the charts to see where we were. We crouched over them, aware after a moment that Tossa was not with us. We found her on a pinnacle, staring back the way we had come, frowning.

"Men on the way," she said. "Numbers of them." She put the glass back to her eyes and searched among the trees we had only lately left. "Trail following. Riddle didn't think they'd follow you!" She sounded frightened.

Chance borrowed the glass. "They've stopped for the night? Can't tell. No sign of fire, but they've not come from under the trees yet. Ah. An Armiger, lads. And a Tragamor."

Tossa exclaimed, "But they are powerless within the boundaries." Still, she was frightened.

Chance nodded. "Yes, but they have blades and spears and fustigars to smell us out. They have more strength than we. And the boundaries are too close. The river marks them, doesn't it?"

She nodded. Yarrel was thinking, his face knotted. "Let the girl go away to the side," he suggested, "while we take to the river. They aren't following her. The river will confuse the fustigars. They have no Seer with them? No Pursuivant?"

Chance told him he saw none, but Tossa would have none of it. She had been sent to guide us out, and she would guide us out. "We will all go by the river, quickly, before they can get up here to see which way we went."

Strangely, as we went down the hogback and into the river, I began to think of the boundaries and what they meant to the people who lived there. They were all pawns here, I thought, with no strength in them except their arms and their wits. In this land the Armiger could not rise into the air like a hawk on the wind; the Tragamor could not move the stones beneath our feet so that we stumbled and fell. In this land, we were almost their equals; no chill Demesne would grow around us, blooming like a hideous flower with us at its center. Almost, I smiled. Now I recoil when I remember that almost smile, that sudden, unconsidered belief that we and those who followed were on equal footing. We galloped down the slope and into the river as dusk came, almost gaily, Chance muttering that we would run down the river then cut back into the Immutable land. The water splattered up beneath our feet; Tossa reached out to seize my hand in hers and hasten me along. When she fell, I thought she had stumbled. I mocked her clumsiness, teasingly, and only when I had prodded her impatiently with a foot did I see the feathered shaft protruding from her back. Then I screamed, the sound hovering in the air around us like a smell. Chance came and lifted her and there was no more smiling as we raced down that stream for our lives, angling away into a creek which fed it at a curve of the river, praying those who followed would go on down the flow rather than up the little stream, running, running, until at last we came to earth among trees in a swampy place, Tossa beside us, barely breathing.

I could feel the shaft in me, through the lung, feel the bubbling breath, the slow well of blood into my nostrils, the burning pain of it as though it were hot iron. I sobbed with it, clutching at my own chest until Chance shook me silent. "Be still," he hissed at me. "You are not hurt. Be still or we are dead."

The pain was still there, but I knew then that it was not from the arrow but from some other hurt. I hurt because Tossa hurt; it was as though I were she. There was no reason for this. I didn't even blame it upon "love," for I had loved Mandor and had never felt his hurts as my own. This spun in my head as I gulped hot tears into my throat and choked upon them, smothering sound. Away to the south we could hear the baying of the fustigars, a dwindling cacophony following the river away, toward the border. The soil we lay on was wet and cold; the smell of rot and fungus was heavy. I heard Yarrel ask, "Is she dead?" and Chance reply that she breathed, but barely.

"A Healer," I said. "Chance, I must find a Healer. Where?"

He muttered something I couldn't hear, so I shook him, demanding once again. "Where? I've got to find someone . . ."

"That ruin," he gargled. "Back where we came into the river. The chart showed a hand there, a hand, an orb, and a trumpet . . ."

A hand was the symbol for Healer. The orb betokened a Priest, and the trumpet a Herald.

"Let me go!" Yarrel was already dropping his pack. I thrust him back onto the earth beside her.

"Help her if you can. I cannot. I hurt too much. I must go or I'll die. They won't be looking for one person, alone . . ."

"Your bandages," Yarrel said. "One glimpse of you and the pawners will know."

"They will not," I hissed. I ripped the pad of gauze from my head and dropped it into the muddy water, sloshing it about before unwinding it to spiral it around my head, covering my face. "Your cloak," I demanded of Chance, taking it from him before he could object.

"Oh, High King of the Game," he protested, "take it off, Peter. Of all forbidden things, this is most forbidden."

"And still, we do them," I quoted at him furiously. "Quickly, give me soot from the lantern for the face . . ."

He fumbled fingers into the chimney of the dark lantern, cursing as he burned them on the hot glass, cursing again as he drew sooty fingers across the muddied gauze to make the eyes, nose, and slitted mouth shape of a Necromancer. "Oh, by the cold but you're doing a terrible thing."

I turned from them, from *her* where she lay so helpless beside them, telling them to bring her near the river and across it as soon as they saw me return. It would do no good to bring a Healer into the land of the Immutables. Then I ran, not knowing that I ran, not thinking of anything except the hand in the ruins, the Healer there.

The waters of the river fountained beneath my feet. The hard meadow of the farther shore fled behind me until the ruins loomed close on their rocky hill. I felt a chill, and with the chill came a measure of sanity which said, "You will do her no good if you are caught in some Game, no good if you are hasty." The truth of that stopped me. Shuddering, I circled the hill to measure the Demesne, keeping the chill upon my right hand, six hundred paces, more or less. A small Demesne, someone at the center of it pulling only so much power as it might take to rise into the air (as Heralds can) to spy out the land around. I crept toward the ruin's center, searching the skyline from moment to moment. Shattered corridors led into roofless rooms, and at last I found a wall with slitted windows overlooking a courtyard.

Of the three gathered there I saw only the Healer at first, her pale robes spread upon the mossy stones, half in shadow, half in light from the fiery pillar which rose and fell in a languorous dance. Beside it stood a Priestess, gesturing in time with the firelight. One glance was enough to tell me what she was, for such beauty and glamor are unreal, passing all natural loveliness. The Herald sat near her, bright tabard gleaming, raising and lowering his finger to make the fire move. They were within sound of my breath, and it seemed to me they must have heard my heart. Close as they were, it would do me no good unless I could get the Healer away from them and to the river's side.

Even as I struggled to find a plan, the fire sank from its dancing column into an ordinary blaze, a small campfire. The Priestess sighed, complaining, "So I build a fiery web, Borold, with none to see and admire . . ."

He rose to put a cloak around her shoulders, stroking her arms gently. "I admire, Dazzle. Always . . ."

The Healer moved in a gesture of exasperation. "You have only made the place cold. Why can't you be content to leave well enough alone and give up these children's tricks?"

The Herald objected. "Give over, Silkhands. She has made a pillar of fire and I have made it dance. Together we have pulled no more power than you might use to heal a sparrow. Why should she not do something for her own amusement?"

"When has she ever done anything not for her own amusement?" the Healer countered. "We are sent here to sit like badgers upon an earth because Dazzle insisted upon amusement."

When the Priestess turned toward her I saw again that matchless face, curled now into spiteful mockery. "You will not be content until you destroy me, Healer-maid. You are disloyal to me now as always, hating and jealous of my following." The woman preened in the firelight, stretching like a cat in satisfied self-absorption. "We will not be here long, only until Himaggery decides that he misses me, which he will, and sends word for me to return to the Bright Demesne. The Wizard will bring us back soon."

"I have never been disloyal," said the Healer in a low voice, full of strain. Though I could not see her face, I thought she was fighting tears. "But I would rather live where I can use my skills to heal. Here I can do nothing, nothing."

I thought I would give her something to do as I turned from the slit window to approach them from below. I had gone only a pace or two before turning back in a fit of inspiration to strip off my white shirt and hang it within the window. The breeze moved it slightly there, pale in the firelight.

Once out of the ruin and on the plain below them, I put my hands to my mouth to make that echoing ghost call with which we boys had frightened each other in the attics of Mertyn's House. As I approached the tumulus the Herald rose above it to stand high upon the air. He called, "Who comes?" but I did not answer. I knew what he saw; black cloak, skull face, a Necromancer. I spread the cloak in a batwinged salute and called in the deepest voice I could make.

"One comes, Herald, bringing a message from a Wizard to one known as Silkhands, the Healer . . ."

There was a little fall of rubble as the Priestess and the Healer climbed onto the piled stone beneath him. I kept eyes unfocused, unseeing of that face, but still I could feel the pull of her eyes. Priests have that quality, and Kings, and Princes—by some called "follow-me," and by others "beguilement." Dazzle had more of it than any I had seen, so I did not look her in the face. She called.

"Come, Necromancer, closer that we may hear this message you bring in comfort . . ."

"Nay, Godspeaker. Let her whom I have named come with me to hear the words of Himaggery." The Healer struggled down the pile toward me. When she was close, I whispered, "You are to come with me, Healer, to do a thing the Wizard desires." She followed me as I turned away, but the Priestess was not of a mind to let us go.

"Oh, come up to me, Necromancer, that I may judge whether this is a true message . . ." Her voice was sweet, sweet as honey, a charm and an enchantment. Almost I turned before I thought. The three of them had no power of far-seeing among them, but the disguise would not stand close inspection, as Chance had well known. I would have to try the trick I had planned. I turned again toward her where she stood above me on the stones.

"My Master, who is your Master also, has warned me that you are not always quick to do his will. Therefore, he has suggested I take the time, if you are troublesome, to show you your dead . . ." I gestured high, letting the sleeve fall away from my pale arm as I pointed at the far slit window behind them. Luck was with me. As they turned, the breeze caught my shirt and moved it as though something living or undead moved among the stones. Once again I gave the ghost call. The Priestess shuddered. I could see it from where I stood and knew then that she was one of those with reason to fear her dead. I led Silkhands away. From behind came a frantic call.

"The shade you have raised remains, Necromancer. Will you not remove it?"

"The shade remains only for a time, Godspeaker. Go to your rest. Come morrow it will be gone." As it would be. I had no intention of letting them discover the trick. The Healer followed me, mute, until we drew near the river. I gestured her ahead to the place where Yarrel and Chance waited, a dark blot upon the earth between them. She ran toward them. I tried to say something to her, command her, but my body had gone dead, as though all the energy which had forced me to the ruin and into the masquerade had drained away leaving me empty. I felt horror, breathlessness, an aching void, then fell, hearing as I did so the Healer's voice crying, "She is dead, dead."

# 3

# The Wizard Himaggery

I WOKE WITH THE HEALER'S HANDS ON MY CHEST, my heart beating as though within them. Some mysterious message seemed to move between my eyes and hers, shadowed against the dawn sky. She said, "Well, this one lives, and he is no Necromancer. Nor, I'll warrant, was it any Wizard's message which sent you to me. Why did you bring me to her?" She gestured with her chin to the place Tossa lay, tight wrapped in her own cloak, a package, nothing more. "I could not have healed her even had she been alive when I came. She is an Immutable, not open to healing."

I struggled away from her hands. "I thought, if we brought her outside their land . . ."

"No, no," she said impatiently, with a gesture of tired exasperation which I was to see often. "No. It is something they carry in them, as we carry our talents in us. Not all of them have it, but this one was armored against any such as I."

"You could tell? Even with her dead?"

"Newly dead. If I had had great strength, and if she had not been what she was—well, it might have been done. But, she was what she was. And you are what you are, which is not a Necromancer from Himaggery's Demesne."

Chance stepped forward to offer her a cup of tea, his old head cocked to one side like that of a disheveled bird, eyes curious as a crow's. He made explanation and apology. I felt no pride at all in the trick I'd managed, but the Healer seemed slightly amused by it, in a weary way. I would have been amused, perhaps, if it had worked. As it was, I felt only empty.

"What happened to me?" I asked.

"It was as though you had been the girl herself," the Healer answered.

"Arrow shot, heart wounded. But, there was no mark on you. Were you close kin? No, of course not. Stupid of me. She was an Immutable. What was she to you?"

I didn't answer for I didn't know. The moment passed. What had Tossa been to me? Chance murmured something by way of identification of her, a guide, a mere acquaintance, daughter of the governor of the Immutables (at which Silkhands drew breath). What had she been to me? I was terrified, for I could remember what she had been but felt nothing at all, nothing. The Healer caught my look and laid her hands upon me. Then it was all back, the agony of loss, the terror of death.

"Will you bear it?" she asked. "Or, shall I heal it?"

In that time it seemed an ultimate horror that I could be healed of the pain while Tossa lay unmourned. I said, "Let me bear it—if I can." I was not certain I could.

They carried her body back to the edge of the trees, wrapped well against birds and beasts, and buried it under a cairn, leaving a message there to her father for those who would come searching. Chance trembled at the thought of that man's anger following us; the Immutables were said to be terrible in wrath. We went off to the ruins as I wept and ached and drew breaths like knives into me. She had been a girl, only a girl. She had been. She was not. I could not understand a world in which this could be true and the pain of it so real. I did not know her at all; I was her only mourner. This was more horrible than her death.

The Healer called out as we approached the ruins. While the others circled it, I went through the tumbled stones to retrieve my shirt. The trickery had been laid bare, but it was a good shirt and I had no intention of leaving it there. The route I had taken on the night before eluded me; I came at the slit windows from a different direction. There was a sharp, premonitory creak, then the earth opened beneath me to dump me unceremoniously into a dusty pit. My head hit the floor with a thump. When I stood up, dazed, it was to find myself in a kind of cellar or lower room which smelled of dust and rats. The walls were lined with slivered remnants of shelves and rotten books. Something small turned under my foot.

I picked it up, saw another, then another, stooped to gather them up. They were tiny—no longer than my littlest finger—game pieces carved from bone or wood, delicate as lace, unharmed by time. Pieces of a rotten game board lay beneath them, and a tiny book. I gathered it up as well, even as I heard Chance calling from above.

I wondered afterward why I had moved so quickly to hide them and put them away in my belt pouch. It would have been more natural to call out, to show them as a prize. Later I thought it was because of the way we had lived in the School House. There had never been any privacy, anything of one's own. There were few secrets, virtually no private belongings. Secret things were wonderful things, and these were truly marvelous, so I gathered them as a squirrel does nuts, hiding them as quickly. They were not paying any attention to me at any rate, for the Healer had attracted it all. She had found all her belongings gone, Borold and Dazzle gone, and was in full lament.

"My clothes," she wailed. "My boots. My box of herbs. Everything. Why would they do that?"

"Probably because they thought they were following you," said Yarrel, sensibly. "To that Wizard Peter pretended the message came from . . ."

"Oh, by the ice and the wind and the seven hells," she said. "They would be just such fools as to do that." Then she fell silent and we didn't find out for some time what that was all about. There was nothing for us to do but travel together, for the Bright Demesne of the Wizard Himaggery lay south, the way we were going.

We slept before starting out, I crying myself to sleep, hurting because of Tossa, saying to myself, "This is what love is." It was not love, not at all, but I did not know that then. When we woke it was with a high riding moon to light our way south.

During the way south I learned something more of women. Yarrel taught me. He did not see the Healer as anything mysterious or strange. He saw her as a woman and treated her, so far as I could see, as he had treated Tossa, with a certain teasing respect which had much laughter in it. The first village we came to he insisted we buy her a pagne to wear, she having nothing with her but the one dress and light robe, both becoming raggedy from the road. Once the people saw a Healer was come, however, nothing would do but that they stoke the oven in the market place and bring the sick to lie about it. She, all glittering-eyed and distant, walked among them touching this one and that until, when she was finished, most had risen on their feet and the oven was cooled no warmer than my hand from her draw of power from it. They paid her well, and she insisted on repaying us for the pagne, though I argued it was small pay for healing me.

"I have your company," she said simply, for once not going on like a coven of crows gabbing all at once. She was tired. I could see it in her face. "It is good to have company on the road, even pawns and boys, if you take no offense at that."

We told her we were not offended by truth. Later, when we stopped for the night, she wrapped herself in the bright pagne and combed out her hair. I thought once again of birds, but this time of the clamorous, unpredictable parrots with their sudden laughter and wise eyes. Her hair was the color of silver wood ash, and her eyes were green as leaves in her pale, oval face. Chance was once more gloating over his charts, and she leaned on his shoulder to trace our way south among the hills. "Dazzle has gone to the Bright Demesne," she said. "She and Borold, thinking Himaggery sent for me. Oh, she will be a jealous witch, Dazzle, thinking anyone has sent for me." She sounded very tired. I thought of Dazzle's beauty and shivered. How could one such as that be jealous of anyone? Silkhands went on. "She believes she loves him, you see, the Wizard. But Himaggery is proof against her, and it drives her to excess. Ah, well, we will get there soon after her and no doubt bring her away again. She will be very angry."

Yarrel asked, "Why do you care? Are you her leman?"

"Half sister, rather. Our father was the same, but she was born to another mother than Borold's and mine. I am oldest, by six years."

"Why were you sent away?"

"Because Dazzle stirs trouble as a cook stirs soup. You called her Godspeaker, Priestess, but she is no Priestess. She is a witch, as uncontrollable as storm."

"Where is this Bright Demesne?" asked Chance. "I can't find it here what should be so sizable."

She helped him search, but there was no sign of it upon the chart. Chance puffed his cheeks in complaint. "No trust, lads, that's what it comes to. Pay gold, or healing, or laughter if you're a clown, and get nothing but tricks and lies. This chart was said to be *complete,* and look at it—some old thing dusted off and sold with pretense." He folded it sadly, stroking the parchment with a callused hand. I knew how he felt.

It was a godlike feeling to spread the charts and trace one's way softly along a crease of hill, imagining the way, learning the names and aspects of the land. It was less wonderful if one knew that the charts lied. Then it was only pretend, not true game.

That night I lay awake after the others slept, mazed by a lucific moon, and set out the tiny Gamesmen I had found. For the first time I noted they were not like those I had played with as a child. Of the white pieces, the tallest was a Queen, but there was no King beside her. Instead there was a white Healer. There were two Seers, two Armigers, two Sentinels, but no Churchmen. Of the black pieces the tallest was a Necromancer. There was a Sorcerer almost as tall, then two Tragamors, two Elators, two Demons. I could not tell what the little men were, crouchy and fuzzed in the moonlight. In the first morning light I looked again. They were crouchy indeed, Shapeshifters all, of the same ilk but differing in detail. Each piece had the same fascination in the hand I had felt when I first held them. Unwillingly, I put them away, each wrapped in a scrap of cloth and buried under my needfuls.

Traveling south, sun and rain, forest and meadow, Silkhand's chatter, Yarrel's silences, Chance's wry commentary upon the world, no chill, no menace. Silkhands said that Himaggery had taken much of the land around Lake Yost and assembled thousands of Gamesmen there. Chance laughed, but she claimed it was true. How so many could find power to exist, she did not say. We did not ask. It was only a tall tale, we thought. Hum of bees, quiet sough of wind. Then, suddenly, as we climbed a high ridge of stone, a cold gust from above, chill as winter, without warning. We ran for overhanging stone and peered from beneath it like badgers.

"Dragon," whispered Yarrel. I saw it then, planing across the valley beyond, great wings outspread, long neck stretched like an arrow, tail behind, straight as a spear. Fire bloomed around its jaws. I was the first to see the other, higher, diving out of the sun. It was something I had never seen before. "Cold Drake," someone said in a hiss. The cold intensified. We huddled close, pulling clothing from the packs to wrap with our blankets around us, to keep our heat in. Neither of the Gamesmen knew we were there or cared. They would soak our heat for their play just as they would that from the sun-hot stones. All we could do was wait in the shelter of the stones, praying they would fly on before it grew too cold for us.

I wondered as we lay there how many thousands of pawns—and lesser Gamesmen, too—had died thus, lying helpless under stones or trees or in their houses while Gamesmen drew their heat away, slow degree by slow degree, until they fell into that last sleep. We had seen bones here and there as we traveled, littering the roadside, heaped around the ruins where Silkhands had been, all those who had stayed quiet and cold while Gamesmen played. Even so, it was a wondrous thing to watch the Dragon and the Cold Drake fight.

The one was all sinuous movement, twisting coil, black on black with frosty breath; the other all arrow darting, climb and dive, amber on gold with the breath of fire. As it grew colder around us, it grew more difficult for the Gamesmen to draw heat as well, and their movement slowed. We kept expecting them to move away, over the sunwarmed plains, but they did not. We knew then that they dueled, that they had set the boundaries of their Game and would not leave them until one or both were dead.

The end came as suddenly as the beginning. The Cold Drake caught the Dragon full in a looping coil which tightened, tightened. The Dragon screamed. They fell together, linked, faster and faster, wings unmoving, a blur in the clear air. Then they were upon the plain before us, lost in a stirred cloud of frigid dust which erupted into the wind and was gone. The Healer sobbed and moved into the open, stumbling toward those distant bodies, we after her. She paused at one body only a moment, then went on to the other. He breathed feebly, back in his own form, a slender youth looking scarcely older than I, pale of skin with black hair and the long ears of the southern people. He tried to focus his agonized gaze upon the Healer, said "Healer . . . please . . ." Silkhands reached out as though to touch him then turned away.

"Too cold," she said. "Oh, there is nothing to make into a fire. If we could have fire swiftly . . ." We all looked around, but there was nothing to burn upon the hard-packed earth. The youth gave a bubbling cry and was silent. I turned to find Silkhands weeping. "Too cold, always too cold and I can do nothing. No power, no way to get power. Oh, Lords of the seven hells, but I wish you were a Tragamor . . ." She sobbed upon Chance's chest like a child. Looking toward the far line of forest I, too, wished I were a Tragamor, though with the cold as it was I doubted even a Tragamor could have ported wood from that forest in time. My eyes caught a glitter there; we all stared at the procession which came. It was not lengthy but puissant, the tall figure on the high red horse most of all. I knew him by the fur-collared robe embroidered with moonstar signs, even before Silkhands sank to her knees murmuring, "The Wizard Himaggery." My eyes did not stay long on the Wizard, for behind him rode one whose face I well remembered, that pawner from the Gathered Waters who had sought me, followed me. Well, I thought, run as we might he had found me. Blood gathered behind my eyes and I launched myself at him, shouting.

The next thing I knew I was on the ground with two men sitting on me. There had been a sudden burst of heat from someone in the train, a Sorcerer mostlike. The Elators sitting on me had not needed it, however. They had needed only their own strength and my clumsiness. The Wizard sounded amused.

"And what occasions this animosity, my good pawner? Is this the one you have been telling me about?" There was a mumbled reply before the Wizard spoke again. "Let him up, but keep your eyes on him. This is no time nor place to sort out such matters. We must look upon the bodies of our foolish young." And with that he rode forward, almost over me where I struggled with the Elators, unwilling to give up. He stopped by the youth's body and spoke to Silkhands. A Sorcerer rode out of the train and offered her his hand so that she might draw upon his stored power if she would. She shook her head. Too late. The Wizard turned his mount and came toward us again. "Oh, stop squirming, boy. You will not be dealt with unfairly," and rode away toward the forest.

There were extra horses, evidently brought in the hope the duelers could ride home. Chance and Silkhands had one, Yarrel and I the other. Behind us the bodies of the duelers rose into the air to float behind us, a Tragamor riding before each with a Sorcerer between. Even irritated as I was, I admired the crisp way it was done, each knowing what to do and doing it. Yarrel did not notice. His face was glorious. There would never be anything in the world as important to Yarrel as horses.

The Gamesman who rode beside me, one I could not identify—gold tunic embroidered with cobweb pattern, magpie helm and gray cloak— began to talk of the ones who floated behind. "Young Yvery and even younger Yniod," he said, "both having conceived a passion for the Seer, Yillen of Pouws, and having studied the madness of courtly love (much studied by them and some other few fools in Himaggery's realm) did each claim the other had insulted the lady. She, having been in trance this seven month, could not intervene. So was challenge uttered, and by none could they be dissuaded. Himaggery demands that all may have free choice, and so did this occur.''

I found my voice somewhere beneath my giblets and got it out. ''Which of them did the Seer love?''

''Neither. She knew neither of them. They had only seen her sleeping.''

''What is this courtly love you speak of?''

The Gamesman gestured to Silkhands. ''Ask your Healer friend, she knows.''

Silkhands turned a miserable, shamed face to me. ''Oh, yes, the Rancelman is right. I know. It is some factitious wickedness which Dazzle thought up and spread among the impressionable young. She may have read of it in some ancient book or come upon it in amusements for herself, and none will do unless there is combat and ill feeling.

''That is why we were banished to the ruin. Three times we have lived in the Bright Demesne, and each time Dazzle has started up some such foolishness. It does nothing but cause trouble, dueling, death, stupidity. Each time Himaggery has sent her away . . .''

''Her? Not you?''

''No.'' She seemed almost angry that I had asked. ''Not I. Not Borold. But we cannot let her live alone . . .''

''I would,'' snorted Yarrel. Of course, he had not seen Dazzle. ''So long as she has you to comfort her, why should she mend her behavior?''

''So says Himaggery,'' she admitted. ''But this last thing must have started ages ago. Dazzle could not have begun any new mischief. There has not been time.''

I mumbled something intended for comfort. We went on through the fringe of forest and out into the clear, blue shining of the lake's edge. For a moment I did not understand what I saw rising from the earth. Fogs spiraled from steaming springs which fed the waters. The town was scattered among these mists, and I knew why Himaggery had taken the Lake of Yost and how it was that thousands could gather here.

''There is power here,'' I said as I felt the heat.

''Yes,'' Silkhands agreed. ''There is plenty of power here, and not much is needed here. There is none out there, and that is where it is always needed. It is never where I need it!'' Her voice rose in a pained cry.

I said, "It hurts you! When you need to heal and have not the power, it hurts you!'' The idea was quite new to me.

"Yes. That is true for all Healers. And for all Seers, and all Demons, too. We who are the children of Gamesmother Didir have this pain." She was speaking of the legendary grandmother of our race. Didir was progenitress of the mental powers, Gamesfather Tamor the progenitor of the material ones. Religion has it that all of us are descended from these two. I was not thinking so much of that, however, as of the idea of pain.

When Tossa had been wounded, I had felt her pain, felt her death. When Silkhands had felt pain, I, too, had felt it. What did this pattern mean? Understand, for boys of my age—and, I suppose, for girls too, though I had no way of knowing—the most important thing is to know what name, what talent we will have. We search for signs of it, hints, even for auspices. We beg Seers to look ahead for us (they never will, it is forbidden). What did this mean? Was I a Demon emergent, reading the feelings of others? But, no, this was foolishness. Tossa could not have been read in this fashion. It spun in my head endlessly, so I tried not to think about it.

So, we were given food and water and proper amenities and brushed up to be presented to Himaggery in his audience hall as soon as might be. I heard water under the floor, the warmth of the stones telling their own tale of power. Dazzle was there, and the pawner. When they had been heard, Chance took our let-pass from his breast and gave it to the Wizard who perused it.

"All right, lad," the Wizard said. "You've heard the pawner say he was hired to find you, hired by a Demon and paid well for his work. You've heard Silkhands say you played a forbidden game to get a Healer to a wounded Immutable, something anyone could have told you wouldn't work. I've heard complaining from Dazzle, as usual, but you merit no punishment on that account. Now, let me hear from you. Why does this Demon want you?"

"I do not know, sir. I have met only one Demon in my life, at the last Festival, and I don't even remember his name."

"Well, easy tested by a Demon of my own." He gestured to a tall Demon who stood at his left, and that one fixed his eyes upon me. There

43

was a tickling in my head, a fleeting kaleidoscope of colors and smells, quickly gone. The Demon shook his head and said to Himaggery, "He speaks only truth. He is only what he seems, a student, a boy, nothing more."

"Ah. So. Well then, why did you try to kill this pawner? He was, after all, in my protection."

"He killed Tossa," I grated. "He killed her or had her killed. What had she done to him? Nothing. Nothing! And he killed her."

The pawner squirmed. "An accident, Lord. A . . . misunderstanding. It was not my intent to kill anyone, but one of the men in my train . . . he was caught up in the chase . . ."

The Wizard said, "It seems to be explained. The boy has committed no wrong except for a bit of forbidden disguise. The pawner, however, has killed the governor's daughter, an Immutable. It is likely he won't live long to regret that. We'll cry you to them, pawner. I'll not have blame laid on me or mine."

"But, Lord . . ."

"Be still. If you anger me more, I'll give you to them rather than merely cry you to them. As for you, Silkhands, you've done nothing ill except exercise poor choice in certain matters we've discussed before. And Dazzle is with us again . . ."

He had stepped close to me as he spoke, putting his hand on my shoulder. I felt the solid weight of it, smelled the mixed leather and herb scent of his clothing, and followed his glance to the window where Dazzle was posing like some exotic bird or silken cat. I saw her, then saw her again and turned sick with horror. One eye socket gaped empty. One side of her nose was gone, eaten away. From her jaw jagged splinters of bone and tooth jabbed through multiple scars, all as though one half of her face had been chewed away by some monster. I choked. Himaggery removed his hand, and the horror was abruptly gone. I reached out to him for support, and the vision returned. He saw the sick terror on my face, stooped toward me to whisper, "You saw?" then drew away, eyes narrowed in thought as I nodded, unable to speak.

"Say nothing," he whispered. "Be still." He caught curious glances around us. "Tell them I am forbidding you to pretend to Necromancy." Then he left me tottering there. I could not leave the room quickly enough to suit me. Even in my own room, I retched and was sick. When I had settled myself somewhat, I went out onto the little balcony and sat there, hunched against the wall, trying not to think of anything. I saw the pawner in the courtyard below me with some other men. In a few moments they mounted and rode away, turning south along the lake shore. At the moment it meant nothing to me. Later I was to wonder, why south? The Gathered Waters and the pawner's ship lay north of us. I had not long to brood over anything, for Silkhands came to fetch me to the Wizard.

We found him in his own rooms, out of dress, Wizardly costume laid aside in favor of a soft shirt and trousers which could have clad anyone. He was examining a fruit tree in the enclosed garden.

"They will not ordinarily grow this far north," he told us. "Except that they find eternal summer among these mists. We have fruit when others have none, power when others have none. If we can find our way into the heart of life—within the Game or, likely, out of it—we may build a great people from this place."

I think I started at this heresy, not sure I wanted to hear it, but he pretended not to notice, grinning at me over his beard, blue eyes glittering with humor and understanding. He went on.

"And you, Healer. Are you ready to admit that your presence does nothing to help Dazzle, indeed, only makes her worse?"

"Lord, certainly I make her no better."

"Did you know this lad *saw* her?" Silkhands turned a shocked face to mine, was convinced by the expression she found there.

"But how? None can. Except you, Lord, and I."

"He can," said Himaggery, "though I cannot think why. Well, life is full of such mysteries, but it were better for you, boy, if you forgot this one. Am I right that you saw through my eyes? I thought so. Well then, it may be emerging talent of some kind, and no point in worrying about it."

"How did she . . . why is she . . . I . . ." I couldn't get the question out.

"Why is she a hideously maimed person? Why does no one know it? Why? Ah, boy, it's one of those mysteries I spoke of. But, I don't think Silkhands will mind my telling you." He looked to her for permission, and she nodded, eyes fixed upon her twisting hands. He patted her shoulder and told me the story.

"There were two children of Finler the Seer and his loved wife, a Tragamor woman out of the east: Silkhands, here, and her full brother,

Borold, born two years apart. When they were still children, their mother died, and Finler took another woman, a Tragamor from Guiles whose name was Tilde. They had a daughter, some six years younger than Silkhands. Dazzle.

"Silkhands and Borold manifested talent quite young, when they were about fifteen. Silkhands, being a Healer, was much respected in the place they lived as Healers often are, whether they merit it or not, though from everything I have learned I would judge that Silkhands merited it more than most. Borold showed flying early, and then moving, and was named Sentinel. Dazzle was a beauty, even as a tiny thing, and grew more beautiful than any in the place had ever seen. But she was not fond of Silkhands . . ."

"It was Tilde's fault, somewhat," interjected Silkhands. "She resented my mother even though mother was long dead. She was jealous of her reputation in the town, and of the fact that I, her daughter, was a Healer. We cannot blame Dazzle . . ."

"Be that as it may," the Wizard went on, "Dazzle deeply resented her half sister. And, when at last she manifested a talent of her own, it was along the lines she had first laid down, glamor, beguilement, power-holding, and fire—the measure of a Priestess or Witch. Because she was a power-holder, Silkhands sought her help in healing, for Dazzle could have carried power with which Silkhands could have healed many . . ."

"She wouldn't," cried Silkhands. "She would not do it. She would not carry power for anything except her own amusement and delight. If there were sick, she would turn away saying, 'They are nothing to me. They stink, besides. It is better if they die.' "

The Wizard nodded. "So. And Borold fell under the spell of the girl and turned away from Silkhands and would not help her in healing, though at one time he had carried her through the air in search of the sick and wounded. He stopped that and flew only for Dazzle's amusement."

"Then came a Game," said Silkhands in a monotone, as though reciting scripture. "A very great Game, the armies of it massing near the place we lived. And the Tragamors of that Game rained stones upon the opposing armies directed by the Seers and Demons of that Game, but something went awry and the stones fell upon the town and upon our house and upon us.

"And my father died, at once. And Tilde lay with her legs beneath a stone, screaming. And the Game had pulled all the power so that I had none with which to heal her, so I called to Dazzle, as Borold and I tried to roll the stone away. 'Dazzle, your mother is sorely hurt. Give me power to heal her or she'll die.' But Dazzle said, 'I am old enough to need no mother now. I need my power for myself, to keep me safe . . .' and she cowered in the corner weaving a beguilement for *herself,* about *herself,* that she was safe . . .

"Then another stone came, shattering the roof, and a huge tile of the roof came down like a knife, shearing her face. Borold did not see. I saw and screamed at the horror of it. Her mind was not touched, only her face, and I begged her for power to heal her, but she only said, 'Don't try your tricks on me, Silkhands, I'm all right. Let me be. Don't try to get my juice for that old woman.'

"And she went on weaving the glamor around her with all her power so that Borold could not see the wound and she herself could not see it when she sought her mirror, and so has she woven since Tilde died. I could do nothing but ease the pain a little. It was very cold. Shortly the Game was over and help came, but it was too late. And Dazzle went on beguiling . . .''

"Then she doesn't even *know?*" I asked, astonished.

Himaggery made a sour face. "She does not know. She leches after me from time to time and is in perpetual annoyance that I do not return her lusts, but I cannot. Would not, even were she whole, for there is a deeper maiming there than the face."

"Can't she be truly healed, here, where so much power is?"

Silkhands answered sadly. "The power of healing works through the mind, Peter, as all our powers do. If an old wound is long healed, the mind accepts it and will not help me fight it. I am no Necromancer to raise dead tissue to a mockery of life."

"So, boy," said Himaggery. "I will appoint you judge of this matter. Sometimes we do this in the Bright Demesne—appoint a pawn judge of some issue or other . . .''

"But, no," I exclaimed. "Such a one would not know the rules."

"Exactly. You have the heart of the matter there. Well, since you do not know the rules, what would you rule in this case? I believe Silkhands

47

should go away, that staying with Dazzle only makes matters worse. What say you?''

Since there were no rules, I could only use what sense I had. Though Chance had never thought me overburdened in that respect, I had sometimes resented his opinion, so did my best. I thought of the young Dragon and the young Cold Drake, dead because of Dazzle's machinations. I thought of Mandor as I had last seen him, full of envy, ready to destroy me because of it. I thought of Silkhands and her pain that she could not heal more . . . and I said,

''She should go away. If Dazzle is like one I have known, she will not hesitate to destroy you, Silkhands. If you are gone away, then part of the cause of her anger will be gone.''

''Exactly!'' Himaggery beamed at me. ''I need her to carry a message for me; she needs to go away. You need company upon the road, so does she, you go the same place. See how neatly it works out.'' He turned to her. ''I want you to go with the lad to the High Demesne at Evenor. He is not half healed yet, and you can rid him of those scars along the way.''

''Why me?'' she muttered, wiping tears.

''Because you'll be welcome there; Healers always are. Because if I sent a Seer or Demon they would think I sent a spy. Because you are to go to an old friend of mine who needs your help and care; I hope to bring him back here with you. The High King will not want to let him go, and you must use all your wiles as honestly as you can—which you will, because you are honest and cannot think thoughts which would seem treasonable. Are those enough reasons?''

She cried, and he comforted, and I listened, and the hours went by while they talked of other things. They talked of heterotelics (I wrote it down) and an animal in the wastes of Bleer which makes scazonic attacks (I wrote that down, too) and of great Gamesmen of the past—Dodir of the Seven Hands, the Greatest Tragamor ever known, and Mavin Many-shaped. That name seemed familiar to me, but I could not remember where I had heard it before. And they talked more of that one to whom she was being sent, an old man, a Gamesmaster, but something more or other than that as well. They talked long, and I fell asleep. When I woke, Himaggery was brooding by the fire and Silkhands had gone.

I was moved to thank him. The occasion demanded something from me, something more than mere words. I took the pouch from my belt and placed it in his hands, saying, "I have nothing worth giving you, Lord, except perhaps these things I found. If they please you, will you keep them with my thanks for your kindness?" When he opened the pouch, his face went drear and empty, and he took one of the pieces in his hand as though it were made of fire. He asked me where I had come by them, and when I had answered him, he said, "There, in a place I would not go because of her I had sent there. So, they were not meant for me, and it does no good to think about them.

"Boy, I would have given the Bright Demesne for these if I could have found them myself. However, they did not come to my hand and they are not to be given away. I may not tell you what they are—indeed, it may be I do not truly know. I may not take them from you. I can say to you take them, put them under your clothes, keep them safe, keep them secret. I will remember you kindly without the gift."

I wanted to ask him . . . plead with him to tell me something, anything, but his face forbade it. The next morning we left the Bright Demesne, and only then did I realize how strange a place it was. There had been no Gaming while I had been there. I had not seen a single pile of bones. I had no idea what talent the Wizard held. "Strange talents make the Wizard" they say, but his were not merely strange, they were undetectable. Later, of course, I wondered what talent enabled him to see Dazzle as she was. Later, of course, I wondered what talent enabled me to see through his eyes.

# 4

# The Road to Evenor

Just before we left the Bright Demesne, Dazzle saw fit to throw an unpleasant scene during which she accused Silkhands of every evil she could think of—of being Himaggery's leman, of being his treasonous servant, of plotting against her and Borold, of abandoning one whom she had been unable to compete with because her powers were pulish and weak, of being envious—childish, evil, acid words. Neither Dazzle nor Borold saw us off, though Himaggery did. Silkhands was drawn and tired, looking years older than herself, and she only bit her lip when Himaggery told her to put it out of her mind, that he would take care of Dazzle. So, we rode off mired and surrounded in Silkhand's pain. I could feel it. The others could see it well enough.

As I could feel her pain, so I could feel Yarrel's joy. We were mounted on tall, red horses from Himaggery's stable, and Yarrel beamed as though he had sired them himself. As for me, Silkhands bade me leave the bandages off, and as we rode she held my hand and led me to think myself unmarred once more. There was one deep wound which could not be healed, a puckered mark on my brow. Silkhands said my mind held to the spot for a remembrance. Certainly, I did not want to forget what had happened in Schooltown.

She led me to think of Tossa and speak of her until that hurt began to heal as well. I learned that what I had felt was not love. It was some deeper thing than that, some fascination which reaches toward a particular one, toward a dream and thus toward all who manifest that dream. She made me talk of the earliest memories I had, before Mertyn's House (though until that moment I had not known of any memories before Mertyn's House) and I found memory there: scents, feelings, the movement of graceful arms in the sun, light on a fall of yellow hair. So, Tossa had been more than I knew, and less. Even as I grieved at her loss, I grieved that I could not remember who the one had been so long ago, before Mertyn's House. I could not have been more than two or three. I tried desperately, but there were only pictures without words. Tossa had matched an inexplicable creation, an unnamed past.

As well as being Healer, Silkhands became Schoolmistress. Believing Yarrel and I had been too long without study, she began to drill us in the Index as we rode, day by day. It was something to do while the leagues passed, so we learned.

"Seer," she would say. "Give me the Index for Seer."

Obediently, I would begin. "The dress of a Seer is gray, the mask gray gauze, patterned with moth wings, the head covered with a hood. The move of a Seer is the future or some distant place brought near. The Demesne absolute of a Seer is small, a few paces across, and the power use is erratic. Seers are classified among the lesser durables; they may be solitary or oath bound to some larger Game..." Then she would ask another.

"The form of the Dragon is winged ... breathing fire ... and the move is flight through a wide Demesne. Dragons are among the greater ephemera ... the dress of a Sentinel is red ... of a Demon is silver, half-helmed ... of a Tragamor is black, helmed with fangs ... of a Sorcerer is white and red, with a spiked crown..." and so and so and so. Some of the names she knew I had never heard of. What was an Oneiromancer, a Keratinor, a Hierophant? What was a Dervish? I didn't know. Silkhands knew, however, the dress, the form, the move, the Demesne, the Power, the classification.

"When I was a child," she said, "there was little enough to do in the village. But there were books, some, an Index among them. I learned it by heart for want of anything else to do. I think many of the names I learned are very rare. Some I have never seen anywhere in life." Still, she kept me at it.

"Of a Rancelman is cobwebbed gold, magpie helmed ... of an Elator is blue, with herons' wings ... of an Armiger is black and rust, armed with spear and bow ... of a King is true gold, with a jeweled crown..."

"And Shapeshifter," she said. "What is the Index of a Shapeshifter?"

I said I did not know, did not care, was too hungry to go one pace further. She let us stop for food but continued teaching even as we ate.

"The Shapeshifter is garbed in fur when in its own shape. Otherwise, of course, it is clad in the form it takes. The Demesne of a Shifter is very small but very intense, and it goes away quickly. It takes little power to make the change and almost none to maintain it. They are classified among the most durable of all Gamesmen, almost impossible to kill. They are rare, and terrible, and the most famous of all is Mavin Manyshaped.''

"Why Manyshaped?" asked Yarrel. "Can she be more than one thing at a time?"

"No. But she can become many different things, unlike most shifters who can take one other shape, or two, three at most. But Mavin—it is said she can become anything, even other Gamesmen. That, of course, is impossible. It couldn't happen.''

When we had eaten, we went on again, silent for a time while we digested. Yarrel stopped us several times to examine tracks on the road before us. "A party of horsemen," he said, "some four or five. Not far ahead of us." For the first time I thought of the pawner who had ridden away south.

"How far ahead?" I asked. I did not want the man near me and was suddenly sorry I had not asked Himaggery to hold him or send him back to his ship under guard. "How far?"

"A day. We will not ride onto their tails, Peter. You think the pawner rides ahead?"

"I think, somehow, he knew where we were going."

"We made no secret of it.''

"Perhaps we should have done." I was depressed at my own ignorance and naivete. Why had I thought the man had given up? All our ruminations were interrupted, however, by a blast of chill from above. Silkhands threw one glance behind her, cried "Afrit," and rode madly for the timber, we after her in our seemingly permanent state of confusion.

"Is it looking for us?" I asked. She shook her head. Another blast of chill came from another direction. She frowned.

"What is going on up there?" She led us toward rising land from which we might see the countryside around. We found a rocky knuckle at last and climbed it to peer away across a wide valley. Our way led there, straight across, to a notch in the hills at the other side. It was not a way we would take. Drawn up upon the meadows were the serried ranks of a monstrous Game, files of Sorcerers and Warlocks standing at either side, glowing with stored power. Wagons full of wood lined the areas of command where pawns struggled beneath the whip to erect heavy sections of great war ovens. Above the command posts Armigers stood in the air, erect, their war capes billowing about them, rising and falling like spiders upon silk as they reported to those below.

"Lord of the seven hells," said Chance. "Let's get away from this place."

Silkhands looked helplessly across the valley. Our way was there. Our way was blocked. We could not wait until the Game was over. Games of this dimension sometimes went on for years. We could not go around too closely or we risked being frozen in the fury of battle. Silkhands had no power to pull from those mighty ovens and thus protect us in the midst of war. "Borold," she cried, "why are you not here when I need you?" Her brother could have tapped that distant power. We were forced to a fateful decision which meant that we were to come to the High Demesne. Had we gone across the plain, we would have gone no farther. We did not know it, but we were awaited in that far notch of hills. Strange, how all plays into the hands of mordacious fate. Mertyn used to say that.

"We'll go far around," said Silkhands, and Chance agreed. It was all we could do. And we would not have done well at it except for Yarrel.

It was he who read the maps, who found the trails, who found camp sites sheltered from the wind and rain, who kept the horses from going lame and us from being poisoned by bad food or worse water. He bloomed before my eyes, growing taller and broader each day. I woke one morning to find him standing beneath a tall tree looking out across the land, his face shining like those pictures one sees of the ancient pictures of Gamesmother Didir with the glory around her head. "Yarrel," I said, "why were you ever in Schooltown? What was there for you?"

He hugged me even as he answered. "Nothing, Peter. Except a few years during which my mother needed not worry about me. We pawns sometimes have short lives. My beloved sister was *used* in a Game, 'lost in play' by some Shapeshifter who needed a pawn and cared not who it was. We are not considered important, you know, among the Gamesmen. If they wish to eat a few hundred of us in battle, they do it. Or use up a few of our women in some nasty game, they do that. By buying my way into the House, they protected me for a time."

"Bought your way in?"

"With horses. Fine horses. Paid for my rearing, my schooling. Who knows. It may have done me good. Certainly, I know more than my family does about Gamesmen. And Games. And what can and cannot happen. To most of us the Game is a true mystery. If I get back to them, I will have a school of my own—for pawns. To teach them how to survive."

"Then you never expected to develop talent."

"No. To get me into the School, mother had to lie, had to say I was Festival got, by a Gamesman. I never believed that. My father is my father, like me as fox is like fox, no more talent than a badger has, to be strong, to dig deep."

"You could live among the Immutables, be safe there."

"Yes," he replied somberly. "I have thought about that in recent days."

Yarrel my friend, Yarrel the pawn. Yarrel Horse-lover, my own Yarrel. Yarrel who had helped me and guided me. I saw him as in a mist, struggling beneath the whip to assemble war ovens, to cut the monstrous wagon loads of wood. Yarrel. "How you must hate us," I said. "For all you've lived among us since you were tiny . . ."

"I suppose I did. Still do, sometimes. But then, I learned you are the same as us. You want to live, too, and eat when you are hungry and make love to girls—oh, yes, though you may not have done so yet—and sleep warm. The only thing different is that you will grow to have something I have not. And that something will change you into something I am not. And from that time on, I may hate you." He was thoughtful, staring out across the fog-lined vales, the furred hills, the rocky scarps of the range we traveled toward. When he went on it was with that intrinsic generosity he had always shown. "But I do not hate Silkhands. Nor Himaggery. And it may be I will go on liking you, as well."

"There were no games at the Bright Demesne." I don't know why I said that. It seemed important.

"No. There were no games, and I have thought much about that. All those Gamesmen. All that power. And no games at all. What did happen, the Dragon, I mean, was regretted. It means something. In Mertyn's House we never learned . . . never learned that there was any . . . choice."

Choice. I knew the word. The applications of it seemed small. One glass of wine or none. Bread or gruel. Stealing meat from the kitchens or not. Choice. I had never had any.

"It is hard to imagine . . . choice." I said. He turned to me with a face as remote as those far scarps, eyes seeing other times.

"Try, Peter," he said. "I have tried. I think sometimes how many of us there are, so many pawns, so many Immutables, all of us living on this land, and we have no Game. Yet, for most of us the Game rules us. We let it rule us. Imagine what might happen if we did not. That's all. Just imagine."

I was no good at imagining. Yarrel knew that well. For a time I thought he was mocking me. I was nettled, angry a little. We worked our way more deeply into the mountains, struggling always toward a certain peak which marked the pass into Evenor, and the way was hard. We talked little, for we were all weary. Far behind us in the valley were still smokes and confusions of battle. Ahead were only mountains and more mountains. I went on being angry until it seemed boring and foolish, and then I tried to do as Yarrel had asked and imagine. I tried really hard, harder than I had ever tried in Mertyn's House. It was no good. I could not think of choices and pawns and all that. And then in the night . . .

I found myself standing beside my horse on a low hill overlooking the field of battle. I could see the ovens red with heat, the Armigers filling the air like flies, raining their spears and arrows down onto the Gamesmen below. I could hear the great whump, whump of boulders levered out of the ground and launched by teams of Tragamors and Sorcerers, hand-linked as they combined their power to raise the mighty rocks with their minds. Behind enemy lines I could see the flicker as Elators twinked into being, struck about them with double daggers, then disappeared only to flick into being again behind their own lines. On the heights Demons and Seers called directions to the Tragamors and Armigers while Sorcerers strode among the Gamesmen to give them power. Shifterbeasts ran through the ranks, slashing with fangs or tusks, or dropped from the air on feathered wings to strike with blinding talons.

And on each side, at the center of the Game, stood the King and the Princes and the other charismatics to whose beguilement the armies rallied. Among the wounded walked Healers, each with a Sorcerer to hand. I could see it as though it were happening before me.

And I saw more. At the edges of the battle, beyond the Demesne, stolid files of pawns. They stood with stones in their hands, and flails, and hay forks, sharp as needles. And it came to me in the dream, for it was a dream, what would happen when the war ovens grew cold and the Sorcerers were empty of power, the Armigers grounded, the Tragamors helpless, the Elators unable to flick themselves in and out of otherspace. What then? I heard the growl of the pawns and saw the flails raised and felt the battlefield grow cold . . .

And woke. For a time, then, it remained as clear to me as a picture painted upon plaster, the colors bright as gems. Then it began to dwindle away, as dreams do, only bits remembered. How can I tell it now? Because I dreamed it again, and again as time passed. Then, on the wild-track to Evenor I saw it only for a brief time in the chill dawn and lost it thereafter. But for what time I was cold in fear, thinking I felt the mute anger of the pawns and the touch of hay forks on my flesh.

# 5

# Windlow

I HAVE SEEN no place more beautiful in the world than the high lakes at Tarnoch. There is a wild grandeur about them which caught me hard at first sight of them and held me speechless for long hours as we wound our way down the precipitous drop from the high pass we had crossed at noon. When I say that Silkhands the Chatter-bird was silent also, you will know that it was not only a boy's romanticism that was stirred. At noon the lakes were sapphires laid upon green velvet, the velvet ripped by alabaster cliffs spread with rainbows. As the afternoon wore on, shadows lengthened to soak the green with shade, and still more as evening came so that the whole shone like a diadem of dark and light under the westering sun, the lakes now scarlet with sunset.

The High Demesne stood upon one of the white cliffs over a cataract of water which spun its falling veil eternally into the gem-bright pools below. We came onto the approach road at starshine, the gates of the bridge before us crouching like fustigars, great stony buttresses of paws in the dust and tower tops staring at us from lamp-lit eyes. We were expected. Each of us had felt the brain tickle of a Demon's rummaging, had seen the flare of a Sentinel's signal fire as we rounded the final curve. I found myself hoping that they Read my hunger and thirst and would be hospitable.

I need not have worried. There was no formality to our welcome, only a busy hall-wife escorting us to rooms where baths and food came as quickly as we could be ready for them. "The High King will see you tomorrow," she told us, making off with our boots and cloaks to see what could be done with them, for they were sorely stained with travel. She left us to hot, savory food, generous jugs of wine, and the utter joy of clean, soft beds.

Such was done, I suppose, to put us at our ease, for in the night we were examined more than once. Why I lay awake when the others slept, I don't know. Silkhands was in a room of her own, but Chance, Yarrel, and I shared a room, one equipped with several beds and large enough for a Festival Hall. Perhaps it was Chance's snoring—he did that, trumpeting at times like a Herald and betimes a long, rattling roar like drummers on a field of battle so that I woke in the night listening, waiting for the fifes to join in. So it was I felt the Demon tickling in my brain again and again, deeper, and deeper yet, so that my arms and legs jerked and twitched, and I fought down the desire to scratch. What they were looking for, I don't know, except that Silkhands was wakened by it, too, and came to my bed like a wraith, slim and white in her sleep-robe, rubbing her head as though it ached.

"Oh, they will be at me and at me," she complained. "I carry everything I know and think on the top of my head like a jar of water, but they will go digging and digging as though I could hide a thought away, somewhere."

"Can that be done?" I asked. "Can anyone hide thoughts from a Demon?"

"Oh, some say they can recite a jingly rhyme or think hard on a game or a saying or on reciting the Index or some such and it will hide deeper intents beneath. I have never tried it, and I've never asked a Demon about it. But this digging at me and digging at me means *they* think it is possible at least. I wish they would let me sleep."

"What was it Himaggery said? That the High King might suspect someone was spying on him unless it was a Healer. Maybe they think it anyhow."

"Well, so let them think it. Good sense should tell them better, and I wish they'd give over until morning and let me sleep. Here, let me share your bed, and you can rub my bones."

So she lay down beside me on her belly to have me rub her ribs and backbone. I had done this for Mandor, and it was no different with Silkhands, save her hips swelled as his had not and she made little purring sounds as he had not, and we ended up asleep side by side like two kittens. Yarrel was full of teasing in the morning until she told him to lace his lips and be still. His teasing set me in mind that perhaps, next time, I would not sleep so soon, Silkhands willing, but no more than that.

*     *     *

The Seer was at our breakfast, gauzy masked and all, staring at us with glittering eyes from behind his painted wings. We sighed and tried to ignore him—or her; it could have been a her for it said not a word to us but stared and stared and went away. And, after that an Examiner came to ask us about Himaggery, and about our trip, and about the battle on the plain, and about everything we had thought or done forever. And after that, lunch, and after that an audience with the High King who had decided, it seemed, that we were not intent on damage to himself or his Demesne.

I did not take to him as I had to Himaggery. The High King was a tall man, stern, with deep lines from nose to chin, bracketing his mouth like ditches. His nose was large and long, his eyes hooded under lids which looked bruised. He was not joyed to see us, and all his questing in our heads had not allayed his suspicions, for the first thing we had to do was tell him once more all that had happened to us since we were weaned.

"And you have come from the Wizard Himaggery?" he asked again. "Who is still up to his nonsense, is he? Saying that those who are Kings perhaps should not be Kings, that's one of Himaggery's sayings. Those of us who were born to be Kings do not agree, of course." He watched us narrowly, as though to see how we would react to this. Then he went on, "And you come for what reason?" His voice was as harsh as a crow's, and deep.

"To visit Himaggery's old teacher, the Seer Windlow. Because Himaggery wishes me to use my skill on the old man's behalf, High King, if that would be useful to his aged weakness. Also, I bear messages of regard and kindness and am told to ask if the Seer Windlow would visit Himaggery in the Bright Demesne." All the while she spoke the King nodded and nodded, and behind him his Seer and Demon and Examiner nodded and nodded, so that I thought we were in one of those Festival booths which sell chances to knock the nodding heads from manikins with leather balls, five chances for a coin. Someone Read me, for the King glared in my direction, and all of them stopped moving their heads. I blushed, embarrassed.

"Ah," the High King responded. "Windlow is old. Far too old for such a journey. The thought will please him, however. He welcomes visits or messages from his old students. But—no. He could not leave us. It would be too dangerous for him to attempt it. We would miss him too greatly. But the thought, yes, the thought is kind. You must tell him of that kind thought, even though it is impossible . . ."

He turned to me abruptly. "And you, boy. A special student of my old colleague, Mertyn, eh? Caught up in a bit of dangerous play during Festival, you say, and given let-pass by the Town Council? To come to Windlow's house." He sighed, a deep, breathy sigh which was meant to sound sorrowful but was too full of satisfaction for that. "Windlow's House is much diminished since Mertyn knew of it. I wonder if he would have sent you had he known how diminished it is. No students left, these days. My sons all grown, not that I would have bothered Windlow with their education, the sons of my people gone. I doubt there is one student left there now, but you are welcome to go, you and your servants . . ."

Beside me, I felt Yarrel stiffen. I laid my hand upon his arm and said firmly, "Not my servants, King. My friends. My guides. We could not have come this way without their skills and great courage." The King nodded, waved me away. He did not care. The distinction meant nothing to him. Still, I felt Yarrel's muscles relax beneath my hands, and he smiled at me as we left the hall.

Windlow's House was evidently some distance away through the forest, but the High King was not prepared to let us go there at once. We were to spend several days in the company of his people, his Invigilators, his Divulgers (though we were not threatened with actual torture), his Pursuivants. He was still not sure of us, and he would not let us away from his protectors until he was convinced we could do him no damage. I complained of this and was mocked once more for being naive.

"Why, it's the way of the Game, lad," said Chance. "And the way a great Game often begins. First a trickle of little people across a border, a flow of them bearing tales here and there, bringing back word of this or that. Then the spies go in, or close enough to read the Demesne . . ."

"The High King has Borderers well out," said Yarrel. "I noticed them when we rode in. I doubt a Demon from outside could get close enough to read anyone at the High Demesne. You see how it's placed, too, high on these scarps where no Armiger can overfly it. No, this High King is wise in the ways of the Game and well protected."

"And not inhospitable," said Silkhands, firmly. I was reminded once more that everything I thought and said would be brought to the High King and that it would be better to think of something else. It was not difficult to do, for the High King had done more than set his palace in a place of great natural beauty. He had added to that beauty with gardens and orchards of surpassing loveliness and peopled them with pawns of exotic kinds, dancers and jugglers and animal trainers. At first their entertainments did not seem fantastic or difficult until one understood that it was all done by patience and training, not by Talent. When the dancers leapt, it was their own muscles took them hovering over the grass, not Armiger's power of flight. When the jugglers kept seven balls whirling between their hands and the heavens, it was training let them do it, not a Tragamor's Talent of moving. Once one knew that, there was endless fascination in watching them. Seeing I had no Talent yet, they accepted me almost as one of them, and a band of acrobats taught me a few simple tricks in which I took an inordinate pride. I began to notice the grace with which they moved. Talents are not graceful. Or, I should say, often are not. I have seen some Gamesmen who were graceful in their exercise of Talents, but not many. These pawns, however, moved like water or wind on grass, flowing. It made me wonder why Talents should not be used so.

"Silkhands uses her Talent with grace," Yarrel said, dryly.

I thought about that, and of course it was true. "Himaggery also," I said. "Though I am not sure what his Talent is."

"Perhaps he is not using Talent at all."

Now that was a thought. Like many of Yarrel's comments, it was troubling and dissatisfying and went in circles. So, I thought about learning to do cartwheels and walking upon my hands. Remember, I was only a boy.

Finally, after some nine or ten days of amusement and fattening on the High King's excellent meals, we were summoned to him once more. He was doing several kinds of business on the morning; receiving a delegation from some merchant group or other, buying some exotics from a bird-dealer, and disposing of our visit. He did them all with dispatch and sent us off to Windlow's house with some potted herbs and a caged bird as gifts for the old man. The bird was said to be able to talk, though it did nothing on the journey except eat fruit and mess the bottom of its cage. It was very pretty, but I did not like the way it smelled.

The way to Windlow's House led through forest which had never been burned or cut within memory. The trees loomed like towers, vast as clouds. The trail was needle-strewn and redolent of resin, sharp and soft in the nostrils. Flowers bloomed in the shade, their secret faces turned down toward the mosses, and the trickle of water was around us. We led a considerable pack train from which I understood that Windlow's House was supplied from the High Demesne, unlike the Schooltown I had known with its own farms and merchants. We asked if this were so, and the guide replied that except for garden stuff, meat, milk, and wool, and firewood, which was cut by the School's own servants, all supplies came from the King.

The place was a day away from the High Demesne, set at the top of a south sloping valley, a single white tower with some lower buildings clustered at its foot. It looked very lonely there. However, when we arrived we found the place well staffed. The kitchens were bustling, the stables clean and swept, the courtyard gleaming with fresh washed stones. The men who had come with us unloaded the train, received a meal, and went back the way they had come. Only we were left, with some three or four Gamesmen from the High Demesne who evidently rotated duty in keeping watch on Windlow's House. Of Windlow, we had seen nothing yet. Nor did we until the following morning. Then we found him in the garden behind the tower, wrapped in a thick blanket in the warmth of the early sun.

I had never seen anyone so old before. He was frail, tottery, his face wrinkled like an apple dried in the barrel. But, when he smiled at us we knew his mind was not dulled, for his glance twinkled at us in full knowledge of who we were.

"So, released by my old student the High King at last, are you? I wondered how long he would hold my guests this time. Last time I was lucky to get to see them at all. He protects me, you know." He winked outrageously and drew a serious face. "He says he believes I much need his protection." And his eyes sought heaven in a clown's mockery.

Silkhands laughed and sat down beside him, taking his hand in hers. The rest of us simply sat around soaking up the sunlight, waiting for him to be ready to question us or speak to us, as he chose. It was very peaceful there, and I amended my earlier thought of loneliness. Peace, rather. Content. A vast quiet which was not at all disrupted by the cackle of fowls in the yard or the bustle of the laundress crossing the yard.

"Now," said the old man, "tell me everything about everywhere. My

Talent was never large, and of late it has reached no further than the kitchen garden. I see a plague of moth there, but not until late summer." Once again he winked and drew that clown's face, and this time I knew it for what it was, a cover for more serious things, a nothing to hide thoughts that were deep as oceans. He caught my eye and said, very quietly, "You may speak, lad. Your thoughts are not spied upon here and now. In my garden today, no Demon intrudes."

So, as Silkhands held him by his wrist and worked her way with his aged arteries (so she later said) we told him everything that we knew and guessed about the world outside. We told him especially of the Bright Demesne and of Himaggery's invitation. "He needs you, Sir," we said. "He says to tell you that he needs you, to come to him for now is a time when you should . . ."

At this he was quiet before beginning to talk in his gentle voice about the distance, the time it would take, the weariness of the journey, and of the High King. We all knew that none of it meant anything except his talk of the High King, and we all knew the High King did not intend to let him go. "He was once my student, a proud, haughty boy, Prionde," Windlow said. "He wanted my love, my adoration. What is the Talent of a King, after all, if it cannot inspire adoration? Even then, I think he knew he would be a King. But, what good is a Master who can be summoned and sent like a little tame bunwit? What good a Seer who is blinded to the qualities of those around him? So, I could only give him my teaching. He gave me respect, but no understanding. He would not understand what I so much wanted him to learn, so when the time came that he could, he held me captive to his ignorance, as though to say, 'See, I have power over this Gamesmaster! What are his teachings worth? I command his obedience, and what I do not understand is not worthy of understanding.' So, he preens in his possession of me, for others respect me and he believes his possession gives him prestige. He does not know that he possesses nothing. Nothing. This rack of bones is nothing . . ." He fell asleep with that word, the sudden sleep of the very old. Silkhands stayed beside him, but the others of us wandered about the garden, looking at the thousand varieties of potted herbs, from the tiniest to some the size of small trees. Their combined fragrance in the sunwarmed space made us dizzy.

Later there was more of the same kind of conversation, but Windlow seemed more alert than before. In the evening Yarrel and I chased fireflies in the meadow. I had never seen them before, and we took immoderate pleasure in behaving like infants. Chance drank a great deal of wine and traded tall tales with the kitchen people. It was a generous and pleasant time.

By the third day, Silkhands' work with the old man had made a difference we could all see. He was more alert, more erect, and his questioning of us was quick and incisive. Silkhands said she had made small changes in the flow of blood to his brain, had added a chemical here or there, dissolved bits of cloggy tissue in one place and another, and built small walls other places. "It is only small repair," she said. "I cannot stop age nor forestall death. It will come, still, inevitably. But the small weaknesses and pains of age, those I can ameliorate, and to do it for him is a pleasure. His mind in mine feels like sunshine and rain."

With his incisive questioning came also his own dialogue with himself. We heard for the first time about his own life, about who and what he was.

"They named me Seer," he ruminated, remembering a time long past. "They named me Seer for I knew, as Seers do, what would happen in future times. Small things. A fall of rain here. A wager won there. The outcome of a Game. The life or death of a man. As a Talent it is seldom controllable, never dependable, and yet when it happens, it is unmistakable. Well. Every Demesne must have a Seer or two, or six, or a dozen. The more the better coverage, so they say. And so I became a Seer, attached to a King. That's the best place for a Seer. At least the meals are dependable. Well, Seers have a lot of time on their hands. Seeing doesn't require time. I began to read. Books. Old books, mostly. There aren't many new ones except among certain classes of pawns and the Immutables. I read those, too. Everything. Old books half rotten. Old books all moldy. Old books in pieces. Old books about still older books. You would not believe the trash which accumulates in the cellars of old School Houses or in old towns the Immutables no longer use or in some old ruins. I stopped thinking of myself as a Seer and began to think of myself as a Reader. Well, what one reads, one learns, of course, and it was not too many decades before I realized that all those books were the bits and pieces of a puzzle, shards of a broken pot, clues to a great mystery. It was all there, boys, in the past. Something shaped differently from the way things are shaped today.''

"Were you the only one," asked Yarrel. "The only one reading? How did you get about? All those travels?"

The old man smiled. "Oh, told small lies and begged small favors. Whenever there was a particularly good Seeing, I'd beg a boon of the King, or the Prince, of whomever it happened to be at the time." He smiled to himself at some ancient, innocent villainy. "Seers wander about a good deal, anyhow. It is said to improve the quality of the vision. And, as to your question, boy, no I was not the only one. Most of the others were Necromancers, however, or Shapeshifters, or Rancelmen. You don't know Rancelmen? A little like Pursuivants. Their Talent is finding things which are lost.

"Well, I believed that there was a mystery in the past, far back, in the time of Didir and Tamor perhaps, at the beginning of things. I came to believe there would be a document, a book, a certain book . . . called the Onomasticon, the Dictionary of True Names. I came to believe I would find it, that I needed to find it. Once I could learn the right names for things, you understand, I would be able to decipher the puzzle. You understand?''

"You mean that if there had been different names for things once and we knew what those names were we could . . . know how things started?'' Yarrel seemed bemused by this idea. "But we wouldn't even understand those words.''

Windlow was patient. "We might. They might not be strange words, you see, only words used differently. Or, so I think. And as I read the old books, then older ones and older still, I saw that the meanings of words did change. I stopped being a Seer and became a Historian." He mocked himself with pursed lips, as though we should not take him too seriously. Silkhands, however, took everything seriously.

"That is not a name in the Index, sir. I know all the names in the Index, every one, and that one is not among them . . .''

"I know," he hushed her. "Of course, I know. But it could be there. It isn't a strange word, you see. All of you know immediately what it means.''

Yarrel said, "Well, yes. Among the pawns there are vegetarians who believe in eating only vegetables. And librarians who believe in keeping books. So, a historian would be . . . someone who believes in . . . keeping history?''

"But it isn't in the Index," complained Silkhands. "It has nothing to do with Talents . . .''

"It really does," said the old man. "It takes certain talents to read and study and remember.''

"Those aren't *Talents*," she said.

He shrugged. "Not in today's world, no. But, in History they may have been talents. History. Of the Game. Of the world. Why is a King a King? Why are Sorcerers what they are? Who was the first Immutable, and why?''

"That's religion," I objected. "All of that is religion.''

"Well, lad, I thought not, you see. I thought that if one asked a question and then found a definite answer to that question it was most certainly not religion. I thought it was History. But then, most Gamesmen believe precisely as you do, so it turned out I was not a Historian, after all. I was a Heretic.''

I made the diagonal ward to reflect evil. I didn't believe for a moment he was a Heretic, but it was the automatic thing to do. He didn't have horns, for one thing, and his teeth didn't drip with acid. Everyone knew that Heretics were like that. I found him smiling at me in a pitying sort of way which made me squirm. "I don't think you're a Heretic," I said. "I don't.''

"That's kind of you," he said dryly. "I do appreciate that. I wish the High King would accept your opinion as fact, but he is a very religious man. Still, perhaps if one sends enough Rancelmen into the world to find what is lost, one may come up with some answers. Now, I find myself suddenly very tired . . .''

So, we went away to let him nap in the sunshine among the herb-scent and the birdsong and the laundrywoman's slap, slap, slap of wet clothes and the far-off call of the herdboys in the meadow.

"You know, I understand what he means about words meaning different things," said Yarrel. "In the village when I was a child, when the Gamesmen marched in Game Array we called it 'trampling death.' In Mertyn's House we learned to call it a Battle Demesne of the True Game.''

"I learned to call it True Game as a child," said Silkhands. "But when the stones came through the roof of our house, I called it 'death.' "

What they said was true. If it had been Yarrel beneath the whip, stoking the war ovens, I would not have called it "True Game." When Mandor played me at the Festival, I did not think of it as "True Game." I called it "betrayal" in my head. But still, I was baffled by one thing. "How does he know there is such a book as the one he is searching for?" I asked. "To send all those Rancelmen searching? How does he know?"

"Peter, sometimes I think you do not think," complained Yarrel. "The old one is a *Seer*. He told us so. He has *Seen* the thing he searches for, probably Seen it in his own hands at some time in his future, maybe here in this place which is another reason why he will not come with us to Himaggery."

The old man had been so gentle with us, so twinkly in his glances and humorous in his speech, I had not thought of him as a Seer, not even when he had said it was his Talent. Then, too, he had not the gauze mask with moth wings or any of those appurtenances which lend awe to the Seer's presence. This led me to the thought that it might be easy to pretend to be a Seer. After all, if one pretended to have visions of the far distant future, how would anyone know if they came true or not? This idea was exciting, for it was the first time I could remember myself "imagining." By evening, I had thought up several other ideas which were interesting and quite original. When I tried them out on Yarrel, it seems he had thought of most of them first, and I was embarrassed. Still, I was at least getting the idea.

The next day in Windlow's garden he said, "If I talk heresy to you, you may become tainted and some Demon will pick it from your heads and tell someone, perhaps the High King, who will feel he should do something dramatic about it such as flaying you all, or selling you to pawners for transport to the southern isles or something else equally unpleasant. So, let us talk religion instead."

"Sir," I interrupted him, "did not Mertyn send us to you for Schooling? If we are to be Schooled, surely there is some work we should be doing. If we are not to be Schooled, then we must be careful not to impose upon your hospitality . . ."

He gave me a look which saw through me to the bones of my feet. I felt it distinctly; my soles tingled. "My School House is much diminished, boy. The High King's sons are long gone into the Game, not that they were allowed to learn much from me. The sons of the followers are gone out into the world as well. There are few young at Evenor. The High Lakes of Tarnoch echo no more with childish laughter and the splash of boyish play. I know this. Am I not a Seer? Long since I told Prionde that his Kingdom would dwindle, that he would crow at last like an old cock upon nothing but a dung heap, ashes and broken crockery. So I told him, but I made the mistake of telling him why. History, I said. Not Seeing. Since that time, the visions have come, but he chose to disbelieve them. I tell you, lad, that men will believe if one says, 'The Gods say . . . ' They will believe if one says, 'I had a Vision . . . ' They will believe if one says, 'It was told me on a tablet of hidden gold . . . ' But, if one says, 'History teaches,' then they will not believe.

"Mertyn sent you here for Schooling. So, I'll school you. Himaggery sent you here for his own reasons. They will be fulfilled. So, be patient. Talk to me here in my garden while the sun shines. Chase the firebugs of the meadow in the evening. Flirt with the maidens who keep the tower clean and prepare our meals. Be at peace. The other will come soon enough!"

So, he taught us. "Do you remember the chart of descent from Didir and Tamor?" he asked us. "Can you recite it?" I told him I could not. We had seen it, of course. It hung upon the wall in Mertyn's own rooms, and I had seen it there on the day he had warned me against Mandor, but we had never learned much about it. We had not studied religion much, in Mertyn's House.

"I want you to learn it," he told us, then quoted it off to us line by line for the first of ten or a dozen times.

"In the time of the ancestors was born Didir, and she had the Talent to Read what lay in the minds of all about her, so they named her Demon and she was taken from them. And in that same time was born Tamor, and he had the Talent to rise into the air and fly so that he looked down upon the habitations of men so that they named him Ayrman, which is to say Armiger, and he was taken from them to another place. And from the union of Didir and Tamor was born a son, Hafnor, an Elator. And from the family of Didir after many generations came Sorah, named Seer, daughter of that line. And from the line of Didir and the line of Hafnor came a son, Wafnor, who was the first Tragamor. And of a son of Hafnor and a daughter of Sorah was the first Healer born, a daughter, Dealpas.

"And of the family of Dealpas and the line of Sorah came a son, Thandbar, the Shapeshifter, and of his line Shapeshifters forever to the current time. And from the line of Wafnor came Buinel, Sentinel, and of that line Sentinels to the current time. And of a mating between Wafnor's line and Hafnor's line came Shattnir, Sorceress, and of her line and the line of Sorah came a daughter, Trandilar, a Great Queen, and of her line Kings and Princes to the present time. And, of that line after many generations, came Dorn, a Necromancer, and of his line Necromancers to the present time.

"And of the pawns who served our forefathers was bred a new people, the Immutables, which was planned and done by Barish and Vulpas, Wizards of the twelfth generation of the Game, and from that line have come Immutables to the current time. But Barish and Vulpas were sought by the Council for they had committed heresy in creating these Immutables. So did the Council claim them pawnish and forfeit and sent to have Barish and Vulpas slain.

"But the Immutables which they had made fled into the mountains and the caves and bred there a numerous people, so that when they came among the Gamesmen once more in a later time they could no longer be used and were proof against all the Gamesmen could do."

Silkhands had been writing down as much of this as she could, and I saw Yarrel mouthing it to himself to commit it to memory. That noon we figured it out and put it into a chart on a piece of parchment like the one I remembered on Mertyn's wall. We showed it to Windlow in the afternoon, and he chuckled at it. "Very good," he told us, "but learn it the way I told it to you, for that is the way it is written in the books of religion. If you think of it in that way, the Demons will not think you are fulminating heresy."

That night we were saying that we could not see what all this nonsense was about "heresy." He had not told us anything so very wonderful or different. Chance heard us and said, "Well, do not dwell upon difference, boy, if you want to stay living. A little heresy may be all right in his garden among the pet birdies and the pot plants with the guards half asleep and leagues between this place and the world. You may think what you like here, but how do you unthink it before we go away again? Hmm? And you would have to unthink it, lad, or you would not last a handful of days.''

So we stopped talking about it altogether and got on with what Windlow called our schooling. We reviewed the different sorts of games; games of two, that is, ''dueling,'' and games of intrigue such as that one Mandor had played during Festival, and Battle Games of all sizes from little to great, and hidden games played by Gamesmen for their own purposes with no others knowing of it, and games of amusement, and art games, and the game of desperation. And we reviewed the language of True Game, the labels of risk, King's Blood, Dragon's Fire, Armiger's Flight, Sorcerer's Power, Healer's Hand—all of them. One says ''King's Blood'' to mean that the King is at risk in the play. If the risk is small, one says, ''King's Blood One.'' If the risk is great, if the King will be killed or taken, one says, ''King's Blood Ten.'' I asked Windlow why we did not simply say, ''King's Risk'' or ''Dragon's Risk,'' the same for all of them. It would be much simpler.

''The nature of the artificer is to make things complex, not simple,'' he said, his mouth frowning at me while his eyes smiled. ''We invent different labels for things which are not different and so we distinguish among them. I have read that in the utter past people did this with groups of animals. One would use a different name for each type of animal. It persists still today. We say, 'a coven of crows' or 'a follow of fustigars.' It makes us sound learned. We who are Gamesmen wish to seem learned in all aspects of the Game. So, we use the proper titles for the risks we run. It is more dramatic and satisfying to say, 'Sorcerer's Power Nine' than it would be to say, 'I'm about to smash your Sorcerer . . .' '' We laughed. He asked if we understood. I told him solemnly that I understood well enough. King's Blood Four meant that the King was not seriously threatened, but that some other Gamespiece might be.

''Oh, yes,'' he shrugged. ''There are always throwaway pieces. Talismen. Totems. Fetish pieces of one kind or another. Pawns or minor pieces used as sacrifices because the Game requires a play and the Player is unready or unwilling to play a major piece. And then there are Ghost pieces . . .''

''I thought they were only stories,'' said Yarrel. ''To scare children . . .''

"Oh, no. They are real enough." The old man rearranged the blanket around his shoulders, shifted to a more comfortable slouch in the woven basket chair. "After all, when Necromancers raise up the dead, the dead were once Gamesmen. They would be Ghost Gamesmen, with Ghost talents." At which point, just as we wanted to ask a hundred questions, he fell asleep. Before he woke to continue our lessons, the tower Sentinel cried warning to the House, and we looked up to see a cloud of dust on the long road down from the forest edge through the valley. I was standing beside Windlow when the cry came, and he woke suddenly, his eyes full of pain and deep awareness.

"The High King, Prionde, has sent these men," he said. "He has been made deeply suspicious of us. Someone has come to him bearing tales of guilt and treachery. Guardsmen come to take us all prisoner." I saw tears in his eyes. "Poor Prionde. Oh, pitiful, that my old student should come to this."

Silkhands, who had been sitting beside him, holding his hand as she did for hours each day said, "Dazzle. Dazzle and Borold. They are the ones." She said it with enormous conviction. It was not Seeing, of course. She had no Talent of that kind, but she knew, nonetheless. We all heard her and believed her, and we were not totally unprepared when the dusty guardsmen rode in to gather us up as though we had been livestock, handling the old man with no more courtesy than a sheep, and shut us within the Tower to await some further happening. Silkhands spoke softly to one of them, asking if a Priestess had come to the High Demesne. Yes, one said. A very beautiful Priestess with her brother, a Herald and a group of pawners had come to the Demesne the day before. This was enough for Silkhands. She sat in a corner and wept away the morning.

"But all they need to do is send a Demon to Read us," I protested. "They did it often enough when we were there! They *know* we have no plots against the High King."

Old Windlow spoke softly to us from the cot where we had laid him. "My son, be schooled by me. If your people taught you when you were a child that there are monsters in the wood, you would have believed them. Then, later, if a woodsman had come and said to you, leading you among the trees, 'See, there is nothing here but shadow and light, leaf and trunk, bird and beast. See, I show you. Look with your own eyes.' Though you would look and see nothing, still you would believe there were monsters there. You would believe them invisible, or behind you, or hiding beneath the stones, or within the trees somehow. No matter what the woodsman said, you would believe your fear. Men always believe their fear. Only the strong, the brave, the curious—only they can overcome their fear to peer and poke and pry at life to find what is truly there . . .

"Prionde believes his fear. His Demons tell him we are harmless to him, but he is afraid we have discovered some way to fool the Demons, some way to avoid the Seers, some way to trick the Tragamors. He believes his fear . . ."

There were tears in the old man's eyes, and with both Windlow and Silkhands mourning, Yarrel, Chance, and I did not know what to do except be still and let the day wear out. The guardsmen did feed us and bring us wine and a chamber pot, which we did not need for there were old closets built into the wall of the tower, unused for many years.

The day diminished. We lit the lanterns and sat in the fireglow of evening as the stars pricked the sky above the lightning bugs in the meadow. We grew very bored and sad. There was a gameboard set into the top of an old table in the room where we all were, and I thought it might make things more bearable to play an old two-space game with Chance as we had done when I was a child. I took the pouch from my belt and set the pieces and the little book out, quite forgetting what Himaggery had said about them. After all, I was among friends. Chance was curious at once, full of questions about where I had found them. After a time, Windlow got up and tottered over to have a look while I went on chattering about the ancient room in the ruins. Something in the quality of the silence elsewhere in the room made me look up, words drying in my mouth. Everyone was looking at Windlow, and he at the table, face shining as though lit from within. Perhaps it was a trick of the lantern light, but I think not. He shone, truly.

He touched the carved Demon. "Didir," he said. Then he lifted the Armiger. "Tamor." He laid a trembling hand upon my shoulder, leaning to touch the Elator. "Hafnor," he said, "Wafnor," as he laid his finger upon the Tragamor. He named each of them, "Sorah, Dealpas, Buinel, Shattnir, Trandilar, Dorn." Last he picked up one of the little Shapeshifters and said, "And Thandbar and his kindred. How wonderful. How ancient and how wonderful."

I mumbled something, as did Silkhands, and the old man saw our confusion. "But don't you understand? It is *History!* The eleven!"

Yarrel said, "We are stupid today, Sir. We do not understand what is special about these eleven."

"Not *these* eleven, boy, or *those* eleven. *The* eleven. The eleven Gamesmen who are spoken of in the books of religion. The first eleven . . ."

We looked at one another, half embarrassed, not sharing his excitement. Yes, there had been eleven mentioned in the books of religion. Yes, there were thousands of types of Gamesmen, each mentioned in the Index, each different. What did it matter that these tiny, carved figures were of the first eleven. As we watched him, his wonder turned to caution. He said, "Who knows of these?"

I replied, "Only those of us here, and Himaggery. I showed them to him, and the book as well . . ." I put the little volume into Windlow's hands, half hoping to distract him from this strange passion, for he looked very distraught. It did not have the desired effect. It was only a little glossary, directions for a Game, I thought, written in an archaic lettering, much faded. I had not paid it much attention. Windlow, however, took it as though he took the gift of life from the hands of a god. He peered at it, opened it, caressed the page, raised it to his face to smell of it. He leafed through it, leaning so close to the lantern I thought he would burn himself.

When he murmured, "The Onomasticon . . ." the word meant nothing to me. "All those Rancelmen . . ." he said. "Year after year, hundreds of them sent into the world, to search, search, always looking for it, and it is put into my hands by an ignorant boy—beg pardon, lad, no reflection upon you personally—who does not know what he gives me. Ah. Life is full of these jokes. Full of jest . . ."

Then I understood. This was *the* book, the one he had been searching for. At least, he believed it to be the book. I remembered he was a Seer. If this was the book he had Seen himself having, then it surely was *the* book. He went on talking, almost to himself.

"See. The word *Festival.* In the Onomasticon it carries the meaning 'opportunity for reproduction.' We talk of *School House,* but the book says, 'Protection of Genetic Potential.' We say *True Game.* The book says 'Population control.' We say *King.* The book says . . ."

Yarrel leaned forward to put a hand over his lips. "Sir, is it safe to speak so?" Windlow looked up, dazed, lips still moving. Then he became still, as though listening.

"No. No, lad, not safe to speak so. Not safe to say what I have said, not even to those I have spoken to. I would not go from this place before, for I had Seen myself having the book here, in the old Tower. Also, I have been fond of Prionde as though he were my own sister's son. Now, however, the book is here and my love is a foolish thing, for Prionde has turned against me. Let us leave. Let us get out."

# 6

# Escape

"Out?"

I think Chance said it, though it may have been Yarrel. We were all equally astonished, not at the thought, for each of us had probably considered the idea since we had been shut up in the tower. We were astonished at the matter-of-fact way Windlow stated it.

"Out?" I repeated. "How do you propose that we do that?"

"Why, I have no idea," Windlow said. "Though I do know that we are to get out, or at least that I am, for I have Seen myself with the Book in another place than this. I have the Book, and there seems little reason for delay if we can think of a way to go now . . ."

None of us could think of a reason for delay either, but this did not help us think of a way to get out. The guards who had been sent by the High King showed no signs of relaxing their alert stance. There was an Invigilator among them who, while not quite as thorough in pursuit as a Pursuivant might be, was nonetheless to be reckoned with. At least one of them was an Armiger, which meant we could be seen from above if we succeeded in leaving the Tower but needed to cross the meadows. We had no Armiger of our own to carry us through the air. I wondered if it might be possible to burrow under the ground and said something of the kind to the others. At once Yarrel fastened upon the idea and began wandering about the tower with an abstracted look of concentration.

"That old earth closet," he asked Windlow, "does it go into a pit? Do you know?"

"Why, no." The old man searched his memory. "There is a stream up the valley which was diverted, yes, I recall when the builders were at it. They brought it underground so that it would not freeze in winter. It comes into a tank above the cookhouse and laundry. Then the drains and the rest of it run down under the Tower, here, and the closet empties into it.''

"How?" Yarrel sketched a circular dimension with his arms. "Like a pipe, small? Or a tunnel? How did they build it?"

"Why, a tunnel, small as tunnels go, I suppose. About as high as your shoulders. The walls and floor were laid in stones, I remember, with beams over the top and earth on that.''

"And it comes out where?''

"I don't know.'' He looked almost ashamed, as though he were guilty of some obscure sin. "I didn't pay attention. Do you think it might join the stream again, further down?''

"It would make sense to do that," said Chance. "I've seen it done that way many a time. Probably dumps out into a pool somewhere to overflow into the old riverbed. So I've seen it done.''

Yarrel's eyes were glinting with an adventurous spark. He said, "Well, easy enough to find out. Shall we go together, Peter? You and I? Exploring once more?'' He was remembering when we were very small boys searching the crannies of the attics in Mertyn's House. The memory brought back smells of dust and sunwarmed wood and the look of bats hung on old rafters like black laundry.

We cut a blanket into strips and made rope out of that. Chance lowered us one at a time down the old closet. It hadn't been used in a long time, so it smelled no worse than an old barnyard midden, musty and rank, but not actually foul. Once at the bottom with our little lantern, we kicked away piled rubbish to disclose the turgid flow of water which crept from one side of the shaft to the other.

"I'll wager it's broken or plugged further up," said Yarrel. "Which is lucky for us. There's hardly any water at all.''

Still, there was enough to make the place slimy with mold and greeny slickness on the walls. In places the old beams had broken or half broken to sag down into the already low ceiling of the place and drop clods of mud and things with legs onto our necks. The way turned and swerved inexplicably, but Yarrel said it was probably that they had dug it in a way to miss large outcroppings of rock. Whatever the builder's reasons, it made a confusing way, and I soon lost any sense of the direction in which we moved. However, it was only a short time until we saw a glimmer of light ahead and came up to an opening all overgrown with brush through which the trickle wandered out and down a little slope into a mire. I could hear the river but not see it. We were surrounded by trees.

"Thank the Game Lords, Peter. We are in the trees and behind the stables. We may go from this place undiscovered and mounted, all else willing."

I left him where he was and went plodding back up the little tunnel to be hauled up into the light once more, blinking and filthy. Silkhands wrinkled her nose at me, and old Windlow said, apropos of nothing at all, "I have always wondered how moles keep clean . . ." He did not seem at all surprised when I told them the way was clear and we needed only wait until dusk to meet Yarrel at the tunnel entrance. We then spent some time in devising a way to carry Windlow through the tunnel, for Silkhands demanded that he not be forced to huddle and crouch like the rest of us. In the end we slung him into an uncut blanket, and Chance and I carried him between us. Before we went, however, nothing would do but he must scurry around like a tottery old heron and pack up bits of herb and grass about himself, bladders full of this and wraps of that. By that time the warders were bringing our evening meal, so we shut the closet door and pretended Yarrel was within. When they had gone, we ate two bites and packed up the rest before lowering Windlow into Silkhand's waiting arms. I went down, then Chance, pulling the makeshift rope after him. We abandoned it in the tunnel.

The second trip down the little tunnel was easier for me, for I knew where it ended. Yarrel was not at the entrance, but three saddles were, together with other tack. He had even managed to steal some water bottles from somewhere. We had brought such clothing as we thought we would need, and now waited impatiently for Yarrel to come while Windlow lay upon his back making learned comments about the stars. He seemed to know much about them, as he did about everything, from all that Reading, no doubt. I could hear whickering of horses in the meadow, that coughing noise they make when they are quite contented, but interested in something. It was not long until they came, three of them, following Yarrel as though he had been their herd leader.

"There were only these three loose," he said. "I do not want to risk being discovered in the courtyard where they have stabled the others. These came after me like lambs, no commotion at all, but it means we will have to ride double. Chance, you and Silkhands take the roan, he's a sturdy beast. I will take Windlow upon the gray. That will leave the white for you, Peter. You're among the lightest of us, and it's a small beast. I should not wonder if it had not some onager blood. Still, even double is quicker than afoot.''

We agreed, saddled the animals and led them away through the trees as quietly as owls' flight. Only when we had come over the ridge separating the Tower from the forest did we mount. As we mounted we heard a braying from the south, as of a brazen trumpet, but it sounded only once and was blown away on the wind. We held still for long moment waiting for it to be repeated. There was only an uneasy silence. At last we rode away in the belief our departure was yet unnoticed, leaving it to Yarrel to find us our way in the wilderness—that long way north to Lake Yost and the Bright Demesne.

We would have ridden faster had we known of the tumult behind us. A cavalcade had arrived from the High Demesne; Dazzle and Borold with it, the pawner I had escaped twice before, and a Demon of some considerable power. The trumpet we had heard summoned warders from the surrounding hills. We were pursued long before we knew of it, and we rode through moonlight and shade down the dark hours, guided by what Yarrel could learn of the slope we traveled, marking our way by the river's edge, waiting for enough light to sight some landmark which would set us more firmly upon our way.

Before we had left the Tower, Chance had puzzled over the charts so that he could tell Yarrel of them now; what lay north, what ranges and valleys. All of us knew that this study may have been useless. The charts might be true or false, true as any man's skill could make them, or false as a man's need might draw them. One never knew in buying charts what Game the maker played.

The Demon behind us could not see us or touch us, therefore he could not pick out our thoughts from the countryside. He could only throw his net into the void to skim whatever vagrant pulses were there, to recognize fear, perhaps, or some thought of the pursuer in the mind of the pursued which would tell him that those he sought were in one direction only. Though we did not know it, he did not find us for some time, for we had dropped below the rocky ridge of hills, out of his line of search. Then, at the bottom of the first long slope, we dropped down once more into a maze of little canyons which twined themselves down the long incline like a twisted rope, joining and rejoining among high, flood-washed walls. Once we were into the twisting way we were doubly hidden. He had to leave the search and climb the highest mountain to our west in order to Read us. Once he had done so, however, he found us soon enough, and the pursuers came behind us at twice our speed.

Morning came. We stopped to eat the little food we had brought, and when Yarrel laid the old man down, his eyes opened in surprised alertness. "I see," he said. "They are coming behind us. We are pursued." There was almost panic in his voice.

Silkhands shook him gently, touched his face. "Have you Seen our arrival at the Bright Demesne? Have you Seen us with Himaggery?"

He nodded, still in surprise and with something of shame. "I have seen myself there, dearest girl. So, I assumed . . . Oh, wrong to assume. Wicked to do so. Having seen myself in safety, I did not think for you, not any of you. How vain and mean to let you come this way with so little protection . . ."

We hushed him, comforted him, but I was fearful. They might pursue him, true, but I thought he needed fear little more than being taken back to his garden and his birds. Me? Well, someone wanted me for something, but I did not think I had offended anyone enough that I was seriously in danger. But Silkhands was another matter. Her fate would be a dire one, denounced by her envious sister, accused of treachery by sister and brother to one who would kill at a word and mourn his error later. Windlow had been right. The High King was a bare, hard man who would believe his fear first. I did not want Silkhands lost to him.

Windlow pulled himself together and we made plans, hasty plans, plans with perhaps too little chance of success. Still, it was better than doing nothing and falling meekly into their claws. It was decided that we would split up, each horse would take a separate way down the twisting canyons. As we went, we would each concentrate on playing a game of two-space-jumper in our heads. It was an infants' game, one we all knew, played with two Armigers on an otherwise empty board. If we could keep our concentration clean, uncorrupted by other thought or fear, the Demon following us could not tell us apart. We would all be alike to him, and perhaps the searchers would split up, as well, or failing that, would choose one way and ignore the others.

Then, when we had gone in this way until noon—and it would not be easy to keep only those thoughts for so long a time—we would sit quietly upon the slope of the canyon, wherever we happened to be, chew a certain leaf which Windlow gave us, and "become as one with wind and leaf." I had no great confidence in being able to do this, but Windlow said the herb would do it if we did not fight it. "Let go," he said. "Let everything go. And if you are pursued, they will lose you and pass you by."

If we did it well, there was a chance the pursuit would pass us by and we could hide behind them, protected from their searching minds by a thousand rocky walls. This was the hasty plan, depending much upon luck and resolution rather than on skill, for we had no practice of this deep meditation while the hunters came after us on swift feet.

"Ill prepared or no, we must go on," said Windlow. "If we had waited another day, we could not have escaped at all. We *must* go on." So we did. Yarrel and Windlow went down the middle way, the widest and smoothest. Chance and Silkhands took the western branch, narrow and deep. I went down the easternmost way. If the chart told true, all these ways would spill into the Long Valley sooner or later and we would meet there if we met at all. As we left one another, I was not at all confident of it, and Yarrel's half-pitying glance over his shoulder at me did little to reassure me.

My way led among rocky heaps full of whistling burrowers who marked my passage with alarm sounds. I paid them no attention, being intent upon the Armiger game, jump by jump, trying to keep the whole board in my head and remember which squares had been ticked off. This thought had to be interrupted only a few times to remind the horse that he was expected to keep moving. Once or twice I checked the place of the sun in the sky. I lost myself in the game, truly, able to keep that and only that in mind far better than I would have thought possible.

So—I did something foolish. Only later did I realize what it had been. The canyon I was in was a twisting one. The sun was only a little before noon, in the corner of my right eye. Much later, oh, much, much later I caught it still in the corner of my right eye and said to myself, see, the very sun is standing still. It had not. Nor had I. The way had turned upon itself, the sun had moved past noon, and I was still thinking the Armiger game in my head. It took a moment to realize what had happened. By then, of course, mine had been the only mind which the pursuers could have followed for a very long time.

I knew it was probably too late to do any good, but losing myself in the herb and the silence could at least do no further harm. If anyone had been Reading during the past hour, only my thoughts would have been there. Perhaps I had decoyed some pursuit away from the others. I tried to convince myself this was a good thing if it had happened. The white horse and I went up the slope to hide among the trees where I sat beneath a fragrant, needled tree and chewed Windlow's leaves, concentrating the while upon the grasses around me which moved so gently in the sun and air. In a little time it was as though the world dropped away, and I was me no longer. I was grass. I was air, perhaps, as well, but certainly grass, moved by the wind, gloriously green and flexible in the sun. So time passed and I was not.

Even as I became the grass upon the hillside, they came down the canyon after me. All the others had vanished at noon, gone into nothingness. I had not. The Demon had tracked me as a fustigar does a bunwit. They came down the canyon below me, would have gone on by me into the great valley without seeing me, precisely as planned. Except for the little, white horse.

From wherever I was, whatever I was, the noise of the little horse was no more than a bird call, a beast cry, a little "whicker, whicker, here I am, abandoned and left all alone upon the hillside . . ." The noise which followed, however, was more than that; shouting, calling of men, whistles blown shrill into echoes. Something deep within me wrenched, and I was myself upon the hillside as men clambered toward me. The little white horse had been lonely, no doubt, had thought himself abused, had called out to the mounts of the men who passed below. At that moment somewhere deep inside me it seemed that I knew a way of escape but had forgotten it. I longed to become as the grass again, then mocked myself for so foolish a desire. No matter how convinced my mind might be, the men would see me for what I really was. All this occurred to me within seconds, and without abating that strange notion that escape was there, within reach, if I could only remember . . .

And then they surrounded me. Dazzle was there, Borold fiercely smiling, the lean and villainous pawner, and a Demon. Now I knew the Demon. I had seen him last on Festival night in School Town: Mandor's friend from Bannerwell. I was not afraid, only confused. What could this assemblage want with me? Despite all Yarrel's imaginings, I could not be convinced that I was the real object of their search, could not be, would not be.

Part of the puzzle unraveled at once. The expression of fury on Dazzle's face told me that I had not been her quarry. She was infuriated that Silkhands was not with me, demanded to know where she was. My thoughts said, gone, down the valley, safe to Himaggery's. So I thought, and so they believed. Why should they not? I believed it. Some in the train had been sent in search for old Windlow. I put my head into my hands and thanked the Gamelords that Silkhands was well gone. If she had been found with Windlow, the two escaping together, it would have been considered proof enough of that treachery which the High King so feared. What did it really matter if his old teacher ran away to a better place? It did not, save to the High King, and for no good reason. I turned my thoughts from this as they clambered around me and over me, searching the rocks and trees, sure that the others were not there and yet bound to search for them, bound by the same terror which chained the High King. Doubt. Doubt and more doubt. Fear and more fear. I sighed. The little white horse whickered at me, and I cursed him and his lineage for several generations.

I sat in the landwrack of my dreams and cursed a horse, doing the dreams no good and the horse no harm. So it is with much of life, as old Windlow had said, a jest. We stand at the side of the board and are overrun by the Game of others. When I was younger, I would not have believed that.

# 7

## Mandor Again

THERE WAS A SHRILL, HISSING ARGUMENT, among the Demon, the pawner, and Dazzle. Dazzle, backed by Borold and the High King's men, demanded aid in seeking Silkhands. The Demon refused. Silkhands was no part of his bother. The pawner, meantime, felt ill used since he had not been paid for finding me. Of the three, the only one with any dignity was the Demon, and him I could almost have admired though, at last, even his patience broke upon the shoals of Dazzle's temper.

"If you would dispute, then ride with me to Bannerwell, for it is not my will I do, but the will of another. If you would dispute, then bring your disputation to Bannerwell and submit them there to my Lord and Prince, Mandor."

Ah, said my inner self, so he is not dead after all. I waited for love to well up in me, for gladness to occur, for some emotion to flow as it had used to do and felt nothing. Within was only the memory of grass and wind and a longing for peace. Well, I said to myself, you are tired after all. Tired from all that riding and concentration. Later you will feel something. I saw Dazzle, still screaming at the Demon, saw her real face, at which I shuddered, gulped, so deeply sick I had to put my head between my feet to gulp for air. The pawner mocked at me.

"Well, boy, and what is it with you? You need fear nothing. They mean you no harm."

I told him I knew, I knew, but the feeling of sickness and sorrow did not abate even when we had mounted and ridden off along the twisting canyon in its winding way north. Some good spirit was with me, for I did not think of the others at all but only of my own internal miseries. As a result, the others were not further sought. Wherever they were, they escaped the notice of my captors, and when we reached the long, east-west valley Dazzle and Borold turned eastward and left us. I did not notice they were gone as we turned west and rode up into the hills. It was a winding way, a climbing way, but it was definitely a road leading up and over the high scarp which was the southeasterly end of the Hidaman Mountains, those most lofty of peaks, tonsured in ice, beyond which lay Bannerwell. The setting of the High Demesne in the same range had been beautiful, but the way we traveled was simply wild; fearsome, grim and deep the chasms, remote and chill the peaks. I was glad of the road and felt that the white horse would be punished enough by the time we arrived anywhere. So, that first day while I rode I did not think of anything at all.

At about sunset we reached a way station where horses were kept. I was chained. I had never been manacled before, and I did not like it. They did nothing more than link my ankles with light bonds and that to a tree, but it made me feel less than human. When I complained, the Demon was half kindly about it. "It is only for your own protection," he said. "You are not with us of your own free will, after all. You might decide to wander away in the night. If you were to end up in these mountains alone, well—there are beasts, quadrumanna, chasms. We mean you no harm, and you will be safer with us."

They fed me well. There was water from the snow melt which smelt of pine, fragrant as tea. There were camp buns baked in the ashes and slices of meat from the day's hunt. The Armiger had brought down a small, hoofed animal which I did not know. The beast was called "Mountain zeller," but the meat was named "thorp."

I thought I would not sleep, not for a moment, and woke in the chill dawn thinking that only moments had passed. I had slept the whole night, not feeling the chain, so tired that nothing had moved me during the black hours. So, I thought some about Silkhands and Windlow, wondering if they were well and had gone far on the road to the Bright Demesne. The Demon gave me a puzzled glance, as though what I thought of was not what he expected. Well, what did he expect? I did not even know why I was sought, much less what expectations they might hold. Nothing would be lost in trying to find out. When we were on the way, I kicked the white horse into a clumsy canter and came up to the Demon's side. It was like riding beside a giant. The horse he had taken from the way station was one of those great, feather-footed monsters Yarrel had known at once as Bannerwell bred. I felt that running so dwarfed was good for the white horse. An exercise in humility. I had not yet forgiven him.

"I would feel less distressed, sir, if you could tell me why I was sought? Why we are going to Bannerwell? I have done nothing to warrant enmity from anyone . . ." I let my voice trail off, not quite pleadingly. His jaw was set, and for a moment I thought he would not answer me at all. Then he did, grudgingly.

"You are not sought in enmity, boy. Were you not close friend to my Prince Mandor? Did you know he was hurt?" He cast a curious glance at me out of the corner of his eye, almost covert, as though to see what I thought of that.

"I was told so." It seemed wisest not to say much. "I, too, was hurt." I would not have been human had my voice not hinted asperity. Had it not been for Mertyn, I would have been more than hurt. I would have been damn near killed.

He jerked angrily, the little muscles along his jaw bunching and jumping as though he were chewing on something tough. "Yes. Well, you are better healed than he. There were no Healers in the Schooltown during Festival. It was long before one could be found and longer yet before we found one who was competent." The little muscle jumped, jumped. "He is not healed of his hurt. Perhaps you can aid him in that."

"I am no Healer!" I said in astonishment. "So far, I'm nothing at all."

Jump, jump went his jaw, face turned from me, stony. At last, "Well, your presence may comfort him. As a friend. He has need of his friends."

I could not stop the thought. It bloomed angrily in me as fire blooms on grassland. "He who sought my death claims my friendship! A fine friend indeed!" The Demon caught it, had been waiting for it. He could not have missed it, and he looked down at me out of a glaring face, eyes like polished stone set into that face, enmity and anger wished upon me. I felt it like a blow and shuddered beneath it.

"You were friends once, boy. Remember it. Remember it well, and be not false to what once was. Or regret be thy companion . . ." He spurred his horse and went on before me. I did not see him again until we camped that night. Then he was as before, calm, but did not speak to me nor I to him. In his absence I had thought of Mandor, of how I had once felt about Mandor. No echo of that feeling remained. It was impossible to remember what once had been. For the first time I began to be afraid.

By the time we had come over the last of the high passes of the Hidamans and down the last stretch of road to Bannerwell, I was more frightened yet. I had also forgiven the white horse. He had carried me without complaint or balk, growing noticeably thinner in the process. The sight of my own hand and wrist protruding from my sleeve for a handsbreadth told me some of the reason. While mind and emotion may have been disturbed by all the journeys since Schooltown, body had gone on growing. Measuring my trouser legs against my shins, I guessed myself a full hand higher than when we had left Mertyn's House. My hand shook as I lengthened the leathers to a more appropriate stretch, and my eyes brooded over the close-knotted forest of oaks which fell away from us down the long hills to Bannerwell itself, a fortress upon a cliff, surrounded on three sides by the brown waters of a river.

"The River Banner," said the Demon, reading my question before it was asked. "From which Bannerwell takes its name. The ancient well lies within the fortress walls, sweet water for harsh times, so it is said." He cast me one of his enigmatic looks before rounding up the train with his eyes, counting the men off, arranging us all to his satisfaction. I noted the silence among the retainers, the gravity each seemed to show at our approach. The Demon said, "I was to have returned with you a season ago, boy. I rode from this place due east on a straight road to Schooltown only to find you gone."

I knew he could Read my question, but I felt less invaded if I asked it aloud. "Why, sir Demon? It is not for friendship. You know that as well as I. Won't you tell me why?"

For a time I thought he would not answer as he had not when I had asked before. This time, however, he parted reluctant lips and said, "Because of your mother, boy."

"I have none. I am Festival born." I felt the deep tickle in my head as I said it and knew that he had plunged deep enough into me to Read my inmost thoughts. His face changed, half angry, half frustrated.

"You have. Or had. Her name is Mavin Manyshaped, and she is full sister to Mertyn, *King* Mertyn in whose House you schooled. I Read it in Mertyn's mind at the Festival. There is no mistake. He saw you at risk and knew you for close kin in that moment. He called you thalan, sister's son.''

Turmoil. We approached Bannerwell, but it was someone else seeing those walls through my eyes; someone else heard the thud of the bridge dropping across the moat, the screeching rattle of chains drawing the screen-gates upward to let us through. I suppose mind saw and heard, but *I* did not. Inside me was only a whirling pool of black and bright, drawing me down into it, full of some darting gladnesses and more many-toothed furies, voiced and silent, leaving me virtually unaware of the world outside. There was only an impression of lounging gamesmen in the paved courtyard; the gardens glimpsed through gates of knotted iron, light falling through tall windows to lay jeweled patterns on dark, gleaming wood. The smell of herbs. And meat and flowers and horses, mingled. Someone said, ''What's wrong with him?'' and the Demon answered, ''Leave him a while. He has been surprised.''

Surprised. Well. That is a word for it. Astonished, perhaps. Shocked. Perhaps that word was best, for it was like a tingling half deadness in which nothing connected to anything else. I think I fell asleep—or, perhaps, merely became unconscious. Much later, long after the lamps were lit, I realized that I, Peter, was sitting against a wall in an alcove half behind a thick curtain. The shadow of a halberd lay on the floor before me, and I looked at it for a long, long time trying to decide what it was. Then the word came, halberd, and with it the knowledge of myself and where I was. Someone was standing just outside the alcove; beyond was the dining hall of Bannerwell full of tumult and people coming and going, smells of food, servants carrying platters and flagons. Well. I watched them for some time without curiosity until one of them saw me and went running off to tell someone. Then it was the Demon standing over me, reaching down with rough hands to turn my face upward.

''I did not know it would take you so. I had hoped you knew—that you are thalan to Mertyn, as Mandor is to me . . .''

Thalan. Full sister's son. The closest kin except for mother and child were thalani. The Demon was tickling at my mind and finding nothing, as usual. I almost laughed. If I could not tell what I was thinking, how could he?

He said, ''Do you often do this? This going blank and sitting staring at nothing?''

87

"Sometimes," I admitted from a dry throat. It was true. Whenever things happened which were too complex, too much to bear, there was an empty interior space into which I could go, a place of vast quiet. I seldom had any recollection of it afterward. Perhaps it was not the kind of place one could remember, only a sort of featureless emptiness. I resented his question.

Perhaps the resentment showed, for he made a face. "I can remember that feeling from my own youth, lad. There is little enough we can do until our Talent manifests itself. Before that, there is always the fear that there will be no Talent at all." I nodded, and he went on. "I remember it well. When we are impotent to do anything consequential, it seems better not to exist than to live in such turmoil. If I were not thalan to Mandor, if he were not dear to me as my own soul, I would pity you and let you go. But, I cannot."

"What good will it do to keep me here?" I begged. "I have no power. You tell me I am the son of a Shapeshifter, a famous one at that, one whose name I know. You tell me this and I must believe you, but it does you no good. I have no such power, and if I had, what would it profit you?"

"Perhaps nothing. Perhaps it is no more than a mad idea born out of pain. I have said you will not be harmed, you will not. But Mandor has it in his head you can help him, or get help for him. It may be you can do nothing, and the whole matter will be forgotten, but for now I have done what he begged of me. I have brought you to Bannerwell where hospitality awaits you. Let Mandor himself tell you more . . ."

I had to be satisfied with that. Mandor was not in the dining hall. He was not waiting for me in the room I was given, nor was he in the kitchens in the morning when the Demon and I took early meal together. The Demon asked me to call him Huld, and I did so with some reluctance. We went together up the River Banner to a horse breeder's farm to fetch two animals for the fortress stables, and Mandor was not with us. During all this ride, I longed for Yarrel and was as lonely as I have ever been in my life. Huld was garrulous, a little, trying to make me comfortable, to make me feel relaxed and kindly. I could not. The warmth came no nearer me than the length of his glance, covert and measuring. I did not feel him in my head that day, but I knew I could not prevent his Reading me when he chose. I thanked the Gamelords I was a clumsy boy, a bobble-head, a dreamer with no Talent. If he found my dreams, I would hate it. It would be like being taken for sex, without consent, but he could hurt no one else with what I knew or dreamed, for I knew so little.

To realize that one knows nothing, that one is helpless, that one's highest hope is to be ravished alone without injury to others, that is a lonely feeling. Then even that hope was taken from me.

"I have long admired King Mertyn," said Huld. "He would be sorry to know his mind betrayed you into a Game against your will . . ."

So that was my value! That in my destruction, Mertyn might be wounded! I laughed, a sound like a bray, and Huld turned his face to me, full of surprise and sudden offense. "No, lad. No, I swear. Such a thought had not occurred to me, nor to Mandor . . ."

I brayed again, and when we returned to the fortress I went to the room they had given me and curled on the bed, willing myself to silence. If it were possible, I would have willed myself to death. I felt the tickle in my head and paid it no attention. Let him seek my misery and find it. Let him feel it and know I did not believe him. I think I may have cried like a child. At last I slept.

And in the morning I saw Mandor again.

# 8

# Hostage

HE WAS IN A TOWER ROOM, a room not unlike the one Mertyn had occupied in Schooltown, windowed and well lit. Mandor, however, was surrounded with a luxury which Mertyn would not have allowed: carpets of deep plush, couches and heavy draperies to shut out the evening cold. Mandor's familiar form was posed against the jeweled light of an eastern window. I saw his profile, more familiar to me than my own, the long lashes lying upon his silken cheek, mouth curved into that sensuous bow, his long, elegant hand stroking the silk of his gown. Huld spoke from behind me, "Peter is here, Mandor." No answer. It might have been a form of wax or marble which stood against the light. I waited to feel something and felt nothing.

Until he turned.

Then I thought there had been a masquerade, and they had put Dazzle into Mandor's clothes, for the face which looked at me was one I had seen before, hideous, a gap-faced monstrosity, a noseless, cheekless horror. Vomit boiled into my throat, and I turned away, feeling the Demon's intrusion into my mind, hearing him say, "He sees you, Mandor." I heard a sob, as well, and knew it came from the Prince.

"How?" The word was almost gargled, and my brain formed the unwelcome image of shattered teeth and tongue bending and probing to form articulate speech. "How?"

"He doesn't know." There was a silence during which I swallowed and swallowed, staring at the stones of the wall, not thinking. "Truly, Mandor. He does not know. He simply sees you, that's all."

"Talen'. Bahr?"

"Not any Talent or Power he knows of."

"I was some time among the Immutables," I said, bitterly. "Perhaps I have caught it from them."

"It is not unknown," Huld said to Mandor. "There are some who cannot be beguiled. Or who can be beguiled for a time, but not thereafter. You know it is true."

I turned to confront the horror, but he had turned away, and it was only that matchless profile which I saw. The lips moved. "Nus helb . . ."

"I have told Peter he must help, Mandor. If he can."

"I would help you if I could," I choked. "I would help anyone like you, if I could. But there is nothing I can do. I cannot see you as once I did, feel for you as once I did. I have no Talent, no Power. I have learned from Huld that I am a Shapeshifter's son, but I do not know how that would help you."

"Get her here!" The three words were perfectly clear, not at all garbled.

I laughed. "Get her here? Mavin? For my sake? I've never seen her. I don't know her. If I did, what then?"

"Go out, boy," said Huld, opening the door for me. "Now that Mandor has seen you, and you him, we need to talk, we kindred. I'll come to you later."

I brayed again, that meaningless laugh, that pawn's laugh at the foolishness and stupidity of the world, and I went out into the gardens of Bannerwell to lie beside a fountain and think of Tossa. I summoned her up out of nothing, her colt's grace and great sheaf of gold hair, her warm brown arms stretched wide against the sky. I dreamed her into reality, then I went with her into a world unlike our own and built a place there—built it, furnished it, plowed the soil of it and planted an orchard. I summoned Yarrel to live there, with horses and a bride for him, and Silkhands as well . . .

Only to have the world vanish when Huld came into the place and sat down beside me. "I will tell you what is in his mind," he said, hoarsely. I did not reply, only begged earnestly for him to go away, to leave me alone. He did not, only sighed deeply and began to talk.

"You have seen him. There were no Healers in Schooltown at Festival time. None. It is unimaginable that it should have been the case, but it happened. We took him away, burned as he was. I sent men in all directions to find a Healer; they found one. He was drunk, incapable. All he did was make matters worse. There was no competent Healer to be found.

Days passed. The tissues died. When we found a good Healer at last, it was too late. He was as you see him . . .

"He would not believe. We have brought Healers from as far away as Morninghill, beside the Southern Sea, summoned by relays of Elators and carried here by Tragamors. None could help him appear as once he did without his Talent, his beguilement. That is still as powerful as ever. His people see him as they always have, except for a few of us, except for himself . . .

"After a time, he began to believe he could have a new body, a new face . . ."

"A new body?"

"He began to believe that, perhaps, a Healer could take another body, a healthy, unscarred body, and somehow place Mandor's mind within it."

"That's impossible."

"So they told him. Then he twisted that thought a little. He began to believe that his own body could be *changed,* into another form . . ."

"By a Shapeshifter? But, that's foolish. A Shapeshifter can only change himself, into a fustigar, perhaps, or a nighthorse, or some other animal shape. Shapeshifters cannot take human form other than their own."

"Mavin is said to do so."

"*Said* to do so. And, what difference, said or real? Does he mean to have Mavin pretend to be Mandor? Take Mandor's shape? Move about as Mandor while Mandor stands in his Tower room and pulls the strings?"

"It was his intention to have me Read him, guide the Shapeshifter in changing, guide one to take not only the form, but also the thought . . ."

"To have you what? Read Mandor and the 'shifter at the same time? To somehow impress one upon the other? That's evil nonsense. Where did he get such an idea?"

"Out of desperation," said Huld. "Out of fury and pain and refusal to die or to live as he is."

"And what would happen to Mavin, did she come? Would she be one more Gamesman used up, lost in play? As I would have been lost in play?"

Huld flushed, only a little. "All of us are lost sooner or later. It has never been tried. Who is to say it would not work."

I sneered. "If I were Mavin put to such a test, I would try my best to shift into the form of a waddle-hog."

"She would not if she cared for you, or cared for Mertyn. For, if she did, you would die, and Mertyn as well, and all others whom she might hold dear." He was hard as metal. For the first time I realized that he was quite serious. He might not believe in it, but he intended to do what he could to make it happen. I turned from him, sickened. He went on as though he had not noticed. "Unfortunately, you do not know where Mavin is, or even whether she still lives. Which means we cannot use you to find her. However, it is probable that Mertyn knows, and we do know where he is."

I left him there, unable to bear any more of his talk, his quiet exposition of villainy, treachery, and evil. It was Talisman to King's Blood one if Mertyn did not love me, Talisman to King's Blood ten if he did. We were thalani, and I had never known it. Did he love me? Since that was the condition which would lead to the most pain and confusion, undoubtedly he did. Had Yarrel been with me, he would have accused me of cynicism. What I felt was utter despair, which was not lightened when I found a letter from Mandor on my bed. It was not long.

As Mertyn's love for you led him to protect you, so was I turned into this monster. So, let his love for you be used to turn me back again . . .
You are not Gamesman, now or ever. You are pawn, mine, to throw into the Game as I will. Mavin will come, or you will die . . .

I laughed until the tears ran down my face. So Mandor had not thought such a treacherous thing, according to Huld. By the seven hells and the hundred devils, he had done. He had thought every wickedness, every pain which could be put upon me, and he was bound by his rakshasa to bind me with each one and every one until I was dead. Well, if I were dead, they could not put anything upon me. I left the room as silently as possible, creeping through the still halls to the twisting stair which led into the Tower. The stair went past Mandor's rooms and on, up onto the parapet, twenty manheights above the rocks at the river's edge. It was all

I could think of which could be done swiftly, and I prayed that someone would know I had not killed myself out of dishonor.

At Mandor's door I paused. Huld's voice was raised within, almost shouting, and I could hear it clearly. "And I tell you once more, Mandor, that he knows nothing of help to you, nothing. Do you think I would lie to you if there were any hope? Do you not dishonor yourself in this treacherous use of one who loved you? You dishonor me!"

Ah, I thought, the Demon may do Mandor's will, but he gets no joy of it. I went on, up past the little spiraling windows, out through the low door onto the lead roof, covered with slates. I did not see the figure leaning upon the parapet until I had thrown my own leg over and was ready to leap out into waiting oblivion. By then it was too late. I was caught in huge arms and held tightly as eyes glittered at me through winds of paint. A Seer. His shout went up. Armsmen of one kind and another came in answer. I was carried down the stairs to confront Huld where he stood just outside Mandor's door.

"That was foolish, lad," he said sadly.

"I thought not," I answered him. "Death is easier than this ugliness you do."

The huge Seer behind me thrust past to kneel at Mandor's feet. I could tell from the way he did it that he saw Mandor as Mandor had been. Strange. One who could see into the future could not see clearly in the present. "My Prince," he said, "I have Seen this boy . . ."

There was an inarticulate shout from Mandor. The Seer reacted as though he had heard it as a question.

"Yes, my Prince. I have Seen the boy in a form other than the one he now wears, Seen him crowned, as a Prince . . ."

Huld turned a burning face on me, flushed red with a great surfeit of blood. Was he angry? I could not tell. Some emotion burned there which I could not read even as I felt him digging in my head, deeply enough to hurt. I cried out and he withdrew.

"There is no knowledge of it in him . . ."

"There 'ill ve," Mandor said.

"Yes, my Prince. There will be," agreed the Seer.

Mandor turned into his room, slamming the door behind him so that it raised echoes down the stair, sounds beating upon our ears like the buffeting of bat wings. Huld motioned the guards who were holding me, and they followed him down into the depths of Bannerwell, below the pleasant gardens, into the stone of the cliff itself to a place where they chained me in a room of stone. I sat stupidly, staring at the chain.

Huld said, "You will not be able to harm yourself here. A guardsman outside the door will watch you always. This place is warm and dry and you will be well fed. You will not suffer. The Seer has Seen your future, Seen you in the guise of the Prince. This means his hope is not false, not impossible. Somehow through Mavin or through your inheritance of her Talent, Mandor's hope will be brought to fruition. You understand?"

I did not say because I did not understand. It was all foolishness, stupidity.

"For your own good, I would suggest you focus your attention upon that Talent. For the good of others as well. Mandor is impatient. He will apply every encouragement he can."

I will not weary myself with telling of the next days. I did not know what passage of time it was. There was only torchlight there, and no time except the changing of the guard and the bringing of food and the emptying of the bucket into which I emptied myself. There were quiet times during which I forgot who I was, where I was, why I was. There were terrible times when Mandor came, his face unveiled, and sat looking at me, simply looking at me for what seemed hours. There were times when he spoke and I could not understand him, and he was maddened by that. There were times when he struck me, enough to cause pain, though not enough to wound me permanently.

There were times when Huld came, came to argue, remonstrate, dig into my head to see what went on in there. Little enough, the Gameslords knew. There was little enough to find. When I was let alone I made long, dreamy memories of Tossa, summoned her up beside me and made lovers' tales and poems to her. I did not think of Mertyn or of Mavin. I did not think of Himaggery or Windlow. I did not think, in fact, more than necessary to keep me alive.

There were times when the torches went out and I was left in darkness. There was one time when I refused to eat, and they brought men to hold me down while a Tragamor forced food down my throat. After that, I ate. There was the time that Mandor—no, I do not need to remember that. He had to tie me, and I do not think he got any pleasure of it.

I will not tell of that time, for it was the same over and over for a long while. Instead, I will tell of what happened at the Bright Demesne. I did not learn of it until later, but it fits the tale here, so why should it not be told:

When those who captured me turned west down the great valley, they were seen by Yarrel and Windlow from a post high on a canyon wall. When we had gone, they sought Silkhands and Chance, finding them about eventime. They did not wait on morning, but rode swiftly east toward the Bright Demesne. At first light Yarrel told them they rode hard upon the tracks of two other horses, and they knew at once it was Dazzle and Borold. The four of them together would have been no match for Dazzle and Borold in a rage, so they took pains not to ride on the heels of those who went before. They left the road and made their way slowly through the forests, arriving warily among the outlyers of the Bright Demesne a full day after Dazzle and Borold had come there. This was about at the same time that I rode on the laboring little horse over the highest pass of the Hidamans on my way to Bannerwell. Once within Himaggery's protection, Silkhands feared no more but went to him as swiftly as she could with the tale of Dazzle's perfidy and my capture upon her lips.

I was told later that Himaggery's meeting with old Windlow was joyous, full of tender feeling and gratitude for the old man's safety, the meeting marred only by the story of my capture and of Dazzle's infamy. Dazzle had already been sent away once more by Himaggery, sent into the eastern forests on a contrived "errand" and could not now be found without great effort. As it was, they knew only that I had been seen in company with a pawner and a Demon and some others, riding westward to some unknown destination. The horses had been of the common type which are ridden by all the mountain people, so Yarrel was of no help.

They conferred at great length about finding me, discussing this possibility and that. Had I been taken for ransom? If so, by whom? Had I been taken for some other reason? If so, what? They engaged in recriminations of themselves that Dazzle had not been Read when she returned, but Himaggery had only thought to be rid of her, not where she had been in the interim.

"My fault," he said, not once but many times. "I should have realized that she would have been involved in any mischief or wickedness which she could find or create. Why did I not have the sense to examine her, to question Borold. He would not have had the wits to oppose me . . .''

Yarrel, impatient at this long delay, simply demanded help in finding me. Himself a pawn, though that was not generally known, he summoned the courage to demand that Himaggery exert the utmost effort in finding me and aiding me if that were needed. No, I have not put that right. Yarrel did not need to summon courage. He simply was courageous. I miss him greatly in these later days.

Then was the full power of the Bright Demesne assembled to the service of Himaggery. I have visualized it so many times. It happened in that great room, the audience hall, where we had first sat for our stories. Beneath the floor the hot waters of the springs flowed in channels, making the stones mist with steam, for they had been recently mopped for the occasion. The walls of that room are white, mighty blocks of stone polished to a high gloss set in curving bays, each bay lighted with tall windows, one above the other, each bay separated from its neighbor by a marble pillar on which vines are carved, and little beasts and birds, the whole inlaid with gems and gold and other precious materials so that it glitters in the light. Six or seven manheights above, the dome curves up in a sweep of polished white toward the Eye, a lens set in the center of the dome. It is cut in a way to break the light, making small rainbows move across the floor and walls as the world tilts. At one side are a pair of shimmering doors, and at the other is Himaggery's seat, a simple stone chair pillowed with bright cushions and set only high enough that he may be seen and heard by all. On this morning he had summoned all the Seers, Demons, and Pursuivants of his Demesne and dependencies, and with them the Rancelmen and others whose Talent it is to seek and find. They came into that great room, a wide circle of them, with another circle inside that, and inside that a third, each Gamesman seated upon a cushion, his hands linked to those on either side, or her hands linked it may be, for many were women. In the center were a group of Elators. Silkhands, who had been keeping to her room until Dazzle was gone, Chance, and Yarrel were there a little behind Himaggery where they would not be in the way. Beside the seat was a bronze gong in a carved frame, and Himaggery took the striker between his hands as he spoke to the assembled Gamesmen.

"These two, Yarrel and Silkhands, know Peter well. Chance has known him since he was a babe. You may take the pattern from them and then search wide. The boy was seen last some three days ago, in company with a pawner and Demon and some company of other Gamesmen, riding west down the Long Valley. Seek well, for this Demesne is honor bound to find him . . ."

He struck the gong. Under the assembly the floors shuddered as workmen below shifted gates to allow the boiling water of the springs to surge beneath the stones. It grew hot, hotter, but only for the moment. In that moment the linked Gamesmen began to seek, each tied to another, each pulling the power of the springs below him, each sending mind into the vast forests of the Hidaman Mountains, west and north, west and south, seeking, seeking. But first . . .

To Silkhands it felt as though she had been struck by some gigantic wing, monstrous yet soft. There was none of the normal Demon tickle in her head. Instead there was a feeling that her mind was taken from her and unfolded, laid out like a linen for the ironing, spread, smoothed, almost as though multiple hands stroked it to take out each wrinkle. Then it was folded up again, just as it had been, and put away.

Yarrel and Chance did not describe it so. To them the search came as water, as though a stream ran into and away from them, bearing with it all manner of thought and memory so that they were stunned and silent when it was done, unable for many moments to think who they were or why they were in that place. This was "taking the pattern" as Himaggery had said, directing his searchers to go on the trail, like fustigars on the scent. They, with the scent of me in their nostrils, went out into the world to find me.

Later no one remembered who found the first sign. It might have been a Rancelman, one used to seeking the lost, or more likely a Pursuivant who saw through Yarrel's mind the site of that canyon entrance. In the center of the audience hall sat the Elators. When a place could be sufficiently identified to guide her there, one would flisk out of sight, gone, directed by that linked Talent and her own to that distant place. There she searched, found the tracks which the Pursuivant said must be there, saw the direction they went, looked there for a landmark and returned. The landmark was passed through some Demon to another Elator who went as the first had gone, this time to the farther point.

At one point a Seer called out as a sudden Vision interrupted the slower jump, jump, jump of Elators. "Further North," he cried, "toward the White Peaks." Thus the search leaped forward until an Elator found the road once more. There were false landmarks as well as true ones. Sometimes the Elators overshot the mark and came out in places far from the road, sometimes the road branched and they guessed wrong. Sometimes the picture was dim and confused as it came from one into the minds of the others. The pace became slower. The room became hotter. There was no lack of power, but the bodies which used it were growing weary. Himaggery struck the gong once more, and the water-gates beneath the floor shuddered closed.

"Eat," ordered the Wizard. "Sleep. Walk in the gardens. We will meet once more in this room at dusk."

He invited Silkhands and Yarrel to join him with old Windlow in his own rooms for the meal. Silkhands was full of comment and chatter, as always.

"I do not understand how this is done? What Game is this? I have not heard of this."

"No Game, Healer. We are not playing. We are seeking a reality, a truth. We have not done it often, not often enough to become truly practiced at it. We have done it only in secret, not when mischief makers were about. If you had not insisted in being always with Dazzle, you might have taken part before this time."

"But what is it? How is it done?"

"To understand, you must first understand a Heresy . . ."

"Oh, you two and your Heresies. I have yet to understand what either of you mean by Heresy. You have said nothing I have not learned or thought a thousand times . . ."

"There are eleven Talents," said Himaggery.

"Nonsense," she contradicted him. "There are thousands. All in the Index, all of them. Each type of Gamesman has his own Talent."

"No, there are only eleven."

"But . . ."

"You have asked, now be still and let me say. There are only eleven, Silkhands, twelve if you count the Immutables."

"The Immutables have no Talent!"

99

"Indeed? They have the power to mute our Talents, to be themselves unchanged no matter what we attempt to do. Is that not a Talent?"

"But, that's not what we mean when we say Talent . . ."

"No. But it is what is true. It is in Windlow's book."

"The Index lists thousands. I have learned their names, their dress, their types, how they move, their Demesnes, all . . ."

He turned from her to the mists and the fruit trees which mingled outside his windows. "Healer, your Talent is one of the eleven. You can name the others if you would. They are those which you have recently learned at Windlow's House."

"You mean what Windlow said about the First Eleven, from the religious books? What has that to do with . . ."

He laughed. "Silkhands, you are such a child. Do you know that elsewhere in this world there is a group of very powerful Wizards who are known, collectively, as the Council? Did you know that they have taken upon themselves to assure that there are no heretics in our world? None who speak of arrangements not found in the Index? None who talk of the Immutables having Talent? You are so innocent. Here, we can talk of it. Here you are safe, in the Bright Demesne. But you will not thank me for it.

"It was Windlow who saw it, long years ago, and taught it to me, quietly, so that it should not come to the attention of the Guardians, those of the Council whose interest it is to maintain things always as they are. It was Windlow who saw that the books of religion are actually books of history, that what was said about the descent of our forebears was indeed true.

"We are told of Didir, a Demon. Imagine, Silkhands, imagine Yarrel, a world in which there were no Talents. It will be easy for you, Yarrel. Imagine a world all pawns. No power but the power of muscle and voice, persuasion and blows, nothing else. Perhaps some power of intelligence, too. Windlow and I argue about that."

"There would be intelligence," said Yarrel. "There is power in intelligence. I know. I can imagine your world."

"Very well. Then, imagine that into this world is born one woman who can read the thoughts of others. Didir. Why is it that we call them Demons? Those who read thoughts? Hmmm? We speak of evil godlets as demons, wicked spirits are demons. Why, then, is a Reader a Demon?"

"Because they would have considered her an evil spirit, an evil force," said Yarrel. "They could not have helped but feel that way. It would have been terrible for them to have their thoughts wrenched out into the open, laid before others . . ."

"Ah, yes. Even so. And the books of religion go on. They say that one was born named Tamor, an Armiger. The oldest books say Ayrman. Why is that do you suppose?"

"Because he could fly," said Silkhands. "Armigers can fly."

"And what would the world of pawns think of that?"

"They would wonder at him," said Yarrel. "And fear him, and perhaps hate him. I wonder that they did not kill him."

"Windlow says not," Himaggery went on. Old Windlow nodded where he sat. "Windlow says that *they,* the pawns of that world took Tamor and Didir to some other place, away from the world of the pawn."

"What other place?" said Silkhands. "What place is there?"

Himaggery shook his head. "Who knows? But Windlow believes this because he says it makes sense out of much he has read. He says that Didir and Tamor were sent away, and that thereafter they mated with one another, and either they or their offspring mated with some of the pawns who went with them. From their mating came Hafnor, an Elator. The Talent of an Elator is to transport himself, or herself, from place to place. Generations later, from the family and lineage of Didir came the first Seer, Sorah. And so forth. And when you have listed them all, you have eleven."

"But there *are* more. There are Heralds, and Witches, and Rancelmen, and . . ."

"The Witch has three of the eleven," said Himaggery, patiently. "Firemaking, beguilement, and the power to store power, as Sorcerers do. A Witch has none of these in the strength that those who hold them singly do, but the witch has all three."

"And Heralds?"

"Heralds have the power of flight, but only in small, and the power of Seeing, also in small, and a slight ability to move things with their minds, as Tragamors do."

"And Rancelmen?"

"Seeing, Reading the thoughts of others, both in small, and a natural curiosity which seems to have little to do with Talent."

Yarrel said slowly, "Reading, Seeing, Flying, Transporting, Moving, Storing, Healing, Firemaking, then—what would you call it?"

"Beguilement, the power of Kings and Princes. A power to make others believe in one, follow one. Sometimes the Talent is called 'follow-me.' And this leaves two more: Shapeshifting and Necromancy. Those are the eleven. There are no others, except for the one held by the Immutables."

"Which the books of religion say was created purposefully by two Wizards, Barish and Vulpas." Yarrel was very thoughtful. "I can imagine why they did it. They probably saw all the people without Talents being eaten up in the Game, and they felt it was wrong. So, they created a power which would protect the pawns from harm, and they gave it away. But only to some," he concluded bitterly.

"Perhaps there was not time to give it to all," Silkhands said.

"Perhaps they were prevented from doing so," said Windlow. "When first I read of that act, I wondered why two Wizards would behave so. Then, at last, I knew. A Wizard would do such a thing when he learned the word *Justice*. It is a very old word. It is in my book. It means to do what is right, to correct what is wrong, to find the correct way."

"Correct?" asked Silkhands. "I do not understand correct."

"No, we do not know the word," Himaggery agreed. "In the Game it is only the rules which matter. The rules are always broken, and there are few penalties for that, but it is still the rules which matter. Few care for what is honorable. None cares for what is right or just. They care only for the rules. Windlow says the rules were created to bring some order out of chaos, but over the centuries the rules became more important than anything else. They became the end rather than the means. Now, I have taught you heresy. There are those in the world who wish the Game to continue as it has been played for generation upon generation. There are those who do not care for the idea of justice—and well they might not. Thus far we have been fortunate, the Bright Demesne has been fortunate. We have not been challenged in a Great Game. We have made common fortune with some few Immutables and spoken with them from time to time on neutral ground. Much do they suspect us, however. We hold a tenuous peace. It cannot last forever, and it may be that Peter's abduction is the falling pebble which starts the avalanche.

"Windlow Sees, and he tells me to have good heart. I trust him with my life and love him with my soul, as though we were thalani. But I am not courageous always," confessed Himaggery. "I have not that Talent."

"Lord," asked Silkhands, "what Talent do you have? What is the Talent of Wizards?"

He laughed at her and rumpled her hair but did not answer. "If I have any, it is to link Gamesmen together to pursue this word, this justice. If I have any at all, it is that."

# 9

# Shapeshifter

THE ASSEMBLED TALENTS OF THE BRIGHT DEMESNE went at it again at dusk, and again on the morning following. By noon of the second day they had tracked me to Bannerwell, and one Seer at least told them I was alive within its walls. It took them a day or two to send a Pursuivant to a place nearby, for though Pursuivants have the power of transporting themselves, as Elators do, it is not as potent a Talent. They have the power of Reading, as Demons do, as well, but again it is not as intense. Thus, my friends were not really surprised when the Pursuivant returned to say he could pick up thoughts which he believed were mine, but he could not be sure. He had, however, picked up a clear reference to Mertyn from several sources in and around Bannerwell, and this was enough to make some in the assembly turn their attention toward Mertyn's House in Schooltown.

From that moment it was not long until they discovered my parent-age—or should it be motherage. Strange, I had not thought of that before. I knew that Talents were inherited, that they might be traced both from the female and male parent, but even when I had heard that I was Mavin's son, I had had no curiosity about my father. It was, even when I thought of it, only a passing thought, and that was much later. As soon as Himaggery was told of it, he sent an Elator to Mertyn, begging him to travel to the Bright Demesne. He broke the rules in doing so. Elators do not, by the rules, carry messages from one Demesne to another. That is left to Heralds or, on occasion, Ambassadors. Though none of us knew it, it was fortunate Himaggery held the rules so in contempt. Mandor's own Heralds were even then on the road to Schooltown.

They arrived to find Mertyn gone. He had taken a swift ship from Schooltown to sail across the Gathered Waters and down the Middle River to Lake Yost. He had not left word with any in Mertyn's House where he had gone. Himaggery's Elator, who had set Mertyn on the road, offered no help to Mandor's Heralds, who had no choice but to take lodging in Schooltown and await Mertyn's return. Eventually they gave up and returned to Bannerwell to face Mandor's wrath. The day they returned was a day I do not wish to remember.

Meantime, each day Himaggery would seek out Windlow, who sat in his pleasant rooms over the garden reading my book, to ask him what should be done next. The old man would close his wrinkly eyes and lean back against the side of the window, the sun falling sweetly on his face in quiet warmth, the mists drifting up and away as they always did, and invoke a long silence during which he searched for Seeings. Then at last he would open his eyes and say what he could.

On one day it was, "Peter is not in immediate danger, Himaggery. However, he is desperate, and very lonely, and without hope."

Silkhands was in the room. She said at once, "We must go to him. Now. While the rest of you figure out what it is you will do . . ." Himaggery began to object, but was interrupted by the old man.

"No. Don't forbid her, Himaggery. That may be a very good idea. Healers are generally respected, almost always safe. If she goes with Yarrel and Chance—a Healer riding with two servants? Can you pretend to be servants?" He asked it of Yarrel, knowing Yarrel's pride.

"I can't pretend," said Yarrel. "I can be." And he bowed before Silkhands as though he were her groom. "If Silkhands will learn her part."

"Oh, I will do," she pledged.

So, the three of them set out for Bannerwell, not over the high passes of the Hidamans, as I had come there, but up the western side of Middle River and then along the foothills west in the valley of the Banner itself. Before they left, Himaggery took Yarrel aside and told him of other Seeings which Windlow had had recently.

"There is to be a Grand Demesne, lad. A great Game. Silkhands must not know of it, for they will Read her in Bannerwell. They will not bother you or Chance. Pawns are not considered in such matters. But you must know, in order to plan . . ."

While those three left the Bright Demesne, Himaggery plotted and plotted again, and Mertyn sailed toward him, and Mandor raged, and I sat in the rocky cell and dreamed myself elsewhere or hoped I could die. All of us were thinking of me. No one was thinking of Dazzle.

She, however, returned from her errand to learn that Silkhands had come and gone, which threw Dazzle into a compelling fury. She was full of wrath, full of vengeance against all those she fancied had wronged her, with Borold offering a willing ear to all her fancies. Thus, in a quiet dark hour, Dazzle and Borold rode out on Silkhands's trail. Perhaps they had murder in mind. Perhaps she feared what Himaggery would do if Silkhands were hurt directly and so plotted some more indirect revenge. No one knows now what she thought then, save only that she meant Silkhands no good.

Time passed. I knew none of this. I knew nothing save my own continuing sorrow and despair.

Then, one time I was sitting on the cot in the cell where they chained me, the room dim and shadowed from the torch which burned smokily in the corridor outside the grilled door; the guard who stood there half nodding, catching himself, then nodding again; the place silent as the moon, when there was a flicker of movement at the edge of my eye. There was only stone there, nothing could have moved, so I turned my head, surprised, to see an Elator framed for an instant against the rock. He gave me one sharp look and was gone. I thought I had imagined it, had imagined the slim form in its tight wash-leather garb, close-hooded, appearing almost naked in silhouette. But, could I have imagined that furtive, hasty glare? The matter was resolved at once, for the guardsman shouted and ran away down the hall. He had seen it, too.

They came then, Huld and Mandor, Huld to trample through my mind with heavy feet, scuffing and scraping, trying to find what was not there once more, Mandor to rail and spit and rage, his horrible face made more hideous still in wrath. I choked and was silent and let them do it. What else could I do? Each time it happened, I was amazed anew that the guards did not see Mandor as I did. I knew from their conversation that none in Bannerwell saw him as I did except Huld. To them all he was still the shining Prince, the elegant Lord. I had one guard tell me that he envied me, *me,* for it was said abroad that the Prince had loved me.

"He does not know," Huld told Mandor for perhaps the thousandth time. "There may have been an Elator, but Peter does not know him or whence he came or for what reason."

There was an inarticulate shout from Mandor which Huld seemed to understand perfectly. "No, Mandor, I cannot be mistaken. If someone searches for the boy, then he does so—or *she* does so without the boy's knowledge. How should he know? How long have you kept him like this? Who would have informed him of anything? Surely you do not think he has become a Seer. Let our preparations for Great Game go forward! I doubt not we will be challenged, and soon, but let the boy alone!"

There was another slather of spitting words. Mandor's attempts at speech sounded to me like fighting tree cats, all yowls and hissing. Huld replied again, "It is possible that Mertyn searches for him, possible that Mavin searches for him, possible even that the High King searches for him, if we are to believe that Witch we brought with us from the High Demesne. All that is possible. But it is *certain,* your Seers tell us, that someone has started a Great Game and Bannerwell is being moved upon. What then? Direct me. I am your thalan and your servant."

"Get Divulger," said Mandor. Once in a great while his words were very clear, and this was one of those times. "Get Divulger."

Huld shouted. "He cannot tell you if he does not know, not even under torture."

"He can shif'," said Mandor, stalking away down the echoing corridor. "Shif' or die."

Huld said nothing, swallowed. Bared his teeth as though in a snarl, but it was not at me. At length, he said, "This is not honorable, Peter. I would not command it were I not commanded to do so. He orders you put to torture in the vain hope that pain will force Talent to come forth, if there is any to come forth. Some say that Talents emerge when needed to save us. I do not know if that is true. I beg your pardon . . ."

And he left me. Vain wish, I thought, oh Huld who has no honor. Vain wish if you will do as you are bid no matter what you are bid. My mind was afire, thinking up and discarding a hundred schemes. What might I do? What might I say? I did not want to meet torture, knowing as I did what it meant. I had seen much from my rocky cell, more than needful, for the torture dungeons lay below and men had been dragged to and fro before my eyes. I thought of Mertyn, of Himaggery, wondered if they would send help, knew it would come too late. I thought of Chance and Yarrel, wished they could comfort me. I thought of old Windlow, Windlow and his birds and his herbs . . . and remembered. Windlow's herbs. I had still in my pocket leaves of that herb he had given us in the canyons, that herb which had let us leave our bodies to become as grass.

I tugged out the scrap of cloth, heard men coming, fumbled the leaves out and into my mouth, returning a few to my pocket. If I could keep my head and there were a few moments of peace, perhaps I could separate myself from my body enough not to feel pain. Footsteps approached. The Divulger peered in through the grill, a hairy man, arms bare to the shoulder, black hood across his eyes, leather-shirted with high boots.

"Come out," he said, and I came, following him like a lamb, like a lamb. We passed the guard. We were alone. He at my side, face set in contempt. He of the hard body, heavy body, muscular arms, hairy neck, slope of shoulder, flat skull, small eyes peering through the half hood, heavy, the feet slap, slap, slap, the feel of the soles as they hit the stone, the curve of a toenail biting into the flesh with a sullen pain, the broken skin on the knuckle of the right hand, memory of the taste of morning grain furring the square, yellow teeth, running my tongue across them to feel the broken one where a victim had lashed out with a stone in his hand, not like this boy, only a baby, wouldn't last a minute on the rack, would come to pieces like a stewed fowl . . . and turned to look at the victim to see himself as in a mirror, himself looming hugely in the corridor, to feel the torch crash down across his brow, the metal band crushing out thought, life. Then there was only one of us in the corridor alive, and one of us dead, and both of us the same, the same.

It was not until I saw my hand holding the snatched up torch that I realized something had happened; not until I turned to see my face reflected in the metal plate over a cell peek-hole that I knew what had happened. It was true. I had a Talent. I had inherited from Mavin Many-shaped who was said to take human form other than her own. Oh, yes. Indeed. As I had done.

And not only the form. For there, open to me as though in a book, were all the memories of that morning, the man's own name, faces of those he knew, bits and pieces of the fortress laid out as though on a map. I tried to remember something further back, his childhood, his parents, but there was nothing there. No. Only a few, loose thoughts, a sufficient baggage to carry about for a few hours, names, places, faces, and one's own job. I had been thinking of that with anticipation, I the Divulger. I, Peter, was only frightened by it. What now? We two still occupied the corridor, one alive, one dead.

Well, I would be safe so long as they thought me the Divulger, one Grimpt by name. Thus, they must not find the other one, the original Grimpt. I caught the body beneath the arms and tugged it along the corridor. The memories which I had taken over with the body were enough to guide me. The torture dungeon lay this way, and in it were pits, oubliettes, places where bodies might be hidden for a time or lost forever. Before I disposed of him, however, I took inventory of my own form because something was not . . . ah, my clothing. I had taken the Grimpt form well enough, but not the form of the clothing. My own rags still hung on me, the trousers ripped at the seams by a sudden excess of flesh. I peeled them off and stripped him to put his clothes on me over my shirt. Never mind the stains of blood. There were others, older, dried to crusts of brown. That, seemingly, was part of the costume. I remember the herb which Windlow had given me. There was a little of it left, not much. Perhaps enough to make another shift, I thought, and then it might not be needed after that.

Come to, I encouraged myself. There will be time enough to think of such things later. Now it is time to assure safety. So, dead Grimpt went down the oubliette. Live Grimpt went back up the corridor to a place where he might call to the Guardsman outside Peter's cell door.

"Hey. You there, what's yer name, Bossle is it? Well, run on up t'the kitchen and bring us a mug. I'll put what's left of this'un back to bed. G'won now, it's thirsty work enough." The man was only a common guardsman in a rust-splotched hauberk with little more Talent than a pawn, a Flugleman perhaps. He opened his mouth to argue, decided against it, leaned his weapon against the wall and went clattering up the stairs. I moved to the open cell, went in, curled the thin mattress beneath the blanket as though someone lay there, put Peter's shoes beside the cot and his trousers under the blanket, showing a little at the edge, came out of the place and locked it. I met the guardsman at the foot of the stairs, gave him the key, told him a filthy story which I found in Grimpt's mind ready to be recounted, drank the beer, slapped him heavily upon his back and went up the stairs whistling tunelessly.

Huld was waiting for me at the top of the stairs. Grimpt's mind said ''bow,'' so I bowed.

''Well?'' he asked.

I shrugged. ''He didn't say nothing . . . except what they all say,'' I sniggered. Huld made an expression of distaste which I feigned not to notice. ''I put 'im away. Y'wan it done again today?'' The question was automatic, requiring no thought.

''No.'' He shuddered. ''No.'' He turned and left me, the expression of distaste more pronounced as though he smelled something. I, too, smelled something, and realized that it was the smell of a Divulger's clothing— old blood, and smoke, and sweat. Grimpt had a place, a place with a door on it, a filthy place. I went there. Once inside with the door locked behind me, I spent some time in thought.

When they discovered that Peter was gone, they would question the guard. He would know nothing, but he would turn attention to Grimpt. Then they would question Grimpt. My surface thoughts were Grimpt's, well enough, but they held recent memories which would not stand up to examination. No. I could not remain Grimpt. It would be necessary to become something else, take some other form—something unimportant, beneath notice. I left the filthy little cubby and wandered out toward the courtyard, full of the tumult of men hauling the sections of the Great Game ovens onto the paving stones, the screech and clangor of hammers and wheels, the rumbling rush of wagons crossing the bridge bringing wood for the ovens. The bridge was down, the gate up to allow the wagons to move in and out, but each crew was guarded and there were more guards at the bridge. It would not be easy to leave the fortress, so much was clear. A Divulger would have no reason to go into the forest; any attempt to do so would cause suspicion.

The lounging guardsmen were all alert, scanning the high dike to the east through which the Banner flowed. They had been told to expect challenge or attack and were keyed up by recent admonitions from their leaders. One man was much preoccupied with the pain of a sore foot. From inside an iron gate came a gardener's thoughts, mixed irritation and anger that the help he had been promised had not come. It was a natural thing, so natural that long moments passed before I realized what was happening. Grimpt was able to *Read.* I tried to find something more in the minds of the guardsmen or the gardener, but could not. Seemingly, the Talent was a small one, able to pick up only surface thoughts. Quite enough for a torturer, I thought. The thoughts of his victims were probably very much surface thoughts. What else could a Divulger do? The question brought its own answer as a gate swung toward my hand. Yes, of course. The Divulger would be able to Move things, slightly. I tried to lift a paving stone and felt only a dull ache. No, this too was a small Talent. Well, it was one which might be helpful.

The gardener was a pawn, he had no Talent. He was a little angry, but unsuspicious. So, let the man have the help he had been promised. Let the gardener have his boy. I slipped into a niche of the wall where it extended out over the moat into a privy used by the servants of the courtyard, and the grooms. No one had noticed me. The guardsmen had begun a straggling procession toward the kitchens; the remaining ones were looking away toward the hills. I took one leaf of the herb, only one, and bit down on it as I thought about a boy, a vacant-eyed boy, a boy dressed only in a dirty shirt, a brown-legged boy with greasy, brownish hair and no-colored eyes, an unremarkable boy with a gap in his teeth. I thought of the boy, the boy, how he would feel about helping the gardener, harder work than he liked, but they told him to help or no food, so he'd help, damn them all anyways.

The boy put Grimpt's boots and clothing down the privy, belted Peter's shirt tightly around his slim waist and stepped out of the privy and into the garden where he stood sullenly at the gardener's elbow.

"They told me off to help you," he said.

"Oh, they did, did they? Well, it's about time. Promised me help this morning, they did, and not a sign of it. You take that barrow, there, and go fill it up at the dung heap. Dig down good, now, you understand. I don't want any fresh. I want old stuff that's all rotten down. And be quick about it." As the boy turned away, the man asked, "And what's your name?"

"What's it matter?" the boy muttered.

"What's it matter? Well, it don't matter. But I got to call you something, don't I? Can't go around yelling 'boy' or I'd have half the young ones in the place buggering around. I need something to lay a tongue to . . ."

"Name's Swallow," the boy said. "Y'can call me Swall; they mostly do."

# 10

## Swallow

SWALLOW HAD A DIRTY FACE and could spit through the gap in his teeth. There had been a boy once at Mertyn's House who could do that; Peter had envied him. Swallow had lice in his hair, or at least he scratched as though he did, and an evil, empty-headed leer. When the gardener received a noon meal, Swallow received one as well, a large bowl of meat and grain and root vegetables, the same again at night with the addition of a mug of bitter beer and a lump of cheese the size of his fist.

The gardener had a hut beside the fortress wall, near the kitchen gardens. The cooks had a place near the kitchen. Others had cubbies and corners here and there, closets and niches hidden in the thick walls behind tapestries. Swallow found a place in the hay loft above the stables, a good enough place, both warm and dry. He was to every intent and eye invisible. No one in the place noticed him, and no one in the place except the gardener could have said who he was or how long he had been there. Swallow was one of them, the pawns, the unconsidered. When, in the middle of the afternoon, there was a great tumult in the castle with men running to and fro and a confused trumpeting of voices as a search for Grimpt was conducted, no one thought of Swallow. No one spoke to him, or asked him anything. Swallow watched them running about, his mouth hanging open and his face vacant, but they did not see him.

All night long while Swallow slept burrowed deep in the warm hay, the castle hummed with men coming and going, wagons rumbling toward and away from the sound of axes in the forest. He may have wakened briefly at the noise, but went to sleep at once again. Swallow had worked hard all day. What was this confusion to him?

Thus he could be completely surprised the next morning when he listened to the whispers of the guardsmen as they ate their first meal in the early sunlight of the yard.

"The Prisoner is gone, they say. Gone right out of his clothes. Nothing left of him at all."

"And Grimpt gone, too? Filthy sot. I'll believe that when bunwits lay eggs."

"No. It's true. He's gone right enough. They've searched every corner for him. It's said now he went down the privy and over the moat."

"Down the privy. Ay. That's the place for old Grimpt, right enough."

"They found his boots in the moat. Fished them out."

"What's it all about? Do they say Grimpt took the prisoner with him?"

"No. There's talk of a Great Game coming. The prisoner was taken out by Powers, by a Wizard, they say. Or burned up in his clothes by a Firedrake."

"The clothes 'ud burn, too."

"They say not."

"Ah, well. They'll say anything."

The gardener had been listening also, came to himself and shut his mouth with an audible snap, caught Swallow by an arm and spun him around. "Enough of this loll-bagging about. Great Game or no, there's lawn to level, and we'd best at it."

Swallow spent the better part of the day rolling a heavy cylinder of stone over clipped grass, muttering the whole time to anyone within ear shot. The gardener wasn't listening, but Swallow let no opportunity for complaint pass by. Huld came through the garden at noon, his face drawn and tired. He did not notice the boy. Swallow saw Huld but kept his eyes resolutely upon the stone roller. It was not his business to draw the attention of Demons. Mandor, too, came into the garden, but by that time Swallow was having his lunch in the courtyard, almost out of sight around the corner of the iron gate. Mandor saw nothing. His eyes were fixed and glazed, and there was dried foam upon the corners of his mouth. Swallow looked up from his bowl to see adoration upon the faces around him. His own face became adoring at once, and he did not start eating again until those around him did so.

Late in the afternoon two Armigers rode in, bringing with them two pawns and a Healer. Swallow watched them ride in, as did everyone else in the place, his mouth open, his fingers busy scratching himself. The Healer was escorted into the castle, and the pawns were told to stand by the wall until they were summoned. It seemed to Swallow that they looked almost familiar, and he turned away to continue his work as Peter said to him softly, "Swallow, that is my friend Yarrel and my friend Chance." Hearing the voice from within frightened Swallow, and it was a long moment before Peter could fight his way to the surface again.

"There is more to this business than I thought," I said to myself. I had created a reality, a half-person who grew more real with each passing hour, more real than myself. And yet, to be safe, it had to be so. Swallow had to be more real than Peter, without any thoughts which would attract attention. I sank below the surface of me, thinking of myself as a fish.

Fish, fish. I could set a hook into this fish, a hook which would pull it up to the surface when it was needed but would let it swim down into the darkness otherwise. A hook. The faces of my friends, the names of Mertyn and Himaggery and Windlow. These would be my hooks. When these pulled, I would rise to peek above the water only to sink again quickly out of sight. I imagined the hook, barbed, silver, tough as steel. I set it deep into Peter and let him go.

Along toward evening a very beautiful woman and a Herald rode into Bannerwell escorted by guardsmen. Swallow saw them, though they did not see Swallow. The beautiful woman demanded an audience with Prince Mandor, and she spoke of Silkhands. The hook set and Peter rose. I said to Swallow, "When night falls, get up into those vines along the side of the hall and find a window." Then I went away again. Swallow listened. He heard me, but showed no signs of having done so. He went on his gap-toothed way, spitting and scratching and slobbering over his food as though the evening bowl had been the last he would ever receive, then off to his hay loft to fall into empty sleep.

When the moon had risen, and the place was quiet except for the pacing of the guardsmen upon the battlements, Swallow woke and sneaked through black shadow into the vines on the castle wall, century old vines with trunks thick as his body. He was hidden within them as he climbed, empty-headed, high above the paved courtyard into a night land of roofs and across silvered slates to a high window which looked down into the great hall. He picked out pieces of bent lead to make a gap in that window larger, pulling out fragments of glass, softly, softly, a thief in the night. Then he could see and hear what went on below.

Silkhands was there, and Peter rose to that hook, fished up out of liquid darkness to watch and listen.

"I have come, Prince Mandor, because the Wizard Himaggery has traced a young friend of his here, Peter, former student of King Mertyn at Mertyn's House. You knew him there." It was not precisely a question. I heard Mandor's gargle and wondered how Silkhands understood it. Then I found that if I listened, without looking at him, letting the sound enter my ears without judging it, I, too, could almost understand it. Almost it was the voice of someone I had once cared for . . . But Silkhands went on, "The Wizard, Himaggery, believes that the boy may not have come to Bannerwell of his own will. He sends me to ascertain whether he is well."

"Oh, he is well. Quite well. He is not here just now, gone off for a day or two on a hunting expedition. He'll undoubtedly be back within a few days. You are welcome to wait for him, Healer. You need not worry about Peter. He's well taken care of."

If Silkhands had spoken with the Elator who saw me in the dungeons, she knew Mandor lied. If she had spoken with that Elator then she would not have come to Bannerwell with this transparent story, for she would know that Mandor's Demons would Read her. No. She knew I was in Bannerwell, but she did not know under what conditions. She did not know exactly where I was, or she would not have dared come to ask for me in such innocence.

Another voice floated up to the high window from which I watched, silvery sweet and deadly. "Oh, Sister, why do you tell such lies? You know that you were not sent for any such reason. The Wizard cares nothing for the boy, nothing. If he has sent you, it is for some treacherous purpose of his own."

It was Dazzle. I peered down to see her standing against a tapestry, posed there like a statue. Her pose was almost exactly the one which Mandor had assumed when I first saw him in his rooms, profile limned against a background, pale, graceful hands displayed to advantage. Mandor was regarding her with fixed attention. Silkhands had become as still as some small wild thing, surprised too much by a predator to move. When she spoke, her voice was tight with strain.

"The Wizard cares much for Peter, Dazzle. As he has cared for you, and for Borold, and for all who have come to the Bright Demesne. The Prince needs only have his Gamesmen Read my thought to know I do not lie . . ."

"Or to know you have found some way to hide a lie, Sister. I am of the opinion that the Wizard is clever enough to have found such a way. He is very clever, and ambitious . . ." She cast a lingering look at Mandor, turning away from him so that the look came over her shoulder. It was all pose, pose, pose, each posture more perfect than the last. Only I could see the horror of her skull's head, her ravaged features confronting that other skull's head across the room. Mandor did not see. Dazzle did not see. Oh, Gamelords, I thought, they are using beguilement on one another, and neither sees what is there. She went on in that voice of poisonous sweetness, "Borold will bear me out. He, too, is of the same opinion." As, of course, he was. Borold had no opinion Dazzle had not given him.

"Well," Mandor said, his voice cold and hard, "Time will undoubtedly make all plain. Until then, you will be my guest, Healer. And you, Priestess. Both. If there is some Game at large in the countryside, we would not want to risk your lovely lives by letting you leave these protecting walls untimely."

From the height I saw Silkhands shiver. Dazzle only preened, posed, ran long fingers through her hair. "As you will, Prince Mandor. I appreciate such hospitality, as would anyone who had come for any honest reason . . ."

Mandor gestured to servants who led them both away, each in a different direction. I watched the way Silkhands went. I might need to find her later.

Then Mandor was joined by Huld, and the two of them spoke together while I still listened.

"Have the guardsmen found Divulger? Any sign of him?"

"Only the boots in the moat, Lord. There is no discernible reason he should have made off with the boy."

"Oh, don't be a fool, Huld. He didn't make off with the boy. He killed the boy. That's why he fled, in fear of his life."

"We've found no body."

"When the moat is drained, the body may appear. Or, he may have hidden it deep, Huld, in the Caves of Bannerwell. If you wanted to hide a body, or yourself, what better place than the tombs and catacombs of Bannerwell. Things lost there may never be found again . . ."

I sneaked away across the slates, summoning Swallow back and telling him to do this and that and then another thing. Which he did. He went to the kitchens and sat about within hearing of the cooks and stewards until one entered the place saying that the Healer in the corner rooms on the third floor had had no evening meal and needed food. There was tsking from the cooks, kind words about Healers in general, and vying between two sufferers as to which of them should take the meal to her when it was ready. Enough.

The two pawns who had come with her were still in the courtyard, crouched along the wall. Swallow slouched toward them, spoke to the guard nearby. "They c'n sleep in the stable hay along of me if they'd mind to . . ." The guard ignored him. He had not been told to watch these two inconsiderable creatures. Swallow kicked at Chance's boots. "Softer there than here, and you c'n bring your things."

The two rose and followed him to the loft to lay themselves wearily down, with many grunts and sighs. Swallow sat in the dark away from them, letting the sight of their faces fish Peter up out of the dark waters to whisper, "Yarrel. Yarrel, listen to me. It's Peter."

He sat up, staring wildly about. "Peter? Where are you?"

"Shhh. I am here in the shadow."

"Come out here, into the moonlight. We expected to find you in the dungeons." I did not move, and he said warily, "Is this some trickery?"

I was very tired. I did not want to use any more of Windlow's herb, there was so little left. At that moment I could not remember the "how" of changing back, and I was too tired to try. Instead I said, "No trick, Yarrel. Listen, you and I stood on the parapet of Mertyn's House and saw a Demon and two Tragamors riding to Festival. You said the horses came from Bannerwell, remember? You said it to me. No one would know of that but us."

"A Demon might have Read it," he said coldly.

"Oh, a Demon might, but wouldn't. Think of something to ask me, then . . ."

"I ask you one thing only. Come into the light!"

Sighing, I moved forward. He seized me roughly by the shoulder and shook me. "You. You are not Peter."

It was Chance who said, "Yarrel. Look at his eyes, his face. This is Peter right enough." Evidently even in my weariness, I had let my own form come forward a little, my own face. Still, Chance had been very quick. I wondered at that moment whether he had not known all along who my mother was, whether he had not perhaps expected something of the kind. The thought was driven away by Yarrel's chilly, hostile voice.

"Shifter. You're a Shifter."

I slumped down, head on knees. He who had been my friend for so long was now so unfriendly. "I am the son of Mavin Manyshaped," I confessed. "She is full sister to Mertyn. I was told this by Huld, thalan to Mandor, as Mertyn is to me. He Read it in Mertyn's mind at Festival time." There were tears running down my legs, tears from tiredness. "Oh, Yarrel, I would rather have been a pawn in a quiet place, but that isn't what I am . . ."

Chance reached forward to stroke my arm, and I intercepted a stern look he directed at Yarrel. "Well, lad, if there has to be a Talent, why not a biggun, that's what I say. If you're going to make a noise, might as well make it with a trumpet as with a pot-lid, right?"

Yarrel had moved away from us, spoke now from some distance in that same cold voice. "Pot-lid or trumpet, Chance, but a Shifter, still. Shifty in one, shifty in all, or so I have always learned. Not Peter any more, at least. I am certain of that."

"That's not the way it is," I screamed at him in an agonized whisper. "You don't understand *anything!*" I knew this was a mistake as soon as I had said it, for his voice was even more hostile when he answered.

"Perhaps you will enlighten us. Perhaps you will tell us 'how it is,' and what you intend to do . . ."

"I don't know," I hissed. "If I knew what to do, I'd have done it by now. I know I have to get Silkhands and you two out of this place, somehow. Mandor is mad and if he can use her in any way to do evil against those he imagines are his enemies, he will do so. And Dazzle is here to make sure he imagines enemies. He could easily give Silkhands to the Divulgers, as he did me . . ."

But it was not Yarrel who calmed me and comforted me and told me all that I have recounted about Himaggery's Demesne and the surety of a Great Game building around Bannerwell. No, it was Chance, comfortable Chance, dependable Chance. Only when I spoke of Mandor's wild plan to link some various Talents together to get himself a new body did Yarrel speak, saying roughly, "More minds than one on that idea. Himaggery works along that line as well, to link the Talents of the Bright

Demesne. In Himaggery's hands it might not go ill for my people, but in Mandor's . . .''

"Himaggery marches against Mandor for your sake, Peter," said Chance. "What will you do?"

"I hoped you would help me. I don't know what to do next. I don't really understand how this Shifting works. I've only done it twice. The first time it just happened, not even intended. I thought you and Yarrel . . .''

Yarrel interrupted, firmly, coldly, "The Talent is yours. I will not take responsibility for it. It is yours by birth, yours by rearing. We are no longer schoolfellows to plot together. You have gone beyond that . . .''

"But, Yarrel . . .'' I stopped. I didn't know what to say to him. This chance was unexpected, sudden. I remembered his saying to me on the way to the High Demesne that I might gain a Talent which would make us un-friends, but surely he would not pre-judge me in this fashion. Except that . . . it had been a Shapeshifter who had done great harm to his family. Except that. Oh, Yarrel.

Chance said, "We're as good as rat's meat if Mandor knows who we are, lad. From what you say, Silkhands should be out and away from here as soon as may be. If this Talent of yours can help us, time it did so, I'd say. Great Game is coming. It would be better not to be caught in the middle of it."

"A Great Game," I said miserably. I turned away from them to lie curled on my side, hurt at Yarrel's coldness. After a time, I slept. I dreamed of a Grand Demesne, a Great Game gathering around Bannerwell. The ovens in the courtyard were red hot, their mouths gaping like monstrous mouths come to eat the people of Bannerwell. Stokers labored beside them, black against the flame. Once more I saw the flicker of Shifters in and out of the press of battle, Elators in and out of the lines of Armigers upon the battlements, saw fire raining from the sky, a sky full of Dragons and Firedrakes and enormous forms I had not seen before. And there, far at the edge of vision, gathered at the forest edges, were the pawns with their hayforks and scythes, stones in their hands. I woke sweating, gasping for air. The dark hours were upon the place. I rose wearily and went from the stables through the garden down to the little orchard which grew behind low walls over the abrupt fall to the River.

I needed someone with more knowledge than I had. If I found

someone, however, what would I do? Kill him for whatever thoughts were on the surface of his brain? Likely they would be only about his dinner or his mistress or his gout, and I'd be no better off. I needed to know what I could do and had no idea how to begin. So, there in the darkness among the trees I tried to use my Talent.

After a time, it was no longer difficult. I found I could become anything I could invent or visualize, any number of empty-headed creatures like Swallow, male or female, though there were things about the female form which were uncertain at best. I could turn myself back into Grimpt, or into something else which didn't look or smell like Grimpt but had Grimpt's small Talents. The kitchen cat meauwed at me from the orchard grass, and I laid my hands on it to try to take that shape, only to burst out of the attempt with heart pounding in a wild panic. The cat's brain was so small. As soon as I began to be in it, it began to close in from all sides, pressing me smaller and smaller to crush me. Was it only that it was small? Let others find out. I would not try a creature that size again.

By the time I heard the cock gargling at the false dawn from atop the dung heap, I knew why it was that Shifters were said not to take human form. Had it not been for the panic, Windlow's herb, and my own inheritance, I would not have been able to do so when I changed to Grimpt. Only ignorance had let me make up the person of Swallow. In the dark hours I had learned that I could change only if the pattern were there, only if I could lay hands upon it and somehow "read" it. So much for easy dreams of shifting into an Elator and flicking outside the walls, or shifting into an Armiger to carry Silkhands to safety through the air from her window. I could not become a Dragon because I had no pattern for it, nor a Prince, nor a Tragamor. Not unless I could lay hands upon a real one. Which it would be death for Peter to do and highly dangerous for Swallow to attempt. Grimpt? I could, perhaps, go back to that. There were undoubtedly other clothes in the filthy hidey-hole the man had lived in.

But there were other creatures larger than a cat on whom Swallow might lay hands. Horses. The great hunting fustigars from the kennels. There were possibilities there. Well enough. I went back to the loft and spoke to Chance, telling him that I needed to sleep. I said it in a firm voice without begging for help. My pride would not let me do that. If Yarrel would not help me, I would help myself.

Still, the last thought I had was a memory of Yarrel saying that I might get a Talent which would make him hate me. I knew I had already done so, and there was no comfort from that thought. I let Peter sink away from it into swallowing darkness, let Swallow come up again into the quiet of sleep. A few hours until day. It would come soon enough.

# 11

# The Caves of Bannerwell

WE AWOKE to the smell of smoke and food, the clamor of guards and grooms, the pawnish people of the fortress about the business of breakfast, the cackle of fowls, the growling of hungry fustigars. When we had received our slabs of bread and mugs of tea, we sat on the sun-warmed stones while I told Chance and Yarrel what I could do. More important, what I could not. I saw Chance's look of disappointment, but Yarrel's face was as stony as it had been the night before, almost as though he were forbidding himself to have any part in my difficulties. Well, if he would not, he would not. I did not beg him for pity or assistance. If he would be my friend again, he would when he would. I could only wait upon him, and this I owed him for the many times he had waited upon me. So and so and so. It wasn't comforting, but it was all I could do.

"Well then," said Chance. "We'll busy ourselves around the stables. Likely no one will bother us if we are seen grooming horses and mucking out. That will give you time to think more . . ."

"We haven't time," I said. "And I have already thought as much as I can. They gave me to the Divulger because they saw an Elator flick into my dungeon, give me a looking over, then disappear. Would that have been Himaggery's man?"

Chance said, "Himaggery knew where you were. He had a Pursuivant close enough to Read you. He wouldn't have risked your life so—no. It would have to be someone else."

"Then who? Mandor knew where I was. It was none of his doing, obviously. Mertyn?"

"Unlikely," said Yarrel in a distant voice. "Himaggery had already sent word to Mertyn. He would not have risked your life either, as you well know."

"Then again, who?"

"The High King," said Chance. I stared at him in astonishment. I had never thought of the High King.

"But why? What am I to the High King?"

"You are a person who was with Windlow, that's who. You are a person who was with Silkhands. The Elator may have been looking for her, for Windlow, not for you at all. But the High King would look, wouldn't he? He's a suspecter, that one."

"Having found, what would he do?"

Chance mused. "Get himself into the midst of us one way or another, I'd say. He was set on keeping old Windlow captive, most set. Like a fustigar pup with his teeth in a lure, not going to let go even though there's nothing in it but fur. Likely he's wanting Windlow back again and come here looking for him."

"Windlow will be here," said Yarrel. "When Himaggery comes, Windlow will be with him."

I was dizzy with the thought of it. "So, Himaggery comes from the east, with Mertyn, in such might as they can muster. And the High King comes from the south, also in might. Are there no contingents moving upon us from other directions as well . . ."

Yarrel said coldly, "From what direction might Mavin come, knowing her son is held captive by Mandor?"

I refused to rise to this bait. Being Mavin's son was no fault of mine. I would not be twitted about it. Remembering the dream of the pawns with hayforks, I tried to sympathize with his feelings. "The end of it all will be only blood and fury," I said, as softly and kindly as I could. "First the Gamesmen will kill one another, and then perhaps the pawns will come to kill those of us who are left, if any are left, and there will be more Mandors and more Dazzles to turn death's faces upon the world." I saw their incomprehension. They had not seen Dazzle and Mandor as I had. I tried again. "The Great Game will be a monstrous Death. In which we may all perish. This is not the way to do things. There must be something better."

"Justice," said Yarrel. "Himaggery says we might try that."

"I do not know the word." Indeed, I had never heard it.

"Few do," he answered. "It means simply that the rules do not matter, the Game does not matter so much as that thing which stands above both rules and Game.'' He went on, becoming passionate as he described what Himaggery had said and what he, himself, had been thinking and dreaming in all his journey from the Bright Demesne—perhaps in his journey since birth. I understood one tenth of it. That tenth, however, was enough to give me an important thought. How important, even I did not know.

"Yarrel, if you believe in this, then why do we not try to do it—try to stop the Game.''

"Surely," he sneered. "Ask Mandor to let you and Silkhands go. Ask him to let you both go to Himaggery without Mandor's plotting against Himaggery. Ask the High King to leave Windlow alone. Ask Dazzle to stop building conspiracies against Silkhands. Ask the world to change. Ask that my people be given Justice. All that.'' His voice was bitter.

"There are those who could not need to ask," I pleaded. "The Immutables, Yarrel. They wouldn't need to ask. If *they* came, then there could be no Game.''

There was a long silence. "Why would they come?" he asked at last.

"Perhaps because of this 'Justice' you speak of. Perhaps because their leader's daughter was killed by Mandor and Huld and the pawner. The killers are here. Perhaps because we beg it of them. I don't know why they would come, but I know they will not unless someone asks them, begs them . . .''

"And how may we beg them, we who are prisoners here?''

That piece I had already worked out. "I have an idea," I said, and told them about it. Chance objected to certain things about it, and Yarrel offered a suggestion or two. By the time we were done with our bread and tea, which we had made last longer than any of those around us, we had a plan and my heart was a little lighter. Yarrel had looked at me once without enmity, almost as he used to do. They went off to the stables and I went to offer myself to my taskmaster, the gardener, who was furious that I had not been with him since before dawn. Swallow gaped a witless grin at him and let the words of fury slide away. Within moments he was at the barrow handles once more, on his way to the dung heap.

When he went to get the second barrow-load of the day, Chance signaled from the stable door and Peter rose. I let the barrow rest near the privy, as though I might be inside, and slipped away to the kennels. One of the fustigars lay against the fence, drowsing in the sun, and I laid hands upon her body for long moments before she roused to challenge me. It was enough. I skulked away behind the kennels and went over the fence in the shape of a fustigar, opened the kennel gates in that guise (easy enough even with paws, when the mind inside the beast knew how to do it) and then went among the great, drowsy beasts like a hunter among bunwits. I was mad. My mouth frothed, my growls were deafening as I snapped at flanks, howled, bit, drove them into panic and from panic into wild flight out the open gate. From the stables came the high, screaming whinny of horses similarly driven into fear and flight, and I knew that Chance and Yarrel were at their work getting the horses to the same frenzied pitch as the hunting animals. The fustigars burst across the courtyard in a howling mob, me among them still snapping at hind legs; the horses came out of the stables in a maddened herd, both groups headed straight for the bridge. The lounging Tragamors who guarded it dived out of the way as the animals plunged past them pursued by Yarrel and Chance, pitchforks in their hands, shouting, "Get the horses, don't let the horses get away, grab those horses . . ."

By the time some surly guardsmen were sent in pursuit, Chance and Yarrel were hidden within the forest whistling up their own saddled and laden beasts who had gone unnoticed among the stampeding animals. No one had realized that the two pawns pursuing the horses were not grooms from Mandor's own people. It was true what Yarrel had said. No one paid much attention to pawns.

One fustigar had not gone out with the others. That one slipped behind the kennels from which Swallow emerged, grinning and scratching, so amused by the spectacle that he stayed overlong in the courtyard and had to be summoned back to the gardener.

Armigers went aloft to seek the animals. A Tracker strolled out of the barracks to join others on the bridge. By early afternoon the horses and fustigars were back where they belonged except for two. No one missed the two, or the two pawns who had gone after them. During all this, Peter stayed well down just in case anyone should take it into his head to discover the source of the animals' panic. Distracted as they were by the threat of challenge and Great Game, no one did. There was no hurry, now. The Gathered Waters lay two days' journey east along a good road from Bannerwell. There were little ships crossing it almost daily. Or, one could travel around it to the place of the Immutables on the far side. It would be days before Chance and Yarrel would get there, days more before they could return—or not.

That afternoon Swallow stole some clothing from a washline, the clothing of a steward. He tucked it away where it could be found later and promptly forgot about it. That afternoon the fortress gossiped about an Elator who had appeared in the audience hall and after that in the dungeons. There was much talk of this, and a great deal of movement among the Borderers and other guardsmen. Throughout it all, Swallow fetched manure. When he had eaten his evening meal, he slept, much in need of sleep, and then repeated the previous day's activities. That evening he went to the roof, but saw nothing of importance going on. The third day the same, and on that evening Swallow ceased to be.

On that evening Swallow heard Mandor say to Silkhands that she would be sent to the Divulgers upon the morrow. "To learn who it is who sends these spies among us." Dazzle, leaning against a pillar, heard this threat with enormous and obvious satisfaction. Huld attempted to argue, half-heartedly, as though he knew it would do no good. Silkhands was pale and shaking. As a Healer she knew that they need only leave her in a chill room without sufficient food and she would be unable to Heal herself.

"Why do you do this?" she whispered. "Your thalan knows I make no plot against you! The High King's Demons knew it as well. Yet there is this idiocy among you! What is this madness?"

"If it is madness," Mandor lisped, "then it is what I choose. I *choose* that you be sent to the Divulgers, *Healer*." His voice was full of contempt and anger, and it was then I knew why he hated Silkhands and why he had hated me. He did not believe that she had secrets or conspiracies against him any more than he had believed it of me. He simply hated her because she was a Healer who could not Heal him, hated me because I had once loved him and could not love him now. The talk of conspiracies was only talk, only surface, only something to say so that Huld would have an excuse to forgive him without despising him utterly.

The reasons no longer mattered, however. Peter had come up to the surface. Swallow had ceased to be. The half-made plan I had made for the rescue of Silkhands would have to go forward at once, ready or not.

I had observed the stewards as they went about the place bearing food or linens or running errands for Gamesmen of rank. Each wore a coat of dull gray piped in violet and black, Mandor's colors. Swallow had stolen such a coat together with a pair of trousers and soft shoes. I changed into these garments in the orchard as I changed myself to match them, becoming an anonymous steward with an ordinary face. Then I had to watch until the kitchen was almost empty before going into it to pick up a tray with bottle and wine-cup. Only one of the pawnish wenches saw me, and I prayed the face I wore was ordinary enough that one would not notice me particularly. I walked away, staying to the side of the corridors, standing against the wall with my head decently down when Gamesmen went past, bearing the tray as evidence that I belonged where I was, doing what I was doing. When I came to the door of Silkhands' room, it was barred and guarded by a yawning Halberdier. He looked me over casually, without really seeing me, and turned to unbar the door. He did not get up after I hit him with the bottle. It didn't even break. I dragged him behind an arras to take his clothes. He would have a vast headache when awoken, but I was as glad not to have killed him as I was not sorry to have killed Grimpt. He was a simple man with a very small Talent for firemaking and a tiny bit of follow-me. This made him popular among his fellows, but was no reason to wish him ill.

When I went in to Silkhands and told her to come with me, she was hideously frightened. I wanted to tell her not to be afraid, but it was necessary that she feel fear if anyone saw us and felt curious about her. Only if she were truly afraid would the thing work at all, so I put Peter well down into the depths of the Halberdier and let that man escort her into the corridor. We went down a back flight of stairs, along corridors and down yet another flight which brought us into a short hallway off the dining hall. There was still much coming and going though it was very late. Catching Silkhands by the shoulder, I told her roughly to stand quiet. She did so, whimpering. I cursed inside as a group of Gamesmen went past, laughing and quarreling after some late play at cards. Three of them stopped to talk, and I thought they would never go. Then, when they went through the door and away, as I was mentally rehearsing the way to a side door and down through the gardens to the wall, there was an alarm from above. I knew at once they had found the Halberdier.

There was no time left to attempt the escape through the gardens and orchard to the rope over the wall. They would be guarding the walls at the first sound of the alarm. I pulled Silkhands to me and hissed, "If you wish to live, be silent. If you truly wish to live, think of being grass as once you did upon a canyon side with Chance beside you . . ."

She searched my face, then said, "Peter." I do not know how she could have known so quickly who it was, except that my hands were on her and she could see into the body I wore. Perhaps it had some distinctive feel to it that she recognized. She was quick and compliant, however, for she stopped gaping at once and let her face go blank. I knew she was doing everything she could to be invisible if Huld sought her.

The surface mind of the Halberdier knew the castle well, but I could find no sure hiding place in those memories. Then I remembered the words of Huld and Mandor when they spoke of Grimpt. The Caves of Bannerwell. Where? The Halberdier did not know, but Grimpt knew. I sought the pattern of that memory once more, pulled it back into being. Oh, yes, Grimpt had known well. There was the way, the rusty door, the key, the cobweb hung tunnels . . .

I did not wait to explore the memory or understand it. Instead, I turned back the way we had come and tugged Silkhands into a stumbling run. Here was a panel which opened to a secret pressure. Here was a door hidden behind a tapestry. Here were cobwebby stairs hidden within walls which led downward to that same torture dungeon toward which Grimpt had led Peter those long days before.

We did not stay to examine the instruments there. The place was empty though a torch burned smokily on the wall. The way in Grimpt's memory lay through a half-hidden door, its metal surface splotched with corruption, the hinges red with rust, the key in the lock. It opened protestingly, the hinges screaming, and we stepped within to lock the door behind us. I had known the way would be dark so had taken up the torch to light our way down into the belly of the earth. There was no sound. Our footsteps were pillowed in dust and our panting breaths lost themselves in the vaulted height above. Silkhands followed, her face still carefully blank until I shook her and said, "There is stone between us and the world, Silkhands. We cannot be Read here." Then she sighed and almost fainted upon my arm, and I knew it was from holding her breath for endless moments.

"How did you find this place?" she whispered. "Where does it go?"

"I don't know," I confessed.

"You're a Shifter," she said, almost accusingly. I was reminded of Yarrel's tone. "You did turn out to be a Shifter, like your mother."

"You knew about my mother?"

"Himaggery found out. Before we came after you. He said it would make no difference if I knew, for Mandor already knew of it. How did you find this place?"

"I took the shape of one who knew. The memory came with the form."

"Ah," she said. "It's like Healing, then."

"Is it? I suppose it must be. Like Healing. Like Reading. It feels to me as though several of those things are going on, all at once."

"Where do we go now?"

I laughed, then wanted to cry. "Silkhands, I don't know. I don't know what this place is, or why Huld thought of it as a hiding place or why Grimpt knew of it. I only knew we needed to get away, and this was available. It seemed better than being given to the Divulgers."

"Well," she offered, "if you don't know, then we must find out."

So we explored. We did not fear losing our way for we could always follow our own footprints in the dust to go back the way we had come. That dust, undisturbed for ages, indicated that we were in no frequently traveled place. It was almost a maze, winding corridors with niches and side aisles and rooms. After a very long time, during which we went down and then up and then down again, we came to an opening into a great open space filled with tombs, a veritable city of tombs. They stretched away from the torchlight in an endless series to a high, far line of lights, dim, fiery, as though of windows into a firelighted place.

"Could we have come under the walls?" Silkhands asked me. "If this is the place Bannerwell gives its dead, then there must be another entrance, one better suited to processions."

She was right. Funeral pomp and display would require a ceremonial entrance of some kind, something with ornamental gates and wide corridors. "If we could find it," I whispered, "it would probably be well guarded. And I don't feel that we are outside the walls . . ."

"How had you planned to get us out?" She laughed when I told her. "Down a rope? Well, it might have worked. I was fearful enough to risk my life down a rope. Why did you not shift into an Armiger and carry us away?"

I told her that I did not because I could not, and she became very curious, full of questions, while we both stood in the land of tombs and the torch burned low. I wanted to hug her and slap her at once. There was no time for this, for this chatter, no time and I couldn't decide what was best to do. As was often the case, while I dithered and Silkhands talked, events moved upon us. There was a booming noise from the far, high firelit spaces, an enormous gonging sound, then a creaking of hinges. One of the firelit spaces began to enlarge, torches starring the space behind it.

"There is your ceremonial gate," I said. "They've come to search for us."

"And we've left prints in the dust a blind man could follow!"

"No," I said. "We'll leave nothing behind us. Turn and see." Grimpt's small Talent for moving was enough. The dust rose in little fountains and settled once more, even as a carpet. We turned and ran, little dust puffs following us like the footfalls of a ghost. I thought of Ghost Pieces and of the surrounding dead and shuddered, glad I had seen no Necromancer in Bannerwell. "Try to remember which turns we make," I panted. "When they have gone, if they go, we'll try to find our way back." She saved her breath for running, but I knew she heard me. We twisted, backtracked down a parallel way, then down a branching hall, into a small tomb chamber, then into an alcove behind a carved cenotaph. "The torch must go out," I said. "Else they'll find us by the light."

"Gamelords," she sighed. "I hate the dark."

"It's all right. I can light it again." I blessed the Halberdier and was glad once more that I had not killed him. He knew enough to light the torch, thus I could do it when I had to. We crouched in the blanketing dark. They would not be able to Read us through the stone, or track us by eye, but they might use fustigars. Indeed, we heard baying rise and fade, rise and fade again. "They cannot smell our way in this dust," I said. "Our tracks are gone. They cannot find us . . ."

I had spoken too soon. The sound of the animals grew nearer, and we waited, poised to run. As I rose to my feet, I caught the string of my pouch on a stone and it snapped. Some half-dozen of the tiny Gamesmen fell to the floor. I felt for them with my hands, cursing the darkness, gathering them up one by one. I had heard one of them fall to my left, groped for it, found it at last and gripped it tightly just as a beam of light went by the entrance to the tomb chamber out of which our alcove opened. It grew warm in my grasp, warmer, hot. Almost I dropped it, then opened my hand to find it shining in the dark, the tiny Necromancer glowing like a small star on my palm.

I closed my hand to hide the light. It spoke to me. It said, "I am Dorn, Raiser of the Dead, Master of all my kind..." A pattern was there, complex as a tapestry, knotted and interwoven, vast and ramified as root and branch of a mighty tree. It did not wait for me to Read it or take it. It flowed into me and would have done even if I had tried to stop it or dam it away. Silkhands gasped, for the Gamespiece shone between my fingers so that the flesh seemed transparent. Far away was the yammer of voices and animals. I only half heard it as I dropped the piece back into the pouch. It was no longer glowing.

The searchers were returning. They paused at the entrance to the tomb room and began to come inside. I heard Huld calling to them from a distance. "Search every room. Mark every corridor to show you have searched..." They could not fail to see us if they came inside as those obedient forms began to do, long shadows reaching ahead of them in the torchlight. Something within me sighed, deeply.

Between us and the searchers were seven tombs, cubes of marble set with golden crowns. Here lay some past rulers of Bannerwell, some Princes or Kings of time long gone. I sighed once more, the Dorn pattern within me beginning to Read time, back and back again, taking measure from the stone in which the dead Kings lay, back into their lives, taking up their dust, their bones, the rotted threads in which they were clad, making all whole again as though living, to rise up, up from the sepulcher into the air, a shade, a spirit, a ghastly King peering down upon these intruders out of shadowy eyes, speaking with a voice in which the centuries cried like lost children in a barren place, "Who comes, who comes, who comes..."

Beside me Silkhands hid her face and screamed silently into her hands. Before me the searchers drew up, eyes wide, each mouth stretched into a rictus of fear. The fustigars cowered, and the spirit confronted them, "Who comes, who comes, who comes," as yet another rose beside him, and then one more, and yet again and again.

The searchers fled and the spirit heads began to turn toward the place we hid. Within me came the sigh, and Dorn let them rest once more.

Now I knew why Dazzle had so feared the threat of her dead. These had been no dead of mine, and yet I feared, for out of these had come a hungering and a thirst which my life would not have slaked. One who raised these dead raised terror. And yet, even as I knew this, I knew that Dorn could hold them so they did no harm, or loose them, as Dorn would.

I comforted Silkhands, blindly, babbling. "Himaggery told me to keep the Gamespieces safe. To keep them to myself. Well did he say so. I wish I had buried them back once more in the earth."

"We are alive," she whispered, practical and fearful at once. "I would rather be alive, even sweating like this. Having seen death, I would rather be alive."

"I can raise them up again, if we need to . . ."

"Not now," she begged. "I am so tired. I have been afraid for so long. Not now."

We lit the torch and followed the footprints of those who had fled, but the hope of escape was vain. The great room of tombs was lit with a thousand torches and there were watchers at every corner of it. I could Read Mandor in the room, glowing with anger. I could read Dazzle there, as well, writhing thoughts, like a nest of serpents twining upon one another in incestuous frenzy. A telltale tickle at the edge of my mind pushed me back behind a towering midfeather which held up the groined ceiling. I hugged Silkhands to me. "We can't stay here. Huld is searching for us. We need stone between us and him . . ."

My words were interrupted by a fury of sound, drums throbbing, a wild clatter of wheels, and a thunder upon the bridge. Trumpets called. Silkhands said, "So, someone has come to give Mandor a Great Game. Those are the last of the wood wagons being driven across the bridge with fuel for the ovens . . ."

We heard Mandor scream instructions at the guards. The doors clanged shut and there was a scurry of purposeful movement. We withdrew into the shadows of the corridor. "I have not slept in days," said Silkhands. "If we may not get out, let us hide away and rest. I cannot Heal myself of this weariness much longer, and I am hungry . . ."

I was hungry, too, and we had nothing with us to eat or drink. As for sleep, however, that we could do. We went from squared and vaulted rooms into dim bat-hung halls where dawn light filtered down from grilled shafts twenty manheights above us, and from there into darker corridors lined with vaults bearing each the sign and legend of him who slept there. At last we found a high, dry shelf three-quarters hidden behind hanging stone pillars down which water dripped endlessly in a mournful cadence. There we would be hidden by stone in all directions, hidden by shadow, hidden by sleep. We shared the last of Windlow's herb and fixed our minds upon peace. Lost in the darkness of the place of tombs, we slept.

# 12

# Mavin

I WOKE TO A CLICKING SOUND, a small, almost intimate sound in the vastness of that stone pillared cave. It reminded me of the death beetle we had often heard in the long nights in School House, busy in the rafters, the click, click, click timing the life of the Tower as might the ticking of a clock. I was still half asleep when I peered over the edge of the ledge we lay upon. The cavern drifted in pale light, mist strewn, and at the center of it a woman was sitting in a tall, wooden chair, knitting.

She had not been there before. I had not heard her arrive. For the moment I thought it was a dream and pinched myself hard enough to bring an involuntary exclamation, half throttled. Silkhands heard it, wakened to it, sat up suddenly, saying, "What is it? Oh, what is it?" Then she, too, heard the sound and peered at the distant figure, her expression of blank astonishment mirroring my own.

Before I could answer her, if I had had any answer to give, the woman looked up toward us and called, "You may as well come down. It will make conversation easier." Then she returned to her work, the needles in her hands flashing with a hard, metallic light. I stared away in the direction we had entered this vault. Nothing. All was silence, peace, no trumpets, no drums, no torches. Finally, I heaved myself down from the ledge and helped Silkhands as we climbed down to the uneven floor of the cave. The clicking was now interspersed with a creaking sound, the sound of the chair in which the woman sat, rocking to and fro. Once, long, long ago I had seen some such chair. I could not remember when. The yarn she used frothed between her hands as though alive, pouring from the needles in a flood which spread its loose loops over her knees and cascaded to the stone. The speed of her knitting increased to a whirling rattle, the creaking of the chair faster and faster, like a bellows breathing, until she was finished all at once. She flung the completed work onto the stone before her where it lay like a pile of woolen snow.

"What have you made?" asked Silkhands, doubtfully. I knew she was unable to think of anything else to say. I could think of nothing at all. The woman fixed us with great, inhuman eyes, yellow and bright as those of a bird.

"I have knitted a Morfus," she said in a deep voice. "Soon it will get up and go about its work, but just now it is resting from the pain of being created." The piled fabric before her shivered as she spoke, and I thought it moaned. "Would you care for some cabbage?" the woman asked.

Silkhands said, "I would be very grateful for anything to eat, madam. I am very hungry." When she spoke, my mouth filled with saliva, even though I hated cabbage raw or cooked and always had. The woman found a cabbage somewhere beside herself in the chair and offered it. Silkhands tore off a handful of leaves.

The woman said, "It is better than nothing. Although I do not like it as it is." She stared intently at the vegetable in her hand, turning it this way and that. It fuzzed before my eyes, fuzzed, misted, became a roasted fowl. The pile of fabric moaned once more, sat up, extended long, knitted tentacles and pushed itself erect. Vaguely manshaped, it swayed where it stood, featureless and without much substance. I could see through it in spots. An impatient snort from the woman brought my attention back to her. She had given the fowl to Silkhands. "Try this instead. Tell me if it tastes right."

Silkhands tore a leg from the fowl and took a bite of it, wiping her face on her arm, nodding. "It tastes . . . only a little like cabbage."

"Ah. Well, then, it's an improvement. Still, you could do much better, being a Healer, if that lazy youth would help you."

"I don't understand," said Silkhands, remembering at last to offer me some of the fowl. "What do you mean, I could do better?"

"Have you ever Healed a chicken?" the woman asked.

"Never."

"Ah. Well then, perhaps you could not do as well as I have done. If you had ever Healed a chicken, you would know how the flesh is made. And if that boy were to Read you as you thought about that, then he could change the cabbage far better than I have done."

"Pardon, madam," I said. "But I have not that Talent."

"Nonsense. You have all the Talents there are, from Dorn to Didir, or from Didir to Dorn, as the case may be. You have the Gamesmen of Barish, I know it. Even if I had not felt the spirit of Dorn moving in the corridors of the earth like a waking thunder I would still have known. Was it not Seen? Was it not foretold? Why else am I here and are you where you are?"

"The Gamesmen of Barish?" By this time I was certain that I still slept, dreaming in the high stone wall on the little ledge. "I don't know what you . . ."

"These," she flicked a knitting needle at me, catching the loop of my pouch and rattling the Gamesmen within it. "These. You have already taken Dorn into being. Soon you must take others, or if not soon then late. By the seven hells, you're not afraid of them, are you, boy?"

"Afraid? Of *them?* Them . . . who?"

"Witless," she commented acidly, looking me over from head to foot as though she could not believe what she saw. "Witless and spitless, no more juice than a parsnip. By the seven hells, boy, you raised up the ancient Kings of Bannerwell. How did you think you did that? Did you perhaps whittle them up out of a bit of wood and your little knife? Or whistle them up like a wind? Or brew them, perhaps, like tea? How did you do it, gormless son of an unnamed creation? Hmmm? Answer me!"

I was beginning to be very angry. As I grew wider awake and even slightly less hungry (the fowl was filling, though it did taste like cabbage), I became angrier by the moment. I was distracted, however, for at that moment the Morfus decided to do whatever it was a Morfus did. Moaning shrilly, it staggered off toward one side of the great cavern and began to climb the stone. It lurched and flapped like laundry upon a slack line, wavering and lashing itself upward.

"At this rate, it'll never get there," she commented as she took up the needles and the wool once more to pour out another long confusion of knitting upon her lap. "You haven't answered me," she said. 'How did you think you raised them up, boy? By what means?"

"I raised them up by using the pattern I found in one of the Games-pieces," I said, stiffly. "By accident."

"No more by accident than trees grow by accident. Trees grow because it is their nature to do so. The Gamespieces of Barish were designed to have a nature of their own—to lie long hidden until a time when they would fall into the hands of one who could use them." There was a long pause and then she said in a slightly altered tone, "No. That is not quite correct. They would fall into the hands of one who would use them *well.* That is tricky. Perhaps a bit of fear and confusion would not be amiss under those circumstances." The knitting poured from her lap onto the floor and lay there, quivering. Then the knitted creature heaved itself upward to stagger toward its companion which still struggled upward against the far rock wall.

Silkhands had been observing the woman narrowly, and now she seated herself at the knitter's feet and laid hand upon her knee. The woman started, then composed herself and smiled. "Ah, so you'd find out what goes on, would you, Healer? Well, stay out of my head and the rest of me be thy play-pen. There's probably some work or other needs doing in there."

"What are the Gamesmen of Barish?" I asked. "Please stop confusing me. I think you're doing it purposely, and it doesn't help me. Just tell me. What are the Gamesmen of Barish?"

She rose, incredibly tall and thin, like a lath, I thought, then changed that thought. Like a sword, lean and keen-edged and pointed. She laughed as though she Read that thought. "Long ago," she chanted, "in a time forgotten by all save those who read books, were two Wizards named Barish and Vulpas. You've heard of them? Ah, of course. You've heard of them from the self-styled Historian." She laughed, almost kindly. "These two had a Talent which was rare. They called it Wisdom. Or, so it is said by some. They caused the Immutables, you know. They learned the true nature of the Talents. They codified many things which had been governed until then, in approximately equal parts, by convention and superstition. Those who lived by convention and superstition could not bear that matters of this kind be brought into the light, and so they sought out Barish and Vulpas with every intention of killing them.

"Later the Guardians announced that Barish and Vulpas were dead. There was much quiet rejoicing. However, there are books which one may read today (if one knows where to find them) which were written by Barish and Vulpas many years after the Guardians announced their deaths. Could it be the Guardians lied? Who is to say. It was long ago, after all . . ."

"The Gamesmen," I said firmly.

"Barish claimed," she went on, "that the pattern of a Talent—nay, of a whole personality, could be encoded into a physical object and then Read from that object as it could be Read in a man, by one with the ability to do so."

"That would be utter magic," said Silkhands.

"Some may say so," the knitter said. "While others would say otherwise. Nonetheless, the *books* say that Barish made his claim manifest in the creation of a set of Gamesmen. There are eleven *different* pieces in the set, embodying, so it is written, the Talents of the forebears."

"Why?" I breathed, ideas surging into my head all at once. "Why would he have done this thing? It's true, Silkhands. I know it's true. It was exactly like Reading a person. I felt Dorn, felt him sigh. It was he who raised the specters up, not me. How terrible and wonderful. But why would he do it?" I babbled this nonsense while the knitter fixed me with her yellow eyes and the Morfuses clambered ever higher against the stones.

"If Barish was able to code the Talents in this way, then he must also have been able to perceive them for himself. In which case, he would have perceived the Talent of Sorah, Seer. Perhaps through Sorah he saw something in the future. Who can say? It was very long ago."

"You are saying that the Wizard did this thing long ago so that someone—Peter—could use these Talents now?" Silkhands seemed to be asking a question, but it was directed more at me than at the knitter, sounded more like a demand than a query. "So that Peter can use them," she repeated. What did she want me to do? Gamelords! She seemed to want something, Yarrel wanted something else, Mertyn another thing, Mandor something else again. While I . . . what in the name of the seven devils did I want? Nothing. I wanted to do nothing. Nothing at all. Doing things was frightening. Every time I had done anything at all decisive, I had been terrified.

I said it to Silkhands, praying she would understand. "When I heard Dorn sigh within me, I was afraid . . ."

The knitter interrupted. "But you knew Dorn could control the Ghosts. You knew you could do it."

"I knew someone could. Someone. But it didn't feel like me."

"Aha," she chortled, rocking so hard that the wood of the chair began to creak in ominous protest. "You felt you were someone else, did you?

And when Grimpt cracked Grimpt's skull and put him down the oubliette? Hmmm? Who did that?''

"No one knows about that," I said, horrified. "No one at all.''

"No one except those who *do* know about it. Watchers. Morfuses. Seers. Bitty things with eyes that peer from crannies and cracks.''

Silkhands said, "Who is Grimpt?''

"Ahh, shh, shh, we've upset him enough. Poor boy. All this Talent throbbing away at his fingertips and he doesn't know where to put his hands.''

What was I to say. She was right. I had the Talent in my mind or in the pouch at my belt to fling Mandor and all his house into the nethermost north, into the deepest gorge of the Hidamans. All I needed was a source of power great enough . . . and even with ordinary power, the heat in the stone beneath me, I could summon up legions of the dead and was afraid to do so. "You've a poor tool in me," I said. "A poor tool indeed. Dorn terrified me. Sorah would probably petrify me. Why couldn't I have been a pawn, like Yarrel. I'd have been a good pawn, moved about by others . . .''

"Better a poor tool than an evil one," she said. Then she reached out to touch me for the first time, and it was as though I had been lightning struck. "You've been too long in the nursery, boy. Too long with lads and dreamers and cooks. Come out, come out wherever you are! The cock crows morning, and the Great Game is toward! Play it or be swept from the board.''

From high above came a keening howl, a ghost noise, like wind down a chimney. We looked up to see the Morfuses' black shapes against a glow of sky. They had found a way out and called to us of their discovery.

"There it is," said the knitter. "The way out. You can go that way if you like. Sit on a pile of stone up there on Malplace Mountain and watch the Game. Or, you can go out through the funeral doors to the tombs, out with a host behind you." She was across the floor and up the wall like a spider, arms, legs, head all a blur as she moved toward those two figures high on the wall. "It's your choice, boy. Mothers should not force their young. It's bad for personal development . . .''

"Who," I rasped, choking. "Who . . . who are you . . .''

"Mavin Manyshaped, boy. Here to cheer you with two of your cousins.''

The Morfus shapes before the light flickered and changed before us. Now there were only two slim youths grinning down at us out of glittering eyes, flame-red hair falling across their faces. Then they were out of the hole and gone, her behind them, so quickly gone there was no time to say anything. Mavin—Mother. And two Shapeshifter cousins, children, that meant, of Mavin's sister or sisters. And a way out. High and pure through that sunny hole came the sound of a trumpet calling "To Air, To Air" for the Armigers. A drum answered from a hillside, "Thawum, Thawum," signal to the Tragamors, "move, move."

"Oh, hells," I giggled hysterically. "Who is doing battle with whom? Is it Himaggery? Or the High King? Or merely some trickery of a Shape-changer who says she bore me . . ."

Silkhands cried, "Oh, Peter, if you're going to go all sensitive and nervous, this isn't a good time for it at all."

I screamed at her, screamed at her like a market stall woman or a mule driver, thrust her before me up the rocky slope until she was pushed half out of the opening, half laughing, half crying at me. "Be damned, Healer," I shouted at her. "It isn't you has to do the things you expect me to do. Go out there and watch the Game, you silly thing, you chatter-bird. Go, go out, out of here and leave me alone . . ."

Then I tumbled back down the rock wall into the bottom of the cavern to lie face down on the stones, weeping miserably and feeling that never, never in my fifteen years of life had I been understood by anyone at all.

After which I went and raised up the dead.

# 13

# The Great Game

I MUST LEAVE MYSELF AGAIN to tell you what I later learned had happened to others. I must go back to Himaggery's realm, back to the fourteenth day of my captivity. An Elator arrived from Schooltown to tell of Mertyn's arrival only hours before he himself arrived.

I have visualized that arrival many times. King Mertyn, in a dusty cloak, his travel hat stained with rain, beard floured with the dirt of the road, riding into the courtyard of the High Demesne among the mists and the blossoms. They offered him time to bathe before he came to Himaggery, and he refused it. He came into the audience hall to find Himaggery awaiting him, not seated upon his chair, elevated, but standing alone without servitors by the door. The two had not met before.

And the King used his Talent. He used Beguilement upon Himaggery, a fatal charm, a deadly charisma. Standing in that room of power, where no chill might rob him of the full use of that Talent which was his, he used it as he had not used it in his life theretofore. So he has told me, his thalan, since that time. He wagered his life upon being able to charm Himaggery into doing what the King wished.

And Himaggery laughed. He laughed, clasped Mertyn by the hand, and led him to a table where he offered him a wash basin full of hot water, a towel, and foods steaming from the kitchens.

"You need not beguile me, King. I will help you without all that charm. I will help you because I believe it is right to do so, though I am less sure of that than of some few other things. Our cause, however, seems to be the cause of Justice."

Mertyn was better educated than many of his fellows. He had, after all, been a student of Windlow, as had Himaggery. Unlike Prionde, the High King, he had listened to Windlow, had even understood some of what he was taught. Thus, when he heard Himaggery use the word "justice'' he recognized the word, and with that recognition came a sense of peace.

"My friend," he said solemnly, "forgive me. I thought to protect my thalan, Peter, through his early years. Who knows? Perhaps I hoped to protect him throughout his life, though we know that in the Game such things are impossible. I have broken many rules. I am paying for that now, perhaps, in being consumed with fear for the boy. I never called him by any name of kinship. I tried to warn him away from that kindermar, Mandor. At the end, I only tried to save him, and I might as well have thrust him into Mandor's hands. Have you any news of him?" Despite all dignity, I am told, his eyes were wet.

"Shh, shh, I understand," said Himaggery. "I had no sisters, thus have had no thalan, but there are young ones I have loved and cared for and fretted over in the dark hours. Yes. I have word brought by an Elator from Bannerwell who has it from a Pursuivant I have stationed there. The boy is imprisoned. He has been harshly treated, but he is not seriously hurt. Which is not to say he may not be hurt at some future time, though the Seers of this Demesne think not. Windlow thinks not, Mertyn."

"Windlow? Here? Oh, how did he come here? How did he manage to escape from Prionde? How wonderful. I wish to see him, Wizard, soon. What a wonderful thing . . ."

And see him he did. Do not think that they were all careless of me, but they were not willing to take impetuous action which might endanger me further. They knew where I was, that I was watched hour on hour, and that I was in great despair, but they knew I wouldn't die of it. Each of them had been equally despairing at one time or another, and each of them had survived it. So, while they plotted and planned to come to Bannerwell for my sake, they plotted and planned for other reasons as well.

"Whether Peter were held by Mandor or not, it would still be necessary to wage Great Game against him, Mertyn." So said Windlow. "We have learned from his mind and from Peter's that the Prince is thinking of linkages . . ."

Mertyn looked thoughtful and curious at once, nodding for the Wizard to say on.

"Mandor believes he can get himself a new body through some use of linkages. So my spies Read. He has in mind a linkage of Demon and

Shapechanger. He has not thought it through. He has not studied or read, for which we may be grateful. Instinct guides him, and it guides him too far. If he had thought more, he would have included a Healer in the group as the Talent most likely to manipulate the tissues of a brain to accommodate him. *We are grateful that he has not thought,* King. He has as yet had no success. Even a small success may show him how limited his imagination has been.''

''I seem to remember that you mentioned linkages to me long and long ago,'' Mertyn said to Windlow. ''It was something you believed was possible . . .''

''It is something I know is possible,'' the old man replied. ''Himaggery has done it. You should have seen it, Mertyn. It was quite wonderful. Demon linked to Pursuivant linked to Elator—with a few Rancelmen mixed in for flavor. They found Peter in Bannerwell in two days. If we had not allowed ourselves to be misled by a few false handmarks, we would have found him in one day. Truly remarkable. And it is only one of an infinite number of things we can do . . .''

''Only one of many things which are possible,'' corrected Himaggery. ''We have done only a few. The possibilities are wide, as Windlow says, and terrifying. Half the things I dream up frighten me out of my wits. But I trust me more than I trust this Mandor, though that, too, is terrifying.''

''Believe me,'' said Mertyn, ''you are wise to do so. I have known of Prince Mandor since he was a child. If there was a simple way to do a thing which would not hurt or kill, he would eschew it in favor of some complex scheme which would maim and mutilate. If there was an honorable thing to do, he would do the opposite. He so conducted himself in the Games of his youth that he had a dozen sworn enemies of great power by the time he was twenty-seven. They were ready to descend upon Bannerwell, to obliterate it forever, with all its long history and the tombs of its lineage. Then Mandor's thalan, Huld, a Demon of good reputation, a Gamesman of honor, prevailed upon the young Prince to go into the Schooltown as a Gamesmaster for a time. It was thought that this sequestering of the young man in a place where he was honor bound not to use his Talent would allow matters time to cool, insults to be forgotten, enemies to become merely un-friends rather than rabid warriors. So it might have done.

143

"But Mandor could not occupy the post of Gamesmaster with honor, or even patience, though it was needful to save his life. He behaved toward Peter as he had always behaved, as he will always behave. There is something warped in him . . ." Mertyn sighed.

"There is nothing more warped in him than in many," said Himaggery heatedly. "Any Gamesman who eats up a dozen pawns during an evening's Game has no more honor than Mandor . . ."

Mertyn nodded. "You say it. I might say it. Windlow, you, I know, would say it. Does the world say it? No. Pawns are pawns for the eating. That is what the world says."

"I am in my own world," said Himaggery. "You, Mertyn, may follow the outer world, but I will make my own. And the knowledge of what can be done with linkages must not come into Mandor's hands. So. It is necessary that Great Game be called. He must be distracted from this obsession. If necessary, he must be destroyed."

"And how will you mount Game against him? He is in his home place. Undoubtedly his battle ovens are erected, his fuel wagons running to and fro from dawn to dawn. You will be far from your home, far from this source of power. He will have an advantage."

"*I* will have the advantage," whispered Himaggery. "And I will use only a hundredth of it. If I were to use it all, the world could not stand against me."

"'Ware, Himaggery," said Windlow, sternly. "'Ware the demands of pride."

"Oh, I am safe enough, old one. For now, at least." He laughed, a little bitterly. "Though you may need to watch me in the future."

Then it was that Himaggery, Windlow, and the King began their work. From all the surrounding area Gamesmen were summoned by Elators to attend upon the Bright Demesne. The Tragamors and Sorcerers who came were many, more than King Mertyn had ever seen in one place.

"Why Tragamors?" he asked. "I can understand Sorcerers, but most Games of this kind depend more heavily upon Armigers than upon Tragamors . . ."

"We will have Armigers when we need them," Himaggery replied in a grim voice. "But we do not need them here. They go toward Bannerwell even now, in small groups, within the forest. As do other Tragamors than those you see here and other Sorcerers, as well. Every one I have been able to recruit during the last decade.''

"I did not know your Demesne counted so many Gamesmen among its followers.''

"It were better that none knew, and well that as few were aware as possible. For that reason, we have had no panoply, no Gamely exercises. What we have learned to do, we have learned in private, and only those safe from the needs of pride have learned with us. It would take only one braggart in a Festival town to have given our secret to the world.''

"What is it you have learned?''

"You will see soon enough. It is easier to see than to explain. We have not yet had enough practice at any part of it. I have been at some pains to keep triflers and troublemakers far from this Demesne. Some, like Dazzle and Borold, two I tolerated out of affection for Silkhands, were sent away on errands of one kind or another if they insisted upon attaching themselves to me. Others I have sent on long journeys. Still, I have always had the fear we would be betrayed.''

"And where is Dazzle now?'' asked Windlow.

"Gone. Gone after Silkhands, still seeking to do harm to her who would only have wished her well. I should have stopped her, should have . . . well. I was thinking of other things.''

And he went on thinking of other things, though not for long, for on that afternoon, the eighteenth of my captivity, an Elator arrived from Bannerwell to tell them that Silkhands had been taken prisoner after being denounced by Dazzle and Borold. And on the day after that, still another messenger arrived to say that Chance and Yarrel had fled from Bannerwell, but that Silkhands was still held there.

It was on that day that Himaggery's legions began the march to Bannerwell, though it was like no march Mertyn had seen before. There was a monstrous wagon piled with many huge, curved shields of metal, polished to a mirror gleam. And there were all those Tragamors in the train. And the way was always starting and stopping, with a curved shield taken off the wagon each place the march stopped, each with a Sorcerer to attend it and at least two Tragamors, though in places there were three or even four. In each spot was a wait while the shield was "tested" while Mertyn fretted and old Windlow lay in his wagon, soft pillowed in quilts, watching the sky. This testing seemed to take eternities, and Mertyn grumbled and sweated, furious that Himaggery would not tell him what was being done.

"I cannot," said Himaggery. "You might well think about it if I told you, and Mandor may have Demons Reading the road."

"Aren't you thinking about it?"

Himaggery laughed. "Does the stonemason think of cutting stone as he does so? His hands know what to do. He thinks of his dinner or of going fishing. That's what I think of. Going fishing."

It was true that all those in the train seemed well practiced at what they did. Their road lay straight across the Middle River, with the first stop made across the lake from the Bright Demesne. Then, each successive stop was in a straight line from the previous one. Where there were hills, a mirror was placed atop each. The nineteenth day of my captivity passed (for I still counted the captivity as I later numbered it for all the time I was in Bannerwell), and the twentieth, and the twenty-first.

During all this time the legions of Himaggery drew closer to Bannerwell, but slowly, a crawling pace which wearied and fretted all within the train. On each morning and evening came a messenger from Bannerwell to say that the ovens were built, that the wood wagons thundered in across the bridge, that the fortress was furnished against siege, that Armigers, Sorcerers, Elators, and Tragamors were assembled with more still coming in. And still Himaggery did not hurry, did not increase his pace. They went on, the shield wagon growing less and less heavily laden, the vast number of Sorcerers and Tragamors dwindling day by day.

And on the evening of the twenty-second day of my captivity, word arrived at Himaggery's tent that Silkhands was to be given to the Divulgers but that she had thwarted Mandor by disappearing.

"I should think," Windlow told them thoughtfully, "that Peter is involved in this. Though my Talent grows dim with age and faulty with time, I seem to See something of that boy in this whole affair. He is all mixed up somehow with Divulgers and manure piles, but the feel of him is still unmistakably Peter, moving about in Bannerwell or beneath it. I am sure of it."

Himaggery laughed silently until tears came to his eyes. "You would advise us not to worry?"

"Oh, worry by all means," said Windlow. "By all means. Yes. It sharpens the wits. A good worry does wonders for the defensive capabilities of the brain. However, I should not advise you to do without sleep.''

Mertyn said, "Somehow, that doesn't help, old teacher. I think it will affect my ability to sleep . . .''

To which Windlow replied, "I think I have an herb here somewhere which will . . .'' And so they slept that night, not overlong, but well.

On the morning came yet another messenger to tell them the most astonishing news. The trumpets and drums of Bannerwell beat summons to air, to move, because upon the surrounding hills had come a mighty host to call Great Game upon Bannerwell, no other than the followers of the High Demesne and the High King himself. It was those same drums and trumpets which I heard as I drove Silkhands out of the caves in a fury. The High King had come to Bannerwell. And why?

Why, he had come to take Windlow back with him, for he believed the old man was held captive in the Bannerwell dungeons.

What followed was something Silkhands saw from her place on Malplace Mountain, watching the Game as Mavin had suggested, crying to herself, and talking, as she watched.

You must see Bannerwell as she saw it. Below Malplace Mountain the river curves down from the north, swoops into a graceful loop before swinging north once more, then turning eastward through Havajor Dike and across the fertile plains to the Gathered Waters. In that loop of river stands a low, curved cliff upon which the walls of the fortress are built to follow the same line, so that cliff and wall are one. On the west the Tower rises from the wall in one unbroken height, on the south the green of the orchard close feathers the walltop with the roofs and spires behind it. From her place on Malplace Mountain, Silkhands could look down into the courtyard to see it packed full of Gamesmen with more upon the walls and the roofs. On the north, hidden by the bulk of the castle, was the shield wall and bridge, and outside that the moat which extended from the Banner on one side to the Banner on the other side, across the whole neck of the looped river. The bridge was up, the gate was down. Any further messages would be carried by Heralds; there was no further need for a bridge.

Then, see upon the hills to the north of Bannerwell a great host of Gamesmen and horses and machines centered upon a cluster of tents with a high, red tent in the midst of them. Here was the High King among his people. Between the moat and the hills was another host under the banner of some tributary Prince to the High King, and still more allies were assembled between these multitudes and the stony dike. This great host had come upon Bannerwell from the north, an unexpected direction, and waited now as Game was called upon Prince Mandor. The trumpets were still shivering when Silkhands came onto the ledge.

It is part of the Talent of a Herald to Move the air about him in such a way that all within the Demesne may hear each word which is spoken. So Silkhands, even at that distance, could hear plainly when the Herald of the High King rode to the edge of the moat and cried:

"All within reach of my voice pay heed, all within reach of my voice give ear, for I speak for the High King, he of the High Demesne, most puissant, most terrible, who comes now in might to call Great Game against Mandor, styled Prince of Bannerwell, who has in most unprincely fashion given sanctuary to traitorous and miscreant pawns, abductors of the old, holders for base ransom the valued friend of Prionde, High King.

"I speak of Windlow the Seer, formerly of Windlow's House, School-house to the High Demesne.

"So says the High King: That Windlow shall be sent forth with honor and in good array, that those who abducted him shall be put forth, dis-honored and bound, and that Mandor, styled Prince, shall pay the cost of all the array here massed against him and his Demesne, else shall Great Game proceed . . ."

"Gamelords," whispered Silkhands. "It's Borold with Mandor." She could see Mandor on the battlement, three figures beside him. Huld, Bor-old, and Dazzle. Now the trumpets of Mandor sounded and Borold rose higher than the tower to look down upon the High King's host as he cried the response of Bannerwell.

"All within sound of my voice pay heed, all within reach of my voice give ear, for I speak for Prince Mandor of Bannerwell. My Prince is not unwilling to meet Great Game with those who have challenged him or those whom he has taken pains to offend. But he begs of the High King an indulgence, that they may speak together with their attendant Demons in order that the High King be sure of the grounds of his offense e'er Game is called . . ."

Then was a long silence during which the Herald of the High Demesne spoke with the High King, as did others of his train, until at last the drums on the hills beat thrice, "thawum, thawum, thawum," and were answered from the castle, "bom, bom, bom." The bridge rattled down, raising a cloud of dust as it struck the far edge of the moat. The gates went up with a creaking clatter of chains, and Mandor rode forth, Huld at his side, Dazzle just behind them. Before them floating in air, went Borold, stately, just at the level of the heads of the horses. "Oh, Borold," lamented Silkhands. "How silly. How silly you are."

From her place Silkhands could hear nothing of what went on between Mandor and the High King. She saw it all. She saw Huld salute the Demon of the High King, saw Dazzle summoned forward to bow and pose and talk and gesture. Even from that great distance the whole was unmistakable. She could even have put the words into their mouths, the suspicious whine of the High King, the assertion by Mandor that Windlow was not in Bannerwell, the testimony of Dazzle that the old man was in the Bright Demesne, that some of the culprits who had taken him were possibly even now on their way to challenge Bannerwell while another of them was probably hiding in the caves beneath the fortress. Smile, smile, pose, pose. The Demons frowned, spoke, spoke again.

At last the High King nodded his head, snarled something from one side of his mouth, and rode forward, some of his company behind him, though the greater part still covered the hills to the north. Silkhands saw Signalers flicking from place to place, saw the host to the east begin to scurry and shift to meet a new threat from that direction, finally saw the High King and his close attendants ride within Bannerwell's walls, and the great gate close behind him.

"Allies," Silkhands whispered to herself. "From challengers to allies, within the hour. Oh, Himaggery, I hope you know what it is you are doing."

Had she looked upward at that moment she would have seen an Elator poised above her on a stony prominence, watching the scene as she herself had done and with no less understanding. This was Himaggery's spy, gone to him in that instant to warn him of the unexpected alliance. But Silkhands fretted upon the mountain, thinking perhaps to come warn me, or trudge off through the forest looking for someone else to tell, or hope to intercept Himaggery, or perhaps just curl up in a ball where she was and pray that the world would not notice her until it had stopped its foolishness. As it was, she did none of these things. She simply sat where she was and waited to see what would happen. . . .

I, of course, knew none of this. I had gone from fury to martyred sulkiness, from rage to wounded sensitivity in the space of an hour or so. I had decided that Mavin was my mother and that I hated her, and then that she could not be my mother to have spoken to me as she had, and then that it didn't matter. I had cursed Mertyn, briefly, before remembering it was Mandor who had injured me, after which I cursed him. The echoing caverns accepted all this without making any response. Rage or sobs were all one to the cave. It amplified each equally and sent it back to me from a dozen directions in solemn mockery until I was tired of the whole thing. Even while all this emotion was going on, some cold part of my brain began to plan what I would do next and why and whether this or that option might be a good thing to consider. So, when I was done making insufferable noises for my own benefit, what needed to be done next was already there in my brain, ready to be accomplished.

Windlow had spoken of Ghost Pieces and Ghost Talents. It was apparent that the caves contained ghosts enough to make a great host, among them most of the Talents which would have been available in a sizable Demesne. If Dorn could command such Talents, then I could do it as well. However, Ghosts alone might not be enough. The other Talents were there in the pouch at my belt, waiting to be taken. I could have taken Sorcerer, but did not. The mere holding of power would not suit my need. Seer? For what? What would happen would happen within hours, perhaps moments. There would be no need to See more than I might see with my eyes. Demon? Grimpt's small Talent in that direction seemed enough for the present circumstances. I had no useful thoughts about an Armiger's flight or a Sentinel's fire. No. Moved by some adolescent sense of the fitness of things, some desire to win at least some Game of my own, I chose to meet Mandor upon his own ground. I took into my left hand and clutched fast the tiny carved figure of Trandilar, First of the line of Queens and Kings and all lesser nobility.

It came upon me like the warmth of the sun, like the wooing of the wind, gentle, insistent, inexorable. She spoke to me in a voice of rolling stars, heavenly, a huge beneficence to hold smaller souls in thrall. She took me as a lover, as a child, as a beloved spouse, exalted me. Adoration swept over me, then was incorporated within me so that it was I who was loved, the world one which loved me, followed me, adored me. All, all would follow me if I but used this beguilement upon them. Within was the sound of a chuckle, a satisfied breath, not the weary sigh of Dorn but a total satiety of love, love, love. "Trandilar," I said, speaking her name in homage and obeisance.

"Peter . . ." came the spirit voice in reply. Oh, surely Barish had done more than merely force a pattern onto some inanimate matter when he had made these Gamesmen. For the moment I could not move or think as myself. For that moment I was some halfway being, not myself, not Trandilar.

And then it passed, as Dorn had passed, leaving behind all the knowledge and Talent of that so ancient being. I had no fear, now, of Mandor's minions. Compared to this . . . this, his was a puny Talent, fit only for Fluglemen and Pigherders.

From that moment I was no longer a boy. Why should one raise up the dead and remain innocent, but raise up love and fear death? I leave that to you to figure out. I only learned in that moment that it was true.

So, I went back down the dusty corridors, following the prints which Silkhands and I had left toward the end of our journey, then relying upon memory and some instinct to guide me to that same cavern in which the dead kings had so recently been raised. Once there I did that thing which Dorn had taught me how to do, heard that spectral voice once more call into time, "Who comes, who comes, who comes . . ."

And answered it. "One who calls you forth, oh King, you and your forebears and your kin and your children, your followers and your minions, your Armigers, Sorcerers, Demons and Tragamors, your Sentinels and Elators, come forth, come forth at my command; rise up and do my will."

The King spoke to me, like a little chill wind in my ear, softly crying, "Call thy Game, oh spirit. Call thy Game and we will follow thee . . ."

# 14

# Challenge and Game

THE OUTFLUNG RAMPARTS OF MALPLACE MOUNTAIN STRETCH far
from the summit to east and north, opening in one place to permit the
River Banner to loop around Bannerwell, thrusting out both east and west
of that fortress to push the river north and, on the east, making a long
ridge of stone through which the river washed its way in time long past.
It cuts now through that ridge like a silver knife, and the place is named
the Cutting of Havajor Dike, or often just "The Cut." From the eastern
side of this dike one may see the bannerets on the spires of Bannerwell,
but the whole of it and its surroundings cannot be seen until the dike
itself is mounted. So it was that Himaggery saw it first from the top of
the dike, saw the assembled hosts inside and out of it, the moat and river
around it. What he saw was not unexpected. His Elators had kept him
advised of all, of the High King's arrival, of the Game Call, the negotiations, the unexpected alliance. Thus when he had ridden to the top of
the dike and dismounted, he did not waste a moment in open-mouthed
staring. He knew well enough what it would look like.

Some of those with him were not so sanguine. Indeed, the host before
them was mightier than any could recall in memory. The tents of the
High King's array spread north and west like a mushroom plot fruiting
after rain. Between the dike and the Banner the level plain was filled
with smaller contingents grouped around their ovens, and the sound of
axes still rang from the forested slopes of Malplace Mountain above the
ferry barges moored upon the river. Mertyn stared. Even Windlow sat up
in his wagon and looked at the horde, bemused. "If I had not Seen it
already," he is reported to have said, "I would have been amazed."

Himaggery was busy with the last of the huge curved mirrors, setting
it in place upon the dike, bracing it well with strong metal stanchions
and setting men ready to hold it or prop it up if it were overthrown. "It

must withstand Tragamor push,'' he told them. ''Brace yourselves and be ready . . .''

''Ware, Himaggery,'' said a Demon, close at hand. ''Herald comes . . .''

And it was Borold once again, Borold showing off for Dazzle who stood resplendent upon the tower top of Bannerwell, Borold in his pride, glowing with it. He cast a look over his shoulder as he floated up the dike toward Himaggery, one long look to see her standing there. Windlow thought that in that look was such love and uncritical adoration as a god might instill into a new creation. ''Except, how boring at last,'' he thought. ''To have one always, always adoring one. But, perhaps gods do not get bored . . .'' (You may wonder how I knew what he thought, what he said, what happened. Never mind. Eventually, I knew everything that had happened to everyone. Eventually I knew too much.)

It was Borold who trumpeted the Challenge to Game, Borold who spoke not only for Mandor but for Prionde, as well. Turning his head slightly so that his words could be heard behind him on the fortress walls, he cried, ''All within sound of my voice pay heed: I speak for Mandor of Bannerwell, most adored, most jealously guarded, and for the High King, Prionde, of the High Demesne, most puissant, most terrible. I speak for these two in alliance here assembled to call Great Game and make unanswerable Challenge upon Himaggery, styled Wizard, who has in treacherous fashion betrayed the hospitality shown his followers by the High King by stealing away one dependent, the Seer Windlow, and who has betrayed the good will of Mandor by sending into his Demesne a spy, the Healer Silkhands. For these reasons and others, more numerous than the leaves upon the trees, all reasons of ill faith and betrayal, treachery and all ungameliness, do my Lords cry Challenge upon this Himaggery and wait his move. We cry True Game!''

Borold awaited answer, at first imperiously, then impatiently, finally doubtfully. Himaggery had paid him no attention, but had gone on fiddling with the great mirror. It was some time before Himaggery looked up and gave a signal to an Elator near him. By this time Borold was casting little glances over his shoulder as though to get some signal from the castle. The Elator vanished. Himaggery signaled once more and a Herald rose lazily from the ground, walked to confront Borold. He did not rise in air. He merely stood there and made the far mountains ring with his words.

"Hear the words of Himaggery, Wizard of the Bright Demesne. The Wizard does not cry True Game. The Wizard cries Death, Pain, Horror, Mutilation, Wounds, Blood, Agony, Destruction. The Wizard calls all these and more. HE IS NOT PLAYING!"

And with that there came a great light and a smell of fire moving like a little sun, hurtling out of the east, spreading somewhat as it came, driving toward the great mirror where it stopped, coalesced and was taken up by a Sorcerer who stood there, ready. The Sorcerer turned and released the little sun once more. The quiet troop of Tragamors who had been crouched on the stone stiffened, twisted in unison, bent their heads toward Bannerwell, and sent the bolt of force against the walls of the fortress. Even as it burst there with a shattering impact and a sound of thunder, another little sun shot into the waiting mirror, was caught, was sent after the first, and yet again and again.

Mertyn whispered in awe. "Gamelords, what is it? How have you done this . . ."

To which Himaggery replied, "We have only done what could have been done at any time during the last thousand years. We have used Tragamors, working in teams, to Move the power from place to place. The mirrors are only to catch it, focus it, make it easier for the Sorcerers to pull it in without losing it . . ."

"Ahh," said Mertyn, almost sadly, watching the walls where the lightning bolts struck and struck again. Those walls trembled, melted, powdered, fell to dust. All before them fell to dust. The Gamesmen before them blazed like tiny stars and were gone. The tents blossomed, died. "Where does it come from, this power?"

"From various places," Himaggery answered him, somewhat evasively.

"It is better not to know," whispered Windlow. "Better not to think of it. Better merely to make an end to Bannerwell's pride and Prionde's vainglory, then go. Go on to something better."

But the end was not to be so quick in coming. A struggle broke out near the great mirror. It tipped, moved, and one of the hurtling suns sped past to splash against the far mountain in a cloud of flowing dust. Elators had materialized near the mirror and were trying to overturn it. Among the struggling Gamesmen the forms of fustigars slashed with white fangs, slashed, ran, turned to slash again—Shapeshifters, come up the dike in the guise of beasts.

'' 'Ware, Himaggery,'' cried the watching Demon, and thrust him aside as an arrow flashed from above. They looked up into the faces of Armigers who had come upon them from the wooded sides of the mountain. The Demon signaled. A hurtling ball of fire flew in from the east, was sloppily intercepted by two Sorcerers without benefit of the focusing mirror, was released again, and tossed upward by the Tragamor. The Armigers fell screaming from the sky like clots of ambient ash. Once more the mirror stood upright and the balls of fire struck at the walls of the fortress.

And those walls fell. Himaggery held up his hand, a drum sounded. Far back to the east the sound echoed, relayed back, and back, beyond hearing. The hurtling fires came no more. He waited, poised, watching intently to see what would happen to that great horde before him.

Through the rent in the castle wall the assembled Gamesmen poured out like water, those who could fly darting across the Banner, others leaping into the flood to be carried away to the north, struggling to come to the flat banks there and flee away across the plains. There was a struggle going on in the courtyard which could be seen from the dike: Gamesmen of Bannerwell fighting against those of the High Demesne, red plumes against purple, the red plumes overcoming the purple to release the chains and let the bridge fall. Then the red clad followers of the High King fled the fortress, out across the bridge and the grassy plain, toward the red tents which stood upon the northern heights, running toward them as though safety might be found under that fragile covering.

Himaggery gestured once more. Once more the bolts came into the mirror and were cast forward, this time onto those red tents which burned and were gone. The fleeing Gamesmen turned, milled about, some fleeing to the west, others making for the fringes of the forest, still others turning back to throw themselves into the waters of the Banner. It was not long before Himaggery's men could look down the Cut and see the bodies of those who had drowned in the attempt to swim the Banner, panoplied in sodden glory, dead.

"Prionde?" whispered Windlow. "Was he in that rout?"

"Who could tell, old friend," said Himaggery. "Should we withhold our fire to save one King?"

"No," said Windlow, weeping. "No. We agreed. It shall be as quick and sure as can be done. No long, drawn out Game to make the weaker hope and hope and refuse to surrender. No. Do it quickly, Himaggery."

He answered through clenched teeth. "I'm trying."

Once more the bombardment stopped and Himaggery watched to see what was happening below. There was no movement in the fortress. There were no watchers on the battlements.

"How long?" Himaggery asked.

Windlow answered him, "Soon. When I Saw it in my vision, the sun was just at that place in the sky. They will come forth soon. Wait. Destroy no more . . ."

So they waited. Mertyn asked what they waited for, and Himaggery answered, "For the fulfillment of a vision, King. Windlow has Seen this place, this time. Your thalan is up to something there. See. See that gateway within the wall of the Fortress!"

It was the gateway to the place of tombs, the ceremonial gateway to the Caves of Bannerwell. It opened within the walls of the fortress. It could be seen clearly through the shattered walls from the dike as the guardians of those tombs fled outward, fleeing in horror from something which pursued them. And behind those fleeing Guardsmen came a horde, an array, a Ghost Demesne pouring out of their graves and sepulchers, the catacombs giving up their dead, an army of dust, of dreams, of undying memory; battalions of bones, regiments of rags and rust, spear points red with corruption and time, swords eaten by age, bodies through which the wind moved, inspirited by shadow, tottering, clattering, moaning, sighing as the wind sighs, and calling as with one voice an ultimate horror, "We come, we come, we come . . . to take revenge upon the living, we who no longer live . . ."

They passed through the gateway, across the courtyard like moving shade, and through the great oaken doors of the castle, as though those doors were curtains of gauze. The Guardsmen who had stayed to guard the caves fled through the shattered walls of the fortress and into Himaggery's hands. An enemy held no terror for those who had seen the dead march. I came behind them. They could not be led, only sent, so I had sent them into the castle and stood waiting for them in the castle yard.

They would return again, but they would not return alone. I had commanded it.

I felt the eyes of Himaggery's men on my back. Though I did not turn, I knew well they were there. I had seen them when the gates flew open, had seen the great rent in the fortress wall, knew that others Moved even as I Moved, that all came to a point at this hour. I waited, calm now. Time was done for any foolish blathering. There were no questions now. Only answers, at last.

Then it happened. The doors to the castle burst wide, and the followers of Mandor fled forth, white and trembling, falling, crawling, vomiting on the stones, clutching their way across those slimed stones like crippled creatures, crabwise slithering away, away from what came behind. I saw Dazzle, and Huld, and a hundred faces I had seen in Mandor's halls, the High King, and followers of his. They came forth in a flood and saw me, and seeing me they knelt down or fell down before me and cried to me for help. "King," "Prince," they cried, bending their knees to me, leaning upon their hands and beating their foreheads upon the stone.

And I told them to be still and wait. Be still, I said, for Mandor comes.

As at last he did. No less white than they, no less horrified, and yet with some dignity yet and a pathetic attempt at beguilement. Even now, even now he tried to use Talent upon *me* and still he wound it about himself.

I motioned him to kneel. I said, "I have shown you your dead, Mandor. I have brought you your dead. The ancient ones you have dishonored. The newly dead you have robbed of life. Some among them have Game to call against you, so they tell me . . ."

If it were possible for him to grow more pale, he did so. I looked from him to Dazzle. "And there are other dead, Dazzle. Your mother, I think, and others perhaps. Would you have them brought here to join those we have brought from the Caves of Bannerwell?"

She did not answer me. I had not thought she would. She was too busy clutching the power to herself, weaving, weaving as Mandor was. Well, let them weave. The Ghost army crowded out of the castle door, moving toward these pitiful mortals, moving to trample them, take them up, inhabit them, clothe themselves in life again . . . Dorn within me cautioned me. Before they grew stronger, it was time to send them back . . . back . . .

And then, of a sudden, it was as though someone lifted a great heaviness from me. Before me the Ghosts began to waver. They cried softly, once, twice, and were gone. A sound swept through my head like wind in pines and the smell of rain. Dazzle looked up at me, horrid that face. Mandor saw her, screamed, and screamed again as his people looked upon him and scrawled away from him, away and away, clutching at one another like survivors of some great flood, and casting glances backwards at him in horror. Then it was that Mandor and Dazzle flew at one another, clawing, striking with their hands, locked in a battle of ultimate despair.

Behind me someone spoke my name. "Peter. Enough. We have come to Bannerwell as you have asked."

I turned. It was that lean man, Riddle, the Immutable, the leader of the Immutables, Tossa's father.

"I have been told what you tried to do," he said. "For Tossa. I thank you."

"It was useless," I wept. "Useless, as this has been. But I tried to . . ."

"I know," he touched my arm. Then I saw others behind him, Chance, Yarrel.

"You got there," I said stupidly. "You got back."

Yarrel's eyes were on Mandor and Dazzle, not upon me. His expression was one I dreaded, full of horror and contempt. I knew what he was thinking and did not want him to say it, but he did. "See there," he whispered. "This is what Talents do. This is all that they do, and I have had enough of it . . ."

"Shhh," said Riddle. "We have agreed. Part of the blame is ours. We have allowed it to go on. And we are agreed that it must end . . ."

"While you are here, they cannot use their *Talents*," he spit the word at me. "But when you are gone, Riddle, they will use them once more. And again. And again." He turned away and went through the shattered wall, his shoulders heaving. Once he turned to look back and saw my face, saw something there, perhaps, which moved him for a moment. His hand moved as though he would have gestured to me in friendship, but his face hardened in that moment and he turned away.

I knew what I could do. I could follow him. Soon we would be away from Riddle's force or power or Talent and my own would be usable once more. Then I could evoke Trandilar, and Yarrel would love me as once he had done—more, more. He would adore me. As Mandor's people had done. Oh, for the moment I wanted that. Yes. For that moment I wanted that.

And then I did not want that at all, never, not Yarrel.

I miss him. I have not seen him, but I know he is well. Some days I need him greatly, greatly, more than I can say. Perhaps, someday . . . well. All time is full of somedays.

After a long time full of many confusions, we came away from Bannerwell. Dazzle and Mandor stayed behind, together with Huld and a few others—and the Immutables. Neither of them can hide what they are any longer. They are what they are.

I imagine them there, inhabiting the corridors and stairways of Bannerwell, drifting like shadows down long, silent staircases, vanishing behind hangings, seen at a distance upon a crenellated battlement, dark shadows, moving blots, heard in the long nights as the wind is heard, a ceaseless moan, never encountering one another except to see a shade vanish from a lighted room, to hear a cry down a chimney stack from some long unused place within that mountain of stone which is Bannerwell.

I imagine them awake in the dark hours, veiled by night, hidden in gloom, plodding endless aisles of opulent dust in the Caves of Bannerwell to look upon the tombs, to dream of such a silence, such a healing as that, for on the tombs the marble dead sleep whole and unblemished, softly gleaming in torchlight, forever safe except to one such as I—such as I.

I think of Huld, hopeless and without honor, committed to his endless servitude, his mordacious kinship with horror, and I imagine that he follows them there, down those endless halls, watering the sterile dust with his tears.

Will we meet again, Mandor and I? I do not think he will live long. I would not if I were he.

But—I am not he.

And I—I returned with Himaggery to the Bright Demesne. We found Silkhands upon the mountain and brought her with us. She was changed by it all. She does not talk as much now as she used to. But then, neither do I.

Windlow is here with us. Riddle comes to meet with Himaggery now and again. Our part of the world is only a small part of the world. Elsewhere there are Guardians and Councils and Wizardly doings and much persecution of Heresy. There are plans afoot. When a little time has passed, I may have heart to take part in them.

Just now I do not take part in much. Himaggery says he is sure there is a way Talents such as mine can be fitted into a world which Yarrel would approve, a way in which a Peter and a Yarrel may continue to be friends. Just now, however, that world seems far away and long into the future.

So, I think on that and "imagine" what such a world might be like. What might my place in it be? I am such an animal as they have not known before, a Shifter-King-Necromancer who may, if he chooses, become Sorcerer, Seer, Sentinel—and every other thing as well. I must leave here to decide about that, I think. I must find Mavin. I think she knows something which all these solemn men have not yet thought of.

The fruit trees bloom in the mists of the Bright Demesne. Soon it will be Festival time. I shall no longer sew ribbons upon my tunic to run the streets as a boy. King's blood one. King's blood ten. King's blood, and the world waits.

# NECROMANCER NINE

# 1

# Necromancer Nine

I HAD DECIDED to change myself into a Dragon and go looking for my mother despite all argument to the contrary.

Himaggery the Wizard and old Windlow the Seer were determined otherwise. They had been after me for almost a year, ever since the great battle at Bannerwell. Having seen what I did there, they had decided that my "Talent" could not be wasted, and between them they had thought of at least a dozen things they wanted done with it. I, on the other hand, simply wanted to forget the whole thing. I wanted to forget I had become the owner—can I say "owner"?—of the Gamesmen of Barish, forget I had ever called upon the terrible Talents of those Gamesmen. I'd only done it to save my life, or so I told myself, and I wanted to forget about it.

Himaggery and Windlow wouldn't let me.

We were in one of the shining rooms at the Bright Demesne, a room full of the fragrance of blossoms and ubiquitous wisps of mist. Old Windlow was looking at me pathetically, eyes three-quarters buried in delicate wrinkles and mouth turned down in that expression of sweet reproach. Gamelords! One would think he was my mother. No. My own mother would not have been guilty of that expression, not that wildly eccentric person. Himaggery was as bad, stalking the floor as he often did, hands rooting his hair up into devil's horns, spiky with irritation.

"I don't understand you, boy," he said in that plaintive thunder of his. "We're at the edge of a new age. Change rushes upon us. Great things are about to happen; Justice is to be enthroned at last. We invite you to help, to participate, to plan with us. You won't. You go hide in the orchards. You mope and slope about like some halfwitted pawn of a groom, and then when I twit you a bit for behaving like a perennial adolescent, you merely say you will change into a Dragon and go off to find Mavin Manyshaped. Why? We need you. Why won't you help us?''

I readied my answers for the tenth time. I behave as an adolescent, I would say, because I am one—barely sixteen and puzzled over things which would puzzle men twice my age. I mope because I am apprehensive. I hide in orchards because I am tired of argument. I got ready to say these things. . . .

"And why," he thundered at me unexpectedly, "go as a Dragon?"

The question caught me totally by surprise. "I thought it would be rather fun," I said, weakly.

"Fun!" He shrugged this away as the trifle it was.

"Well, all right," I answered with some heat. "Then it would be quick. And likely no one would bother me."

"Wrong on both counts," he said. "You go flying off across the purlieus and demesnes as a Dragon, and every stripling Firedrake or baby Armiger able to get three man-heights off the ground will be challenging you to Games of Two. You'll spend more time dueling than looking for Mavin Manyshaped, and from what your thalan, Mertyn, tells me, she will take a good bit of finding." He made a gesture of frustrated annoyance, oddly compassionate.

"You have others," I muttered. "You have thousands of followers here. Armigers ready to fly through the air on your missions. Elators ready to flick themselves across the lands if you raise an eyebrow at them. Demons ready to Read the thoughts of any who come within leagues of the Bright Demesne. You don't need me. Can't you let one young person find out something about himself before you eat him up in your plots. . . ."

Windlow said, "If you were just any young person, we'd let you alone, my boy. You aren't just any young person. You know that. Himaggery knows it. I know it. Isn't that right?"

"I don't care," I said, trying not to sound merely contentious.

"You should care. You have a Talent such as any in the world might envy. Talents, I should say. Why, there's almost nothing you can't do, or cause, or bring into being. . . ."

"*I* can't," I shouted at them. "Himaggery, Windlow, *I* can't. It isn't me who does all those things."

I pulled the pouch from my belt and emptied it upon the table between us, the tiny carved Gamesmen rolling out onto the oiled wood in clattering profusion. I set two of them upon their bases, the taller ones, a black Necromancer and a white Queen, Dorn and Trandilar. They sat there, like stone or wood, giving no hint of the powers and wonders which would come from them if I gripped them in my hand. "I tried to give them to you once, Himaggery. Remember? You wouldn't take them. You said, 'No, Peter, they came to you. They belong to you, Peter.' Well, they're mine, Himaggery, but they aren't *mine*. I wish you'd understand."

"Explain it to me," he said, blank faced.

I tried. "When I first took the figure of Dorn into my hand, there in the caves under Bannerwell, Dorn came into my mind. He was . . . is an old man, Himaggery. Very wise. Very powerful. His mind has sharp edges; he has seen strange things, and his mind echoes with them— resonates to them. He can do strange, very marvelous things. It is *he* who does them. I am only a kind of . . ."

"Host," suggested Windlow. "Housing? Vehicle?"

I laughed without humor. They knew so much but understood so little. "Perhaps. Later, I took Queen Trandilar, Mistress of Beguilement. First of all the Rulers. Younger than Dorn, but still, far older than I am. She had lived . . . fully. She had understanding I did not of . . . erotic things. She does wonderful things, too, but it is she who does them." I pointed to the other Gamesmen on the table. "There are nine other types there. Dealpas, eidolon of Healers. Sorah, mightiest of Seers. Shattnir, most powerful of Sorcerers. I suppose I could take them all into myself, become a kind of . . . inn, hotel for them. If that is all I am to be. Ever."

Windlow was looking out the window, his face sad. He began to chant, a child's rhyme, one used for jump rope. "Night-dark, dust-old, bony Dorn, grave-cold; Flesh-queen, love-star, lust-pale, Trandilar; Shifted, fetched, sent-far, trickiest is Thandbar." He turned to Himaggery and shook his head slowly, side to side. "Let the boy alone," he said.

Himaggery met the stare, held it, finally flushed and looked away. "Very well, old man. I have said everything I can say. If Peter will not, he will not. Better he do as he will, if that will content him."

Windlow tottered over to me and patted my shoulder. He had to reach up to do it. I had been growing rather a lot. "It may be you will make these Talents your own someday, boy. It may be you cannot wield a

Talent well unless it is your own. In time, you may make Dorn's Talent yours, and Trandilar's as well.''

I did not think that likely, but did not say so.

Himaggery said, "When you go, keep your ears open. Perhaps you can learn something about the disappearances which will help us.''

"What disappearances?'' I asked guardedly.

"The ones we have been discussing for a season,'' he said. "The disappearances which have been happening for decades now. A vanishment of Wizards. Disappearances of Kings. They go, as into nothing. No one knows how, or where, or why. Among those who go, too many were our allies.''

"You're trying to make me curious,'' I accused. "Trying to make me stay.''

He flushed angrily. "Of course I want you to stay, boy. I've begged you. Of course I wish you were curious enough to offer your help. But if you won't, you won't. If Windlow says not to badger you, I won't. Go find your mother. Though why you should want to do so is beyond me. . . .'' and his voice faded away under Windlow's quelling glare.

I gathered the Gamesmen, the taller ones no longer than my littlest finger, delicate as lace, incorruptible as stone. I could have told him why I wanted to find Mavin, but I chose not to. I had seen her only once since infancy, only once, under conditions of terror and high drama. She had said nothing personal to me, and yet there was something in her manner, in her strangeness, which was attractive to me. As though, perhaps, she had answers to questions. But it was all equivocal, flimsy. There were no hard reasons which Himaggery would accept.

"Let it be only that I have a need,'' I whispered. "A need which is Peter's, not Dorn's, not Trandilar's. I have a Talent which is mine, also, inherited from her. I am the son of Mavin Manyshaped, and I want to see her. Leave it at that.''

"So be it, boy. So I will leave it.''

He was as good as his word. He said not another word to me about staying. He took time from his meetings and plottings to pick horses for me from his own stables and to see I was well outfitted for the trip north to Schooltown. If I was to find Mavin, the search would begin with Mertyn, her brother, my thalan. Once Himaggery had taken care of these details, he ignored me. Perversely, this annoyed me. It was obvious that no one was going to blow trumpets for me when I left, and this hurt my feelings. As I had done since I was four or five years old, I went down to the kitchens to complain to Brother Chance.

"Well, boy, you didn't expect a testimony dinner, did you? Those are both wise old heads, and they wouldn't call attention to you wandering off. Too dangerous for you, and they know it."

This shamed me. They had been thinking of me after all. I changed the subject. "I thought of going as a Dragon. . . ."

"Fool thing to do," Chance commented. "Can't think of anything more gomerous than that. What you want is all that fire and speed and the feel of wind on your wings. All that power and swooping about. Well, that might last half a day, if you was lucky." He grimaced at me to show what he thought of the notion, as though his words had not conveyed quite enough. I flinched. I had learned to deal with Himaggery and Windlow, even to some extent with Mertyn, who had taught me and arranged for my care and protection by setting Chance to look after me, but I had never succeeded in dealing with Chance himself. Every time I began to take myself seriously, he let me know how small a vegetable I was in his particular stew. Whenever he spoke to me it brought back the feel of the kitchen and his horny hands pressing cookies into mine. Well. No one liked the Dragon idea but me.

"Well, fetch-it, Chance. I am a Shifter."

"Well, fetch-it, yourself, boy. Shift into something sensible. If you're going to go find your mama, we got to go all the way to Schooltown to ask Mertyn where to look, don't we? Change yourself into a baggage horse. That'll be useful." He went on with our packing, interrupting himself to suggest, "You got the Talent of that there Dorn. Why not use him. Go as a Necromancer."

"Why Dorn?" I asked and shivered. "Why not Trandilar?" Of the two, she was the more comfortable, though that says little for comfort.

"Because if you go traveling around as a Prince or King or any one of the Rulers, you'll catch followers like a net catches fish, and you'll be up to your gullet in Games before we get to the River. You got three Talents, boy. You can Shift, but you don't want to Shift into something in-con-spic-u-ous. You can Rule, but that's dangerous, being a Prince or a King. Or you can . . . well, Necromancers travel all over all the time and nobody bothers them. They don't need to *use* the Talent. Just having it is enough.''

In the end he had his way. I wore the black, broad-brimmed hat, the full cloak, the gauze mask smeared with the death's head. It was no more uncomfortable than any other guise, but it put a weight upon my heart. Windlow may have guessed that, for he came tottering down from his tower in the chill morning to tell us good-bye. ''You are not pretty, my boy, but you will travel with fewer complications this way.''

''I know, Old One. Thank you for coming down to wave me away.''

''Oh, I came for more than that, lad. A message for your thalan, Mertyn. Tell him we will need his help soon, and he will have word from the Bright Demesne.'' There was still that awful, pathetic look in his eyes.

''What do you mean, Windlow? Why will you need his help?''

''There, boy. There isn't time to explain. You would have known more or less if you'd been paying attention to what's been going on. Now is no time to become interested. Journey well.'' He turned and went away without my farewell kiss, which made me grumpy. All at once, having gained my own way, I was not sure I wanted it.

We stopped for a moment before turning onto the high road. Away to the south a Traders' train made a plume of dust in the early sky, a line of wagons approaching the Bright Demesne.

''Traders.'' Chance snorted. ''As though Himaggery didn't have enough problems.''

It was true that Traders seemed to take up more time than their merchandise was worth, and true that Himaggery seemed to spend a great deal of time talking with them. I wasn't thinking of that, however, but of the choice of routes which confronted us. We could go up the eastern side of the Middle River, through the forests east of the Gathered Waters and the lands of the Immutables. Chance and I had come that way before, though not intentionally. This time I chose the western side of the River, through farmlands and meadowlands wet with spring floods and over a hundred hump-backed, clattering bridges. There was little traffic in any direction; woodwagons moving from forest to village, water oxen shuffling from mire to meadow, a gooseherd keeping his hissing flock in order with a long, blossomy wand. Along the ditches webwillows whispered a note of sharp gold against the dark woodlands, their downy kittens ready to burst into bloom. Rain breathed across windrows of dried leaves; greening now with upthrust grasses and the greeny-bronze of curled fern. There was no hurry in our going. I was sure Himaggery had sent an Elator to let Mertyn know I was on the way.

That first day we saw only a few pawns plowing in the fields, making the diagonal ward-of-evil sign when they saw me but willing enough to sell Chance fresh eggs and greens for all that. The second day we caught up to a party of merchants and traveled just behind them into Vestertown where they and we spent the night at the same inn. They no more than the pawns were joyed to see me, but they were traveled men and made no larger matter of my presence among them. Had they known it, they had less to fear from me than from Chance. I would take nothing from them but their courtesy, but Chance would get them gambling if he could. They were poorer the next day for their night's recreation, and Chance was humming a victory song as we went along the lake in the morning light.

The Gathered Waters were calm and glittering, a smiling face which gave no indication of the storms which often troubled it. Chance reminded me of our last traveling by water, fleeing before the wind and from a ship full of pawners sent by Mandor of Bannerwell to capture me.

"I don't want to think about that," I told him. "And of that time."

"I thought you was rather fond of that girl," he said. "That Immutable girl."

"Tossa. Yes. I was fond of her, Chance, but she died. I was fond of Mandor, too, once, and he is as good as dead, locked up in Bannerwell for all he is Prince of the place. It seems the people I am fond of do not profit by it much."

"Ahh, that's nonsense, lad. You're fond of Silkhands, and she's Gamesmistress down in Xammer now, far better off than when you met her. Windlow, too. You helped him away from the High King, Prionde, and I'd say that's better off. It was the luck of the Game did Tossa, and I'm sorry for it. She was a pretty thing."

"She was. But that was most of a year ago, Chance. I grieved over her, but that's done now. Time to go on to something else."

"Well, you speak the truth there. It's always time for something new."

So we rode along, engaged at times in such desultory conversation, other times silent. This was country I had not seen before. When I had come from Bannerwell to the Bright Demesne after the battle, it had been across the purlieus rather than by the long road. In any case, I had not been paying attention then.

We came to the River Banner very late on the third day of travel, found no inn there but did find a ferrymaster willing to have us sleep in the shed where the ferries were kept. We hauled across at first light, spent that night camped above a tiny hamlet no bigger than my fist, and rode into Schooltown the following noon.

Somehow I had expected it to be changed, but it was exactly the same: little houses humped up the hills, shops and Festival halls bulking along the streets, cobbles and walls and crooked roofs, chimneys twisting up to breathe smoke into the hazy sky, and the School Houses on the ridge above. Havad's House, where Mandor had been Gamesmaster. Dorcan's House across the way. Bilme's House, where it was said Wizards were taught. Mertyn's House where my thalan was chief Gamesmaster, where I had grown up in the nurseries to be bullied by Karl Pig-face and to love Mandor and to depart. A sick, sweet feeling went through me, half nausea, half delight, together with the crazy idea that I would ask Mertyn to let me stay at the House, be a student again. Most students did not leave until they were twenty-five. I could have almost a decade here, in the peace of Schooltown. I came to myself to find Chance clutching my horse's bridle and staring at me in concern.

"What is it, boy? You look as though you'd been ghost bit."

"Nothing." I laughed, a bit unsteadily. "A crazy idea, Brother Chance."

"You haven't called me that since we left here."

"No. But we're back, now, aren't we? Don't worry, Chance. I'm all right." We turned the horses over to a stable pawn and went in through the small side door beside the kitchens. It was second nature to do so, habit, habit to remove my hat, to go off along the corridor behind Chance, habit to hear a familiar voice rise tauntingly behind me.

"Why, if it isn't old Fat Chance and Prissy Pete, come back to go to School with us again."

I stopped dead in savage delight. So, Karl Pig-face was still here. Of course he was still here, along with all his fellow tormentors. He had not seen my face. Slowly I put the broad black hat upon my head, turned to face them where they hovered in the side corridor, lips wet and slack with anticipation of another bullying. I was only a shadow to them where

I stood. I shook Chance's restraining hand from my shoulder, moved toward the lantern which hung always just at that turning.

"Yes, Karl," I whispered in Dorn's voice. "It is Peter come to School again, but not with you...." Stepping into the light on the last word, letting them see the death's-head mask, hearing the indrawn breath, the retching gulp which was all Karl could get out. Then they were gone, yelping away like whipped pups, away to the corridors and attics. I laughed silently, overcome.

"That wasn't nice," said Chance sanctimoniously.

"Aaah, Chance." I poked him in his purse, where the merchants' coins still clinked fulsomely. "We have our little failings, don't we? It was you who told me to travel as a Necromancer, Chance. I cannot help it if it scares small boys witless." My feelings of sick sweet nostalgia had turned to ones of delighted vengeance. Karl might think twice before bullying a smaller boy again. I planned how, before I left, I might drive the point home.

In order to reach Mertyn's tower room we had to climb past the schoolrooms, the rooms of the other Masters. Gamesmaster Gervaise met us on the landing outside his own classroom, and he knew me at once, seeming totally unawed by the mask.

"Peter, my boy. Mertyn said you'd be coming to visit. He's down in the garden, talking to a tradesman just now. Come in and have wine with me while you wait for him. Come in, Chance. I have some of your favorite here to drown the dust of the road. I remember we had trouble keeping it when you were here, Chance. No less trouble now, but it's I who drink it." He led us through the cold classroom where the Game-model swam in its haze of blue to his own sitting room, warm with firelight and sun. "Brrrr." He shivered as he shut the door. "The older I get, the harder it becomes to bear the cold of the game model. But you remember. All you boys have chapped hands and faces from it."

I shivered in sympathy and remembrance, accepting the wine he poured. "You always had us work with the model when it was snowing out, Master Gervaise. And in the heat of summer, we never did."

"Well, that seems perverse, doesn't it? It wasn't for that reason, of course. In the summer it's simply too difficult to keep the models cold. We lock them away down in the ice cellar. It will soon be too warm this year. Not like last season where winter went on almost to midsummer."

He poured wine for himself, sat before the fire. "Now, tell me what you've been doing since Bannerwell. Mertyn told me all about that." He shook his head regretfully. "Pity about Mandor. Never trusted him, though. Too pretty."

I twirled my glass, watching the wine swirl into a spiral and climb the edges. "I haven't been doing much."

"No Games?" He seemed surprised.

"No, sir. There is very little Gaming in the Bright Demesne."

"Well, that comes with consorting with Wizards. I told Mertyn you should get out, travel a bit, try your Talent. But it seems you're doing that." He nodded and sipped. "Strange are the Talents of Wizards. That's an old saying, you know. I have never known one well, myself. Is Himaggery easy to work with?"

"Yes, sir. I think he is. Very open. Very honest."

"Ah." He laid a finger along his nose and winked. "Open and honest covers a world of strategy, no doubt. Well. Who would have thought a year ago you would manifest such a Talent as Necromancy. Rare. Very rare. We have not had a student here in the last twenty years who manifested Necromancy."

"There are Talents I would have preferred," I said. Chance was looking modestly at his feet, saying nothing. This fact more than anything else made me cautious. I had been going to say that Necromancy was not my own or only Talent, but decided to leave the subject alone.

"I don't think I even have a Gamespiece of a Necromancer," he said, brow furrowed. "Let me see whether I do...." He was up, through the door into the classroom. I followed him as seemed courteous. He was rooting about in the cold chest which housed the Gamespieces, itself covered with frost and humming as its internal mechanism labored to retain the cold. "Armigers," he said. "Plenty of Armigers. Seers, Shifters, Rancelmen, Pursuivants, quite an array here. Minor pieces; Totem, Talisman, Fetish. Here's an Afrit, forgotten I had that. Here's a whole set of air serpents, Dragon, Firedrake, Colddrake, all in one box. Well. No Necromancer. I didn't think I had one."

I picked up a handful of the little Gamespieces, dropped them quickly as their chill bit my fingers. They were the same size as the ones I carried so secretly, perhaps less detailed. Under the frost, I couldn't be sure.

"Gamesmaster Gervaise," I asked, "where do you get them? I never thought to ask when I was a student, but where do they come from?"

"The Gamespieces? Oh, there's a Demesne of magicians, I think, off to the west somewhere, where they are fashioned. Traders bring them. Most of them are give-aways, lagniappe when we buy supplies. I got that set of air serpents when I bought some tools for the stables. Give-aways, as I said."

"But how can they give them away? To just anyone? How could they be kept cold?"

Gervaise shook his head at me. "No, no, my boy. They don't give Gamespieces to anyone but Gamesmasters. Who else would want them? They do it to solicit custom. They give other things to other people. Some merchants I know receive nice gifts of spices, things from the northern jungles. All to solicit custom." He patted the cold chest and led the way back to Chance. The level of wine in the bottle was considerably lower, and I smiled. He gave me that blank, "Who, me?" stare, but I smiled nonetheless.

"I hear Mertyn's tread on the stairs," I said. "I take leave of you, Gamesmaster Gervaise. We will talk again before I leave." And we bowed ourselves out, onto the stair. I said to Chance, "You were very silent."

"Gervaise is very talkative among his colleagues, among the tradesmen in the town, among farmers. . . ." Chance said. "You may be sure anything you said to him will be repeated thrice tomorrow."

"Ah," I said. "Well, we gave him little enough to talk of."

"That's so," he agreed owlishly. "As is often best. You go up to Mertyn, lad. I'm for the kitchens to see what can be scratched up for our lunch."

So it was I knocked on Mertyn's door and was admitted to his rooms by Mertyn himself. I did not know quite what to say. It was the first time I had seen him in this place since I had learned we were thalan. I have heard that in distant places there are some people who care greatly about their fathers. It is true here among some of the pawns. My friend Yarrel, for example. Well, among Gamesmen, that emotion is between thalan, between male children and mother's full brother; between female children and mother's full sister. Here is it such a bond that women who have no siblings may choose from among their intimate friends those who will stand in such stead. But our relationship, Mertyn's and mine, had never been acknowledged within this house.

He solved it all for me. "Thalan," he said, embracing me and taking the cloak from my shoulders. "Here, give me your hood, your mask. Pfah! What an ugly get-up. Still, very wise to wear it. Chance's choice, no doubt? He was always a wary one. I did better than I knew when I set him to watch over you."

I was suddenly happy, contented, able to smile full in his face without worrying what he would say or think when I told him why I came. "Why did you pick Chance?" I asked.

"Oh, he was a rascal of a sailor, left here by a boat which plied up and down the lakes and rivers to the Southern Seas. I liked him. No nonsense about him and much about survival. So, I said, you stay here in this House as cook or groom or what you will, but your job is to watch over this little one and see he grows well."

"He did that," I said.

"He did that. Fed you cookies until your eyes bulged. Stood you up against the bullies and let you fight it out. Speaking of which, I recall you often had a bit of trouble with Karl? Had a habit of finding whatever would hurt the most, didn't he?"

"Oh," I said and laughed bitterly, "he did, indeed. Probably still does."

"Does, yes. Early Talent showing there. Something to do with digging out secrets, finding hidden things. Unpleasant boy. Will be no less unpleasant in the True Game I should think. Well, Chance stood you up to him."

"I'm grateful to you for Chance," I said. "I . . . I understand why you did not call me thalan before."

"I didn't want to endanger you, Peter. If it had been known you were my full sister's son, some oaf would have tried to use you against me. Some oaf did it anyhow, though unwittingly." He sat silent for a moment. "Well, lad, what brings you back to Mertyn's House? I had word you were coming, but no word of the reason."

"I want to find Mavin."

"Ah. Are you quite sure that is what you want to do?"

"Quite sure."

"I'll help you then, if I can. You understand that I do not know where she is?"

I nodded, though until that moment I had hoped he would simply tell me where to find her. Still.

He went on, "If I knew where she was, any Demon who wanted to find her could simply Read her whereabouts in my head and pass the word along to whatever Gamesman might be wanting to challenge her. No. She's too secret an animal for that. She gives me sets of directions from time to time. That's all. If I need to find her, I have to try to decipher them."

"But you'll tell me what they are?"

"Oh, I've written down a copy for you. She gave them to me outside Bannerwell, where we were camped on Havajor Dike. You remember the place? Well, she came to my tent that night, after the battle, and gave them to me. Then she pointed away north—which is important to remember, Peter, north—and then she vanished."

"Vanished?"

"Went. Away. Slipped out of the tent and was gone. Took the shape of an owl and flew away, for all I know. Vanished."

"Doesn't she ever stay? You must have grown up together as children?"

"Oh, well, by the time I was of an age to understand anything, she was almost grown, already Talented. Still, I remember her as she was then. She was very lovely in her own person, very strange, liking children, liking me, others my age. She did tricks and changes for us, things to make us laugh. . . ."

"And she brought me to you?"

"Yes. When you were only a toddler. She said she had carried you unchanging, and nursed you, unchanging, all those long months never changing, so that you would have something real to know and love. But the time had come for you to be schooled, and she preferred for some reason not to do that among Shifters. I never knew exactly why, except that she felt you would learn more and be safer here. So, she brought you here to me, in Mertyn's House, and I lied to everyone. I said you were Festival-get I'd found wrapped in a blanket on the doorstep. Then I tried never to think about you when there were Demons about."

"And I never knew. No one ever knew."

"No. I was a good liar. But not a good Gamesman. I couldn't keep you away from Mandor."

"He beguiled me," I mused. "Why me? There were smarter boys, better-looking boys."

"He was clever. Perhaps he noticed something, some little indication of our relationship. Well. It doesn't matter now. You're past all that. Mandor is shut up in Bannerwell, and you want to find Mavin Many-shaped. It will be difficult. You'll have to go alone."

I had not considered that. I had assumed Chance would go with me wherever I went.

"No, you can't take Chance. Mavin may make it somewhat easier for you to find her, but she will not trust anyone else. Here," he said and handed me a fold of parchment. "I've written out the directions."

*Periplus of a city which fears the unborn.*
*Hear of a stupration incorporeal.*
*In that place a garment defiled*
*and an eyeless Seer.*
*Ask him the name of the place from which he came and the way*
*   from it.*
*Go not that way.*
*Befriend the shadows and beware of friends.*
*Walk on fire but do not swim in water.*
*Seek out sent-far's monument, but do not look upon it.*
*In looking away, find me.*

"It makes no sense," I cried, outraged. "No sense at all!"

"Go to Havajor Dike," he said soothingly. "Then north from there. She would not have made the directions too difficult for either of us, Peter. She does not want to be lost forever, only very difficult to find. You'll be able to ravel it out, line by line. There is only one caution I must give you."

He waited until he saw that he had my full attention, then made his warning, several times. "Do not go near Pfarb Durim. If you go to the north or northwest, do not go near that place, nor near the place they call Poffle which is, in truth, known as Hell's Maw." He patted me on the shoulder, and when I asked curious questions, as he must have known I would, said, "It is an evil place. It has been evil for centuries. We thought it might change when old Blourbast was gone, but it remains evil today. Mavin would not send you near it—simply avoid it!" And that was all he would say about that.

We went down into the kitchens, sat there in the warmth of that familiar place, eating grole sausage and cheese with bread warm from the baking. It was a comforting time, a sweet time, and it lasted only a little while. For Gervaise came bustling in, his iron-tipped staff making a clatter upon the stones.

"An Elator has come, Mertyn," he cried. "He demands to see you at once. He comes from the Bright Demesne...."

So we went up as quickly as possible to find an Elator there, one I knew well, Himaggery's trusted messenger.

"Gamesmaster," he said, "the Wizard Himaggery and the old Seer, Windlow, have vanished."

"Vanished?" It was an echo of my own voice saying that word, but this time we were not talking of Shifters. Mertyn asked again, "What do you mean, vanished?"

"They went to Windlow's rooms after the evening meal, sir, asking that wine be sent to them there. When the steward arrived, the room was disturbed but empty. We searched the Demesne, but they are both gone...."

"Why have you come first to me?"

"Gamesmaster, I was told by the Wizard some time since that if anything untoward should happen, I was to come to you."

"Windlow told me," I cried. "Just before I left. That's what he meant when he said they would need your help soon. That word would reach you ..."

"I warned them," Mertyn grated. "I warned them they might be next if they went on with it."

"Next?" The word faltered in my throat.

"Next to disappear. Next to vanish. Next to be gone, as too many of our colleagues and allies now are gone."

"I might have stopped it," I cried. "Himaggery told me he needed me, but I wouldn't listen...."

He shook me, took me by my shoulders and shook me as though I had been seven or eight years old. "This is no time for dramatics, my boy, or flights of guilt. Be still. Let me think."

So I was still, but it was a guilty stillness. If I had been there? If I had been willing to take up the Gamesmen of Barish and use them, use the Talents? Would Himaggery and Windlow still be there? I wanted to cry, but Mertyn's grip on my shoulder did not loosen, so I stood silent and blamed myself for whatever it was that had happened.

| **The Skip-rope Chant** | **The Gamesmen of Barish, their Talents.** |
|---|---|
| Mind's mistress, moon's wheel, Cobweb Didir, shadow-steel. | Grandmother Didir, First Demon. Talent, Telepathy. |
| Mighty wing, lord of sky, lofty Tamor, hover high. | Grandfather Tamor, First Armiger. Talent, Levitation. |
| Night-dark, dust-old, bony Dorn, grave-cold. | Dorn, First Necromancer. Talent, Raising of Ghosts. |
| Flesh-queen, love-star, lust-pale, Trandilar. | Trandilar, First Ruler. Talent, Beguilement. |
| Pain's maid, broken leaf, Dealpas, heart's grief. | Dealpas, First Healer. Talent, Healing. |
| Cheer's face, trust's clasp, far and strong is Wafnor's grasp. | Wafnor, First Tragamor. Talent, Telekinesis. |
| Far-eyed Sorah, worshipper, many gods who never were. | Sorah, First Seer. Talent, Clairvoyance. |
| Here and gone, flashing fast, Hafnor is trusted last. | Hafnor, First Elator. Talent, Teleportation. |
| Chilly Shattnir, power's store, calling Game forevermore. | Shattnir, First Sorcerer. Talent, Power storage. |

Fire and smoke, horn and bell,
messages of Buinel.

Buinel, First Sentinel.
Talent, Fire starting.

Shifted, fetched, sent-far,
trickiest is Thandbar.

Thandbar, First Shifter.
Talent, Shapeshifting.

When all time is past,
eleven first, eleven last.

The eleven represent the pantheon
of elders, the ''respected ones'' of
the religion of Gameworld.

NOTE: There are short verses for every Gamesman in some issues of
the Index of Gamesmen, over four thousand different titles. In some
areas, skip-rope competitions are held during which young men and
women attempt the recitation of the entire Index. The last person to
complete this task successfully was Minery Mindcaster, in her eighteenth year, at the competition in Hilbervale.

# 2

# A City Which Fears
## the Unborn

At the end of the short time which followed, it was Mertyn who left me, not I who left him. I had never seen him in this kind of flurry, this Kingly bustle with all the House at his command and no nonsense about not using Talents in a Schooltown. He simply ordered and it was done, a horse, packing, certain books from the library, foodstuffs, two Armigers and a young Demon to accompany him. I did nothing but get in his way, each time trying to tell him that I would go back with him to the Bright Demesne to do what I should have done in the first place. He would have none of it.

"For the love of Divine Didir, Peter, sit down and be still. If there were anything you could do, I would have you do it in a moment. There is nothing. Believe me, nothing. Just now the most important thing you can do is what you were intending to do anyhow, find Mavin and tell her what has happened here. Give me a moment with these people and I'll talk to you about it. . . ."

So I sat and waited, with ill grace and badly concealed hurt. It was quite bad enough to remember that I had come away when I was needed; it was worse now to be denied return when I was eager to help. At last Mertyn had all his minions scattered to his satisfaction, and he came back to me, sitting beside me to take my hand.

"Thalan, put your feelings aside. No—I know how you feel. You could not have failed to love old Windlow. All who know him do. As for Himaggery, it is hard not to like him, admire him, even when he is most infuriating. So, you want to help. You can. Hear me, and pay utmost attention.

"For some time there have been disappearances. Gamesmen of high rank. Wizards. Almost always from among those we would call 'progressive.' Many have been Windlow's students over the years. It can't be mere happenstance, coincidence. We suspect the cause but have no proof.

"Are those who have vanished dead? If they are, then some among the powerful Necromancers should be able to raise them, query them, find out what has happened. So, Necromancer after Necromancer has called into the dust of time, but none of the vanished rise. Instead, for some few of the searchers, it has been Necromancer Nine, highest risk, and they have vanished as well. Gone. Not dead, Or, if dead, dead in a way no others have ever died." He shivered as though cold. "If not dead, then where? Demon after Demon has sought them, and for some of them it has been Demon's Eyes Nine; they have disappeared as well. Are they imprisoned? Pursuivant after Pursuivant has searched, Rancelmen have delved. We find nothing. Those who vanish are simply *gone*.

"Yet still we pursue our goal, our studies. Himaggery. His allies. Windlow's old students. Though our allies vanish, our numbers continue to grow—slowly, too slowly. I warned Himaggery to draw no attention to himself. Bannerwell was a mistake, though we had to do it. As Windlow would say, it was morally correct but tactically wrong. So it has happened. Old Windlow evidently had some foreknowledge of it; he told you I would be needed. Well, I will go and try to hold things together while you seek out Mavin because we need her. We need her clever mind, her hidden ways, her sense of strategy. You can help most by finding her, which you would have done in any case."

I could not be so discourteous as to argue against that. He meant what he said. It was no mere sop for my comfort. I swallowed my pride and assented, sorrowing that I had refused help earlier and that it was now too late. He pulled me close, whispering.

"Thalan, mark me. You have the eidolon of Dorn. I know you dislike using it, but if you have chance to do so, query among the dead for Himaggery and Windlow. If you—by any chance—use others of those Talents—no, don't say anything, boy—seek for Himaggery and Windlow. Even half answers are better than no answers at all."

He kissed me and went. I was left in his aerie alone, among the tumble of packing, things half out of boxes, paper scattered upon his table, maps curling out of their cases, a disorder which spoke more harshly than words of his state of mind. I spent an hour setting it right, then went to make my own preparations and to take farewell of Chance.

It was not easy. He did not accept that I would have to go alone. He could accept only that Mertyn had so ordered, and he was as bound by that order as I. At the end he told me he would go back to the Bright Demesne to await my return. He said that two or three times, to await my return, as though by saying it he could assure it would be so. It comforted me more than it did him, I'm sure. Perhaps he intended it so. I was very uncertain of what was to happen next, so preoccupied I paid no attention at all to Karl Pig-face and by my contemptuous silence (for so he and his followers interpreted it) did his unpleasant reputation grave and permanent harm. At the time, I didn't think of him at all.

I rode out of Schooltown at first light. It was a three-day trip to Bannerwell from the town. I made it in two, riding late and rising early, paying no attention to the scenery and eating in the saddle.

Havajor Dike lay just east of the fortress of Bannerwell. I came upon it at evening, late, with only an afterglow in the sky where the high clouds still shed a little reflected light. A star shone above the clouds, only one, trembling like a tear in the sadness of dusk with its blue-brown scent of dark, bat-twittered and hesitant. I saw one lonely figure upon the Dike, black against the glow, and rode up to ask what housing might be available for the night. As I came closer, I saw that it was Riddle, Tossa's father, that lean Immutable who had come to Bannerwell with Chance and Yarrel at the very end of the battle, making battle unnecessary.

It struck me when he turned to face me that he showed no fear at all. No stranger had confronted me since I had left the Bright Demesne without showing some shrinking from me, perhaps a curious, awed stare followed, more times than not, by the ''ward-of-evil,'' by an over-the-shoulder stare as he hurried away. Riddle had no fear, but it was a few moments before I realized that he did not know who I was and that it did not matter. He was an Immutable. They did not fear the Talents of Gamesmen, not even of Necromancers.

''Do I know you?'' he asked, leaning on the wall, gaze burrowing at my gauze-wrapped face. ''Have we met?''

''It's Peter, Riddle,'' I said, pulling the hood from my head and running dirty fingers through my dirtier hair. ''I should have spoken.''

''Peter.'' He gave me his oddly kind smile, reached out to touch my face as though I had been his child or close friend. "To see you dressed so. I had forgotten you had this . . . Talent. I thought it was something to do with . . . changing shape."

I started to say something about the Gamesmen of Barish, caught myself and said nothing. No one knew of the Gamesmen but Windlow and Himaggery, Silkhands, Chance—one or two others who would say nothing about them. Instead of explaining, I shrugged the question away. "Small reason for you to remember. I did not stay long here at Havajor Dike once Bannerwell was overthrown. Have you played jailor here alone since then?" I knew the Immutables had intended to stay at Bannerwell long enough to assure there would be no more of Mandor's particular kind of threat, but I had not expected Riddle himself to stay among them. He was said to be their leader, though I had never heard him claim any such title.

"No," he replied. "They sent for me after Mandor died."

"Dead? Mandor?" I could not imagine it, even though I had foretold it myself. I had known he could not long withstand the pain of a disfigurement visible to everyone, of loss of power, of the absence of adoration, not he who had lived for power and adoration and had adored himself not least among them. And yet . . . it was strange to think of him dead. "How did he die?"

"From the tower." Riddle indicated the finger of stone which gestured rudely from the western edge of the keep. "He stood there often. We saw him in the dusk, or at dawn, a black blot against the sky. Then one morning he was not there, and his body was found among the stones at the river's side. They sent for me then, and I arrived in time to learn that Huld had gone as well."

"Dead?"

"I fear not." He looked angry, biting off the words as though they tasted bad. "Himaggery had left Demons here, around the edges of the place, to Read if any tried to escape. They did not Read Huld. I theorize that he drugged himself into unconsciousness after hiding in a wood wagon or some such. Certainly he went past us all without betraying his presence."

I said nothing. I did not like the idea of Huld loose in the world. I shivered, and Riddle reached out to me again.

*183*

"So, my boy. What brings you to the Dike? Was it to meet with Mandor again?"

I shivered once more. "Never. I have an errand away north of here, and the Dike is a convenient place to begin the northern journey. . . ."

"Ah. Well, you will not begin that road tonight, will you? There is time for hot food, and for a bath? Some talk, perhaps. I have not had news of the south for some time. . . ."

So I went with him to his camp, a sturdy stone house near the mill, once almost in ruins but reroofed and made solid by the Immutables and those pawns released from Bannerwell. We were waited on by quiet people with faces I thought I recognized from the time of my captivity. At my unspoken question, Riddle explained.

"These were Mandor's people, yes. Once his powers were nullified by our being here, he could not beguile them any longer. None would stay. They saw him, feared him, gradually learned what he had done to them and so began to hate him, I think. He could not bear it."

"What had he done to them?" I asked cynically. "More than any Gamesman does?"

"More," he said. "Though perhaps it was not he who conceived it. . . . No. I will say no more about it."

I wanted to hear no more about it, though later I was to wish I had insisted. I told him of the disappearance of Windlow and of Himaggery. He withdrew into startled silence, but then told me of other vanishments he knew of. He speculated, almost in a whisper. I drank wine and tried not to fall asleep. Others of the Immutables came in and greeted me kindly enough. They murmured among themselves while I yawned. Then we were alone and Riddle was leaning across the table to put his face close to mine.

"I have no right to ask it, Peter, but I beg a service of you. One you may be loath to give."

"I will do what I can," I murmured, half asleep.

"We need to speak with Mandor's spirit. . . ."

The sickness rose in me so that I choked on it, retching, tears pouring from my eyes as I tried not to vomit upon the table. In a moment he was putting cool water on my face, giving me a cup to drink. "How can you ask it," I gargled at him. "And why? What would you know that his ghost can tell you?"

"We have found certain . . . things in Bannerwell. After Huld had gone, our people found them and summoned me. They are . . . things which some of these pawns have reason to remember with great pain. We have studied them as best we may. We need to know what they are, how used, but more important, from whence they came. Mandor would have known. We believe they belonged to him."

"Certain things. . . ." He showed them to me. They were stored in a back room of the stone house, strange things, crystal linkages, wires, boards on which wires and crystals together made patterns full of winking lights which told me nothing. They reminded me of something . . . something. Suddenly I had it. "Riddle. Long ago—ah, not long ago. About a year. Mertyn sought to protect me from being eaten up in a Game. His servant, Nitch, sewed a thing into my tunic, a thing of wires and beads, a thing like these things. If you would know of them, ask Mertyn."

"We have done. It was Nitch who knew the doing of it, not Mertyn. Nitch has gone, gone in the night without a word."

"Vanished? Like the others?"

"No. Simply gone. Have you heard of 'magicians'?"

Where had I heard of . . . yes. "Gamesmaster Gervaise. He said the little blue Gamesmen were made by magicians, west somewhere. I had not heard of magicians before, save as we all have. At Festivals, doing tricks with birds and making flowers appear out of nothing."

"I do not think a Festival magician made these." He shut the door upon them and led me back to the table before the fire. I knew he would ask me again. I wanted to refuse. How could I refuse? Oh, Gamelords, in what guise might the spirit of Mandor rise to greet the eidolon of Dorn?

"By Towering Tamor, Riddle, you ask a hard thing."

"I know. But it is said your Talent is great. I would not ask it, save you come so fortuitously to our need. I thought of it when I saw your mask, at first, and I would not ask it if I thought it endangered you."

How could I tell him that it did endanger me? It sickened me, yes. Brought nightmares and horrors, but endangerment? Well, I would lose no blood nor flesh over it. Perhaps that was the only endangerment which counted. Riddle's daughter, Tossa, had lost her life in aiding me. I could not refuse him.

"In the morning," I begged. "Not at night."

"Certainly, in the morning," he agreed. I might just as well have done it in the dark for all the sleep I had.

We went to the pit in the gray dawn. They had not laid Mandor with his ancestors and predecessors in the catacombs beneath the fortress, and I was thankful of that. There the ghosts were as thick as fleas on a lazy dog, and I had no wish to raise a host on this day. No, Mandor lay beneath the sod in a kind of declivity a little to the north of the walls, a place fragrant and grassy, silent except for the sigh of wind in the dark firs which bounded it. Riddle let me go into the place alone, staying well away from me in order that his own, strange "Talent" not impede mine . . . or Dorn's. As I left him, he said, "We need to know whence these things came. What their purpose is. By whom made. Can you ask these things?"

I tried to explain. "Riddle, I have not heretofore questioned phantoms to know what knowledge they may have. Those discarnate ones I raised on this land before were ancient, long past human knowledge, only creatures of dust and hunger, fetches to my need."

"It is said that Necromancers are full of subtlety."

"I will be as subtle as I can." Though it would be Dorn being subtle, rather than Peter. I took the little Gamesman into my hand, fingers finding it at once in the pouch as though it had struggled through the crowd to come into my grasp. He came into me like heat, burning my skin at first, then scalding deeper and deeper, nothing wraithy or indistinct about it, rather a man come home into a familiar place. I was not surprised when he greeted me, "Peter."

"Dorn," I whispered. Before, I had been fearful. This time I was less so, and perhaps this accounted for my courtesy to him, as though he were my guest. I explained what we were to do, and he became my tutor.

"Here and here," he said. "Thus and thus." My hand reached out, but it was Dorn who pointed the finger at the grass, Dorn who called the dust and bones within to rise. Mandor had not been long dead. The ground cracked and horror came forth, little by little, the worms dropping from it as it rose. I heard Riddle on the hill behind me choking back a gasp, whether awe or fear I could not tell.

"Thus and thus," Dorn went on. "So and so."

The bones became clad in flesh, the flesh in robes of state. The head became more than a skull, then was crowned once more, until at last what had been so horrible at the end of Mandor's life became the beauty I had known in Schooltown, bright and lovely as the sun, graceful as grass, and looking at me from death's eyes.

From this uncanny fetch came a cry of such eerie gladness that my heart chilled. "Whole," it cried in a spectral voice. "Oh, I am risen whole again. . . ."

I could have wept. This wholeness was not an intended gift, and yet . . . it was one I would have made him during life if I had known how. "So and so," said with Dorn within me. "You could not have made him so or kept him so in life for any length of time."

Riddle called from the hillside, reminding me of our purpose there. So I asked it, or Dorn did, of those strange crystalline contrivances which Riddle was so concerned about. The phantom seemed not to understand.

"These are not things which Mandor knew. These are things of Huld. Playthings for Huld. Magicians made them. Huld understood them, not Mandor. Oh, Mandor, whole, whole again . . ."

I heard Riddle cursing, then he called to me, "I'm sorry, Peter. Let the pathetic thing go back to its grave."

But I was not ready to do that. I had remembered Mertyn's words concerning those who had vanished.

"Mandor, do you speak with others . . . where you are? Do the dead talk together?"

The fetch stared at me with dead eyes, eyes in which a brief, horrible flame flickered, a firefly awareness, a last kindling.

"In Hell's Maw," it screamed at me. "They speak, the dead who linger speak, before they fall to dust, in the pits. When all is dust, we go, we go. . . ."

"Have you spoken to Himaggery?" I asked. "To Windlow the Seer?" I remembered the names of others Riddle had told me of and asked for them, but the apparition sighed no, no, none of these.

Then it drew itself up and that brief flame lit the empty eyes once more. "Words come where Mandor is . . . troubling . . . all . . . seeking those you seek . . . not there . . . not in the place . . . Peter . . . let me be whole, whole, whole. . . ."

I sobbed to Dorn. "Let him be whole, Dorn, as he goes to rest." And so it was the phantom sank into the earth in the guise he had once worn, the kingly crown disappearing at last, in appearance as whole as he had been in Schooltown before his own treachery maimed him.

And I was left alone, Dorn gone, Mandor gone, only Riddle standing high upon the rim as the wind sighed through the black firs and the grasses waved endless farewell on Mandor's grave. Inside me a small dam seemed to break, a place of swampy fear drained away, and I could turn to Riddle with my face almost calm to go with him back to the millhouse. He was no more given to talk than I, and we had a silent breakfast, both of us thinking thoughts of old anguish and, I believe, new understanding.

When we had eaten he said, "Peter, I will go with you a way north. I have an errand in that general direction, and it is better never to travel alone. That is, if I am welcome and my own attributes will not inhibit your . . . business."

I laughed a little. "Riddle, my business is a simple one. I am going in search of my mother who has . . . left word of her whereabouts in a place known as 'a city which fears the unborn.' All I know of the place is that it is north of here."

"But, my boy, I know the place," he exclaimed. "Or, I should say, I've heard of it. It is the city of Betand, between the upper reaches of the Banner and . . . what is the name of that river? . . . well, another river to the west. I will go with you almost that far. My business will take me east at the wilderness pass."

"Why is it called a city which fears the unborn?"

"It seems to me I heard the story, but I've forgotten the details of it. Something to do with a haunting, some mischance by a wandering Necromancer. Your Talent is not generally loved, Peter, though I can see that it may be useful."

He was being kind, and I helped him by changing the subject. I was glad enough of his company, gladder still when he proved to be a better cook than Chance and almost as good a companion as my friend Yarrel had been when we were friends. On the road we talked of a thousand things, most of them things I had wondered at for years.

One of the things that became apparent was that the Immutables cared little for Gamesmen. Riddle's toleration of me and of a few others such as Himaggery was not typical. I asked him why they let Gamesmen exercise Talents at all, feeling as they did.

"We are not numerous enough to do otherwise," he said. "There are fewer Immutables than there are Gamesmen, many fewer. We do not bear many children, our numbers remain small and our own skills remain unchanging through time—Immutable, as you would say. Each of us can suppress the Talent of any Gamesman for some distance around us. I can be safe from Demons Reading my thoughts or Armigers Flying from above, but I am not safe from an arrow shot from a distance or a flung spear, as you well know."

I nodded. Tossa had died from an arrow wound.

"So, those of us with the ability find it safer to band together in towns and enclaves with our own farms and crafters. Thus we can protect ourselves and our families from any danger save force of simple arms, and this we can oppose with arms of our own. We could be overrun, I suppose, if any group of Gamesmen chose to do so, but Gamesmen depend too much upon their Talents. Without the Talent of Beguilement, few if any of their Rulers would be able to lead men into battle. And, of course, the pawns will not fight us. They turn to us for help from time to time."

"I would think all pawns would flock to you for protection."

"We could not protect them. We are too few."

"What do they want, you want, Riddle? The Immutables?"

"We want what any people want, Peter. We want to feel secure, to live. We want to be free to admire the work of our own hands. Even Gamesmen do the same. Why else their 'schools' and their 'festivals'? The Gamesmen depend upon the pawns for labor, for the production of grain, fruit, meat. If we were numerous enough to protect the pawns, and if they came to us, then . . . then the Gamesmen would fight, even without their Talents."

"They could till the soil themselves," I offered, somewhat doubtfully.

"Would they?" asked Riddle. Both he and I knew the answer to that. Some few would. Some few probably did, out of preference. As for the others in their hundreds of thousands, they would rather die in battle than engage in "pawnish" behavior.

So we rode together, I in the circle of his protection, he in the circle of fear which came with the Necromancer's garb. No one bothered us. There was little traffic upon the road in any case, and those we encountered left a long distance between themselves and us.

"The things you found in Bannerwell," I asked. "Why are you so curious about them?"

"I am curious about anything subtle and secret, Peter. It is difficult to keep secrets among Gamesmen. A powerful Demon can learn almost anything one knows, can dig out thoughts one does not know one has. How then are secrets kept? You would not deny that they are kept?"

"One has one's own Demons to guard against thought theft by outsiders. One stays in one's own purlieus, in one's own Demesne. . . ."

"Ah, but walls of that kind can be breached, or sapped. No. Sometimes secrets are kept, even by those who go about the world in the guise of ordinary Gamesmen. There were secrets kept in Bannerwell. Someone there *knew* things that others do not. Huld, it seems. How did he manage that . . . ?

"Do you know," he went on, suddenly confidential, "as a child I envied the Gamesmen. Yes. I was much enamored of Sorah. A Seer. How wonderful to see the invisible, the inscrutable, the future . . . how wonderful to know *everything!*"

"I don't think that's quite how it works," I said, remembering old Windlow and his frustration at partial visions of uncertain futures.

"Perhaps not. Still. There are many things I want to know. For example, does the name 'Barish' mean anything to you?" His tone was casual, but he watched me from the corner of his eye.

I took a deep breath, hiding it, wondering what to say. "Barish? Why, it's a name from religion. A Wizard, wasn't he? Did something very secret and subtle—I forget what. . . ." I waited, scarcely able to breathe. "Is it a name I should know?"

"Secret and subtle." He mused. "No. Everyone knows that much, and seemingly no one knows more than that." He smiled. "I am merely interested in secret and subtle things, and I ask those who may know. I have heard, recently, of this Barish."

I turned my hand over to let his words run out. "I do not know, Riddle. You riddle me as you must riddle others. Do you always ask such questions?"

"I talk to hear my voice, boy. I tie words on a journey as a woman ties ribbons on her hat."

"Do they?" I asked, interested. "I have only seen ribbons on students' tunics, come Festival."

"Oh, well, Peter. You have not seen much." And with that, he lapsed into a long, comfortable silence. It had rained betimes and we found lung-mushrooms all along the sides of fallen trees. Riddle cut away a nice bunch of them, glistening ivory in the dusk, and rolled them in meal to fry up for our supper. He told me about living off the countryside, more even than Yarrel had done. Riddle spoke of roots and shoots, berries and nuts, how to cook the curled fronds of certain ferns with a bit of smoked meat, how to bake earth-fruits in their skins by wrapping them first in the leaves of the rain-hat bush, then in mud, then burying the whole in the coals at evening to have warm and tender for the morrow's breakfast.

Our road cut across country between loops of the River until the land began to rise more steeply. Then the River ran straight or in long jogs between outcroppings, plunging over these in an hysteria of white water and furious spray. Our horses climbed, and we strode beside them for part of each morning and each afternoon so they would not tire or become lame. Stone lanterns along the way began to appear, at first only broken, old ones, half crumbled to gravel, but later newer ones, and then ones lit with votive lights.

"What are these?" I asked. "Burning good candles here in the day-light?"

"Wards against the Gifters," said Riddle. "The people hereabouts are most wary of Gifters and what Gifts they may make to the unsuspecting."

"Why have I never heard of them until now?"

"Because students hear of very little." He did not make it a rebuke, but I was offended nonetheless.

"We were taught morning to evening. They did nothing but teach us of things. . . ."

"They did nothing but teach you of *certain* things," Riddle replied sternly. "And they told you nothing of other things. They told you noth-ing of the Gifters, though the world north of the Great Bowl goes in constant fear of them. You are told nothing of the nations and places of this world, but only of the small part you inhabit. . . ."

"Riddle." I was caught up in a curious excitement. "Why do you say 'this world'? Do you believe it is true what the fablers say, that there are more worlds than this?"

"There are stories of others. Not that the stories are necessarily true.

But that is part of what I mean. In the Schools you are all taught so little about what really is and what may truly be.''

"Why would they do that? Why would my own thalan, for example, fail to teach me things I would need to know?''

"Because they do not believe you do need to know,'' he replied in exasperation. "They think the least told, the least troubled. If you do not hear of the Northern Lands, you will not venture there. If you do not hear of Gifters, you will not fall prey to one. It is all arrant nonsense, of course. Pawner caravans pick up a hundred ignorant youths and carry them away north for every one who adventures there on his own. Gifters make between-meal bites of the naive, while the well-taught escape with their lives. I have even heard old Gamesmen speak with tears in their throats of the 'innocence' of youth. 'Innocence,' indeed. They should say arrant ignorance and be done with it.'' He fumed for another league and I did not interrupt him, for I often learned much by letting him burble. Thus it was I did not ask him more about Gifters when I should have done.

"There is a pawnish settlement in the south,'' he said at last, "in which they do not teach their children anything of sex. It is kept a great mystery. The belief of this sect is that this ignorance will keep their children from harm. As a result, they value virginity highly and it is virtually unknown among them.''

I did not believe this, but allowed it to stand unchallenged as we rode on. I didn't ask about Gifters, or the northlands, or anything else. Ah well. Yestersight is perfect, so they say.

We had been several days on the road when we came to a rolling range of hills and began to track upward by repeated switchbacks, higher and higher, the way becoming more rocky and precipitous as we went. I was reminded a bit of the road from Windlow's House to Bannerwell, except that this one did not seem to run through wilderness. There were villages all along the way, cut into the sides of the mountains with meadows the size of handkerchiefs spread upon the ledges, and a constant procession of lanterns, little ones and big ones, never seeming to run out of candles. At last we came to a high pass at which the road split, one fork leading downward to the north, the other winding to the east among the crags.

"Well,'' he said to me. "We are near Betand. We come to the parting of ways, Peter. I am thankful for your company thus far. If you will slit your eyes you will see the roofs of the city away to the northwest, and I wish you well in your journey.''

I was sorry to part from him. Truth to tell, I had never been really alone before the brief trip from Schooltown to Bannerwell, and I did not like it much. It was not fear I felt, but something else. A kind of lostness, of being singular of my kind. As though there were none near to greet me as fellow. Of course, the Necromancer's hood had much to do with that. Nonetheless, I had been grateful for his company and said so. We sat a time there on the pass, saying nothing much except to let one another know we would be less comfortable on the journey after we parted. At last, as I was about to run out of polite phrases and begin to choke, he patted me upon one shoulder.

''I go east from here, to Kiquo, and to the high bridge only recently restored though it was eighty years ago in the great cataclysm that it fell. I go to seek mysteries, my boy. You go to seek mysteries of your own. Well, then, good journey and good chance to you.'' And he went away, not looking back, leaving me to press down the further slope toward the city I could see beneath me in the westering sun of late afternoon.

Smoke lay above it like a pall through which the towers reached, like the snouts of beasts seeking upward for air. My eyes watered, just looking at it. If there were not wind before evening, it would be thick as soup in that bowl which held the city of Betand, the City Which Fears the Unborn.

# 3

# Periplus

IT TOOK SEVERAL HOURS TO REACH THE CITY, and a wind had come softly from the north to greet me as I rode by the outskirts of the place, inns and caravansaries, stables and eating houses, taverns and stews. I decided to have a meal before entering the city. There was a place there called the Devil's Uncle, and it seemed as good as any other from the point of cleanliness and better than most from its smell. The stable boy took my beast without making any signs at all, which I took either as a sign of sophistication or of total ignorance. Either many Necromancers came here or none did. It did not matter much which.

Once within, I saw a few curious faces, one or two downturned mouths, but no ward-of-evil signs. I ordered wine and roast fowl and a dish of those same stewed ferns Riddle had fed me on the outward journey, evidently a local delicacy. They were not laggard with the food, nor was I in eating it. No one there paid me much attention until I was almost finished and had only half a glass left in the jug. Then a wide-mouthed Trader sat opposite me and showed me his palms. I raised mine courteously, and let him talk.

"Laggy Nap, fellow-traveler," he greeted me. "Trader by Talent, philosopher by inclination. What brings one so young and horridsome to the city of Betand?"

I did not know whether to be offended, which I was, or pretend to be amused. I chose the latter as having the lesser consequence.

"Merely one who would travel through Betand on his way to somewhere else," I said. At which he laughed, repeating my remark to some others who also laughed. I supposed there was something entertaining in the intent to travel through Betand, so ordered wine for those around and asked, all innocence, if the city were accounted so amusing by all who went there.

"Oh, sir," said the Trader, "it is my amusement to ask new wanderers whether they intend to go through Betand, and then to offer them a meal at my expense at the Travelers' Joy, which is on the other side of the city. You can tell me then whether you were amused, and I will be entertained by your account." He fixed a glittering eye upon me, seeming to look further than I would have wished. He was a man with down-slanting brows and deep furrows between his eyes, wide-mouthed, as I have said, with a long, angry-looking nose against which his eyes snuggled a bit too closely. His eyes belied his mouth, the one being all motion and laughter while the others were cold and full of accounts.

"You do not wish to tell me why I will be . . . amused?" I asked him. He merely chuckled, elbowed some of those around him, and together they engaged in laughter of a mocking sort. Almost my hand sought Dorn in the pouch at my belt, but I decided against it. No point in stirring up trouble. I took my leave of them and went on toward the walls, a gaping gate full of torchlight before me.

I began to identify myself, to give some sort of name such as "Urburd of Dowes" or "Dornish of Calber." Chance and I had made up a whole list of them to be used as needed. The guardsman gave me no time. He laid a hand upon my arm and said intently, "Sir, you are nobody here. If you would not be charged with a grave offense, remember that. You are nobody."

He passed me on to another guardsman who gazed me in the eye with equal intensity, seeming unafraid of the death's-head. "Who are you now, sir?"

"I am . . . nobody?" I said, wondering what fools' game they played and whether I was the fool for playing it with them.

"Surely, surely," said the second guardsman. "Go through this gate, sir. Leave your horse in the stables there. The matron will meet you."

He had no sooner spoken, directing me to a little postern gate in the rough wall, when there came a howling out of the night as though a chase pack of fustigars was lost in a lonely place and crying for their kind and kindred. He blanched, made the sign of evil-ward, thrust his hands over his ears. I, too, sought to block my ears, for the cry went up in a keening scream, up and up into an excruciating silence. "Quickly." He pushed me. "Go!"

I went. The woman who met me on the other side was plump and motherly, hands thrust beneath her apron, chivvying me along as though I had been her pet goose.

"Well sir," she said. "What kind of woman would you prefer? There are several in the waitinghouse tonight. Three I would call a bit matronly for you, for you walk like a lad no matter the horrid face on you. Necromancer or no, boy you are, or I'll eat my muffin pan. Well, not them, then. I've one virgin girl scared out of her wits. You'd do me a favor, you would, to take that one. Nice enough she is, but as unschooled as any nit and vocal along of it. . . ."

I had no idea what she was speaking of. "I would be glad to do you any service, madam."

"Good enough, then," she said, stopping at the first door and opening it only long enough to call within. "Sylbie, come out here, lass. Nobody is here."

A small time passed before the girl came out, a pale girl with soft brown hair and eyes swollen with crying. She gave me one glance and shrieked as though ghost bit.

"Oh, stuff and foolishness," said the Matron. "Sylbie, it is only a guise. Come now, you've seen Gamesmen all your life. Must you scritch at the lad, and him only a boy (as I can tell by his walk) to make him sorry he said he'd favor you? You could go back and wait for one of those drovers to quit drinking in the Devil's Uncle would you rather. . . ."

"N-n-no, Madam Wilderly," she stuttered. "It's only that it was very unexpected. . . ."

At that the howling began again, and we all leaned against the stone as it rushed on us out of the empty streets, shrieking and moaning, then dwindling away down the throbbing alleys once more. It was a horrid sound.

"The unborn," said the Matron in explanation. "We are haunted, sir, as you must have heard."

"I had heard," I said weakly. I had, too, but the reality made the stories dim. I would have gone mad if I had had to listen to that howling for more than a short time. These thoughts were halted by the matron's instructions.

"Just in there, sir, Sylbie. You'll find a nice room to the left at the top of the stairs. Wine all warm by the fire and a bit of supper to help you get acquainted. The Midwife will be around in the morning, just to check has the law been complied with." And with that she was off down the street in the direction we had come.

The girl led me up the stairs, I still wondering what went on. The girl seemed to know, and I assumed she would tell me. Besides, once within a room I could take off the death's-head mask and wash my face, thus showing her a face which would not frighten her. I did so, and when I took the towel away, she handed me a cup of wine. She was no longer crying, but she looked frightened still.

"Well," I said. "Suppose you tell me what all this Game is, Sylbie. I will not harm you, so you need not make dove's eyes at me."

"Don't you know?" she asked. "About Betand? I thought everyone for a thousand leagues around must know about Betand."

"Well, I did not. Even the man I was traveling with, who had heard of Betand, was not sure of the cause of its fame. You are referred to in our part of the world as 'The City Which Fears the Unborn.' Not very explanatory."

"Oh, but very descriptive, sir. It is the unborn you heard howling in the streets. It has driven some mad and others into despair. My own mother tried to drown herself from the constant horror of it. We cannot sleep by night because of the howling, and we cannot sleep by day or we will all starve. I, myself, think it might be better to starve. My father said he would rather starve than have me raped, but my mother said nonsense, the girl must be raped because it is the law."

I dropped the cup and heard it echo hollowly from under the bed where it rocked to and fro making clanking sounds. "Raped! By whom?"

"By you, sir. Or, rather, by nobody."

I sat upon the side of the bed and reached for the cup with my foot. "Sylbie, pour more wine. Then sit here beside me and tell me what you have just said. I am quite young, and I do not understand anything you have said."

"Oh, sir," she said, falling to her knees to fetch the cup, "truly you are very stupid. I have already told you. But I will tell you again.

"It was two years ago last Festival that the Necromancer came to Betand. He was an old man, and he amused the crowd at the Festival by raising small spirits (some said it was forbidden for him to do so during Festival, and was the cause of all our woe) which danced and sang like little windy shadows. Well, one night he was drinking at the Dirty Girdle, a tavern which, my mother says, has a well-deserved reputation, and he got into an argument with the tavernkeeper, a man as foul of mouth as his kitchen floor, so says my mother. Doryon, the Necromancer, would not take besting in any battle of words, so my father says, and so decided to place a haunting upon the tavern. He was very drunk, sir, very drunk.

"So he rose to his feet and made some gestures, speaking some certain words, at which, so my father says, the whole company within the place trembled, for he had summoned up a monstrous spirit which fulminated and gorbled in the middle of the air, spinning. Then, so my father says, did the old Necromancer clutch at his chest and fall like an axed tree down, straight, stiff as a dried fish and dead as one, too.

"But the haunting he had raised up went on boiling and fetching, sir, growing darker and more roily until at last it began to howl, and it howled its way out of the tavern and into the streets of Betand where it has howled and howled until this night."

"But," I said, "why was not some other Necromancer brought to settle the revenant? What one can raise, surely another can put down. Or so I have always been taught."

"Sir, it was thought so. But Doryon was very drunk, and the Necromancers who came after said he had raised no dead spirit from the past but had, instead, raised up some spirit yet unborn, twisted in time and brought untimely to Betand. None of them knew how to twist it out of being and into the future again."

"So. And so. And so what is the what of that?" I was baffled, mystified. "What has that to do with being raped because it is the law?"

She shook her head at me as though I should have seen the whole matter clearly by this time. "If it is the spirit of one unborn, then it is in the interest of the city that it become born as soon as possible. Which means that every woman of Betand able to bear must bear at every opportunity."

"But rape," I protested feebly. "Why?"

"Because all sexual congress except between married persons is defined as rape in the laws of Betand. Marriages cannot be entered into lightly for mere convenience. There are matters of property, of family, of alliance. It takes years, sometimes, to work out the agreements and settlements and the contracts."

"So they expect *me* to rape you, to break the laws of the city?"

"Oh, truly you are *very* stupid, sir. *Nobody* will break the laws. Did they not say you were *nobody?* How can nobody break a law? It is manifestly impossible, so says my mother. We of Betand do not change our laws readily, so says my father, but we interpret them to our needs."

"I see. At least, I think I see." I was not sure, but it had begun to make a weird kind of sense.

"I hope so," she said, wearily taking off her jacket. "You look far less dirty than the drover." Removing her blouse, "That is, if one may choose among nobodies."

My throat was dry. I could think of nothing to say to her, nothing at all. While I poured wine and drank it, she removed all of her clothing except a filmy thing which began halfway down her front and ended above her knees. It did little to hide the rest of her. Knowing my history, you will believe it when I say she was the first female person I had seen so unclothed. Silkhands the Healer, even when she traveled across the country with us, had never been so unclad. Now that she was bare, Sylbie seemed not to know what to do next. I offered her wine, and we gulped at it together, each as uncomfortable as the other.

"Have you had lots of women?" she whispered in a voice which seemed hopeful of an affirmative answer.

I managed to say, "Ummm," in a vaguely encouraging tone.

"I didn't want to be—fumbled at," she said through tears.

"Ummm," sympathetically.

"I think it might help if I knew your name."

"P—Peter."

"Well, Peter, it's a comfort that you know about . . . everything. My mother says that will make it much easier," she said, then she threw herself sobbing onto the pillows.

I was—am a fearfully stupid person. Until that instant I had not considered the Gamesmen of Barish which were in the pouch at my belt. Among them was the eidolon of Trandilar, great Queen, Goddess of beguilement and passion. I had taken that eidolon once before, outside the shattered walls of Bannerwell. I had not thought of it since, had rejected use of it, had tried to pretend it had never happened. Now, faced with the sodden misery before me, I could not in conscience ignore Trandilar longer. Peter, rude boy, would indeed "fumble at her." Only Trandilar offered any hope for something less than agony for us both. My hand found the Gamespiece without trying, as though it rushed into my hand. I knew then what to do and how to do it as the lizard knows the sun.

"Come," I said to the girl, laughing. "Let us have some of this good supper the matron has left us. Tell me about your family. Eyes like yours are too lovely to spoil with tears." (Was this Peter speaking? Surely. If not Peter, then who? Nobody?)

Tears were wiped away. Wine was drunk and food eaten; fire allowed to warm skin to a roseate gleaming. Bodies allowed to huddle together for comfort when the howling came, to seek the softness of the mattresses and quilts, to burrow, explore, touch, wonder at, murmur at. Alone, I would have made all stiff, complex, and hateful, but with Trandilar all merely occurred. I seem to recall some howls from within the room, but I cannot be sure. It was of no matter.

When I awoke, I found her staring at me, the tears running down her cheeks once again.

"Why are you crying? What's the matter?"

"They will arrange a marriage for me," she sobbed, "with someone awful, and it will never be like this again."

Oh, Trandilar. Is nothing ever as it should be?

Later that morning the Midwife came to the door of our room, as the matron had said she would. The dress of a midwife is red, with a white cowl and owl's feathers in a crest. She stared at me, then laid hands upon Sylbie with an expression of fierce concentration before shaking her head and turning away without a word. At which Sylbie turned unwontedly cheerful, as suddenly as she had become teary before.

"You must stay another night," she crowed. "Nothing happened."

I replied, somewhat stiffly, that I felt a good deal had happened, at which she was properly giggly. I had not known before that girls were giggly. Boys are, young boys, that is, in the dormitories of the schools. Perhaps girls are allowed to retain some childhood habits and joys which boys are not. Or perhaps it is only that male Gamesmen are so driven by Talent—but no. The whole matter was too complex to think out. At any rate, the matron came again to give us leave to go into the market while she arranged for the room to be cleaned and food brought in. So the day went by and another night during which I had no real need of Trandilar, and another morning with Sylbie weeping, for this time the Midwife nodded, the owl feathers bobbing upon her head. A child would be forthcoming, it seemed, and the purpose of my being a nobody had been fulfilled. We sat in the window above the street as she shed tears all down the front of my tunic.

"There is no reason to believe you will not have great pleasure with your husband," I said. Privately, I thought it unlikely unless he had been taught by Trandilar, until I remembered that Trandilar herself had been taught by someone. "Don't cry, Sylbie. This is foolishness!"

"You don't understand," she cried. "They will marry me off to someone I don't even know. Someone old, or bald, or fat as a stuffed goose. Young men don't get wives with settlements as good as I have, or so my mother says. They have not the wherewithal. Only old men have enough of the world's wealth to afford a wealthy wife. Oh, Peter, I shall die, die, die. . . ."

She was such a pretty thing, soft as a kitten, warm as a muffin. I was moved to do something for her, saying to myself as I did so that the occasion for doing helpful things should not pass me by again while I mumbled and mowed and made faces at the moon. So much I had done when Himaggery asked my help. I would not be so laggard in the future.

"Shh, shh," I said. "Be still. If I fix it so that you may marry whom you will, will you leave off crying? Sylbie, tell me you will stop crying, and I will work a magic for you."

There were kisses, and promises, after which I went off to see the master of that place, a great fat pombi of a merchant Duke with more Armigers around him than any Gamesman needs if he is honest. It was not easy to get to see him. I needed all the Necromancer's guise to do it. He greeted me coldly, and I resolved therefore to make the matter harder on him than I had intended.

"I am told that Necromancers have tried heretofore to rid Betand of its specter," I intoned. "Without success. I come to do what others have not done, if the price be to my liking."

He shifted in the high seat, staring over my shoulder in the way they do. He would not meet the eyes behind the death mask, as though he were afraid I would take out his life and transmit it to another realm before time.

"What price would you ask?" His voice was all oil and musk, slippery as thrilp skins.

"One request. Not gold nor treasure. Merely that one of the people of

Betand shall be governed according to my will. For that person's lifetime." I made my voice sinister. He would assume I wanted torture and death as my portion, being of that kind which would sooner kill anyone than give a woman joy. I know his kind—or Trandilar knew them. Yes. Perhaps that was the way of it.

"One of my people?" He oozed for a moment, thoughtfully. "Will you say which one?"

"Not one close to you, Great Duke. I would not be so bold. Merely an insignificant one who has attracted . . . my attention."

He glanced at his counselors, seeing here a nod, there a covert glance. "What makes you believe you can do what others have not?"

I shrugged, let a little anger play in my voice. "If I do not, you will not give me my price. If I do, you will pay me. Or I will return worse thrice over. Is this reason enough?"

At which he gave grudging agreement. I insisted it be put upon parchment, signed before witnesses with the Gamesmen oath. I trusted him as far as I could kick him up a chimney.

Sylbie and I spent the day together. When evening came I went into the center of the city and called up Dorn, explaining the problem of Betand. There was deep, mocking laughter in my head, a sound as though I had my head in a bell which someone struck softly. When he had done laughing, I became his student once again. "Inside out." He showed me. "What we would have done, inverted, so, tug, pull, twist so that it becomes this shape instead of that. Oh, this would be good sport if we were drunk. See, over there, under and through, down and over, and under once more—there is your unborn, Peter. It will be born in nine months in any case. Are you sure you want to let it rest? Ah. Well then, down and over and through once more, dismissing it thus: *Away, away into time unspent. Away, away into life unused. Be still. At peace. In quiet. And done.*" Indeed, when I let Dorn go and walked forth into the streets there was only stillness, peace, and quiet.

So I went to the Duke and waited with him while his counselors wandered about listening to the stillness. Even then he would have cheated me if he could, saying that none knew whether my Talent would hold. I told him we would let my Talent summon up something else as a demonstration, and he agreed to payment.

"There is in this city the daughter of a merchant, one Sylbie, well dowered. Last night nobody begot upon her a child which she will bear, come proper season. It is my will that she be allowed to marry as she will, or not as she chooses, no matter what the cost.''

He bloated like a frog. I thought he would burst, he was so red and purple, and murmurs behind me told me that the Duke had thought of Sylbie for himself. Well and good. If she willed it, good. If she willed it not, then devil take him. I took her the parchment he had signed and told her the names of the witnesses and took oath to lay upon kindred of mine the obligation to see that the Duke's oath was fulfilled. Then there were more kisses, and more promises to remember, and I left her.

Well, it was time to make the ''periplus of a city,'' so I walked all the way around it on the ring-road inside the walls. The ''stupration incorporeal'' had been attended to, a mere word play on rape by nobody. Now I was in search of a ''garment defiled.'' In the entire journey, I found only one place that fit, the Dirty Girdle, that same tavern Sylbie had told me of. So, it being almost time for supper, I went in. The name was far worse than the place. It was a drinking place near the vegetable markets and took its name from the farmers' habit of wiping earthy hands upon the ends of their knotted girdles. The food was good, not expensive, and the people in an ebullient mood, toasting the end of the haunting, for which the Duke had been careful to take credit. When I asked whether ''an eyeless Seer'' frequented the place, they told me Old Vibelo would be in at dusk. So I drank and listened to the talk and waited for whomever Old Vibelo might be.

There was some talk of disappearances. A Wizard from a town away east had vanished, as well as a respected Armiger from among his people. This talk reminded me of Himaggery and Windlow, so my earlier feelings of accomplishment and self-satisfaction were much dwindled by the time the blind Seer tapped his way through the door. I greeted him kindly and offered him a meal in exchange for his company. This seemed to surprise him, but he was nothing loath to take advantage of the offer. After a few mugs I could not have stopped the flow of talk had I willed to. So, I asked him the name of the place from which he came, and how he had first come to Betand.

''Ah, that is a story.'' He raised his head and his toothless gums showed between curly lips. ''For a man with time to listen, that is a story indeed.''

I told him I had time. Since I had no idea what the next phrases of Mavin's enigmatic directions meant, it would be wisest to listen to anything he might offer, hoping that sense would come out of it. "Say away," I said. "I'll keep your glass filled."

He began talking at once, stopping only long enough to gulp more beer or put more food into his mouth.

"I was reared in Levilan," he said, "beside the shores of the Glistening Sea where Games are mostly in fun and Seers see nothing but peace. That is east of here some considerable way, Gamesman, some considerable way indeed. We have not so many of the Schools there, you understand, and many of us grow up in our own homes with family, it being a peaceful place.

"Well, peaceful is well enough, but dull, if you take my meaning. For a young fellow with molten iron in his veins and a heart set for adventure, peaceful is duller than bearable. So, when I was some twenty years in growth, with Talent as good as it was likely to get (not to say it was too great a one, ever, but good enough for some purposes) I made a pact with an Explorer to go into the northlands to the headwaters of the River Flish and all the lands beyond. Have you seen an Explorer, Gamesman? Dressed all in bright leathers with a spy glass on the shoulder and a hat made of fur? Fine. Oh, my, yes but I thought that was fine. The moth wings on a Seer's mask are well enough, but for adventure I would have had an Explorer's skins every time."

He spilled a little beer on the table and traced it with a finger into a long, wavering line. "This would be the River Flish coming from the north into the Glistening Sea. The mountains start up there a ways. There are wild tribes there, pawns who were never tamed since day the first, giant Gifters full of malice, shadow men, oh, you think of something wonderful and you'll find it there, Gamesman, be sure you will.

"So we went along and we went along, not greatly discommoded by the travel for we were young fellows all. The land got steep and then steeper yet, so that there were places we were heaving the horses up the rocks with tackle and spending a day to go a league. But at last we came to the headwaters of the river, a great swamp full of reeds and birds and scaly things that came out of the reeds at night to leave horridsome tracks. And there were biting things there, flying things, big as a finger. Twasn't long before I had been bitten near the eye, and the eye swelled shut so that I could not see on that side. Well, I was not overconcerned. A bite is a bite, and they heal, you know. Save this one did not.

"So, the way north was blocked by the swamp, so we turned away toward the west, following the sides of the hills, with me getting blinder in the eye as time went on and feverish from it, too. We had no Healer with us, more's the shame, and many a night as I lay there heaving and sweating I longed for one. Was then we were attacked by the shadow men. I never saw one, only heard their piping and fluting in the trees and felt the darts whirring by my head. Some of us they got, and some of us they missed, and those they got were dead and those they missed went on, me among them.

"Well, soon after we came upon a camp full of big men who took us in and gave us food, and seeing how shabby we were and in what bad health, gave us a chart to lead us out of trouble. While they were at it, they gave me stuff to put on the eye which they said would fix it. Came morning they went on away north to wherever they were going, and we took the chart to begin working our way back into civilized lands.

"We were fools, Gamesman, fools. Young and inexperienced and without the sense to save our necks. The chart was false and the salve for my eye was false, and when we had done with both I was blind and we were lost in the Dorbor Range somewhere, so lost we thought we'd never come out again. They'd been Gifters, you see."

"Gifters?" I murmured.

"Aye. Gifters. Devils in the guise of humankind, generous with gifts which lead only to destruction. Well, we didn't want to die, not even me, blind as a cave newt. So we worked our way south as best we could. There was stuff to eat enough. We killed mountain zeller and ate berries, and the cliffs were full of springs and streams, so it wasn't that we hungered. Then we came upon a sizable river running away south. We built ourselves a raft and let the few horses go—poor beasts, they might be living there yet if the pombis didn't get them—and floated away south.

"Then it was hell, Gamesman, sheer hell for days on end. There were rocks in the river, and falls, and taking the raft apart and hauling it around obstacles and putting it together again. Once or twice my companions spotted smoke off in the woods, but we didn't dare see who was there for fear it might be Gifters again. We just went on and went on until we came to a long, placid stretch of river, and then we curled up on the raft and slept. I think we may have slept for some days, because when we came to ourselves we were coming to the town of Zebit, some ways south of here.''

"South of here," I said, puzzled. "Bannerwell is south of here."

"No, no, Gamesman. Bannerwell is south and a little east. If you go down the *west* side of the mountains, you'll come to Zebit, and it is south of here, right enough. The river makes a long curve, so we had floated by Betand in the darkness. The river I speak of flows just west of the city, here, over a low swell of hills.

"Well, they had all had enough exploring to last them a time, and I wanted only to have a Healer do something with my eyes. Those in Zebit said there was nothing they could do, but they recommended a Healer here in Betand who was said to be very powerful. So I bought a small pawnish boy to be my guide, and we crossed the river there at Zebit and found the trail into the mountains and then north to Betand. It was all nonsense about the Healer. She could do no more than the others. So, here I've stayed since, evoking small visions in return for a place to sleep or a bite to eat. The end of my great adventure, the only one I am ever to have. . . .''

I shook my head, musing, as he nodded, lost in memory and the flow of his own voice. "So," I said at last, "you came here from the south." That didn't help me at all.

"Oh, you might say so, Gamesman. But I came from the east, you know, and from the north as well. Twas my whole adventure brought me to Betand, and it was in all directions from here. . . .''

"Save west," I said, suddenly enlightened.

"True," he murmured, saddened. "I slept in the west, but I did not see it. Oh, I've seen it in visions, the sounds of metal, the green lights, the great defenders. . . .''

Would I had paid him more attention, but I did not. My question had been answered, and I was on fire to be away. So I pressed coins into his hands and left him without hearing what he was going on about. He had come to Betand from every direction except the west, therefore west was the direction I should go. I wondered briefly what guise Mavin had taken to hear the old man's tale. She may have sat in the same place, buying beer as I had done and listening to him tell the well-rehearsed story. Well.

Enough of that and time to be off. I did not even really listen to his tale of the perfidious Gifters.

I left the city through the northern gate and would have ridden on at speed save for a voice hailing me from among tents and wains at the side of the road.

"Ho, traveler. And were you amused by the city of Betand?"

It was that same wide-mouthed trader I had met in the tavern to the south of the city. I remembered he had said he would meet me, but I had paid little attention. Cursing silently, I reined in and waited for him to come up to me.

"Was it interesting, Necromancer?"

"The city was not a bad city, Trader."

"Nap, friend. Laggy Nap. Oh, yes, Betand is interesting," he said and again came that lewd laughter I remembered. "Interesting to get for no cost what one must pay for in other places, hmmm?" When I did not reply, he went on, "Well, have you a story to tell?"

"None, Trader Nap. I have accomplished my business in Betand and now ride west of here. Thank you for your interest."

"Oh, more than interest, friend! Much more. Concern. Yes, true concern. We make it a practice, my fellows and I, to befriend any Gamesman traveling alone. It is a wicked world, young sir, an unconscionable world. It takes no account of youth or business. No, only with numbers does protection come. If you ride west, then you ride as we do. Come, let me introduce you to my people."

I should have ridden away, simply ignored the fellow and gone, but the habit of courtesy was still too fresh in me. Fretting at the delay, I dismounted and walked with him to the line of wains at the roadside.

"Izia," he called. "Come out and greet a Gamesman who travels alone."

She came from behind one of the wagons, came like a vision, a Priestess, a Princess, a Goddess. I am sure my mouth dropped open. We had statues in the public square in Schooltown which embodied the ideal of female grace and form. If one of them had come to life and walked, thus was Izia's walk. Her hair was black without any light in it at all. Her eyes were smudged with deep shadow. Her lips curved downward and upward in the center in that most sensuous of lines, that half smile which is a silent evocation of passion. A few days before I would not have noticed. Now I did. So much had I learned in Betand. She walked with grace, but with a slight . . . what was it? A kind of hesitation, a tentative placement of her feet, as though she had some reluctance. So she came beside the wide-mouthed man and said in a soft, neutral voice, "Welcome, traveler. Would you desire food or drink?"

"Not for me," I said hastily. I felt I had done nothing but eat and drink for several days. "Truly, and thank you. I must ride on."

"We will not hear of it." The Trader had a firm arm about my shoulders, fingers dug into my upper arm in what might have been a friendly grip but felt like the talons of a bird of prey. "Never. You will ride with us, and we with you, for our mutual protection. If you need to go now, then so will we." And with that he called instructions to some of the people in the shade of the wagons and provoked a swift turmoil of harnessing and packing. I tried vainly to remonstrate with him, to no avail. Each argument was met with firm, smiling denial, while all the time his eyes looked into my soul without smiling at all. I had never before met one who would, on no acquaintance, call me friend so often in so insistent a voice.

Well, what could I do? They were moving out onto the road, going in the way I intended to go. It was with no good grace I accompanied them, but accompany them I did. All the while the woman, Izia, moved among the horses, as I watched her broodingly, clucking to them, speaking softly to them, fingers going to the harness as she murmured into their cocked ears, submitted to the nuzzling of their muzzles. When Nap came near, the animals shied away, but they responded to her as though she had been one of them. She was dressed in a swinging, wide skirt, a tightly-laced bodice over a wide-sleeved shirt, and high gray boots of some strange metallic weave. From time to time she would bend to stroke the boots, or more—to stroke her legs through the boots, first one and then the other, almost without seeming to know she did it. I wondered, once more, at the hesitancy in her step, then decided it must be a thing common to her people, for several of those in the train walked in the same way. Probably, I thought, it was a habit peculiar to whatever land they had come from.

I cast my mind back to the time when Silkhands the Healer had spent hours and days teaching me all the Gamesmen in the Index. It had been boring at the time, but now I searched the memories to find what type of creature this Laggy Nap might be. "Trader" had been in the Index. I recalled the Talents of a Trader, to hold power, some, and to have beguilement. The dress of a Trader was leather boots, trousers of striped brown and red, wide-sleeved shirt, and over all loose cap and tunic broidered with symbols of whatever stuff was traded. Laggy Nap's tunic was covered with embroidered pictures of everything from pans and lids to horses' heads; tinner to horse dealer, he seemed a man of many trades. None of the others wore the guise of Gamesmen. They were dressed much as the woman was, full short trousers over the gray boots, wide shirts and laced vests. I wondered where they came from but forbore to ask. I did not want to talk to the Trader more than necessary. I did not know why, could not have explained why, but the feeling was strong. It was as though I felt he could hear more in my words than I meant, see more in my face than I cared to show. I smiled, therefore, and nodded as he spoke to me, saying little in return. So are fools sometimes protected by instinct when they are too stupid to do it by wit.

So we rode out, me silent as could be, spending most of my time watching the woman. At first it was because I thought her so beautiful, but after a time I saw that she was not so lovely as first glance had told me. Her nose was too long. Her mouth too wide. One eye was a little higher than the other, and she seemed always to have her head cocked as though waiting for the reply to some forgotten question. Still, I could not stop watching her, and I rode so that wherever she was in the train, I would see her as I rode. She drew my eyes as a treasure draws a miser.

She saw that I watched her and turned her head away, not as if displeased, but as though saddened. I had done nothing to make her sad. There was another reason for that, and I resolved to learn it. Whenever we stopped, she was quick among some of the silent men to bring drink or prepare food, and I tried to talk with her about one thing or another. It was as though she had never learned to speak more than three words at a time. Yes. No. May I bring? Take some . . . Her distress at being addressed was so patent that I stopped at last, pretending what I should have pretended from the first—disinterest. It was good I did. Nap was scowling at me when he did not think I saw him.

There were some eight wains in the train, most of them open wagons loaded high with crates and covered with waterproofs. One or two were fitted up as living places in which the persons of the train might sleep and prepare their food. One was a chilly, small wagon which breathed vapor like a dragon and contained, so Laggy Nap said, perishable food-stuffs accounted great delicacies in the west. The wagons creaked along behind their teams, some of horses and some of water oxen, and the persons driving were silent. Izia was silent. I was silent while Laggy Nap talked and talked and talked of everything and anything and the world.

So went a day, a night, another day, and in the evening of the second day, as I went to relieve myself in a copse at the side of the road, I realized that I was being guarded. One of the persons in the train walked by the copse, and I recalled that every time I had ridden a little ahead or lagged a little behind, someone had been beside me within moments. Yes, I told myself, you knew it before. It is this which has made you uncom-fortable all along. These people are not simply offering you company on the way, they are keeping you, guarding you, and would not let you go away if you tried to escape. I was as certain of it as if I had been told it by Laggy Nap himself. I lingered in the copse, within sight of the man who watched me, giving no sign I was disturbed, going over and over in my head the words Mavin had left for my guide.

"Befriend the shadows and beware of friends." She had warned me, and I had not been alert to the warning. Well. So and so. Time enough to be wary now. I adjusted my clothing and wandered back to the wagons, pausing now and then to look at a tree or a bush. Were there shadows? If so, where? I saw none, could find none, and was greeted by Laggy Nap at the fire as though I had been away for a year and we were lovers. My throat was dry as autumn grass, and I was afraid. Well, I would learn nothing to help me by silence. It was time to play their Game and hope I had time to yet win something to my benefit.

So that evening I drank with him, talked with him, told him long tales of Betand, including three thousand things which had not happened there with at least a hundred maidens who did not exist. All the while his wide mouth smiled while his eyes looked coldly into my heart. All the while I kept my eyes away from Izia, praying I had not already harmed her by my interest. Finally, I pretended drunkenness, asked him about this and that. "Have you heard of magicians?" I hiccuped to show that the ques-tion was not of importance. "In Betand they talk of . . . hic . . . magi-cians."

His hand twitched. I saw the jaw tighten over his smile and Izia, where she crouched by the fire, started touching her legs as though wounded, looking up as though she had heard an ugly voice call her name. I put my nose in the cup and made gulping sounds. Something wrong. Well, I would take time to consider it later.

"Magicians," he said cheerfully. "No. I don't think I've heard of magicians."

"Nor I before," I babbled, all bibulous naivete. "But there in Betand they talk much of magicians. Why is that, do you think?"

"Oh, well, it's a parochial place, after all. Most of the people there are ignorant, superstitious. They must talk of something, and it is amusing to talk of wonders, freaks, Gifters . . . yes, Gifters. They talk much of Gifters, but has any one of them ever *seen* a Gifter?" His eyes watched me over the top of his cup. I met them with a stare in which no glimmer of intelligence showed.

"No, you know, you're right!" I slapped my knee, laughed. "No Gifters either, you think? Wonderful. Everyone lighting candles to something which doesn't exist . . . marvelous." I laughed myself into a long stretching movement which let me see Izia. Yes. She still stroked her legs, still frowned into the fire as though in pain. Well. Cold certainty seeped into me. The man meant me no good, no good at all.

I knew I was right when he came to my blanket to offer me a wineskin, saying, "Some of the vintage we carry to the cities away west. Not that stuff we've been drinking. No. Something very special. Thought you'd enjoy it." Smile, smile, smile. I smiled stuporously in return, took the wineskin and laid it beside me.

"Generous of you, Trader. Generous. I'll have a sip of it in a bit. Oh, yes, soon as this last bit settles." I laughed a little, let my eyes close as though I were too drowsy to stay awake, watching him from beneath my lids. The smiling mouth of him snarled, then took up its perpetual cheer.

"Sleep well," he wished me. "Drink deep, and sleep well."

"Ah, yes, yes, I will. I will, indeed." If I drank his gift, I would probably not wake, I told myself. How in the name of Towering Tamor was I to get out of this?

A little time went by. Darkness settled. I heard someone going by the place I lay and reached out to catch an ankle. It was Izia, and she crouched beside me saying, "What would you, fool?"

"Izia, I may be a fool indeed to ask you, but—am I in danger?"

211

"Oh, poor fool, you are. And I may not aid you unless I die in more agony than you have ever felt." She took my hand and laid it upon her boot, high upon her leg, and held it there. Long moments went by. Then I heard Laggy Nap call from the wain, call her name, once, again, and beneath my hand the boot began to burn like fire. I drew my hand away with a harsh exclamation.

"I come," she called in a clear voice, then knelt to hiss into my ear. "You see, fool. We obey. We obey, obey, obey. Or we burn."

# 4

# Befriend the Shadows

WHEN THE CAMP CAME AWAKE in the morning, I pretended a headache and staggering incompetence. During the long waking hours I had decided that Laggy Nap was unsure of my powers, my Talents, and would therefore probably (though not certainly) decide not to attack me directly. No, he would attempt something else, something sly and sneaking like the drugged wine I was sure he had already offered me or, if he wanted me dead, some sneaking murder. So, I decided to appear no threat to him while I found a little time to design some strategy to protect my life. I knew Izia would say nothing. In this I was correct. For the first time I was able to interpret the discipline around me correctly. It was all fear and pain, simply that. Laggy Nap had some mental link or some other control of the boots they wore. The wearer of those boots did Nap's will or burned. I was led to a remembrance of the devices which Nitch had sewn into my tunic the year before. Were not these torture boots something of the same kind? And were both not similar to the things Mandor had said were Huld's?

Well, the provenance of the things did not matter at the moment. My life did. Therefore I staggered and sweated and even managed to vomit in the bushes. Truth to tell, I felt sick enough, though it was not wine-sickness but strain and fear. Oh, yes, I was fearful. In the night hours I had reached for Dorn. He had come into my mind slowly, reluctantly, murmuring "Necromancer nine, Peter, Necromancer nine." I could get nothing else out of him, and I had not needed that warning that I was at grave risk. I had already figured that out for myself.

It was not long until Nap confronted me with a false smile and prying questions. Had I drunk the special wine he had given me last night? I answered with vague noddings, sick grins, avowals that one more drop of anything would have killed me indeed. He got no satisfaction, and I knew it would not be more than a few hours before he would try something again. Let him think me an idiot. I did not think much better of myself.

I needed some other Talent, and this made me fretful, weighing and discarding notion after notion. I could shift into some other form if I left my horse and all belongings behind me. I was reluctant to do that. There was a great distance still to travel, I thought. Instinct told me that Trandilar would not move Nap. He was of a kind impervious to the beguilement of others. He was also of a kind who would not be fearful of the dead. Therefore some other Talent. Not Elator, as that would lose me horse and gear, and Elators could only move themselves between known locations. I knew no location forward on the journey, so any move would lose me leagues already traveled. Armiger? Again, horse and gear lost if I flew away. The Talents of Fire? Or Healing? What good were these to me? A Demon's Talent for Reading? Perhaps, if that would let me know what was in Nap's mind. Musing thus, I rode along beside the icy little wagon, seeing the mist rise from it like the mists far behind me in the Bright Demesne. Nothing presented itself as a good strategy. All seemed forced, difficult, possibly dangerous. . . .

Then I saw the cliffs ahead of us, looming against the lowering sky, for it had been chill and rainy during the early hours and was only now clearing. Cliffs, crumbly at the rim, trailing away in long talus slopes at their bases. An idea began to form, slowly, only bones of thought still to become fleshed and finished. The sun came from behind the clouds, hot and impatient. I reached into the pouch at my belt and found the little image of Shattnir, First Sorcerer, great lady of Power. She did not speak to me as the others had done. Instead, she flowed into my veins and across my skin, bound me around with her net, tied me into her being, and began to take the heat from the sun and place it—somewhere within. I could feel it building within me, a tightness, as though my skin were stretched and swollen. I knew my eyes were bulging and my lips turning outward, puffed, but my reflection in the polished harness plate between the horse's ears showed no change in my appearance. ''Not too much,'' I begged silently. ''Enough, Shattnir, but not too much.'' She did not listen but went on taking the power from the bright sky, more and more and more, until at last I gave up waiting to explode and let her find room for it all. When I quit holding my breath, the swollen feeling abated slightly, and evidently there was room for it all for we rode so until the mountains rose across the sun to make a long, violet-gray shade for our stopping place.

The fires were lit, the silent pawns began their evening chores and routines. Izia moved among the horses, examining their hooves, stroking their glossy hides, murmuring to them. I excused myself to go away from the camp, unsurprised when one of the booted men followed me. I did not go into the copse, however, but up the rocky slope against the cliff, stumbling a little on the scree, seeing loose bits of it slide and rattle beneath my feet with hopeful satisfaction. There was a hollow there, a place where a piece of the cliff had broken away from the main mass leaving a narrow space behind it, no larger than a closet. I eased myself within, watching my follower peering after me. Well enough.

I reached into the pouch and took the image of Wafnor into my hand, first and greatest Tragamor. I became a room into which a man with a cheerful face entered, laughing, grasping the hands of those there with a fond greeting. Almost I could hear him, "Dorn, Trandilar, Shattnir, how well you all look. Oh, it is good to see my friends again." And then he was at my side saying, "And what have we to do?"

Perhaps I told him, perhaps he simply knew. I cannot really describe what it is like. Sometimes it is like telling another person something, sometimes it is like talking to oneself, sometimes simply like knowing. Within me I felt his arms reach up, up along the cliff face, higher and higher to the rimrock fifty manheights or more above, to grasp the stones there and move them, one, two, a dozen, slowly down and down until they began to roll and fall, to tumble clacking against others, knocking, more and more, down, an avalanche of stone, toward my hidden closet behind the stone, a rumbling roar as I shrieked to the man who watched me, "Look out! Rock fall!" One glimpse of his face, a white oval around the round hole of a dark scream.

Then I could feel nothing and hear nothing except the grating roar of the stones. Still Wafnor reached out to them, stacking this one and that one as they fell, arranging them over me, over and around like a cave while outside the shuddering cave the stones still fell for long moments into a shattered silence.

There were cracks among the stones around me, little crevices to let in the air and the sound. Through these I could hear the whinnying of beasts, snorts, cries of men, Izia's scream as she tugged animals away from the tumbling stones. Wafnor reached out once more, across the camp to the place my horse was tethered with my pack and saddle still upon him, urged him away into the trees, out of sight of the camp, calmed the horse there to wait for me. Then Wafnor did nothing, I did nothing, and we merely waited and listened to the sounds.

"Where is he?" Laggy Nap, raging.

A voice in answer, shaky, almost hysterical. "I don't know. He was against the rock, up in there, and it came down on top of him. He screamed at me to look out. You heard him scream. It came down right on top of him . . . buried . . . covered over . . ."

"Devils take it," Nap screamed. "What started the fall?"

"Just started. Nothing. Didn't see anything. No people, nothing moving. No thunder, nothing like that. Just started . . ."

"Shadow men? Did you see shadow men?"

"Nothing, sir. Nothing at all. He screamed, and the rocks were coming down. . . ."

Nap once more, this time strident, calling in his servitors. "Get up here, you lot. We'll have to dig him out!" He sounded frantic. Dig me out? And why? This was unexpected, but Wafnor did not seem disturbed. He reached high once again, sent a few small stones cascading at Nap's feet, followed by a medium-sized boulder or two. High above I could feel Wafnor's hands upon the megalith, swaying it.

"Get back, get back. The whole wall looks to come down. Oh, why did he come up here against the wall. Izia! Did he say anything to you?"

Her voice. "You know he did not, sir. He has said nothing to me out of your hearing. And now he is dead. . . ."

"I was told to bring him," Nap snarled. "Bring him to the west, to Tallman and the mumble-mouths. How can I go empty-handed?"

"Why would they do anything to you? It is not your fault the cliff fell. It is ill luck, but not your doing. . . ."

"I have had ill luck since the Shifter sold you to me, fool. Ill luck all the years of our travel. I wish you were dead beneath that rock instead of the one I was told to bring." I heard the sound of a blow, a scream, then long silence.

A man's voice at last. "Surely even they understand things that happen which are not foreseen."

"Which are nor foreseen! Yes! But which should have been foreseen. I will demand they give a Seer to serve me. Perhaps more than one. When we arrive, I will demand . . ."

"Do we continue on this road, sir?"

"No. This road goes nowhere. We came this way only to follow that troublesome Necromancer, that death's-head, that son of a loathsome toad. Oh, I came this way only to trap him, and now he is trapped too deep for me to reach! We go back to River Haws, and north almost to Hell's Maw, then west by Cagihiggy water. We can take no time for food. We go now!"

I heard a voice saying something weary and hopeless about Hell's Maw, and the sound of another blow. Then were the rattle of harness, the creaking of wheels, the voices of men and one woman dying away to the east, gone. Then long gone. I waited, not moving. Nap was tricky. He might think to leave someone to watch. Night came. I slept. Morning came, and Wafnor moved the stones aside. I was born into the world like a revenant to a Necromancer's call, squinting in the sun. When I whistled, my horse came from the trees where Wafnor had held him throughout the night. We needed water, he and I, and only when that was taken care of did we ride on to the west. I should have been cheered, but was not. My escape, my safety were shadowed by Izia's continuing captivity, and she was in my mind during the morning hours, so much so that at last I decided it would do her no good, nor me, this brooding. So, I set my mind firmly upon Mavin's words, "Befriend the shadows." Come evening, I would try to do her bidding.

The way led upward. From a lonely height I could look back along the trail to see a small trail of dust on the eastern horizon. Was that Laggy Nap? Izia? Was there something I should have done which I had not? Within me was a kind of consultation, and voices came to tell me there was nothing I could have done, not then, that there were more urgent things for me to do. Still, I felt the queasiness of one who leaves a needful task undone. Though I tried not to think of her, she was much in my mind.

And still in my mind in the evening. I watched from beside my fire, waiting for evidence of shadow men. I saw nothing, heard nothing except an occasional interruption of insect sounds as though something might have walked among them. Morning came, gray and dripping, and I rode on west to another evening and another fire. I reached out to Trandilar, begged her for a blandishment, a beguilement to charm birds, small beasts, whatever might be within sight or smell of me. She let it flow through me and breathe into the air, a perfume, a subtle fragrance of desire. Watching quiet greeted it, a silent attention. I could not say how I knew they were there, but I knew it. I slept at last, weary with waiting for them to come to me.

In the morning I journeyed beside a stream which became a small river. I had come high onto a tilted upland that slanted down toward the west, and the river I followed was fed from all sides by swiftly flowing rivulets making conversational noises over the polished stones of their beds. By day's end I began to smell something strange, a vast wetness, like that of the Gathered Waters, but different in some way I could not describe. Suddenly, the air before me was full of rainbows, the river plunged away through a notch in the land, and I could see the waters below, a mighty sea stretching beyond sight into the west. The evening wind was in my face, thrusting the waters onto the beach below in long combers of white. A twisting path wound down the face of the cliffs, and at the bottom the beaches reached away north and south in a smooth curve into which the elevated land behind me dropped and vanished. Some little distance to the north was an inlet bordered with trees, a grassy bank, a pool of still water over which white flowers nodded their heads and devil's needles dipped glassy wings. The horse stumbled with tiredness; I licked lips wet with salt and almost fell when I dismounted. There was no sound but water talk, yet I knew something was watching me, had been watching me for days. I was too weary to eat so only pulled the saddle from the horse and rolled myself into a blanket to sleep dreamlessly.

It was dark when I woke, dark lit by a half moon. Some sound had wakened me, some cry. I stared across the moonlit waters to see a boat, a long, low boat like those carried on larger ships. It seemed empty, but I had heard a cry. The boat showed only as an outline against a kind of glow, a subtle luminescence, nebulous and equivocal. It drifted toward me, grated on the pebbles of the beach and rocked there, each wave threatening to carry it out once more. In my sleep-befuddled mind it seemed fortuitous, a boat to carry me west. I stumbled out of my blanket, still half asleep, intending to pull the boat further onto the shore.

Then, as I stumbled toward the boat, an anguished keening came out of the dark, and I was stopped, unable to move further. There were little arms about my legs, thrusting me back, tugging at me, moving me away from the boat. Between me and the impalpable glow, I could see their figures outlined. Two or three of them carried something among them, a balk of timber perhaps—something bulky. They went close to the boat, heaved their burden high and ran wildly away. The bulky burden fell within the boat. . . .

And the boat tilted upward, rose into the air, became the end of an enormous pillar to which it was attached, a monstrous, flexible arm upon which it was only a leaf-shaped tip, one among many mighty tentacles thrashing upward in a maelstrom of sinew to tangle themselves around the ''boat'' and carry it beneath the surface. The little fingers pushed me back, back, and from the waters those tentacles came once more, questing across the pebbles with palpable anger to find the prey they had been denied. Against the watery glow I thought I saw a nimbus outlining an eye, rounder than the moon and as cold, peering enormously at the small shadowy figures which capered on the pebbled shore and hooted as they danced.

They were quadrumanna, the four-handed ones, shadow people, silky-furred, with ears like delicate wings upon their heads and sharp little teeth which glinted in the half light of the stars. All through the hooting and warbling they never ceased to tug at me, back away from the water's edge, back to the place I had slept. As we went they acted out the rage of the water creature, letting their long, supple arms twist like the tentacles, dropping them onto the pebbles in an excess of artful rage. ''Hoo, hoo, hoor, oor, oor.'' Others gathered from the streamside until I was surrounded by a jigging multitude. All sleep had been driven away. I fed sticks into a hastily kindled fire, watching the celebration.

One of them brought me a fruit, which I ate, and this moved others to bring me bits of this and that, some of which smelled and tasted good, others which I could not bring myself to put in my mouth. They learned quickly. If I rejected a thing, they brought no more of it. After a time the excitement dwindled, and they gathered in crouching rows to watch me. I reached to the nearest, patted him (or her, or it) saying, ''Friend.'' They liked that. Several mimicked my word in my own voice, and others took it up, "Friend, rend, end, end, end." At this, a silvery one from among them was moved to stand and come to my side, to strike his chest with an open hand. "Proom," he said. "Proom. Proom."

I tapped his chest, said "Proom," then struck my own. "Peter."

"Peter, eater, ter, ter," they murmured, enchanted.

The grizzled one waved at the waters, at the tremulous surface, mimed a swimming stroke, raised his hands in the writhing mime of tentacles. "D'bor."

I pointed to the waves and repeated the word. He nodded. It seemed to be going well from his point of view.

"D'bor, nonononononono," he said proudly, miming swimming once more. "Nonononono."

I laughed. "Nonononono," I agreed, at which we both nodded, satisfied. Mavin's words came to me. "Walk on fire, but do not swim in water." Surely. Water was a nonononono.

Well then, walk on fire I would, if I could find any. I fed sticks to the fire, building the blaze high, then stood to point both hands toward it in a hierarchic gesture before walking around it, one hand over my eyes, peering into the darkness north, west, south, and east, then pointing to the fire once more. They conferred among themselves, a quiet gabble. The gray one pointed to the fire. "Thruf," he said. Then he turned toward the north. "Thruf," he said again, indicating something big, bigger, huge.

I mimicked his mime, used his word. "Thruf," made walking motions. The soft gabbling continued among them, and several got up to come after me, following, walky-walky in the soft grass, going nowhere. They giggled. Evidently several would go with me, when I went. Time enough to go when the sun came up, or so I thought. They thought otherwise. The ones who had appointed themselves, or had been appointed, for all I knew, took up my belongings and went to get my horse, standing nose to nose with the beast as each made whiffling noises of intimate interrogation and reply. Nothing would do but that I mount the animal and go along quietly as they led him. Well enough. If I put my mind to it, I could almost sleep in the saddle. So we went, along the pebbled shoreline of the waters—though well back from the edge— toward the north. The sky grew dim, milky with dawn, and my guides showed consternation amounting almost to agitation. There was an abrupt halt to forward movement, a casting about from place to place, then a long "hoor-oor-oor" from a forested slope. The others followed it and brought me to a cavelet, dark as a nostril in the side of the mountain. They laid my belongings down, made quick forays into the wood for dry branches and twigs, piled these beside the wall of the hill, then vanished within the darkness to a trailing "hoor-oor-oor-oor." I decided this meant hello, goodbye, and here-I-am. I called softly after them. The answer was silence.

So. I was abandoned for the daylight hours. Their huge eyes and wing-like ears should have told me they were creatures of the dark. I had the day before me and was not sleepy, so I went fishing. It took half the day to make a proper fish spear and half the afternoon to spear fish enough for the troop. I had a nap and built the fire up before they appeared at dusk. I was not long in doubt whether they liked fish, for there was much smacking of narrow lips, rubbing of round bellies, and hooting of a me-lodious kind. When they had eaten every scrap of skin and sniffed the bones several times, they urged me into the saddle once more to ride throughout the night. Again, they led while I slept, waking only a little now and again to see a changed horizon, a mountain moved from before me to behind me. I told off the days of my journey, counted them, named them over. Tomorrow, I told myself, would be rabbit day. I had little food left in the saddle bags and we had left the stream behind us.

So it went, rabbit day succeeded by dove day, succeeded by fish day II, succeeded by the day we ate greens and nuts. The little people were mightily disappointed at this, but I had had no luck at all in the hunt. We had come to a stretch of moorland crossed by tiny rivulets. There was greenery aplenty, but nothing seemed to be feeding on it but us. That night, halfway through the dark hours' travel, I saw the glow of fire upon the horizon, half hidden behind a bulk of hill. Before morning it stood plain before us, fountains of fire, and behind them more fountains yet to the limits of vision. "Thruf," gabbled my escort in great satisfaction. "Thrufarufarufaruf." I presumed that this meant more fires than one.

As there were. Soon we walked among them, the glowing hills around us closer and more difficult to avoid. Flames erupted from hidden vents in the stone, liquid fire ran into crevasses to glow and breathe like embers, nearer and nearer. Soon we came to a place where there was no avoidance possible. Directly before the horse's nose a wide strip of glowing lava

lay, shining scarlet in the light wind, crusted and scabbed with cinder.
The horse shuddered and refused to go further. "Chirrup," said one of
the shadow people importantly, pulling at my leg. "Chirrup." They
pulled my things from the horse's back, handing me some of them to
carry, carrying others themselves. Then, without hesitation, the chirruping
four-handed one set his furry feet onto the glowing stone. Others followed, one remaining behind to hold the horse. "Walk on fire," I told
myself, sweating, waiting for the pain to burn upward through the soles
of my boots. Nothing. Around me the crackle of flames, but my feet were
cool. "Chirrup," my guide called. "Thrufarufarufarufaruf."

We walked as on a road of glass. The appearance of fire was only
reflection from the geysers and fountains to either side. Rivers of fire ran
beside us. Heaped mountains of half molten stuff built into fantastic
shapes. From these came heat as from a furnace, but upon the road we
walked it was cool. We seemed to be crossing a narrow neck of the fiery
land between two towering heights crowned with spouting smoke which
boiled upward toward the bloody cloud, hideous and heavy with ash and
rain. Before me the little ones began to run, gamboling from side to side
of the way. "Chirrup, chirrup, Peter, eater, ter, ter."

An answering call came from ahead. We ventured between the last
flaming fountains to emerge upon a hillside, green and cool, with a steady
wind blowing the heat away and a glint of water showing among the
trees. The little ones leapt on, me laboring after them, wishing I had taken
time to pack properly and roll my blankets so they would not fall around
my feet. As it was, I arrived in a shambling rush, half tripped up by
trailing bedstuffs, red-faced from the heat and the hurry, to fall on my
face before the one who awaited us. She did me the discourtesy of laughing rudely.

"Rise, Sir Gamesman," she said, sneering at the tumbled stuff around
me. She turned away to hold a multisyllabled conversation with the quadrumanna which seemed to much delight them, for they giggled endlessly
and rolled upon the ground clutching at themselves.

"I have asked them," she said, "if you are one of the mythical tumble-
bats who roll themselves endlessly through the world not knowing their
heads from their tails. They are inclined to believe this, though they say
you are a good provider and are, possibly, the one whose travel was
arranged for by Mavin Manyshaped. Are you indeed he?"

"She is my mother," I said wearily.

"Ah. Well then, you are he. Mavin has not so many sons that we would mistake one of them for another. Your name would be Peter?"

"Yes. And yours?"

"You may call me Thynbel, or Sambeline. Or anything else you would rather."

I grasped at the last name. "Sambeline. Did my mother arrange for you to meet me?"

"Indeed, no. She arranged for me to meet the people of Proom to pay them for their trouble in guiding you here. Though they say they are already well paid since they have your horse."

"My horse? What will they do with my horse?"

"It may be they will sell him, but I think they will eat him."

I could think of no reply to this. It was not a horse I had loved or cared for, but still, it was a good horse. A well-trained horse. A horse which had served me well. "If you pay them, would they consent not to eat the horse?"

"It may be. Or I may pay them and they may eat the horse regardless. But I will try for you."

So she did, engaging in a lengthy and intricate argument, full of words which echoed themselves endlessly. At last the little people giggled a final round, held out their hands for their pay, and had put into those hands a wealth of silvery bells and metal flutes, bright as the sun. They clasped my legs, slapped my sides, called me "Peter, eater, ter, ter" one last time and went capering back down the trail of false fire into the distant dawn.

Sambeline waved at them, turned to me, saying, "They say they will turn the horse loose in the meadows until you return, Peter. They may do that. They may forget. They may do it and then forget and eat it later. They forget a lot, those little ones. They forget where they put their bells and flutes. They lose them by the dozens. So they are always eager for more and are willing to be paid. If they did not lose things, they would not work for us at all. Now they will have music for a time and sing many long songs of their trip to the firelands with the son of Mavin Manyshaped."

I finished packing my things into more compact bundles and strapped them together into a pack I could carry. She made no offer to help, merely sneered at these efforts. I said, "I must needs go further, but you say you are not my guide?"

"No. I will go with you a short way. You are in the land of Schlaizy Noithn, the land of the Shifters. None can guide you here. This is Schlaizy Noithn and no roads run the same here. Not for long. Where do you want to go?"

I sat upon the pack. The dawn had uncovered a green land, forested, flowing with rivers and spotted with pools and lakes. It lay beneath the height on which we stood, stretching north and west in a lovely bowl which cupped at the edge of vision to other heights. "I seek the monument of Thandbar," I said. "Can you tell me where to find it?"

"You think unshifterish," she commented, "when you ask where in Schlaizy Noithn you would find the monument of Thandbar."

I thought on this. It made a certain kind of sense. Thandbar had been the first and greatest of Shifters. Surely his memorial would not be a stable, unchanging thing. It would change, move, shift. "If you had to find it," I asked her, "where would you look?"

"Up and down, here and there, among, between, around, in and out of," she said.

"Upon," I offered. "Within, beneath, through and over . . ."

"Exactly," she replied. "That is more shifterish. There may be hope for Mavin's outland son."

# 5

# Schlaizy Noithn

DURING THE TIME THAT FOLLOWED I learned of shifterish behavior, and thoughts, and habits. How could this be summed up so that you will understand, you of the world in which mountains do not walk and roadways do not run; you of the world in which you wake in the same place you have slept, find your way by landmarks, travel by maps and charts? Having made one journey in the little lake ship, I had seen, though learned nothing of the art of, guidance by the stars. In Schlaizy Noithn, that is what I did, for nothing but the stars remained unchanging through the nights and days of travel. I despair of explaining ''shifterish'' to you except to say that it is difficult for one reared in a Schooltown. And yet, from what I learned later, that rearing had been a mercy my mother had given me which many young Shifters would have been glad to receive. Well, there is no better way to tell it than to tell it, as Chance would have said. So I will tell.

I entered the country of Schlaizy Noithn with Sambeline walking beside me. I said something or other, and she replied, making a remark about Mavin being much respected there, and after a short silence I turned to say something to her but found a huge, shambling pombi walking beside me, its monstrous head swinging to and fro with each step, long tongue lolloped between fangs of curved ivory. I was too frightened to do anything. My first thought was that this beast had killed Sambeline and left her bleeding body somewhere behind us, but when the beast looked up at me abstractedly before leaving the path to climb a hollow tree, to which it clung with one great, clawed foot while dipping into the hollow with the other to suck the honey-dripping paw with every evidence of pleasure, I began to guess that pombi and Sambeline were one. When the pombi blurred, shifted, and flew away through the trees on wide wings of softest white, calling a two pitched ooo-ooo as it went, when the honey tree shook itself and moved away through the forest on roots suddenly as flexible as fingers, leaving me alone, then I began to know what shifterish meant. I began to understand why it was that Sambeline had sneered at my belongings. Does a pombi need a blanket? A cookpot? A firestarter? I put down the pack and stared at it, unwilling to leave it and yet sure it marked me as nothing else could—stranger, outsider, outlander. Was this dangerous or otherwise? I could not tell.

Among the Gamesmen of Barish there were sixteen tiny figures representing Shifters. In an ordinary set of Gamesmen, such as are given to children for their little two-space games, these would be the pawns. In my set, Shifters; and one of them, or perhaps all of them held the persona of Thandbar, old sent-far himself, shiftiest of all. Presumably none of this would have been strange to *him,* and yet I never thought of taking a Shifter figure into my hand, never considered it. Later I wondered why I had not done. It was simple enough: pride. Shifting was my own talent, the one to which I had been born. I wanted no instruction in it from another. I wanted it to be mine. So, out of ignorance and pride, all unprepared for what I would meet or see or be required to do, I went on into the country of Schlaizy Noithn quite alone.

So.

I sat upon a hill beside a grotesque pile of stones, twisted and warped as though shaped thus when molten, making an uneasy meal of fish. These were unusual fish in that they had not howled and climbed up the fish spear to engulf my hands with a maw of ravening fury before melting into a swarm of butterflies and scattering into impalpability against the sky. Because these fish were quiet, these fish, reason said, were real fish, edible fish. Reason said that. Stomach was uncertain.

Beside me the warped stones grated into speech, moving slowly as lips might if they were as wide and tall as a man.

"Whoooo suuuups in Schlaaaaaizeee Noiiiiithnnnn?"

I said, "Peter, the son of Mavin Manyshaped," while trying to keep my heart from leaping out of my breast. The stone said nothing more. However, a long spit of earth began to grow from beside me, upward and outward like a curving branch of the living hill, out to turn again and look at me, opening from its tip a curious eye of milky blue, lashed with grasses, which blinked, blinked, blinked at me, staring. It stared while the fish cooked, while I ate them, while I scrubbed my knife and put it away, while I put out the fire, then turned to stare after me still as I walked away. When I looked back at the crest of the next hill, the eye had grown a bit taller to keep me in view.

Sometimes the road moved. Sometimes it moved in the direction I was going, sometimes sideways, sometimes backwards. Sometimes it jumped, like a cranky horse hopping when it is first saddled. When the road went against my direction, I got off as soon as possible, always apologizing for doing so—or for having been on it in the first place. It was hard to walk unless there was a road, for the land was full of impassable tangles. Sometimes the roads spoke to me, sometimes they cursed me. Once a road held fast to my feet while it carried me back a full day's journey. Will you understand my stupidity when I tell you that I walked the day's journey again on my own two feet, carrying my pack?

They—whoever they were—grew impatient.

I stopped when it grew dark, took my firelighter out of the pack and laid kindling beneath it, ready for the spark. The kindling reached up and flipped it out of my hands to be caught by a bird sitting on a stone. The bird flew away, carrying the firelighter in her claws, and I seemed to hear small, cawing laughter from the air. I cursed, cursed the place, the inhabitants, myself. Nothing seemed to hear me or care, save that the tops of the trees moved in a wind I had not felt till then and clouds began to boil in the sunset, so many puffy gray dumplings in a red soup of sky. Within moments it began to rain. My kindling grew legs and walked into the brush. I rolled myself into my blankets and nibbled on a handful of nuts collected during the day's travel. A stag came out of the forest, trumpeted challenge to another which appeared from behind me; the two charged one another over my body. I rolled, frantic, scraped across stones which left me bleeding, sat up to see the two stags running into the trees, my blankets caught upon their antlers.

I sat beneath a tree, water dripping down my neck, without blankets, without fire, the rain continuing in an endless, mocking stream. Whenever I moved, it found me. There was no shelter near except a hollow high in the tree into which wings flickered from time to time, outlined against flashes of lightning. I was cold. My clothes were little use except to hold some warmth against my body. I felt a little tug at one ankle. The next lightning flash showed a small, razor edged vine cutting the seams of my trousers while a tendril sifted a kind of powder on my boots. Two lightning flashes later and the boots were sprouting fungus from every surface, huge, soggy sponges covering my feet. Wings flickered into the hollow five manheights above me, an opening as wide as my armspan into the great tree.

A kind of dull fury began to pound in me, a discomfort so great that my body rebelled against it. There was no thought connected to it at all. Something deeper and more ancient than thought did as it wished, and Peter did nothing to oppose it.

My claws struck deep into the corky bark of the tree. My long, curved fangs gleamed in the lightning. Above me was a consternation of birds, and my pombi-self smiled in anticipation. I came through the opening into the hollow in a rush, a crunch of jaws, a flap of great paws catching this and that flutterer, to make a leisurely meal of warm flesh as I spat feathers out of the opening and watched the storm move away across the far hills. When it was quiet, I curled into the dry hollow, pausing only to rip out a strip of rotted wood which made a small discomfort against my hide. I slept. It was warm within the tree, and the fury passed as the storm passed.

I woke remembering this dimly, in my own body shape, naked as an egg. Below me the remains of my pack lay on the ground. A few straps and buckles. A knife. Beside me in the hole was the pouch in which the Gamesmen of Barish were stored. Evidently even in fury I had not let them go. I went down the tree as I had come up it, pombi-style, the pouch between my teeth. Once on the ground, however, I became Peter once more, furred-Peter, with a pocket in the fur to hold the Gamesmen. It was no great matter. I wondered then, as I have since, why it took so long to think of it or decide to do it. The knife would have fitted into the pocket as well, but I left it where it lay. The pombi claws would cut as well.

As the sun rose higher and warmer, my fur grew shorter except upon the legs and feet where it was needed as protection against the stones and briars. When it grew cool with evening, the fur became long again. The body did it. Peter did not need to think of it. The body thought of longer legs on occasion, as well, and of arms which were variably long to pick whatever fruits were ripe. That day I ate better than in many days past. No fruit tore itself screaming from my hands. No fish or bird turned into a monster over my fire. Some things I let alone, and the body knew which. After a time, the eyes knew, also, and then the brain.

There were trees one did not approach, hills one stayed away from, roads one did not step upon. There were others which were hospitable, or merely "real." There were artifacts in Schlaizy Noithn. Monuments. Cenotaphs. Monstrous menhirs which looked as though they had been erected in the dawn of time. Some had been put there by—people. Gamesmen, perhaps. Or pawns. Some were Shifters, beings like myself (or so I thought) in the act of creation. I learned to trust the body's feeling about these places. If they were "real" then I might explore or take shelter there. If they were not, it were far better to stay a comfortable distance away. I did not yet know of other kinds of things, neither real nor Shifter, kinds of things my body would not warn me of. What betrayed me to one of these was simply loneliness.

Days had gone by. I had lost count of them. I had quartered the valley in search of the monument of Thandbar. I had searched and had begun to despair, for who was to say the monument had not moved always before me, or behind me? I had not seen a human form since Sambeline had flown away. I had wondered from time to time whether they used the human form only on some ceremonial occasions for some purpose of high ritual in the pursuance of their religion, whatever that might be. In any case, they did not show human form to me. I saw animals which were not animals, things apparently of stone and earth which were not, trees and plants which never sprouted from seed or tuber, but I did not see mankind. Even furred-Peter was far closer to his reality than many others there.

So, when I came upon the Castle, lit from a hundred windows, with a soft breath of music stirring from it into the airs of the night, I was needful more than I could say of that refreshment which comes from one's own kind. I was growing unsure of who I was, what I was. Was I only furred-Peter, running wild in the wilderness, an animal among others, gradually forgetting why I had come and to what end? I needed to be more than that.

So it called me where it stood upon its hill, brooding there over the silvered meadows, its great ornamental pillars contorted into bulbous asymmetries, casting lakes of shadow onto the grasses before me, making swamps of darkness within its courts. Its doors were open, welcoming. There was no warning. It was grotesque, misshapen, abnormal, but not fearsome. I was too lonely to be fearful. I shifted into a more civilized form, relishing the feel of clothing again, the weight of a cloak upon my shoulders. I had learned that clothing was no problem. One simply made it of the same stuff one used to make one's skin.

I walked under the arch, hands empty to show I was no enemy. Here was no portcullis to grind gratingly into stone pockets, no bridge to fall thunderingly upon the pavement. No, only an open way, the floor a mosaic design which swirled and warped, leading away in unexpected directions, returning from unexpected shifts and erratic lines. Looking at it made my head swim, but I told myself it was hunger for talk, for people, for a fire, for food that was cooked, for the trappings of humanity. The name of the place was carved over the great door. "Castle Lament." Well, a name without cheer, but not for that reason damnable. I had been in other places with sad names.

The door swung wider before me, and I went through.

Then it shut behind me.

How can I describe that sound? The door was not huge, no larger than in many great halls. It shut softly but with the *sound* of a door twenty times its size, a monstrous slam as of a mighty hammer, slightly clamoring, briefly echoing, fading into a silence which still reverberated with that sound, and all down the monstrous bulk of that place came the sound of other doors shutting with an equal finality, an inevitable shutting which I could not have imagined until that moment. I was shut in. I turned to beat my hands against the door, then stopped, afraid of what might come in answer to that knocking, for the sound of closing had been like jaws snapping shut, like hands clapping around fluttering wings, to hold, and hold, and hold until hope went, and life. It was the sound teeth might make, fastening in a throat.

I was terribly afraid, so afraid that I did nothing for a long moment, scarcely breathed, crouched where I was, peering into the place, seeing it as in a nightmare. At last I moved.

There were stairs which climbed from the audience hall over bottomless pits of black, arching against pillars to coil, snakelike, about them and climb upward to high pavements littered with a thousand half carven heads of stone which smiled at me and begged me in the voices of children for food, for the light of the sun, for escape. They rolled after me as I walked among them, pleading. I slipped through a door and shut it against their clamor, against the insistent knocking of the stone heads against the door.

There were roofless rooms with walls which seemed to go forever upward into darkness and at the top of that darkness the sound of something poised enormously and rocking, rocking, rocking. There were prodigious arches, windows leading into enclosed gardens in which stone beasts looked at me from wild eyes as though they wanted desperately to move. There were great halls in which fires burned and tables were set with steaming foods. I did not eat. I did not drink. But Shattnir within me drew the heat of those fires and stored it.

When I could go no further, it was beside one of the incredible hearths that I sat, hunkered upon a carpet woven with patterns of serpents and quadrumanna in intricate chase and capture. Shattnir drew power, and drew, and drew. Half sleeping, I let her draw, let her make me one great vessel of power. Far off through the halls of that place I could hear sounds once more, as of doors softly opening and closing, and I was afraid of what might be coming. My hand went into the pocket at my side. "Come, Grandmother," I whispered. "Divine Didir, come. . . ."

What came in answer to that clutching invitation was old, so old that my mouth turned dry and my skin felt crumbled and dusty. Ages settled on me, a thousand years or more. It was only a skin, a shriveled shell. There was nothing there, nothing—and then the skin began to fill, drawing from me, from Shattnir, from the world around us, began to swell, to grow, to push me from within until I thought there would be no place left for me to stand, and I cried in panic, "Stay, stay. Leave me room!" Then there came a cessation, a withdrawing, and a voice which whispered out of ancient years, "I see, I see, I see. . . ."

I sensed Dorn within, and Dorn's awe; Trandilar, bowing down; Wafnor, head up, smiling; Shattnir offering her hand to that One I had raised from the ages. Grandmother Didir, Demon, First of all Gamesmen of the dim past, She who could Read the mind of this place, this monstrous place, if She would. If I had known the awe those others would feel, I would not have had the effrontery to raise Her up. I am glad, now, that I did not know. My other inhabitants had not been ignorant of my fear, now She was not ignorant of it. I heard all their voices, hers rising above them like a whisper of steel, infinitely fine, infinitely strong.

"Well, child. You have found a dangerous place."

"Sorcerer's Power Nine," whispered Shattnir.

"Necromancer Nine," said Dorn.

"Nonsense," she said. "Dangerous, not deadly. We old ones do not easily admit to 'deadly,' do we, child?"

I did not move, for she was reaching out from me, using the power Shattnir had gathered, reaching out through the very fabric of that labyrinthine construction to find its center, its mind. I felt the search go on and on, felt the blank incomprehension of the mighty walls, the stony ignorance of the pillars and stairs while she still searched, outward and outward from me to the very edges of the place. Nothing.

Down the corridor, a door opened.

"Below," she whispered, sending that seeking thought out and down, through mosaic floors and damp vaults, down to bottomless dungeons and endless catacombs which stretched beyond the walls away into lost silences. Nothing.

The door shut.

It seemed to me that I could hear Didir grit her teeth, a tiny grinding itch in my brain. "Up," and the mind went once more, more slowly, painstakingly, sifting each volume of air, each rising stair, climbing as the structure climbed into the lowering sky, wrapping each rising tower as a vine might wrap it, penetrating it with tiny thoughts like rootlet feet, to the summit of it all, the wide and vacant roofs. Nothing.

Just outside the room in which we were, not twenty paces down that great corridor, we heard a door open, heard the waiting pause, then heard it shut once more with that great, muffled sound as of an explosion heard at a distance. Oh, Lords of all Creation, we stirred in fear. Those within me gave shouted warning, but I needed none of them. I *flowed* up the wall, calling upon the power Shattnir had stored, flowed like climbing water, until I lay upon that wall no thicker than a fingernail, stretched fine and thin and transparent as glass, seeing through my skin, feeling through my skin, knowing and hearing with every fiber as the door into the room opened and something came through. The door shut once more.

But within the room something hissed, something ancient and malevolent. I could feel it, sense it, knew that it was there, but it was not there to any known sense of seeing. Protogenic and invisible, it filled the room, pressed against the walls, pressed against me in a fury of ownership of that space, that structure. Then slowly, infinitely slowly, without relinquishing any of the threatening quality, a door at the far side of the room opened and that which had inhabited the room flowed away. Behind it the door shut with that absolute finality I had heard over and over again.

"It knew someone was here," whispered Didir within. "But it did not know where you were."

I slid down the wall to lie in a puddle at its base, a puddle in which the little pouch which held the Gamesmen of Barish seemed the only solid thing. "Pull yourself together, boy," said Didir sternly. "Give me a shape I can think in!" She slapped at me, a quiver of electric pain which cared nothing for the shape I was in. I struggled into the form of furred-Peter, placed the Gamesmen in my pocket and waited. Far off and receding came the clamor of the great doors.

I eavesdropped then upon a conversation among ghosts. Dorn and Didir, Wafnor and Shattnir, with Trandilar as an interested observer, all talking at once, or trying to, as I tried to stay out of my own head enough to give them room. It went on for a long time, too long, for down the echoing corridors the sounds of the doors returned.

"Enough," I snapped, patience worn thin. "None of you is listening to the others. Be still. Let me have the use of my head!" There was a surprised silence and a sense almost of withdrawal, perhaps amused withdrawal. I didn't care. Let them laugh at me as they would. It was my body I needed to protect.

I set out my findings as Gamesmaster Gervaise had once taught me, high in the cold aeries of Schooltown, setting out the known, the extrapolated, the merely guessed. "Didir finds no mind in this place. If there were a mind, Didir would find it, therefore, there is no mind here. Nonetheless, we are in a place which shows evidence of intelligence, of design, a place which probably did not occur by accident or out of confusion. Therefore, if there is no mind now, at one time there was. If it is not here, it is gone—or elsewhere." I waited to be contradicted, but those within kept silent.

I went on obstinately, "Despite all this, there is something in the place, something primordial and evil, which allows outsiders to come in but will not let them out again. It is a trap, a mindless trap, inhabited by what?"

"A devil?" The voice was Wafnor's, doubtful.

"What are devils?" asked Didir.

Silence.

"What is left when the mind dies?" This was Dorn, thoughtful. "If the body were to go on living, after the mind were dead. . . ."

I thought. Beneath Bannerwell, in the dungeons there, after the great battle, we had found several Gamesmen with living bodies whom Silk-hands the Healer had cried over, saying they should be allowed to die for their minds were already dead, root-Read, burned out, leaving only what she called living meat. They had breathed, swallowed, stared with sightless eyes at nothing. Himaggery had let her have her way, and she had sent them into kind sleep. Didir read my memory of this.

"What mind does the lizard have upon the rock?" she asked. "What mind the crocodilian in the mire? Mind enough to eat, to breathe, to fight, to hold its own territory against others of its kind—of any kind. So much, no more. No reason, no imagination. . . ."

"How long," breathed Dorn. "How long could it survive?"

"Forever," whispered Didir. "Why not? What enemies could stand against it?"

"So," I questioned them, "the creator of this place is . . . dead? Perhaps long dead? But something of . . . it . . . survives, some ancient, very primitive part?" Outside the room the hissing began, the door began to open. I flowed across the wall once more, quickly, for *it* entered the room in one hideous rush of fury. I sensed *something* which sought the intruder, *something* ready to rend and tear. This time it stayed within the room for a long, restless time, turning again and again to examine the room, the surfaces of it, the smell and taste of it. Terrified time passed until at last it flowed away again, out the other door, away down the corridors of the place.

"How do we stop it?" They did not answer me. "Come," I demanded. "Help me think! Was the place built? Or is it rather like that hillside I sat upon which spoke to me? Are we within the body of a Shifter?"

"It doesn't matter," said Wafnor. "Call upon my ancestor, Hafnor, the Elator, who is among the Gamesmen. Call upon him and we will be transported from this place. . . ."

I gritted my teeth at the temptation. "Had I desired that, I would have called him rather than Grandmother Didir. Think of the stone heads. The beasts in the gardens. Shall we leave them here forever to cry out their pain?" This was presumptuous of me, but I had resolved that no cry for help would find me wanting in the future. The fate of Himaggery and

Windlow—and, perhaps, Izia—burned too deep within me, the guilt too fresh to allow another yet fresher. I felt them move within me, uneasily, and it made me feel dizzy and weak, depleted of power.

"Ah, well," said Wafnor from within. "If we cannot find the mind, then we must attack the body."

I felt him reaching out with his arms of force, out and out to a far, slender tower upon the boundary of the building, felt him push at it using all the power Shattnir had built up for him. The tower swayed, rocked, began to fall. From somewhere in that vast bulk came a screaming hiss, a horrid cacophony of furious sound, a drum roll of doors opening and closing down the long corridors toward that tower. Like a whip, Wafnor's power came back to us, reached once more, this time in the opposite direction. He found a curtain wall over a precipice and began to hollow the earth from beneath it, swiftly, letting the stone and soil tumble downward as the bottom layers weakened. I felt the wall begin to go, slowly, leaning outward in one vast sheet which cracked and shattered onto the stones far below. Within the castle the sound of fury redoubled, a rushing of wind went through the place from end to end, seeking us, searching for us. The hissing grew to a roar, a frenzied tumult.

"The thing is hurt," said Didir. "See the doors. . . ."

Indeed, the doors stood open into the corridor, open here and there up and down that corridor, moving as though in a wind, uncertain whether to open further or close tight. Wafnor reached out once more, this time to a point of the wall midway between his two former assaults, once more undermining the wall to let it shatter onto the mosaic paving in a thunder of broken stone. The door before us began to bang, again and again, a cannonade of sound. Between one bang and the next came a long, rumbling roar, and the stone heads burst through the open door to ricochet from wall to wall, side to side, screaming, eyes open, stone lips pouring forth guttural agonies. The clamor increased, and they rolled away, still shrieking, as Wafnor began to work on the fourth side of the castle. The walls of the room began to buckle.

"It is striking at itself," whispered Didir. I pulled myself across the room, onto the opposite wall, watching and listening with every fiber. The wall opposite me breathed inward, bulging, broke into fragments upon the floor and through it into the endless halls below. Then Wafnor came back to me, and we did not move, did not need to move, for around us Castle Lament pursued its angry self-destruction, biting at itself, striking at itself in suicidal frenzy. Walls crumbled, ceilings fell, great beams cracked in two to thrust shattered ends at the sky like broken bones. Then, suddenly, beam and stone and plaster began to fade, to blur, to stink with the stink of corruption. Gouts of putrescence fell upon us, rottenness boiled around us. I rolled into myself, made a shell, floated upon that corruption like a nut, waited, heard the scream of that which died with Castle Lament fade into silence, gone, gone.

When the silence was broken by the songs of birds, I unrolled myself into furred-Peter once more. I stood upon a blasted hill, upon a soil of ash and cinder, gray and hard, upon which nothing grew. Here and there one stone stood upon another, wrenched and shattered, like skeletal remains. Elsewhere nothing, nothing except the stone heads, the stone beasts, silent now, with dead eyes. I kicked at one of them and it fell into powder to reveal the skull within. It, too, stared at me with vacant sockets, and I wept. "Shhh," said Didir within. "It does not suffer."

At the foot of the hill, two trees shivered and became two persons, youths, fair-haired and solemn. A pombi walked from the forest, stood upon its hind legs and became Sambeline. A bird roosted upon one of the stone heads, crossed its legs and leaned head upon hand to look at me with the eyes of a middle-aged man. Slowly they assembled, some of the Shifters of Schlaizy Noithn, to stare at me and at the ruins, curiously—and curiously unmoved.

At length I looked up and demanded of them, "How long was this place here?"

The bird man cocked his head, mused, said, "Some thousand years, I have heard."

"What was it? It was a Shifter, wasn't it?"

"I have heard it was one called Thadigor. He was mad. Quite mad."

"He was not mad." I forced them to meet my eyes. "He was dead."

"That could not be," said Sambeline. "If he had been dead, Castle Lament would have gone. . . ."

"No," I swore at them all. "The Shifter was dead. His mind had died long ago. Only some vestige of the body remained, some primitive, compulsive nerve center which kept things ticking over, the fires lit, the walls mended, doors opening and closing, holding and hating. Only that." I waited, but they said nothing. "How many of you has it taken . . . captured . . . killed?"

"Few . . . of us," said the bird man.

"Ah. So you warned your own? But you let others learn for themselves. Or die for themselves. How many went in?"

"Thousands," said Sambeline moodily.

"And how many came out?"

"None," said the bird man.

"Wrong," I said. "They have all come out. All. And now, I demand of you an answer which I have earned from you. Where is the monument of Thandbar?"

They looked at one another, shifty looks, gazes which glanced away from eyes and over shoulders to focus on distant things.

"I can do to others what I did to Castle Lament," I threatened, softly. "No matter what shape you take, I will find you. . . ."

It was Sambeline who spoke, placatingly. "Schlaizy Noithn is the monument to Thandbar," she said. "All of it. The whole valley."

Almost I laughed. Oh, Mavin, I thought. Mother, are you of this shifty kindred, this collection of lick-spittle do-nothings? And, if so, do I want to find you at all? My eyes went to the heights. "Look not upon it," she had written. Well, if I look not upon Schlaizy Noithn, I would look upon the heights. Somewhere up there.

I did not speak to those who still stood in the wreckage. I turned from them all and went away toward the heights. Behind me I heard voices raised briefly in argument. When I looked down from the trail they had gone. The valley was as I had seen it first, green, wooded, garlanded with rivers and jeweled with lakes. At the edge of the valley nearest me was a scar of gray. "Become grass, and cover it," I whispered to them. "To hide your shame." Within me, Didir stirred. "Never mind," I said. Let them look upon the scarred earth for a while. Perhaps it would make them think of something they should have done. Or would have done, had they learned any of the words old Windlow taught me.

In that moment I would not have given a worm-eaten fruit for all the Shifters in Schlaizy Noithn.

# 6

# Mavin's Seat

AT THE TOP OF THE SLOPE a trail led around the valley. I turned toward the west since this was the direction opposite the one from which I had come into Schlaizy Noithn. The way led higher and higher, ending at last at a pinnacle which speared out westward over the lands beyond. I leaned against a tree, staring at the far horizons from ice-topped mountains in the south to a far, mist-shrouded land in the north where the jungly swamps were to be found. I leaned, thinking of nothing much, until a movement caught my eye. There upon the pinnacle was Mavin, crouched above a fire over which several plump birds were roasting. My mouth filled so in anticipation of the taste of them that I could not speak as I approached.

She looked up at me and snarled, "What kept you? I expected you long since."

It was too much. I felt the hot fury build in me and blow up my backbone like a hard wind. "How could you allow an abomination like that to exist?" I screamed at her. "Centuries of it. Festering like a sore! And you did nothing. Nothing! I came close to being killed. Like the thousands who were killed! Who were they? Little people? Pawns? People of no consequence? Eaten up in play? How could you let your own flesh fall into that trap? How could you . . ." I sputtered out, made mute by rage.

She did not seem to have listened. She plopped one of the birds upon a wooden trencher, dumped a spoonful of something else at its side, added a hunk of bread and set it all on a stone beside me. "You'll be hungry," she said. "Exorcism is hard work."

I screamed at her again. She bit neatly into a leg of fowl, using one finger to tuck in a bit of crispy skin. The smell ravished me. She said, "Your dinner will get cold."

I raged, howled, strode back and forth in a perfect frenzy of extemporaneous eloquence. She went on eating. At last the exertion of the day, the long rage, and sheer weariness caught up with me. I choked, gagging on my own words. At this, she put a wooden mug into my hand. I thought it was water, drank half of it in a gulp, then choked myself into silence. It was pure spirit of wine, wineghost, and it burned away my fury, sweeping through me like a broom through a midden. "Allllg," I said. "Allllg."

"Exactly." She placed the trencher in my hands. "If you have done with your peroration, my son, I will answer your charges. How old do you think I am? No. Never mind. Surely you do not think me a thousand years old? No. I thought not. Well, then, I can disclaim any responsibility for that place you speak of for at least nine hundred years. Since I became aware of it as a curse upon the valley of Schlaizy Noithn, I have tried three times to correct the matter. I tried first to get some of those stiff-necked Immutables to come into the valley. I was sure the Shifter was mad, and I told the Immutables so, but they would not come. None of their affair, they said, whether it ate a thousand Gamesmen or a thousand thousand. Later, I tried to get a noted Healer to come with me into the valley. He refused me, saying he felt the chance of success was small. My third attempt succeeded. Castle Lament is gone, and you are here, eating roast fowl and none the worse for it."

I stared at her, unbelieving. She had meant me to fall into that . . . that . . .

"I was right, wasn't I?" she asked. "It was mad?"

"It was dead," I mumbled. "Dead, and I could've been killed. . . ."

"Nonsense. You are my son. You are a Shifter. Shifters of Mavin's line do not 'get killed.' We are too shifty, too clever, too sly. . . . Besides, you have help."

The wineghost had seeped into my fingers and toes, warming and tickling them into a feeling almost of comfort. The food slid down my throat. I could not summon the energy for anger. "You got me drunk," I accused.

"I know how to deal with hysteria," she said stiffly. "You did take your time in coming to visit me. Did the invitation confuse you?"

"No . . . no. I wanted to come. But others wanted me to stay. Time went by."

"The journey? Was it easy?"

"The worst was the Trader. I did think I might be killed there. He tried. . . ."

"Nap? A smallish man with a wide mouth? Mouth all full of smiles and easy words? Eyes full of flint and old ice? That one?"

I nodded yes. "Stupid. I was stupid to fall in with him. But he was persistent. . . ."

"He is that." Her voice grated.

"It took me a while to figure out he wanted to kill me. Or something else. I'm not really sure."

"What did he try?"

"Drugged wine. Or poisoned. No, I think drugged, because he was wild when I convinced him I was dead." I went on to tell her in fits and starts what had occurred during the journey, leaving out nothing except what had set me off in haste to her in the first place. Well, I was full of wineghost. When I told her of my long trials in Schlaizy Noithn, she shook her head.

"We call it the monument of Thandbar, true. Howsomever, it is as much a nursery as anything else. Many of those there are new come to their Talents, or very young, or limited. Sambeline has only three shapes, her own, a pombi, and an owl. Many there are were-owls or were-pombis. Some there are experimentalists, madmen or women who cannot adapt to the Talent at all, who shift and become locked into strangeness. Roads which move. Speaking hillocks. Some experiment themselves into shapes they cannot get out of. I think Castle Lament was one such. I have long thought it would be worthwhile to have a few Immutables available to unlock them, but I have been unable to convince the Immutables of that."

"They have no fondness for Gamesmen." I yawned. "Though Riddle has been very kind to me."

"Well, perhaps we can call upon that kindness come someday. Tell me of my kindred? Is Mertyn well? Does he plot still with Himaggery and old Windlow?"

I cursed myself. She didn't know. I had sat by her fire eating and drinking for an hour, and she did not know. I blurted it all out, the disappearances, Himaggery gone, Windlow gone, Mertyn in the Bright Demesne. She looked at me frozen-faced with suspicious wetness at the corner of one eye.

"Himaggery vanished! Oh, Gameslords, but I feared it would happen. He is a sweet man, full of juice as ripe fruit." She paused, and then said, "He is your father. I remember him kindly always, though he does not so remember me. He would have had me stay with him and live with him like some pawnish wife of a farrier; me, Mavin Manyshaped, for whom the world is not too large! So I left him against his will and he likes me no longer."

"Does he know? Did he . . . I mean, that he is my father?"

"Oh, knowing I am your mother and what your age is, he should have figured it out. Yes. I should think so. Not that it matters. Which is what I told him, but he was full of pawnish ideas. Enough. Whether he likes me well or not at all, still I would not have him vanished into the shadows like so many of our friends. Mertyn did well to send you to me. Now. What's to do about this. . . ."

"Mertyn wanted me to find them, search for them. He told me to ask for them wherever I went, as Necromancer. . . ."

"Tush. Those who are vanished in this way are not dead. We had figured that out a decade ago. Nor do they live, for the Pursuivants cannot find them. No, it is into the Land of Dingold they have gone, the place of shadows, and it is there we must Shift to find them. Nap, now, he knows something, you may be sure."

This abrupt change of subject caught me by surprise, and seeing this, she pointed down from the height we sat upon to the place below, slowly emerging into the light as the shadow of the precipice grew shorter. I peered down at strangeness, stranger even than Schlaizy Noithn, for it looked like nothing I had seen before that time, a weirdness lying below us at the foot of the cliff.

If a giant child had built a mud-spider out of shreds and threads, rat fur and murk, then set it upon a stone dish with its legs arrayed full circle around it and its eyes glittering in all directions, this might have been likened to what I saw. Then, if the child had built bulky mud towers between the spider's legs, each tower with doors at the bottom in the shape of faces, each face a maw opening into the dark—why then, that might have been likened to what I saw. Then, if the child had surrounded it all with a saw-edged wall and set the whole thing in quivering motion— well, that was the place. Smoke rose from it. Clangor sounded from it, soft with distance. The faces upon the tower doors grimaced, eyes first open then shut. The spider turned its eyes this way and that, the whole a clot, a bulk of dark in the light of morning.

"What is it?" I whispered, unbelieving.

"The Blot," she said. "To which Gifters come. Nap among them."

"Gifters!"

"Traders. They call themselves Traders. They are Gifters nonetheless. They bring certain things here, they take certain things from here. The things they take from here they sell, sometimes. Often they give."

"Is this—the place of magicians?"

"What do you know of magicians?" she demanded.

"Only what is said in the marketplace. What Gamesmaster Gervaise said. What Laggy Nap said. That there may be, perhaps, a place of magicians to the west. Gervaise says the little cold Gamespieces come from there. Nap says no such thing, but we both know he is a liar."

"Some call the place below there a place of magicians. But there are no Gamesmen there. No Immutables. Only a few very strange beings which stay there and other strange creatures which come and go. And soon now, Nap again. He comes regularly, and last time he came here, he left here with your cousins in his train."

"My cousins?" I remembered two grinning faces under flame-red hair, peering down at me from a height before the battle at Bannerwell. "My cousins? With Nap?"

"Your cousins. Swolwys and Dolwys. Twins. Scamps. But better Shifters than any you met in Schlaizy Noithn. They have not your advantages, no Gamesmen of Barish to call upon (as I presume you did in Castle Lament, as I intended) but good boys for all that. I sent them to join Nap's train the last time he came to the Blot, and I let them go and return by that road to the north. If we had no other evidence, the fact that Nap travels *that* road would tell us what he is. Past Poffle. Too close. But they should return soon."

She was staring away to the north where a pair of ruts wound around the edge of the plateau and disappeared. Following her gaze I could see a plume of dust there. Someone was upon that road, certainly, and it came in only the one direction, toward the place below.

"There they are. Still some hours away, coming no faster than the pace of their water oxen. So, if I were you, my son, I'd sleep a while. Drink the rest of your wineghost and take your full stomach into my cavern yonder. I will call you when they come.'' She gestured toward a half hidden entrance I had not noticed before. I was too weary to argue, so let her push me in that direction.

When I came to the cave entrance, I looked back expecting to see her still watching from the prominence, but it was bare. High above me circled a huge bird with wings as long as I am tall. It cried my name and dipped toward me, then caught a current of air to carry it north. It was very beautiful in the sun, white and gleaming, trailing plumes graceful as smoke. I went into the cave with a feeling of exquisite sadness, as though ridden by a memory I could not identify. Had I seen her so before? Or was it something in her voice as she cried to me? Perhaps it was only the spirit in my blood, the aftermath of anger. I was asleep as soon as I lay down.

She woke me in the late afternoon, shaking me and offering some warm brew from a simmering pot by the fire. "They have stopped," she said. "It is as though Nap is not eager to come to the Blot. They have come almost to the wall, however, and you can see them easily from the pinnacle."

So I went onto the pinnacle once more to watch the compact circle of wagons near the cinereous walls. The animals were unhitched and led away to a patch of tall meadow grass near the bottom of the long slope. Mavin watched the animals with curious intensity. Until that moment I had given no thought as to what guise my cousins had taken in Nap's train. Now her focused gaze told me where they were and in what shape. A pair of oxen grazed away from the others, toward a stony place heavy with obscuring shadows, grazed around, behind them, and was gone. A rustle among small trees marked their passage.

"They will be here momentarily," she said with satisfaction. "Perhaps we may learn something. . . ." There was the sound of plodding on the trail, silence, and then they appeared around the high stone, precisely as I remembered them. Broad-faced, red-haired, with grins of the same width on lips of the same shape. One of them had an interesting scar over one eye. Otherwise they were identical. The scarred one pointed to his identifying mark.

"Swolwys," he said. "I keep the scar to make it easier for others to address me by name. It is easier than Shifting into something unique."

"Our similarity is uniqueness enough," said the other. "Why should we not be known for that fact as well as any other? I am Dolwys. Those mental midgets in the wagon train did not even notice that they had two identical water oxen. We did it to see if they were alert. They are not, or at least, not very. They even believed you dead, Cousin Peter.''

I swallowed. They looked very young to be so insouciant, younger even than I. ''I take it you were not convinced.''

Swolwys considered this. ''Ah, had we not known who and what you are, it is possible we would have been taken in. It was very well done. Except that we could not figure out why you did not simply Shift and slide away.''

''There was a woman in the train,'' I said.

''Ah,'' said Dolwys. ''Izia.''

''Lovely Izia,'' commented his twin. ''Not a type attractive to me, but still, fair. Very fair.''

Mavin's head had come up like a questing fustigar's. ''A woman? What is she to you?''

''She is nothing to me.'' I laughed, somewhat bitterly. ''Why this concern? She is a pawn, a servant. She is in durance, held unwillingly, captive by some device I have not seen or heard of before. Boots. Metal boots, high on the leg, which grow hot at Nap's will. Had I simply vanished, Nap might have thought the woman involved in my disappearance, for I had been stupid enough to let him see me watching her. As you say, she is very fair.''

''But she is nothing to you?''

I began to bridle at this repeated question. ''Not quite nothing, no! She is a captive. As were those in Castle Lament. I have told you my feelings about such matters.''

''Ah. Well. Perhaps we can do something about it.''

At that moment, I was glad there was no Demon among them. I had not been able to say she was nothing to me with an honest heart. She was a good deal to me, and the fact that she was now almost within reach of my voice made me tremble. Izia. I could not leave her to Nap's malevolence. I would have to find a way to free her. I did not understand the compulsion, for it was not merely pity, but I welcomed it as I now supposed I had welcomed Sylbie and Castle Lament. They were all problems, problems to be solved, wrongs to be righted. I thought again of Windlow's curious word: Justice. It was odd how many satisfying things could be done under that rubric. So, I ruminated while my cousins and mother leaned upon the stone to watch the wagons below.

"There," whispered Mavin. "Nap has decided to wait until morning to enter the Blot." It was true. The camp had settled; Nap was seated beside his fire as others moved about the endless duties of the train. I saw Izia at once, moving among the animals, searching for the missing pair, her skirted figure plain among the trousered ones of the men, all walking with that strange hesitation which I now, too well, understood.

"Is there some way we can free them?" I asked the twins. "From Nap, or from the boots?"

"If it becomes important, we must find a way," said Swolwys. "However, those boots are locked on in a way we do not understand. I have heard Nap say that an Elator in those boots could not move out of them. A Tragamor could not move them from himself. A Shifter could not change out of them. They transcend Talent, so says Nap. Nap controls them, but he must return to the Blot every season to have that power renewed. It is growing weaker even now, and I think it is only that which brings him back to the Blot. Without his power, control of his servants wanes. The last day or two we have seen indications of rebellion among the pawns, particularly the newest ones. We went far to the south, you know, looking for you, I suppose, cousin. We stopped near the Bright Demesne. You were not there, but Nap bought pawns from a pawner, young, strong ones who look at him with mutiny in their eyes."

"Izia? Is she likely to mutiny?"

"No. Nap has had her since she was a child. He taunts her with that fact. He tells her that she was sold to him by a Shifter because she was worthless, that only Nap's kindness and forbearance have kept her alive these years. He has had her in the boots since she was seven or eight years old, for ten years, at least. Those years have bent her. She does not mutiny. She scarcely lives."

"Why does he hold her so? Why?"

The twins gave me a curious look, and Mavin speared me with one of her imperious stares, but Swolwys replied readily enough. "She comes of a line of horsebreeders and farriers from the South. Skill with animals is bred into that line as Talent is with us. She can do anything with horses, with almost any animal, and she is worth a thousand times her price to Nap. Also, she is fair...."

I did not want to hear about that. The thought of her in Nap's sleazy embrace was more than I could bear. "What now?" I asked.

"Now you will take Swolwys' place," said Mavin. "You will go down to Nap's camp. We need to know what happens inside those walls on the morrow." She gave me another look, daring me to disagree, but I had no thought of that. No, I would have begged to go. I needed to see that Izia still lived . . . as I remembered her.

# 7

## The Blot

I WAS ACCEPTED AMONG THE WATER OXEN as a water ox, that is, after I had laid hands upon the real beast enough to know how one was made. I had already learned it was easier to become something entirely imaginary than to become something which had a recognized form and movement of its own. Thus, for the first few hours of wateroxship, it was necessary to admonish myself to keep my head down, my tail in motion against the flies, my floppy feet out from under one another. Being a fustigar had been easier for me, once, but then I had seen fustigars every day of my life. Water oxen were more rural animals, certainly smellier ones. Dolwys whispered to me that I could stop monitoring my own behavior when the smell no longer seemed foreign. It did not take as long as I had expected.

I learned in the transformation to pick up bulk, a thing I had not known before. At first inert, as one maintained a form the excess bulk became incorporated gradually into the flesh of the creature. When one shifted back, there was a certain bulk left over. Some Shifters, as the hillock had in Schlaizy Noithn, simply gained and gained until that network of fibers which made Shifters what they were was stretched so far it could not assume its original form. It was all in this network, so Mavin said. She had already harvested the flesh left over when Dolwys and Swolwys had Shifted back into human form. It was too scattered to make chops, she said, but it would make good soup. I confess a certain queasiness about this. I did not like the thought of eating what had once been a part of my cousins. They laughed at me when I said this, making me feel very young and foolish. Nonetheless, I did not like the idea and was glad it was not put to the test. Instead of soup, I learned to eat grass.

I learned that Shifters had a jargon of their own, almost a language. Changing back into an original form was called "pulling the net," evidently from that network of fibers which transferred more or less intact from creature to creature, from form to form. One could "be" a bird with only about half the network. One could "be" a water ox with about two-thirds of it. What was left over simply lay about inside, doing nothing, available to "become" other things, clothing or whatever. It was all very interesting.

At any rate, by morning I was an unremarkable water ox, driven from my graze to a wagon and hitched there, able to see Izia whenever I swung my head in her direction. Laggy Nap had at last decided to go the final few paces of his journey, into the shadowy courts of the Blot. The gates were open when we approached. They looked as though they had been open for a generation or more, hinges rusted and hanging, metal doors bent and sagging, grass pushing up between the stones. Inside the gates the shadows of the huge, spidery arches fell upon us, and a Tower-face mumbled at us from across the pavement. Dolwys whiffled as though startled, and I remembered that I was a water ox which would have been startled at such a sight and whiffled with him, hearing Izia's voice, "Shaaa, shaaa, shaa, still now, nothing to bother about, my strong ones. Shaaa, shaaa." The sound of her voice made me shiver involuntarily; perhaps any water ox would have shivered at it.

We saw the first inhabitant of the place as it came mincing across the pavement, and for a moment I thought I had not managed the Shift of my eyes properly. Something was monstrously wrong with the shape which confronted us, and it stood before us for some time before my mind believed what my eyes saw. This was no Shifter. It was a true-person, or perhaps two persons. From the waist up it was two, two heads, two sets of shoulders, four arms, two chests tapering into one waist, one set of hips and legs. It chortled, "Dupey one," out of one mouth as the other mouth said in a deeper voice, "Dupey two." I looked up to see Izia trembling upon her seat and Laggy Nap striding forward with every expression of confidence.

"Oyah, Dupies. Will you stable the beasts in the yard, or would you rather we stake them outside the walls?" His voice was ingratiating, a tone I had not heard him use except when he had sought to seduce me into his train outside Betrand.

The tenor head answered, "Oh, here, here, Laggy Nap, here. Where Dupies can watch them, feed them, brush their pretty hides. You let

Dupies have them. We'll love them all to bits, nice things, great, wonderful beasties.''

Besides me Dolwys trembled. I, too, at the lustful endearments which sounded to me much like hunger. The deeper voice said, ''Oh, see how it shivers, pretty beasty is cold, all cold from the shadow. Bring it in the sun, Dupey, where it is warm. . . .''

''Fine,'' said Nap heartily. ''You take them along into the sun and bring them food and water, Dupies. They'll love you for that.''

''Ooooh, love us all to bits, the big things will.''

''Love us, yes they will.'' The two led us off, the one led us off, caroling their—its pleasure. Beside me Dolwys trembled again and again. I wondered what he was thinking. We were too much in evidence to talk. It would have to wait. We were taken to a sunny spot near a trough of water, and a cart of hay was pushed near to us. We swished our tails and swung our muzzles under the pattering hands and constant voices of the Dupies, trying to see through them or around them to what Nap and the others were doing.

''Where is Fatman? Dupies, where is Fatman?'' Nap was persistent in the question, as he needed to be to draw the monster's attention away from us.

''Fatman? Oh, Fatman is here. Maybe in a little while, Laggy Nap. He was here a while ago. Patience, patience. He will be here.''

''Tallman? Is Tallman here as well?''

''Oh, yes. Tallman is always here. Always sometimes. He goes and comes, Laggy Nap. Patience, patience.'' The two heads turned to one another, kissed passionately, hugged one another fiercely and went back to their patting and brushing of the horses. They had not groomed us yet. I found myself begging that they would not. This was not to be, however, and I was thoroughly fondled as was Dolwys at my side, with such hungry tenderness that we were both shaking by the time the Dupies had made off and left us. At last we could watch the people of the train, but they might have been made of stone, slumped as they were on the shadowy pavement of the place near one of the great, mouthy doors. None moved except Nap, striding among them, slapping his hands along his thighs, clicking his heels upon the stone, toc, toc, toc, an erratic rhythm. From some hidey hole we could hear the Dupey voices calling, ''Patience, patience, Laggy Nap.''

The first evidence of other inhabitants came in a shrill, premonitory shrieking, like a tortured hinge crying stress into the quiet of the place. It came from within one of the towers, behind the mumble lips of the doors. The shriek became a rumble, the rumble a clatter and one of the mouths began to open, reluctantly, wider and wider until the eyes disappeared in wrinkles and the teeth gaped wide above a metal tongue extending outward, toward us. Down this ramp rolled a figure as strange in its way as the Dupies were in theirs, round, so fat that the shoulders bulged upward and the cheeks outward to make a single convex line which blended into a spherical form, a balloon, a ball, an egg of a man. He rode in a kind of cup, like an eggcup on wheels, and it was this vehicle which made the extraordinary shrieking noise.

"Oil, Dupies," it cried. "Oil for the Fatwagon. Oh, she screams, doesn't she. Makes a terrible racket. Laggy Nap, walla, wallo, holla hello, listen to me come screaming at you. Oil! Oil! Dupies!"

"Patience, patience, Fatman," came the answering call, evidently the standard reply to all happenings in this place. The Fatman rolled his eggcup backward and forward, sending all the animals into frenzies at the high-pitched sound, until the Dupies ran from whatever place they had been hiding. They bore a can of oil, and a kind of tag game ensued during which the sounds gradually diminished into almost quiet. It was only then that Laggy Nap came forward once more.

"I greet you, Fatman."

"Oh, I greet you as well, Laggy Nap. Have you a fine cargo for us this time? Something to please *them?* Something to make the great, tall things happy? I do hope so. They become difficult, Laggy Nap. Sensitive. Given to fits and hurling things at us for no reason. Oh, my, my, my, yes. They need distractions, Laggy Nap, indeed yes."

"I have most of what I was sent for, yes."

"Most? Do you say 'most,' Laggy Nap? Ah, to have only *most* may not be enough. It is far better to have *more,* not most. Well, he will be in a temper, you may be sure. Tallman will be in a temper, Laggy Nap. All the Tallmen. All. He'll tell you so, even if I don't." And the Fatwagon rolled away among the towering arches and the mumbling door-faces, exclaiming to itself as it went, careening here and there, light glistening again and again in the gloom from the bald pate of Fatman where he wheeled his way into the shadows.

I heard Izia say to Laggy Nap, "Why will you not let us go outside? We are no good to you here. Let us take the animals outside the walls. We will wait for you there." Her voice was hopeless, even as she begged.

"I want you here!" he hissed, fingers jumping along the seam of his trousers, tap tap, full of an energy and rhythm of their own. "Here."

"We sicken," she murmured. "All of us, animals, all. In here. In the gloom of this place, we cannot help it. We sicken."

"So, sicken. I care not whether you sicken. Sicken silently. I swear, I will find that Shifter who sold you to me and sell you back to him or have vengeance upon him for cheating me as he did."

"You were not cheated, Laggy Nap! I have driven your animals across this world a dozen times in the ten years you have had me. Who treats your team beasts when they are injured or ill? Who gets them across fords they will not cross and up trails they will not climb? Who but me, Laggy Nap? You were not cheated."

"I say I was because you do not give me peace. Now be silent or burn a little." His fingers tapped a different rhythm, and she caught her breath in sudden pain.

I moved, and Dolwys immediately put one of his great, floppy feet upon mine, half tripping me in the process. I heard him sigh, "wait," or some such word, blown through his water ox throat. I subsided, frustrated, unable to do more than ache at her hurt. In any case, Nap did no more than twinge at her, perhaps because his powers were much dwindled and perhaps because the careening Fatwagon came barreling out of the dusk into our midst, its occupant caroling madly.

"Tallman's coming, Laggy Nap. I sent the call, just as I knew you'd want me to, and he's coming swiftly. Watch the big mouth, now, Laggy Nap, he's on his way. Come, Dupies, come and watch. Tallman's coming."

The Dupies emerged from twilight places, chattering at one another like sparrows, patting at one another with their swift little hands, eyebrows cocked and mouths moving, all the time stroking at one another, pausing only to hug and kiss with that same greedy passion they had displayed toward the animals. They paused before one of the mumbling Tower mouths, waited in hushed expectancy. Reluctantly, Laggy Nap took up a position beside them and the Fatwagon rolled to one side. There was a long hush, then the sound of far off machinery in motion, a rumbling which vibrated the ground beneath us and sent all the Tower mouths into fits of grimaces.

The mouth before us turned downward, an introspective frown, followed by an expression of alertness, wonder, and then it opened to vomit out its own metal tongue, an endless tongue which extruded itself into a platform a little raised above the surface on which we stood. Onto this platform rolled a little car, somewhat like those I have seen used in some pawnish mines to transport ore, except this one was flat. From its prow there stuck up a tall beam, narrow and high. The beam broke itself into angles and stepped down from the car, its top section bending to look down upon us all.

"Tallman," cried the Dupies.

"Tallman," Fatman warbled in the same tone.

"Tallman," said Laggy Nap, his fingers jerking along the seams of his trousers. As for the rest of us, we animals, we pawns and animals, we said nothing but stared and stared. The voice, when it came, was a wood-wind sound, a reed sound, deep and narrow-edged.

"Well, Laggy Nap. You have returned. Have you fulfilled the orders I gave you?"

Fumble, fumble, fingers tap tap along trouser seams, feet shuffle back and forth, pale as paper, Laggy Nap. "I have most of what I was sent for, Tallman. The youth, Peter—the Necromancer, he was killed on the journey. . . ."

A long, long pause during which that narrow, hooded head bent above Laggy Nap as some great serpent head might bend above its prey. "Killed? How killed? By you?"

"No, Tallman! Never! It was a rockslide on the southern route, in the canyons there. He would go that way, and mindful of your orders, we went with him until we could be sure to take him without injuring him. He went to the canyon wall to relieve himself, Tallman, and the wall broke over him. More rock than the train could move in a season, Tall-man. His body, under all that rock . . ." Nap's voice faded into uncertainty, and the head above him never moved but brooded still in that unrelenting scrutiny.

"How long ago?"

"How long? Ah, let me think. We have been thirty-five days on the northern route, Izia, wasn't it thirty-five days? Then there was a space of three days getting back to Betand. Less than forty days, Tallman. Thirty-eight, I would say."

"Not so long, then, that you could not take a Necromancer there and raise him. Raise this Peter. Find out from his spirit what it was he knew. Not too long for that?"

"Oh, I could do that. Yes." He gave a little hop, as though eager to be on his way. "I need only to have my power renewed, Tallman. And to unload the cargo."

There was a silence, a silence which drew out into a swamp of stillness in which no one moved. Laggy Nap himself did not seem to breathe. He might have forgotten how to breathe, so still he was, and when Tallman spoke at last the air came out of Nap as out of a balloon. "No, Laggy Nap. No power renewal this time. We will give you power when you return."

"But, but . . ." Teeth chattering, face like melting ice. "How will I keep the pawns in order? How keep the beasts in order, the work done? How keep Izia doing her work. . . ."

The impossibly tall figure straightened itself. "You will leave the pawns here. *They* need some pawns. To make blues. For a ceremony. You will leave the woman here. I need a woman for . . . something. You will take one wagon and go. And you will wear the boots to be sure you return."

Fatman burbled, chortled, "Boots, Tallman. Whose boots for Laggy Nap? Does Tallman have extra boots he wishes to be used for Laggy Nap?"

And the Dupies, "Patience, patience, Laggy Nap. We will find boots for him. . . ."

Tallman growled something, beckoned to Izia where she crouched ashen-faced against a pillar. She sidled toward him fearfully, and he bent above her. "Take off the boots."

"They will not come off," she whispered, hysterical, panting.

"Fool! They would not come off until now. They will come off now. Take them off."

So, she drew them from her legs almost before my eyes, and I could see what had happened to her legs from the years she had worn them, old scars and lines of festering red, a scaly peeling surface where there should have been maiden smoothness. She saw her own legs and crawled away, retching and gasping. Dolwys put his foot upon mine once more, and again I heard that same, sighed word. "Wait."

It was the Dupies who put the boots upon Laggy Nap, one of them holding him while the other drew them on. When it was done, Tallman tapped at his sides and Laggy Nap screamed.

"So," said the Tallman, "you will be able to feel my impatience even to the ends of the world, Laggy Nap. Now, unload your cargo and get you gone to do what I have ordered. Go to Betand. Find a Necromancer there. Promise him what you must to go with you to the place Peter was killed. Raise Peter and find out what he knew."

"What he knew about what, Tallman? Do not be angry. Tell me what is needed so that I may not fail you again. Please, Tallman, tell your good servant what to do. . . ."

The polelike form turned impatiently. "What did the youth know of 'magicians'? What did he know about 'Council'? What was he plotting with the wizards? Find out, Laggy Nap. Return here as soon as may be or burn, Laggy Nap. I will not be patient."

I watched him retreat through the sagging gates, slumping, watched him take the small wain which the Dupies had already hitched for him and mount to the seat, there to hold the reins laxly in his hands as though he had never seen them before. He turned to call rebelliously, "Tallman. Give me Izia, at least. She is good with the beasts and will make sure I reach Betand in time. . . ."

"Go, Laggy Nap. I have another use in mind for Izia."

The little wagon rolled out through the gates and away down the long line of hills toward the north. Still Dolwys' foot was upon my own, his jaw next to mine chewing endlessly at nothing. It was hard, hard with Izia lying there not five paces from me, weeping upon her hands, the Dupies capering about her as they made sorcerous motions with their plump little hands.

"Oh, pretty, pretty, all for Dupies, this one. Oh, we will love it to death, pretty legs, pretty legs . . ."

I shuddered, somehow aware of what it was the Tallman planned, so hideous a thing, and yet it came into my mind as though Didir had plucked it from the Tallman's head. I would stop it, stop it, but the need was not yet, for Tallman called the Dupies away to unload the wagons which Nap had left behind. They called into play a kind of metal creature with arms and a clattering track for feet which helped them, and Fatman carried some things to and fro. There was ore of a kind so special that they picked up even tiny fragments of it dropped from the sacks; bottles and jars of stuff I did not recognize; long bundles of herbs with an odor which reminded me of Windlow's herb garden in that land far to the south. Soon they had unloaded all the wagons except the little cold-cart which Nap had told me contained perishable fruits. All the sacks and bundles were heaped on that strange flat car which Tallman had arrived upon.

Now came a strange hiatus.

Tallman went to the cold-cart, walked around it, lifted its covering, touched it here and there. Behind him the monsters wheeled and capered, silent as shadows. The hood hid whatever passed for Tallman's face, but the angle of his head spoke of concentration. At last he spoke.

"You are a good hitch, you Fatman, you Dupies. I chose well to choose you from the monster pits as my hitch. You did well to warn me that the Trader had not brought everything, Fatman. I had time to find out what to do . . . what questions to ask."

The tenor Dupey said, "Tallman? Will *they* be angry? *They* will be angry, won't they?"

The lofty head nodded, once, twice.

"But Dupey still gets the legs, don't we, Tallman? Dupey gets the pretty legs to have. Oh, we'll put them in the coldwagon, Tallman. They'll last a long time in the coldwagon."

The lofty head turned toward Izia, spoke softly. "I said you would be rewarded, Dupey. So you shall." Then, voice raised, "Do you know your fate, woman? Dupey does not care whether you know or not, but I enjoy it more when the fate is known and the one shaped like *them* can suffer in knowing what will happen." The polelike form shifted from side to side, as though blown by an unfelt wind. "Dupey has two heads, as you have observed. Two sets of arms, two upper bodies. However, he has only one set of hips and legs. He needs another set, obviously. He prefers a female set, for reasons of his own, eh, Dupey?" The monster capered, patted his cheeks, kissed himself, busied himself about his lower body with both sets of hands. Peter, water ox, could not watch. Dolwys's foot pressed upon me.

"Give me," cried Dupey in two voices. "Give me."

"He has various ways of removing the top half," mused the Tallman. "Dupey is original, innovative. I have been much amused by watching Dupey."

"Dupey was saved," the monster cried. "Saved from the horrid mid-wifes. Saved to serve Tallman and *them*. Weren't we, Tallman? Oh, give me . . ."

"Patience, patience, Dupies. First you must unload the coldwagon. Otherwise you will have nowhere to keep the pretty legs. . . ." Some other sound came from Tallman, some sound of humor. Compared to that sound, laughter is the song of angels. Such a sound devils might make.

But with that sound the cover was thrown back from the chill wagon, and long bundles were brought from it and laid in a single, close layer upon the car. Something about the size and shape of those bundles picked at a mind horrified by Tallman, petrified by monsters, picked at a mind without result. But then Dupey turned too quickly from his work, and the covering of one of the bundles caught upon his belt. He turned to cover the contents of the bundle again, quickly, but the water ox which was Peter had seen, seen, seen. It was Windlow, old Windlow lying there, ash gray with cold, unmoving. It all happened too fast, too fast for Peter or Dolwys to react, for Tallman was once more on the car, the pawns were summoned to sit upon its edges, and it was moving away through the tower mouth which had rumbled open. Fatman was watching Dupey. Dupey was approaching Izia. Peter fought to be in two places at once, but it was too late. The tower door mumbled shut.

Water oxen have horns, usually blunted. They have huge, slow feet. They are ponderous, quiet, seldom moved to anger. Therefore, what Dol-wys and I became might not have been called water oxen but something else, not totally unlike. Our horns were needle sharp, our feet hard and hooved, our anger real. Dupey never reached the place where Izia lay. Fatman was spilled from his wagon long before he reached the tower door he wheeled for. Beneath the trampling hooves they became mere broken clots of shadow upon the hard pavement within the darkness of the spidery arches. When we had done my heart was pounding as though we had fought a great battle, and it was almost with surprise that I turned to see Izia still upon the ground, mouth open in bleak astonishment.

It was furred-Peter and long-legged Dolwys who brought her up the steep slopes to the pinnacle where Mavin waited. Perhaps she had been watching us from her bird form, for it needed little explanation to tell her what had happened. Izia fell away from our supporting arms to curl upon the stone, turned into herself as a snail turns, tight against the world. The seared, horrid skin of her legs lay bare, an obscene statement of her life with Laggy Nap. Dolwys and I sat panting until I could speak.

"Windlow's body, Mavin. Brought by Nap, in the wagon. The Tallman took it. Through those doors. We didn't have time to . . . I'll have to go back."

"But we need a Healer for her," said Dolwys. "We must do something for the girl!"

"We have a Healer," said Mavin, fixing me with her raptor's eyes. "That is, we have one if Peter chooses to use it. . . ."

I was so breathless, so senseless, that it took me a time to realize what she meant. Dealpas. First among Healers. Among the Gamesman of Barish in my pocket.

"Of course," I stuttered. "At once, I'll . . ."

"Shhh," she said. "Take a moment to get your breath. She will not perish in the next moment what she has survived for the past years." She went to the woman and knelt beside her, urging Izia to her feet, into the cave and onto the bed there, pressing a hot brew into her hands, all despite Izia's incomprehension and blank-eyed apathy. The sight of her legs had done what all the years of Laggy Nap had not, driven her into a kind of madness.

"What if Dealpas cannot heal her?" I murmured, to no one in particular. It was Swolwys who answered me as he brought me some of that same brew which Mavin was spooning into Izia.

"Well, and what if the Healer cannot? Or you cannot? Then she must live or die with what is, as we all must. It will not lie upon your shoulders, Peter. If blame be found, let it be found on Nap's hands."

"You could go further back than that," I said bitterly. "To the Shifter who sold Izia when she was only a child. She could not have been more than seven or eight then. Taken from Game knows where; sold for Game knows what reason."

"Do not say 'Shifter' in that tone," Swolwys demanded. "It could have been a Seer, or a Tragamor, or a pawn, for all that. Each plays his Game, and Games eat men. They eat children, also, but it is the Game does it, not the Gamesman."

*257*

"Some Gamesmen do," I said, thinking of Mandor, and Nap, and the fat Duke of Betand. Swolwys was right, though. I did tend to think ill of Shifters, both because of Schlaizy Noithn and because of . . . Yarrel. What brought Yarrel to mind? I had not seen him since he walked away from me outside Bannerwell, giving up our friendship, turning his back on me. His face swam into my mind, dark hair, level brows, large-nosed and generous-lipped. I pressed my hands to my face and shook myself. Now was not the time to indulge in this bitter-sweet nostalgia. I went into the cave.

"Let me try Dealpas," I said to Mavin. "Though it may not work. Silkhands the Healer told me that tissue, once dead, cannot be healed."

Mavin had uncovered Izia's legs and was studying them as I spoke. The boots had come high upon her thighs, almost to the crotch, and there was a line around her thighs there, healthy pink glow of flesh above, gray scabrous hide below, like a diseased lizard. "I do not think the tissue is dead," she said. "I think the boots did not really burn at all, but acted directly upon the nerves. This flesh is abnormal, but it lives. . . ."

"Well, let us hope Dealpas will know." I reached into the pocket to find the little Gamesman. I had to search among them. Dealpas did not come into my hand readily. My fingers chased her among the other pieces, catching her finally against my flesh. She came reluctantly, slowly, with infinite regret.

"I thought I had left all this," I felt her say. "Pain. Suffering. I thought I was done with it. . . ."

"There is never an end," said Didir.

"Never," echoed Dorn.

And from the others within I heard agreement, according to their natures. There was Wafnor's sturdy cheer, Shattnir's cold challenge, Trandilar's passion. And among them Dealpas stood as one weeping.

I was firm. "Come, there is work here."

"There is always work." But she came, regretfully, until I laid my hands on Izia's flesh, and then she was as a rushing stream.

I could not follow what it was she did. It was like Shifting in a way, for filaments seemed to flow from my own hands into the flesh of Izia. It was like Moving, in a way, for once there the filaments stretched and tasted and smelled at things, chased down long white bundles of fiber, paddled through blood, marched unerringly along great columns of bone.

It was easy to find the wrongness, less easy to set it right. Expeditions went out into far-flung territories of gut and fluid, into intimate halls of gland, bubbling hotly in wrinkled caverns, to return with this and that thing, to pump and build and stretch, to open cell walls and herd things, as a herdsman his flock, which twinkled and spun like stars, to clamp upon sparkling nerves so that no hint of pain could move past the place it originated. I watched, sniffed, tasted, and was one with Dealpas. I learned. I would have to have been witless not to have learned, but withal that learning I could tell there was a universe she knew and I never would.

Until, after a long time, she separated herself from me and became what she had been, a withdrawing presence, a mind which demanded to be let alone, to rest, to sleep, never to be wakened.

The others let her go. I let her go. Before me on the pallet, Izia's flesh appeared not greatly different from what it had been before, but my hands told me healing was begun. Enough. She slept. I knew she would sleep long. Her face had relaxed into quiet, and she lay with mouth a little open, faintly snoring, a little bubble at the corner of her mouth. I knew with unshakable certainty where I had seen that face before and why it was I had been so drawn to her.

"She is so like Yarrel," I whispered. "So like that she can be no one other than his sister, his lost sister, the one he thought dead, gone in the Game, lost to a Shifter. He hated me for that. But she is not dead. No."

"Are you certain?" Mavin asked. Her words were nonsense. I had just said I was certain.

I stroked the hot forehead, pushed the dark hair back from her face. Yarrel had worn his so, brushed back from his face.

"She must go back to him," I said. "To her family. As soon as possible."

"So long ago. Will she remember her family at all?"

"No matter. What she cannot remember, she will relearn. But she must go back, at once."

"You can take her," said Mavin. "When she wakes."

"No. Swolwys may take her, or Dolwys, or both. In fact, they must, for she must be kept utterly safe, beyond all possibility of harm. I cannot take her myself. I must go after Windlow."

For if anything was certain, it was sure that I could not fail Windlow and Himaggery again. I had failed them once in the Bright Demesne, once in the Blot. But not again.

259

# 8

# The Magicians

I WAS SURPRISED when Mavin said she would go with me. I had always thought of her, when I thought of her, as elsewhere, not with me. When I had met her on the pinnacle, it had been with no thought that she would accompany me anywhere. If I had had any expectations of that meeting, it would have been to spend some time with her, in her own place, and learn what I could from her to make my Shifterish soul more comfortable. So, when she said very calmly that the twins would escort Izia to her childhood home and she would come with me, I was speechless for a time. Remnants of courtly training suggested I should protect her by refusing her company. Good sense told me how silly that was. Of the two of us, she was probably better able to take care of herself. Certainly she had had far more experience than I. At the end, I said nothing, not even thanks.

"I would have gone eventually anyhow," she said, over Izia's sleeping form. "The time has come to find out what happens beyond the Blot. Many of us have known for a long time that strangeness and disturbance comes from there. If you saw Windlow's body, then it is certain Himaggery is there as well. Do you think they are alive?" She did not wait for my nod, we had been over this before. "Himaggery, yes, and probably Throsset of Dowes, that great Sorcerer, and Mind-Healer Talley, one of the few Healers ever to have great skill in healing sick minds, and who knows—a thousand more who have disappeared. Pawns as well, I suppose. I have seen them go by the dozens into that place like dazed sheep. Into the mumble mouths, riding the little cars. Many of us know, have known, but we have not been organized. . . . No. We have simply been too fearful to go into that place."

"You? Fearful?" I doubted this.

"Do not mistake my arrogance for courage, my son. It is true that I am renowned for what I can do. But I am afraid of the unknown, as are most men, Gamesmen or pawns alike. My sisters and I were told as children that monsters dwelt in the West, that night creatures would come from there to take us if we were naughty, that all dark dreams came from the West. When I grew older, I learned that there was truth in that. Of course I fear it. We should both fear it, but there is at least one place worse than this!''

"And we will go?"

"Of course."

Swolwys and Dolwys were not so sure. They gave her arguments which extended into the night, all the while that Izia slept. I went now and then to see that she was covered and to look at her legs. The grayness was fading. There were patches of smooth skin behind her knees and along the ankles. I gave thanks to Dealpas in my heart, but did not summon her. I remembered the skipping chant which the children of School-town used to sing beneath the windows of Mertyn's House, as they sang in every village of the world. "Pain's maid, broken leaf, Dealpas, heart's grief." There was a verse for each of the eleven, so familiar to all children that we did not even think of it as anything religious or special. I thought of others. "Mind's mistress, moon's wheel, cobweb Didir, shadow-steel." That one was right enough, a web of adamant woven from moonlight and shadow. "Only-free and sent-far, trickiest is Thandbar." I hoped that one was right, too, for we two of Thandbar's kindred. From what Mavin had said about the Blot, we would need to be tricky. I was frightened, too, but I did not hesitate except to stroke Izia's hair and touch her cheek. I knew then that I loved her, but I was not sure whether I loved her because she was Yarrel's sister or because she was herself. It did not matter. I might never see her again after the morrow.

When she woke, I sat at her side and held her hands in mine, though she cowered and tried to jerk them away. I made her look at her legs, at the places which were healing, made her listen as I told her that she was healing, healing, that all of the years with Laggy Nap were past, gone, done with, forever dissolved in time. She shivered and sobbed, at last letting her hands lie in mine. Only then I asked, "Do you remember a time before Laggy Nap? Do you remember when you were a child?"

"I remember horses," she said.

I laughed to myself. Oh, assuredly this was Yarrel's sister.

"Do you remember a boy, your own age? A brother?" I wanted her to name him. Oh, I held my breath wanting her to name him.

"I remember Dorbie," she said. "Dorbie was my fusty."

"No, Izia. Not a fustigar. A boy. A brother. What was his name?"

Her eyes became unfocused, concentrating. "It was . . . was Yarry," she said at last. "Yarry was my brother. Twin. Twins we were." Tears welled to spill down her cheeks. "I lost him. I lost everything."

"No." I squeezed her hands, kept myself from hugging her, for I knew it would only frighten her and remind her of Laggy Nap. "No, Izia. They aren't lost. Tomorrow you will travel with my cousins to find Yarry, and your parents." Later I cursed myself for mentioning her parents. I had not heard of Yarrel's family in a year. One or both might be dead. Well, it was too late to change the words. "Your family are still there, Izia, and they have never ceased thinking of you."

"Oh, fool, fool," she said, singsong. "They sold me to the Shifter. They did not care for me." The sobbing commenced again.

"Shhh. Izia, that was Laggy Nap's lies, all lies. You were not sold to the Shifter. He took you, by guile, by trickery. Try to remember how he took you! It was the Shifter who did it, Izia, no one else."

She subsided onto the pallet, and I gave way to Mavin who brought yet another cup of hot broth from the fire, her cure for all ills, to be spooned down the girl's throat a few drops at a time. She shook her head, made a bitter face as though she tasted gall when she saw Izia crying. Later she said much to me about Gamesmen who prey upon children. She needed have said none of it. I already had my opinions, and she could not have made them worse.

By noon Izia was enough recovered to finger the healing places on her legs with trembling hands, to seem to understand when we told her she was to return to Yarrel, even to be eager to depart. Mavin took some time, more than I thought necessary, to tell her that Dolwys and Swolwys were "good Shifters" who would see that she was kept safe. She also spent some time with my cousins, instructing them how they should behave toward her to avoid hurting her further. Swolwys went into the plains to fetch horses. When he returned, Izia became herself once more, walking about the animals, picking up a foot to examine a hoof, all the actions I had seen her perform in Nap's camp. So, they went away, and Mavin and I were left alone.

"I had thought," she began with a brooding stare into the darkness of the Blot, "that we would take the shape of those two creatures you dispatched down there. I can manage the duplicate creature if you can manage the shape of the Fatman."

I considered it. When we had destroyed Fatman, we had not much damaged the Fatwagon, and I thought I could figure out how to run it. I could not imagine taking the shape of the Dupies, however, and I asked Mavin how she would manage that.

"I will keep myself low, in the belly, I should think, with bony plates around my brain. The heads of the creature will have to be managed like puppets. With practice, I should be able to make both of them speak at once, though that may not be necessary." Still she brooded, finally swearing a horrible oath and stepping from her perch. "I don't like it. It is like taking a shape of shame. The Guild of Midwives has much to answer for."

"Not their fault," I said. "The Dupies said they had been 'saved from the horrible Midwives.' I did not understand what they meant at the time. . . ."

She shook her head. "It has to do with the oaths the Midwives take, Peter. With their religion, if you will. I find myself more in sympathy with it, the older I grow." She saw my puzzled look and went on. "Do you think you have a—a soul?"

Windlow, Silkhands, Yarrel and I had discussed this at Windlow's tower in the southlands, in a recent time which seemed very long ago. It was old Windlow who had pointed out that each of us was conscious of being two persons, one which did and one which observed the doing. He had told us it was this which made mankind different from the animals we knew. So, I considered Mavin's question and said, "I have more, perhaps, than a fustigar. Or so Windlow thought."

"The Midwives believe in the soul. However, they do not believe that it is inborn in mankind. They believe it comes partly with the learning of language (which mankind alone of the animals seems to have) and partly from our fellowmen, a gift of human society to each child. Do you think that sensible?"

"I'm not sure I follow," I said. "You mean, if I had been born among fustigars, and reared by fustigars, learning no language, I would be more fustigar than human?"

"Something like that. But more. The Midwives believe that only those who perceive their own humanity and perceive that *others* have the same become ensouled. Some who look like men can never believe that others are like themselves. They do not believe that others are real. One such was Mandor. . . ."

I nodded. I believed her. Mandor had seen the whole world as his fingernail, to be cut at will and the parings thrown away.

"Huld, too," she went on. "Though he talks a mockery of manners. The soulless ones can be well-mannered, as a beast may be well-mannered. Or so say the midwives who have studied the matter."

"What has this to do with Dupey?"

"Ah." She came to herself with a start. "The Midwives take an oath, very solemn and binding, that they will look into the future of each child born, and if they do not see that one gaining a soul, then they do not let it live. It is the Talent of the Midwives to see the future in that way, more narrowly than do Seers, and more reliably. It is called the Mercy-gift, the gift the Midwife gives the child, to look into the future and find there that it will have gained a soul."

"How explain Mandor, then, or Huld?"

"The great Houses want no Midwife at their childbeds. No. They care nothing for 'souls.' They care only for manners, and this they can train into any if they be but strict enough. However, I do not think the Dupey was the offshoot of any great House. More likely he was scavenged from the Midwives, or born in some House where Midwives did not go." This last was said with a hesitating fall, as though she knew where that might have been. The talk was depressing me, but it had raised a question I had to ask.

"And did the Midwives deliver me, Mother?"

She smiled such a smile, a dawning on her face. "Oh, they did, Peter. And you have had all the gifts we could give you, Mertyn and I. No fear. You are no Mandor. Nor any Dupey. If men all were better, perhaps even a Dupey could be given a soul, but it would take holymen and women to do it. No simple mother could do it. The horror would be too great, and the pain of the child too monstrous to bear. How did he live? And why? While it is true that monstrous things are sometimes born, it takes something more monstrous, evil, and prideful yet to keep them alive. . . ."

"And the Fatman?" I asked. "Legless, he was, with no lower body at all. Had he been born that way, he would have died unless someone intervened. Why? How and why? Well, perhaps Windlow can tell us, for he is very wise. . . .''

"If we can find him. If we can free him. If he yet lives. Well, we will not do it standing here. It is time to go.''

We stayed only long enough to set a boulder before Mavin's cave. There were things inside which she treasured. We went empty-handed, clad only in our fur until we reached the puddled shadows of the Blot. There clouds of flies rose from the remnants of Dupey and Fatman. There we took those shapes and moved about in them, trying them. They were hateful. They were *wrong*. There was no logic or kindness in those shapes, and I began to understand what Mavin had tried to say about souls. One could not exist in those shapes without becoming compressed, warped, envenomed. There was pain intrinsic to the shape, and I began to think what it would be like to live with that pain forever. I began to modify the shape to shut the pain away, and I heard Mavin panting.

"I cannot inhabit it,'' she said. "I must carry it upon me like a rigging. . . .''

"Perhaps we should try something else,'' I offered.

"No,'' she said. "My mistake was in trying to take the identity of the creature. We must only *appear* to be these creatures. We must not *be* these things or we will become monstrously changed.''

So, we were warned, and I was glad for the time spent in moving and trying that body. It took time, but at last we were able to make an appearance not unlike what had been before while still maintaining our own identities untouched. I was as weary as though I had run twelve leagues.

"Rest,'' said Mavin. "Here is food. We will carry some with us, for Gamelords know what will be found within.''

Even in those few moments rest, we found that we shifted away from those shapes. Mavin barked a short laugh.

"Mavin Manyshaped,'' she mocked herself. "I do not deserve the name.''

I thought of the shapes I had taken easily, almost without trying. "It is not lack of Talent,'' I told her, sure that I was right, feeling it through some internal shrinking as though my spirit shrank from what I was. "The shapes are evil, Mavin. Moreover, they were meant to be evil.''

She did not contradict me, and we went toward the mumble mouth in those evil shapes, building within ourselves certain barriers against becoming what we appeared to be. I do not know how Mavin managed. For myself, I built a kind of shell between me and the image of Fatman, and within that shell dwelt Peter and the Gamesmen of Barish, within and yet no part of that thing.

Mavin had evidently observed the Blot for some time, for she knew how to open the mouths by striking them sharply with a stick, crying in the Dupey's voice, "Open, open, old silly thing. Open and let Dupies come in. . . ."

There were shriekings and clatterings from within, and then the mouth opened to extrude its long metal tongue. Grooved tracks divided it lengthwise, tracks into which the flatcar had fit. The Fatwagon did not fit these, but I managed to straddle them with my own wheels as I followed the Dupey shape up the ramp and into the place beyond. I had expected a tunnel, a place not unlike the catacombs beneath Bannerwell. This place was not what I had expected.

The walls were metal, long sheets of it, dim and slightly glossy, polished at one time but now faintly fogged with time. At intervals the metal was interrupted by panels of glass, many of them broken, the shards lying upon the floor of the way. Behind some of the intact glasses were greenish lights, feeble, sickly lights. It was enough to find one's way by, not truly enough to see by, so we strained to see, pushed at the dimness with our minds, grew fractious and annoyed in the effort. Above us the metal panels extended to a high, curved ceiling, and in this were screened holes emitting sighs and drips, moody winds and dampness smelling of rot. Something in the place tried to help us by lighting the way ahead, darkening the way behind. Each effort was accompanied by frustrated clicks and whirrings, often with no result except to plunge us into darkness. Then there would be running noises, hummings, squeals as of slaughtered belts or gears, and light would come again, only to go off again when it was most inconvenient.

"Gamelords," said Mavin in fury. "Why can't the place ignore us and let us be." At the sound of her voice the clickings and hummings redoubled in inefficient clatter. She stopped, forehead furrowed. "It hears me."

"Tell it to turn the lights on and leave them on," I grated between my teeth. At my words the spotty lights went on down the whole length of the corridor and all the noises stopped. We looked at one another, expecting some other thing to happen, but silence succeeded silence, dripping water fell behind us, small breezes beat damply into our faces. We went on. The lights stayed on and there were no more of the noises. "Someone heard us," I said.

"Something heard us," she corrected. "This is a place of magicians. A place of mechanisms. Like the machine which unloaded the cargo, things created to fulfill special functions. . . ."

"They do not do it well," I commented, half angrily. The wheels of the Fatwagon had begun to squeal. Mavin reached over with the can of oil she had taken from Dupey's body and the squeak faded to a high shriek at the very limits of perception. It set my teeth on edge. Our journey was not helped by the fact that we had come to side corridors, branching ways, each helpfully lit into dim distances.

"The tracks," Mavin said, noting my confusion. I saw then that the grooves in the floor did not go into the side corridors. I flushed. I should have seen that, as she had. We went on, as quietly as we could, the endless corridor fading behind us into phosphorescent distance, an equal tunnel always ahead, no change, no variation except in the pattern of broken glass or the shape of the puddles under the dripping vents. We had brought food with us. Twice we stopped to fetch it forth and nibble as we went on. My internal clock said that half a day had gone, or more. The corridor did not seem to curve, and we had walked far enough to come under the mountains which had been visible from the pinnacle.

"Snowfast Range," Mavin said. "We call them the Forbidden Mountains, full of glaciers and crevasses. We have a long history of explorers going into the Snowfasts and not returning. . . ."

Then we stopped, confused. The tracks divided into three before us, one going on down the endless corridor, another swerving right down a long declivity, one going left up a long slope into the dark. I could not kneel, so Mavin did, peering at the tracks to see which ones evidenced wear, which were dimmed with corrosion. She gestured us off to the left. When we entered that way, the lights came on, fewer of them than in the way we had left, but still enough that we could avoid stumbling over the fragments of ceiling which littered the middle of the way.

Now side corridors led off with increasing frequency. We began to hear sounds, murmurs, buzzing as of machinery or distant voices in conversation. Mavin began a little song, silly and repetitive, the kind of thing the Dupies would have sung for themselves, discordantly twin-voiced. She had mastered the shape at last and was able to make both heads move and speak. From deep within me the voice of Didir came in a faint sigh, "Persons, nearing, beware. . . ." I passed the warning on to Mavin, who needed it not. Neither of us were surprised when we were confronted, though both of us took pains to simulate paroxysms of hysteria as we knew our shapes would have done.

Black they were, pale faces showing like moons against the dark, bodies and limbs hidden beneath the straight black dresses they wore, hair and ears hidden beneath square black caps which rode upon their heads like balanced boxes, held there by tight cloths which came down over the ears, under the throat, down the back of the neck. Around each wrist was a metal band, and upon each hand a fingerless glove. Against all that black the fingers squirmed like worms in gravesoil, and the faces peered at us without expression. We backed away, gibbering in our pretended fright, and one of them spoke.

"Well, Shear, monsters escaped from the pits? How come here? And why?"

"I have no idea, Dean Manacle. None. But they are not going from the pits, you will note, but toward them. . . ."

Mavin chose this moment to say, "Oh, Dupies need to talk to Tallman, good Tallman will help Dupies. Dupies got into the mumble mouths, we did, came to find Tallman. . . ."

"Oh, do not be in a temper, great sirs," I managed to gulp. "The calling machine did not function, and we have word. . . ."

"Dupies say 'Patience, patience,' " Mavin went on, wickedly. "Fatman says we must find Tallman, oh, good Tallman, to tell Dupies what to do. . . ."

"Creatures from some portal," said the one called Shear. "That is why they go toward the pits. Creatures from some portal who have come into the base in search of their hitch."

"An inescapable hypothesis, Shear. Also, an interesting occurrence. One worthy of note. Perhaps a small monograph? However, practicality dictates that they not be allowed to remain *here*. Will you call for removers?"

"Certainly, Dean Manacle. As you wish."

It was as though they heard nothing we said, as though we had chirped

like birds or howled like fustigars to make some general noise without
content. Mavin realized it as soon as I did, and we both subsided into
meaningless babble. They took no notice of this, either. The one called
Shear fiddled with a wrist band, poking at tiny knobs upon it with a fierce
display of concentration which even I could recognize as mannered. Who
were these strange ones? Mavin made a face at me from Dupey's left
head and went on with the nonsense sound she was making. The two
before us continued to converse as though we were not there.

We had not long to play this game. A shrill shrieking set Fatman's
ears on edge. I damped the sound, a sound which seemed to accompany
every machine which moved in this place. A little cart came gravely
around a corner, ridden by two replicas of Tallman, or perhaps by one
replica and Tallman himself. It did not matter, for the one called Manacle
made it clear there was no difference, no distinction.

"Tallmen! There are two monsters here, probably from a portal. See
they are removed and that the Tallman responsible is sent to the pits. . . ."

The Tallmen did not reply. I began to understand that the black-dressed
ones, who must be those magicians we had heard so much of, did not
hear words unless spoken by one of their own kind. The treelike figures
merely unfolded themselves from the cart and reached toward us with
their hands. A bolt of force, small and controlled, but nonetheless painful,
struck us both. We cried out, both Dupey heads in unison and Fatman in
shock and surprise, a long harmonic of anguish. We moved in the direction indicated.

"Tallman," I cried, "Fatman has news, news, listen, Tallman, to what
Fatman has to say. . . ."

One of them spoke, not quite the voice I had heard before. "Hold your
noise, monsters. We are not your hitch. He will be found, you may be
sure, and disciplined beside you in the pits. Were you not told never to
enter the labyrinth! You were told. All the hitches are told. Now you
have made *them* angry." Another, totally gratuitous, bolt struck us from
behind though we were moving as rapidly as possible. I conceived a
hatred for the Tallmen in that moment. Vengeance would have to come
later, however, for now it was enough that we were being escorted into
the maze. I comforted myself with this while Shifting my burned flesh
about. The bolts had been painful enough, but they had not done any real
damage.

The Tallmen did not speak between themselves. All was quiet except for the shrieking wheels of the cart, the drip of water from the ceiling, the moody sighing of the ducts. Soon the ceilings began to rise; we came to larger spaces; we encountered other carts and other black-clad magicians striding along the corridors without seeming to notice what went on around them. Then, almost without warning, we were at the pits. They opened before us, broad and deep as quarries, sheer walls dropping into a swarm of ceaseless movement as of a hive of insects overturned. A cage of metal stood at the pit wall, tall metal beams which reached from the pit floor to the ceiling far above, and within this square of beams a smaller cage was suspended. We were forced inside; the door was shut behind us; the endless machine shriek began as we were lowered into the swarm where a thousand creatures like ourselves flurried in ceaseless agitation. The door opened to let us out, and we moved hesitantly into nightmare. Beside me I heard Mavin's voice from Dupey's throat. "Gamelords! What madness is this?"

They crawled about us, oozed, flopped, hopped or stumbled, by every means of locomotion and by none. Some had one leg and some had none, or three, or six. Some were one-headed, some had two, or none, or four. There were blobs which lay while features chased themselves across their surfaces; some attached to mechanisms which made the Fatwagon seem a model of simplicity. There were howlers, moaners, silent ones whose thoughts beat at me in a tide of agony. The place stank of refuse, and excrement, and blood. Some things, dead and half eaten, lay against the walls of the place. Instinctively Mavin and I moved to the wall and put our backs against it. I looked up to see the hooded heads of the Tallmen peering down at us. I had never seen a Tallman's face, and I wondered in that instant if they had faces. Some of the creatures around us did not. Something crawled across my feet and lay there, rippling at me. Deep within, I heard Didir recoil. "Wrongness, Peter. Wrongness. Beware, beware."

The walls of the pit were pierced with black arches, screens behind which we could discern faint shadows, black on black. A bell rang somewhere, and the creatures began to edge toward these arches. There were troughs beneath them which began to flow with half liquid soup. The creatures fed. I watched, feeling the place with my skin. It was like being in a waking dream, a dream from which one knows one should be able to waken. The cage rattled upward, then down once more. Inside it was a Tallman and great bundles of solid food, stinking sides of meat, sacks of beaten grain. The Tallman came from the cage before it tipped to spill the food upon the floor. When the cage rattled upward again, the monsters broke from the arches, howling, to descend upon the scattered food. The Tallman kept away from them, turning, turning until glittering eyes from beneath the concealing hood met mine.

"Fatman," he breathed. "I will kill you. . . ." He moved toward me. I let him come close, close enough that he could not be seen from above. Then Wafnor reached out and held him, bound him about with arms of steel, held him fast while I looked under that hood at his eyes. Tallmen had faces, of a sort. At least, this one did. The face burned hatred at me and at Dupey behind me. "Who are you?" it asked at last. "You are not Fatman."

"No," I admitted. "I am not Fatman. I am one who will hear you talk, Tallman. Tell me of this place, of these magicians, of these pits. . . ."

He was not willing to do so, but it did not matter. Didir Read him; Wafnor shook words out of him; Trandilar entranced him. The bell rang again. The creatures assembled before the arches once again, and I looked with a Shifter's eyes through that dark glass to the shadows beyond. Pale, moon faces were there under their square hats; younglings were there, dressed in black but with soft caps covering their heads, eyes wide and fingers busy as they wrote on little pads of paper, wrote and peered, wrote and peered.

"What are they doing?" I demanded.

"Monster watching," Tallman gasped. "It is what they do. It is why they say they are here."

I thought this a lie, and yet Didir said Tallman believed it to be true. Since they were watching us, we behaved as monsters should, howled, bubbled, rocked and capered, all the while holding Tallman fast so that he could not move. Those watching would have only seen him stand, head down, face obscured. After a time the bell rang once more, the monsters left the arches to resume their endless movement in the pit.

We questioned. At last, we knew all the Tallman knew and let him go. He backed away from us to the center of the pit, staring about him with wild, glittering eyes, maddened by shadows. They were not shadows who came after him, however, but things of the pit which seemed to bear

Tallmen some malice. He had a weapon of some kind, and he did some damage to them before he was buried beneath their bodies. Mavin and I did not watch. We were intent upon those other Tallmen who hovered at the edge of the pit, far above.

"He did not harm his hitch," said one. "I would have killed mine had they disobeyed me. Why did he not kill his hitch?"

"Mad," said the other. "He was mad. Sometimes we go mad, you know. They say so."

"I would have killed them," replied the first. "Mad or not." They moved away from the pit and were gone. I caught a Dupey eye upon me with Mavin's keen intelligence behind it.

"We have spent time enough here," she hissed.

There was the matter of the Fatwagon, which should be left in a place it would not attract attention. There was the matter of the arches behind which the watchers lurked. She knew this as well as I, and we sought a solution to the dilemma. We found it at the base of the metal cage, a slight declivity in the pit wall, a space large enough to hide us as we Shifted. When next the movable cage fell and rose, we rose with it, hidden beneath it like a false bottom to the thing. Once the space around the pit was empty, two Tallmen came into being and moved away to the fringing corridors.

When we had found a secluded place, we stopped to set some plan of action. Tallman had believed what he had told us. He had not known the name "Himaggery" or "Windlow." He knew only that a certain cargo was ordered for *them,* that it would go behind the inner doors to *them,* to be used in certain ceremonies which were to happen soon. He knew only that the monsters were created by *them,* in order that the monsters could be watched by *them.*

*They* made things, things which were sent out into the world to be sold or given away by the Gifters. *They* needed pawns to serve them, so pawns were brought in through the mumble mouths. Tallmen were created by *them* to maintain the corridors, to maintain the portals, to repair things which broke. "But we cannot," he had said pitiably. "No one knows how to fix them. . . ."

*They* did not talk to Tallmen, except to give instructions. This Tallman had not been through the inner doors; he did not know what happened there. We asked what friends he had? None. What acquaintances? None.

Surely he slept somewhere, in some company? No. At most, they could gather in pairs. Why sleep in company? Why eat in company? One slept wherever one was. . . .

We had asked him how he had learned to speak? Surely he remembered a childhood?

At that his eyes had rolled back in his head and he had trembled like a drumhead. Mavin had said sadly, "Let it go, Peter. I do not know whether it was born of humankind, but it has been changed beyond recognition. This is only an empty vessel, drained of all but limited speech and directed action and fear of pain. Let it go."

That was when we had let him go.

Now we leaned against a wall and considered. Somewhere in this tangled, underground labyrinth were the inner doors the Tallman had spoken of. Somewhere in this web of a place we would find some answers, but we would not find them standing against a wall. We would have to follow some of *them*. "I will not do this," Mavin said with asperity, "mock that unfortunate creature by saying *them*. They are magicians, and so I will say."

"Say away," I commented. "Particularly if it will help some."

Easier conceived of than accomplished. There were none of the magicians about. Perhaps it was not a time they moved about. Perhaps the earlier occurrence had been a random happening with little chance of repetition. We wandered, baffled and frustrated. Bells rang. Machines wheezed and gulped. Tallmen moved quietly past. Silence came.

"Perhaps it is night outside," said Mavin. "These beings must once have lived beneath the sun. Perhaps they keep its time still."

"If that is so, they may be sleeping rather than watching what goes on around them. And if that is so, then we might risk other bodies than these." We hesitated, wondering whether it was wise to take the risk.

At last she said, "If it finds us anything, it is worth it. I will go left, you right, as fast and as far as possible. Meet here when they begin to move about again."

So we agreed, and I set out as furred-Peter once more, on legs as swift as I could Shift them. I had no luck, none, and returned to the place heavy with anger and disappointment. Mavin was there already, curled against the wall half asleep, and I knew at once she had been luckier than I.

"I found them," she said. "Found the inner doors. Sleep now, and when we have rested, we will find a way through them."

We were well hidden. I gave up anger in favor of sleep and dreamed long, too well, of Izia.

# 9

## The Inner Doors

THE PLACE OF THE MAGICIANS was full of niches and corners, almost
as though they provided space for invisible beings, Tallmen and servants
whom they did not see. We found such a niche, a place from which we
could see the doors Mavin had found without being seen ourselves. The
doors were quite ordinary, a wide pair of time-blotched panels without
handles or knobs, and beside them a little booth of glass, though I suspected it was of a material more durable than that. We had not long to
wait before one of the magicians came into the booth, an old one, jowls
jiggling and pouches beneath his eyes, a nose which, had I seen it in a
tavern in Betand, I would have considered evidence of much wine toping.
He hawked and mumbled to himself for a time, his voice carried out to
us through some contrivance or other which made it echo and boom.

"Huskpaw here," he mumbled. "On duty, Huskpaw. Huskpaw is *on*
duty. Doors unlocked. Oh, tum to tum, boredom, weariness, and ennui,
clutches and concatenations of all tedium. . . ." Then he must have heard
a sound because he stiffened, sat himself down before the glass and took
a pose of watchfulness.

We heard the voice of Manacle. "Doctor Manacle, here, Proctor Huskpaw. Desirous of egress . . ."

"What business have you among the monsters?" rapped Huskpaw, so
rapidly I knew it was rote, even as he reached for whatever thing it was
controlled the doors.

He received a giggle in response, the voice of Shear. "Doctor Manacle
goes forth to select monsters for consecration, Proctor Huskpaw. It is
time. The ceremonies will not wait. . . ."

"Lecturer Shear," Manacle's voice, cold as a battlefield after Great
Game. "I can make my own explanations, if you please! Huskpaw, give
your handle a twist there, my good fellow. Your Dean goes forth among

monsters to select a few for consecration. Write me down as upon the business of the college.''

"Certainly, Dean Manacle. At once, sir. Written as upon the business of the college. Surely. Proctor Huskpaw at your convenience, sir. . . .'' opening the doors through which Manacle and Shear emerged, Shear still in a high good humor, obviously unsuppressed. Mavin twitched at me, and we followed them, hearing Huskpaw's voice behind us as we went, ''Oh, certainly, Dean, certainly, Doctor, Dean Manacle, Dean Mumble-head, Dean monster-lover. Blast and confusion upon him and his lickass Shear, old stuff-sox. May he rot. . . .''

We followed the two on a circuitous route before they stopped at last beside one of the monster pits, whether the one we had been in or some other, I could not tell. They leaned at ease upon a railing, looked at the farther wall without letting their eyes move downward, and discussed the grotesques which seethed below.

"Nothing here worth consecration, eh, Shear? Not for us, at any rate. Perhaps for Quench? Now, I have the idea that Quench would select some of these for consecration, don't you?'' Titter, giggle, elbow into the ribs of the shorter magician. ''But nothing for us. Pity. That's what comes of being discriminating. Bother and overwork, all to maintain one's standards. . . .'' They wandered off along the corridors, Mavin and I still close behind them in our Tallmen guises. They might have seen us if they had turned, but they did not. They were oblivious to our presence as though they were the only living creatures in all that vast place.

They came to a second pit, or perhaps the same one from another side. Mavin shifted uneasily at my side. The two magicians leaned upon the railing once more and stared at the ceiling fifty manheights above them.

"Now, there are some likely ones here, aren't there, Shear? That three-legged one, yonder, with the tentacles? Most interesting. I must remember to bring that to the attention of my son, Tutor Flogshoulder, to be included in his research. Ah, yes, that one would make interesting watching. One could get a decent footnote out of that. Somehow, however, I do not feel it would be . . . quite . . . right for consecration, do you, Shear?''

Shear, tittering, responding with a shaken head, a flurry of expostulation. ''Not at all, my dear Dean. At least, not for one of your taste and standards. No. Certainly not. For Quench, perhaps. Or for Hurlbar. Not for you. Certainly not . . .''

They were off again. Again we followed. Three times more the scene was repeated. I watched them carefully. They never looked into the pits they talked over. They never saw anything except the featureless walls of the place. It was some kind of Game, perhaps a ritual. I could sense Mavin's impatience, but the play was nearing its close. They had come to a different kind of pit, shallower, cleaner, in a place where the dismal hooting of the ventilators was somewhat muted, the drip from the ceilings somehow stopped. This time the two looked down, and this time they were silent as they looked. Mavin and I faded into an alcove.

"Oh, here are some who will do!" Manacle, greedy as a child seeing sweets. "Not well, but better than the others we have examined."

"Yes." Shear in agreement. "Not perfect, but then, who can expect perfection in these difficult times? Still, better than any of the others we have seen. . . ."

Manacle whistled sharply, and a Tallman materialized at his side out of some corner or cross corridor. There were murmured instructions. The Tallman entered the cage, dropped below my sight. The creak of the rising cage riveted our attention as it squealed its way upward. In it the Tallman stood, surrounded by four little girls.

"No, no, no," Manacle cried, full of shrill anger. "Not that one, idiot. *That* one, over there in the corner. Take this one back and get me *that* one." The cage dropped again to return with some exchange made which I could not detect. The little girls were clad in white kilts, not entirely clean, above which their slender chests were as breastless as any baby's. Shear and Manacle gazed at them with greedy satisfaction. "Oh, these will do very well, won't they, Shear? Bring them along, Tallman. We will consecrate these monsters at the doors." With that they were off, nodding and bubbling in mutual satisfaction and congratulation.

"Monsters?" I whispered to Mavin.

"Females," she said harshly. "Have you seen any female here, anywhere? The magicians, their servants, the Tallmen, all are male. These children are the first females I have seen."

"But why 'monsters'? They look perfectly normal to me."

"I think not," she said. "Come, this is our chance to get through the doors."

She carried out her plan so swiftly I had barely time to make the shifts with her. First she showed herself to the two children who were last in

277

line behind the shambling Tallman, cutting them away from the others and sending them wandering down a side corridor. Then, we became those children, "conserving bulk" as she hastily directed, following the Tallman as he strode along mindlessly, his shadowed face betraying nothing of interior thought or confusion or misapprehension. I felt heavy, squeezed into the smaller form, but we managed it well.

At the doors, Huskpaw was instructed to assemble a group of magicians. There was a good deal of coming and going, lengthy chanting and waving of papers. The ceremony seemed to be called "conferring honorary degrees." The two real children did not respond except to move where they were pushed; Mavin and I did likewise. The eyes of the real girls showed only a kind of vacancy, like that of the Tallmen, only more so. I knew then that they were not normal children but were something else, perhaps monsters, perhaps something I could not name. Eventually the magicians dropped a robe over each of us, black as their own, and the ceremony appeared to be over. We were ushered through the doors and into a wide reception chamber where the group was joined by others to be served with wine and sweet cakes by a pair of costumed pawns as silent and vacant as the little girls. The girls, we among them, stood in a loose huddle at one side of the room, largely ignored except for occasional lascivious glances from Manacle. I was to be grateful for this seeming invisibility. I had expected to see only strangers in this place, and the entrance of someone I knew brought a sudden terror.

He came through an arched door, dressed much as I had seen him last at Bannerwell, half helmed as a Demon, clad in silver. Huld. Thalan to Mandor. My tormentor in Bannerwell; him I had conquered and imprisoned in turn. Now, here. In this place. I could not stop an involuntary shudder. He had no reason to suspect I might be here, but I shuddered nonetheless. If he had any cause to suspect, his questing mind would Read me among this multitude and find me in moments. Only the clutter of thoughts in the room hid me now. Within me Didir stirred, whispered, "I will shield you, Peter. Go deep, deep, as you have done before. . . ." I could not take her advice. I had to warn Mavin.

The two little girls were holding hands, clinging together as two kittens might in a strange place. I copied the action, caught Mavin's hand in mine to spell letters into her palm. She stiffened, began to swing her eyes toward him even as I moved before her to screen her from his gaze. Then she saw the Demon helm, and that was enough. Her face went blank, and I knew she was focusing upon some nonsense rhyme, some jibble tune to keep her thoughts busy on the surface, invisible beneath. Didir spoke from within once more, "Go deep, Peter. I will shield you. Watch, listen, but do not be. . . ."

I had done it before, in Bannerwell, had become a witless nothing which wandered about with no more surface thought than a kitchen cat. So I did it now. I became the child whose body I mimicked, became a girl without a mind, a passive body, sank deep into that soft vacancy and listened. Words flowed through my head like water, meaningless as ripples. It did not matter what they meant. When the proper time came, I would remember, or Didir would tell me.

"Huld, my dear fellow." Thus Manacle engaging in rough shoulder pats which caused Huld to tighten his lips and smile angrily. Manacle, not noticing. "Dear fellow. So nice of you to join us. This is an occasion, you know. Signal Day is only two days hence, and it is time to rededicate ourselves to our historic mission. We bring in a few new monsters to serve as breeders, properly consecrated, of course. My position requires me to be first, to set an example. Not the most enjoyable of our duties, but"—manly chuckle—"not the least. Will you join us?"

"May I hope, Dean Manacle, that in the flurry of preparations you have not forgotten why I am here?" Huld, stiff, angry, but with something behind the anger—a kind of gleefulness? Something out of place, something conniving. Didir heard it.

"Certainly not, dear fellow. Of course not. I have transmitted your warnings to several of my colleagues. They are concerned, most concerned. They consider your request quite appropriate, under the circumstances. The Committee will meet tonight, and we will bring the matter before them at that time."

"And you've received the cargo? All of it? That Seer, Windlow, and Himaggery, so-called Wizard? Most important, the young Necromancer, Peter?"

Manacle shifted uncomfortably. "Well now, there's a bit of bother about that. We have two of them, brought in only a few days ago. Yes. But one seems to have been killed en route, so to speak, at least so I am told. The Tallman believed so. He sent the Gifter back to find one of those gamespeople who are supposed to be able to raise the dead. Nothing to that supposition, of course. Impossible to raise the dead. Not like your own talent, my dear Huld, which we have studied and find some signtific basis for. At any rate, the young one isn't in the cargo. . . .''

Huld glared, heat coming off his skin to make Manacle move back from his blazing. "I do not believe he was killed."

"My dear man, the Tallman was quite explicit. The Gifter said a rockfall had completely buried him. No chance of his having survived. Shear, come over here and tell our friend what the Tallman said about that boy who was killed. . . .''

"I don't care what your Tallman said." Huld in fury. "Haven't you understood anything I've said to you? Let me say it again. The Council plots against you, against the magicians. I came to warn you, out of friendship, in return for past favors. The Council works through certain Gamesmen in the outer world. They have done so for decades. Now, they move beyond that. They *create* Gamesmen. Gamesmen with new Talents, powerful Talents. Peter is one. He is no ordinary Gamesman, no ordinary Talent! I, too, once thought him dead, or as good as! I was wrong. You are wrong now."

Shear interrupted, his mouth full of wine and crumbs which exploded into a little shower upon his black dress. "We do not like being called 'magicians,' Huld. The ignorant Gamesmen may do so, but we expect more courtesy from you. We respect your warnings, but if this Peter is dead, surely . . .''

"You fools, don't you understand? He isn't dead. I don't care what your Gifter said or pretended. Peter is not dead. . . .''

Manacle now, chilly as winter. "I do not appreciate being called a fool. As a direct descendant, unto the thirtieth generation, of the original Searchers, as fifth in a direct line to win the title of Dean, I am not one to be lightly called fool. We bear with you, Huld, though you are a mere Gamesman, because you have been useful. We do not bear with insult, however."

I heard Huld's teeth grind together. To be called a "mere Gamesman" would have been enough. To hear the scorn in Manacle's voice was more than enough.

"You bear with me, *Dean* Manacle, because I am the only one who can warn you of what the Council plots against you, what the Council intends. Without me, you are at the mercy of that strange people, not a tender mercy, Manacle. Now, where are they? Where are the Wizard and the Seer?''

Manacle drew himself up with a trembling hauteur, pompously waving the hovering servitor away. ''They are in the laboratories, Huld. I will take you there tonight, after the meeting. You may see for yourself. I will tell you then what the Committee has decided about your request, your request to have access to our defenders. I do not think they will be sympathetic, Huld. They believe that the Council and the Committee are effective counterweights to one another. They believe it is so we keep the world in balance.''

''Until the Council grows tired of balance.'' It was said very quietly, but with enormous menace. With that utterance the room became perfectly still. One of the little girls whimpered, the sound falling into quiet as a pebble into a pool, the ripples spreading ever wider to rebound from the walls, an astonishment of sound. Manacle stared at Huld with eyes grown suddenly wary.

''Why would they wish to destroy the historic balance?'' he quavered.

''Why would they not? They grow proud, powerful. They long for new things. Why else would they have created this 'Peter,' this new Talent? For what other purpose than to change the balance?''

One of the magicians who had stood silent during this exchange, one taller than most, with a face the color of ash, said, ''Do you know this to be true?''

''Professor Quench, I know it almost surely. The likelihood disturbs me greatly. And it should disturb you.''

''We must know,'' said Quench in a voice of lava, flowing, hardening, roughening the room with its splash and flow. ''We must know, Manacle. We must know, Shear. Likely isn't good enough. We must know.''

Manacle dithered, shifted his feet, picked at an invisible spot of lint. ''The Committee of the Faculty,'' he offered, ''the subject is to be brought before the Committee when it meets tonight.''

Quench stared him long in the face, then nodded. ''See that it is,'' he said, walking out of the room, voice splattering behind him. ''See that it is. I will be there.''

Manacle now very much on his dignity, feeling diminished by ashy Quench and burning Huld, flutters at Shear. ''Take the consecrated monsters away, Shear. This has quite disordered my day. If we are to have questions raised like this, out of order, before the Committee has had a chance to consider, well. I have much to prepare.'' He bustled away in the direction Quench had gone. Shear herded the girls away, and my last glimpse of Huld was of his fiery eyes watching Manacle to the end of sight. We went, Mavin and I, quiet as bunwits, down the carpeted hallway and into the place designated. There were pallets there for sleeping, and spigots for a kind of gruel, and a pool for bathing. There was nothing of interest save the tall, barred door which led into Manacle's quarters. Once Shear had gone, it would be no trick to shape a finger into a key, to go out and lock the door behind us.

So we did. ''What will he think when he finds two of us gone?'' I whispered to Mavin.

''He will think the two remaining ate the two who are missing,'' she snarled at me. ''Don't be a fool, boy. Leave the door open as though Shear forgot to lock it. Then he may wonder where his breeders are, but he will not suspect a spy in his own place.''

Shamefaced, I went back to unlock the door. Inside the room the two little girls had settled upon one of the pallets and were engaged in a game of a curious kind. I turned my face away, flushing. Evidently they were not totally mindless. They had been trained to do at least one thing. ''What now?'' I asked Mavin.

''Now I need to think,'' she rasped. I could not understand her anger until she spoke again. ''What is he up to, that fustigar-vomit? What does he mean saying you were created by the Council? I know better than he how you were created, and it was in the usual way. No Council had part in it save the counsel between man and woman. He seeks to trick these magicians in some way for some reason. What is the reason?

''Who are these people, these magicians who do not like to be called magicians? They say they are 'faculty' of a 'college.' Well, I know what a college is. It is only another word for school. Windlow had a college. So did Mertyn. What are faculty except schoolmasters. Hm? Except these seem strangely preoccupied with signs and rituals, speaking often of sign-tists and Searchers. Is this some kind of religion? Manacle claims himself descended from original Searchers. Well enough. Searchers after what? They hold Gamesmen in contempt. There are no women among them. They seem to admit only four kinds of beings: themselves, monsters, Gamesmen, and pawns. . . .''

"Tallmen," I offered.

"Only a lesser kind of monster, or perhaps I should say a superior kind of monster. What is this Council that Huld uses to frighten them with, as a nursemaid uses night-bogies to frighten naughty children?"

"Himaggery spoke of a Council. I thought he said it was a group of very powerful Gamesmen—I think he said Gamesmen. They search out heresy. . . ."

"Some such group has been rumored, yes. But is it that group which Huld speaks of? And meantime we know nothing about Himaggery and Windlow except that they are 'in the laboratories.' Where are the 'laboratories'? What are they? We are rattling around in here like seeds in a dry gourd, making a slithering noise with no sense. Come, son, set a plan for us."

To hear Mavin say this in such noise and frustration amused me. There was no time to be amused, no time to treasure that moment, but I stored it away to gloat over later. Of such moments are adulthood made. I almost said "manhood," but thought better of that. "We must not be misled by the puzzle," I told her. "Whatever the Council is, whatever this place may be, whatever the history of the place or its reasons for existence— none of these are more important than Himaggery and Windlow. Manacle will meet Huld after tonight's meeting. So we will go to the meeting and hear what is said. After that we will follow Manacle to his meeting with Huld, and Didir must protect me as best she can. If we are inconspicuous, we will likely pass unnoticed." When I said the word, *inconspicuous*, it made me think of Chance, and for a moment I was overcome with a terrible homesickness for him, for Schooltown, for the known and familiar and sure. I gasped, but Mavin had not noticed.

"I will be inconspicuous," she growled. "And I will be patient, but this place itches me."

It itched me, too, as I tried to find the place of the meeting. No mind I sought through knew of the meeting or where it might be held. "An exclusive group," murmured Mavin, when I told her this. "Do you suppose the room is never cleaned?"

This took me a moment to puzzle out. Then I understood that the room would undoubtedly be cleaned by someone, a pawn. I began to search among pawnish minds, Didir dipping here and there as we moved above the place. On the sixth or seventh try, we found a mind which had once known of the place. We went to it. All of this had taken so much time that we were there only a moment before the magicians began to arrive, only time to find a dark corner in a kind of balcony over the main room where two additional chair-like shapes would go unnoticed. The place was under a duct which brought in heat, and Mavin settled into it with a tired sigh.

"One more shift and I would have started to eat myself," she confessed. "I cannot store as you do, my son."

I realized with some guilt that Shattnir had gone on storing power for me at every opportunity. It had begun to feel as natural as breathing. I let power bleed between us. "Take from me," I whispered to her. "I feel we will not move from this place for some time."

One wall of the place below was made up of hundreds of tiny windows, blank and black, except that on one or two a light crawled wormlike and green. One end of the long table had a slanted surface with buttons and knobs on it. There had been many surfaces like that in this place, controls for the contrivances of the magicians. Both the windows and the control surface looked dusty, unused. A side wall held rows of portraits, face after face, mushroom pale above black garb, gold plates identifying each in letters too small for me to read. The last portrait in the bottom row was of Manacle, however, which told us enough. The tops of the higher frames were black with dust. The carpet of the place was worn through in spots. At each chair was set an empty bottle and a drinking glass, a pad of yellowed paper and a writing implement. At one place the writing implement had been shifted in position, and I could see a pale pattern of it where it had once lain upon the paper. Whoever might once have cleaned the place had not done so recently, perhaps not for years. Dust lay upon everything in a thick, gray film.

Quench came in to sit at the place where the writing implement had been moved. He moved it back onto its shadow, carefully, centering it upon its image before settling into the chair, arms folded across his wide torso. The lines of his boxlike hat seemed to continue downward through his head, obdurately square.

Others entered. There were whispers, mumbling conversations. I risked a questing thought to get pictures of long, half ruined corridors, tumbled portals far to the north and south, ramified networks of dusty catacombs, buried in decay. One of those who entered had white tabs at his throat.

Others bowed toward him, murmured "Rector." Time passed. Some fifty were assembled before Manacle entered. Well, now we would learn what we would learn.

"Evening, gentlemen. Evening. Glad to see everyone is here so promptly. Well, we have a considerable agenda this evening. Let's call the meeting to order and get started. Will the Rector give the invocation."

The tab-fronted one rose, stared upward and intoned, "Oh, Lord, we your children have pursued your purposes for thirty generations upon this planet. For a thousand years we have been faithful to your commandments. We have watched the monsters in this place, have kept ourselves separated from them, have kept your sacred ordinances to research and record everything that the monsters do. Now, as we approach the holy season of Contact With Home, be with us as we consider grave matters which are brought before us. Let us be mindful of your ordinances as we consecrate monsters to our use in order that your will may be continued unto future generations. Keep us safe from the vile seducements of Gamesmen and the connivances of the Council. We ask this as faithful sons. Amen."

During this pronouncement, the others in the room had peered restlessly about themselves as though someone else were expected to enter, but no one did. There was a brief silence when the man finished speaking. Manacle sat in his chair with head forward, as though he were asleep. Quench cleared his throat with a hacking noise, and Dean Manacle jerked upright.

"Hmmm," he mumbled. "We will move to the minutes of the last meeting." He rose and pushed one of the buttons on the table before him, saying as he did so, "I am Manacle of Monsters, son of Scythe of Sinners, Dean of the Executive Committee of the Faculty of the College of Searchers. Will Central Control please read the minutes of the last meeting." He tilted his head to one side and seemed to be counting. Around the room the others stared at their fingers or murmured to one another, bored. When a slow count of fifty had passed, Manacle went on, "Since Central Control does not think it necessary to read the minutes of the last meeting, may I have a motion to approve them as unread."

"So move," said Quench. He did not move, however, which was confusing. Again, I knew it must be ritual.

"Seconded," said an anonymous voice from the end of the long table.

"It has been moved by Professor Quench, seconded by Professor Musclejaw, that we approve the minutes of the last meeting as unread. All those in favor . . ." A chorus of grunts and snarls greeted this. "Opposed? Hearing none the motion is passed." There was a pause while Dean Manacle collected himself and shuffled through the papers before him. "We shall move to subcommittee reports . . . the subcommittee on portal repair . . ."

"Nonsense," said Quench.

"I beg your pardon." Manacle looked up, bristling. "The agenda calls for . . ."

"Nonsense. The agenda calls for nonsense. Stupidity. Obtuseness. Obfuscation. Let's talk about the Council. Let's talk about this Gamesman, Huld, who wants access to the defenders!"

Grunts of surprise, voices raised in anger. "The defenders? We don't allow access to the defenders! What did he say?"

"We will have the report on portal repair," Manacle shouted. "And the report on the problems at the monster labs, and on the food stocks brought in by Gifters. These are important matters, Quench. Vital matters . . ."

"How vital?" boomed Quench. "If the Council is planning to destroy us all, how vital is it that the monster labs shall or shall not meet quota? If we are all killed, how important that the northern portal cannot be repaired, as we know it cannot, as the southern portal could not in its time. If there are none left to have appetite, how vital is it that the Gifters bring in their full cargoes of grain and meat? Vital? Manacle, you're a fool and your father before you was a fool."

I had not seen until then the little hammer which Manacle picked up from before him. He whapped it upon the table, raising a cloud of dust at which several members began to sneeze and wipe their eyes. If this was meant to restore order, it failed its purpose. A trembling oldster was shouting at Quench who was bellowing in reply. Elsewhere in the room confusion multiplied as small groups and individuals rose in gesticulating argument. Manacle thrashed with his little hammer, voices rose, until at last Quench shouted down all who would have opposed him.

"Sit down, you blasted idiots. Now you all listen to me for a while. If you choose to do nothing after I've spoken, well, it will be no less than you've done about anything for fifty years. I will speak. I'm a full professor, entitled to my position, and I will be heard, though I am a doddering Emeritus.

"Most of you in this room recall the meeting a generation ago when Dean Scythe admitted to this Committee that the techs could not repair the portal machines, or the air machines, or most of the others, so far as that goes. You recall that we had before us at that time a suggestion, made by me, that we set some of our brighter young men to studying the old machines and the old books in order to learn about them. You recall that my suggestion was met with typical revulsion and obstinate lack of understanding. No, you all said, we wouldn't deny our sons their chance at earning their degrees by asking them to be mere *techs*." Quench spat the word at them bitterly. "Oh, no. Every one of us had been assistant, associate, tutor, lecturer, assistant professor—all of it. Each of you wanted the same for his boys. So, old Scythe suggested we pick some *Gamesmen* and bring them in to learn about the machines, that we give some *Gamesmen* the old books, that we turn our future over to the Gamesmen because we were too proud to be techs. So we brought some of them in. There was that fellow Nitch, came and went for a decade. Where is he now? Gone to use what he learned for his own profit, I have no doubt. And there were others. Fixed a few things, but not for long. Now there's this fellow Huld, threatening us with the Council. Telling us the Council is going to destroy us—the Council we've cooperated with for hundreds of years by taking up dangerous Gamesmen and putting them away when the Council told us to. Now here's Huld telling us the Council is *creating* Gamesmen with dangerous new talents. Here's Huld saying *he* will protect us if we only give him access to the defenders. And idiot Manacle has half told him we'd do it. And, while all that's going on, Manacle wants us to sit here talking about repairing the north portal which has been in ruins for five generations. Outrageous piffle!" He subsided into seething silence, picked up the writing implement before him and broke it in two. There was a horrified gasp from others in the room.

"You broke the pencil." Manacle trembled. "They've been here since my great-grandfather's time, and you broke one. . . ."

"Piffle," repeated Quench. The angry silence was not broken until an old voice quavered in treble confusion.

"Excuse me, but what are you suggesting, Professor Quench? Are you saying we should not listen to Huld? Or should listen to Huld? Do we now distrust our colleagues of the Council . . . ?''

"I'm suggesting," said Quench, "that we do now what we should have done generations ago. Get some of the young assistants and associates out of the watching labs. Let them put their 'search' aside for the moment. There's nothing new in it anyway. Hasn't been anything new in it for ten generations. We can create monsters until we're sick of it and watch them till we're bored to death, and there'll be nothing new in it. Why, a year's watch doesn't produce a footnote. No, let's create a degree in machinery, for College's sake. Create a degree in repair. Let the young men 'search' in the old books. Stop depending upon these Gamesmen . . .''

"Heresy," thundered the Rector. "Professor Quench, you speak heresy of the most pernicious sort. Our forefathers made a sacred covenant with Home to search and record information about monsters. To think of creating a degree in some other discipline . . .''

"Oh, monster offal," snarled Quench. "You pray that we be kept safe from the vile seducements of the Gamesmen, and then you fall right into their vile seducements yourself."

"Holy Scripture . . .''

"Holy Scripture be shat upon. You read it your way, Rector, and I'll read it mine. When we're all dead, what will be the sense of Holy Scripture? You know what I think of your sacred covenants? They don't make sense!''

"Sir, you question the very basis of our history, the foundations of our faith. . . .''

"I question your data, Rector." There was a shocked intake of breath. This was evidently a serious charge, though I could not tell why. "I question whether our forefathers ever agreed to do what you say they did. In any case, it's susceptible of proof. Ask Home."

The shocked silence extended, built, was broken at last by Manacle. "Ask Home? What do you mean, sir?"

"I mean, ask Home. Two days now, isn't it? Aren't we getting the blues assembled for the ceremony? Getting ready for the rigamarole? Going to send the Signal? Right? Signal says we're all spandy-dandy, doing well, following the sacred covenants, right? This time let's tell them we've got some religious questions and would appreciate clarification of the scriptures." He glared at the open mouths around the table. "I dare you. And, while we're at it, it might be a good idea to find out if the defenders still work. Lord knows the portals don't.''

"The defenders are self-repairing," said Manacle. "If the Council were to strike at us for any reason, it would be at their peril. I would release the defenders in a moment, Quench, and they would work as they did a thousand years ago. Depend upon it.''

"I don't depend upon it," he replied. "I depend upon rust and decay, spoilation and corrosion, that's what I depend upon. And on my memory. I remember that we need food and fuel from outside. There are Gamesmen out there who would limit our access to those, and the Council has helped us with that by identifying the rogues and removing them, sending them in to us to be made into blues. In return, we supply drugs to make them live long. Balance, Manacle. Balance. Mutual advantage. Why would they change all that? I think this Gamesman of yours may be full of vile seducements, all right, and the evil intentions may not come from the Council!''

The Rector, sneering, said, "Does our respected Professor Emeritus postulate a fifth force? Some mythological concept?''

"Maybe," replied Quench, with a sneer of his own. "Have you heard of Wizards, Rector? Not your field, hmmm? Haven't heard of Immutables, either, I suppose? Not your field. No, I thought not. Well, an aged Emeritus can prowl around outside a little, as I have done—no, no, don't look horrified—I said I can prowl around out there without compromising my academic dignity, even if it isn't my field. There may be a fifth force, Rector. And I'd like to move we find out . . .''

"You're out of order." Manacle hammered, raising another cloud of dust with every blow. "The Agenda says . . .''

"Get your head out of your backside, Manacle! I move we get some of the young men working on the old books, if they have wits enough. . . .''

"Is there a second? Motion dies for lack of a second," gabbled Manacle, his voice a shriek which cut through the babble around him. "I will appoint a subcommittee to study the matter which the Gamesman Huld has warned us of. Is there further business to be brought before this committee; hearing none this meeting is adjourned." He collapsed momentarily into his chair, lips moving in and out like a fish's.

"Piffle," shouted Quench. "There's no hope for you.''

Mavin and I did not move. There seemed little hope for us either. We had understood hardly a word of what had been said, and below us in the meeting room, Manacle rose and fled through the door as though to escape Quench's words.

# 10

## The Labs

"DON'T LET MANACLE OUT OF OUR SIGHT," Mavin whispered as we slithered out of our chair shapes and into the guise of ubiquitous, invisible Tallmen. Her warning came late, for we had already lost sight of him, and it was only the sound of his voice echoing back from a twisting corridor which led us in the right direction. He had been joined by Shear, who was receiving a Manacle harangue with obsequious little cries of outrage and acclaim.

"You know why he does it!" asserted Manacle, beating Shear upon the shoulder to emphasize his point. "That Quench! He does it because he never begot a son on his breeders, not one. Only monsters. Dozens of them. Why, the pits are full of his get, but not one boy to carry on the academic tradition. Why should he care whether our boys get their professorships? Not him! 'Get the boys out of the monster labs. Create a degree in machinery,'" he mimicked viciously. "Emeritus or not, he ought to be stripped of his membership on the Committee. He ought to be driven off the Faculty. . . ."

"He has some followers," Shear said nervously. "Some who believe he may be right."

"*Right?* The man's a fool. Wants us to turn out the only person who's capable of helping us. Wants us to send Huld away empty-handed. Scared to death Huld will learn something that will endanger us. Poof. I could give Huld the keys to the defenders this minute, and it wouldn't hurt us as much as making an enemy of him. Well, I have no intention of sending Huld away in a fury. Quench can blather all he likes, but I think we need the man, and I'll tell him how highly we regard him when we meet him. . . ."

"You're meeting Huld?" Shear stared guiltily about, afraid he might be seen. His eyes slid across Mavin and me, but we did not exist in his vision. "Do you think that's wise?"

"I wouldn't do it otherwise," snarled Manacle. "I've had enough, Shear, now don't you start on me. Just trot along here to the labs where I'm meeting Huld and we'll have a talk. My son, Flogshoulder, is supervisor of the transformation labs this term. We'll have privacy, and you can watch them make the blues. That always amuses you."

"Yes. But should Huld see that? I mean, it's private . . . part of the ritual . . ."

"Oh, poof. I know it's part of the ritual, but what does Huld care about that? He knows, in any case. What's he going to do? Steal the bodies?"

I stole a glance at Mavin to find her watching me, puzzlement meeting puzzlement. "What are blues?" I whispered. She crossed her eyes at me in answer.

It was not far to the anteroom where Huld waited, a glossy, much used area beside a high transparent wall. We stared at the place beyond that wall, a lofty area of tall glittering machines, lights which spun and danced, wormcrawls of green light upon a hundred black screens. Greenclad figures moved in this exotic milieu with strange devices in their hands or clamped upon their heads, or both. Manacle greeted Huld, took him by the arm, and tapped upon the glass wall to attract the attention of one of those inside. That one bowed and came to slide a portion of the wall aside.

"Dean Manacle," he said.

"Now, now, no formality, my boy. You've met our good friend, Huld? Huld, my son, Tutor Flogshoulder. He is supervisor of the term here in the transformation labs. You wanted to see the cargo for yourself? Well, Flogshoulder will be glad to take us through and explain the process. If it's convenient, my dear boy."

The dear boy, who suffered from an unfortunate superfluity of teeth, gaped, then covered this gaucherie with a self-conscious giggle. "Oh, it's quite convenient, Father. Most interesting for guests, too. Just come through here. Don't mind the techs, they haven't the wits of a bunwit and don't understand anything but machines. . . ." He led the way into the polished room, Mavin and I following. I believed they would stop us, see us, forbid us entry. They did not. Across the room a pair of Tallmen pushed brooms along the aisles, as invisible as we.

At the first sight of Huld, I had gone deep into myself and now was letting Didir guide me by small promptings from within as the words of those in the room flowed through and away. The sight of the two bodies upon the chill dark slab at the center of the place almost broke my composure. Mavin's was destroyed. I saw her stumble and turn pale before catching herself, to continue the endless recitation of some nonsense rhyme. The bodies were Windlow and Himaggery, cold and gray as when I had seen Windlow at the Blot. I let Didir tune my eyes to their keenest and watched, to see the slow, slow rise of chests over the shallowest of breaths. They were alive, alive but laid out like meat on that dark slab.

Huld approached the slab and hung over the bodies like some predatory bird, his nose stabbing at them beakwise, peering and peering until he was satisfied and returned to Manacle's side.

"So, you have two of them," he said. "If you had the boy, I would have cheered you, Manacle. As it is, you have only delayed the time of ruin, not forestalled it."

"Oh, come, come, my dear fellow. The situation is not that grave."

"Grave enough. If you are not to perish with all your colleagues, measures must be taken. Still, having these two is better than nothing. What do you do with them now?"

"We're getting ready for the ceremony, dear fellow. We'll use these to make blues and bodies for the occasion, two bunwits with one arrow, so they say. That will remove the threat of these two, permanently, just as it has removed the threat of thousands in the past, and it will give us trade goods for the Gifters. Would you like to see the process?"

I do not know why Mavin and I did not act then. Surely we did not understand what was to occur, or we did not realize it would happen at once. Perhaps we had concentrated so on being unseen and unnoticed that we had not allowed for the need for sudden intervention. In any case, we did nothing. Flogshoulder gestured imperiously at one of the greenclad "techs." That man leaned forward to move a long, silver lever. At that the dark slab rotated, dropped, and moved beneath a contorted mass of metal and glass with wires and tubes protruding from it which had been making a low humming sound. The hum ascended into a scream; lights flickered; there was a smell of burning and a cloud of acrid smoke. One of the techs coughed, shouted, pumped a piece of equipment to produce a puff of bad smelling mist. The fire went out; the scream dropped into a hum once more; the slab twisted and returned to its former position.

Himaggery and Windlow were still there, still there, but I knew before Manacle reached forward to tap old Windlow's arm what sound I would hear—the sound of ice, faintly ringing, bell-like, metallic, dead. Beside each frozen skull rested a Gamespiece, tiny, blue. I looked upon them with my Shifter's eyes, eyes which can be those of a hawk to see the beetle upon the grass from a league's height. These "blues" were no crude carvings, no anonymous, featureless gamespieces. These were Himaggery and Windlow in small, each in his appropriate guise, and even the moth wing mask of the Seer could not hide the glitter of Windlow's eyes. If this thing did not weep, I was blind. I started to move forward, but Mavin caught my arm to hold me. If Huld had been alert and Reading at that moment, we would have been discovered. Huld, however, was listening with avid attention to Manacle. If Huld thought the information important, then I did also.

"The contrivance," said Manacle in a pompous, didactic tone which reminded me a little of Gamesmaster Gervaise, "was used by our forefathers when we came to this place. Evidently the length of the journey, or the time it took, did not allow persons to travel while awake and alive in the ordinary way. No, the fleshy part was preserved, as you see, for storage. They can be kept forever, these bodies, or so the techs say. However, when resurrected, these bodies would have no memory, no intelligence—all of that is wiped clean by the process, so we are told. So a record was made. A record containing all thought and memory, and this record was embodied in the form you see. Blues. That is what we call them. We make a few hundred each year to use in the Calling Home ceremony. Then we give them to the Gifters to use in trade. . . ."

"I have seen them," said Huld. "Kept in cold chests. Why are they kept cold?"

"Well—I am not certain. Perhaps one of the techs would know. The techs make the gameboards, after all, don't they, Flogshoulder?"

"I will ask a tech, Father. It is not something which interests me. Hardly in our field, you know." He went away to return in a moment with an old, pleat-faced man with tired eyes. "Tech, why are the blues kept in cold chests? And are the gameboards made here? You have a word for it, I think. Micro—micro something?"

"Microcircuitry, Supervisor. The gameboards are made with microcir-cuitry. To make the Gamespieces move. They are kept cold because they are supposed to last longer that way. The manuals say they break down very rapidly if they get warm."

"There are manuals?" Huld, greedy-voiced. Too greedy-voiced, for Manacle gave him a sharp look before taking him by the arm to guide him away. "So. Interesting, isn't it, Huld? And now you need worry about those two no more. Their bodies will be stored in the caves, used in the ceremony, then put into the caves once more and forever. Their blues will go into some Trader's wagon to be given to some Gamesmaster as a giftie. I sometimes wonder if they feel anything, those bodies. They seem very dead."

Huld, pretending a disinterest I knew he did not feel, "How are the bodies and the blues joined together again?"

"Oh, my dear fellow. Who knows? I wouldn't know. We haven't done that in a thousand years. There may be a book about it somewhere, but I doubt the machinery to do it even works. Why would one care?" They went out the way they had come, still chatting, leaving Mavin and me behind, hidden among the sighing machines. When they had put a little distance between them and us, I hissed at her.

"One of us must go after them. One must stay here to see where they put Windlow and Himaggery. Which?"

She thrust me away. "You must go after Huld. I have no Didir to protect my mind, and I cannot keep up this rhyming and jiggy song forever. You go. I will stay. I will meet you in that place they held the meeting, soon as may be. Go!" And I went.

I went in a fever of impatience and anger, anger at myself, at Huld, at the silly, fatuous Manacle and his idiot son. If we were to save Himaggery and Windlow now, we would have to restore them to wholeness, put their two halves together, body and spirit, and who knew how to do that? The books? What books and where? I was reaching the end of my ability to slink and sly about, the limit of my self-control. It was Didir and Dorn who saved me, who soothed me into sleep like a fretful child and held me there, barely ticking, while they followed Huld, Manacle, Shear and toothy Flogshoulder deeper into the labyrinth while Huld sought infor-mation.

"These books, Manacle. The ones which tell about rejoining the bodies. Have you seen them? Read them? What did they say about . . . the blues?''

"I don't recall seeing anything about them in books. But then, I recall what my father said about them. A pattern, he said. The pattern of a personality. Yes. That was well put. The pattern of a personality. In ancient times, of course, the pattern was reunited with the body when both had reached their destination. It is this process we reenact during the ceremony. We don't really *do* it, of course. Some of the younger men act the part of bodies, and we use the blues symbolically. It's only a ritual, but very impressive for all that. But then I've told you all this before.''

"Why don't you actually *do* it?'' Huld asked. Didir could detect an avidity in this question though the tone of voice was deliberately casual. ''That would be even more impressive.''

"Why, ah . . . I'm not sure,'' began Manacle, only to be interrupted by his unfortunate son.

"Because no one knows how, the techs say. The manuals aren't there, not where they belong. Of course, all techs are fools, as we all know, but that's what they say. . . .''

"Do they think the books were lost?'' Huld, pursuing. ''Or destroyed, perhaps? Or taken away?''

Flogshoulder put on a thoughtful face, marred by the obvious vacancy within his skull. ''I should know. Truly I should. I've heard them talking about it often enough. They say Quench asked for the same books, and they've been looking for them. . . .''

"Quench.'' Manacle turned red, blustering. ''Quench!''

"Yes, Father. Quench thinks it was Nitch who took the books; that's it. You remember Nitch? The books have been gone since he went.''

"Went?'' asked Huld softly, so softly. ''Went?''

"Away. He went away. At least, I think he went away. Didn't he go away, Father?''

Manacle nodded angrily, muttering and counting under his breath as he walked along. ''Quench, thirteen fourteen. Damn Quench. Fifteen. Mind his own business, keep to his place. Sixteen. He and Nitch two of a kind, ungrateful wretches. Seventeen. Ah, this is it. The seventeenth door from the corner, on the right. You wanted to see the defenders, Huld. Well, here we are. I'll just find the key here, somewhere, among all these little ones I think. Gracious, haven't looked in here almost since my investiture. Yes. This one.''

The door swung wide. They went through it, leaving it open behind them. I faded into the wall surface, unseen, unheeded. The room was empty save for one of those control surfaces which abounded in the place, this one with a large red lever and five covered keyholes, all bearing legends in archaic letters of a kind I had seen only once before—in that old book which Windlow had so coveted, the one I had found with the Gamesmen of Barish.

"They are self-repairing," said Manacle in a self-important tone. "Requiring no maintenance, no techs, for which we may rejoice. Should we need to activate them, I have only to turn these keys in those holes, five of them. At one time each key was kept by a separate member of the faculty, but upon my investiture, I brought them all together in the interest of efficiency. There are times when ritual must give way to convenience, don't you agree? So, I have only to insert them thus, and thus, and thus, here, and here, turning each one, so. Now, if any of us were to move the lever, the defenders would be activated at once. We will not do that, of course. There is no need. However, I will leave the keys here and turned, just in case. No point in wasting time later, if your warnings, dear Huld, were to prove accurate and immediate.''

"What—ah, what form do the defenders take?" This in Huld's sweetest voice. Peter, who had been Huld's captive in the dungeons of Bannerwell, did not trust that voice.

"I do not recall ever having heard what form the defenders take. What is that phrase in the ritual, Flogshoulder? You have learned it more recently than I—gracious, I have not thought of that in fifty years. Something about 'Defense of the home, to hold inviolate—' ''

"No, Father. It goes, 'Should they gain power to the extent that the base is threatened, in order that Home be held inviolate the defenders shall be activated that the signtists and searchers be held in glorious memory.' ''

"That's not how I learned it," objected Shear. "I learned it when I was only a boy, before I could read. It went, 'Should their power and extent again threaten the base, the defenders will assure that Home is inviolate through the selfless action of signtists and searchers held forever in glorious memory.' ''

"Glorious memory," said Manacle happily. "I think of that whenever we have the ceremony. The base. That's where the shiptower is, dear Huld, and therefore the ceremony is held there. It's very impressive, quite my favorite occasion. Let me tell you about it.

"We begin by placing a number of the bodies in the shiptower, along with some of the young fellows who play the part. We put some blues there, as well, for verisimilitude. The unloading machines are all polished and garlanded with flowers.

"Then I, as Dean, have the honor to take the part of Capan. I emerge from the shiptower and recite the inspiring words of dedication. All the Faculty is there, of course, down to the least boychild. I recite the words, then I start the unloading machines and they bring out the bodies and the blues. We put the young men into the rejoining machine, together with some blues to make it look real, and they emerge at once, all glowing and eager. Then I give them the Capan gown. This is symbolic, you understand, of our continuation in the academic tradition from the time of Capan to the present. We still wear the Capan gown in his honor. It is moving, my dear Huld, very moving. Then the machines take the rest of the bodies and the blues, the real ones, away to the caverns while Capan (I still have that part, of course) brings a monster out of the ship and puts her in the pit. This is symbolic too. It symbolizes our mission to search the monsters and record everything about them. Everyone cheers.

"Then, I go back in the shiptower and do the 'Calling Home' or 'Signal Home' as it's sometimes called. I go alone into the shiptower and instruct the instrument to contact Home with our message, then I come out and tell everybody what message has been called Home and what Home said. Everyone gets very choked up at that, and the choir sings, and the techs serve special cake, and we all drink wine. A very happy time, Huld. A very happy time." He wiped his eyes on the corner of his robe, looking all at once grave and grandfatherly, eyes full of an old and childlike joy. I wanted to kick him, but he went on in happy ignorance of my intent. "We give each other gifts, too, in honor of the occasion. I still have some gifts my father gave me, years ago."

"You bring a monster out of the ship?" said Huld. "Does this mean that in that long ago time your forefathers brought the monsters to this place?"

"Oh, yes. Certainly. Our forefathers came. With the monsters. To keep Home inviolate, to watch and record."

"Gamesmen were here, then, when your forefathers came?"

"Oh, I suppose so, Huld. Yes. They must have been, how else would they be here now? Your people. And the pawns, of course."

"And the monsters in your pits are the descendants of those your forefathers brought?"

"Oh, no, sir," babbled Flogshoulder, eager with his tiny bits of information. "They do not reproduce at all well, sir. No, many of the monsters in the pits are made in the monster labs. I will be supervisor there, next term. Also, we pay the Gifters to bring some from outside. And some . . . well, some . . ."

"You may say it, my boy," said Manacle, still kindly with his nostalgic glow. "Some are born to our own consecrated monsters, to be reared in special pits and adapted properly for our use. Waste not, want not." He made a high pitched little obscenity of laughter.

"Interesting," said Huld. "Very interesting. Well. If you will just show me whatever books there are which describe the defenders, our business may be concluded for a time."

"Oh, my dear Huld. I thought you understood. There are no manuals for the defenders! Either there never were any, and that may well be the case, or Nitch took them when he went. In any case, it doesn't matter. They are self-repairing, my dear fellow. You needn't concern yourself about them. If we need them, we have only to press that lever down. Everything else has been done."

I could feel Huld's baffled fury from across the room, feel his heat. "Dean Manacle. What will happen when the lever is thrust down? Do you know?"

"Well, of course. We will be defended. Haven't I said so again and again. Really, Huld, sometimes you are very trying."

Didir and Dorn pushed me deep into the corner, perhaps to avoid touching Huld as he stormed away, followed by the others who were full of twittered commiseration. "Gamesmen!" said Shear. "They have no manners."

"After all our courtesies to him. Well. He was simply furious to see that we didn't need his warnings as much as he had thought we would.

Dreadful blow to his ego. Full of pride, that one is. Still. He'll get over it.'' Manacle, comfortably full of his own view of his world.

In a moment they were gone. Didir let me come to the surface of myself, drove me to the surface of myself like a volcano exploding within me. I saw shattering lights, felt electric burning and shock, heard her voice, loud, "They are wrong, Peter. Wrong. That is not the way it was. I was there. I was there, I know how it was." Bits of her memory fled across my mind.

A babble erupted inside me, Dorn and Trandilar, Wafnor's hearty cheer dimmed in a wild crosstalk which felt like panic, like fury, like fear. Finally Dorn's voice, dark and heavy as velvet, "Turn the keys back, Peter. Turn the keys back and take them away. . . ." only to hear Didir once more, "No! It must be done in a certain order, a certain order or it goes . . ."

I trembled with vertigo, sick, thrust this way and that by those inside me, without balance or direction. I screamed silently, "Stop! Stop!" and the interior babble ceased. Then Didir's voice, thrumming like a tight bowstring, held from panic by her ancient will, "Did you see the order in which the keys were turned, Peter? Did you observe?" At which I laughed. She herself had kept me submerged during all that time. I had only heard what came to my ears. I felt that tight bowstring thrum, thrum, begin to ravel. "Then leave them alone. Can you lock the door into the corridor?" she shrieked at me.

I could do that, and did, before she broke in a shower of fiery sparks which shook every fiber of me, went down every nerve, dropped me to the floor to lie twitching like some maddened or dying thing while I knew what it was that Didir knew. If the lever in that quiet room behind me were pushed down, something huge and horrible would happen—something final and irretrievable. And Didir believed it would happen to all the place we were in, to the corridors, the mountains, caverns, to all the black-clad magicians and their servants, to their monsters, their machines, and perhaps—perhaps to the world as well.

# 11

## Calling Home

I CONVULSED, there on the floor, thrashing like a fresh-caught fish. If anyone had come by, they would have found me there in my own shape, naked as an egg and helpless as any fledgling. The presence within which had been Didir became a scattered shower of sparkling half-thoughts, fleeting memories; pictures of herself going to this place or that; pictures of someone else I did not know, tall and dark, gold-decked; premonitions of disaster which unmanned me to leave me gasping without ever making connected sense. Then there was a time, long or short, I never knew, of darkness. When I came to myself again it was to feel the hard, cold floor beneath my wet cheek where I had lain in my own drool.

After a little time, I was more or less myself again. I recognized what had happened—panic. Through all the confusion, I found myself wondering how one of the Gamesmen of Barish could feel panic. But then, I told myself, they were more than mere constructs. They had reality, though they had to use my head to express it—a head which was still splitting with an excruciating pain, pain enough to have panicked *me* and shut down all the places which the Gamesmen had occupied. Didir was gone, but so were Dorn and Trandilar, Shattnir and Wafnor. My head felt empty, vacant and echoing. The pain diminished almost at once, and I lay against the door of that dreadful room, frightened and quite alone. I wondered almost hysterically whether they would come back to me again, so felt for Shattnir because she was the one who was hardest, least vulnerable. Nothing. Her figure lay in my fingers like a doll, wooden, slightly chill. Well, there was no time to experiment or wonder. I had no knowledge of the time which had passed. I had to find Mavin, quickly, and tell her what I knew.

Furred-Peter grew a pair of wide, fragile ears upon his head, like those of the shadow people, and fled through the halls listening for any movement. There was no Didir to warn me, and I was vulnerable in those metal corridors. I fled, promptly losing myself in the maze, unable to fish for thoughts to help me locate myself, following this one and that one at a distance until at last I came to a familiar place from which the committee room could be found. I got there, got in—and found it empty. Mavin was not there. Whether she had been there, I could not tell.

I was alone there for a long time, time enough to get hungry, to find my way to a place food was stored for Tallmen, Tallmen who came and went, saying nothing to me in the guise of a Tallman as I also came and went. The food was tasteless stuff, but it sustained me. I slept a time. I strode back and forth through the committee room, looking at the portraits of Deans from ancient times to the present. Perhaps it was my imagination, but they seemed to grow more and more foolish-looking at either end of the time. Some in the middle looked hard and competent—rather like Himaggery. I thought about that for a while, without reaching any conclusions. Then I had a fit of apprehension about Mavin. Had she been caught? Perhaps killed? Was she lying somewhere wounded, waiting for me to rescue her? I cursed the panic which had driven Didir out of my head and tried to get her back. Nothing. The little figure lay in my hand like a stick. Not a quiver. No, perhaps a quiver, but remote. I tried Shattnir once more. Only a far, faint tingling. Well, whether it was something in the Gamesmen or something in myself, I could not tell. My head felt as though it had been struck by lightning. Perhaps there were fibers there which could be temporarily severed, synapses which could be shocked into quiescence. I waited. I walked about. I chewed my fingernails off, grew others and chewed them off as well.

I was about ready to give up and go on searching alone when she arrived, breathless and weary, desperately glad of the food I had hidden in the balcony of that dusty room.

"Lords, Peter, but that was a journey," she said, falling into long silence while she chewed the tasteless food, eyes closed, body swaying with fatigue. "The techs in that place fiddled about for hours, talking among themselves, mostly about old Quench. It seems that ancient firebrand has been preaching revolution and rebellion to the techs, along with his other strange activities. The techs are mere pawns, Peter, brought in here, put in boots, forced to maintain the place. Some of them are clever.

They have learned a lot though they are not given the chance to learn enough.'' She swayed, chewed, sighed.

"At last they put Himaggery and Windlow upon a kind of cart and wheeled it into a corridor where the cart was attached to a train of similar carts, all loaded with bodies and blues and crates of one thing or another. I hid myself on one of the carts, and a group of pawns rode it as well. Most of them are older men. I believe there have been no young techs trained for some time.'' She stopped to sip some of the bottled water I had found. "Lords, what a journey. We went north and west, I think, though it is hard to say because of the ways the corridors curve and join. Whatever the direction, we went far and long to the place they keep the bodies, distant and high, lying under some great glacier, I think—some source of endless cold. They are stacked there, Peter, thousands of them, piled like wood for the war-ovens. Endless aisles of them. I saw Throsset of Dowes. He was on top of a pile, like a carving. I saw Minery Mindcaster. I knew her when I was a child and she a marvelous, twinned Talent. They drove the carts into a side room and left them, then they all got on the one little machine which had hauled the rest and went away. There was no place on it for me to hide, and they all knew one another.'' She put her hand on mine, still shaking with cold. "So, I followed them on foot, and became lost, and took endless time to return.'' I let the food and drink restore her before I told her what I had learned. When I had done, she questioned me.

"What is Huld up to? You knew him. What do you guess?''

"I guess he is up to gaining power,'' I said. I knew this to be true, though I was not sure what power Huld sought in this strange haunt of magicians who seemingly were not magicians at all but merely bad custodians of ancient skills and knowledge. "Huld is not content to be merely Demon, merely Gamesman. He has no wish, I think, to be willingly followed. It is power he wants, power over the unwilling. He wants to be worshipped, yes, but out of fear and trembling, not out of beguilement. He had that, through Mandor, and it was something, but not enough for him. Still, that is why he hates me. Because I conquered Mandor and held Huld against his will, even for that little time.''

"And he came to this place—how?''

"I think he learned, somehow, how I had been protected in Schooltown, how Mertyn and Nitch had protected me. He could have Read that from me, easy enough, when I was captive there. I think Huld sought Nitch, sought him and found him—perhaps killed him for what he knew. This is only supposition, but I know Huld, and the idea hangs together.'' Surprisingly, the idea did hang together, though I had not known until that instant that I had figured it out. ''So Huld came here, seeking power, and found Manacle.''

''And Nitch had taken certain books?''

''Perhaps. And perhaps Huld had not thought to Read Nitch concerning books, so perhaps the books are gone forever.''

''Or perhaps they were lost half a thousand years ago.''

''Perhaps.''

''So there may be nothing we can find to tell us about these defenders, nothing we can find to tell us how to restore Himaggery and Windlow and a thousand, thousand more. . . .''

''About the defenders, I know only what I caught from Didir's mind before she fled me in panic—or, before I drove her out in a panic of my own. She knew of the defenders. Originally there were five keys, kept by five persons, one of whom was . . . someone near to Didir. The reason for this was to prevent the defenders being accidentally released. Now Manacle has unlocked all the bonds. Any one who gets into that room needs only press a lever down, and whatever it is the defenders do will occur. The idea of this drove Didir into panic, the others as well, and it burst my head with them. Now I cannot raise them.''

''You locked the door?''

''I locked the door. Manacle has a key. I have no helpful thoughts about that. Let us think of Himaggery and Windlow instead. So far we have failed horribly at everything we tried to do.''

She replied with some asperity. ''Who would have thought that rescuing them would have entailed putting them back together? It is difficult to go into a place such as this to set someone free if that person is able to walk and think and assist in the process. I have done that, in one Game or another. It is more difficult if the prisoner is unconscious or wounded, and I have played that Game too, in my time. But to have a prisoner who must be reassembled prior to rescue denies logic and sets all sense awry. I did, however, try to make our process somewhat simpler. I have half of them with me.'' And she reached into some interior pocket to bring forth the two blues, Himaggery the Wizard, Windlow the Seer, tiny and impeccable, cold and hard. They were only patterns, as Manacle had said. Patterns of personality. Mavin waved at me to keep them, saying, "I have been thinking all the way back how we might put them together again. It may be that the machine used to separate them is the same machine used to reassemble them. In which case, we need only bring the bodies to that laboratory place."

I remembered something Manacle had said. "We need not do that. The bodies are to be brought to a machine, Mavin. Not to the laboratory, but to the 'base' where the ceremony is held. There will be a machine there, too. They will pretend to use it to restore those who play the part of voyagers. The ship thing is there. Manacle called it a shiptower. At any rate, the bodies will be brought there, and there we should be waiting for them."

When she asked me where that might be, I shook my head. I could not use Didir to fish for answers. We knew that Manacle would go there, however, and he was easy enough to find—we knew where his quarters were. "Manacle," commented Mavin, as we went toward his rooms. "The techs hate Manacle. I think some kind of mutiny brews there, my son, an old mutiny."

I thought of Laggy Nap and his power over the boots. "Perhaps the contrivance which controls the boots has fallen into disrepair. Perhaps, if techs are expected to repair things and techs are also controlled by the boots, they have found a way to disrepair it."

"As I said," she murmured, "mutiny. Something brews."

Though I had not seen Huld since he had stormed away from us outside the room of the defenders, I felt his presence still like a weight upon my lungs. Without Didir to protect me, I had to be more sly and secretive then heretofore. Thus, it took a sneaking time to come to Manacle's place and hear his rumbling whine through the open door. Shear came out, then went in again, several times. Flogshoulder, too, went in and out, bearing garments of some ceremonial type. They emerged together to go to a dining place, from which we later stole food which was of better quality than that given to Tallmen.

"How long until this ceremony?" I muttered. "How long must we lurk in this way?"

"We are so far underground time is without meaning," she said. "Nonetheless, if Manacle said 'two days' when we came into this place, then it cannot be long now. We have blundered about in here for the better part of two days at least. Time grows short, and I am glad of it. I could not bear much more of this.''

I felt it, too, the being without sunlight, without passage of day and night. I wondered if this was how ghosts felt in the grave, separated not only from life but from time as well. This led to other thoughts of gloom and destruction, from which Mavin had to rouse me when Manacle came from his quarters for the final time.

We had no doubt he came out prepared for ceremony. There were stripes of gold upon his sleeves and his high square cap was splattered with gold as well. Shear and Flogshoulder came behind, also decorated, and we went in procession down and down corridors toward a distant gate. It was truly down, as though toward a valley, and it was into a valley we came to see the first light of dawn rouging the heights before us, brightening the cliffs with morning while the forests lay still in night below. Here was a green meadow crisscrossed with metal tracks, heaped with mounds of wrack and jetsam (or so they appeared), with a blackened tower standing at its center, silvered at its tip. A tiny opening gaped high in the side of the tower, like a missing tooth, and a tall spidery ladder stood beneath it. Upon the valley floor small groups of techs removed covers from machines which had been covered against the depredations of time and weather. Near the tower was a machine similar in every respect to that one which had so changed Himaggery and Windlow.

''The blues,'' whispered Mavin. ''See, they are carrying the blues into the tower.''

She was right. Some of the techs were carrying boxes of the blues to the tower where a lower section had been opened into some large cargo space. There were no Tallmen on the field. We would have to take the form of techs, and I looked at them closely with my Shifter's eyes before fading back into the shadows to take their shape. Even as we emerged onto the field, the wagons of bodies came out of the tunnels to clatter their way toward the tower. We went purposefully after it, looking neither right nor left, intent upon our pawnish, techish duties.

When we arrived at the tower, we began helping with the loading. Mavin went up into that cargo space, then I. We lifted body after body into it, stacking them, within moments ceasing to think of them as bodies at all. They were only things. When the tech outside put Windlow's feet into my hands for a moment I forgot what I was doing. Mavin brought me to myself.

"Here, pass him to me. I have found a place to hide them."

So then I did double duty while she dragged Windlow away somewhere, then Himaggery, when he emerged from the general pile.

When the tech outside thrust up the last body to me where I stood inside the tower, he said, "Those who follow Quench, in the southeast portal, as soon as the ceremony starts . . ." then turned away from me as though he had not spoken, waiting for no answer. I had sense enough to step back out of the light. When I turned, Mavin was there, nodding.

"I heard him," she said. "I told you, Peter. Mutiny. It will happen during the ceremony, when all the magicians are here. Mark me, it will happen. Now come see where I have put them."

The tower seemed small from outside, but from within it was a warren of twisting halls and tiny cubbies, many no bigger than closets, with mattressed shelves which were obviously beds. So it was a ship. A ship. How could it be? I turned to Mavin with the question on my lips.

"Not a water-going ship, Peter. Think! Put together the pieces. You spent long enough with Himaggery to have learned to do that. . . ."

She showed me where she had put them, in one of the little cubbies, half hidden behind a huge pipe which seemed to run the entire height of the place, from tip to base. At that moment I wanted only to lie down beside the cold bodies and sleep, but she dragged me around the pipe and into it, where stairs wound up and up to some dizzying termination.

"We need to find a place to watch from," she said, dragging me along behind her. So we went, up and up, coming at last to that open place we had seen from the tunnel mouth. The spidery stairs were just outside. Far below on the grass the magicians were assembling.

Now, how can I make you see what we saw, Mavin and I? I must, for in what we saw was much of old Windlow's conjecture and Himaggery's purpose, much of my confusion and Mavin's effort. It was in that ceremony we learned what we were, and why, and I, all unwitting of what was to come, was only sleepy, lonely, and a little afraid of what might happen at any time. So let me step outside of that and tell you what you would have seen, had you been there.

On a grassy hill were rows of the young magicians, ordered inexplicably by one who stood before them, each holding a book before him.

Here and there upon the grass groups of the magicians stood about, chatting with one another. The sun came down, lighting all with a kind of innocent glory. The young magicians began to sing. I had never heard music like that before. It soared and pierced, made me want to laugh and cry. Some of the voices were as high, almost, as women's voices, others a rumbling bass, muttering like drums. I had thought these magicians wholly without honor or sense. Now I had to revise my opinion. Whatever they lacked, they did not lack art. Perhaps it was this art that had kept them alive. I looked down from my high perch to see Manacle at the foot of the ladder, the tears flowing down his face, a face lit from within with a kind of exaltation.

After the singing came a blare of trumpets. This came from a machine somewhere. The sound was inglorious compared to what had gone before. Manacle came up the ladder, slowly, puffing a little as he climbed. Below him the groups of magicians drew away to seat themselves. I counted them while he climbed, perhaps a thousand. Not many to rattle in a place of such size. Of that thousand, there were only fifty or sixty young ones, and one or two were very young indeed, being carried by their fathers who pointed out each step of the ceremony.

Mavin and I took the shapes of the place around us, were invisible when Manacle stepped from the high ladder into the tower. Once there he closed the door behind him, then waited for some signal from without. It came in a second blare of trumpets, and a hideous, monstrous machine-like roaring which built into an unbearable level of sound before fading away. I heard Manacle murmur, "The sound of the ship landing. Now. The ship has landed." He thrust the door before him open and went out onto the ladder.

See it now, this tiny man upon this high place, all in gold-decked black, his fellows gathered below and staring upward, pale faces like saucers there, silence, and respect from every eye. Hear him cry out in a voice changed and made dramatic, "Behold the planet. I, Capan Barish, have brought signtists and Searchers from afar upon a sacred mission. Come forth! Come forth!"

Then see the machines reach into the shiptower and remove the bodies of the young magicians who were playing the part, all covered with paint to appear gray and hard. See the machines take blues from the ship, clatter and clamor across the grass to the great, garlanded resurrection contrivance, decked with flowers and fluttering with ribbons of silver and gold, all dancing in the light wind of morning. See the young magicians laid upon the slab with the blues, from which they leap up, shouting, wiping the paint from their faces as Manacle comes down from his high place, slow step by slow step, all in dignity and purpose to greet each one of them and drop a black gown over each clean-wiped head. Then see them move away across the meadow while the machine goes on unloading, real bodies this time, and Manacle begins his slow climb up the spidery ladder once more. As he climbed, the singing began again, and I found myself wishing he would not climb so fast if the singing might go on while he climbed forever. Silly. Yes, but it was what I thought and what you would have thought had you heard it.

Then was an unexpected interruption. Manacle came through the entry and back into the ship to make inexplicable clicks and bangs, opening and shutting something. In a short time he was back, leading by the hand one of the consecrated monsters. . . .

No. Leading by the hand a young woman. She was naked to the waist, her high breasts tilted and goosefleshed in the chill, her empty face staring outward at nothing. Manacle led her out upon the ladder, crying, "Behold, the monster! Toward which all your Search shall be that Home be kept inviolate!" Then he took her down the stairs to a pit they had prepared for her somewhere below. I did not see that, could not. When he had led her out, I had remembered. They were Didir's memories, burned into me outside that room of the defenders, as real to me as my own. I remembered the landing, the huge sound of the engines, fires guttering blackly at the base of the ship, green hills in early light. I had been half naked, just wakened by Captain, as he had promised, before any of the others. He supported me with one arm, gesturing out at the world, "Behold, little monster. A world for you, and for me, and for our children and our children's children. . . ." And I, Didir, had said, "The researchers will not let us have this world," and he had replied, "Some day . . ."

It had been the sight of the girl's body and the gold-striped uniform which had stormed the old memory, the sound of a male voice, lustful, adoring, confident. It was only a memory, but it collapsed me, and I came to myself with Mavin shaking me, saying, "Peter! What ails you? Come to, boy. Manacle is coming back up the ladder." So, I drew myself together and we hid ourselves once more, fortuitously, as it happened. Before Manacle arrived, someone else came up the hidden stair. Quench.

Quench, scuttering into the place and hiding himself all in one swift motion as though he had practiced it twenty times before. I heard Manacle arriving, heard the singing begin again, slow, ceremonial, mighty and premonitory. Some great climactic thing was to happen now. The music made that clear.

But all that happened was that Manacle shut the door behind him and sat down, disconsolately, upon the metal floor. He took a writing implement from a pocket, with a piece of paper, and sat there, alternately chewing the one and jotting upon the other.

The singing built into a climax, slowed, and dwindled to silence. Still he sat. After a time the singing began again, and it went as before. At this, he stood up and sighed, murmuring to himself. "Well, well. That will do as well as any message. I used it five years ago, but it will do as well as any." And reached to open the door.

"Do as well as what, Manacle?" It was Quench, leaning against a shiny panel, boring into Manacle with eyes which could have burned holes in stone. "Why have you not Called Home, Manacle? That is what you are supposed to have done. Call Home. I wish to hear what Home has to say!"

"Oh, Quench. Quench, you monster. What are you doing here? Why have you come? You are disrupting the ceremony. Get out of my way. I have to tell them. . . ."

"Tell them what? That you did not Call Home? That there was no message from Home? That there has not been any message from Home for—for how long, Manacle? How long, you little, insignificant dribble. How long?" He shook Manacle, waving him like a flag. "Tell me, or I'll break your bones."

"Don't be a fool, Quench. You know it's only a ceremony. We all know it's only a ceremony. The message from Home is only a ritual. We all know . . ."

"We don't all know. We all may suspect, but we don't all know. How long has it been, Manacle. I *want* to know. Now!"

"My . . . my great-grandfather's time. Not since then. Not since then to Call Home. And no message received from Home long before that.

The machines stopped working, Quench. It wasn't anyone's fault. They just stopped working.''

"So it's all a mockery and a deceit. All of it. The monster watching, and the Faculty—all of it.''

"No, no, Quench. You know that isn't true. It's worth something, worth preserving. You mustn't, mustn't . . .''

"I mustn't, mustn't I? Manacle, for the sake of those poor fools down there, I won't drag you out on the platform and expose you for what you are, an empty sack of nothing. I'll leave you to go to them, Manacle, with your lies and your ceremonial message. You! I remember a time when being Capan meant something. As for me, I'm off to the Council. . . .''

"What—where—what are you going to do?''

"I'm leaving, Manacle. I'm leaving with all the techs who want to leave with me, and that means almost all of them. We disabled the power machine for the boots this morning. You can't hold them, and they won't be held. We're going. Some of the younger men may go with us, and if not—well, be that as it may. I'm sorry for you all, Manacle, but there's nothing I can do to save you, and I won't perish with you.''

And he was gone, clattering down the spiraling stairs. Mavin and I could hear him, down and down until the sound faded, and I knew he had come to the cargo space at the bottom and gone out through it. Manacle was crying before us, great tears oozing down his face. The singing outside had reached its climax once more. He gulped, made a little heartbroken sound, then wiped his face upon his sleeve, leaving long red welts upon it from the harsh gold trim. Unconscious of this he stepped to the door, straightened himself, and opened it. As Mavin and I slipped away to follow Quench, we heard his voice crying to the world, "Message, message from Home . . .''

# 12

# Huld Again

WE ARRIVED AT THE CARGO SPACE near the bottom of the tower— the "ship"—only moments before Manacle himself came down. He wore a forced, fixed smile as he met Flogshoulder and Shear near the ladder. I heard Shear say, "Where are the techs? They should be here to unload the bodies and take them back to . . ." and Flogshoulder interrupting, as always, with some inconsequentiality. Manacle did not hear either of them.

He laid hands upon Flogshoulder and said, "Quiet, my boy. Be still. Now listen to me, for all your life is worth. Remember the room where we were yesterday? The room which controls the defenders? Good. That's a good boy. Now, I want you to go there. I left it unlocked for you. I want you to press the lever *down*. Just do that, my boy. Then come back and tell me." He patted Flogshoulder, almost absentmindedly, as he turned to Shear with that same fixed smile.

"Shear. There's a minor emergency. Nothing we can't take care of, but I think the Committee should be advised. Can you go among the celebrants and suggest that we move the celebration indoors? Hmm? And tell the Committee members we will meet them in the Committee room. Have you seen Huld? No. Well, that was more than I could hope for, perhaps. . . ."

Shear and Manacle began a slow circling movement among those gathered in the grassy space. I remembered Manacle saying that the techs would serve cakes and wine. There were no techs, and the magicians were looking about themselves with pursed lips and expressions of annoyance. A mutter began, grew in volume as the celebrants moved away, away toward the doors. We waited for the last dawdlers to leave before emerging from the ship with the bodies of Windlow and Himaggery carried before us. We staggered across the grass to the machine. When we came close, I was horrified to see that the ribbons and garlands covered areas of corrosion. Wires and tubes appeared fused together into a blackened mass. We stared at each other for a moment. "What can we do but try?" asked Mavin. "We must."

We laid Himaggery upon the slab, placed the tiny blue in the recess beside his head, and Mavin went to the long, silver lever which protruded at the side. Her eyes were shut, her lips moving. I don't know whom she invoked, what godling or devil. Perhaps it was only herself she counseled. Her hands were steady when she thrust the lever up, in the opposite direction we had seen it moved in the laboratories, and I knew she had been thinking of that, puzzling it out. Could it be that simple? I could not dare to hope it was.

The machine screamed. I bit my lips until the blood came. The slab moved, turned, swung beneath the blackened mass which towered above it. I smelled smoke, burning oil. There was no device here to put out fire. I only held my breath and waited, waited while the scream rose to an agonized howl before diminishing to silence. The slab had not returned. Mavin jiggled the lever, once, twice. Slowly the slab dropped from beneath the machine, down, twisting, out and back toward us once again. The blue was gone. Himaggery looked like Himaggery once more. I could see his chest move, tiny, tiny movements, the shallowest of breaths. We pulled him from the slab and put Windlow in his place.

I knelt above Himaggery while Mavin went to the lever again. I heard the ascending howl, smelled burning once more. This time there was smoke, harsh and biting. I coughed. Himaggery coughed. His head moved, his hand. I found myself patting him, stroking him, mumbling nonsense into his ear. Then Mavin's cry from behind me brought me to my feet.

The machine was on fire. Below the contorted mass, the slab moved out slowly, too slowly. Already I could see that the blue was still there. Nothing had happened. Then, when it came further into view, I knew that something had happened—Windlow's body had been . . . changed. Was it the heat of the machine? Some ancient device which had broken at last, irretrievably? It didn't matter. What lay upon the slab could not support life again, and I knew this with every cell which Dealpas had inhabited. "Dead," I whispered, unable to believe it. "Dead . . ."

"Dead?" The voice behind me was Himaggery's. I turned to see him trying to sit up, failing, and trying once again. His eyes were unfocused, blind. Mavin was beside him in that instant, ready with one of the black dresses which Manacle had used in his ceremony, ready to wrap him and coerce him back into life once more. I reached over the slab and took Windlow's blue into my hands, hands sticky with tears. I tried not to look at the slab again, but could not stop the thought that this, this is what old Windlow had foreseen and begged for my help against.

Perhaps Mavin read my mind, or my face. She snapped at me. "There is no time for guilt, Peter. We must get out of this place. What Didir feared will happen very soon. . . ."

"The door is locked," I said stupidly. "Flogshoulder will find the door locked. He will have to return to get the key. We have a little time."

"We have no time. Didir warned of some general catastrophe. Game-lords know how far we would have to go to escape it, but the farthest, the soonest would be best." She leaned across Himaggery once more, urging him to his feet. I do not know how he did it, but the man lurched upright, mouth open in anguish as he did so. She went on even as she urged him toward the tunnels. "The cars that brought the bodies to this place are still there, still on the track. I watched them when they ran them. They will take us away."

I followed her, placing Windlow's blue tenderly in my pocket as I went. The carts were there, just as she had said. Himaggery and I climbed into the foremost one as Mavin fumbled with the controls. It shuddered, made a grating noise, then began to run forward into the mountains.

"Where?" I asked her, seeing the daylight vanish behind us. "Where will you take us?"

"Where the tracks go," she replied. "The carts came from those cold caverns, they should return there. We need distance between us and this place, and any other way would take too long. . . ."

So we ran off into a half darkness.

There were no magicians. There were no techs. We saw one or two Tallmen from time to time, but they stood by the walls as still and silent as trees, but unalive. It was then I began to know that they had not truly been living things—or not entirely living things. I thought of Tallmen, and I thought of music, and I wondered how those who made the one could make the other. I have not yet made an answer to that.

Somewhere early in the journey, Himaggery began to regain his wits.

He wanted to know what had happened, and in order to tell him that I had to tell him everything, Laggy Nap, my journey, Mavin, Izia, the Tallmen, Manacle, Quench . . . and Didir. We passed one of those dining places once, and Mavin stopped while we raided it. After that, Himaggery seemed to be better, though still rather disoriented and weak. When he asked about Windlow, I could not answer him. I could only look back the way we had come and let the tears run down my face. So it was Mavin who told him, and then there was a silence which seemed without end.

Finally he broke it. "So what is happening now?"

"Now we are trying to get away," I answered. "Flogshoulder will go to the room. He will find it locked. He will return to Manacle, and one way or another, with Committee approval or without it, Manacle will give him the key. Or Manacle will go himself. Whatever occurs, it will not take long. Manacle will believe that Quench is more of a threat than he ever believed the Council was. The defenders are to be used against a threat. So, he will use the defenders."

"What will happen?" whispered Himaggery from a dry throat.

"I don't know for sure. I *believe* that the defenders were never designed to defend the magicians. They were designed to defend Home, wherever that may be. Another world, somewhere."

"So you've figured that out," said Mavin, dryly.

"Yes. The defenders were designed to defend Home against the monsters."

"Monsters?" asked Himaggery. "What monsters? Who?"

"Oh, Himaggery." I laughed and cried all at once. "You. Me. Mavin. All the children of Didir. *She* was the monster, the girl monster, the one the ship brought. Only she. And all those others to watch her and write down everything she did. All of it, the defenders, everything. Just to keep one little woman monster from threatening Home."

"I thought so," said Mavin. "I thought that was the way of it."

"Well, if you thought so, I wish to heaven you had told me!" I said.

"So what will the defenders do?" Himaggery went on, tenacious as always.

"Destroy the place," said Mavin with finality. "Destroy Manacle and stupid Flogshoulder and sycophantic Shear, all the Tallmen and the pits, all the monsters—the real ones—and machines. Everything. Or so I believe.''

''So do I,'' I said. ''And we had best be far away when that happens.''

''How far away?''

I couldn't tell him. Didir had thought only of danger, danger to everything. She had not limited it to a certain circle, a Demesne which could be measured for chill. ''Far,'' I said. ''As far as possible.''

''At least to the end of these tracks,'' said Mavin, practical as always. So we rode along the tracks, deeper and deeper under the mountains as Himaggery grew stronger and I felt more the pain of Windlow's death. Once I thought of asking Mavin whether there was some way out of the place she was taking us, but decided she would not appreciate the question. If there was a way out, there would be a way out. If not, not. My asking would not change it.

The way to the caverns was a long way. When we arrived there, I wished we had not come. The bodies around us lay in piles as high as my shoulders, five or six bodies high, men and women together, stacked in endless rows. In one area to the side of the entry, Mavin and Himaggery found body after body of those they had known. Here were those Mavin had mentioned to me, but many others as well.

''And all of their minds—their memories, all, gone? Out there? In the aeries of Gamesmasters, to be used as teaching aids for children?'' Himaggery sounded unbelieving, but we assured him it was true.

''Then what threatened us and worked against us was not the Council at all? It was these old men in this moldy place? Abducting us one by one and storing us away like fish?'' Again we assured him this was true.

''Then we have only to tell the world what has gone on here, and it will stop. The Traders can be watched.''

''That may be true,'' I said. ''But there may be more to it than that. It was these old men who abducted and kept you, true. But Quench said it was the Council told them *who* to take and keep. And it is to the Council that Quench has gone, gone with every tech in the place.''

''And,'' said Mavin, ''I would wager with every book they could lay hands on.''

We had not yet gone into the largest part of the cavern, a place from which a chill wind came to assure us of egress somewhere. It was then, as we were readying ourselves to find it, that the first rumble came, shivering the rock about us and dropping dust and ice onto our heads from far above. The shaking went on. Rock grated and twisted beneath us.

"We have taken too long," shouted Mavin. "Through the large cavern, quickly. . . ."

But we were not allowed to go.

We had no sooner stepped within the large cavern than he came from behind a pile of bodies, Demon helmed, all in silver, a strange device cradled in his arms, its ominous tip pointed toward me. "Peter, the Necromancer," he said. "I told them you were not dead! I would not let you be dead! Not you, Peter. Not until I could do it myself! I call Game, and Move. Necromancer Nine!"

Himaggery leapt to one side, behind a pile of bodies. Well, he was older than I. He had more experience with this kind of thing. On the other side, Mavin Shifted into something quick and fierce, and the corner of my eye saw her fade into an aisle. Well, she, too, was a more experienced Shifter than I. I did not move. The tip of the thing which pointed at me said *do not move,* and I understood its language. "What have you there, Huld?" I asked him, almost conversationally. I was not unafraid. I was simply too surprised to act frightened.

"A thing Nitch made for me, Peter. Was that not kind of him? It was when you all thought me bottled up in Bannerwell. Do not trust Immutables to do your bottling for you, Peter. They do not do it well. They have no skill in foxing or outfoxing; any Gamesman could outwit them, as I did. I had another place to go, a better place. I found Nitch as he traveled between Schooltown and that place of the magicians. Nitch. It was Nitch who was responsible for what happened to Mandor, Peter. Remember that. What happened to him was just."

"What happened to him?" I had put one hand into my pocket, feeling desperately for—for what? Shattnir could do me no good in this cold place. Those around me were not dead to be raised by Dorn. And neither would come to me in any case. . . .

"Why, he died," he said, pretending surprise. "After he had made me the things I wanted, told me the things I wanted to know, given me the books he had. He made this shield, like the one you had in Schooltown. This weapon, like no other you have ever seen. Oh, Peter, with this weapon there will be no Gaming against Huld. No. All the Gaming will

be as *I* choose." He stroked the thing exultantly. "After I dispose of your
... family ..." He drew out the word to make it an obscenity. Until that
moment, I had not thought of them as my family, but they were. Himaggery. Mavin. My own kind. My fingers still groped in my pocket. Habit,
not hope.

And closed around a Gamesman, closed to feel a warm, wonderful
certainty rise through me, soft and gentle, kind as summer, the voice
whispering as familiar, almost, as my own. "Peter. Why are you standing
here? Valor is all well and good, but shouldn't you be elsewhere if you
can manage it?"

It was Windlow.

I almost laughed aloud before remembering the threat. Yes, I know
that is foolish. It was only an instant thing, as quickly suppressed. I let
Windlow go and burrowed deep to close around a figure I had not tried
until then. Old as Didir, powerful as she, her mate and coeval, Tamor.
Grandfather Tamor. Towering Tamor.

There was no hesitation. The block, whatever it might have been, had
been healed. Perhaps Windlow had healed it. Tamor came into me like
a hawk stooping, and I was looking down on Huld as he peered at the
place I had been. There was no sensation of flying as I had often thought
there would be. No, I was simply lying high upon the air, above Huld,
seeing Mavin and Himaggery moving stealthily toward him around barriers of chill bodies.

"Huld!" I cried.

He pointed the device up, released a bolt of force which blistered past
me and melted stone and hanging ice from the arched ceiling far above.
Liquid rock fell past me, hardening as it came, and Huld ran from the
lethal rain even as I swooped away to another part of the cavern. More
stone and ice rained down. This was no result of Huld's weapon. This
was more of the same quaking we had felt before. Mavin waved to attract
my attention, pointed to the far end of the great cavern. I nodded to show
her that I understood.

I should have watched Huld, not Mavin, for another bolt from the
weapon came toward me, touched me agonizingly, and splashed against
the ice. "All right," said Tamor from within. "Keep your eyes open,
boy. Shall we rescue your friend?" Himaggery did look lonely and lost,
sprawled out below me between two piles of bodies. We swooped down,

not at all birdlike, to grab him and lift him high in a long shallow glide which took us toward the cavern end. I heard Huld screaming in fury. He had known of some of my Talents. He had not known of them all. Well, how could he have done? I had not known of them myself.

"You will not get away," he was screaming at me. "I've closed that way out. I knew you'd come here, come where the bodies of your allies lay. I knew you'd try to get them. It's the kind of Gamish stupidity they taught you, boy. . . .

"Even if you escape, it won't stop me. I'll come after you again, and yet again. I have allies, too. And plans. And the world will not hold us both as Masters, so you will serve my Game. . . ."

"Tchuck." Tamor made a tsking sound in my head. "That kind of hysterical threat is unbecoming, undignified. I do not like being called Grandfather to that." We were away on another long, swooping glide that broke twice to escape bolts from Huld's weapon. A great slab of stone turned red behind us and slid toward the floor, half flowing. Without thinking, I reached for Shattnir and felt her run into me like wine, reaching out toward the melted stone to draw its heat and power into every fiber. We stayed there, hidden behind the bodies, until I heard Huld coming, then rose once more, lying flat, skimming like an arrow behind the stacked bodies toward the chill wind. Himaggery gasped. I was holding him under one Shifted arm, huge and hairy as a pombi's leg. Well, he should have been used to Shifter ways. In order to get me upon my mother he should have known her rather well.

The shaking of the cavern was constant. I heard Huld shout something, away behind me, then another shout which sounded like fear. He had either been under a falling chunk of rock or had been narrowly missed. I didn't care which. The opening of the cavern was before me. Mavin was already there. The entrance was covered by a narrow grill which sizzled with the same force Huld's weapons had used. Mavin spread her hands wide in consternation. She could not Shift to go through the narrow openings without frying herself. Within me, Shattnir laughed. The laughter of Shattnir had nothing of humor in it. It was not an experience, then or thereafter, which I greatly enjoyed.

All the heat of the great melted slab went into the bolt which broke the grill, melted it in its turn, and spread its broken shards over half the mountainside. Mavin fled through the opening, out and down, knowing

I would follow. Around us the earth clamored, no longer quivering but heaving to and fro in long, hideous waves. I flew through the opening into nubilous air, high into gray cloud to see the white wings of a huge bird slide through the gloom beneath me.

Then we saw it, Himaggery and I. Away to the southeast, where the shiptower might have been, a ball of flame, swelling, swelling into a little sun, a cloud rising from it lit from below, bloody and skull-shaped in the murk, fires within it, lightnings playing upon its top. The wind took us then, tumbling us over and over in the high air on the face of a hot wind which Shattnir merely sucked into me and stored away. The earth roared, heaved, and fell in mighty undulations. I saw a mountain tremble, throw back its head and laugh into roaring fragments as we spun through the air again, rolling on the wind. Wild fire licked and crackled and eventually died.

After a time we came down, onto a green hill which sat quietly beneath us, steady as a chair. Wind from the north whipped the bloody clouds to tatters and away. The sun broke through, midway down the western sky. It was not a day, yet, since we had hidden in the shiptower to see the Ceremony of Calling Home. Beside me, Himaggery picked up a straw and closed trembling lips upon it.

"Well, lad. What do you think we should do now?"

I picked up a straw of my own.

"I don't know what you want to do, Himaggery," I said. "But I'm going to change myself into a Dragon and go looking for my mother."

# 13

## Bright Demesne

We found Mavin on her pinnacle, just where I had thought she would be, and she was properly admiring of the most splendid Dragon she or anyone in the world had ever seen. It was exactly as Chance had said, a foolish idea. The fire and speed and wind in the wings were all very well, but there was still Windlow in my pocket and the bodies of ten thousand great Gamesmen (as well as a few pawns) lying in the cavern under the snows. Oh, we had gone back, Himaggery and I, just to be sure. The cavern was quite intact except for a little fallen ice and melted stone. Huld was not there, dead nor alive, which meant he was still at large in the world, hunting me. I was growing tired of that.

So, once I had done my gomerousing around as a Dragon, I settled with Himaggery and Mavin on the pinnacle, to await the arrival of my cousins. We sat about Mavin's fire, me watching Himaggery be excruciatingly polite to her while she twitted him at every opportunity. I finally took her aside and told her to let him alone. If she truly did not want to be the man's pawnish mate, I told her, then she should not keep saying so so vehemently, which would just make him believe the opposite. I don't know how I figured that out, except that Trandilar probably had something to do with it. At any rate, it bought us some peace and we got along better.

Swolwys and Dolwys arrived in good time. They had delivered Izia, improved in both health and spirits by the time they arrived. More important, when they had come to Izia's home, Yarrel had been there and she had remembered him. The cousins did not say much about that meeting. I hoped for their sakes that Yarrel had not treated them as coldly as he had treated me when last we met. His rejection of me still hurt, and I hoped that Izia's return might make him feel more kindly, though I knew that if he learned all she had gone through in the intervening years, he might hate all Gamesmen even more.

And this line of thought brought me to thoughts of Windlow. I figured that matter out in the privacy of the cave, unwilling to talk about it with anyone. I simply chipped at the corner of the tiny Didir figure with my thumbnail until the white covering flaked away to show the blue beneath. The Gamesmen of Barish were blues, simply (simply!) blues, made in the long past for some reason I could not know, though I was beginning to make some rather astonishing guesses. The Gamesmen themselves did not tell me, though whether they could not or would not, I did not know. At the moment I was content to let things be. Except for one thing.

At one time or another, casually, over a period of several days, I handed one or another of the Gamesmen to my cousins, to Mavin, even to Himaggery. They handled them as I had done, with bare hands, but they gave no indication that they felt anything or experienced anything at all. So. "Blues" could not be Read by anyone who handled them. It was a particular Talent which I had, seemingly I alone of all the world. So again. No one had seen me take the Windlow blue. No one knew I had it. I doubt that either Mavin or Himaggery ever thought about it, and I did nothing at all to remind them.

We traveled to the Bright Demesne together, three horses and two horsemen. We younger ones were the horses, two for riding, one for baggage. I thought of Chance when I did it. He would have approved mightily of how inconspicuous I was.

I could not help but overhear the long conversations between my mother and—Himaggery (I could not think of him as "Father"). As the hours of our travel wore on, they spoke more and more often of certain Gamesmen they had known. I heard again the name of Throsset of Dowes. I heard again the name of Minery Mindcaster. Himaggery spoke of the High Wizard Chamferton, and Bartelmy of the Ban. They were cataloging all those they had seen in the cavern or suspected might be there.

And they were making plans to bring all the blues of all the world to the Bright Demesne. "There will be a way," Himaggery insisted. "A way to do it without the machines. Or to build a new machine to do it. So many, so great. We cannot leave them there, stacked like stove wood."

And then they would talk more, list more names, and end by saying the same thing again. Peter in the horse's head nodded wisely. We were no sooner out of one mess than we would get into another.

And, of course, they talked about the Council. The mysterious Council. The wonderful Council. The probably threatening Council. They could not decide whether it was totally inimical, perhaps beneficial, or, possibly, nonexistent. Peter inside the horse's head nodded again. Such questions could not be left unanswered, not by one like Himaggery. Peter inside the horse's head had other thoughts, about Quench, Huld, books, about what several hundred or thousand pawns who had been "techs" might do when loosed into a world which did not know they existed.

And we came at last to the Bright Demesne. Word having been sent ahead, we were expected. There was a certain amount of orderly rejoicing, and Mertyn seemed to have some trouble letting me out of his sight for several days. Chance, on the other hand, behaved as though I had only been gone on a day-long mushroom hunt and was no different on my return than on my going. Only the quantity and quality of the food which kept appearing before me told me that he had worried about me. I helped him by pretending I did not notice.

There was mourning, too, for Windlow. I wept with the rest and kept my mouth shut.

And then Izia arrived—with Yarrel.

They rode into the kitchen court about noon. I was in the kitchen garden with Chance, pulling carrots. There is no Talented way to do this easier than simply stooping over and yanking them out by their tops. So I was muddy and sweating and unsuspecting when the clatter of hooves came from the cobbled yard. I looked up, wiping my eyes with my shirt-tail, and saw Izia looking at me, very pale and very beautiful. She reached one hand to the person beside her, and then I saw Yarrel. He was looking at me, too, but with an expression in which resentment and eagerness seemed equally combined. He slid from the horse's back, helped Izia down, and they came together toward me. All I could think of was that I wanted to hide, not to have him angry or hateful to me again.

Perhaps he saw this emotion on my face, for he stopped and smiled, almost shyly. "Peter . . ."

Was there something of a plea in that voice? I gritted my teeth and stepped forward, the shirttail still between my hands, wiping away the mud so that I could offer him a clean hand. He did not wait for that, but took both muddy fists in his own and drew me within the circle of his arms.

It was only a moment, a moment before he stepped back, his face calm again as he raised his hand to Chance and let me guide them into the kitchens. We sat there in the fireglow as we had sat year on year, within hands' clasp of one another, eating Chance's baking and telling one another of all that had happened in our worlds. It would be good to write that all was as it once had been, the old friendship, the old closeness. But that would be a sentimental story, not true. It was not as it had been; it was only better than it was before he came.

And Izia sat there, sometimes smiling a little, a tiny smile, tight and tentative, but a smile, nonetheless. Once she even laughed, a short little hoot of laughter, like a surprised owl. I knew then that I had loved her for herself, and because she resembled him, and because I had rescued her. I knew in that same way that she would never know it, that it would only be a burden to her. She could accept Yarrel's touch, and only his, a gentling, animal-handler's touch, with nothing in it of lust or human ardor. She would grow more secure, less frightened, as the years went by. But—no, she would never accept what might remind her of Laggy Nap. Nap. I had not thought of him or wondered where he had come to. I wondered now, idly, whether it would be worth the trouble to avenge myself and her.

So I rejoiced that Yarrel had come, and grieved that Yarrel had come bringing Izia, and then simply stopped feeling and *was* while they were there.

And after they had gone, I went to Himaggery, where he sat in his high, mist-filled room and asked him whether he would still accept my help, my Talents and my help, in whatever it was he intended to do. Mertyn was there with him. It was being said that Mertyn would stay, would not return to the Schooltown, so I thought the matter might well be discussed with them both.

"Ah, you see," said Himaggery to my thalan. "It is precisely as Windlow said." Then, turning to me, "Windlow told me you would come into this very room and say that very thing, Peter. He did not know when it would be. Ah. Ah—but his vision was wrong in one thing. He thought he would be here, too. Tshah. I shall miss him."

"As I will, also," I said. Oh, Windlow, I thought, why did you not simply tell me before I left the Bright Demesne! If you saw the threat, knew the danger, why didn't you tell me. . . . But there was no answer to that. He rested softly in my mind and did not answer though he was present, as he had foreseen.

So I asked the question of Himaggery again, and this time he told me, yes, he would accept my help with great pleasure. It was precisely as I thought, of course. We were to locate the Council. We were to bring the blues to the Bright Demesne. We were to find a way to reunite the body and spirit of ten thousand Gamesmen. We were to pursue Justice, for Windlow had desired that. We were, in short, to do enough things to take a lifetime or two, most of them complicated, some of them dangerous, all of them exciting.

And, I had an agenda of my own. Huld, for example, who had called Necromancer Nine on me, Huld who did not know that he had been right. He had called Necromancer Nine on the young Necromancer, Peter; it was his intention that Peter die, and *that* Peter had died indeed. I did not quite know who the Peter who survived would be, but he would not be Dorn, or Didir, or Trandilar.

So I smiled on Himaggery and offered him my hand. Time alone and the Seers knew what would come next. Highest risk, Necromancer Nine. I was not afraid.

# WIZARD'S ELEVEN

# A FEW HELPFUL NOTES

## The Gamesmen of Barish

1. Dorn, Necromancer Talent: Deadraising
2. Trandilar, Ruler Talent: Beguilement
3. Shattnir, Sorcerer Talent: Power Holding
4. Wafnor, Tragamor Talent: Moving
5. Didir, Demon Talent: Mind Reading
6. Dealpas, Healer Talent: Healing
7. Tamor, Armiger Talent: Flying
8. Hafnor, Elator Talent: Traveling
9. Buinel, Sentinel Talent: Firestarting
10. Sorah, Seer Talent: Seeing the Future
11. Thandbar, Shifter Talent: Shapechanging

In addition, the Immutables were reckoned to have Talent Twelve, and Peter was found to have Talent Thirteen. The Talent of Wizards is never specified. "Strange are the Talents of Wizards."

## Notes on the Fauna of the World of the True Game

The animals, birds, and water creatures originally native to the world of the True Game lack a backbone and have evolved from a vaguely starfish-shaped creature. The basic skeleton is in the form of a jointed pentacle, or star, often elongated, with the limbs and head at the points of the star. Despite this very different evolutionary pattern, the bioengineers among the magicians succeeded in meshing the genetic material of the new world and that from which they came. Among the creatures now native to the world of the True Game are:

BUNWITS: Any of a variety of herbivorous animals with long hind legs and flat, surprised-looking faces under erect, triangular ears. Like all animals native to the world, bunwits are tailless. They eat young grasses and the leaves of webwillows.

FLITCHHAWKS: Swift, high-flying birds which prey mostly upon bunwits of the smaller varieties. Noted for their keen eyes.

FUSTIGARS: Pack-hunting predators, some varieties of which have been extensively inbred and domesticated.

GNARLIBARS: A huge animal which lives in the high wastes below the Dorbor Range. It feeds upon anything it can catch, including old or ailing krylobos. The gnarlibar has a ground-shaking roar which has earned it the name of "avalanche animal." Gnarlibars always pack in fours, two females and two males; females always bear twins, one male and one female. A set of Gnarlibars is called a "leat" or crossroads, because of their invariable habit of attacking from four directions at once. It is thought that the gnarlibar is the descendant of a prehistoric race of animals so prodigious in size as to be considered mythical.

GROLE: A long, blind, legless animal with multiple rows of teeth which lives by burrowing into soil, stone, or other inorganic materials, utilizing the light metals in its metabolism. The teeth are of adamant and can be used as grinding tools. The so-called "sausage groles" are not related to rockeater groles but are smaller creatures of similar configuration which eat only organic materials, notably the meat of the ground nut.

KRYLOBOS: A giant, flightless bird with well-developed wing fingers, capable of very high running speeds. The krylobos dance contests are among the most exciting of spectacles for adventurous zoologists, as the birds are extremely agile and powerful.

POMBIS: Carnivores distinguished by clawed feet and the ability to climb tall trees or nest in virtually inaccessible locations. Pombis are irritable and have a reputation for unprovoked belligerence.

THRISPAT: A small omnivore which bears its young alive, lives in trees or upon precipitous mountain slopes, and mimics the calls of other animals and the human voice. Small thrispats are favorite pets in the jungle cities where breeders vie in extending the vocabularies of their animals. A good thrispat can speak up to a hundred words and phrases with some indication of understanding their meaning. Thrispats are particularly fond of ripe thrilps, whence the name.

WARNETS: A stinging, flying insect of minuscule size and legendary bad temper, which lives in hordes. Called "saber-tail" by some. It is said that krylobos will take warnet nests and drop them into the nests of gnarlibars during territorial disputes.

# Native Peoples

At least two peoples are known to occupy the lands around the area of the True Game.

SHADOWPEOPLE: Small, carnivorous (omnivorous when necessary) nocturnal people delighting in music and song. They are extremely fond of festivals, dance contests, song contests and the like and have been seen to assemble by hundreds within sound of the annual contests at the Minchery in Leamer. While Shadowpeople eat bunwits of any size, it is notable that they do not attack krylobos and are not attacked by pombis, gnarlibars, or warnets.

EESTIES: A people said by some to be aloof and withdrawn, by others to be friendly and helpful. Seen most often as solitary individuals. Native language unknown. Habits unknown. In appearance, star-shaped, moving as Armigers do or rolling upon the extremities.

# 1

# Wizard's Eleven

MAVIN MANYSHAPED, my mother, had told me that when a Shape-shifter is not Shifting—that is, when he is not involved in a Game—it is considered polite for the Shifter to wear real clothing and act, insofar as is possible, like any normal Demon or Necromancer or Tragamor. I like to humor Mavin when I can. The proper dress of a Shifter includes a beast-head helm and a fur cloak, so I had had a pombi-head helm made up, all lolloping red tongue and glittering eyes, with huge jowls and ears—fake, of course. A real pombi head would have weighed like lead. My fur mantle was real enough, however, and welcome for warmth on the chill day which found me midway between the Bright Demesne and the town of Xammer. I was mounted on a tall black horse I had picked for myself from Himaggery's stables, and Chance sulked along behind on something less ostentatious. We were on our way to visit Silkhands the Healer, not at her invitation and not because of any idea of mine.

Chance was sulking because he had recently learned of a large exotic beast said to live in the far Northern Lands, and he wanted me to Shift into one so that he might ride me through the town of Thisp near the Bright Demesne. It seemed there was a widow there . . .

I had said no, no, too undignified, and wasn't Chance the one who had always urged me to be inconspicuous? To which he had made a bad-tempered reply to do with ungrateful brats.

"If she had seen you mounted on a gnarlibar, Chance, she would never have let you in her house again. She would have felt you too proud, too puissant for a plumpish widow."

" 'Twould not be too warlike for that one, Peter. She's widow of an Armiger and daughter of another. Great high ones, too, from the telling of it."

"But she has no Talent, Chance."

"Well. That's as may be. Boys don't know everything." And he went back to his sulks.

Whoops, Peter, I said to myself. Chance is in love and you have been uncooperative. Thinking upon the bouncy widow, I could imagine what Talents she might have which Chance would value. I sighed. My own history, brief though it was, was mainly of love unrequited. I resolved to make it up to him. Somehow. Later. Certainly not before I found out what a gnarlibar might look like. This rumination was interrupted by more muttering from Chance to the effect that he couldn't see why we were going to Xammer anyhow, there being nothing whatever in Xammer of any interest.

"Silkhands is there, Chance." I didn't mention the blues which were the ostensible reason for my trip.

"Well, except for her there's nothing."

Right enough. Except for her there was probably little, but between the blues and old Windlow the Seer, I had reason for going.

The Bright Demesne had been like a nest of warnets since Mavin, Himaggery, and I had returned from the place of the magicians in the north. Those two and Mertyn had great deeds aflight, and all the coming and going in pursuit of them was dizzying. They had been horrified to learn of the bodies of great Gamesmen stacked in their thousands in the icy caverns of the north and had resolved to reunite those bodies with the personalities which had once occupied them, personalities now scattered among the lands and Demesnes in the form of blues, tiny Gamespieces used in the School Houses in the instruction of students. Mavin had appointed herself in charge of locating all the blues and bringing them to the Bright Demesne, though how she planned to reunite them with the bodies was unknown unless she was depending upon the last of the magicians, Quench, to make it possible. In any case, uncertainty was not standing in the way of action. Pursuivants were dashing about, Elators were flicking in and out like whipcracks; the place was fairly screaming with arrivals and departures.

Coincident with all this was a quiet search for my enemy, Huld. We were all eager to find him, accounting him a great danger loose in the world and ourselves unable to rest in safety until he was in some deep dungeon or safely dead.

And, of course, there was still much conjecture and looking into the matter of that mysterious Council which was rumored to be managing or mismanaging our affairs from some far, hidden place of power. Anyone not otherwise occupied was trying to solve that enigma. Meantime, I traveled about, collected blues, spent little time at the Bright Demesne. Standing about under the eyes of an eccentric mother, a father who kept looking at me like a gander who has hatched a flitchhawk chick, *and* of my thalan, Mertyn, who persisted in treating me like a schoolboy, made me short-tempered and openly rebellious in a few short days. I said as much to the three of them, but I don't think they heard me. They considered me a treasure beyond price until it came time to listen to me, and then I might as well have been a froglet going *oh-ab, oh-ab, oh-ab* in the ditches. I would like to have been involved at the center of things, but—well. It would have done no good to talk to Mavin about it. She was a tricksy one, my mother, and though I would have trusted her implicitly with my life, I could not trust her at all with my sanity. Matchless in times of trouble, as a day-to-day companion she had remarkable quirks. Himaggery and Mertyn were preoccupied. Chance was courting the widow in Thisp. There were no other young people at the Bright Demesne—all locked up in School Houses. What was there to do?

Given the state of my pockets, I had decided to go swimming. During my travels in Schlaizy Noithn, I had learned to do without clothing most of the time, growing pockets in my hide for the things I really wanted to carry about. When one can grow fangs and claws at will, it is remarkable how few things one really needs. Well, pockets in one's skin sound all very well, but they accumulate flurb just as ordinary pockets do, and accumulated flurb itches. A good cure for this is to empty the pockets, turn them inside out and go swimming in one of the hot pools with the mists winding back and forth overhead and the wind breathing fragrance from the orchards. All very calm and pastoral and sweetly melancholy.

Well, enough of that was enough of that in short order. I sat on the grassy bank with the contents of my pockets spread out, sorting through them as one does, deciding what to do with a strange coin or an odd-shaped stone. While I was at it, I dumped out the little leather pouch which held the Gamesmen of Barish.

There had been thirty-two of the little figures when I had found them. Only eleven had been "real." The others were merely copies and carvings made by some excellent craftsman in a long ago time in order to fill out a set of Gamespieces. The ones which were only carvings were in my room. The eleven real ones were becoming as familiar to me as the lines in my own hand.

There was Dorn, the Necromancer, death's-head mask in one hand, dark visaged and lean. I could almost hear his voice, insinuating, dry, full of cold humor, an actorish voice. There was voluptuous Trandilar, Great Ruler, silver-blonde and sensual, lips endlessly pursed in erotic suggestion. There was Didir, face half hidden beneath the Demon's helm, one hand extended in concentration, the feel of her like a knife blade worn thin as paper, able to cut to inmost thoughts and Read the minds of others.

There was stocky Wafnor the Tragamor, clear-eyed and smiling, his very shape expressing the strength with which he could Move things— mountains, if necessary. He had done that once for me. There was Shattnir, androgynous, cold, menacing, challenging, the most competitive of them all, the spikes of her Sorcerer's crown alive with power. Beside her lay the robed form of Dealpas the Healer, tragic face hidden, consumed with suffering, her they called "Broken leaf." And, last of those I knew well, Tamor the Armiger, Towering Tamor, poised upon the balls of his feet as though about to take flight, Grandfather Tamor, strong and dependable, quick in judgment, instant in action. I knew these seven, knew the feel of their minds in mine, the sound of their voices, the touch of their bodies as each of them remembered their own bodies. I could, if I concentrated, almost summon the patterns of them into my head without touching the images.

There were four others I had not held. Sorah, the Seer, face shadowed behind the moth-wing mask, future-knower, visionary. There was fussy Buinel, the Sentinel, Fire-maker, much concerned with protocol and propriety, full of worry, holding his flaming shield aloft. There was Hafnor, the Elator, wings on his heels, quicksilver, able to flick from one place to another in an instant. And, lastly, there was Thandbar the Shifter whose talent was the same as my own, tricksy Thandbar in his beast-head helm and mantle of pelts. They lay there, the eleven, upon the grass.

And one more.

One not disguised by paint as the Gamesmen were. One icy blue. Windlow. I had not taken him often into my hand, and there was reason for that, but I took him then beside the warm pools and held him in my palm out of loneliness and boredom and the desire to be with a friend.

He came into my head like good wine and we had a long time of peace-fulness during which I sat with my legs in the water and thought of nothing at all.

Then it was as though someone said "Ah" in a surprised tone of voice. My mind went dreamy and distant, with images running through it, dis-solving one into another. My body sat up straight and began to breathe very fast; then it was over, and I heard Windlow saying inside my head, "Ah, Peter, I have had a Vision! Did you see it? Could you catch it?"

And I was saying, to myself, as it were, "A vision, Windlow? Just now? I couldn't see anything. Just colors."

"It is difficult to know," he said. "Your head does not feel as mine did. It doesn't work in the same way at all. How strange to remember that one once thought quite differently! It is like living in a new House and remembering the old one. Fascinating, the difference. I could wander about in here for years—ah. The vision. I saw you and Silkhands. And a place, far to the north, called—'Wind's eye.' Important. Where is Silk-hands?"

"You and Himaggery sent her to Xammer." This was true. It had happened well over a year before, after the great battle at Bannerwell. Though Silkhands had long known that her sister and brother, Dazzle and Borold, were kin unworthy of her sorrow, when the end came at Ban-nerwell which sent Dazzle into long imprisonment and Borold to his death—for he had died there at the walls, posturing for Dazzle's approval to the very end—it had been more than Silkhands could bear. She had cried to Himaggery and to old Windlow (this was long before Windlow had been captured by the traders and taken away) and they had sent her off to Xammer to be Gamesmistress at Vorbold's House. She had gone to seek peace and, I had told her at the time, perpetual boredom. I had given her a brotherly kiss and told her she would be sorry she had left me. Well. Who knows. Perhaps she had been.

"Ah. Then she is still in Xammer. Nothing has changed with Silkhands since I—passed into this state of being."

It was a nice phrase. I knew he had started to say, "Since I died," and had decided against it. After all, one cannot consider oneself truly dead while one can still think and speak and have visions, even if one must use someone else's head to do it with. "She is still there, Windlow, so far as I know. You're sure Silkhands was in your vision?"

"I think you should go to her, boy. I think that would be a very good idea. North. Somewhere. Not somewhere you have been before, I think. A giant? Perhaps. A bridge. Ah, I've lost it. Well, you must go. And you must take me along . . . and the Gamesmen of Barish."

I asked him a question then, one I had wanted to ask for a very long time. "Windlow, why are they called that? You called them that, Himaggery called them that. But neither of you had seen them before I found them."

There was a long and uncomfortable silence inside me. Almost I would have said that Windlow would have preferred that I not ask that question. Silly. Nonetheless, when he answered me, he was not open and forthcoming. "I must have read of them, lad. In some old book or other. That must be it."

I did not press him. I felt his discomfort, and laid the blue back into the pouch with the others, let him go back to his sleep, if it was sleep. Sometimes in the dark hours I was terrified at the thought of the blues in my pocket, waiting, waiting, living only through me when I took them into my hand, going back to that indefinable nothingness between times. It did not bear thinking of.

Now, since I had never told anyone about having Windlow's blue, I could not now go to them and say that Windlow directed me to visit Silkhands. A fiction was necessary. I made it as true as possible. I reminded them of the School House at Xammer, of the blues which were undoubtedly there, of the fact that Silkhands was there and that I longed to see her. At which point they gave one another meaningful glances and adopted a kindly but jocular tone of voice. Besides, said I, Himaggery always had messages to send to the Immutables, so I would take the messages. I could even go on to a few of the Schooltowns farther north, combining all needs in a single journey. What good sense! How clever of me! I would leave in the morning and might I take my own pick from the stable, please, Himaggery, because I have grown another handswidth.

To all of which they said yes, yes, for the sake of peace, yes, take Chance with you and stay in touch in case we find Quench.

Which explains why Chance and I were on the frosted road to Xammer on a fall morning full of blown leaves and the smoke of cold. We had been several hours upon the road, not long enough to be tired, almost long enough to lose stiffness and ride easy. The ease was disturbed by Chance's whisper.

" 'Ware, Peter. Look at those riders ahead."

I had seen them, more or less subconsciously. Now I looked more closely to see what had attracted Chance's attention. There was an Armiger, the rust red of his helm and the black of his cloak seeming somehow dusty, even at that distance. The man rode slouched in an awkward way, crabwise upon his mount. Beside him I saw a slouch hat over a high, wide collar, a wide-skirted coat, the whole cut with pockets and pockets. A Pursuivant. Those who worked with Himaggery had given up that archaic dress in favor of something more comfortable. Beside the Pursuivant rode a Witch in tawdry finery, and next to her an Invigilator, lean in form-fitting leathers painted with cat stripes. What was it about them? Of course. The crabwise slouch of the Armiger permitted him to stare back at us as he rode.

"Watching us?" I asked Chance. "How long?"

"Since we came up to 'em, lad. And they wasn't far ahead. Could have started out from the hill outside the gate, just enough advance of us to make it look accidental like."

"Why?"

"Why?" He snorted under his breath. "Why is sky blue and grass green. Why is Himaggery full of plots. Why is Mertyn bothered about a Shifter boy with more Talent than sense. 'Tisn't me they're bothered over."

"Me?" I considered that. Ever since I had left Schooltown I had been pursued by one group or another, on behalf of Huld the Demon, on behalf of Prionde the High King, on behalf of the magicians. Well, the magicians were probably all dead but one, so far as I knew, but both Huld and Prionde were alive in the world. Unless I had attracted another opponent I knew nothing of.

If someone had put the group together to win a Game against me—the me I appeared to be—then they had selected well enough. Both the Pursuivant and the Invigilator had Reading, though not at any great distance. Both the Armiger and the Invigilator could Fly. Both the Invigilator and the Witch could store some power. In addition, the Pursuivant would be able to flick from place to place—not far and not as quickly as an Elator would have done, but unpredictably—and he would have limited

Seeing. Add to this the Witch's ability as a Firestarter (her Talent of Beguilement didn't worry me) and they were a formidable Game Set.

I wondered how much they knew about me. If Huld had sent them, they knew too much. If Prionde had sent them, they might not know enough to cause me trouble. And if someone else? Well, that was an interesting thought.

" 'Their aim, what Game?' " I quoted softly for Chance's ears alone.

"No Game this close to Himaggery, boy. Later on, it'll be either kill or take, wouldn't it? Why Game else?"

"I wonder what I should do," I mused, mostly to myself, but Chance snorted.

"You went to School, boy, not me. Fifteen years of it you had, more or less, and much good it did you if you didn't learn anything. What's the rule in a case like this?"

"The rule is take out the Pursuivant," I replied. "But no point chopping away at them if they're only innocent travelers. I'd like to be sure."

"Wait to hear them call Game and you'll wait too long." He shut his mouth firmly and glared at me. He did that when he was worried.

"There's other ways," I said. Under cover of the heavy fur mantle, I reached into the pouch which held the Gamesmen. I needed Didir. She came into my fingers and I felt the sharp dryness of her pour up my arm and into me. Lately she had dropped the formality of "speaking" in my head in favor of just Reading what she found there. I let her Read what I saw. A moment went by.

Then, "I will Read the Witch," she whispered in my brain. "Small mind, large ego, no Talent for Reading to betray us. Just ride along while I reach her. . . ."

So I rode along, pointing out this bit of scenery and that interesting bird for all the world like a curious merchant with nothing more on his mind than his next meal and the day's profits. Covertly I examined the Witch in the group ahead. Shifters have an advantage, after all. They, and I, can sharpen vision to read the pimples on a chilled buttock a league away. I had no trouble seeing the Witch, therefore, and I did not like what I saw. She was sallow, with bulging eyes surrounded by heavy painted lines of black. Her mouth was small and succulent as a poison fruit, and her hair radiated from her head in a vast frizzy mass through which she moved her fingers from time to time, the finger-long nails painted black as her eyes. The clinging silks she wore revealed a waistless pudginess. Overall was a Beguilement which denied the eyes and told the watcher that she was desirable, wonderful, marvelous.

"Pretty Witch," I said to Chance.

"Beautiful," he sighed.

Oh, my. She was using it upon both of us, not knowing my immunity to it. Or, perhaps knowing my immunity but testing it? The possible ramifications were endless.

"She's a Witch, Chance," I said sternly. "A perfect horror. Black fingernails as long as your arm, frog eyes, hair like a briar patch and a figure like a pillow."

His mouth dropped open a little, but he was well schooled to the ways of Gamesmen. "I'll keep it in mind, Peter," he said with considerable dignity. "Be sure I'll keep it in mind."

"But if you act like you know," I added sweetly, "she'll know I told you. Better pretend you think she's gorgeous."

He gave me a hurt look. "I'm not a fool, boy. Had that figured out for myself." And he went back to staring at her with his mouth open. If I had not known about the widow back in Thisp, I would have sworn he was smitten.

It wasn't long before Didir spoke to me again. "They seek to take you, Peter, as agents for some other. The Witch does not know for whom. The Invigilator has something dangerous in his pocket, however, something to make you helpless. Be careful." And she was gone once more. The Gamesmen did not stay in my head. I wondered, not for the first time, if this was courtesy or discomfort. Did they refuse to invade me out of kindness or because my brain was unpleasant for them? As conjecture, it served to keep me humble.

"The rule is to take the Pursuivant out, Chance, but we will break the rule, I think. Since we are warned, let them move first. I'll see what the Demesne feels like. I think the Witch intends to move soon. Can you carry on a flirtation at this distance?"

"Game is announced, is it?" He mumbled something I couldn't hear, then, "Well, if she makes a beckon at me, I can manage to stir my bones in motion." And nodded, satisfied with himself. Old rogue. He was right. Game was announced.

In a formal Game, Great Game, the announcement had to be done in

340

accordance with the rules of Great Game, by Heralds calling the reasons and causes, the consequences and outcomes. In Great Game everyone knew who was Gaming, for what reasons, and what quarter might be given. Then there were Games of Two which were almost as formal. Game would be called by one and responded to by another before their friends and compatriots. Then there was secret Game, covert Game, but even there (if one played according to the rules) Game had to be announced. The announcement, however, could be part of the Game. If the opponent were a Demon, the announcement might be merely thought of. If the opponent were a Rancelman, then the announcement might be hidden. If the opponent were a Seer, then deciding upon the Game was considered announcement enough. A true Seer, it was reasoned, would See it in his future. The variations were endless. In this case the Armiger had called attention to himself and the Witch had thought of the Game. Announcement enough. The only question in my mind was whether the group ahead knew that I could do what Didir had just done. Oh well, tra-la. Game is announced. On with it.

We continued our journey, the group ahead moving only slightly slower than we so that we gained upon them as the leagues went by. The Witch was closer and closer yet, and Chance looked in her direction ever more frequently. We were not within Reading distance by the Pursuivant and Invigilator yet, and I wanted the first encounter over before they tried to Read me and failed. Chance and I stopped and made as if to go into the bushes on personal business, watching them from cover. When the distance had widened a little, we came after them, all innocence. If they really intended to use the Witch, she would make her Move soon.

And she did.

We watched them pull up, saw the broadly acted consternation as the Witch searched through her clothing, miming something lost. My, oh, my, what had she lost upon the road? Something important. Oh, yes; wide gestures of loss and concern; equally wide gestures to the others to go on, go on, she would ride back and then catch up to them. "Watch her," I said to Chance. "She'll head back toward us pretending to search the road for something lost."

"What did you say she looks like?" panted Chance.

"Black nails, black painted eyes, body like a bolster and hair like wires. 'Ware, Chance. She'll eat you."

"Up to you to prevent it, boy."

When she was a hundred paces from us, she turned to us, smiling, blazing. Lord, she was beautiful. My mouth almost dropped open, but then I felt around for the pattern that let me see clear even while my fingers fumbled for Wafnor in the pouch. Far ahead on the road the Armiger's horse was now riderless. I trusted not, tra-la. The Witch pouted, prettily.

"Oh, Sir Shifter, I beg your assistance. I know that Shifters can make their eyes keen like those of the flitchhawk to see a coin dropped in a canyon from a league away. Can you find for me the bracelet I dropped along the way here, perhaps at the edge of the trees?"

Then she turned to Chance, casting that smile on him like the light of a torch. Almost I saw him melt, but then I caught the tucks in his face where he had his cheeks between his teeth, biting down. "Pawn," she said, "would you help your master find my bracelet by walking along the trees. What he can see, you can retrieve, and have my thanks as he will. . . ."

Chance's eyes were out a finger's width, and he gave every appearance of being about to fall off his horse. Meantime, I smiled, bowed, and oozed desire in her direction while I called up Didir to sit in her head and tell me what she planned. I knew the Armiger was above us, somewhere, ready to fall upon us when we came within the trees. I gave a gulping prayer that I had enough power to do what I intended, then turned my eyes to the grassy verge of the road as the Witch came nearer. Under my fingers Wafnor came alive and reached up into the branches. I worked my way almost to the forest.

"Oh, lovely one," I called. "Here. Could it have caught on a branch? See the sparkling there where the sun catches it, not so bright as your beauty, but able to adorn it. . . ."

Witches are, for the most part, stupid. They tend to come into their Talent early, and this early accession to beguilement gives them too easy success in their formative years. At least so Gamesmaster Gervaise was wont to say. This particular Witch could have served as an object lesson. She came into the trees after me, still glittering and beguiling for everything she was worth. I was reminded of Dazzle, and, yes, of Mandor, and when I turned toward her she must have seen it in my face, for she flew at me with a scream of rage and those black nails aimed for my eyes.

There was no time for thought. I grabbed her wrist, ducked, twisted, and felt her fly over my head to land with a whoosh of expelled breath on the leaf-littered ground behind me. Then Didir did something quick and clever inside her head and the Witch lay there unconscious. Physical combat is not something we ever learned in a School House, but Himaggery believed in it. He had pawnish instructors giving classes every afternoon in the Bright Demesne. I hadn't seen the sense of it until now.

Chance looked at her where she lay. "Ugly," he said.

"I told you," I muttered.

"What now?" Chance always asks me what now when I have no idea what now. I shook my head, put my finger to my lips, concentrating on what Wafnor was doing. Fingers of force fluttered the bright leaves above us. The noise would be the Armiger. I could feel Wafnor searching, then there was a harsh "oof" as though someone had been roughly squeezed. I felt a shaking in my head, then Wafnor speaking in a cheerful grumble. "Stuck. Got him between two branches, and he's stuck!" One of the tree tops began to whip to and fro as Wafnor continued growling cheerily. "Won't come loose. Stupid Armiger . . ."

"Whoa," I said, weary of the whole thing. "Chance, hold the horses while I climb the tree."

I found the Armiger hanging by one badly bruised foot in the cleft of a tallish tree. Wafnor assisting me, we thrust one limb aside to let the Gamesman fall, none too gently, into the forest litter. He lay there beside the Witch, the two of them scruffy minor Gamesmen, not young, not well fed. The idea of killing them did not appeal to me. They were not players of quality. I said as much to Chance.

"They haven't the look of Huld about them somehow. He has more sense than to send such minor Talents."

"Maybe, lad. And maybe they were hired as supernumeraries by those up ahead. Hired fingers to touch you with, see if you sizzle."

Chance's remark had merit. I explored with Didir a possibility which would allow us to let them live, something she might plant in their heads which would take them away. After a short time the Witch and Armiger picked themselves up, dusted themselves off, and limped away to the south leading the Witch's horse. "They will believe they are going to meet others of their company," whispered Didir. "The notion will leave them in a day or two, but by that time they will be far distant from this place.''

"Now," I said, "we can ride in a wide circle south which will take us around those two ahead. We'll leave them behind us. . . .''

"Oh, lad, lad," sighed Chance. "Go around 'em and they're behind you. Lose a Pursuivant and he'll find you. What are you playing at?''

I sighed, pulled up my boots, looked at the sky, sucked a tooth. He was right. One doesn't "lose" a Pursuivant easily, and the trick of sending the other two away south wouldn't fool anyone long. Besides, if Chance's notions were correct, the two ahead of us were the real threat and came from a real opponent. The more I thought of it, the more I wondered if Huld was behind it. It didn't feel like Huld, but undoubtedly Huld would have to be dealt with sooner or later. I struck Chance a sharp blow on one shoulder. "Right you are, Brother Chance. Well then, it's back to the road, ride on, and let them wonder.''

Which we did. The Pursuivant and the Invigilator had moved on a little, leading the Armiger's horse. I went through a dumb show of waving as though taking leave of someone hidden in the trees. They wouldn't believe it, but it might confuse the issue still further.

We were a moving Demesne, the Game was not joined. Between the two men ahead of us on the road were five Talents and not inconsiderable ones. This reminded me of my own depleted state, and I fingered Shattnir, feeling the warmth of the sun beginning to build in me. I might need all I could get. The two ahead might be as shoddy as the two just defeated, but they might be the real foe, the true opponent, the True Game. If so, then what? What did I want to happen?

"Young sirs," Gamesmaster Gervaise had often said. "When you confront True Game in the outmost world, remember what you have been taught. Remember the rules. Forget them at your peril.'' Well, so, there was time during this slow jog along the road to remember the rules.

Game had been announced in two ways. By the Witch thinking of it and by the Armiger riding awkwardly. The Witch would have thought what she thought whether ordered to do so or not, but the Armiger would have ridden in that fashion only to attract attention. Therefore, the announcement was directed to one who would see the announcement with his eyes, not Read it. So presumably they had announced Game to a Shifter—which was, after all, what I seemed to be.

Now the Armiger was gone. Presumably, therefore, they knew that their opponent, the Shifter, had played. They knew I was in the Game. I knew they were in the Game because of what Didir had Read in the Witch's head, but *they* did not know that *I* knew what was in the Witch's head, therefore . . .

"I never had any head for covert Games," I complained to Chance. "Whenever I get to the third or fourth level of what I know and they know, I lose track."

"Look, lad. They know you're a Shifter. They're expecting that. They may have been *told* you're something else as well, but nobody knows exactly what, so they can't expect everything. Just be original and surprising. My granddad, the actor, used to say that. Original and surprising."

"Follow the rules." I sighed again. The rule was to take out the Pursuivant first, because he had the power to change place in an instant, and one might find him behind one with a knife before one could take a deep breath. Two of the Gamesmen of Barish and I had a little conference, waiting for a turn in the road. It might have been quicker to use Hafnor the Elator, but I had never 'ported from one place to another. The thought made me queasy, like being seasick. Besides, I didn't know the area ahead, and those with that Talent could only flick to places they could visualize. Which was another reason they were moving ahead of us. They had seen the road we traveled, but we hadn't seen the road they were on. No. I would use Tamor and Didir. I was used to them. And Shattnir, of course, to provide power, which she'd been doing for the last hour or so. It was moving toward evening before the road set as I wished it to.

We were moving between close set copses, dark trunks still half masked in drying leaves. One could not see far into them, a few paces perhaps. Just ahead of us the road swung around a huge rocky outcropping to make a loop to the left. Shortly before the riders ahead of us reached this place, Chance and I began a conversation which turned into a loud argument—Chance's voice much louder than mine. Old rogue. He was an actor as much as his granddad had ever been. As soon as the two ahead had ridden out of sight, I grasped the figure of Tamor and flew up from my saddle, darting away through the trees like an owl among the close trunks while Chance's voice rose behind me in impassioned debate. From time to time a softer voice would reply, Chance again, but those ahead would have no reason to think it was not me, Peter the Shifter, riding along behind them.

I had to intercept them before they had any opportunity to become suspicious. The trees were close, too close for easy flight, but I came to the edge of the road silently only a few paces behind them. I drew my knife and threw it, launching myself at the same moment, Shifting in midair. The Pursuivant went down, skewered, even as my pombi claws swept the Invigilator from his saddle. Then I sat on him. Beneath me he screamed, struggled, tried to fly. I let him struggle while I drooled menacingly into his face. He screamed a little more, then fainted. At least Didir said he really fainted, sure I was going to eat him. Shattnir drained him of any power he had left, and then we tied him up after going through his pockets. I found the thing almost at once. It was another of those constructions of glittering beads and wires like the one Nitch had sewn into my tunic in Schooltown, like the things Riddle had shown me outside Bannerwell. It was rather like the thing Huld had used against me in the cavern of the bodies, away north. It was shaped like a hood or cap, with a strap to go beneath the chin.

"What does it do?" asked Chance.

Didir sought in the Invigilator's unconscious mind even as I started to say I did not know. The man stirred in discomfort. She was not being gentle with him. I repeated to Chance what she told me.

"It guarantees docility," I said. "If they had put it on my head and fastened the strap, I would have obeyed anything they told me to do." I stood there for a time, thinking, then asked Didir to search further. Did the man know who sent him? Once I was "docile," where would they have taken me?

Whispering, she told me, "There are some ruins near the river which bounds the land of the Immutables. Old ruins. North of here. He would have taken you there."

Ah. I knew the place. I had found the Gamesmen of Barish there. Dazzle and Borold and Silkhands had stayed there. Well, I would go there. It would be original and surprising.

"Put the cap on him," I told Chance. "I'm going to get into the Pursuivant's clothing." So much for my fine fur cloak and my pombi head, lost in the mad flight through the trees. I stripped the Pursuivant and put his clothes on, sorrowing for him as I did so. I had not intended to kill him. The knife had turned in flight. When I had done, I carried him into the woods and laid him in a shallow scrape and covered him over with leaves before we rode away.

In a little time three men rode on: an Invigilator, very silent, the strange cap hidden beneath his leather garb; a Pursuivant, whose clothes fit none too well; and a pawnish servant who rode along behind leading two extra horses.

"Do we go on to Xammer, then?" the servant asked, humming to himself.

The Pursuivant, I, merely nodded. We were indeed going on to Xammer, to meet Silkhands, and then we were going farther on to those ruins I had visited once before. Behind us in the forest the real Pursuivant's body was food for ants, and before us was food for thought. I hoped it would not give me indigestion.

# 2

# Xammer

WE RODE INTO XAMMER, each taking a part in our little play. Chance was playing the grieving servant for all he was worth. The Invigilator, wearing the mysterious contrivance, played himself, though with only such verve as we ordered him to display. I, Peter, played the part of the Pursuivant, trying to convey with every attitude the heartfelt regret I felt at having killed the young Gamesman, Peter, during some unspecified and unfortunate occurrence upon the road. If we were being observed, this bit of acting should have gone further to confuse the observers. We took a room at an inn on the edge of town. I changed aspect and clothing in our rooms and sneaked out the back way, having been able to think of no good excuse for a Pursuivant to visit Silkhands the Healer. Chance was happily immured with a supply of wine and a perfectly biddable audience to listen to his reminiscences. He could have been happier only if the sportive widow from Thisp had been present, so I felt no need to hurry.

It was as well. The town of Xammer may be unique among School-towns. There was much to observe.

There are no Festival Halls in Xammer. Vorbold's House is one which specializes in teaching the daughters of the powerful, daughters of Queens and Sorcerers who have risen to first rank, of eminent female Armigers and Tragamors. They are taught how to play their own Games at Vorbold's House, the game of survival and reproduction. No Festivals for them, to be impregnated by nameless pawns or bear young at random. No. These maidens are the prizes of alliance and are as protected within the walls of Vorbold's House as they might be within a fortress guarded by dragons.

So much I knew, for it had been discussed at the time that Silkhands was sent to the place. I had not considered the implications of it, however, and it was these which made the town unique. It was full of shops, shops dealing in luxuries which were purveyed to the School House and to those who visited there. It was full of inns, not scruffy roadside inns but hostelries built with magnificence as the objective. It was full of travelers, powerful travelers entering the town under death bond that no Talent would be used within the walls. It was full, therefore, of courtesies and veiled malevolence as Gamesmen pursued their strategies through earthbound Heralds forbidden to Fly and a pawnish class of merchants who called themselves negotiators and arbitrators. I had never heard so much talk, not even in Himaggery's council hall.

I had known enough to bring proper dress, a little ostentatious and overdone, and was received with some courtesy for that if for no other reason when I presented myself at Vorbold's House. It had a high graceful gate leading into a sunny courtyard where a cat and kittens made endless play through the flower pots. I expected to be invited into the School but was instead shown to a small audience room off the courtyard and told to wait. The time was made less onerous by the arrival of a pretty waiting girl who brought wine and cakes and lingered to flirt with me. This was enjoyable for both of us, so much so that I almost regretted the sound of Silkhands' step on the tessellated pavement. That is, regretted until I saw her.

She was—yes, still Silkhands, but something more. At first I thought she had somehow Shifted herself to become so lovely, but then I saw it was only a matter of a little more flesh smoothing her face and gracing her neck and arms, a little more sleep in a softer bed than the campgrounds we had shared, less worry and stress and sorrow, a little more silk against the skin to replace the rough rub of traveling clothes. She did not even notice the retreating servant girl—nor did I—but came straight into my arms as though I had been some long lost love. "Peter," she said, "I am so happy to see someone from Home. How is Himaggery? Did they finish the new swimming pool in the orchard? Is your thalan still at the Bright Demesne? How is your mother? I heard about Windlow—ah—" and she was suddenly crying on my neck. I could feel the warm trickling wetness of her tears.

I felt as though two years had disappeared and we were traveling from the ruins where I had found her to the Bright Demesne once more. The best I could manage was a mumbled, "You haven't changed at all, Silkhands,'' while my body and my mind jigged with the notion that she had changed entirely, utterly. Of course, it was not she so much, but I figured that out later.

She asked if I were alone, and I told her that Chance and another fellow were at the inn, giving no details beyond that at first. She asked if I wanted to stay in the Guest House of Vorbold's, and we talked of that. I murmured something about the place being secure, and she looked at me slantwise, a look I remembered from the past.

''I see you have something to tell me, Peter. Well, the Guest House of Vorbold's is as secure a place as exists in all the purlieus and demesnes. We have guards against trifling as you would be astonished at. So. Will you go to the inn for your baggage, or shall I send for it?''

I thought it best to sneak in and out and to tell Chance myself. It was as well I did so, for the Invigilator had fallen into some kind of a trance, and Chance could not make him move or speak. We took the wicked little cap off of his head and put him to bed, bent up as he was in a sitting position. I told Chance to tie him and gag him loosely if Chance left the room, just in case the fellow came around, but otherwise to do as he pleased for the day or two I would spend at Vorbold's. ''Tell anyone who asks that your Pursuivant companion suffers from a flux,'' I suggested, ''and if this fellow hasn't moved in a day or two, I'll ask Silkhands to take a look at him.'' I could have called forth Dealpas, of course. She was preeminent among Healers, but she was so tragic and sorrowful that it was a pity to wake her. The fellow was breathing well enough, and his heart beat steadily. I thought a day or two would not change him greatly if he were kept warm and quiet.

And then I went back to Vorbold's House to find a guest's room made ready for me (not in the House itself) and a servant standing ready to unpack or clean or press or whatever I chose. I was glad to have brought clothes with me and thanked Mavin for so directing me. I had thought of traveling without any. The man advised that dinner would be served in the Hall at the evening bell, and he took himself off. I luxuriated in my bath, listened to the music from the courtyard, and tried to shake off the very uncomfortable feelings Silkhands had stirred up in me. After the bath I leaned in the window to watch the musicians. Vorbold's House collected artists, musicians, and poets from all the lands and demesnes. A representative group of them were gathered in the courtyard below me, all demonstrating their skills. The poets wore their traditional ribbon cloaks, looking something like boys let out of School for Festival, though more ornate and grand. There is some controversy about musicians and artists. Some hold that they are Talented, while others hold that it is merely a skill. In any case, they are not under bond in the town as the more ordinary Talents are. They may use whatever it is they have in a Schooltown or anywhere else, and it is not considered proper to Game against them.

Below me a musician played short phrases of melody over and over while a poet set words to them, and across the yard another poet declaimed a long verse, phrase by phrase, while another musician set notes to that. It seemed there was to be a song contest in the evening on a subject assigned by Gamesmistress Vorbold herself the evening before. In Mertyn's House, where I was reared, we would have disdained such trifles, and I formed the intention of twitting Silkhands about it. That was before I saw the great Hall.

It lay in the area to which guests are admitted, one ceremonial entrance for the guests, one even finer opposite which led into the School. I found my assigned seat and sat back to watch the spectacle which had aspects of Festival and of a bazaar. The guests were almost all male. Many were there on their own behalf, but others were there as agents. The products which they bargained for sat at other tables, on low daises of ivory hued stone, young women clad in silks and flowing velvets, each table of them with a Gamesmistress at its head. Silkhands sat at a table near my own. I could look across the glossy heads between and wink at her. Somehow the intensity of the atmosphere around me—though it was all covert, glances and sighs and whispers—made a wink seem improper. I satisfied myself with an unsatisfactory smirk and bow. I was, by the way, clad most sumptuously and wearing a face not entirely my own. I had cautioned Silkhands against knowing me too well or obviously in this public place. She bowed in return, I thought more coldly than was necessary.

The evening's entertainment began with welcoming words from the Lady Vorbold, Queen Vorbold. She wore the crown of a Ruler, but her dress was much modified. As I looked about the room I noted that all the women of the House were clad in light delicate gowns under robes of heavier richer stuff; that all the young women who were of an age to have manifested Talents wore appropriate helms or crowns or symbols, but all reduced in size and bulk to the status of mere ornaments. The heavy silver bat-winged half helm of a Demon might be expressed as a mere bat-winged circlet, airy as a spray of leaves. I saw a Sorcerer's spiked crown, tiny as a doll's headdress, and a Seer's moth-wing mask reduced to a pair of feathery spectacles drawing attention to the wearer's lovely eyes. It was as though they sought to make the Talents less important than the women who wore them. Well. In this House that was probably the case. Why did I suddenly think of the consecrated monsters which Mavin and I had seen in the caverns of the magicians? Was it some similar blankness of eyes? I did not quite identify the thought.

The song duels began, one against one, the musicians playing and singing in turn while the poets sat at their feet. At the conclusion of each song, the diners tapped their silver goblets upon the table to signify praise, and the judges—a table of elderly Gamesmistresses—conferred among themselves. I heard one of the phrases I had listened to from my room, woven now into a complete fabric of song. The singer was young and handsome, and his voice was pure and sweet. I thought of the singers among the magicians, lost now under the fallen mountains, and grew sad. The song was one which evoked sadness in any case. He finished in a fading fall of strings and was rewarded by a loud clamor of goblets upon wood. He took the prize. It was fitting. His was the most melancholy music of the evening. All the ladies loved it.

After this entertainment came an intermission during which the young women circulated among the tables to talk idly to the guests. One elegant girl wove her way to the table where I sat, body like a willow waving, garments swaying, face showing that smiling emptiness I had noted before. We greeted her, and she sat to take a glass of wine with us. She was obviously interested only in the tall chill Sorcerer who sat with us. He asked her politely what she was studying.

"Oh, ta-ta." She pouted. "It is all about Durables and the Ephemera, and I cannot get it in my head. It stays about one instant and then goes— who knows where."

The Sorcerer smiled but said nothing. Thinking to fill the silence, I said, "My own Gamesmaster gave us a rule which made it easier to remember. If a Talent is continuous, as for example it is with a Ruler or a Sorcerer, then the Gamesman is one of the Greater Durables or Adamants." She smiled. I went on, "Those in whom the Talent is discontinuous but still largely self-originated are among the Lesser Durables. Seers, for example, or Sentinels.''

She cocked her head prettily and looked up into the face of the Sorcerer. Still he said nothing. She made a little kiss with her mouth. ''The Ephemera, then? What is their rule?''

''Those Gamesmen who take their Game and power from others, sporadically, are of the Greater Ephemera,'' I said. ''Demons, for example, who Read the minds of others but only from time to time, not continuously. And finally there are the lesser Ephemera, those who take their only value from being used by other Gamesmen. A Talisman, for example. Or a Totem.''

''I see. You make it sound so interesting.'' She gazed up at the Sorcerer again after a quick ironic glance at me, and in that glance was all I had not understood until then. It was not that she failed to remember, not that she lacked interest in the subject. She *knew,* perhaps better than I, but had been taught not to show that she knew. I caught a sardonic smirk on the face of the Sorcerer and turned away angered. There was not that much difference between these, I thought, and the consecrated monsters of the magicians. I wondered how Silkhands could lend herself to this—this whatever it was. There might be time to ask her later, but now the intermission had ended and we were to be granted another song by the evening's champion.

He stood among us, smiling, relaxed, not touching his instrument until all present had fallen silent. When he touched the strings at last it was to evoke a keening wind, a weeping wind which focused my attention upon him and opened my eyes wide. He faced me as he sang, coming closer.

> ''Who comes to travel Waeneye
> knows what makes the wild-wind cry.
> Whence the only-free goes forth,
> shadow-giant of the north,
> cannot live and may not die,
> sorrowing the wild-wind cry.''

The wind music came again, cold, a lament of air. He was very close to me, singing so softly that it seemed he sang for me alone.

"Wastes lie drear and stone stands tall,
signs are lost and trails are thinned,
abyss opens, mountains fall,
Gamesman, Gamesman, find the wind. . . ."

Then he moved away, walking among the tables, humming, the music reminding me of night and bells and a far, soft crying in caves. He was standing next to Silkhands as he sang:

"Who walks the Wastes of Bleer must know
what causes this ill-wind to blow.
Shadowmen play silver bells,
krylobos move in the fells,
gnarlibars come leat and low,
listening to ill-wind blow."

He looked up to catch my eye again, sang:

"Mountains mock and mystify,
hiding Wizard's ten within.
One more walks the world to cry,
'Healer, Healer, heal the wind.' "

The music ran away as a wind will, leaving only a dying rustle behind it. There was a confused moment, then a barely polite tapping of goblets upon the table. They had not liked it. At once he struck up a lilting dance song with a chorus everyone knew. Within moments virtually everyone in the room had forgotten the wind song, if they had ever heard it, except Silkhands and me and a young woman who sat at Silkhands' table and now regarded me with an expression of total comprehension. She had large dark eyes under level brows, a pale face with a slightly remote expression, and a tight controlled look around her mouth, like one cultivating silence.

I, too, had found the song disquieting, though I could not have said why. All the evening's entertainment had done nothing but leave me irritated and cross. When Silkhands came to my room in the Guest House later, this irritation remained and I made her a free gift of it, not realizing what I was doing. I was speaking about the girl who had come to our table, about what I presumed to call her "dishonesty." Silkhands disagreed with me.

"Ah, Peter, truly you expect too much. Who was it came to your table? Lunette of Pouws? I thought so. Her brother wishes to establish an alliance with the Black Basilisks at Breem. So he seeks to interest Burmor of Breem in Lunette. She is his full sister, and she is no fool. She seems like to manifest a Talent which will fit her well enough among the Basilisks; however, Burmor wants no competitor in Beguilement at the Basilisk Demesne. Thus she plays witless before those he sends to look her over. What would you have her do? Stand upon her dignity and Talent, as yet unproven, and so cause her full brother annoyance and grief? If she goes to Burmor, she will be of value there as symbol of the alliance. She will be protected, and there will be time for her Talent to emerge."

This argument did not sit well with me, and I said so with much reference to the "consecrated monsters" I had seen in the place of the magicians. "They, too, were taught to be passive, or were so changed in the hideous laboratories that they could be nothing else. They, too, existed for nothing except to breed sons. . . ."

"You may recall," she said, "that Windlow once told us of the rules of the Game? How those rules had been made originally to protect; how those rules came to be more important than what they protected; how those rules came to be the Game itself! Well, those rules were made by men, Peter. Lunette chooses to make her own safety and her own justice within the Game. It is her choice."

She was so annoyed with me that I thought it wise to change the subject. "Who was that minstrel who won the prize? Did I mistake him, or did he sing to you and me alone of all that crowd?"

"Ah, one of my students, Jinian, thought the same. He has sung this wind song before. It seems to follow me wherever I go, into the orchards, the gardens. His name is Rupert of Theel, and he is well known among the musicians. Yesterday in my bath I heard 'Wild-wind weeps and ill-wind moans. Has the wind an eye? A hand? Has the wind sinews or bones? Healer, Healer, understand.' It so infuriated me I leaned naked from the window and told him to cease singing 'Healer' or 'wind' in my hearing."

"Well, last night he sang 'Healer,' but he also sang 'Gamesman,' " I commented. "He sang to me as well as you if he sang to either." We wondered at it a bit. What was there in it, after all? A song. There was this much in it: it linked the two of us together as did Windlow's prophecy. Musing on this I reached out to take her into my arms. She sighed upon my shoulder and we sat there for a long time in the candle shine and starlight, lost in our own thoughts. When she drew away at last, I began to tell her what had brought me to Xammer.

Thus Silkhands learned about the blues, and about Windlow's blue, the only person besides myself who knew of it, the first person beside myself to know the sorrow of it.

"I take the blue into my hand," I whispered. "Windlow comes into my mind, a gentle visitor, gentle but insistent. Silkhands, he struggles there. I feel his struggle. He inhabits my mind as a man might inhabit a strange house—no, a strange workshop where nothing is in its accustomed place. I feel him search for words he cannot find, seek explanations for things which are not there—connections and implications which might have been obvious to Windlow in the flesh but which he cannot find in me. He struggles, and it is like watching him drown, unable to save him."

"Not your fault," she soothed me. "Not your doing."

"No," I agreed. And yet it was my doing. "If I do not take him up, then he lies imprisoned in the blue, a living intelligence imprisoned as intelligence is imprisoned in these students of yours who must hide it to protect themselves. Oh, Silkhands, worst of all is when he wants me to read to him."

"Read? As a Demon Reads?"

"No, no. Books. A book. He wants me to read the little book, the one he called the Onomasticon, over and over. As though there were something in it he needs to know and cannot find. Oh, he is gentle, kind, but I can feel the sorrow like a whip."

At that she came into my arms again to comfort me, and we lay there upon the wide windowseat staring at the stars until we fell asleep. When I woke, stiff and sore, it was morning and she had gone. I went out to the necessary house behind the Guest House. (A silly place to have it. We had toilets near our rooms at the Bright Demesne.) The singer was there, Rupert, and I thought to find out about the wind song, perhaps find why it disturbed me so.

"I am interested in the song you sang," I said politely. "The one about the wind?"

"Better you than I, Gamesman," he said, making a face. "Would I could forget the thing."

I evinced surprise, and he laughed a short bark without amusement. "I heard it first at the Minchery in Leamer. They make shift there to train artists up from childhood, and there is a summer songfest at which many of us assemble to lend encouragement and judge the contests. There are always new songs, some written by students, some brought in from the Northern Lands. Many are of a caliginous nature, dark and mysterious, for the students love such. Well, this wind song was one of them. I heard it, and since have been unable to get it out of my head. I find me singing it when I eat, when I bathe, when I . . ." he gestured at the necessary house behind him.

"The places mentioned in the song? Waeneye? The Wastes of Bleer? Where are those?"

"Oh." He seemed puzzled. "I do not know that they exist, Gamesman. I took them for more mysteries. They may exist, certainly, but I know nothing of them." He smiled and bowed. I smiled and bowed. We took leave of one another. I believed he had told me all he knew. Considering how the song ran in my own head, I could believe it had haunted him.

When I saw Silkhands later in the morning, I asked, "Have you a cartographer at the School?"

"Gamesmistress Armiger Joumerie," she said. "A good Gamesmistress. A difficult person."

"Difficult or not, I would like to see her."

And I did see her that afternoon in my room at the Guest House, for no male may enter the School House. As the girls there were much valued for their ephemera they were much protected against its premature bestowal.

I asked the Gamesmistress whether she knew of a place called Bleer, or one called Waeneye. Also did she know of Leamer, or of any place where creatures called krylobos or gnarlibars might live. I had heard, I said, that gnarlibars lived in the north, but that might have been only talk.

"Bleer, Bleer," she mumbled to herself, stroking her upper lip with its considerable moustache as an aid to concentration. She was a big woman, larger than many men, and her face had a hard, no-nonsense look about it. "Yes. That jostles a memory."

"Possibly a mountainous place," I offered. The song had mentioned mountains and stone, an abyss, fells.

"No help, Gamesman," she said tartly. "If one excepts the purlieus around the Gathered Waters and Lake Yost, virtually all the lands and demesnes are mountainous. You are not untraveled! Surely this has struck you. How much flatland have you seen?"

I had to admit having seen little. The valley of the Banner was fairly flat, as were the valley bottoms leading into Long Valley in the southwest. Other than that I could think only of that vast, tilted upland which lay above the River Haws and south of the firehills and Schlaizy Noithn. I would not speak of that to the Gamesmistress, but the thought had reminded me of something. "Shadowpeople!" I said. "Where are shadowpeople said to dwell?"

"Find me a place they are said *not* to dwell," she replied. "They live in the far north and west, in the southern mountains below the High Demesne, in the lands around the Great Dragon purlieu far east of here. No, that is no help to you, Gamesman. Give me a bit of time and I will find it for you. The name Bleer echoes in my mind. I have seen it on a chart before." It echoed in my mind, too, but I could not remember where I had heard of it. Had I asked the right question, I would have had quicker answers.

As it was, Gamesmistress Joumerie returned to me that evening to say she had found the place.

"The Wastes of Bleer," she informed me, licking her lips at the taste of the place, "lie to the north. A highland, the canyons of the Graywater to the west, the vast valley of the River Reave to the east where lies Leamer or Leamers, called variously. If you intend to go there, I could recommend the road to Betand and the eastern route from there over Graywater. There is a high bridge there at Kiquo, the only one for many leagues. Or, River Reave is navigable as far as Reavebridge, or even Leamer in season. There are trails into the high country from there."

"What Games, Gamesmistress?" I asked her. "Is there any troubling there? What Demesnes are active?"

She snorted. "Wary are you? You are young to be so wary. My latest charts show little enough. The Dragon's Fire purlieu lies north on River

Reave, but there is no Game there currently or presently expected. Who knows what hidden Games may be toward? Or games of intrigue or desperation?'' She fixed me with an eye yellow as a flitchhawk's. ''If you are that wary, lad, best enter my School House here and learn to dissemble as these girls do.''

I flushed at that. She went stalking away to the door, making the floor shake. In the doorway she stopped to speak more kindly, seeing she had hit me fair. ''There is a cartographer in Xammer, in Artists' Street, by name one Yggery. He is honest, so far as that goes, by which I mean he will not put anything in a map he knows to be false nor leave out anything he knows to be true. This means his maps are rather more blank than most. Still, if you have treasure enough, buy a map from him before you go north. And if you take Silkhands with you (for I can see the tip of my nose in a mirror in a good light), care for her. She has had more of Gaming than many of us, and has burned herself in caring for others.''

I had not honestly thought of taking Silkhands with me until that moment. I had not thought she would want to leave Vorbold's House. Testing this notion, I asked her and was surprised to hear her say she would have made a trip north in any event.

''I go north to escort Jinian, my student,'' she said. ''I need a time away from Vorbold's House. There are some here who turn their eyes from the students to the Gamesmistresses, and I am . . . weary of that.''

''Have you been molested?'' I was angry and therefore blunt. I should have known better, for she laughed at me.

''In Vorbold's House? Don't be silly. Of course not. I have been sent proposals at intervals, and I have had to listen to a few representatives for the sake of . . . diplomacy. The offers have not been . . . unflattering.'' She fell silent, thinking of something she did not share with me, then, ''Save to those like us who do not value flattery. I know I do not, and I presume you have not changed.''

The expression on her face as she uttered this last was one I knew she used in the classroom, alert, polite, both encouraging and cautionary. I could hear her speaking thus to her students, ''Now, young ladies. We do not value flattery. . . .'' I giggled at the thought.

She stared at me for a moment as though I had lost my wits, then giggled with me. We ended up rolling onto the carpet to end in front of the fire, heads pillowed on various parts of our anatomies as we talked it over.

"I did sound properly Schoolhousy, didn't I?" she asked. "Well, being Gamesmistress does that to you. Perhaps I am too young for it. I am only twenty-one after all. Many of the students are older than I." She did not consider this remark at all important, but to me it came as a revelation. Only twenty-one. I was seventeen, almost eighteen, and she was only four years older? I had thought of her as . . . as . . . well, older-sisterly at least. I was suddenly aware of her thigh beneath my head and of a quickening pulse in my ears. I sat up too hastily, dumping her.

"Come now," I said overheartily, trying to hide the fact that my hands were trembling. "We must make plans. I am going from here to the ruins where I first met you because the men who attacked me on the road would have taken me there."

"Dindindaroo," she said, blinking in the firelight like an owl. "That's the name of the place, or once was. Dindindaroo, the cry of the fustigar. It is said the place was once a main habitation of Immutables."

"Truly? Why was it abandoned?"

"A flood, I think. And a great wind which laid waste to the land about there. At any rate, it was abandoned some three generations ago, perhaps eighty or a hundred years. We used to find old carvings and books when we were there. Himaggery spoke of sending a party of Rancelmen to explore, but he never did."

"So the Immutables once occupied this place, Dindindaroo. Well, some villainy is centered upon it now, and I must go there in the guise of the Pursuivant to see what I can find. After that, however, if no sign of Quench has been found, why should I not go with you to the northlands? Windlow's vision sees us there together, and the song directs us there. Let us go."

She agreed hesitantly. "I must take Jinian to the court of the Dragon King at the Dragon's Fire purlieu. He and another Ruler, Queen someone—I've forgotten her name—set up a Rulership there, a kind of King-Demesne. Having no sisters, he chose to build his strategy around sons rather than upon thalani, but all his sons save one were eaten in Game over the years. He has only one left, at school in Schooltown, Havad's House, I believe. He is desirous of children to replace those lost."

I remembered out of dim mists having heard that name. "Ah. So the Queen died. Or was lost in Game?"

"Died. Of too much childbearing to too little purpose, some say. Now he desires a strong young Gameswoman to bear him sons."

"Who will also die of too many babies?"

She smiled a secret smile at me. "No. Our students learn better than that. We may teach them covert game, Peter, but we teach them to survive at it and their children as well. Jinian will not over-bear."

I did not pursue the matter, though I thought with a pang of the girl who had given me that long, level, understanding look at the dinner. She had not looked like one who would go uncomplaining into such a life. Well. Who could say.

Silkhands went on: "It will be a few days before we are ready to leave. You have your own trip to make. How shall we combine our journeys later?" She looked at me, hopeful and luminous in the firelight. I would have promised to combine a journey with her to the stars, and she seemed to know that, making a pretty mouth at me in mockery. I gestured hopeless and resigned acquiescence, and we spent the remainder of the evening talking of other things. I think both of us thought then that we would become lovers. No. I think she thought it and I hoped it. We did nothing about it except stargazing. There seemed to be time, and no reason occurred to either of us to think time would run out. I can still remember the shape of her in firelight, half of her lit with a soft melon-colored light, the other half in darkness.

So the morning after that found me back in the inn with Chance. The Invigilator had come around to some extent. He would sit up when told, and walk, and eat, and relieve himself. He would do nothing at all unless told to do so, and the strange cap had been on him only one full day. When Didir looked into his head she found an emptiness. "As though untenanted," she said. I was sorry then that we had put the thing on him. "Perhaps if it had not been on him so long," whispered Didir, "the effect would have been less."

We thought this likely. My assailants could not have wanted to make me witless. What good would I have been to them in that condition? I could not even have served as bait. No, the Invigilator had simply been caught in his own trap, but I mourned nonetheless that his body lived while his mind was gone.

Before leaving Xammer, we went to Artists' Street to buy the chart Gamesmistress Joumerie had suggested, and also to the Gamehall to hire a Tragamor. Silkhands had arranged for the few blues held at Vorbold's House to be packed and delivered to the inn. The Tragamor, escorted by an Armiger, took them off to the Bright Demesne along with a message from me.

"I am going north," I wrote, "to stop at the ruins of Dindindaroo. Thence to the land of the Immutables to leave the messages entrusted to me by Himaggery, and thence on the Great North Road in company with Silkhands, traveling to the Dragon's Fire purlieu. Word may be sent to me in the care of the Gamehalls on the way. Let me know if you find Huld, or Quench. I have found something odd I think Quench would know about." By which I meant the cap, of course, a thing made by magicians or techs, if I ever saw one. I sealed the letter, then unsealed it and added a postscript. "All affection to Mavin Manyshaped and to my thalan, Mertyn."

I thought privately that it was a good deal easier to feel affection for them both when I was a good distance from them.

# 3

# Dindindaroo

We rode out of Xammer with me in the guise of the Pursuivant once more. He had been a man with lines in his face all crisscrossed from scowling, hard round cheeks and eyebrows which slanted upward over his nose to give him a falsely mournful expression. It was not a face which pleased me nor on which a smile fit easily, and after a time Chance told me to quit twitching it about and settle on something more comfortable for travel. "You can always gloom it a bit when we come to the ruins, lad," he said. "No sense making me the benefit of it while we're on the way." The Invigilator had no comment. We were still having to tell him when to drink and when to go into the bushes to pee, but Didir said there were glimmers of personality deep within which were beginning to emerge again. Evidently the evil little cap had done the same thing a devilish Demon might have done, wiped out all the normal trails in a brain to leave it without any tracks at all. My conscience still bothered me about that. There are worse things than being dead, and this might be one of them.

Once my face smoothed out into my own once more, it was a more comfortable trip. The ruins—Dindindaroo—were not far from Xammer, a short day's ride, no more. There was a lot of traffic on the road, too, for the comings and goings to and from Xammer were constant. Not only by emissaries of alliance hunters, either, but by merchants who found Xammer a profitable stop and a convenient place to buy luxuries for shipment farther north. One day I would go north on the road, I resolved, and see the jungle cities. Meantime, we amused ourselves, Chance and I, identifying Gamesmen in the trains. I saw a pair of Dragons, the fluttering cloaks painted with patterns of wings and flames and the feather crests snapping in the breeze. They nodded to us as they trotted past, hurrying away somewhere north, perhaps to the Dragon's Fire purlieu which was known for its population of air serpents. There were a good many exotic Gamesmen. I saw a Phantasm, gray and blue, faceplate faceted like a jewel, and a bright yellow Warbler who caroled a greeting at us as he passed, the subsonics and supersonics shivering our horses and making all the fustigars in the forests howl. There was a troop of brown-clad Woodsmen, a common Talent among the Hidaman Mountains where they are much valued to fell timber and fight fires because of their ability to foretell where fires will happen and move earth and start backfires of their own. Though I had heard of a Woodsman taking his troop halfway down the range in pursuit of a fire he had Seen which was accidentally caused by his troop only after they arrived. Even old Windlow had said that Seeing was not dependable, and I considered it a good part flummery. Perhaps it was this opinion which made me reluctant to call up Sorah as I felt it would not make her think well of me.

We saw a Thaumaturge and a Firedancer and a Salamander and then about evening came to the fork in the road where the winding trail led away to Dindindaroo, overgrown with weeds and not appearing to have been traveled at all for many seasons. I did not want to come upon the place in the dusk, even with Didir in my pocket telling me she could not Read any minds at all in the place. So we camped, Chance, the idiot Invigilator, and I, with me doing the cooking. Chance amused himself by having the Invigilator make the fire and gather firewood. I think he was making a pet of the creature. Come morning we were up and on the trail at early light, me with my face carefully shifted into a good likeness of the Pursuivant. I felt my Shifting slip away even before we saw the ruins swarming with men. Chance said, "Immutables," and I knew at once he was right. Well, Riddle might be among them, and he knew Chance, and it probably didn't matter that I could not hide my own face. Let me go as myself and tell part of the truth.

The men working on the ruins had it marked out with pegs and string and were busy digging and hauling loads away in large barrows. We stopped a distance away from the turmoil, waiting to be decently noticed, and a man came down the pile toward us, wiping his forehead and looking oddly familiar to me. When I told him who I was, he started a little and gave me an extremely curious glance which I put down to his not having expected a Gamesman to visit. I took pains to be polite, coming down from the horse and making no extravagant noises.

"Would Riddle be here?" I asked. "I have a message for him from the Bright Demesne."

The man went back up the tumulus, peering at me over his shoulder in a way that reminded me unpleasantly of the way the Armiger had ridden ahead of us on the road. Still, that feeling left me when Riddle himself came from some hideaway and stopped to peer at me nearsightedly as though he couldn't believe what he saw.

"Peter? You? In Pursuivant's dress? But—what does this mean? . . ."

I saved him his puzzlement, not wanting him to start thinking about my Talents or lack of them. He had turned quite pale in his confusion. "We had a bit of trouble on the road," I said. "A Pursuivant was among our attackers. He is dead now, poor fellow, and I put on his clothes to confuse those who had hired him. Whoever it was, they should have been here. So said this Invigilator." I pointed the man out, explaining his lack of interest in what was going on. "He's not very useful at the moment. He had a kind of cap thing in his pocket, a thing like those you showed me at Bannerwell. Well, we put it on him, and it's had this awkward effect. . . ."

Riddle was nodding and nodding at each thing I said, looking very uncomfortable and grim, which I thought still might have been caused by my appearing thus suddenly in the guise of another Talent. At any rate, he collected himself and asked what brought me. I repeated what I had said before, that I had expected to find whoever plotted against me in this place. "Haven't there been any Gamesmen about, Riddle? Have you seen anyone lurking?" To which he mumbled and said something or other about having been too busy to have noticed.

It was obvious he was preoccupied, so I gave him the messages Himaggery had sent (something to do with the search for Quench, in which some Immutables were assisting Himaggery) and told him I would stay in the vicinity for a day or two in case Himaggery sent a message for me. And, finally, he managed to shake off his discomfort, from whatever cause, and become hospitable.

I asked him what they were doing, and he offered us tea while explaining. "We are growing more and more crowded in the purlieu, Peter. Our councilmen decided we should expand our territory, and this ruin marks the southern edge of the lands our people once occupied. They called it Dindindaroo, after the sound of the fustigars who den in the canyons and forests. At any rate, my own grandfather was the leader here in his time. It is our intention to build here once again.''

''Wouldn't it be easier to build to one side of this ruin? Why all this digging and delving?''

He hemmed and hawed for a time before saying, ''Oh, there may be artifacts here which are of interest to our archivists and historians. We thought it a good idea to take a little time to salvage what might be left from a former time.'' Then he changed the subject. His explanations sounded weak to me. They did not seem to be salvaging. They were searching for something particular. At any rate, Chance drew me away to speak privately.

''There seems to be no Gamesman here now, lad, no one to do you harm. So it seems. But there is nothing to keep someone from coming in the night, and even if no Talent may be used with all these Immutables about, still there are knives and arrows that can do a good bit of damage. I'd like it better to be inconspicuous.''

I humored him. We took our leave of Riddle and rode away to the east. Once under the cover of the trees, however, Chance insisted we turn in a large circle which ended us west of the ruins. We found a cavelet well hidden behind tumbled stone, and when we had found the place, Chance asked that Didir look around us to see if anyone lurked. She reported only beast minds and bird thoughts, and I privately thought Chance must be among them to be so concerned. He disabused me of that notion.

''I had a suspicion,'' he said when we had settled down. ''We came to that place expecting to find one there who Games against you, Peter. No one was there but that Riddle and his Immutables. So what if that Riddle had not been a so-called friend of yours? What would we think then? We'd think, well, here is the one who set that Game on us. So what I want to know is, how do we know he didn't?''

''Riddle? Ridiculous.''

''Well, how so ridiculous? I dare say those Immutables have reasons and purposes of their own. Can't you imagine some reason he might want you all quiet and obedient to his will, for him to use some way?''

I could not. I tried. Riddle knew me as a Necromancer. What need or use could he have for me which I would not have fulfilled for him gladly at the asking? I thought of all possible combinations and alliances and strange linkages which could have come about—Huld, Prionde, the

Council, Quench, the techs, Riddle, even the minor Gamesmen such as Laggy Nap and his like. Nothing. I said so. Chance was not satisfied.

"Well, just because we can't think of what it might be doesn't mean it isn't. Would you give me that, lad?" I said yes, I could give him that. He went on, "So 'ware what you say. Don't go telling everything you know about where we're going and what we're about. Say we're going along with Silkhands to that Dragon's Fire purlieu because you and she are—well, give him that idea."

In the lands of the Game it did make sense not to trust too much. The only thing that bothered me was thinking of Riddle as a Gamer. Somehow, because he had no Talent, I expected him to be simple. When I said this to Chance, however, he corrected me with a hoot of laughter.

"Out on the sea, lad, where I spent many a season, we'd know a man by what he proved to be, not by what his mouth claimed for him. A man could be a devil or a good friend, and sometimes one and another time the other. Some Gamesmen are honest enough, I don't doubt, though they have the power to be all else without any to say them no, and some Gamesmen are evil as devils. So I doubt not the Immutables have their good and their bad, their complex and their simple. Well for you to suspect so, anyhow."

And with that, he left me to lie there, aroused by the puzzle but too weary to stay long awake. We went back to Dindindaroo the next morning to see if a message had come from Himaggery and to take leave of Riddle, for if he was what he pretended to be, a simple and honest man, then he would think more kindly of me for the courtesy. And if he was not what he pretended—well. We found him down in a hole, pale and frustrated of face, and he showed such discomfort at my arrival that I thought perhaps Chance was right. I dissembled. For all Riddle could have told, we were still his dearest friends.

"What are you doing down there, Riddle," I demanded. "Burrowing like a grole? Have you lost something? Or found it?" Even as I said it, I realized that the hole he was in was probably the same hole I had fallen into some several seasons ago when I had found the Gamesmen of Barish and the book Windlow called the Onomasticon. I gave him my hand to help him out, and he blinked at me as he brushed dust from his coat.

"I thought for a time we might have found some valuables left here by my grandfather,'' he babbled. ''All the inhabitants of the place fled, leaving everything. There was great loss of life, a flood, a great wind. . . .''

''What exactly are you looking for?'' I asked him, all polite interest and bland lack of concern. ''Would it help to raise up the dead here and ask them?'' Aha, I thought. If you do not want me to know what you are doing here, then you will not accept this offer.

And also aha, said a quiet voice in my head. If Riddle had wanted you to raise up the dead in this place without knowing what you were doing, might he not have arranged for you to be put into that strange cap the Invigilator carried? Hmmm? Chance gave me a look, and I turned away as Riddle shook his head and fussed and said no, no, the only one who had known was his grandfather and his grandfather was said to have died elsewhere, and besides, he doubted a Gamesman could raise Immutable dead. I nodded my acceptance of this while privately thinking that I could do it if I chose. Whatever it was that made them immune to Talents, I wagered it went away when they died.

I shook my head for the benefit of those standing about. ''It is probably just as well, Riddle. The longer they are dead, the less they remember of life. They hunger for life more the older they are, but they remember less. How long ago was the destruction?''

He thought some eighty years. His father had been a young man at the time.

''Well, you have waited a good time to seek what was lost,'' I said, all kindness and concern. ''A good long time.''

He mumbled something. I think the sense of it was that if he had known earlier what was lost, he would have come earlier to look for it. And this told me much. Riddle had lately learned something new. So. I was not of a mind to hang about making the man sweat. There would be better ways to find out. Besides, I was without Talent in this company and had only one man to stand beside me. It could be less dangerous to be elsewhere. I gave Riddle my hand and bade him farewell, putting the Invigilator in his care.

''He will dig for you, if you put the shovel in his hand,'' I said. ''And if any Gamesmen come here who seem to know him, I would be grateful if you would send word to the Bright Demesne.'' I did not want Riddle to think I suspected him of anything. In truth, I still did not know that I *did* suspect him of anything. All I could believe was that Chance was wiser than I, and that I would be wiser—far wiser to be more careful. If only I had remembered that later.

We rode away without talking, both of us preoccupied with our own thoughts. After a time I turned to Chance and said, "I don't necessarily believe it."

"Well, don't then," he said. "But it'd be smart to act as though you do."

"You know what he was looking for back there." I made it a statement, not a question.

"For those things you found, I guess. I notice you didn't offer them to him."

"The thing I noticed was that he said his grandfather left them there. How came his grandfather by them? And why did Riddle not know of them until recently? For I will bet my lost fur cloak that he did not."

Chance shrugged, mumbled to himself. Finally, "Would anyone else among those Immutables know? Or is it only Riddle who knows? What about his family?"

"He had only a daughter," I said. Then there was a long pregnant silence of such a quality that I looked back to find Chance's eyes upon me, brooding and hot. "Oh, no," I said. "I will not."

"She's buried nearby," he remarked. "Almost in sight of the ruins."

"I couldn't do that," I said flatly. It was true. I could not even think of raising the ghost of Tossa. It would have made me feel like a Ghoul, and I said as much.

"I didn't say you should take her with us," Chance said in mild reproof. "I didn't say you should drag her around."

I swallowed bile at the thought. Ghouls did raise certain kinds of recent dead and drag them into a kind of fearful servitude of horror, a thing which no self-respecting Necromancer would think to do. There were others who raised ghosts—Thaumaturges, for example, or Revenants, or Bonedancers. If what old Windlow and Himaggery had told me was true, full half of all Gamesmen would have some Talent at Deadraising. Full half of all Gamesmen would share *any* one Talent. If so, it was not a Talent generally used in the way Ghouls and Bonedancers used it, and I felt unclean at the thought.

"No," I said. "She died, Chance, without ever knowing she was dying. Often the dead do not know they are dead until we raise them up." In that instant I thought of Windlow with a kind of stomach-wrenching panic, then sternly put that thought down. "The ancient dead are only dust; they have forgotten life and possess only a kind of hunger which the act of raising gives them. I do not feel thus about the ancient dead. But the newly dead—ah, Chance, that is a different thing. With Tossa, she would know herself dead, and it would hurt her."

The memory of Mandor's ghost was recently with me. I was prepared to be as stubborn as necessary, but Chance only said, "Well, then we'll have to think up some other way to find out. How about someone dead for eighty years or so?"

"I don't know," I said.

"Do you think you could raise an Immutable?"

"You're thinking of Riddle's grandfather? Riddle said he didn't die in the ruins."

"Riddle said a lot of things. Don't know whether I believe him or not is all."

So we rode along while I thought about that. Riddle was digging in Dindindaroo. He had recently found out that something lay in the ruins which he needed? Wanted? Someone else wanted? Well, which he cared enough about to go to some trouble over, put it that way. Where had he found out, and when? Perhaps on that northern journey he and I had started to make together, when he had turned off toward the east just above Betand? Or in his own land? Perhaps someone had told him? Who? Or he had found old papers?

After a time Chance interrupted this line of thought to say, "You know, these Immutables are just like the rest of us. They drink a little and they talk. Get a little jolly, they do, and they talk. Pawns travel through their land on business. You and me, we could travel there."

Which was an answer, of course. We would need to disguise ourselves. Riddle knew me as a Necromancer only, or so I believed. Chance and I had been seen together once before in the Land of the Immutables, but only briefly. So suppose we went into that land as two pawns, traveling on business. What business? I put this to Chance.

"Well, as you left me to my own devices in that town of Xammer, boy, and without a hello, goodbye, how was your dinner, I got into a little game or two."

"Chance!"

"Now, now. Mustn't react hasty-like. A quiet game with honest folk is always good fun. Anyhow, I took my winnings in various small bits and pieces. A little gold, some gems, fripperies and foolishness. Thought I might turn a profit, up north."

"So that's what's in your saddlebags. I thought you were heavy loaded for having no pack beast."

He nodded to himself happily. I never knew what pleased Chance most—winning a game of cards or dice, finding a woman who was a good cook, or locating a wine cellar put together by a master vintner. Whatever else the world offered, he would choose one or more of those three.

He instructed me: "Enough in the bags to make us legitimate, lad. If you can change your face some and get out of those dusty black clothes. Wouldn't hurt to change horses, too. As may be possible not far from here."

Which was possible with Chance in charge of the trade. He went away leading my lovely tall black horse and came back with a high-stepping mare of an unusual yellow color with nubby shoes such as they use along the River Dourt, or so Yarrel had once told me. It was not an inconspicuous animal. However, he had obtained a pack beast in the trade and had done something to his own face while away from me, stuffed his cheeks to make them fatter and darkened his hair. He looked a different man, and it was easy to disguise myself as a younger version of the same. When we were done with this switching about we turned west to cross the Boundary River into the Immutables' own Land. We had decided to be the Smitheries, father and son, and Chance told me to ride one stride behind and mind my manners toward my elder, which so amused him in the saying he almost choked.

So that night I sat in a tavern and learned a lesson in gossip. Chance talked of the sea, and of horses, and of trading in general, and of the goods he had picked up in Xammer, and of the young women in that city and elsewhere, and of how the world had changed not for the better, and of a strange wine he had tasted once in Morninghill beside the Southern Sea, and of an old friend of his in Vestertown, and of a man he had known once who used to live in Dindindaroo.

"Oh, that makes you a liar indeed," said an oldster, sucking at a glass of rich dark beer which Chance had put into his hand. "If you knew such a one, he was old as a rock. Dindindaroo has been wreck and ruin this hundred year.''

"Not a hundred," interrupted another. "No, Dindindaroo was wreck and ruin in the time of my mother's father when my mother was a girl, and that was no hundred year."

"Oh, you're old as a rock yourself," asserted the first. "For all you're chasing the girlies like a gander after goslings, which you will never catch until the world freezes and Barish comes back. If it were not a hundred, it were near that."

"Ah, now," said Chance. "The man I knew was old indeed. Old and gray as a tree in winter. But he said he was there when ruin came down on the place, he said, like the ice, the wind, and the seven devils. Caught a bunch of the people, the ruin did. Or so he said."

"Oh, it did. Aye, it did. Caught a bunch of 'em."

"Caught old Riddle's grandfather, I heard," said Chance. "That's what the fellow told me."

"Oh, so I've heard. Free and safe he was, out of the place, then nothing would do but he go back for something he'd left there, and then the ruin came. That's the story. Buried in it, they said. Buried in it when the flood came down, and no sign of him and his contrack after that. Oh, a man'll do strange things, won't he, when ruin comes."

"He will, indeed he will," agreed Chance, nodding at me over his beer. At which I nodded, too, and agreed that a man will indeed do strange things.

"What was it he went back for, do you suppose?" asked Chance, as though it didn't matter at all.

"Who knows, who knows," murmured the second oldster, who was growing very tipsy with the unaccustomed quantities of free beer.

"His contrack," the loquacious oldster said. "That's what I heard. Was his contrack from the long ago time of Barish. That's what they kept at Dindindaroo. Charts and books and contracks to keep 'em safe until Barish comes back for 'em. That's what." And he hiccuped softly into his glass before looking hopefully to Chance once more who bought another round and changed the subject. They got into an argument then as to whether Salamanders are really fireproof. After that was a good deal of calling on the seven hells and the hundred devils, after which we went to bed to lie there in the swimming darkness talking.

"So he died there in the ruins, Chance. I have no bad feeling about calling him up. I didn't know him, and he's dead this eighty years, but Dorn himself couldn't call anyone up with all those Immutables about. All of them would have to leave."

"As they may do," suggested Chance, "if they heard that the thing they're looking for had come to light elsewhere."

"Elsewhere?"

"Somewhere far off. Leave it to me, Peter. We'll spend one more night here."

The which we did. And there was more buying of beer and more talk, and this time Chance made the circle of acquaintances larger so that there were more listeners to what was said. Middle of the evening came, together with jollity and general good feeling, and into a pause in the noise, Chance dropped his spear.

"You know, it was odd your mentioning Dindindaroo last night," he said to the oldster at his side.

"Odd? Was it? Did I? Oh, yes. So I did. What was odd?"

"Oh, only that I met a man in Morninghill, not a season gone, and he told me he'd dug up treasures around Dindindaroo."

At this there was general exclamation and interest. Chance turned to me for verification, and I said, "Oh, he said so, Father, yes. Dug up treasures, he said, and was selling them moreover."

Chance nodded, said nothing more, waited. The questions came. What had the man found? The Smitheries, father or son, did not know. Something small and valuable, they thought. Something wonderful and rare, for the man was a famous dealer in such. Old things, certainly. Then, when interest was at its height, Chance led the conversation away from the subject onto something else. I saw two dark-cloaked men leave the place immediately thereafter, and when I went to the window for a bit of air I could hear the pound of hooves going away south.

We slept there that night, and on the morning went out of the Land of the Immutables, riding publicly east toward the Great North Road. Once out of sight, we turned into the forests and began the circle which would bring us into the cover of the trees nearest the ruins of Dindindaroo.

We spied upon the place, I with my Shifter's eyes, keen as any flitchhawk's, and Chance with a seaman's glass he carried with him. Sure enough, there were two dark-cloaked men talking with Riddle, the three of them standing upon a mound of crumbled stone and soil, Riddle gesturing as though he were in a considerable turmoil. Troubled he was. His face was white with frustration. After a time they settled down, and by noon they had reached some decision, for many of them went away north into their own land while others, Riddle among them, rode south. So. He was going to look around in Morninghill, and a long weary journey that would be.

We waited until early evening, until the westering sun threw long golden spears across the tumbled stone, and then we came to the ruins and walked about on them. The industrious diggers had changed them about somewhat. Still, the crumbling walls were there where Dazzle and Borold had sheltered to watch the fire dance, and so was the high slit window where I had hung my shirt to counterfeit a ghost. I stood, looking at it, feeling that deep brown emotion made of dusk and smoke and sorrow which is so piercing as to be sweet beyond enduring. Then I shook myself and took Dorn into my hand.

"Well, Peter," he said to me in my mind. "Here lie many dead. Would you have us raise them all?" He knew what I had thought of, but he was ever courteous, treating himself as a guest. Besides, in clarifying for him, I made clear to myself as well. "A name," he said. "Did you neglect to learn the man's name?"

I uttered an oath, disgusted with myself. If we were to draw out one from among so many, a name would be needed for we did not know precisely where he lay. "What was his name?" I growled to Chance. And he answered me, soft as pudding, well Riddle of course, same as his grandson. So we went with that.

I began to sense the dead about us, the feeling of them, the luxuriant quiet of them. They were at peace in the long slow heat of summer and the long slow cold of winter, the ageless waft of the wind and the high cry of the hawk upon the air. In them the leaves moved and the wavelets of the river danced. In them sorrow had no place; time for sorrow had gone with the turn of the seasons and the fall of the leaves. "Pity," said Dorn, "to disturb this peace."

Still, he called the name of Riddle into the quiet of the place, drawing out and up, and at last we saw a little whirlwind of dust turning itself slowly upon the tumulus before us, spinning and humming a quiet sound into the twilight. Through this whirling dust the sun fell, turning it golden, so that we confronted a shining pillar and spoke as with a Phoenix, for so those Gamesmen whirl into flame and are consumed before rising once again.

We asked, and asked again. This revenant was not so old as those we had raised in the caves beneath Bannerwell, so we had created no monster of dust which hungered for life. Neither was it so short a time after death as the raising of Mandor, so there should have been no remembered agonies. Despite this, it seemed disinclined to speak with us, resisted being raised. I was about to give up when I heard Didir within, unsummoned, feeling—was it excited? Surely not. Impetuous. "Let me." She reached into that whirling cloud and seemed to fumble there as though Reading it, making some tenuous connections of sparkling dust.

Then the humming cloud took the shape of a man, a wavery shape, still resistant, not unlike Riddle in appearance, looking at something I could not see.

"I see Dorn," the phantom said. "Barish promised us immunity, Gamesman. He promised, but I am raised from the dead by Dorn. Ah, but then, I broke my pledge, my oath to Barish. All unwitting, all unwise. Forgive and let go. . . ."

Chance and I looked at one another, a hasty, confused glance. This was not what we had expected. I stuttered, reaching for a question to clarify. "Riddle, tell me of your pledge to Barish."

"Barish . . . Barish. He gave us immunity from your power, Gamesman, for us and our children forever, immutable throughout time, so he said. And in return we must keep his body safe, keep the bodies of his Gamesmen safe where they lie, north, north in the wastes, north in the highlands where the krylobos watch. We must keep the Wizard safe, and the Wizard's eleven. But he went away and did not return. I brought the Gamesmen here, Barish's book here, thinking to find him somewhere, find him and return them, but the waters came, the waters came and I died. . . ." The figure writhed, became the humming cloud once more. From it the voice came in prayer and supplication, "The contract broken, all unwitting . . . and Barish's promise broken as well for I am raised by Dorn to suffer my guilt. Ah. Forgive. Let me lie in peace. . . ."

It was not my voice that said it, and not Dorn's. I thought it was Didir, though I could not be sure. "You are forgiven, Riddle, faithful one. Go to your rest."

The cloud collapsed all at once and was gone. The sun lowered itself below the undulant line of hills. Dark came upon the tumulus and in the forest a fustigar howled, to be joined by another across the river. A star winked at me, and I realized that I saw it through brimming tears. Something had happened. I was not sure what it was, or why, and the Gamesmen in my pocket did not know either. It was as though they and I had listened in upon some conversation from another time, a thing familiar and strange at once—familiar because inevitable and strange because I could not connect it to anything I knew. Chance was watching me with a good deal of concern, and I shook my head at him, unable to speak.

"Well," he said when I could hear him. "What went on there?"

I tried to tell him. All I could get out was that the answers to all our puzzles seemed to lie in the Wastes of Bleer.

"Riddle's grandfather brought some things here from the Wastes of Bleer," I said.

"I think it would help us if we stopped talking around and around," he said thoughtfully. "Let's not say 'things.' What was brought here was those little Gamesmen you found and the little book you gave Windlow."

"I have it with me," I said. "There may have been other things as well."

"No matter. What was lost was the Gamesmen and the book. Now did this Riddle fellow steal them?"

"No!" I was shocked. "No. He was supposed to have them. Supposed to keep them safe—them and the . . . bodies."

The light that engulfed me then seemed to be around me in the world, but it was only inside my head. The bodies. Didir's body. Lying in the northlands, waiting for her. *Her.* Her I had in my pocket, not merely a blue, not merely a Gamespiece, but a person awaiting . . . what? Resurrection? Awakening? Tamor, there in the northlands, Tamor who had saved my life more than once. And tragic Dealpas. And Trandilar. Oh, Gamelords, Trandilar! Voluptuous as boiling cloud and as full of pent energies, erotic, beguiling Trandilar. And Dorn. Dorn who was almost my elder brother in my head, lying there in the northlands, awaiting his renewal.

And all the while that part of me thought yes, oh, yes they must be found and raised up, awakened, another part of my mind said—no. No. They are mine, mine. My power comes from them. *My* Talents. I will not give them up. And the first part of me recoiled as though a serpent had struck at me inside myself so that I gasped, and gagged on the bile that rose in my throat. I struggled while Chance shook me and demanded to know what was wrong, what was wrong. Oh, Gamelords, what was wrong was me!

And then, somehow, I managed to thrust the conflict away, to stop thinking of it. I knew, knew it was there, but I would not think of it. Not then.

"Riddle's grandfather had a covenant with Barish," I choked. "But Barish disappeared, didn't come back. So Riddle's grandfather brought some things here—maybe hoping to find Barish. Maybe for safekeeping. Only wreck and ruin came on Dindindaroo."

Chance objected. "The covenant couldn't have been with Riddle's grandpa only." I shook my head. Obviously not. The contract must have been with the Immutables, father and son and grandson, generation after generation. Chance went on, "Those bodies have been there how long?"

I was careful not to think when I answered. "A thousand years. More or less. And do not ask me how Barish survived or came and went during that time for I don't know, Chance. It does not bear thinking of."

"So now what's our Riddle searching for? What's he up to?"

"Duty," I replied. "The covenant. The contract. The pledge his fore-fathers made to Barish. Oh, Chance, I don't know. I can't think of Riddle as anything but honorable. It's too confusing."

"Well, lad, don't get into an uproar over it," he said, giving me a long measuring look. "Whatever we don't know, we do know more than we did."

"Not enough more," I mourned, thinking of the hundred questions I should have asked the ghost. I could not call him up again. Would not. He had been given absolution by someone, and I would not undo it. I felt tears slide down my face.

"Maybe not enough more," Chance agreed, "but some more." He built a fire then and gave us hot soup, then some wine, and then an interminable story about hunting some sea monster during which I fell asleep. When I woke in the morning, I was able not to think about the disturbing thing, and the day was sharp-edged enough to live in.

# 4

# The Great North Road

I TOLD CHANCE ABOUT THE SINGER in Xammer who had sung about wind to me and Silkhands. A mere song seemed a foolish reason to go exploring the northlands, and I hoped Chance, who was never loath to declaim upon foolishness in general, would say so. This would give me reason not to go, but I did not ask myself, then, why I wanted such a reason. Instead I made excuses. Himaggery and Mavin would need me, I said to myself, waiting for Chance to say something to give substance to my rationalization.

But he said, "What was it made you think the singer sang to you?"

"Only that he sang of the far north," I said without thinking, "and in the Bright Desmesne a Seer told me my future lay there . . . with Silkhands." I did not say the Seer was Windlow.

"Well then, that's twice," said Chance. "And Riddle's grandpa is three times. Remember what I always said about that. Once is the thing itself, twice is a curiosity, but three times is Game."

I did remember. It had always been one of Chance's favorite sayings, particularly when I had committed some childish prank more than twice. "Whose Game? Who would be pulling me north?"

"Well, lad, there's pulling and there's pushing. The ghost was lamenting the loss of those things you carry. And maybe those things you carry are lamenting the loss of their bodies. I would if it was me. Maybe it's them want to get back where they came from."

So Chance was no help, no help at all. The knife of conscience twisted, and the serpent of guilt writhed under the knife. Was it possible? Could they be pushing me without my knowing? I tried to say no. "They have to use my brain to think with, Chance. They are only—what did old Manacle call it—patterns of personality. They are whatever they were when they were made. Didir comes into my head always the same Didir.

She uses my mind, my memories to think with, but she does not carry those memories back into the blue. They stay in my mind, not hers. What I forget, she cannot remember. They couldn't pull or push without my knowing!'' I said this very confidently, but I was not sure. "And I'm not sure that Silkhands and I ought to go north for such a reason. It's probably very dangerous.''

He looked at me in astonishment. "And what do I hear? Peter talking about dangerous? Well, and the daylight may turn pale purple and all the lakes be full of fish stew. I thought never to hear such stuff after Bannerwell. If we are not here to seek out mysteries and answer deep questions, why are we?''

"Why, Chance.'' I laughed uncomfortably. "You're a philosopher.''

"No.'' He rubbed his nose and looked embarrassed. "Actually I was quoting Mertyn.''

I might have known. Oh, Gamelords, I could not turn my back on this thing without feeling cut in half. I could at least pretend to go wholeheartedly, even if I were torn. Why not follow the scent laid down for me as a fustigar follows a bunwit, "Head high and howling,'' as Gamesmaster Gervaise was wont to say. These agonized thoughts were interrupted.

"Where did you and Silkhands arrange to meet?''

"She will be leaving Xammer soon, tomorrow or the next day. I thought it better not to travel together so close to the Bright Demesne. If someone is watching and plotting, let them work at it a little. I told her we would meet her below the Devil's Fork of the River Reave, at the town there. Here, let us see.''

I burrowed out the chart we had been at such pains to buy, spreading it upon the ground with stones at the corner to keep it flat. It was well made, on fine leather, the lettering as tiny and distinct as care and skill could make it. I found where we were, between the ruins and the Great North Road, then traced that road north with my finger to the place it split below the fork in River Reave. The town was there. Reavebridge.

"Well,'' I said, "we can go in disguise, on the road or off it; or in our own guise, on the road or off it. You are the wary one. I leave it to you.''

"Then let us continue as Smitheries, father and son,'' he said. I agreed

379

to that, and we packed up our things to ride away northeast where stretched the Great North Road.

The river which the Immutables call the Boundary came out of the northeast, and we followed it through the pleasant forests and farmlands north of Xammer. Ahead of us we could see the frowning brows of Two Headed Mountain, two days' ride away, which cupped the Phoenix Demesne at its foot. Farther north were the bald stone tops of Three Knob, hazed with smoke from the foundries there. These were both landmarks I remembered from my years at Schooltown, though I had never yet seen either of them much closer than we saw them on our way. Behind Three Knob, between it and the rising range of eastern mountains, was said to be what Himaggery called a Thandbarian Demesne made up of Empaths, Mirrormen, Revenants . . . I couldn't remember the other four Thandbarian Talents by Himaggery's scheme of Indexing. His scheme depended upon listing all the Talents which shared porting as a Talent, first, then all those left which shared Moving, then Reading, and so on. I wasn't sure it was any easier to remember than the old Indexes which listed each Talent as a separate thing, unique of its kind. One didn't seem to make any more sense than the other. There were still thousands of different Gamesmen. If the Talents were evenly distributed, said Himaggery, then half of all Gamesmen would have any one of the Talents. Still, Himaggery was attached to his scheme, and according to him there were seven Thandbarian Talents and over a thousand Elatorian ones. And no Necromantic ones at all except for Necromancers themselves. Which was idiotic, because there *were* Necromantic ones, Ghouls and Bonedancers and even Rancelmen.

Oh well, and foof. Still, since I'd been thinking about them, I asked Chance if he'd ever seen a Mirrorman (I never had), and he gave me a look as though he'd bitten into something rotten. "Yes, lad, but don't ask about it. I was a time being able to sleep at night again, after, and I don't relish the memory." Well. That was interesting.

It was less than a day's ride to the Great North Road where it crossed the Boundary River over a long sturdy bridge which had a look of Xammer about it, the railings being turned and knobbed like the balcony railings I had seen in the town. Its building had undoubtedly been commissioned by the town leaders in order to make travel—and trade—easier. Past the bridge was a campground, a place with a well and toilets and a place providing food and drink and firewood. The night was warm, so we bought food ready cooked and sat in a quiet corner of the place to eat it. Since we had chosen to sit fireless, our eyes were not flame dazzled and we could see who came in. Who came in was a Bonedancer, black and white, helmed with the skull of some ancient animal long extinct. He had either left his train of skeletons outside the place or currently had none, for which I was grateful. Bonedancers have enough Talents, including Necromancy, to raise dry bones and make them dance—or to do other things if moved to malice. Mostly they prey upon pawns in remote villages, telling fortunes and threatening horrors. I wondered how they could do it, wondered if they were ever reluctant to do it, wondered if perhaps there were many Bonedancers who simply did not exercise their Talents at all just as some Ghouls refused. Still, having the Bonedancer there did not upset me much. At first.

Then, however, came three more together: an Exorcist, a Medium, and a Timereacher. Chance drew in breath in a long, aching sigh as the three joined the Bonedancer, all at one fire, all talking together. "Game toward," he murmured. I was inclined to agree with him. Why else so many dealers with the dead in this one place?

"What is it Timereachers do?" I asked. "See the past?"

"It's said so," he whispered to me. "Mediums as well. A combination of Seeing and Deadraising? So I've heard."

"Exorcists too," I said. "Seeing, Healing, Deadraising. Able to settle ghosts, I recall, and perhaps to See where a ghost may trouble before it actually begins haunting. Still, to have all three, plus a Bonedancer? Someone means to raise something great, and he wishes to be sure he can put it to rest again. Who do you think?" The four were taking no notice of anyone around them, but there was something almost familiar about one of the figures. What was it made my skin crawl?

"Do you wish we were away from here?" I whispered.

"Enough to get away from here," he murmured in reply. It needed no discussion. He stood and walked away to the toilets, merely another one in a constant stream of toing and froing. After a moment, I went the same way. We met at the picket line, loosed our horses, and led them quietly into the night. Inasmuch as we had prepared no food for ourselves, nothing had been unpacked. When we had led them far enough for quiet's sake, we mounted and rode northward again, seeing the yellow glows of the little fires dwindle behind us in the dark. I was thinking, suspecting, wondering about the Gamesmen we had seen, the way they had moved and walked, the order of their arrival. Four. A Bonedancer, an Exorcist, a Medium, and a Timereacher. Three with Seeing; two with Healing; one to hold Power; one to raise Fire; and all four to Raise the Dead. I groped for Dorn in my pocket and read him this list.

"If such a four can find a battlefield," he whispered in my mind, "or the site of a great catastrophe in which many died, not so long that bones have fallen to dust yet long enough that flesh has left the bones, why then, were I Gaming, I would guess those four will raise a multitude and will seek, thereby, to do some evil work. . . ." I waited for him to go on. After a long time, he said, "A Healer may Heal. Know also a Healer may Unheal. Do not let the Medium or Exorcist lay hands upon you. . . ."

I had already learned that in School House, the unwisdom of letting those with the power of the flesh (another name for Healing) lay hands upon one. An Exorcist could lay hands on one and leave a bloody hand-print where he had broken every little blood line in one's flesh. It was said, among boys, that Mediums could raise the dead and set them on your trail, and that they would follow forever. I asked Chance if he believed that.

"Well, there are haunts set, lad. You told me you put down one such in Betand. And there are Ghostpieces."

"I have yet to hear one straight word about Ghostpieces," I said with considerable asperity. "Windlow mentioned them once, and others have talked of them. I have never learned what it is they can and cannot do. Perhaps in your wide travels, Chance, you've learned the answers to all this." I was being sarcastic.

He became very dignified at once. "Lad, don't get all exercised at me. So there's Deadraisers on the Great North Road, and so you think they have something to do with you. Well, I'm not ringing any great bell to tell them where you're hid. I don't know a midgin more about Ghost-pieces than the next one; what we've heard is all. We've heard of things raised up which could not be put down again. We've heard of things that turned on those that raise 'em. Himaggery would say to put your reason to work on it, and I can't say better than that."

When Chance got offended like that, there was no use trying to get anything out of him, so I rode along feeling ashamed of myself. Reason said that anything raised had to take power from somewhere. Reason said that, and so did experience, for when Dorn had raised up the dead under Bannerwell, I could feel the power flowing from him—me. But then once they were raised up, they went on their own—at least those in Bannerwell had. It had been like pushing a wagon from the top of a hill, a hard push to get it started, then it rolled of itself. So at least under *some conditions* things raised up would move on their own. Well, reason had not led me far. I would have to think more on it.

Meantime, we had come so far on the road that the Phoenix Demesne stood due east of us. It was time to rest, for us and for the animals. Here and there in the flat farmland, crisscrossed by a thousand little canals which flowed down from the east fork of the River Reave, were small hillocks covered with trees, woodlots left to provide fuel for the farms. In one of these copses we took cover for what remained of the night, tethering the animals so they could not wander out to be seen from the road. I went to sleep in discomfort and foreboding. Gamelords know what I dreamed, but I was so wound up in my blankets that Chance had to help me out of them in the morning, and the sweat had soaked them through.

We breakfasted over a small fire, built smokeless and quickly extinguished when the first travelers appeared on the road. We lay behind a shield of dried fern, peering through. There was an hour or so of usual travel, farm wagons, a herd of water oxen, a girl leading three farm zeller by the rings in their noses, their udders swinging full before milking. Then came a burst of travelers from the south, all riding speedily without looking around them, then another three or four, then a space, then a bunch riding with eyes ahead as though intent upon covering the leagues. There was another little space, then two men riding hard and whipping their animals. After them, the bones.

They came in a horde, a hundred, perhaps more, complete skeletons, so loosely joined that the arms and legs might go off dancing on their own, jerking and rattling, only to come back to the other bones and accumulate once more into more or less complete sets, the grinning skulls bouncing and lunging at the tops of the backbones as though on springs. Behind this clattering aggregation rode the Bonedancer on a shabby black horse, and behind the Bonedancer the Exorcist, the Timereacher, and the Medium—No! It wasn't a Medium. In the firelight the night before I had seen only the dark gray cloak pulled forward, hiding the face. Today the cloak glittered with gold spiderweb embroidery and the hood was thrown back to reveal the magpie helm beneath. A Rancelman—same Talents as a Timereacher, but with Reading added. I sharpened my Shifter's eyes to see more clearly, then muttered an oath as I saw more clearly than I liked.

"It's Karl Pig-face," I said. "A Rancelman!"

"No!" Chance fiddled with his glass, easing it through the dried fern so as not to betray us where we lay. "So it is! But what's wrong with his face? That isn't the Karl you knew!"

I looked again, more carefully. It was Karl Pig-face, right enough, but the face was . . . empty. Pale. Dry, rather than sheened with sweat as I had always seen it. At that instant, his head began to turn toward me, and as his head turned every skull in that endless train of bones began to turn also. Without thinking, I reached for Didir, felt her flow into me, and made my own mind dive down like some depth-dwelling fish to let her shield me. Through my eyes, I felt her watch the skeleton heads swing restlessly to and fro, like pendant fruit, the wormholes of the empty eyes seeking me. Then Karl's head faced forward once more, and they went on, on to the north. I did not move or speak until they were vanished in dust, beyond even a Shifter's ability to see them.

"That one sought you, Peter," whispered Didir. "Sought you out of hate, malice, and because he is forced to do it. He wears a cap, like the other one you are remembering. He felt you, Peter."

"But he did not tell them. . . ." I replied wonderingly.

"They are fools," she said. "Whoever wears the cap will do only what he is told. They told him to find you, not to tell them he had found you. So he found you, lost you, and went on seeking. Their stupidity has saved you, this time."

"Who?" I breathed.

She did not answer. I had not thought she would. Karl had not known who sent him, and for her to attempt to Read any of the others would have been to signal our presence.

"So we are behind them now," said Chance.

"Behind *them*," I said. "But who knows how many have been set on my trail. It began the minute we left the Bright Demesne. I am not such a fool as to think these boneraisers are the end of it. Someone has gone to considerable trouble."

"Ah," said Chance.

"Huld!" I said. I was certain of it. It had all the marks of Huld, all his energy, his relentless malice, his fascination with the mechanisms of the techs. Who else could have learned from Mandor that Karl Pig-face was my enemy? Who else would have known of my association with Silkhands . . . *Silkhands!* "Silkhands is in great danger," I said. "Huld would not let the chance pass to use her against me. He will take her when she leaves Xammer, depend upon it, and she is all unwary of this."

"Well, lad, I wouldn't let him do that if I were you."

Curse the man. No sympathy. No hooraw and horror, no running about squawking. Merely "don't let him do that." Tush. Xammer was more than a hard day's ride south, and she might be leaving at any time. Or have left already.

"There's that Hafnor," said Chance, fixing me with his beady little eyes. "In case you've forgot."

Damn him. Of course I hadn't forgotten. The idea made me sick to my stomach was all. Stopping existing in one place. Flicking away to another place. Starting to exist there. All in an instant. It was worse than the bones. I felt my inner parts lurch and sway, a kind of vertiginous gulping of the guts.

"No other way I can see," said Chance, still staring at me.

With no sense of volition about it at all, I reached into the pouch to find Hafnor, knowing him in the instant by the unfamiliarity of him. I clenched my hand around him and took a deep, aching breath, only to have my mind filled with a gust of mocking laughter. "Well, and where are we here?" I felt someone using my eyes, my nose, my tongue to taste the air, my other hand to feel the ground beneath me. I saw the shape of every tree, the volume of the leaves against the sun, felt the texture of the dried grasses. "That's here," said the laughing voice. "Where do we want to go?" I tried to explain about Silkhands, about Xammer, but felt only a mad, laughing incomprehension and impatience. "Where, where, where? What walls? What smell of the air? What floors? What doors leading in and out? What windows? Draperies? Furniture? What landmarks seen through those windows? Where, where?"

All I could think of was the room in the Guest House, and I tried to remember it in a way that would suit Hafnor. Sudden memories surged up, ones I had not known of, the color and sound of the fire, the feel of the woolen carpet on my hands, the smell of the polish used on the furniture. The memories assailed from every side, and I dropped the tiny figure of Hafnor in panic, to stand heaving like an overridden horse. When I had panted my way back to a kind of sanity, I said to Chance, "If I go, and if I am gone when night comes, then go to . . . to Three Knob. Get rid of that yellow horse and his strange shoes. Tell anyone who seems interested that the young man who was with you has gone away . . . to Vestertown, or Morninghill. But you go to Three Knob and wait there, however long it takes me. We'll meet you there, Silkhands and I."

He did not argue or make any great fuss about it, merely watched me, nodding the while, as I took Hafnor into my hand again. I summoned up the memories of that guest room and saw them take visible shape before me, as though framed in a round window. From the corner of my eye, I saw another window which looked out onto a flame-lit cavern, and another which showed the attics of Mertyn's House in Schooltown, and another which showed the long, half-lit corridors of the magicians' lair beneath the mountains. I spun, seeing these windows open about me, as though I stood at the center of a sponge or a great cheese, all around me holes reaching away to every place I had ever been or known of. "Where?" whispered Hafnor, and I turned to the hole which showed the guest room in Xammer, stepped through it, and stumbled upon the rug before the cold fireplace to fall sprawling.

When I had stopped shaking and had time to get up and brush myself off, for I was still covered with half dried grasses from that hill beside the road, far to the north, I sneaked down to the courtyard and appeared there to the first person I could find from Vorbold's House. It was Games-mistress Joumerie, who looked me over curiously and answered me words I did not like.

"Silkhands? Why, no, Gamesman. She rode out this morning with young Jinian and several servants and two Armigers for safety's sake, riding to King Kelver's purlieu, away north. They will not move over fast, not so far you may not catch them up, ride you swiftly."

I left her with scant courtesies to find a hidden corner and take Hafnor into my hand once more. "What do I do now?" I begged. "I must find her, but I don't know the road well enough to . . ."

"Hoptoad, lad," came the laughing voice with more than a hint of malice at my discomfiture. "Hoptoad. Do you look far ahead, keen as your eyes will go, and I will do the rest." That is what we did. I looked as far down the road as I could see, sharpening my vision to the utmost, spying the place ahead, the trees, the canals, whatever might be about, bit on bit, and then we *flicked*, and I was in that spot. Then I did it again, and flick, and again, and flick, each time scanning the road between to be sure we did not miss her. Until we saw the confusion and heard the screaming and *flicked* to find ourselves among a crowd, all shouting and running about near the unconscious body of one Armiger and the bleeding, perhaps dead, body of another.

I shook one of the bystanders and demanded that he tell me quickly what had happened. He pointed a trembling finger at the forest edge. "Ghoul," he whispered. "Came with a horde of dead out of the trees. The Armigers tried to fight them, but you can't fight that. The Ghoul took the women. Dragged them away into the trees."

Though obviously frightened, he had kept his wits about him. I ran for the forest, knowing that Hafnor could not help me there. It would take Grandfather Tamor, swift flyer, to lift me up where I could see. So it was. He caught me up like a feather, moved me like a swooping hawk to peer this way and that, seeking the movement of leaves or the rustle of undergrowth below, quartering again and yet again, hearing only silence, working slowly westward, a little faster than a man might run.

It was the cold first, then Silkhands' voice which led me to them. The Ghoul could not stop her chatter any more than I had ever been able to do, and her voice went on resolutely, almost as though she knew someone would be searching for her. I came into a tree top to watch them. The Ghoul dragged them along, one on either side of him, his host of dead following in a shamble of rotting flesh. Ghouls do not move clean bones; they have the Talent of Moving, of Power, of Raising the Dead. How much power did this one have? Plenty, it seemed, and was drawing more, for the place was icy as winter. I hung above them judging the distance.

Then as he passed below I stooped upon him, screaming as I flew, "Ghoul's Ghast Nine, I call Game and Move!" as I snatched the two girls from him and launched myself upward toward another tree. . . .

Only to know in one hideous moment that I had played the fool, the utter, absolute and unGamed fool. I had called a risk play, an Imperative, unwise and unready as I was, and the Ghoul would not ignore it. I hung there in the tree, the girls reaching out to cling to the branches as the strength left my arms. There was no power in the place to draw and I was weak . . . weak. I was in the Ghoul's Demesne, and he had drawn it all. Such power as I had I had expended prodigiously in the flick, flick, flick of Elator's hunt in finding them, in the reckless flight and swoop and call. Now there was no more strength in me than enough to move myself away a few yards, myself only, and no way to get more. I gasped, unable even to think what might be done.

I saw him reach for his power. He had more than I would have guessed, for two of the rotting liches staggered to the tree where we clung and began to climb, clotted eyes fixed upon us. They climbed awkwardly, leaving parts of themselves stuck to various small twigs and branches, but they came higher by the moment. Beneath them, others assembled, waiting, lipless mouths gaped in silent grins of amusement at the fruit about to fall into their hands and jaws. I heard Silkhands whimper, saw the girl, Jinian, glaring down at the Ghoul while rumbling curses in her throat. I wanted to close my own eyes, half dead as I was with cold and terror. I could fly myself away to another place, me, alone, with no burden. Or move Silkhands away without me. No more than that, and the place cold, cold.

Below me the Ghoul laughed and screamed into the quiet forest, "Armiger's Flight Ten, fool flyer. Armiger's Flight Ten." He was calling my death and the death of those two with me, and I knew it as did they.

I wondered if I would have the strength to move Silkhands away. My hand clenched in my pocket, clenched, and then gripped again as I felt that other unfamiliar shape in my fingers. Buinel. Sentinel. Firemaker. He came into my mind like a bird onto an unfamiliar nest, fussing and turning. I felt the thousand questions he was about to ask, anticipated the lengthy speech he was about to make. Oh, something within me recognized him, knew him for that Buinel whom Windlow had called Buinel the flutterer.

The branch under my foot swayed. I looked down into the face of one of the liches as it fastened a partly fleshed hand upon my boot. I kicked wildly, and the thing fell away as Jinian shouted shrilly at my side.

"Buinel," I cried silently. "Fire. Or we die, you die, we all die. Forever."

"Who?" he fussed. "Who speaks? What authority? What place is this? Who is that Ghoul? What Game?"

"Buinel," I shouted at the top of my voice, startling a flight of birds out of the trees around us, "if you do not set fire to the Ghoul and to all the liches in this tree, we are dead and you with us."

Something happened. I think it was Tamor, the pattern of Tamor, though it may have been Hafnor. Some pattern in my head issued a command, said something harsh and peremptory to the pattern which was Buinel, and the tree behind the Ghoul burst into flame, all at once, like a torch. The Ghoul turned, startled, but not too startled to begin storing the power of flame. Shattnir was in my hand in the instant drawing from the same source. "More," I demanded. "By the ice and the wind and the seven devils, Buinel, more fire. Burn these liches at my feet." For another of the corpses had reached to lay hands upon me. The cerements on the creature began to smoke, the very bones began to glow and it dropped away silently as other trees went up in explosive conflagration. Meantime, Shattnir and the Ghoul fought it out for the available heat. There was more than was comfortable.

The Ghoul sent up a clamor, "Allies, allies!" into the roar of the flames. I thought I heard a Herald's trumpet away somewhere and turned to catch a sudden dazzle of light reflected off something, but I could not see it and could not wait. I had enough power by then to lift the women and flutter away through the columned forest like a crippled bat, bumping and sliding across branches in a search for water. Behind me I could hear the Ghoul screaming, and I muttered "Ghoul's Ghast Ten," to myself. "Move and Game." I had never planned to die as Armiger's Flight Ten in a strange wood, eaten by liches. But it had been close.

We found a little islet in a pond, and there Silkhands Healed our burns. I drew more power and Searched as the fire burned in all directions, wider and hotter. It would stop at the river on the south, and there were only flat fields to the east, but it would burn long to the north and west unless some sensible Tragamors brought in clouds and wrung them out. I could do nothing about it alone, chose not to in any case, for I wanted to see who ran before those flames. Twice I caught that dazzle of light, but I could find no one. Whoever it might have been had flown away. At last I gave up and returned to the women.

They had made a couch of grasses behind some fallen trees. All three of us lay there in the late afternoon sun to let it quiet us. Later I was to think it strange that I did not inquire what Talent the girl, Jinian, had. Silkhands had not mentioned the matter in my hearing. If she had had any headdress, it had been lost in the attack. In any case, I did not ask and she did not offer. She did ask to borrow my knife in order to set a snare, but I told her I would furnish a meal before I left them to go away and arrange our farther travel. I did it by Shifting into pombi shape and murdering some foolish farm poultry who had wandered into the woods to brood. While the fowl popped over the flames, we spoke of alternatives. I could have gone back to Xammer to procure horses, supplies, a replacement carriage, even guards and servants. We chose not to do so. Instead, when we had eaten, I Shifted myself into a middling ordinary human shape and went off to find some settlement where goods and beasts would be available.

After that was only a weary time of looking and bargaining and going elsewhere for this thing and that thing which no one, ever, would have thought of having when and where it might be wanted or convenient to any other thing which might have been wanted. The evening spent itself into night and the night into morning. It was noon the following day before I led Silkhands and Jinian out of the trees to see what I had accomplished.

"By the pain of Dealpas," said Silkhands reverently, "I have never seen such a tumbletrundle in my life."

I nodded, pleased. The wagon did look as though it might fall apart at any moment, but it would not. I had fixed certain parts of it myself. The animals hitched to it were probably mostly water oxen, though the parentage of either could have been questioned. They were large, ugly, and looked too tough to tempt hunters, too rough to tempt thieves. The clothing in the wagon was of a kind with the rest, ugly and boring.

"No one would want it," said Jinian. I cast her a quick look, thinking it a pity she was so plain-looking, for she had a perceptive mind. "Exactly," I said. "Now we must make sure that no one would want any of us, either."

I believed that we succeeded. Time would prove, the occasion would tell, but we had certainly changed the conditions of our travel more than a little. No one would be interested in the old man or either of the two mabs at his side. All three had dirty faces and gap-toothed smiles. The girls' teeth were blackened out with tar; from an armslength away they appeared to be missing. When evening came of this day after I had left Chance, we were on the Great North Road once more, only a little north of the Boundary bridge. Looking back at it, I sighed. We had spent much time and effort coming a very small way, and there were still twenty leagues between us and Three Knob.

I had only one real satisfaction. The episode with the Ghoul had decided me firmly and finally that Huld was responsible. The earlier episode with the Witch might have been Riddle's doing, but it was Huld who set Bonedancer and Ghoul upon my trail. He had made a fool's call once, in the ice caverns. He had called Necromancer Nine on me, but he could not Play to fulfill it. Now, he was determined to fulfill it, to fulfill it in a way I could not mistake, using Ghoul and Bonedancer, Rancelman and Exorcist—all of them with Necromantic Talents. I had used the dead against Mandor and Huld; now he would use them against me to the death. He had underestimated me before and again this latest time, though not by much. He still did not know what I was or could do.

It was rare to find Gamesmen who did many things well. Sometimes there are children born who, when they reach puberty, seem to have bits and pieces of many Talents. Often they turn into ineffectual idiots who sit in the sun playing with themselves, endlessly moving one stone atop another or floating a handswidth above the earth or porting tiny distances around a circle to the accompaniment of loud laughter. Having more than four or five different abilities seemed to carry destruction with it. Minery Mindcaster was sometimes called a twinned Talent. The way we had all learned to think about Talents made it easier to accept her as being a combination Pursuivant and Afrit than simply as having seven separate Talents. I, who had all eleven chose I to use them, would not be thought of as a possibility by Huld. Not yet. He had known me first as Necromancer, and he was stuck with that notion for some time. Perhaps he knew me as Shifter, but I thought not. He had seen me fly in the ice caverns, but did he think it was my own ability or that some Tragamor lurked out of sight and Moved me? When I blasted out the barrier Huld had set across the exit to that place, did he know I had done it, or did he think some Sorcerer was involved? If he thought I had done it, then he was judging me as an Afrit, for these were the Afrit Talents.

However, he was not a fool. He might be misled for a time. His

## A SAMPLE OF THE INDEXING SYSTEM USED BY WINDLOW

| Power | Elatorians: (sample list) | | | | Tragamorians: | | | | | | | | Demonics: | | |
|---|---|---|---|---|---|---|---|---|---|---|---|---|---|---|---|
| | Pursuivants | Churchman | Phantasm | Archangel | Divulger | Midwives | Heralds | Woodsmen | Warbler | Ghoul | Bonedancer | Afrit | Rancelmen | Invigilator | Basilisk |
| NECROMANTIC — Power of the Dead | | | | | | | | | | × | × | × | × | | |
| HEALING — Power of the Flesh | | | | | | | | | | | | | | | |
| CLAIRVOYANCE — Power of Seeing | × | | | | | × | | × | | | × | | × | | |
| SHIFTING — Power of Shape | | | | | | | | | | | | | | | × |
| FIRESTARTING — Power of Flame | | | × | × | | | × | | | | | | | | |
| SORCERIAN — Power of Storing | | | | | | | | | | × | × | × | × | | |
| BEGUILEMENT — Power of Ruling | | × | | | | | | | × | | | | | | × |
| FLYING — Power of the Air | | | × | | | | × | | | | | × | × | | |
| TELEPATHY — Power of Reading | × | | | × | × | × | | | | | | | × | × | × |
| TELEKINESIS — Power of Moving | | | × | | × | × | × | × | × | × | × | × | | | |
| TELEPORTATION — Power of Travel | × | × | × | × | | | | | | | | | | | |

Armigerians:
- Dragon
- Cold Drake
- Prophet

Trandilarians:
- Talisman
- Thaumaturge
- Firedancer
- Halberdier
- Priest/Witch
- Trader

Shattnijians:
- Phoenix
- Oneiromancer
- Dervish

Buinelians:
- Salamander
- Gazer
- Exorcist

Thandbarians:
- Empath
- Mirrorman
- Revenant

Sorahians:
- Timereacher
- Medium

Dealpasian:
- Mourners

Bonedancer and his Rancelman had not found me on the road. His Ghoul was dead. Nonetheless, Huld was an implacable enemy who grew stronger and more clever with time. Could I lay all my powers down in the northlands and confront him with nothing . . . ? Nothing but myself? Inside me I whimpered and cowered until at last I was sickened at myself. I had been more courageous at Bannerwell than I was being now, and I reflected that a little taste of power could take a reasonably sensible person and make some kind of groveling, cringing thing of him.

# 5

# Three Knob

I HAVE SAID that the land to the east of the Gathered Waters is flat. It was no less flat and unenlivening the second time I traveled it in the space of a few days. The pace of the water oxen may have been as much as a league an hour, when they hurried, which they were inclined to do only toward evening when it grew cool and they sensed water ahead. I had coached both Jinian and Silkhands in the use of jiggly rhymes or songs should any Demon or other Talent with Reading skills come by, and I had set myself a persona, Old Globber, in expectation of some such event. As a matter of fact, one Demon did ride by toward dusk of the second day. So far as I could tell, he cast not even a passing look toward us. We were, indeed, very unattractive.

Boredom began to oppress us early. In midafternoon of the second day, Silkhands and Jinian began to share confidences concerning their emotions and feelings toward those of my sex, and I found myself alternately titillated and embarrassed by their frankness, finally being made so uncomfortable that I sought some way to change the subject. Some idea had been fluttering at the back of my head for several days, and I thought the little book in which Windlow had set such store might net it for me.

"Jinian," I said, thrusting my request into a brief niche in their conversation, "I have something I've been studying, a little book. Would you read it to me?" She said she would, though I could tell that she was surprised at the request. I dug out the Onomasticon and gave it to her. My hope was that hearing it in another voice might let the words fall into some pit of comprehension. Thus Jinian, and when she tired, perhaps Silkhands.

"Shall I start at the beginning?" She was doubtful, having dipped into it and found little sense there.

"Pick a page," I said. "At the beginning, or anywhere. There is supposed to be some deep meaning or content in these pages, so an old friend of Silkhands and mine thought. However, I've been unable to find the key to it. Perhaps you'll find it for me."

She began. " 'When the Wizard returns for the ninth or tenth time, there will be much work to do.' " She stared at the page, then turned to me. "Which Wizard is that?"

"Barish, I suppose," I said. "You've heard it. So have I. People saying, 'When Barish returns.' I heard one codger in a market say he would drop his prices at the twelfth coming of Barish."

She nodded thoughtfully and went on. " 'The greater power these Gamesmen have, the more they are corrupted . . . yet there are still some born in every generation with a sense of justice and the right . . . so few when compared to the others. I would that they become many!' And I say so-be-it to that," said Jinian. "I would there were more like you, Peter, and Silkhands, and fewer like that Ghoul."

I think I may have flushed, conscious as I was of my own struggles to perceive and do the right. Gamelords! It is not hard to risk your life when you have nothing to live for, but it is a hard thing when life is sweet. I tried to catch Silkhands' eyes, hoping for a lover's glance from her, but her eyes were closed and she breathed as though asleep. Jinian went on reading, unaware.

" 'In the meantime, Festivals will provide opportunity for reproduction by young people . . . School Houses will protect them . . . I fear that those at the Base have lost all touch with reality. They are breeding monsters in those caverns and they do not come into the light. . . .

" 'I have met some of the native inhabitants of this place. How foolish to think there were none. They leave us untroubled in this small space but will not do so forever. . . .

" 'I have set this great plan . . . a thousand years in the carrying out . . . centuries of the great contract between us and the people we have set to guard us. . . . ' "

"Read that last part again," I said to her.

" ' . . . a thousand years in the carrying out. It will depend upon a hundred favorable chances, the grace and assistance of fate and those who dwelt in the place before we came, and the perpetuation through the centuries of the great contract between us and the people we have set to guard us.' "

"Nothing ponderous about that," I said in an attempt to be witty. "Lords, but the man took himself seriously."

"What man? Who wrote this? I thought at first it was printed, like some books, but someone wrote it by hand in tiny printing in old style letters. In places it's all smudged, as though the person was tired or confused." She thrust it at me, pointing with one strong finger, and I saw what she meant. Over the years the ink had faded and the paper discolored to make the whole monochromatic and dim. Her question triggered that evasive thought which flickered at the edge of my mind. It was too late; we were too weary. I could hardly see the road verge, much less the pages in the failing light.

"I believe Barish wrote it," I said. "A kind of diary of his thoughts? Though why such a diary should now be considered so important is beyond me. Windlow the Seer searched for this book for decades and read it constantly once he had found it, searching in it for—what? Right now I believe the Immutables are searching for this book. Perhaps others search for it as well. Oh, it's an important book, I'm sure. If I could only find out why. I thought hearing it in your voice might help, but the solution won't come. . . ."

And then, while Silkhands dozed, I told Jinian all that I knew or guessed about this book and about the Gamesmen of Barish while she asked sensible, penetrating questions in a manner which reminded me much of Himaggery on his better days. In the dusk her face had a pale, translucent quality, a kind of romantic haziness, and I remembered I had thought her plain before. Though what was it Chance always said? Any hull looks sound in the dark? Well, her hull was sound enough, dark or light.

"Windlow said something about words changing their meaning over time," I told her. "He said that if we knew the words, then we would know what things once meant—or words to that effect. He mentioned, for example, that in this book the word 'Festival' meant 'opportunity for reproduction,' and he said that was important. I don't know why."

She was a sober little person, very serious and intent. When she considered things, two narrow lines appeared between her eyes and her mouth turned down as though she chewed on the idea. It made me want to laugh to see her so earnest with the dirt on her face and her teeth blacked out.

It was as though she had forgotten how she looked. Silkhands had not. Every time she wakened, she made some petulant remark about it.

"It is true that powerful Gamesmen are careless of the lives of others," Jinian offered. "We all know that, of course. It's part of the Game. So if we did not have School Houses, then young people without Talent yet, or those who don't know how to use their Talents, would be eaten in the Game in great numbers. And if they were shut up always in School Houses, then they would not have babies. We were taught at Vorbold's House that it is easiest for women to bear children when they are young— the women, I mean, not the babies. So, when women are young, they are in School Houses, and if they must have babies then, we must have Festivals. Otherwise there would be few babies and everything would stop." She sighed. "If Barish wrote this, he is saying that School Houses and Festivals are necessary, and further he is saying that he, personally, has invented both. But—that was so long ago. It is a very old book."

"Very," I murmured. "Very old. What was that bit about the native inhabitants?"

She did not answer for some time. I thought she had gone to sleep. I thought of going to sleep myself. The water oxen were now plodding along in starlight, and we had to give serious consideration to stopping for the night they could browse and we could eat and sleep, preparatory to our mad gallop into tomorrow behind the faithful team. When Jinian spoke at last it was conversation extended into dream.

"Did you ever hear the story of faithful-dog?" she asked. I nodded that I had. It was a nursery tale. "Did you ever see a dog?"

"It's just another word for fustigar," I said sleepily.

"No it isn't," she said. "In the story of faithful-dog, the dog wags his tail, his tail, you know? Remember? Fustigars can't wag their tails. They don't have tails."

"Well, maybe at one time they did," I objected. I had never thought of that, though indeed the old story did have a wagging tail in it. That was the point of the story for children, for it was the wag of our bottoms as we acted it out which made it fun.

"Pombis don't have tails," she continued. "Cats do. Mice do. Owls and hawks do, but flitchhawks don't. Horses do. But zellers don't."

"We don't," I said.

"I know. That's what's confusing, because I think we belong with cats and horses and faithful-dog. But we don't have tails and they all do. Anyhow, it's as though there are two kinds of animals and birds and creatures, one kind from here and one kind from somewhere else. Only I don't know if we're the kind from here or the kind from somewhere else. Do you?''

In the place of the magicians, I had learned an answer to this. ''We're from somewhere else.'' She accepted this, as she did almost everything I said, very soberly. ''The shadowpeople are from here, however. And they have no tails.''

''Have you seen them?'' She was as excited as a child seeing the Festival Queen for the first time. I told her I had seen them, and what they were like, and she laughed when I told her of their songs, their flutes, their dances, their huge eyes and wide, winged ears, their appetite for rabbits (which have tails) and bunwits (which don't). I told her of their language, the sound of them crying ''Peter, eater, ter ter ter,'' in the caverns of the firehills. The water oxen had found a convenient wallow at the side of the road where a canal spilled into a little slough, and they refused to plod another step. I shook Silkhands awake, and we burned charcoal in the clay stove I had bought to heat our food. Somewhere to the north of us a shuddering growl came out of the earth, and we felt the vibrations under us. ''Groles,'' said Silkhands. ''Have you ever seen them, Peter?''

I told her I had not, though I had heard the roar often as a child when I had lived in Mertyn's House.

''Sausage groles?'' asked Jinian eagerly, and both Silkhands and I laughed.

''No. Rockeaters. From Three Knob. For sausage groles, one must go on up to Leamer, where the Nutters live. Only rockeaters make that noise, and there will be no fustigars or pombis within sound of it, for it drives them away.''

''Do they have tails?'' This from Jinian, so sleepily that I knew she would not hear the answer. And she did not, making a little sighing noise which told me she was asleep. I covered her with a blanket and let her lie where she was. The ground was at least as soft as the wagon bed, and probably cleaner. I didn't know whether groles had tails or not. I thought not. I went to sleep making an inventory of all those birds and beasts with tails, thinking how odd it was that I had learned this from Jinian when none of my Gamesmasters seemed to have known or thought anything about it.

On the morning, we composed ourselves to ugliness once more and got back into the wagon. If the water oxen could be kept to a steady pace, we would arrive at the Three Knob turn off by midday. I hoped Chance had arrived there safely, and I wondered what guise we might travel in as we went farther north which would not betray us to the Boneraisers. I had no doubt they still searched for me, and I had not yet thought of any convenient way to go through the minions which had been sent against me to reach Huld, who had sent them. It would do no lasting good to Game against mercenaries. Huld could wear me to a nubbin sending bought men against me. So, thinking this and thinking that, we rolled along. Almost I missed seeing the skeleton train ahead, but Jinian thrust a sharp elbow into my ribs and began to sing. Silkhands picked up the song, and they two began nodding their heads in time to their hushed la, la, la as I dived deep and grasped Didir to cover me.

"Larby Lanooly went to sea," they sang. "Hoo di Hi and wamble di dee. Did not matter he would or no, did not matter the winds did blow, put him into the boat to row, Oho for Larby Lanooly." There were at least thirty verses to the song, and Silkhands knew them all. While I drove, letting Didir manage Peter while Globber held the reins, the skeleton train came toward us, back down the road from the north. Old Globber was terrified, as he should have been. He clucked and cried and drove the wagon off the road, almost into a canal. He sat there and shivered in his socks while the bones danced past him, the two women next to him clinging together and singing under their breath, "Larby Lanooly went to farm, Hoo di Hi and wamble di darm. Did not matter he knew not how, put him behind an ox and plow, he'll do well or not enow, Oho for Larby Lanooly."

If Karl Pig-face had been wearing the strange cap before, he was not wearing it now. His face was red again, shiny with sweat, and he tugged angrily at a cord which bound him to the Bonedancer on one side of him. As they passed, Didir heard one of them say, "If you will not do as you are told, we can put the cap back on you, Rancelman."

"I've told you," blustered Karl. "When you had that stupid cap on me, I thought I felt him down the road here. But I couldn't tell you. You need no cap, nor no cord to bind me. Pay me, as you'd pay anyone, and

I'll seek Peter Priss to the end of the lands and purlieus for you. No love between him and me, and I'm glad to do it.''

"Earn our trust, Rancelman. Earn it if you can, and no more sneaking away in the night. Now, stop tugging at the binding and lead us to the place it was you say you felt him last.'' And they went on by us, not looking at us at all. It was many a long moment before Globber got himself together to drive the oxen back onto the road. Meantime we had taken Larby Lanooly from farm to shop to mine to devil-take-it.

"If they have anyone in that group who can track,'' I said at last when the Boneraisers were gone and we were plodding northward once more, "we may see them again. I doubt not that Chance left readable tracks when he came north from the copse.''

"Three days' traffic on the road?'' asked Jinian. "Would that not cover?''

I clenched my teeth, trying to remember. So far as I could recall, only the yellow horse had had distinctive shoes, nubby ones such as they use along the River Dourt, but the yellow horse should have been sold or traded or simply set loose long since. "Perhaps,'' I said. "Though I would feel better about it if there had been rain and a bit of wind.''

"Well, that may happen soon enough,'' said Silkhands. "Watch the sky west of us where the black clouds gather and pour. I doubt not we'll have more rain than is comfortable before nightfall.''

"Before nightfall, we'll be at Three Knob,'' I promised them. We kept that schedule with time to spare, for the sun stood short of noon when we came to the turnoff to the right which led away toward three bald stone hills grouped above the foundry smokes. Stone pillars marked the turn, and we drove between lines of long, low brooder houses where they hatched the groles. There were few of the creatures about during the day, most of them being down below ground, gnawing their way through the stone with their adamant teeth, chewing the rock into gravel and packing it into their endless gut. At night they would digest it, roaring the while, and on the morn the dung gatherers would wash the night's gravel for powder of iron and nuggets of occamy and silver, less only the light metals which the groles had nourished themselves upon. As we drove, we began to see large groles feeding on piles of broken stone and bone and charcoal. These were the toothlings, just growing their teeth of adamant, soon to be promoted to work in the mines. Handlers stood beside each, stroking the creatures with long iron-tipped staffs, crooning grole songs to them. I shuddered. Imagine a great gut, as wide as a man is tall, as long as five men laid end to end, with a dozen rows of teeth and no eyes, and that is a grole. Still, how would we have metal for our axles and weapons did we not have groles?

"Stop," said Jinian. "I want to pet one."

I pulled up the wagon, amazed, and she hobbled over to one of the beasts, staying in character the whole way, to feel its huge side. Nothing would do but that I come as well, and Silkhands, to feel the stony hide of the beast and wonder at its size. The handlers seemed well accustomed to such marveling from travelers, almost uninterested in us.

Then we got back into the wagon and Jinian surprised me further. "You are Shifter, are you not?" Well, of course I had told her I was. "I thought it wise for you to lay hands on the creature. That is how it works, does it not? You must lay hands on it? So I have heard?"

So she thought it wise, did she? She must have seen something of my irritation, for she flushed, then shrugged. "If I have misunderstood, forgive me." She had not misunderstood. That was how it worked, or at least one way it worked. But Shifting into something like that! The bulk, alone, would take hours to build. One could do it by starting small, eating rock and converting it to bulk, then more and more. I thought the process out, step by step, lost in it, and then blushed, embarrassed, to catch her eyes on me. She knew very well what I had been thinking.

"No need for forgiveness," I said. "It is an interesting thought." As it was. I did not ever intend to do anything about it, but it was interesting.

The mines and many small foundries were scattered along the gulches and upon the ridges around the three mountains, but Three Knob itself lay cupped among them like a child's toys spilled upon a dish. I chose not to ride into the town as we were. Instead we would engage in further deception. We found a twist in the road behind a long, crumbling wall, unharnessed the water oxen and drove them away down the slope of the meadow toward a distant line of trees which marked a stream. Then I took the hammer I had brought for the purpose and beat the wagon into several pieces, separating these from the wheels. When stacked along the wall, it looked like what it was. Wood fit for the fire. Perhaps a wheel or two worth salvage by some desperate wagoner. Our rags were buried beneath the wagon, and we cleaned the dirt from our faces and the tar from our teeth before walking into Three Knob as a middle-aged buyer of something or other and his two daughters. I hoped I would not have to look far for Chance.

As it was, I did not have to look far enough. The yellow horse I had told him to get rid of was cavorting in a paddock near an Inn, nubby shoes and all. Chance was toping wine, red of nose and bibulous, full of good cheer and unresponsive to my annoyance.

"Why, my boy, the Bonedancers are all long gone on ahead. He's a good horse. No need to trade him off just yet."

"They're behind us again, Chance. Behind us. They passed us on the road. Karl Pig-face, with his nasty little mind hunting me, and he did feel me back there when you and I lay up in the copse and watched him. Further, he *knows* you!"

I wasn't getting through to him at all until Silkhands reached out to take his hand with an intent expression. She was doing something intricate and intimate to his insides. I saw the flush leave his face and gradual awareness seep in to him. "Ah. Ah, well, lad. I'm sorry about that. Truly, I had not thought they would return. And they may not have one among them who can track."

"Rancelmen do," said Jinian. "They have a skill for it. We must think quickly what to do, for they could be on the start of our trail and back here by evening."

Silkhands nodded agreement to this sadly. Her face was quite drawn, and I felt a quick pity. The way had been hard on her. I could not help her, however, and Chance interrupted the thought.

"It was my doing, so fair it be my undoing. I'll take the animal with much hoorah and ride off on the back roads. Once far enough along, I'll get rid of the animal and continue so far as Reavebridge. You all lay by here until you're rested—Silkhands needs a night's sleep in a bed—then come on north to meet me. Have you barter enough for new mounts, lad?"

I told him truthfully that I did not. The last coin I had had been spent on the wagon and water oxen. So he dug down and gave me a pouch which seemed well filled. Part of his gain from Xammer, no doubt, and he did not deny it. He was generously quick to offer it, and I knew he felt guilty. At the moment, I was in no mood to forgive him, though no great harm had been done if he would ride swiftly away. We had all been talking quietly, so we separated ourselves from him as would any travelers who had made casual talk upon the road and busied ourselves finding lodging. Meantime Chance gathered his string of animals together and got himself gone with much loud joshing and suchlike, to draw attention.

As for the rest of us, we found two rooms adjoining, upstairs above the stable yard, and set about having a bath in deep tin tubs before the fire. Afterwards, wrapped in great, rough towels, we sat in the window to sip warmed wine and watch for the Bonedancer, hoping he would not come. It was after dark that he came, he and his colleagues, but come he did. They did not leave. The bones lay in a drift against the stable wall. The residents of Three Knob cowered in their homes. The Boneraisers, including Karl Pig-face, sat in the common room below, eating and drinking with much cheer. We, Jinian, Silkhands and I, stayed in the rooms above, quiet and inconspicuous.

As for me, I was hung between two pillars. On the one side, I was as angry as I have ever been, angry at Karl Pig-face for sitting below in the common room, undoubtedly eating and drinking his fill without any need to hide or sly about. On the other hand, I remembered clinging to that tree while the Ghoul pranced beneath me, as close to death as I have ever come. I felt no desire for audacity, but I hungered for vengeance against Huld and all his minions. Across the room from me Jinian sat, staring at me, the fire dancing in her eyes. Silkhands slept. I do not know where I got the idea that Jinian knew what I was thinking. There was no Demon tickle in my head, and it wasn't that kind of mind reading anyhow. I simply thought that she knew. I was certain of it when she said, "They don't know me at all. If they ride out tonight, I could lend them a lantern to light them through the dark . . . tunnels."

I was not at all sure I liked her knowing what I thought, but it would work better if she did help. "Tonight would certainly be best," I agreed.

"They must be encouraged to leave soon, then," she said. "Perhaps they would be so encouraged if they heard that the horse they are following is soon to be sold or traded? If they heard this from someone?"

"Someone being you?"

She smiled. "Oh, I don't fear the Bonedancer. I am not pretty enough to attract that kind of attention, either. I can try."

"They may Read you."

"I think not. I will do it simply. But not until you are ready."

I thought about that. "Midnight, then. Or earlier, if it looks like they are going off to sleep." Privately I thought it fairly risky, but better than doing nothing. I slipped out the back way, walked at the side of the road Chance had taken, able to see the prints of the nubby shoes even in the light of the lantern I had brought with me. The road wound and climbed back into the gullies above the town, dodging behind this bank and that hillock. I had not gone far before I found what I was looking for, a narrow defile where the roadway cut through a bank. I put out the lantern and got to work.

As I did so, I visualized what was undoubtedly going on back at the Inn. Silkhands would stay quietly asleep. As a former Gamesmistress of Vorbold's House—to say nothing of her being a Healer—she might be known to someone in the place. Jinian, on the other hand, would be only an anonymous girl, of Gamesman class by her dress. She would go into the common room to the place the Innkeeper sat in the corner adding up his accounts and keeping an eye on the man who poured the beer and wine. She would wait for a lull in the conversation, then say, "Innkeeper? The man who left this afternoon, the one who owned the pretty yellow horse with the nubby shoes? Do you know if he is coming back? He said he intended to sell or trade the horse at once, and I thought I might offer for it."

The Innkeeper would say something about the horse, or about Chance. They would talk of his having ridden north on the back road. Jinian would evince disappointment. "Well, the man will have traded the horse by the time I could catch up to him tomorrow. Ah, well. I will not worry on it further." And then she would take herself off upstairs.

Behind her in the common room, the Bonedancer would snarl at Karl Pig-face. Then, if all went as I thought it might, they would decide to ride out after the man and the horse with the nubby shoes to catch him before the trail was lost. If they hurried, they would say, they might catch him as he slept somewhere, and find they had captured Peter without further effort. I went over this scenario in my head several times, finding it both likely and satisfying. Some time went by. I began to doubt and fidget, never ceasing to chew away at the work I was doing. The moon rode at my back, curved as a blade. In the dim light I saw the shadows at the turn of the road, then heard the clatter, clatter of the bones as they rounded the corner. They had a lantern, for the Bonedancer led them in a puddle of yellow light, Karl trudging sullenly beside him with the others. Then Karl's head came up.

"I Read him," he whispered excitedly. "Petey Priss. I Read him. Not far off. Near us. Oh, what a fool to go sleeping by the road! He's close ahead of us."

"Well then, walk quiet, little Rancelman," a whispered reply from the Bonedancer. "At the end of this tunnel here we'll spread out and seek him. Then you'll be paid as promised and a good job done." I saw the gleam of moonlight in their eyes, then lost the light as they entered the tunnel, Gamesmen first, bones after.

Only then did I shut my mighty grole mouth and let the grole innards grind. In the two hours which had passed, I had managed to add enough bulk to grow a man and a half high and nine men long. I had made a believable tunnel. One without an end, unfortunately for those who entered.

I lay there in the darkness, a great, black bowel in the night, trying to decide whether I felt sadness over Karl Pig-face. I decided that he was more digestible to me dead than alive and hunting me. When I had finished the light metal in the bones (delicious to a grole—they taste with their stomachs, I learned) I pulled the net and gave up bulk, having first heaved myself out of the defile and onto a broader patch of ground. What was left was only a long, vaguely cylindrical pile of rock and some powdered ores. So much for one more of Huld's reaches in my direction. I was not fool enough to think it was the last or the strongest. Next time would not be this easy.

Next time, I thought, he may send a Game I cannot win.

# 6

# The Grole Hills

SINCE JINIAN HAD ALREADY SPOKEN to the Innkeeper about buying horses, it was she who went to the beastmarket the following morning to get mounts for us once again. Silkhands assured me it was wisest in any event, for Jinian had been reared at the southern end of River Jourt, where horses are a religion and a way of life. The whole town was talking of the Bonedancer, visits from such Gamesmen being unusual in Three Knob, and it took her some time to accomplish her business. Meantime, Silkhands and I finished our breakfast, and I taxed her with being a mope and poor companion. Truly, she had been growing quieter and sadder with each step of our journey.

"Oh, Peter," she sighed. "This traveling about is worse than I remembered. I have grown used to luxury at Vorbold's House. The beds are soft, the rooms warm. There are good cooks in the kitchens there, and excellent wines in the cellars. It is a quiet, interesting life, and one need not fear being taken by Ghouls or pursued by monsters. I have grown soft and unwilling to bruise myself upon stones."

"Well," I said heartily, "you'll get used to being rough upon the road again. It will not take long."

There was no enthusiasm in her answering smile. She did not dispute me, but it was plain to see she had no heart for it. The look of her gave me a quick, half despairing sense of loss, and I kissed her. She returned the kiss, but it was more sisterly than our kisses had been in Xammer. I could hardly tax her with not being loverlike when she had never signified she intended to be, so I satisfied myself by swatting her behind. Not, I suppose, the best way to convey the depth of my feelings. Later I thought of that.

When Jinian returned with the horses, she went over them point by point with me, full of enthusiasm, with sparkling eyes and a quickened voice. She pointed out their rough coats, good, she said, for the season, and their common shoes. "They are sturdy, not fast," she said, "as we may travel back roads. What do you think of our going to Reavebridge by way of the Boneview River? I looked at the map last night while you were . . . busy, and if we go overhill from Three Knob to the northeast, we will come into the river valley. Once there we can go west to parallel the Great Road some little way before we must cross it to come to Reavebridge."

Her face was smudged. I had a witless desire to wipe the smudge away. She seemed so eager that I thought, well, why not. It would be easier going on the North Road, but we might be bothered less if we went by back ways.

The women had lost everything they carried in their encounter with the Ghoul, so we had next to replace some garments and cloaks, though Silkhands said there was no selection at all in a place like Three Knob. Well, by judicious use of Chance's winnings, we refitted ourselves for travel. When Silkhands saw the horses, she gave a rueful rub to her backside, and I knew she was regretting the light carriage they had lost on the road. I put my arm around her. "Don't be despondent," I said. "There will be luxury enough when we come to Reavebridge. Chance will have won another fortune, and we will all live on his luck for a few days."

She laughed. "When Chance wins, it isn't luck. No, I am not that concerned at having to lie on the ground for a few nights, Peter. It is this wild, dreamy feeling I have. I woke last night and went to the window for air, only to dream that I saw a misty giant moving across the stars as though he strode at the edge of the world. And the wind song haunts me. And I cannot settle at anything."

Over her head I could see Jinian, watching us and listening intently. I smiled at them both, trying to be light and unconcerned. "Well, that is the way with prophecies. I was told in the Bright Demesne we would go north, and the wind song sings of the north, and in Dindindaroo a ghost spoke to me of the north. Wild and dreamy, indeed, and reason enough for sleepwalking."

"Three times," said Jinian, surprising me with this echo of Chance. "Three times is Gaming. Who Games against you?"

I shook my head. "The minstrel learned the song in Leamer. Perhaps there we'll find the root of it." Jinian frowned at this, as though she might weep, and I could not think why she should be so unhappy at the thought of Leamer. Later I asked Silkhands, and she replied.

"King Kelver is to meet us in Reavebridge. He will take Jinian north from there, so she will not be able to go to Leamer with us. She is undoubtedly disappointed at being left out of the mystery and its solution—if there is one." She sounded very offhand about it, as though it did not matter what Jinian thought. I thought it did matter. If Jinian were disappointed, so was I.

We traveled back through the Grole Hills, leagues of twisty road over which little black tunnel mouths pursed rocky lips, with gravel everywhere. It was the waste product left by the groles after men washed out the heavy metals which the groles don't use. Hooves on the gravel made an endless, sliding crunch, a monotonous grinding sound. There were a few dirty trees in the valley bottoms, so many gray dusters along the scanty water courses. Occasionally a bird would dip from one tree to another with a tremulous, piping call. The air was still, with no smell to it. Men called to one another across the valleys, long echoing sounds fading into silence, and we rode along half asleep with the endless crunch and jog.

Then, all at once, a shadow moved across us from the south, a chilly shade which removed most of the sound and color from the world. The crunch of gravel was still there, but far away as though heard through multiple layers of gauze. The call of the birds became dreamlike. We rode in a world of distance, of—disattachment. Something moved past us, around us, toward the north, and we heard a shred of music and a voice speaking inside us saying, "Kinsman, help." As soon as we heard the words a whip of air struck, and the quiet was gone. Dust swirled up around us, and we coughed, for the air was suddenly cold and smelled of storm.

Jinian gasped, "That was a wild, ill wind," leaning over the neck of her horse and trying to get the dust from her throat.

All three of us had tears running down our faces, all of us were crying as though utterly bereft. The voice we had heard had had no emotion in it at all, and yet we had *heard* it expressing a horrible loneliness and despair. It took us an hour or more to stop the tears, and I cried longer than the women did, almost as though the voice had spoken to me in a way it had not spoken to them. I was not sure I liked that idea or Jinian's compassionate glances toward me. That young woman seemed to understand too much about me already.

It was not long after that the dusk came down, soft and purple. Bird piping gave way to the *oh-ab, oh-ab* of little froggy things in the ditches. I heard a flitchhawk cry from the top of the sky, a sound dizzy with the splendor of high gold where the sun still burned. He made slow, shining circles until the darkness rose about him, and then it was night and we could go no farther. We talked then of the music, the voice, the wind.

"We must be sensible," murmured Jinian. "Things do not occur without purpose, without order, without Gamesense."

"If it is a thing which has occurred," said Silkhands, "and not some mindless ghost."

"A mindless ghost who calls us kinsman?" Jinian doubted.

"Kinsman to us all," I said, "or to only one? And which one?"

"And asking our help," brooded Jinian. "How can we help?"

"We can do nothing except wait," I said. I did not even bother to seek the advice of Didir or the others—not even Windlow. I simply knew that whatever *it* was, *it* would return, and no amount of cogitating or struggling would make anything clearer. I knew.

So we ate the food which had been packed for us in Three Knob, and let our talk wander, and grew more and more depressed.

"All day I have thought of Dazzle," Silkhands said. "When the Ghoul came with his train, the death's heads reminded me of her. Reminded me she may still be alive, there beneath Bannerwell in the ancient corridors. But she is likely dead, young as she was. There are so few old ones of us, Peter. Windlow was old, but he is gone. Himaggery and Mertyn are not old. There are so few old. I was thinking I would like to be able to grow old. . . ."

I tried to make her laugh. "We'll grow old together, sweetling. When you are so old you totter upon your cane, I shall chase you across the hearth until you trip and roll upon the rug." It was evidently not the right thing to say, for she began to weep, the same strong, endless flow of tears we had experienced earlier.

"Will any of us come to that time? Life in Vorbold's House is sweet! Need I lose it in some Ghoul's clutches, be arrow shot by some Armiger at Game? I think of all I knew when I was a child, and so few are left, so very few. . . .''

After that, I could only hold her until she went to sleep, then roll myself in my blankets and do the same, conscious all the while of Jinian's silence in her own blankets across the fire. I knew she had heard each word. And in the morning she told us that she had.

"I did not mean to intrude," she said, flushing a little. "But I have keen hearing, and a keen understanding of what is going on. We are all feeling terribly sad, lonely, and lost. We began to feel so when the whatever-it-was happened yesterday. We must not make the mistake of thinking those emotions are our own."

She sounded very like Himaggery in that instant. I was amazed.

Silkhands shook herself like a river beast coming out of the water, a single hard shudder to shed a weight of wet. "You're right, Jinian. Always good for the instructress to be taught by her student. Well. It is wise and perceptive of you, no doubt, and good of you to tell us so firmly. I am beginning to melt from my own misery."

"You and Peter and I," said Jinian, pouring herself more cider and taking another crisp, oaty cake from the basket, "feel the same, but I know my only reason for sadness is that the two of you have planned to share something in which I was to have no part, that you would go on to an adventure without me. Well, so I have decided I will not let you go on without me. I have heard your story, read your book, felt your wind, heard your music. I know as much of all this as you do. So I will not be left behind."

"But King Kelver will be in Reavebridge," objected Silkhands.

"So," said Jinian. "Let him be in Reavebridge." And we could get nothing further from her, even though Silkhands tried to argue with her several times that morning.

All day we waited for something to happen, another silence, another voice. Nothing. We rode in warm sunlight, bought our noon meal from a farmwife—fresh greens, eggs, and sunwarm fruit just off the trees— and came down to the banks of the Boneview River at sunfall. We were grubby and dusty, and the amber water sliding in endless skeins across the pebbles could not be resisted. We were in it in a moment, nothing on but our smalls, pouring the water over us and scrubbing away at the accumulated dust, when it happened again.

First the silence. River sounds fading. Bird song softening to nothing. Then the fragment of melody, tenuous, fading, at the very edge of hearing. *Kinsman, help.*

Just there the river ran east and west in a long arc before joining the northerly flow. We were near the bank, looking down the glittering aisle of sunset beneath the graying honey glow of the sky. Against that sky moved the shape of a man, moving as a cloud moves when blown by a steady wind, changing as a cloud changes. Time did not pass for us. We watched him against the amber, the rose, the purple gray, the vast swimming form filling the sky until stars shone through its lofty head, arms and legs moving in one tortuous stride after another, slow, slow, inexorably walking the obdurate earth toward the north. Fragments of mist shredded the creature's outline only to be regathered and reformed, again and yet again, held as by some unimaginable will, some remote, dreaming consciousness expressed as form and motion. The idea of this came to all of us at once so that we turned in the direction it moved, toward the north, to stare beyond the lands of the River Reave to the mighty scarps of the Waenbane.

"A god," whispered Silkhands.

I thought not. Or not exactly. Something, surely, beyond my comprehension, and yet at the same time something so familiar I felt I should recognize it, should know what it was—who it was. There was something tragic about it, pathetic for all its monstrous size. We were silent, in awe for the long time that darkness took to cover it. Then—

"Are we going there?" demanded Jinian. "Where it is going? North?"

"Peter and I," began Silkhands wearily.

"All of us," said Jinian. "I won't be left out, Silkhands. I won't."

"King Kelver . . ."

"Devils take King Kelver. I'll spend my whole life weaving an alliance for King Kelver, warming his bed, bearing his children, but not until I've done something for myself. I won't be left behind."

She brushed aside Silkhands' expostulations as though they had been cobweb concerns of no matter. I stifled laughter to see her, so sturdy and independent, so determined not to be left out. Oh, I understood well enough that feeling of being shut up in others' lives. "Let be, Silkhands," I said. "King Kelver will no doubt wait."

"He is to meet us in Reavebridge," Silkhands retorted, obviously annoyed. "He will not be pleased. Nor will your brother be pleased, Jinian. I have heard of the black rages of Armiger Mendost."

"Leave Mendost to me," Jinian said. "He knows how far he may push me and how far he may not. He has no other sisters, but I have other brothers who are fond of me and not overfond of Mendost. They know his black rages, too, and have reason to undo him if he proves unreasonable."

I thought, Aha, she is not so manipulable as I had assumed. And this led me to other thoughts and wonders about Jinian so that for a moment I forgot the giant, forgot the mysteries of our journey, only remembering it all when we had dressed ourselves and gathered at our fire. Then it was only to search the starry sky and wonder whether the misty form still walked north beneath its cover or whether it had come to rest in some far, high place—and in what form. Across the fire, Jinian sat cross-legged with the little book tipped to catch the light of the flames. She was so deep in it that I had to speak to her twice before she heard me.

"What are you finding there, student? You look like a newly named Thaumaturge, trying to figure your life pattern from perusing the Index."

She thought seriously upon this before answering me. "It is not unlike that, Peter. I am taking what you have told me, and what is in this book, and what I have seen and heard, and making an imagining from them."

"A hypothesis," I said. "That is what Windlow called it. A hypothesis; an imagining which might be true."

"Yes." She chuckled, a little bubble of amusement. "Though I had thought of it rather more like a stew. A bit of this and a bit of that, all simmering away in my head, boiling gently so that first one thing comes to the top then another, with the steam roiling and drifting and the smells catching at my nose." She wrinkled that nose at me, making me think of a pet bunwit. "A tasty stew, Peter. Oh, I am eager to go north and see what is there!"

"The song spoke of danger, Jinian. You have been at risk of life once on my account already."

"Well, but it was exciting in a sort of nasty way," she said. "And very surprising. I think I'm more ready for it now, knowing that wonderful things are toward. And, if danger comes, well, it is no little danger to bear children, either. And no one much concerns themselves about that."

Silkhands had retreated into an aggrieved silence which I did not interrupt. When we had lain down to sleep, I did ask, "Will those of Vorbold's House hold you accountable that Jinian chooses to make King Kelver wait upon her pleasure?"

She sighed, turned, and I saw the firelight gleaming in her wide eyes. "Not they, no, Peter. King Kelver himself may spend annoyance on me, but who am I to tell Jinian she must do this or that. The negotiations were complete; she agreed; now she says yes-but-wait-a-while. Who knows who will hold any of us accountable. Do not let it worry you." And she closed her eyes.

When we dropped off to sleep, we were three blanket bundles around the fire. When I woke in the morning, I sat there stupidly, unable to count fewer than four, startled into full wakefulness by a harsh cry from the riverside. There were two monstrous birds drinking from the ripples, spraddle-legged, long necks dipping. Birds. Yes. Two man heights tall from their horny huge feet to the towering topknot of plumes which crowned them, screaming greeting to the morning like some grotesque barnyard fowl, and the fourth blanket bundle across the fire had to be whoever—or whatever—brought them. I began a surreptitious untangling of arms and legs only to be greeted by a cheerful, "Ah, awake are you?" and a small round man tumbled out of the fourth roll of blankets to stand above me, yawning and stretching, as though he had been my dearest friend for years. I saw Jinian's eyes snap open to complete awareness, though Silkhands made only a drowsy *umming* sound and slept on.

He was good humored, that one, bearded a little, almost bald, dressed in a bizarre combination of clothing which led me in one moment to believe he had been valet to an Armiger, or that he was a merchant, or perhaps a madman escaped from keepers and let loose upon the countryside. His boots were one purple, one blue, his cloak striped red and yellow (part of an Afrit's dress) and he wore a complicated hat with a fantastic horn coming out the top, all in black and rust, Armiger colors. Aside from these anomalous accoutrements, he wore a bright green shirt and a pair of soft zellerskin trousers, an aberrant combination, but perhaps not insane.

"Allow me to make myself known to you," he said, stooping over me where I lay in the tangle, taking my hand in his to pump it energetically. "Vitior Queynt. Vitior Vulpas Queynt. I came upon the fading gleam of your fire late in the night and thought to myself, Aha, I thought, Queynt, but here is company for tomorrow's road and the day after that, perhaps. Besides, who can deny that journeys move with a speed which is directly proportional to the number traveling? Hmmm? Four move at least one third faster than three, isn't that so? And a hundred would move like the wind? Ah, hmmm. Ha-ha. Or so it seems, for with every additional traveler is more to distract one from the tedium of jog, jog, jogging along. Isn't that so? Ah, to be alone upon the road is a sadsome, lonesome thing, is it not? Well, I'll get breakfast started.''

Still talking about something else, he turned away to pick up a pot and take it to the river for water, to return, to build up the fire and put the pot to boil, never stopping in all that time his talk to himself or the birds or the river running. I struggled out of my blankets at last and set myself to rights, deciding I did not need to shave myself after a quick stroke at my jaw. I joined our odd visitor at the fire.

"Those . . . birds?" I asked. "Are they . . . I mean, what kind are they?"

"Ah, the krylobos? Surely, surely, great incredible creatures, aren't they? One would not think they could be broken to harness, and, indeed, they have their tricks and ways about them, pretending they have broken a leg, or a wing—not that they use their wings for much save fruit picking and weaving nests—and lying there thrashing about or limping as though about to die, and then comes the predator with his hungry eyes full of dinner, and then old krylobos pops upright with plumes flying and swack, swack, two kicks and a dead pombi or whatever. I've seen them do gnarlibars that way, be the beast not too mature or fearsome bulky. Ah, well, the one on the left is Yittleby and the one on the right is Yattleby. I'll introduce you later so they know they cannot pull any tricks on any friend of old Queynt's. How do you like your egg?"

He had an egg, only one, between his square little hands, but that egg looked enough to feed us four and several fustigars beside.

"They—they laid that?" I asked, awed.

"Oh, not *they*, young sir, no indeed, not *they*. Why, Yattleby would be ashamed at the allegation, for he is a great lord of his roost and his nest and would not bear for an instant such an imputation. No, it is Yittleby who lays the eggs, and Queynt who eats them, from time to time, except when Yittleby goes all broodish and demands time to hatch a family, which is every other year or so and during that time old Queynt must simply do without his wagon, hmmm? Nothing else for it but do without. How do you like your egg?''

I suggested to him that I would be happy to eat egg in any form he cared to offer it, and then I went off into the bushes to think a bit. I sensed no danger in the man, no hostility, but Gamelords, what a surprise! I thought of calling on Didir, but rejected the idea. Was he Gamesman or not? Might he detect—and resent—such inquiry into his state of mind? Better leave it for now, I decided, and wandered back to the fire, stopping on the way to look at the wagon he had mentioned, peaceably parked beneath the trees and as odd a collection of derangement as the man himself. It had a peaked roof and wheels as tall as my shoulder, windows with boxes of herbs growing beneath them, and a cage hung at the back with something in it I had never seen before which addressed me gravely with ''has it got some thrilp? some thrilp?'' before turning head over tailless behind to hang by one foot. No tail, I thought. The krylobos had none, either. Nor, of course, did Queynt, which told me nothing at all.

Jinian was waking Silkhands, murmuring explanations in her ear as I rejoined them. The krylobos were picking nuts from the trees with their wing fingers, cracking them in the huge, metallic-looking beaks which seemed to have some kind of compound leverage at their hinge. Pop, a nut would go into the beak, then crunch, as the bird bit down, then *crrrunch* as it bit down again and the nutmeat fell into the beak or the waiting fingers. ''Kerawh,'' said one of them conversationally to the other. ''Kerawh, whit, herch, kerch.''

''How do you tell them apart?'' I asked Queynt, unable to see any difference between Yittleby and Yattleby at all.

''Ah, my boy, one of the great mysteries of life. How does one tell a male krylobos from a female krylobos? No one knows. Oh, but they manage to do it, the krylobos do. Never make a mistake. A female will tell another female across a wide valley and challenge just like that, but she'll let a male come into her very courtyard, as it were, without a threatening sound. And what's to see in difference between them? Nothing. That's the honest truth. Not a thing. Isn't it so?''

''But you know them apart. You said Yittleby was on the left?''

''Ah, my boy, when they drink or eat or talk with one another, Yittleby is always 'pon the left, indeed yes. When they are hitched to the wagon,

Yittleby is always 'pon the left. Yes, indeed. And when I find an egg, it is always 'pon the left, my boy, certainly, which is how I know it is Yittleby. But if they were not properly arranged, why then, my boy, I could not tell Yittleby from Yattleby or either from the other. And if there were more than two, why, my boy, I would be totally lost among them. Indeed I would.''

Thereafter, I watched them, and it did seem that the same one of them was always to the left, the other to the right, though I could not be sure. Nor could I be sure that the two incredible creatures did not know exactly what I was thinking and were not laughing at me the entire time without opening their beaks.

We had the egg scrambled. Somehow we managed to eat it all, and it was very good, with a mild, nutty flavor. I began to gather our gear, wondering what would happen next, but Queynt soon clarified that. He summoned Silkhands to ride beside him on the wagon seat, holding up the harness so that Yittleby and Yattleby could thrust their long necks through it and pull the traces taut. They were hitched separately, one to each side of the wagon, the harness running across their prodigious chests. I thought it would be a strange, whipsawing way to travel, but when they strode off it was a matched stride, varying not a finger width between them as they went down the road chatting with one another in an endless whit, kerawh, whit, while Queynt lounged on the wagon seat talking to Silkhands who, for the first time since I had known her, could not get a word in edgeways. Smooth as ice they moved along, Jinian and I following, coming up beside when the road widened, falling well back when it was narrow and dusty. So we went, west along the Boneview River toward the Great North Road. When we saw it ahead of us, I suggested to Silkhands that we turn north, avoiding the Great Road and its possible dangers, but she and Queynt forestalled me.

"Why, my boy, this young lady is too weary to go ahorseback another step, not a step will I allow, no, not at all. She may go inside the wagon and the other young lady as well, if you think it necessary which I do not, for as I understand it, no one knows her at all, and as for you, you can Shift a bit not to seem so familiar to any who may be hunting you, and with Yittleby and Yattleby to carry us along, we will go leagues and leagues on the Great North Road in less time than you can imagine.''

If Silkhands were minded to trust this strange one enough to confide in him, which angered me a good deal, then what could I say against it? I would not leave her and turn aside with Jinian, though the thought did go through my head all in an instant. No, if I Shifted a little, we could ride on the Great Road in some safety, I concluded. The wagon and the birds were so outrageously unfamiliar that no one looked at the riders along of it. None who passed failed to turn and stare at the great birds, and to each Queynt called out with a greeting or a jest, all full of words and empty of much sense. The hours went by. Queynt gave us fruit and bread from the wagon, come noon, and we rode on, the birds striding tirelessly, the tall wheels turning, and it was not yet evening when we began to see scattered nut plants and the spires of Reavebridge shining across the silver of River Reave which had been drawing ever closer to the road with the leagues we had traveled.

"We'll make for the Tragamor's Tooth," Queynt told us when we came up beside him. "A fine hostelry with excellent food and a stable which I am happy to say both Yittleby and Yattleby have found to their liking. We have never before been so far south as during this season. We must seem very strange to all these people, who, I must say, seem not far traveled by the looks of them. Why, I'll wager not one in a hundred has been north to the Windgate nor upon the heights of the Waeneye or upon the Waenbane Mountains. 'Windbone,' you know. That's the 'Windbone' Mountains, so called because the wind has carved great skeletons of stone up there, ribs and fingers reaching into the sky as though the very mountain had lain down and lost its flesh upon those heights. Ah, one must go there by way of the Wind's Eye, Waeneye as they say in these parts, if one is to see krylobos which put these two to shame for smallness. There are krylobos there, mark me, which would make you shiver in your boots to see, half again as tall as these, and able to kick gnarlibars to death I have no doubt."

"Wind's Eye," said Jinian. "That's the prophesy you heard in the Bright Demesne. Wind's Eye."

She had remembered it before I had, but her words brought back the sound of Windlow's voice in my head. *"You and Silkhands. A place, far to the north, called Wind's Eye."* I dug out the memory of the other things he had said. *"A giant? Perhaps. And a bridge. You must take me along . . . and the Gamesmen of Barish."* A giant. Perhaps a giant of mist, of cloud, of sadness, a giant seen at dusk who begged for help of his kinsmen. I raised my eyes to the towering scarps which loomed to the west of Reavebridge. Sharpening my Shifter's eyes, I could see the curved spires and organic shapes which Queynt had spoken of, as though some great, unfamiliar beast had laid himself upon those heights to leave his bones.

And behind those bones the outline of a giant, misty and vast, striding, striding to the north. I heard Jinian catch her breath, heard the man, Queynt, fall silent only for an instant before his voice went on in its ceaseless flow. When I turned, it was to find his eyes upon me, insistent and eager, measuring me as though for a suit of clothes—or a coffin—while he told us about the town of Reavebridge and all that lived therein in greater detail and to a greater length than anyone of us could possibly have cared to know.

# 7

# Reavebridge

BEFORE WE ARRIVED AT THE TRAGMOR'S TOOTH, Silkhands busied herself in Queynt's wagon, making herself beautiful. I noted that she did not suggest Jinian do likewise. I put it down to vanity. Silkhands was a little vain, only a little, and not in any sense which was improper or false. She simply liked to appear at her best, and who could argue with that. Jinian, on the other hand, seemed determined to make the King as little sorry for the delay as possible. Knowing that he awaited her at the Tragamor's Tooth, she had drawn her hair, which was plentiful and brown as ripe nuts, back into a single thick braid and had neglected to wipe the road dust from her face. Also, she was dressed for travel and looked as though she had slept in her clothes, which she had. She looked very good to me, very staunch and dependable, but she would have won no prize for style, that one.

So we arrived at the Inn with Silkhands looking a vision, Queynt appearing no less fanciful than he had done at dawn, and Jinian and me, the followers, dirty and sweaty and caring not who cared. Someone must have been watching for Jinian's arrival, for the King, a lean, elegant man, with a curly red beard and eyes that gleamed with intelligence and humor, appeared as we were having our things taken to the rooms we had hired. He came to the place Silkhands stood and called her by Jinian's name, offering his hand and smiling. When she disabused him of the mistaken identity and introduced him to Jinian, his face changed no one whit though his eyes did. I saw a flicker of disappointment there, and Jinian saw it as well. She made her courtesies in a well-schooled manner, however, and her voice was all anyone could have wished, soft and pleasant, without the whine of weariness or rancor at the mistaken recognition.

"I greet you, King Kelver," she said. "Many kind things have been said on your behalf, and though I do not merit your courtesies, I thank you for them.''

He bowed, perhaps a little surprised at her calm and poise. She was not at all girlish, as I have remarked heretofore. I myself sometimes found it surprising.

"I greet you, Jinian. If you have received any courtesies on my behalf, then be assured they were given freely and in pursuance of continued friendship between your people and my own." It was delicately put, and I found myself liking the man. He was telling her that he had not presumed to buy her, that he had only tendered an offer of friendship and the final decision was still hers. Jinian smiled at him, and I saw his eyes lighten. She has a wonderful smile.

Queynt bustled in. "Ah, well then, ladies, young sir, so all friends are met, are they? Good, good. One does not like to stand upon ceremony at the end of a long ride when dust and the day conspire to rob one of whatever youth and spirits one may have hoarded long ago in the dawn—when the skin cries for the waters of the bath and the throat yearns for the marvelous unguents of the vintner's art. Ah, sir, forgive these weary travelers for the moment, and I who have come with them this lengthy way, until we are refreshed and cleansed sufficient to be a credit to the honorable company which you so kindly bestow upon us. . . ." And Queynt bowed us away from the King, who stood with mouth open to watch this aberration lead us to the stairs and whip us upward with the lash of his tongue. "Go now, Peter, to the room at the head of the stairs where a bath will soon be brought, and you, ladies, to the second room where a bath even now awaits, and these lack-a-daisy pawns swift as flitchhawks rise, rise with your burdens that my young friends be not inconvenienced at the lack of any essential garment or lotion or soothing medication which might be contained therein. Ah, when all is sweet again, and pure as the waters of the Waenbain which plunge in eternal silver from the heights, then let us return to this good King Kelver to partake with him of those viands his generosity and foresight cannot but have prepared."

This last faded into silence, and I risked a glance over the banister at that same King to find him with mouth still open but with a laughing look around the eyes. Well then, he was not offended.

I had scarce got into the room before hearing a quiet tap-tap at the door behind me which, when I opened it a crack, disclosed Chance in the get-up of a cook looking for all the world like a major servitor of some proud Demesne. He slipped into the room before I could greet him, stopped my mouth with his fingers, and hissed, "Who is this fellow with you? This clown? Where did you get him?"

I explained that I had not got him, that rather Queynt had got me; that, thus far, the man had done us no harm.

"Harm's known when harm's done," he said portentously, throwing himself into a chair and fanning himself with a towel. Indeed, he looked very hot and harried, and I guessed that the cook's garb was not a disguise. He affirmed this. "Seeing I caused such a hooraw there in Three Knob, I decided to be a little less obvious in future. So, come the outskirts of Reavebridge, I put the mounts in a stable and came into town like any pawn looking for work and well recommended."

"Well recommended?" I didn't mean to twit him, but it did come out that way.

"Well recommended," he announced in a firm voice. "I had foresight enough to have Himaggery and Mertyn write me letters of reference and leave the as-what blank so I could fill it in myself. You'll be pleased to know they recommend me highly as a chef, and chief chef I am in this place since their last one got himself riotous during a recent family observance and hasn't got himself on his feet yet. May not, from what I hear. Terrible stuff, this Reavebridge wine, when drunk with grole sausage, which is mostly how they drink it." He went on fanning himself, pausing only to open the window behind him and lean out to take a deep breath. "I was beginning to give up on you."

"We came the back way," I said.

"Thought you must've come by way of the moon."

"Along the Boneview River, Chance. It was there that Queynt joined us. He's strange, all right, but it seemed less harmful to come along with him rather than make a fuss."

"Silkhands looks tired," said Chance. "Who's the girl?"

"Jinian? A student of Silkhands'. Promised to King Kelver by her brother, Armiger Mendost. However, she's not eager to be given to the King. Wants to come along with Silkhands and me to find the answers to the mystery."

"Oh, ah," said Chance, patting himself all over before finding the crumpled paper he was looking for. "Speaking of mystery, here's a message came by Elator from Himaggery. Says the blues are coming in from all over and they've found Quench. . . ."

"It's directed to me," I said mildly, seeing it was opened.

"Well," he said and shrugged, "you took a time getting here. Himaggery might have wanted an answer."

I unfolded the message, already ragged where Chance had ripped it, to read Himaggery's message. They thought they had found Quench—with the Immutables. "Gamelords," I snarled to myself. "That's why the fellow looked so familiar. It was Quench, Quench all the time."

"Who's that?"

"The fellow who came to meet us at the ruin, the one who went to get Riddle, the long-faced fellow. I'd never seen Quench without that square black hat the magicians wore and the long black robe and mittens. That's who that was: Quench."

"Well, that tells you what that hooraw was on the road. Must have been Quench trying to get you there without your knowing."

I didn't answer him. I was too angry with myself. I went back to the message. Riddle and Quench were being brought to the Bright Demesne together with some others of those who had escaped from the holocaust of the magicians. Riddle had decided he needed help of some kind, and so on and so on. Peter was to feel free to go on to the north if he liked. They sent their affectionate regards.

"Why," I grated at Chance, "why did Riddle do that to me? I would have helped him if he'd asked me. Why! I can't believe he's an evil man."

"Well, if you won't believe him evil, then think up a reason why he's not."

That was Chance. Think of a reason. Before I had a chance to think of anything, we heard someone outside the door and Chance eased himself out with vague words about breakfast as Queynt oozed himself in.

"Well, young sir, so quick to place orders among kitchen staff? Hardly an instant, and breakfast ordered already? Ah, but what it is to be young! Isn't that so? Enormous energy, enormous strength, eat like a fustigar and sleep like a bunwit when one is young. One might ask why not wait to order breakfast until supper has been consumed. One might ask that, but Vitior Vulpas Queynt will not. No! Queynt has learned that each man has his oddities, oh, my yes. Ha-ha. Oddities, which if not questioned can be safely overlooked, but if mentioned must be dealt with, considered, judged! Isn't that so? Now, your tub, young sir, and me off to mine in the instant. Below us, supper soon awaits our pleasure.''

He beamed at me and was gone, giving way to three struggling servitors, one bearing a tub on his back like some kind of half metallic turtle, the other two laden with tall ewers of water, one hot, one cold. All was set down and poured into and arranged to my satisfaction (to my annoyance, rather) before they trooped out to be succeeded by others bearing towels. I had never been so overserved in my life. Whether King Kelver was responsible or Vitior Queynt, I desired most heartily that all of them would leave me alone for a time.

But when I was scarce out of the tub—which the same servitors had come to haul away with much gesticulation and pour with loud shouting down some drain or other—the door was again tap-tapped and Jinian opened it a crack to whisper whether I were dressed or not. I told her I was not, but she came in anyhow. I was decent enough in the towel—more decent than we had been together several times on the road.

"My, you are in a temper," she said, seating herself on the bed and arranging her flounces. "Silkhands made me dress up. She said otherwise would be an affront to the King."

"I am not in a temper," I growled. "I am perfectly all right."

She widened her eyes, played with her hair with one finger, fluttered and pouted. "Oh, ta-ta, Gamesman, but if you go on in this way, I will think I have offended you." She laughed, a high, affected little titter, then spoiled the effect by sneezing with laughter. I could not help it, but laughed with her.

"No," she went on. "You are in a temper. Do you know why?"

"Not really," I growled, "except that Queynt is too sudden an addition to our journey, and Silkhands seems too ready to trust him. She has told him too much, I think. He knew I was a Shifter, though I am not dressed so. He knew we were being hunted. How else did he know but Silkhands told him? She knows better!"

"Put not yourself in another's hands," agreed Jinian. "But she may not have done. You know, Peter, I don't think Silkhands wants to go on with you to Waeneye."

I felt my face turn red. "Nonsense. Of course she does. She's a little

424

tired just now, but Silkhands would not let me go on alone to solve this thing.''

"I think you're wrong," she said, her voice breaking a little at sight of my face. "She would rather not go."

"I have known Silkhands for years," I said, stiffly, and even more angrily. "I don't think it's appropriate for you to attempt to tell me what my friends would or would rather not do as it concerns me. If Silkhands did not want to go to Waeneye, she would tell me. She has not told me. Has she told you?"

"No. Not in so many words."

"Not in any words," I asserted, slamming my hand down on the sill and hurting the thumb. This made me angrier still. "You are *very* young, Jinian. I'm afraid you do not understand the situation at all." The last person I had heard use these honeyed tones was Laggy Nap, trying to poison me.

She did not answer. When I turned at last, it was to see a tear hanging on the fringe of her eyelashes, but she still regarded me steadily, even though her voice shook a little. "No. Perhaps I don't." And she turned to leave the room. In the door, she turned. "However, Peter, it was not that I came to talk to you about. I came to say it is easy to stop listening to Queynt. He talks so very much, to so little purpose. One stops hearing him. However, it would be wise for us to listen to him carefully at all times." And she shut the door behind her, leaving me with my mouth open.

Oh, the ice and the wind and the seven devils, I said to myself. Now why did you do that?

You did that, I answered me, because Jinian is right. Silkhands does not want to go to Waeneye. Moreover, she does not want to journey like this at all. Moreover, her eyes when she looks at King Kelver are calm and considering, like the eyes of a cook choosing fresh vegetables for a banquet on which his reputation will rest. And the time when you and Silkhands might have been lovers is gone, Peter, and that is why you are angry.

That, at least, had the virtue of being true, whether I liked it or not, and I did not. Still, Windlow had seen me in the northlands with Silkhands. So what would she do now?

I could not make my face happy when I went down to the supper which King Kelver had arranged. I bowed to Jinian and apologized for my bad temper. Her lips smiled in response, but there was something distant and dignified in her eyes. So. We went in to dinner.

We had sausage grole, of course. Anyone within fifty leagues of Leamer will eat sausage grole. I do not remember what else we ate. I do remember Chance being much in evidence, in and out of the room, directing this or that servitor; platters in, soup bowls out, flagons in, dessert bowls out. There were candles on the table. I saw Silkhands' face, dazzled in the light, rosy, laughing eyes turned toward the King. I saw Jinian's as well, hearty, simple, regarding me from time to time under level brows. Then we were drinking wineghost from tiny, purple vessels which were only glass though they could have been carved from jewels the way they broke the light, and the King was speaking.

"We are all well met, new friends all, and I have a wish that this friendship be not cut short without good reason. Therefore, as you go toward Leamer on this journey you have set yourself" (and I wondered what Silkhands had told him), "we of the Dragon's Fire Purlieu beg your consent to accompany you." He smiled directly at me. "You will not forbid me, young sir?"

I nodded my courteous permission, gnashing my teeth privately. If there had been any better kept secret, the whole world seemed to know of it now, and it would be difficult to do anything secretly with such a mob gathered about us. Not to be outdone in courtesies, Queynt was talking.

"Ah, how generous an offer, King Kelver. How generous an offer and how kind an intent! Why, I have not seen such courtesy since the time of Barish, when courtesy was an art and sign of true refinement. Things change throughout the centuries, isn't that so? But courtesy remains the same, today as in any century past."

I would not have heard him except for Jinian's warning. As it was, only Jinian and I did hear him. He had not seen such courtesy since the time of Barish, eh? And where had he been in all that time? Was he a dreamer? Madman? Mocker? Or a Gamesman with a deeper Game than we knew? His eager little eyes were upon me, and I let my face seem as slack and wine-flushed as the rest.

The next morn I hired Chance away from the Tragamor's Tooth with much noise and many objections on the part of the innkeeper. We left the town, having seen none of it, to move in slow procession onto the road to Leamer, along the deep, silent flow of River Reave. It took the King out of his way, but not greatly. He could go on north of Leamer and then cut across country to the Dragon's Fire Purlieu, did he choose. Queynt set the pace for us, slower than I would have liked, with Silkhands riding beside him once more and King Kelver on a prancing mount alongside. Two of his Dragons followed behind, mounted, saving their Gaming and displaying for some better time. Far to the rear to avoid the dust came Jinian and I, with Chance and the baggage beast bringing up the tail.

"The King seems willing to follow you to Waeneye," I said to Jinian.

"The King isn't following me," she replied in a steady voice. "Though he is an admirable Gamesman. I had been ready for anger or threats, but he made neither. He is too wise for that. If our agreement is kept—or rather, if his agreement with my brother, to which I assented, is kept—he wants no memory of anger to stain the bed between us."

Hearing her talk in this way put me in a temper again, though I was uncertain why. If it was Silkhands he was courting, why did Jinian's speaking of him thus upset me? It should rather have pleased me as though to say Kelver would not long be seeking Silkhands' company. Looking back on it, it seems that it should have pleased me, but the truth is it did not. I was flustered with myself, eager to fight with someone and ashamed for feeling so. So, we jogged and jogged until the silence grew tight and I sought to break it somehow.

"Have you made your stew yet?" She looked at me with incomprehension, forgetting what she had said on the road from Three Knob. "The stew you said you were making up, your hypothesis?"

"Oh," she said. "That. Why, yes, Peter."

We went on a way farther.

"Are you going to tell us what it is?" I asked, keeping my voice as pleasant as possible. She was very trying, I thought.

"If you like, though it is only to tell you what you already know."

"I? I know too little," I said, sure of it.

"Perhaps. But you know what you are going to find on the top of the Waenbane Mountains. You are going to find Barish's place, his Keep, his hideaway. You will go to find the bodies matching the blues you carry."

"Yes, I suppose so," I gloomed. That much seemed unavoidably clear.

"So much we learned from a whirly ghost," said Chance. "Of that much we may be certain."

"Is there more?" I asked.

"Some more," she said. "I believe I know what plan it was that Barish had, what he intended should be the result of all this mystery and expense of time. We shall see if I am right."

"You think we'll find Barish then?"

She shook her head. "Everything indicates he was awakened last in the time of Riddle's grandfather. He left the northlands then, and he did not return. In which case, we will not find Barish himself. Only the eleven. Your Gamesmen."

"The eleven," I murmured. "Barish's eleven. And a machine to resurrect them." I clutched at the pouch in my pocket. Perhaps, I said to myself, the machine is broken. Perhaps it cannot be used. The other ones, those the magicians had, were broken. If it is there at all, it will be centuries old. Rust and corruption and rot might have spoiled it. The serpent coiled cold upon my heart, and I thought of Windlow.

"Logic says it should be there," she said. "If it was used to wake Barish at intervals, it will be there, where he was."

"And what then?" asked Chance, eager for more mystery.

"And then," she said, serene as the moon in the sky, "we will do whatever it was Barish would have done if he had returned."

That one struck me silent in wonder at her audacity in saying it, even more at her colossal arrogance in thinking it.

"Barish was a Wizard." I laughed at her, the laughter fading as she turned cold eyes upon me.

"Well, certainly, Peter," she said. "But then, so am I."

# 8

# Hell's Maw

ONE OF THE EARLIEST THINGS they had taught me at Mertyn's House in Schooltown was that one does not meddle with Wizards. Himaggery was the only one of the breed I had known, and I couldn't say that I knew or understood him well. Strange are the Talents of Wizards, so we are told, and I could not have told you what they were. Had anyone other than Jinian made claim to Wizardry, I would have laughed to myself, saying "Wizard indeed!" I did not laugh. Jinian did not joke about things. If she said she was a Wizard, then I believed her. Surprisingly, all I could feel was a deep, burning anger at Silkhands that she had not told me and had let me play the fool.

Oh, yes, I had done that right enough. I had said to Jinian that she was very young, that she did not understand. One does not say to a Wizard that the Wizard does not understand. I must have muttered Silkhands' name, for Jinian interrupted my anger with a peremptory, "Silkhands did not know, Peter. Does not know. I would prefer she not. You keep my secret, I will keep yours."

"I have none left," I muttered. "Silkhands has given them all away."

"I think not," she said. "Queynt knows what Queynt knows, but not because Silkhands has told him." Then she smiled me an enigmatic smile and we jogged our way on to Leamer.

So, in the time it took me to consider all this, to feel alternately angry and guilty and intrigued, let me stop this following of myself about in favor of telling you what was happening elsewhere. I did not know it at the time, of course, but I learned of it later. What I did not hear of directly, I have imagined. So, leave Silkhands on the wagon seat beside strange Queynt; leave King Kelver and his men trotting along beside, full of courtesies and graceful talk; leave Jinian there upon the road, calm as ice; leave Chance—Oh, how often I have left Chance; leave Yittleby and

Yattleby in their unvarying stride, their murmured *krerk*ing. Leave me, and lift up, up into the air as though you were an Armiger to lie upon the wind and fly toward those powers which assembled against us and which we knew nothing of.

Go up, up the sheer wall of the Waenbane Mountains, high against that looming and precipitous cliff to the place where they say the wind has carved monstrous, organic forms which they call the Winds' Bones. Do not look north to Bleer. We will travel there soon enough and stay longer than we would wish. Instead, cross the mountain scarp and the high desert to come to that gorge the Graywater has cut between two highlands. There is Kiquo and the high bridge, narrow as a knife edge, and the steely glint of the river, then high cliffs once more and another highland north of Betand.

Find the wide roadway there which leads into the northlands, see the strange monuments built along it, the greeny arches which hang above it. In spring, it is said, they glow with an undomainish light and have been known to drive travelers mad. Follow this road as it approaches the gorges of the River Haws and along the edge of that gorge to the town of Pfarb Durim. Hanging there high above Pfarb Durim, turn your head back toward the east and notice how all the lands between this city and the Wastes of Bleer lie flat and without barrier. A man might walk from one place to the other in two or three days, an Armiger fly it in much less time. Yet it is true that Peter did not think, nor Jinian, nor any in that company of the place called Pfarb Durim along the River Haws.

Look down now at that city. Come down to Pfarb Durim. The walls are high and thick and heavily manned. What do they defend against? What are these mighty gates closed against? Why do the balefires burn upon the parapets of Pfarb Durim? The city seems of an unlikely antiquity. Where else are these strange, keyhole-shaped doors found? Where else these triangular windows which stare at the world like so many jack-o-faces cut into ripe thrilps? Well. Leave it. Go aside from the walls and walk down the road which cuts the edge of the gorge, down to an outthrust stone where one may see what lies below—the place called "Poffle" because the people of Pfarb Durim are afraid to say its name. The place which is Hell's Maw, held now by a certain Gamelord, Huld the Demon.

Let us be invisible, silent, insubstantial as a ghost, to slide down that road to find the truth of what is there.

We will go down a twisting track, graven into the cliffside, sliced into that stony face by the feet of a myriad travelers over a thousand years—more, perhaps. Perhaps the city, the trail, Hell's Maw were there before the Gamesmen came. The trail winds down, deepening as it goes, until it is enclosed by stony walls on either side, shutting off any but a narrow slice of sky. Walk down this darkening gash until the rock edges above close to a silver's width of light; find that dark pocket of stone which nudges the path with a swath of shadow; step in to find yourself at the upper end of a cloaca which bores its echoing way into the bowels of Hell's Maw.

It is dark, and the dark clamors, but as silent feet edge forward, sensible sound intrudes upon the cacophony of echo, and voices converse there in the terrible dark, voices of skeletons fastened to the walls with iron bands and the voice of their warder in hideous conversation.

"Take this torch, old bones. Pass it along there, pass it along. Some one of the high-and-mighties will be along that path soon, and they'll want light whether we need it or not." The warder may have been a Divulger. He is dressed as one, but flabby jowls droop beneath the black mask, flesh wobbles loose on the naked arms protruding from the leather vest. His eyes are blanked almost white with blindness, and he feels the end of the torch to know if it is alight. Behind him in the dark another Gamesman lies stretched upon a filthy cot, dressed black and dirty gray, a Bonedancer, empty face staring at the stone ceiling as acrid numbing smoke pours from his nostrils. "Hey, Dancer," the warder calls. "Kick up the bones there. They're slow as winter!"

The voice, when it comes, is full of sighs and pauses, long unconscious and unwitting moments. "Slow. Always slow. Well, why not? Bones should lie down, Tolp. Lie down. Slow and slow in the summer sun. Summer sun. I remember summer sun."

"I remember summer sun," cries a skeleton from the wall, waving the torch wildly before its empty eyes. "Summer sun. Winter cold. I remember pastures. I remember trees."

"Shush," says the warder, mildly. "Shush, now. Remembering is no good. It only makes you careless with the torches, Bones. Don't remember. Just pass the fire along there, pass it along to the end so the high-and-mighties can see their way."

"Who?" asks an incurious voice from the dark. "Who is it using the way to Hell's Maw, Tolp? They came yesterday, I thought. The legless one and the skull-faced one and the cold one. . . ."

"Came and went and will come again," replies Tolp, lighting yet another torch. "Legless one is a poor Trader, Laggy Nap. They put boots on him, he said, and sent him into the world. When the mountains blew up, so did the boots, and now he has no legs. . . ."

"No legs, no pegs; no arms, no harms. . . ." the bones sing from the dark wall. "No ribs, no jibs . . ."

"Shush. Cold King came yesterday, too. Old Prionde. Not liking what he sees here much. Well, he's not far from bonedom hisself."

"And the Demon, Demon Master, Huld the Horrible?" The Bonedancer laughs, a sound full of choking as the miasma pulses in and out of his cankered lungs.

"Went out, will come in again. Always. Since he was a child. For a while he was in Bannerwell with his pet prince, pretty Mandor, but Mandor's dead so Huld is here now, almost always. Hell's Maw has been Huld's place for a long, long time. . . ."

The Bonedancer sighs, coughs, sits up to spit blood onto the slimed floor. "Huld's been here forty years. Old Ghoul Blourbast brought him here first when Huld was a child, before he was even named Demon. You remember him then, Tolp. Used to help you in the dungeons." The Bonedancer laughs again, a hacking laugh with no joy in it. "Liked the hot irons, he did, specially on women."

"Oh, aye. I remember now. Forgot that was Demon Huld as a child. Mixed him up with Mandor. Well, Huld's only been here really since Blourbast died in the year of the plague in Pfarb Durim. He sent all the way to Morninghill for Healers, I remember. Caught some, too. I got them before he was dead."

"Healer, healer, heal these bones," sing the skulls from the wall. "Call the Healer, broken bones, token lones, spoken moans. . . ." A clattering echo speeds down the line of them into the mysterious, endless dark.

"Hush," says Tolp. "Hush now."

"Wish I had one now," says the Bonedancer. "Any Healer at all."

"There's some up there with flesh power," says Tolp. "One came through here not more'n two days ago."

"Flesh power! That's how I've come to this pass, letting those with flesh power lay hands on me. They may be able to Heal when they're young, Tolp, but when they've laid bloody hands on a few, they forget how to Heal. All they can do is make it worse. No. I mean a real Healer.''

''Been long,'' answers Tolp, ''since a real Healer set foot in Hell's Maw. Those I Divulged for Blourbast was the last.''

''Those you killed, Tolp. Say what's true. You tortured them and you killed them because Blourbast wanted vengeance on them. They wouldn't Heal him. You killed them, and no Healer will lay hands on you ever because of it. Nor on me. Nor on any who's come here of their own will.''

''We could go away,'' says Tolp. ''Travel down to Morninghill ourselfs. They wouldn't know us there.''

''They'd know.'' The Bonedancer lies down with a gasp, takes up the mouthpiece once more to suck numbing smoke and release it into the dank air. ''Don't know how they'd know, but they'd know. Soon as they touched you, they'd know. Left a print in your bones, somewhere. Any time you hurt a Healer, they leave a sign on you. Even if they can't get at you right then, they lay sign on you. I always heard that.''

''Lay sign,'' sing the bones. ''Pray shrine, weigh mine. . . .''

''Hush,'' says Tolp. ''They're coming. I hear them at the end of the tunnel.''

And the light comes nearer as skeleton fingers pass the torch from fleshless hand to fleshless hand keeping pace with those approaching. First legless Laggy Nap on the shoulders of a bearer, a loose mouthed pawn wearing one of the jeweled caps of obedience; then cadaverous Prionde, tall crown scratching the rock above him, deep set eyes scowling over bony cheeks as he draws his robes fastidiously about him; then Huld in trailing velvets which his followers must leap and jitter to avoid. Followers—a Prince or two from the northern realms; a monstrous Ghoul from the lands around Mip; three or four Mirrormen in the guise of other persons; lastly a scarred Medium who drags a limp body behind. Tolp and the Bonedancer crouch in the redolent dark, drawing no attention. Huld does not look at them when he passes, merely calls into the swampy air, ''Let this body be hung with the others.'' To which the hideous Medium grunts a response as he lets his burden fall. Then they go on down the tunnel, the torches following them from bone to bone until they pass from sight and hearing.

''Now it'll stink again,'' says the Bonedancer. ''Stink for days. If he

433

wants bones on the wall, why can't I take them from one of the bone pits? Why put bodies on the wall while they stink?''

"This one isn't even a body, yet," says Tolp. "Still alive." He turns the lax form over with one foot to peer blindly down into a child's unconscious face. "Isn't even grown. What'd he bring us this for?"

"So you can hang him on the wall and listen to him scream and then cry, then whimper, then sigh, then beg, then die," says the Bonedancer in a husky chant. "Then rot, then smell, for he's come to Hell. . . .''

"Why? I just asked why?"

"Because he's Huld," replied the Dancer. "Because this is Hell's Maw." Silent under the pulsing smoke, he reflects for a time and then speaks again. "I think it would be good for you to take the one who isn't dead yet out of here. Up to Pfarb Durim, maybe. Leave it on their doorstep."

"You out of your head, Dancer? Huld'd roast me."

"Huld's got lots on his mind. Might not even think of it again."

"Might not! Might not! And might, just as well. You stick to keeping your bones moving, Dancer. Leave the hanging up to me. Might not! Devils take it."

The Bonedancer shakes with another long spell, half cough, half laugh. "Oh, old Tolp, you'll be hung on that wall yourself, don't you know? You and me. Besides, I'm not keeping the bones moving. Haven't had the strength for that for a long time now. . . ." His words are choked off by Tolp's horny hands upon his throat.

"If you aren't, then who is, Dancer? Who is? Tell me that? Whose power?"

The Bonedancer's head moves restlessly from side to side between the choking hands. When Tolp draws away, growling, the Bonedancer only mumbles. "Ghostpieces, maybe. Who knows whose power?"

"Abuse power," cry the bones. "Blues devour. Choose hour."

Down the black gut of stone the bones cry, gradually subsiding into restless, voiceless motion, finger bones endlessly scratching at the wall, heels clattering on the stones, a ceaseless picking at the iron bands and chains which hold them. One day a skeleton finger will find the keyhole of the lock which binds them, will fiddle with it until the simple pins click and the lock falls open. Until that time, they remain chained to this stone. Pass it by. Go on beyond the last, small skeletons to the oozing stairs. So much I, Peter, have imagined from what I later saw and what Tolp was still able to say. What follows we have been told is true.

At the top of the stairs an anteroom opened to an audience hall, shadow-walled, its ancient stones dimming upward into groined darkness. Many powerful Gamesmen feasted at the lower tables. Huld and Prionde were seated upon a dais, Huld listening to Prionde with a semblance of courtesy, though his impatience could be judged from the hard tap-tap of a finger upon the arm of the massive chair.

"What meat is this?" asked the King.

"The animals are called shadowpeople."

"You eat them?"

Huld gestured at the raised hearth, the fire, the spits, around which were littered the woolly feet and wide ears discarded by the feasters. "Why should I not? There is no flesh forbidden to me, Prionde. Nothing is forbidden to me. Is it forbidden to you?"

"It seems near to human," said the King doubtfully. "Very near to human, in appearance at least."

"Why should that matter? When I hunger, I eat. Meat is meat, human or otherwise. It is all fuel to my fire, Prionde. I think it can be fuel to yours as well."

The King stirred the delicate finger bones on his plate with a finger of his own. Indeed the ones on the plate did look very kin to the finger which stirred them. "Why do you roost here?" he asked at last. "Why in this place, Huld?"

"Because it chills you," the Demon sneered. "You, and any who come here, and any who hear of it. It is the age old place of terror. It was terrible when I was a child and Blourbast brought me here. Mandor found it terrible, and fascinating, as I had in my time. It is the place of ultimate pain and horror, ultimate evil. From what better place may we strike terror into the minds of all? Our task will be easier when the world knows we move upon them from Hell's Maw. This is the place of atrocity, and power!"

"And yet your Ghoul did not return."

Huld shrugged, rubbed his greasy hands upon his velvets in complete indifference. "He was not expected to return. The Phantasm who flew in the trees and observed what happened, though, he did return," and Huld made a gesture of command to one of the Gamesmen sprawled in half drunken abandon in the hall below, a summons which the Phantasm was quick to obey. He knelt at Huld's feet, head bowed, the lantern light flashing from the faceted mask he wore.

"Tell the King what you have reported to me."

The Phantasm began: "I waited as I had been ordered to do, in the forest near where the Ghoul made his foray against the women on the road. When the Ghoul brought them into the forest cover, I followed, staying ahead of him and hidden in the boughs. He had not come far before someone came through the trees behind him. I heard the person cry Game and Move upon him, a risk call. I could not stay hidden and see clearly, but I heard the Ghoul cry out in triumph, as though the pursuer had played Gamefool.

"Then there was a cry from the pursuer, as though to some other Gamesman, words I could not hear clearly. Then a fire came up, all at once, as though a Sentinel had been present. I came closer to see, but the smoke and fire drove me away. I heard someone blunder away through the trees, and it was not the Ghoul. I did not let myself be seen, but came away as instructed to do." The Phantasm remained bowed down, awaiting the King's pleasure. Huld gestured him away.

"The point is," said Huld, "that the pursuer, Peter, arrived too quickly to have Flown. We must assume he Ported. Also, the fire came about because of him."

"What is he? I thought he was Necromancer named?"

"He was named Necromancer inaccurately. It misled me for a time. I believe him to be a twinned Talent. We have seen their like in the past. Minery Mindcaster, for example, was a strong twinned Talent, Pursuivant and Afrit. In my youth I knew of another, Thaumaturge Mirtisap who was, I know, both Thaumaturge and Prophet, though he denied it. Some say they start as twins in the womb, but the stronger swallows the weaker and is born with both Talents. Perhaps Peter is twinned Afrit and Archangel. When I encountered him in the caverns, I thought he was merely Afrit, but Afrits do not have a skill with Fire."

The King sneered beneath his beard, narrow lips curling in a mockery of humor. "You have forgotten that he seemed to have Beguiled Mandor's people at Bannerwell. I never learned that an Archangel has a skill with Beguilement."

Huld waved an impatient hand. "Churchman, then. Churchmen have both Fire and Beguilement. I do not intend to search the Index to find what combination of Gamesmen he is, or what obscure name is given to such a combination. He may be called Shadowmaster for all I care. Enough to know that now we know it, he will not escape me again. No, he will lead us as the arrow flies to that place we want to go, to obtain that which we want to obtain. . . .''

"Which you believe is . . .''

"Barish, King Prionde. Barish of the ancient times. Barish with his knowledge of the old machines, the old weapons, before which the knowledge of the magicians is as nothing. Barish who lies there in the northlands somewhere. Where we have not been able to find him, but where Peter can lead us.''

"And how do you know all this, Demon? Whose head have you rummaged it out of?''

Huld chortled, a nastiness of tongue and mouth as though eating something foully delicious. "No person's head, King. I have put it together out of books, old books, books which lay unread in the tunnels of the magicians. Out of books, legends, and common talk. Out of things Nitch told me before he died, his intellect o'erleaping his pain to find things to tell me. I had an advantage Nitch had not. *I saw the machine.* I saw how the tiny Gamesmen are made! I saw the bodies stored away in caverns like so many blocks of ice. Well, they will not come to life again. The machine which could have brought them to life once more is dead and broken and blown to atoms.''

"Assuming you are correct, then how will Barish be brought to life again? If the machine is gone, buried under the mountains?''

"I think the machine beneath the mountains was not the only one. There will be another, alike or similar, where Barish lies.''

"And what is it makes you think Peter will guide you there? What is he that he should do this thing? What interest has he? His aim, what Game?''

"Only that he was mind-led by the old Seer of yours, King. Windlow the Seer was searching for the same thing I have been searching for, I'm convinced of it. He'd found something. He knew something, or had a Vision of something. Why else does Peter go north now, into the lands of mysteries?'' He laughed, a victorious crow. "Why else does he go north, now, in company with my man? Mine!''

"Nothing more than that? It is all so indefinite and misty, Demon. I would hesitate to commit my men on such a Game had I nothing more than what you have told me. Perhaps it is not Barish who lies hidden in the north. Perhaps it is the Council."

Huld mocked. "There is no Council save ours, King Prionde. When I had worked my way into the confidence of old Manacle, the fool, and his lick-heels, I asked how long it had been since they had heard directly from this Council. Not for seasons, he told me. The machine which brought the words of the Council no longer spoke. And so I told them *I* brought messages from the Council, and they believed me. So judge for yourself."

"You think if the Council still existed, it would not have let its communication be interrupted. Nor would your representations have gone so unquestioned."

"Exactly. Whoever, or whatever, the Council was, its last member has gone, or died, or found something else to play with. No, we are the Council, Prionde. I regret only that we have no more magicians to do our work for us. I found only those few tens of techs, scattered among the valleys." Huld gestured at a far wall where a few forms huddled in sleep. "I would like to find the one who led them, Quench. He knew things others did not. I would not have been surprised to learn that he knew of Barish, that his many times great forefather had passed some such knowledge along to him. Well, we may find him in time. . . .

"And meantime we build terror, Prionde, and utter despair. And when Peter has led us where we want to go, we will descend upon him in horrible power. I do not think he will withstand us. Even a twinned Talent is not immortal."

And so they went on feasting and drinking, while the people of Pfarm Durim kept watch upon their walls lest more innocents be swept up and chained in the endless tunnels of Hell's Maw where Tolp, even then, fastened the iron bands around the kidnapped child. In the blackness, the Bonedancer coughed his life away and lay quiet. When he had not moved for several days, Tolp fastened his body beside that of the child.

# 9

# Nuts, Groles, and
# Mirrormen

THERE HAD BEEN SOME DISCUSSION during the ride between Reave-bridge and Leamer as to the route we might take to reach the top of the Waenbane plateau which hung above us in the west. Certainly, it would not be up the eastern face, a wall as sheer as that of a jug, almost glassy in places. My map showed the long notch coming into that tableland from the north, the way they called Winds' Gate, leading up into Winds' Eye, Waen-eye. Queynt said he had been there, but I was not that trustful of Queynt.

When darkness came up and we had set camp only a league or so outside Leamer, I decided I would ride on into the town and make some general inquiries. It had the advantage of getting me away from Jinian as well. Something in our relationship now made me rather uncomfortable. As I left, I saw King Kelver riding away with a stranger, the King looking very angry and disturbed. I thought to call out, offering assistance, then told myself he had able assistance from his own Dragons if he wished help. I often have these good ideas which are as often ignored. So it was in this case, and I let him go. The results were unpleasant, but then, that's yestersight, which is perfect.

My way led down quiet lanes through the nut orchards. We were well into Nutland by then, so called because of the orchards which pimpled the flats along the river. The ground nuts bulge out of the ground like little hillocks, at first gray-green and shiny, a ring of flat, hairy leaves frilling their bottoms. As they grow wider and higher, the shells turn brown and dull and the leaves squeeze out into multiple ruffles. Some nuts are round, some elongated. When they have ripened, the orchard master drills a hole near the ground into the shell and feeds up to a dozen sausage groles into the hole. This is done at dusk. When they emerge at dawn, as they always do for some obscure reason of their own, their heads are lopped off and a lacing run through the skin of the neck. This is grole sausage, to be smoked or dried or otherwise treated to preserve it. Sausage groles are rather small as groles go, thick through as my thigh and a manheight long or more. Their teeth are formidable, however, for all the small size, and grole growers have terrible tales to tell about being caught inside a nut with unmuzzled groles. At the side of the road were piles of sawn nutshells, stacked like so many great bowls. I asked a nut sawyer what use would be made of his odd shaped pile.

"Why, Gamesman, these go down river to Devil's Fork, then up river again to the very top of the East Fork of Reave, then over the hill to the upper reaches of the Longwater and from there down to the Glistening Sea. We grow the best boatnuts here grown anywhere. It's a special strain my own granddad worked on to get it so long and narrow."

"I knew they made houses of them," I said. "I had not seen boats before."

"Oh, for housenuts you go over the West Fork to the orchards in the north of Nutland. People around there won't live in anything else. Warm and dry and smooth to look at, that's a good housenut. I saw one over there big enough to put three stories high in, five manheights it was, ground to top. There's vatnut groves along the river there, and one fellow had a tiny strain he calls hatnuts. Novelty item is what it is. Merchants buy them. But then, they'll buy anything to sell up north. Well, good evening to you, Gamesman."

And with that he shouldered his nutsaw and walked away into the dark. I smiled at the notion of a hatnut and then stopped smiling as I thought how light it would be in comparison with a metal helm. Nutshells were said to be tough as iron.

I went first to the Minchery, the school for musicians and poets, run by a sensible group of merchants on the same lines as a School House is run, except that the students are pawns, not Gamesmen. Except for that, it was much the same in appearance. The young are very much the young, no matter where they are. Which was not quite true. Mertyn's House had never been so melodious as this place sounded.

I had thought out my story well in advance. A certain song, I said, had won a prize at a Festival in the south. The prize was to be given to the songwriter. I hummed a bit of it, sang a few words, and was taken into a garden to be introduced to a frail, wispy girl whose eyes were misty with dreams and songs. I put the gold into her hand and told her the same tale, glad I had thought of it for it brought her great happiness.

"Did it come to you all at once?" I asked, careful not to seem too interested. "Or did you compose it over a long time?"

"Oh, truth to tell, Gamesman," she piped, "I dreamed it. The tune was in my head when I woke one morning, and the words, too, though they took some working at to fit into the music. It is almost as though I dreamed them in another language."

Well, there was nothing more to be got there, so I thanked her, complimented her skill, and went away to find some place where merchants and traders gathered. It was not difficult. Leamer lies upon the main road between all the fabled lands of the north and south. I came soon enough to a pleasant-smelling place, went inside and sat me down beside a leather skinned man with smile marks around his eyes. He was not averse to conversation, and by luck he had been up the Wind's Gate.

"Curiosity is what I did it for, Gamesman. Nothing up there to buy or sell, far as I knew, nothing to trade for, no people, no orchards, no mines. Curiosity, though, that's a powerful mover."

I told him I thought that was probably so.

"Well, so, I'd traveled along this road between Morninghill and the jungle cities for thirty years, boy and man. Saw these cliffs every time I came this way. Saw those old bone shapes up there. So, one time there wasn't any hurry about the trip south, and when we came to the notch there, the one they call the Wind's Gate, I said, well, fellows, we'll just turn in here and go up this notch to see what's there."

He seemed to expect some congratulations for having made this decision, and I obliged him with another glass and a hearty spate of admiration for his presumption.

"Well, Gamesman, there's a kind of road in there. No real trouble for the wagons save a few stones needing moving where they'd rolled down off that mountain. Little ones, mostly. We moved and we rolled and moved and rolled, and the ground began to go up. Now I'll tell you, Gamesman, there at the end of that notch the ground goes up like a ramp. Like it had been a built road. You'd think it would all be scree and fallen stuff, loose and slidy, but it isn't. It's hard and sure underfoot, just as though somebody put it there and melted it down solid.

"We didn't want to wear out the teams. We left them at the bottom and went on to the top, me and some of the boys. Right up where those bone shapes are, and aren't they something? I'll tell you: Unbelievable until you see them close and then more unbelievable yet. Wind carved, so they say, and that's hard to countenance. Well, we looked around. There's nothing there. Waste. Thorn bush and devil's spear. Flat rock and the Wind's Bones. That's it. Then, not far off, we heard that *krerk*ing noise the krylobos make, and a roar like rock falling, and one of my old boys says, 'Gnarlibar,' just like that, 'Gnarlibar.' Well, we hadn't seen one, but we'd heard about 'em, and we weren't about to stay up there and wait for a foursome to show up, so we turned ourselves around and came back down quick as you please."

"What have you heard about gnarlibars?" I asked. Perhaps I might find out, at last, what the beasts looked like.

"Big," he said. "And bad. Low, wide beasts they are. They come upon you four at a time, from four directions. Always hunt in fours, no such thing as a single gnarlibar. Contradiction in terms, so I've heard. Well, who knows. Somebody told me they're born in fours, twin ones to each female of a four, so every four is always related. It may be story-telling for all I know. We didn't stay to see." And he laughed over the limits to his vaunted curiosity.

I thanked him sincerely and left. There was no traffic at all on the road when I returned, guiding myself by our campfires which gleamed lonely against the dark bulk of the mountain. I found the place quiet, Silkhands busily talking to Queynt. I asked her where Jinian was, and she told me Jinian had ridden out a little time past in company with someone who had brought her a message from her brother Mendost. I went on to the separate fire where Chance squatted over his cookery, readying a bowl for me.

"Well, lad, did you find our way to satisfaction? Did some keen eyed merchant tell you the truth about our journey?"

This led to chaffing him at some length about gnarlibars and his former desire to have me Shift into such a beast. "They come in fours," I said. "You would have been riding an anomaly had I Shifted into a mere single beast, Chance. Your widow would have despised you for lack of knowledge."

"Ah, well, Peter, since you say it's a wide, low beast, it's as well you didn't. There's plenty of tall, dignified beasts what don't require all that company.''

I chewed and gulped and gazed across the fire to the one where Silk-hands sat. There, riding into that light was King Kelver, returning from his errand, face bleary and ill-looking as though he had been stricken with some disease or had been drinking since he left us. Chance saw it, too.

"Ah, now he doesn't look like he's feeling crisp, does he?''

"He doesn't," I agreed. "I wonder what the problem is?" And then, noting her absence, "I wonder why Jinian hasn't returned?"

Chance struck his forehead a resounding blow and fished around in his clothing to bring out a sealed message. "Fuss me purple if I didn't forget it in all this talk of gnarlibars. She left you this message and said give it to you soon as you returned.''

"Chance! I've been sitting here over an hour!"

"Well, you got so stiffy about my opening the last message for yourself that I didn't open this one. What I don't know the contents of, I can't be overconcerned with, can I?" He was getting very righteous, and I knew he was angry at himself.

As well he might. The message read, *Peter, if I have not returned, it is because I cannot. This is a fool's errand, but I must find out. Say nothing to Kelver. Find me quickly, or likely I am dead.*

For a moment it did not enter my mind as making sense, then I screamed at Chance, "Which way did she go? Tell me at once! Which?"

"Which way? Why, lad, I wasn't watching! Somebody came and said they were from Armiger Mendost, and she should come along to the person carrying the message. Though that doesn't make sense.''

It did not make sense. If her brother Mendost had sent a message, it would have been delivered to her in the camp. No need to ride elsewhere. "That was all a trap, a snare," I hissed at him. "Somewhere this minute she may be dying. Did anyone else see her?"

"They paid no more attention than I did, Peter. They were talking among themselves, Silkhands, Queynt, the Dragons.''

"Not the King?"

"No. He'd gone away with some messenger before."

I was frenzied, not questioning the frenzy, not questioning why my heart had speeded or my mouth gone dry. I was lost in a panic of fear for Jinian, not thinking that a Wizard should be able to take care of herself.

It was very dark. No one could follow a trail in this dark, and yet she had said, "Find me quickly." To find her at all was beyond me. "How?" I demanded of him. "I must find her."

"A fustigar," suggested Chance. "Trail her?"

I had never tried to follow scent, was not sure I could. In any case, the fustigar hunts mostly by sight. I shook my head, frantically thinking. Could I use one of the Gamesmen of Barish?

"Not Didir," I mumbled aloud. "No one here knows where she is. She misled them herself, purposely. Not Tamor. Who . . ." Even as I spoke, I fumbled among them. Oh, there was Talent enough to move the world, if one knew what one wanted to do, but I didn't know where, or how, or when. . . .

"If I had only seen which way she went," mourned Chance. "If I'd only seen . . ."

If he had seen. If I could See. I did not much believe in Seeing. It seemed unreliable at best, so much flummery at worst. I had never called upon Sorah, but what choice had I else? I could not find her with my fingers, so dumped the pouch onto the firelit ground, hastily scrabbling the contents back into it before Chance saw the blue piece among the black and white. Sorah was there, at the very bottom, the tiny hooded figure with the moth wings delicately graven upon her mask. For the first time, I wondered how it was that the machine had made blues dressed as Gamesmen when, to my certain knowledge, the bodies they were made from often wore no clothing at all? The question was fleeting. I gave it no time. Instead, I took Sorah into my hand and shut my eyes to demand her presence.

At first I felt nothing. Then there was a sort of rising coolness as though calm flowed up my arm and into my head and then out of it—outward. I seemed to hear a voice, like a mother soothing a fractious child or a huntsman a wounded fustigar. I could feel her stance, arms straight at her sides, shoulders and head thrown back, blind eyes staring into some other place or time, searching.

"What is she like?" the voice asked. "Think for me. What is she? Who is she?"

Likenesses skipped. Jinian in the river pouring water over her head, face rosy with sunset and laughter. Jinian speaking to me seriously on the wagon seat, telling me things I had not thought of before. Jinian angry and chill, turning in my doorway to instruct me. Jinian bent over a book; Jinian beside me laying hands on the great grole; Jinian . . .

Within me, Sorah turned and bent and reached outward once more. Evocation ran in my veins. A net of questions flung outward toward the stars. Jeweled droplets ran upon this net, collected at the knots to fall as rain. An imperative upon the place. "World. Show me this!" Jinian a composite, a puzzle, breaking light like a gem.

And I saw. Jinian, held tight between two men. Dusk. Hard to see. They were beside a ground nut, taking out the plug, thrusting her within. I could hear groles inside, grinding.

Where? High to the west one bright star hung in an arch of Wind's Bones, fainter stars to left and right, above a close, high line of cliff. Around me only scattered hillocks of nuts, stones, wasteland . . .

The vision was gone. Sorah was gone. I dragged Chance off with me to the horses, and we two mounted to ride away. No one called after us to know where we went. It was as well. I do not think I could have answered. I could barely get the words out to instruct Chance what to look for as I sharpened my own Shifter's eyes to scan the rimrock silhouetted against the stars. "North," I hissed. "Closer to the cliffs than here." We galloped into the dark like madmen, our horses stumbling and shying at things they could not see.

I almost missed the arch of bone shapes upon the height. They were smaller than they had seemed in Vision, a slightly different shape seen from the side. Also, the stars had fallen lower against the rimrock but were still unmistakable. One bright, two fainter neighbors. We slowed to pick our way farther north. The nut orchards around us had given way to drier land, the plants themselves were sparse, scattered, oddly misshapen. When I saw the right one, my eyes almost slid over it before noticing the plug. Only that one had a plug cut.

We thundered toward it, dismounted at the run, and hammered at the side of the plug until I thought myself of pombi claws and Shifted some for the job. Then the plug fell to the ground, and I leaned into the dank, nut-smelling dark to call, "Jinian! Jinian!"

There was an answering cry, faint as a breath and hoarse. We began to climb in, but I heard the gnawing of the groles. They cared not what they ate. They loved the taste of bone. I thrust Chance to one side, muttering fiercely at him. "Stay out of here. Do not come in! But, keep calling. I need to hear her to lead me to her." Then I had crawled into the place, all tunneled through with grole holes like the inside of a great cheese, and Shifted.

Do you care to know what it is to be a sausage grole? It is an insatiable hunger coupled to an unending supply of food. It is a happy gnawing which has the same satisfaction as scratching a not unpleasant itch. I began as a rather generalized grolething. Within moments, I encountered a real nut grole, and my long, pulsating body slid over and around that of my fellow in a sensuous, delightful embrace, half dance, half play. After that, I was more sausage grole than before. I heard a shouting noise somewhere, another one somewhere else. Neither mattered. Nothing mattered except the food, the dance.

I suppose it was some remnant of Peter which brought me out of this contented state, some artifice or other he had learned to use in Schlaizy Noithn, perhaps, or the touch of the Gamesmen from within. At any rate, after a little time of this glorious existence, the grole-I-was began to make purposeful munching toward the screaming inside the nut. Groles have no eyes. I remedied this lack. There was no light. I remedied this as well, creating a kind of phosphorescence on my skin. I saw her at last, high on an isolated pillar of nutmeat, crouched beneath the curve of the shell, three groles gnawing away at her support. In light, she might have been able to avoid them. In the dark? I doubted it.

So there was Jinian atop the pillar; there was Peter in shining splendor below. What did one do now? She solved the problem by half falling, half scrambling over the intervening bodies and onto my back where I grew a couple of handholds and a bit of shielding for her. It was no trouble, and I was pleased to think of it. We got out in a writhing, tumbling kind of way, over and under, and I was still not quite full of nutmeat when we slithered out of the shell and I gave up all that bulk to become Peter once more. It lay behind me, steaming in the night air, and I wondered what the grole growers might make of it when they returned at dawn.

Only then did I realize she was crying. I put my arms around her and let her shake against my nakedness, gradually growing quiet as I grew clothes. I did not release her, merely stood there in a kind of unconscious, not un-grolelike content, stroking her hair and murmuring sounds such as people make to small animals and babies.

"I was frightened," she said. "It was dark, and I was afraid you would not come. I was afraid you would not come in time."

I gave Chance a look which should have fried him into his boots, and he had the grace to mumble that it had been his fault. I told her I had used Sorah.

"I knew you would do something," she said. "I knew you would find me because you are clever, Peter, though you often do not seem to know it. But so much time went by, and I became terribly afraid." After which we murmured nonsense things at one another and did not move very much until Chance harumphed at us.

"All well and nice, lad, lass. I'm sure it's gratifying in all its parts, but we don't know who put you there, do we? Or why? What's next? Will they be coming back to find out whether you're sausage or what?"

She stepped away from me to leave a cold place where warm content had been. "It would be better if they think I'm dead, Chance. We must find some place to hide me. Queynt's wagon, I think. The ones who took me must think they succeeded, at least until we find out what's going on!" And she directed us to replace the plug as it was when we found it, turning the pombi-scarred place to the bottom.

She told us what had happened as we rode back. "I saw King Kelver leaving the camp. I thought there was something odd about it, about the way he looked, or the men with him—something. Well, perhaps foolishly, I decided to follow him. After all, it is Kelver I am promised to—if, indeed, he still cares about that promise, which I have doubts over. I followed for a time, then lost them. I searched, quartering about, and was probably seen doing it. I gave up and returned to camp.

"Then in an hour or so, came a fellow saying he came from Armiger Mendost with words I should hear about King Kelver. I knew that was a lie. Mendost sends messengers, but never yet sent any except Heralds or Ambassadors or others in full panoply. Mendost is too proud to do else.

"But I thought even lies lead to the truth, somewhere, if one knows them for what they are, and a lie announces a Game as well as many a truth. So I left word with Chance and went with the fellow. He had another hid nearby, and the two of them bagged me and would have fed me to the groles surely had you not found me in time. As it is, I never saw what Gamesmen they were."

"And all that merely because you followed King Kelver?" I asked, thinking it did not seem like much.

"For no other reason," she said. "Something is toward there, Peter, and whoever Games wants no one to know of it. So I must hide and you must find out what goes on."

She thought to hide in Queynt's wagon. I didn't trust the man. We argued. She won. She thought she could hide even from Silkhands, though Silkhands rode upon the wagon seat all day. Well. What could I do. We hid her away in some brush near the camp, and I returned with Chance. At first light I sought out Queynt and took him aside as quietly as the man would allow me to do so.

"Consult with me, young sir? Ah, but I am flattered that such a proud young Gamesman—for surely pride goes with honor and ability, isn't that so?—would have use for such an old and traveled body as myself. Advise, I often do. Consult, indeed, I often do. Though when advice and consulting are done, who takes any serious regard for the one or puts any faith in the other—why, it would surprise you to learn how seldom words are given even the weight of a fluff-seed. Still, I am flattered to be asked, and would lie did I pretend a false and oleaginous humility . . ."

"Queynt," I said in a firm voice. "Hush this nonsense and listen." His jaw dropped, but I saw a humorous glitter in his eyes. It went away when I told him someone had tried to kill Jinian, that we wanted to find out who, that she needed to hide in his wagon. "No one must know," I said. "Not even Silkhands. And, Queynt, it is Jinian's thought to trust you. I don't. So, if no one knows but you, and anyone finds out or harms her, I will consider my suspicions justified."

He coughed. I thought he did it to hide laughter which was inappropriate for there was no matter of laughter between us. "I will guarantee to hold her beyond all possibility of discovery, young sir. The word of Vitior Vulpas Queynt is as highly valued as are the jewels of Bantipoora of miraculous legend. Say no more. Wait only a bit and then bring her to the camp. I will have sent all eyes to seek another sight that she may come unobserved."

"Queynt," I replied, "I will do so, but I tell you that you talk too much."

"But on what topics, Gamesman? Ask yourself that? On what subjects do I talk not at all?" He smiled at me and went away. In a little time

Kelver and Silkhands and the Dragons rode away toward Leamer. Queynt opened the wagon door at the back of the vehicle, and we brought Jinian to be lifted in. It was a well-fitted place, almost a small house, with arrangements for food and sanitation. "A technish toilet," said Queynt. "Something I obtained from the magicians long ago, when I used to trade with them." He greeted my incredulous stare with equanimity. Jinian took his words at face value.

"Thank you, Queynt," she said. "I will treat your property with respect. If I may lie up within for a few days, we can perhaps discover who means us ill." She gave him her hand, and he bowed over it, eyes fixed sardonically on me. I left them, hoping she would have sense to shut the door in time. I need not have worried. When Silkhands and the others rode back from their expedition to the orchards, the wagon was shut tight. Silkhands, however, was in a fury. She came to visit me and Chance.

"That little fool Jinian. The King tells me she has left us! Without a word to me! Mendost may Game against me, or against the House in Xammer because of this. She did not even tell me goodbye."

Chance blinked at me like an owl and went on stirring as I feigned surprise. "King Kelver told you this? When was that?"

"This morning. Queynt suggested we might like to see the grole sausage made, so we rode over to the orchards. We had gone no distance at all when the King told me she had gone. Gone! It seems she told him she did not like the bargain she had assented to and intended to return to her brother's Demesne."

"The King must be mightily disappointed," I said carefully. "He looks very ill over it."

"I know." She dabbed at her eyes where tears leaked out. "He does look ill. I reached out to help him, Heal him, and he struck my hand away as though I had been a beggar. He is very angry."

"Ah, the King did not want you to help him." I cast another long look at Chance who returned it with a slow, meaningful wink. "I will tell the King we share his distress," I said, rising and walking off to the other fire.

Once there, I bowed to the King where he sat over his breakfast, the bowl largely untouched before him. I murmured condolences in a courteous manner, all the time looking him over carefully beneath my lashes. Oh, he did indeed look very unwell. The crisp curl of his beard was gone, the hard, masculine edges of his countenance were blurred, the lip did not curl, the sparkling eyes were dim. The man who sat there might have been Kelver's elder and dissolute brother.

I returned to our fire, comforted Silkhands as best I could, and waited until she rejoined Queynt upon the wagon seat before saying to Chance, "It isn't Kelver."

"Shifter?" he asked.

"No, I think not. Few Shifters can take the form of other Gamesmen. Mavin can, of course. I can. Most of Mavin's kindred probably can. It isn't easy, but those of us who can do it at all can do it better than it has been done here."

"Perhaps someone less Talented than Mavin's kindred, but more Talented than most Shifters?"

"I think not," I said. "Instinct tells me not. Is there not some other answer?"

Chance nodded, chewing on his cheeks as he did when greatly troubled. "Oh, yes, lad, there's another way it could be done right enough. I like it less than Shifters, though, I'll tell you that."

"Well? Don't make me beg for answers like some child, Chance. What is it?"

"Mirrormen," he said. "Never was a Mirrorman did anything for honorable reason, either. When you find Mirrormen, you find nastiness afoot, evil doings, covert Game, rule breaking. That's always the way with Mirrormen."

I cast frantically back to my Schooldays for what I could remember about Mirrormen. It was little enough. Something . . .

"They will need to keep Kelver close by, and unharmed," I said. "They will need to take his reflection every day or so, so they cannot harm him or keep him at any great distance."

"Oh, that's true enough, so far as it goes," said Chance. "If by 'harmed' you mean maimed or ruined permanent. They'll have done something to him, though, to prevent his using Beguilement on them. He's a King, after all. He can be pretty discomforted, let me tell you, and still give a good reflection."

"There must be two Mirrormen," I said, remembering more from my Schooldays.

"Two," he said. "That's right. One takes the reflection, which is backwards, like seeing your own face in a mirror. Then the second takes the reflection of the first, which makes it come out right. That's what makes it a bit blurry, too. They can't usually get it very crisp. Well, wherever Kelver is, he isn't far from here.''

So we made it up between us to find King Kelver as soon as dark came once more. Meantime, since we had been up through the whole long night, we slept in the saddle throughout the whole long day, nodding in and out of wakefulness as the day wore on. Leamer vanished behind us, the road went on north, and at last we came to the fork where we could look back to the southwest to see the huge notch in the highlands and feel the warm wind rushing out of it into our faces. ''Wind's Gate,'' said Chance.

''Wind's Gate,'' called Queynt from the wagon seat. ''A great and marvelous sight, gentlemen, Healer, where the highlands slope into the lowlands and the wind travels that same road. Oh, many a traveler's tale could be told of the Wind's Gate, many a marvelous story woven. See how Yittleby and Yattleby stride forth, eager to see their kindred upon the heights. Oh, you will be amazed, sirs, Healer, at the wonders which await you there.''

There was no real reason for King Kelver to accompany us, now that Jinian was gone. Some spirit of devilment in me called him to account for his presence.

''It was courteous of you, King, to accompany us thus far in our journey. We understand that it was courtesy offered to young Jinian, promised to you as she was, and that you might feel reluctant to withdraw that courtesy now that she is gone. However, may I express all our thanks and willingness that you feel no obligation to continue. Indeed, sir, you have done enough and more than one might expect.'' There, I thought. That's out-Queynting Queynt himself, and find an answer to that, Mirrorman.

He hemmed and hawed, reminding me of the way Riddle had fumed and fussed when I had called him to account similarly. ''Not at all, Gamesman,'' he finally managed to say. ''I am led by curiosity now. Having come so far, I will not go home again without having seen the heights.'' And he smiled a sick, false smile at me which I returned as falsely. Devil take him.

When we started into the notch, Chance told me to watch to the rear with my Shifter's eyes. ''They have to bring the real King along near,'' he said. "They couldn't try to bring him anyway but by this road—there is no way save this road unless they fly. So you look back there for dust. That'll tell us how far they are behind."

We had gone on for several hours before I saw it, far behind, just then turning at the fork. I could not have seen it had the land not sloped down behind us so that we looked upon the road already traveled. Even then, no eyes but a Shifter's would have seen it. I did not make any great matter out of peering and spying. It was well enough to know that the true King was probably behind us several hours upon the road, which distance would likely be decreased under cover of dark.

So when evening came we built our separate fire once more, and Chance and I made much noise about weariness, how we had not slept the night before out of worry over Jinian and how we must now go early into our blankets. I made up a convincing bundle and slipped away into the dark. Behind me Chance conversed with my blankets. Once away from the light I Shifted into fustigar shape and ate the leagues with my feet, carrying with me only one thing I thought I might need.

I found them without any trouble at all. There were two of them and a closed wagon, not unlike that which Queynt drove. One of the men was an Elator, a cloak thrown over his close leathers against the night's chill. The other was Mirrorman, right enough, got up in King's robes and a feathered hat like Kelver's.

The wagon was shut tight. I had no doubt Kelver was in it. I would learn all I needed by waiting for the other Mirrorman, the false Kelver, to return to his allies. I lay behind a rock and watched the two as they ate and drank, belched and scratched themselves. Finally the false Kelver arrived, riding in out of the darkness, and they unlocked the wagon. I saw where the key was kept, crept close behind them to peer through the crack of the door. The true King was bound and gagged, lying upon a cot. When they took the gag from his mouth, he swayed, obviously drugged. He could not bestir himself to anger, mumbling only.

"You are dishonorable, Gamesmen. Your Game is dishonored. Who Games against me?"

One of the Mirrormen struck him sharply upon the legs with a stick he carried. "Silence, King. Our master cares not for your honor or dishonor, for rules and forbiddings. You may keep your life, perhaps, if you cause us no trouble. Or you may lose your life, certainly, in Hell's Maw."

I had heard Hell's Maw mentioned a time or two, by Mertyn, by Mavin, both with deep distaste and horror. I knelt close to the door crack, not to miss a word.

"Hell's Maw," the King mumbled. "What has Hell's Maw to do with me?"

"Hell's Maw has to do with the world," said the Elator. "Our Master, Huld, moves from the mastery of Hell's Maw to the mastery of the world. You are in the world. Therefore, you are in his Game. Now be silent."

The first Mirrorman took up his position before the true King, stared at him long and long. I saw his flesh ripple and change. When he turned, his was the King's face, but reversed and strange. Now the second Mirrorman, the false King, stared at the first in his turn, the flesh shifting slightly along the jaw, around the eyes. What had been a blurred, sick looking image became slightly better, not unlike King Kelver. Still, while all who knew the King would have accepted this face, they would have thought the King very ill, for it was not the face of health and character which friends who knew the King knew well. They gagged Kelver once more and left him there. I saw where they put the key.

They talked, then, of Hell's Maw. I learned much I would rather not have known, of Laggy Nap and Prionde, of many powerful Princes from the north. I heard of the bone pits and the cellars, the dungeons and bottomless holes. These three talked of all this with weary relish, as though they had been promised some great reward when the ultimate day arrived. Finally the Elator flicked away, was gone a short time, then returned. There were a few further instructions for the false King. He was to signal the Elator if Peter left the others, signal if anything was discovered. The Mirrorman mounted and rode away toward the camp he had left some hours before. Only then did I move after him to take him unaware in the darkness. When a Mirrorman meets a pombi there is no contest between them. The pombi always wins.

I returned then to the Mirrormen's camp, the false King trailing behind me, obedient to the little cap I had brought with me. I had said to him, "*You* are King Kelver, the true King Kelver. You will hear no other voice but mine. You will lie quiet in the wagon, drugged and quiet. You will say nothing at all. You are the true King Kelver, you will hear no voice but mine." Then I laid him behind a stone to wait while the other two drank themselves to sleep.

453

Then it was only quiet sneaking to get the key, to open the wagon, untie the King, hush his mumbling. "You must be silent! Hush, now, or I'll leave you here tied like a zeller for the spit!" At which he subsided, still drooling impotent anger into his beard. I put the false Kelver in his place, cap fastened tight under the feathered hat the King wore. Before we left, I reinforced his orders once more. I intended to come back the following night, perhaps, to take the cap from him before he lapsed into emptiness as the Invigilator had done in Xammer.

When we had come the weary way back to camp, the night was past its depth and swimming up to morning. I took him straight to Silkhands and told her all the story, after which it was only a little time until she had the poison out of him and he sputtering by the fire, angry as a muzzled grole.

"The Elator will probably spy on us," I said. "We must decide how to keep them from knowing."

"They will know in any case," said the King. "When I do not return tomorrow for my reflection."

I snapped at him. "Nonsense. Of course you will return. They will expect to see a Mirrorman come in the likeness of the King, and you will come in the likeness of the King. If you do not, I must, and that is too many Kelvers entirely even for this group." He seemed to be chewing on this, so I gave him reason. "The false Kelver will simply lie there, thinking he is you. The other Mirrorman will do what Mirrormen do, no different. Surely you have guile enough for this? To keep them unsuspecting? To feed information back to Hell's Maw which may be to our liking? If for no other reason, to work vengeance upon them for what they would have done to Jinian."

I was angered that he did not seem as concerned as I about what they had almost done to Jinian.

# 10

## Wind's Eye

HE MAY NOT HAVE BEEN CONCERNED enough about Jinian, but his concern knew no bounds for Silkhands. When I quoted to all of them the words I had heard from the mouth of the Elator concerning Huld and his desire to master the world, Silkhands turned away retching. Kelver went to her, held her, and she cried between saying that Huld had come to her often while she was captive in Bannerwell, had threatened her, invaded her mind, set such fear in her that she had not dared think of it again. Now she was drowning in that same terror. King Kelver began to burn, hot as fire, swearing vengeance against those who had hurt her, mirrored him, Gamed against any of us. "Your enemy is mine," he swore, putting his hand on mine. "We stand allies against those foul beasts."

I had heard more of the Elator's talk than he had, more than I had repeated to any of them. I was glad of any who would stand against terrors I was uncertain I could face myself. We put Silkhands in the wagon with Jinian to let them comfort one another as to what had been misunderstood between them. I needed no further proof that Kelver was no longer interested in Jinian or that Silkhands would never be more than my friend. So I drank with the King and shared objurgations of all enemies with him until we slept at last from inability to do anything else.

On the morning we climbed farther to the endless chattering of the krylobos. Queynt clucked at them indulgently. I asked if he feared to return to the place he had found them, and he shook his head. "It is impossible to say. It was all so very long ago."

"How long ago?" I asked.

"Ummm." He grimaced. "A very long time ago. I was searching for a place. There had been a great catastrophe, and my maps proved useless. You have heard of the cataclysm, flood and wind, storm and ruin? It caused great destruction the length of the River Reave."

"The same catastrophe which destroyed Dindindaroo," I said. "I have been told that was flood and windstorm. Do you know what caused it?"

"Most certainly. When we come to the top, you will see for yourself. A moonlet fell from the heavens, blazing with the light of a little sun. It thrust into the top of this tableland like a flaming spear, causing the ground to shatter for a hundred leagues in all directions, breaking natural dams and letting loose the pent floods of a thousand thousand years, sending forth a hot, dry wind which spread from this center to blow forests into kindling. You may see the destruction in Leamer yet, in certain places.

"Many ancient things were uncovered. And perhaps many other ancient things were covered past discovery." He was quiet then for a little time, loquacity forgotten, before he said, "Perhaps it is only that the signs were lost, the trails thinned. . . ."

If he had been attempting to astonish me, he succeeded. "I have heard a song sung to that effect," I managed to choke.

"Ah, young sir, so have I. It was that song brought me all the way south almost to the Phoenix Demesne searching for a Healer and a Gamesman to whom that song might mean something."

"Our meeting was no accident then," said Silkhands, entering the conversation from her wagon seat. "No accident at all!"

He flushed a little, only a touch of rose at the lobes of his ears. "No, my dear. Not totally accident. But intended for no evil purpose for all that."

It was too much. I was not assured of his honesty and could not fence with him further. I waited until Chance came up to me, then spent a league of our journey complaining about mysteries, Gamesmen in general, an education which had ill fitted me for the present circumstances, and other assorted miseries including a case of saddle chafe.

Chance ignored me, cutting to the heart of my discomfort. "He's a one, that Queynt," he said. "Says more than he cares about and knows more than he says."

"Spare me the epigrams," I begged him. "Can I trust the man? That's all that matters now. He has not seemed to hurt us in any respect, but he has been far from honest with us. . . ."

"As we have been with him," said Chance. "I suppose he's wondering if he can trust us. I would if I was him."

My own honor and trustworthiness was not a topic I chose to think upon. Not then. I could only go on with the journey by not thinking of it, and so I whipped my horse up and rode ahead of all the rest to the top of the notch, seeing the monstrous bone forms edging the rimrock on every side so that I dismounted to stand in amazement while the others caught up to me.

Queynt jumped from the wagon seat to stretch and bend himself, puffing a little in the high air. "They were not here," he said, "these bone forms were not here before the cataclysm. They were buried deep, buried well, buried for a thousand thousand years. When the moonlet fell, the soil which covered them was blown outward to fall upon the orchards of Nutland or was carried by the wild winds to the edges of the world."

The huge shapes were all around us, north, south, west as far as we could see. They were indeed like the skeletons of unimaginably prodigious beasts, pombis or fustigars perhaps. Here and there the shapes were pentagonal, star shaped, like the skeleton of any of our tailless animals, so like a pombi's that I could not believe them wind carved. They felt and sounded, when struck, like stone. Jinian came out of the wagon to lay her small square hands beside my own. The spies were far behind. She could risk this brief escape from the wagon. We remained there, staring, for a long time before turning away.

The King came to us with the Dragons. I had seen them conferring together as they rode, and now he came to ask my advice. "I have two Dragons here who can be sent as messengers. Would you have any thoughts about that?"

I had been worrying the thought of taking Hafnor in my hand and Porting to the Bright Demesne to ask for help. I had not done because I was not sure I could return, not sure I could visualize clearly enough the surroundings where we traveled. This offer was welcome, and I thanked him for it, suddenly wishing most heartily for Mavin and Himaggery, but most of all for Himaggery's host.

"If and when word reaches Huld that we have found what he is seeking," I said, "he will come. We could give up the search and go away. But Huld would move against the world and us, sooner or later. We may find what we may find and keep it secret. But Huld will come, sooner or later. The Elator who follows us says that there are bone pits outside Hell's Maw piled so deep that no man knows where the bottom of them lies. Huld will come with Bonedancers and Ghouls and Princes of the North who share his ambitions. He will come in might with a horrible host. If that host could be met and conquered in this wasteland . . .''

"Or even delayed," whispered Jinian. "Fewer would suffer."

"Except ourselves," said the King.

"Except ourselves," I agreed. "So while we hope for powerful allies before us, let us call upon whatever others we may."

King Kelver examined me narrowly. "What allies before us, Gamesman? I have not been told of any . . . formally."

I flushed and turned from him. Had Silkhands hinted to him? Hoped with him? Well, probably. Behind me, Jinian said, "There may be none, King Kelver. We hope, that is all."

He laughed, not with any great humor, and made some remark about fools living on hope. Well, that was true. Fools did. My hope was in Mavin.

So it was that one scarlet Dragon sped northeast, trailing fire and pennants of smoke to make himself even more conspicuous while another, slate gray with wings of jet, fled south close upon the mountaintop, unseen, to the far off mists of the Bright Demesne. He carried a message from me which said, without any circumlocution, "Help!" Meantime Jinian dressed herself in the Dragon's cloak and brave plumed helm to ride alongside the wagon. If the Elator got a look at us, we were precisely as we should have been: one King, one Queynt, one Chance; one Silkhands, one Dragon, one Peter. One Jinian, gone, eaten by groles. One Dragon gone, flown back to the Dragon's Fire Purlieu with much noise and fire.

Having thus done what we could against the certainty of Huld's coming, we rode forward once more, to the north where Yggery's charts identified the Wastes of Bleer though it was difficult to imagine a place more waste-like than that we traveled already.

We crossed long lines of scattered ash which led away to the south. "There's a hole there that would hold a battle Demesne," said Queynt. "Where the moonlet fell, spewing this ash in trails across the stone. In time the thorn will hide it. . . ."

Little thorn grew on the flat, though the canyons were choked with it and devil's spear grew thickly under shelter of the stones. Else was only flat, gray and drear. The farther north we went, the more fantastic the twisted stone, convoluted, bizarre, no longer looking like isolated bones or joints but like whole skeletons of dream monsters. It was like moving in a nightmare, dreamy and echoing. Had it not been for the wide sky stretching above us to an endless horizon, it would have felt like a prison beyond hope of release.

It was almost dusk when we came to the chasm, knife edged and sheer. At either end of it a mountain had sprawled into an impenetrable tumble of stone. "Abyss opens, mountains fall," sang Queynt under his breath. I knew it was not the first time he had seen it. "It opened at the time of the cataclysm," he said. "Before that time, one could have ridden on into the wastes."

"Tomorrow," I said wearily. "There is no sense worrying at it now. We have other things to do."

And, indeed, there was enough to do for the evening. King Kelver and I would make his obligatory visit to the Mirrormen, he ostentatiously, I secretly to guard him. With many pricked fingers and scratched arms, we hacked enough thorn for a fire. The King had speared two ground-running birds which we roasted and ate with hard bread and dried fruit. The abyss had stopped us early, so that we had finished our meal before dark, the light falling red behind the line of mountains beyond Graywater. We were gazing at the sky thinking our own gloomy thoughts when the giant strode into our view against the bleeding light.

He was coming toward us. As we had seen him from the gentle valley of the Boneview River, so we saw him again, this time from a frontal view. He strode toward us, towering against the sky, shredding and fraying at his edges as though blown by a great wind, ever renewing his outline, his gigantic integrity of shape and purpose. The sun sank behind him; stars showed through him as he stalked toward the place where we sat wordless and awed. There was something so familiar about him, something so close to recognition. I strained at the thought, but it would not come.

At last the giant came so close the shape of him was lost. We felt the cold, ill wind blow around us, heard that agonized voice, "Kinsman, kinsman, find the wind . . ." and then it had gone on past. We turned to follow its progress over the abyss and beyond where it changed, tumbled, seethed into another shape, a tall, whirling funnel of darkness which poured down into some hidden pocket of the world.

In that instant I saw what I had not seen before, how the shredding edges of the great form resembled a furry pelt, ends flying, how the great shape shifted, Shifted . . .

"Thandbar," said two voices at once. Mine, and Queynt's.

There was a long silence full of waiting and strain. Then Queynt said, "It is fitting I should recognize him, Peter. I knew him. Now, how it is that you would know him?"

I was not sure that I should answer. Silkhands gave me no help, merely staring at me owl-like across the fire. It was Jinian who finally said, "Tell him, Peter. If you cannot trust Queynt, you cannot trust any in this world and we may as well give up."

It was there, then, in the dusk of the Waeneye, beside a dying fire that I set the Gamesmen of Barish upon a flat stone, reserving only the blue of Windlow to my secret self. They stood under the eyes of all, but it was only Vitior Vulpas Queynt who leaned above them with tears flowing down his face as he touched them one by one. I wanted to strike him, wanted to seize the Gamesmen and flee into the dark. I could feel the serpent within, knotting and writhing. Only Jinian's eyes upon me, her hand upon my knee, kept me quiet as the man picked them up, turned them, called them by name.

Oh, Gamelords, but they were mine. Mine. Not his.

In a little time, the worst of the feeling faded, and I was able to speak and think again. I had to tell him I could speak with them. Read them, and he looked at me then with such awe I felt uncomfortable.

I tried to explain. "It is my brain they use to think with, Queynt. Otherwise they are as when they were made. I have been under the mountain of the magicians. I have seen how they are made. Have you?"

"Oh, yes, Gamesman," he affirmed, no longer joking or voluble. "I have been beneath the mountain. I went there last some decades ago to search for Barish."

We waited. He seemed to debate with himself whether we should be enlightened or not. At last it was Jinian again who spoke, as she had to me. "Queynt, we've trusted you. You've hinted to us and hinted to us a hundred times asking if we know what you hope we know. Now is time to set all mystery aside. There may have been reasons to stay hidden, but they are in the past. Now we must trust one another."

"Barish and I," he said, "were brothers."

He stood to walk to the side of the abyss, stood there peering northward as he talked, seeming not to like the sight of our faces. "We came to this world together. You know that story. If you do not, it is not important now. . . .

"Well, let it be said. We came, Barish and I, and a host of others. We came to serve a lie. There were wives who were loved and children who were loved and a world approaching war with another world which neither would win—well. Some powerful persons of that world sought to send certain loved ones away to safety. They needed an excuse. A fiction. A lie . . .

"There was a woman, a girl. Didir. Some thought she could read minds. Others thought not. The people of her home place were afraid of her, true, naming her Demon and Devil. The powerful men of the place said they would send researchers away to another place to find out about this strange Talent she had. 'In later time it may prove useful. However, the research may be long, so it will be necessary to send support staff and agriculturists and bio-engineers and technologists and so on and so on.' Their wives were the agriculturists and their children the bio-engineers. Among them were a few, a very few, who really knew something about such matters."

"You," said Jinian. "And Barish."

"I," he admitted, "and Barish. And a few others, though most of the so called scientists were second rate academics caught in a strange web of vanity and ambition. They stayed under the mountain, caught up in their dreams of research—research on 'monsters.' When we would not let them have Didir, they created monsters of their own. And we, the rest of us, came out from the mountain into this new, supposedly uninhabited world. . . ."

"Supposedly," prompted Jinian.

"Well, supposedly. There were living things here. There were intelligent creatures here. There was material the bio-engineers could use, mixes, crosses, deliberate and inadvertent. Children began to be born with many Talents. The Talent of Didir proved to be real. Barish said it was simply evolution, a natural evolution of the race. I said no, it was this world, this place."

He was silent for so long after that that Jinian had to prompt him again.

The rest of us were silent, afraid if we spoke we might stop him, interrupt his disclosure and never learn what he would tell us.

"Well, the poor fools stayed under the mountain. The Talents began to be born, and to grow, and feed on one another. Some were good people. Others were truly monsters. Barish was always an activist. He decided to intervene, to make plans. . . .

"He stole one of the transport machines, disassembled it, brought it here to the wastes. Then he sought out the best of the emerging Talents, seduced them with hope and high promises, and brought them here. There were twelve with Barish, the Council. They made plans. They would accumulate those among the Gamesmen who had notions of justice, accumulate them like seed grain, and when the time came, they would plant that crop for a mighty harvest."

He returned to us by the fire, shivering, though the night was not yet that cold. "It was not enough to plan a great future if one might not be alive to see it. So he asked me to work with him to develop a strain of people who would be immune to the Talents of Gamesmen and immutable through time. Well, we had longevity drugs and maintenance machines as well as the transport machines themselves. It gave us centuries to work. When there were enough of the Immutables, Barish made a contract with them. They were to find the good seed among the Gamesmen and communicate those names to those under the mountain. Those under the mountain would have them picked up, blued, and stored in the ice caverns. He got their agreement very simply, by playing on their fears. He told the 'magicians' that those identified were a danger to them, a danger to be removed but preserved as a later source of power. They believed Barish. Everyone believed Barish.

"And so, the Immutables became the 'Council.' Up until the death of Riddle's grandfather, some eighty years ago. The chain was broken then. We may never know why."

"And Barish himself," prompted Jinian as I was about to do so.

"And Barish himself lay down beside the eleven others he had brought up here to Barish's Keep. Once every hundred years the Immutables were to come and wake him, bringing with them some brain-dead body which he might occupy in order that his own not age, for he wished to save his lifespan for the great utopian time which was to come. And once every hundred years I met him in Leamer, he in one guise or another, I always

462

as Queynt, to talk of this world and its future. Once a century we would argue about the methods he had chosen, I urging him to waken his stored multitudes and learn from those who had been here before he came; he saying that there were not yet enough, to give him just another hundred years. . . ."

"Until?" I asked, knowing the story was almost at an end.

"Until some eighty years ago I came to Leamer to meet him only to find it in ruins. No Barish. Until I came up here to find his Keep, where I had been only once before, to find tumbled stone and Wind's Bones, abysses and fallen mountains. I went to Dindindaroo to ask Riddle—the current Riddle of that time—where Barish was. Dindindaroo was in ruins, Riddle dead, the new Riddle ignorant of the very name of Barish.

"I grieved. I went against my judgment and kept up his work. I became the new Council as Riddle had been before me. I sent my hundreds into the icy caverns. I waited for Barish. He did not return. And then, at last, a year ago the mountain of magicians went up in fire and I knew Barish would not come again of himself.

"He lies upon this mountain, or he is gone. I seek him. You seek him. And we must find him because where he lies is the only machine which can restore Barish's multitude to life once more. If this thing is not done, he will have lived and died to no purpose, and I will have been party to a very grave miscalculation. . . ."

I believed him. We all did. There was no fantastic pretense in him now, no egregious eccentricism. He was only one, like us, driven by old loyalties and a sense of what could be good and right. If Windlow had been there, he would have taken the man by the hand and reassured him, so I did it, wordlessly, hoping he would understand. It seems he did, for he said, "Your purpose is like mine. If you have been guided here by songs, by Seers, by a giant form striding to the north, well—if there is anything of Barish remaining, he will be trying to reach me."

"As Thandbar tries to reach his kindred," I said. "His is the only Gamesman I have never touched. His was my own Talent, so I never called upon him."

"I never knew that any living thing or any known device could reach what lies preserved within the blues," said Queynt. "Though some once said that travelers between the stars sometimes wakened with a memory of dreams. Who knows? I don't. I know very little."

"Do you know how you have lived this thousand years?" asked Jinian. "While I am much inclined to trust you, Vitior Queynt, this is one thing about you I find unbelievable."

"I have lived this long by learning," he said, "from shadowpeople and gnarlibars and krylobos and eestnies. You have not seen eestnies, but they were here before we came and would teach you, too, if you asked. Barish had not the patience for it, so he said. Then, too, he kept thinking I would die. He will be offended I have not."

Well, we had enough to chew on for one night. King Kelver went back along our trail to appear as a Mirrorman. He retrieved the cap at the same time, and my help was not needed. It seemed that the Elator or the Mirrorman suspected nothing.

When morning came, Queynt suggested that Jinian and I take Yittleby and Yattleby and continue the search across the chasm. "The birds can leap the abyss," he said. "If the rest of us stay here or spend some time seeking a trail, it will delay those behind us a bit more. Perhaps we will spend a day or two searching off in different directions while you and Jinian go in the direction we believe correct." It seemed as good an idea as any other, so I Dragoned across, carrying Jinian, then showed myself high in the air to let the followers know that the abyss had been crossed by Dragon. The others were scattered among the rocks, seeming to seek a way through the maze. From my height, I could see several, and I knew they could follow us whenever they felt it wise to do so. Delay, obfuscation, Game and more Game. I was as weary of it as possible to be.

Yittleby and Yattleby had leaped the chasm, galloping to the very edge to launch themselves up and out with ecstatic cries, long legs extended before them, for all the world like boys vying with one another in the long jump. They were saddled, which surprised me, and they knelt at our approach to let us mount. Then it was only necessary to hang on while they lurched upright and began their matched, unvarying stride toward the north. They would bear no bit or bridle. One or two attempts to guide them taught me merely to point in the direction I wanted to go.

Late in the day I saw a fallen stone with a waysign painted upon it. By matching the stone to its broken pedestal, I could see which way the arrow had originally pointed, and I indicated that direction to Yittleby. She ignored me. I tapped her on the neck, sat back in startlement as the huge beak swung around to face me. "Krerk," she said, stamping one taloned foot. "Krerk."

At that moment I heard a harsh, rumbling roar as of a great rockslide. As it went on, rumbling and roaring, I realized it was not the sound of stone. "Gnarlibar?" I whispered.

"Krerk," both birds agreed, turning away from the line I had indicated. When the sound changed in intensity, the birds again changed direction, ascending a pile of rough stones. Halfway up they knelt and shook us off, gesturing with their beaks in an unmistakable communication. "Go on and see," they were saying. "Take a good look." They crouched where they were as we crawled to the top of the pile.

Below us was a kind of natural amphitheatre, broken at each compass point by a road entering the flat. Assembled on the slopes of the place were some hundreds of the shadow-people, their chatter and bell sounds almost inaudible beneath the ceaseless roaring. In the center of the place a single, gigantic krylobos danced, one twice the height of Yittleby or Yattleby, feet kicking high, feather topknot flying, wing-arms extended in a fever of wild leaping and finger snapping. The roaring grew even louder, and through the four road entrances of the place came four beasts.

Jinian clutched at me. My only thought was that this was what Chance had wanted me to Shift to and he had been quite mad. They were like badgers, low, short-legged, very wide. They were furry, had no tails, had a wide head split from side to side by a mouth so enormous either Yittleby or Yattleby would have fit within it as one bite. They came *leat,* that is to say, from the four directions at once, each uttering that mountain-shattering roar. The giant krylobos went on dancing. Queynt's two birds came to crouch beside us, conversing in low krerks of approval, whether at the dance, the dancer, or the attack, I could not tell.

As the gnarlibars reached the center, the krylobos leapt upward, high, wing-fingers snapping, long legs drawn up tight to his body, neck whipping in a circular motion. Yittleby said to Yattleby, "Kerawh," in a tone indicating approval. "Whit kerch," Yattleby agreed, settling himself more comfortably.

The gnarlibars whirled, spinning outward, each counter-clockwise, in an incredible dance as uniform in motion as though they had been four bodies with one mind. The krylobos dropped into the circle they had left among them, spun, cried a long, complicated call, and then launched upward once more as the four completed their turn and collided at the center in a whirling frenzy of fur.

"Krylobos, bos, bos," cried the shadowmen over an ecstasy of flute and bell sounds. "Gnarlibar, bar, bar," called another faction, cheering the beasts as they spun once more and retreated. In the center the enormous bird continued his dance, her dance, wing-fingers snapping like whip cracks, taloned feet spinning and turning. "Bos, bos, bos," said Yittleby, conversationally. I had raised up to get a better view, and she brought her beak down sharply upon my head. "Whit kerch," she instructed. I understood. I was to keep low.

The circus went on. I did not understand the rules, but it was evidently a very fine contest of its kind. When the gnarlibars withdrew after an hour or so, roaring still in a way to shake the stones, Yittleby and Yattleby rose to lead us down into the amphitheatre. Almost at once I heard familiar voices crying, "Peter, eater, ter, ter," and my legs were seized in a tight embrace. Flute sound trilled, there was much shrieking and singing in which I caught a few familiar words of the shadow language. One small figure pounded itself proudly upon its chest and said, "Proom. Proom." I remembered him and introduced Jinian with much ceremony. She was immediately surrounded by her own coterie all crying "Jinian, ian, an an," to her evident discomfort.

"What is it?" she asked. "What's going on?"

"It looks rather like a festival," I suggested. "I was told once that the shadowpeople are fond of such things. Some here have traveled a long way from the place I met them."

I felt a hard tug at one leg and looked down into another familiar little face, fangs glistening in the light. They had never come out into the light when I had traveled with them before. Was it that they felt safe among the krylobos and the gnarlibars? Or that a time of festival was somehow different for them? Whatever the answer, my wide-eared friend was busy communicating in the way he knew, acting it out. He was going walky, walky, pointing to the north, patting me and pointing. I nodded, turned, walky walked myself toward the north, going nowhere. He opened his hands, so human a gesture that Jinian laughed. "What for?" he was saying. "Why?"

Inspiration struck me. I held out a hand, "Wait," then peered into the south, hand over eyes. The shadowpeople turned, peered with me. At first there was nothing as the sun dropped lower. Then, just as I was beginning to think it would not come, there was the giant striding upon the wind toward us once more. I pointed, cried out. Jinian pointed, exclaimed. All the shadowpeople chattered and jumped up and down.

"Andibar, bar, bar," they chanted. "Andibar!"

Jinian and I were astonished. "The sound is so very close," she said. "They mean Thandbar!"

"Andibar," they agreed, nodding their heads. We waited while the giant approached, dissolved into wind and mist around us, then went on to the north. I cried out to the shadowpeople, pointed, made walky, walky. Aha, they cried, louder than words. Aha. They were around me, pushing, running off to the north and returning, indicating by every action that they knew the way well. We went among them, propelled by their eagerness.

Ahead of us we could see the giant twist and change, flowing onto the stony mountain like smoke sucked into a chimney. Yittleby and Yattleby followed us, conversing. We half ran, half walked among the mazes of stone and Wind's Bone to come, starlit at last, to a pocket of darkness into which the shadowpeople poured like water. Jinian and I dropped onto the stone, panting. We could not see well enough to follow them.

They returned, calling my name and Jinian's, querulously demanding why we did not come. Yittleby said something to them, and they darted away to return in moments with branches of dried thorn. One burrowed into my pocket to find the firestarter, emerging triumphantly in a bright shower of sparks. Then we had fire, and from the fire torches, and from the torches light to take us down into the earth.

We needed the fire for only a little time. The clambering among tumbled stone was for only a short distance before we emerged into corridors as smooth as those I had seen beneath the mountains of the magicians. There was light there, cool, green light, and a way which wound deep into a constant flow of clean, dry air. At the end of the way was an open door. . . .

# 11

# The Gamesmen

## of Barish

THE SHADOWPEOPLE OPENED THE DOOR wider as we approached it. The place was not new to them, and I had a moment's horrible suspicion that we might find only ruin and bones within. Such was not the case.

The pawns have places called variously temples or churches in which there are images of Didir or Tamor or of other beings from an earlier time than ours. I had been in one or two of these places on my travels, and they were alike in having a solemn atmosphere, a kind of dusty reverence, and a smell of smoky sweetness lingering upon the air. This place was very like that. There were low pedestals within, clean and polished by the flowing air, on each of which one of my Gamesmen lay.

The shadowpeople had surrounded one pedestal and waited there, beckoning, calling "Andibar, bar, bar," in their high, sweet voices. When Jinian and I came near, they sat down in rows around the recumbent figure and began to sing. The words were in their own language, but the music. . . .

"The wind song," whispered Jinian. "The same melody."

Though the singer in Xammer had played it upon a harp and these little people upon flutes and bells, the song was the same. I knew then where the frail singer in Leamer had heard it first. How she had translated it into our language, I might never know. They sang it through several times, with different words each time, and I had no doubt what they sang and what I had heard differed very little in meaning. When they finished, one very tiny one leaned forward to chew on Thandbar's toe, was plucked up and spanked by another to the accompaniment of scolding words. It did not seem to have damaged Thandbar. He was fully dressed, helm lying beside him, fur cloak drawn about him under a light coverlet. Jinian laid her hand upon him and shivered. "Cold." I already knew that. Except for the ceremonial setting, the careful dignity of his clothing, his body was as cold and hard as those in the ice caverns. And yet, something had left this body to pour into the evening sky, to wander the world and beg his kinsmen for release from this silent cold.

I walked among the others. Tamor and Didir, looking exactly as I had known them; Dorn, piercing eyes closed in endless slumber; stocky Wafnor, half turned on his side as though his great energy had moved him even in that chill sleep. Hafnor bore a mocking smile as though he dreamed; and Trandilar dreamed, likewise, older than I would have expected, but no less lovely for that. Could she Beguile me, even through this sleep?

Shattnir lay rigid, hands at her sides, crown in place, as though she had decided to be her own monument. Dealpas was huddled under her blanket, legs and arms twisted into positions of fret and anxiety. Buinel's mouth was half open. The machine had caught him in mid-word. And, finally, Sorah, the light gauze of her mask hiding her face. I drew it aside to see her there, calm, kindly looking, eyes sunken as though in some inward gaze.

And lastly . . .

Lastly. I gasped, understanding for the first time the implications of what Queynt had told me. "Barish," I said. He lay before me, wrapped in a Wizard's robe embroidered with all the signs and portents, two little lines between his eyes to show his concentration even in this place.

"Barish," Jinian agreed. "He has a good face."

He did have a good face, rather long and bony, with dark bushy brows and a knobby nose over wide, petulant lips.

"I did not expect to find him here," I said.

"Only his body," she replied. "Queynt said he was awakened into different bodies each time."

"Perhaps he wasn't awakened. Perhaps the blue is here, somewhere."

"If it had been," she said soberly, "Riddle's grandfather would have taken it to Dindindaroo with all the rest."

Still, we looked. There were cabinets on the walls, doors leading into other rooms. We found books, machines. In a room we identified as Barish's own there was a glass case which still showed the imprint of a Gameboard which was not there. I fit the Onomasticon into a gap in a bookshelf. This was the place from which Riddle's grandfather had removed the treasures he had sworn to preserve.

We returned to the outer room. The machine was there, behind a low partition, a tiny light blinking slowly upon its control panel.

"There is still power here," I said.

Then I said nothing for a while.

Then, "Let us go out of here. I have to think."

She gave me a long, level look, but did not say anything until we had climbed upward through the tumble to the open air. The little people came with us, chattering among themselves. When we took food from the saddlebags, they clustered around, and I realized there were more of them than we could feed. "I must go hunting," I said. "They will be happy to stay here. Their word for fire is 'thruf.' If you can keep one going, with their help, I'll bring back some kind of meat."

Then she did try to say something to me, but I did not wait to hear. Instead, I Shifted into fustigar shape and loped off into the stones. I did not want to think, and it is perfectly possible not to think at all, if one Shifts. I did not think, merely hunted. There were large, ground-running birds abroad in the night, perhaps some smaller kin of the great krylobos. They were swift, but not swift enough. I caught several of them, snapping their necks with swift, upward tosses of my fustigar head. What was it brought me up, out of mere fustigar to something else?

Perhaps it was the awareness of my bones, the long link bones between my rear legs and forelegs, the shorter link bone between the rear legs, the flat rear space where a tail might have been but was not, the curved link bones between shoulders and head, the arching, flexible ribs which domed this structure and anchored all its muscles. . . .

The starshaped skeleton of this world. Unlike the backboned structure of our world, whatever world it might have been. This world, into which we came, uninvited, surely, to spread ruin and wreck. And yet into which we were welcomed. The shadowpeople waited beside the fire with Jinian for the feast their friend would bring them. They would call Peter, eater, ter, ter into the darkness, play their silver flutes, ring their bells, sniff the bones twice when they had done, and sleep beneath the stones. And they might gnaw a bit on Thandbar and be spanked for it.

And in Hell's Maw they were meat for Huld. So had said the Elator, laughing, as he ate other meat at his campfire.

Some acid burned in my fustigar throat, some pain afflicted my fustigar heart. Ah, well, I could not leave them behind me to flee into a darkness forever.

The animal turned itself about and ran back the way it had come, to stand upon its hind legs and Shift once more. Into Peter once more. Into the same confusion I had left.

They welcomed me with cries of pleasure, assisted in cleaning the birds and spitting them over the fire while others foraged for more thorn and devil's spear. We ate together, bird juice greasing our chins and hands, and sang together in the echoing dark. I saw Jinian's eyes upon me but ignored her as if I did not understand. Tomorrow was time enough for decision.

"I sent Yattleby with a message for Queynt," she said.

"Ah," I replied. "A message for Queynt."

"Written," she said. "I gave it to Yattleby, pointed back the way we had come and said 'Queynt.' He seemed to understand."

"I'm sure he did," I said, fighting down anger. I did not need more pressure on me. Through the thin fabric of my Shifted hide I could feel the pouch I had carried for two years. Inside it were Didir and Tamor. Mine. Shattnir. Mine. Even Dealpas. Mine. "When I give them up," I said in a carefully conversational tone, "I will be powerless to confront Huld. If I had not had them, you would have been meat for groles instead of sitting here beside me, eating roast bird."

"When you saved us from the bones in Three Knob," she said, "it was by your own Talent. If you had not had Sorah to call upon outside Leamer, you would have found another way. You need nothing but yourself, Peter."

"I *do*," I shouted at her, making wild echoes flee from the place. "Without them, I am nothing. Nothing at all . . ."

She wiped her hands fastidiously, poured water from her flask to wash her face, turned that face to me at last, quiet, unsmiling, unfrowning, quiet. "I have told you I am a Wizard, Peter. I will give you Wizardly advice. Think on yourself, Peter. Think on Mavin, and Himaggery and Mertyn. Think on Windlow. Carefully, slowly, on each. Then think on Mandor and Huld. And when you have done, decide with whom you will stand."

Gamelords, I said to myself. Save me from the eloquence of Wizards. She sounded like Himaggery, or rather more like Windlow, though Wind-

471

low had been a Seer, not a Wizard. This abstraction called justice was all very well, but when it meant that one had to give up one's own power. . . . One considered being Huld-like.

"Jinian," I cried. "Do you know what it is you ask?"

"Of course," she said. "Wizards always know what they ask. And they ask everything."

I held out my arms and she came into them to hold me as a mother might hold a child or a Sorceress her crown. When we slept, it was thus twined together, and for a time I did not think of her being a Wizard. The shadowpeople let us sleep. They faded away in the morning light, into the deep caverns of the rock, to return at dusk, I was sure, expecting another feast, another song fest. Well. Perhaps by then we would have more guests to feed. So saying, I took Jinian by the hand and we went back into Barish's Keep.

"Which of them first, Wizard?" I asked. "Shall it be Shattnir or Dealpas? Buinel or Hafnor? I think not Buinel. He would ask us to prove our authority before raising the rest."

"Thandbar," she said. "It is he who has searched for his kinsmen, Peter. It is not fitting he should be raised first?"

I should have thought of it myself. We lifted the rigid body of Thandbar off the pedestal on which it rested, tugged it around the partition to the machine, and spent both our strengths in heaving it onto the metal plate which was precisely like those I had seen on similar machines under the mountain of the magicians. There was even the small, circular receptacle for the blue. I set it in place, stepped back, and thrust down the lever as I had seen Mavin do it.

Nothing happened. There was no hum, no scream, no nothing. No sound. No movement. Jinian looked at me with quick suspicion. I protested: "This is how Mavin did it! There is power here. The light is on. Perhaps it must be set in some way." She helped me wrestle Thandbar to the floor before I began a twisting, pushing, turning circumambulation of the device, moving everything movable upon it. I tried the lever again. Nothing.

I turned to her to expostulate, explain, only to meet her level regard, no longer suspicious. "This is why he never returned. Why Barish never returned."

Seeing my confusion, she drew me away to Thandbar's pedestal where we sat while she puzzled it out. "They would wake Barish every hundred years. They would bring some brain-dead but living body for him, some poor fellow brain-burned by a Demon perhaps, and would put the body in that machine with Barish's blue. Then he, Barish, in a different body each time, would go into the world to meet Queynt, assess the progress of his plan. He would return here after some years—how many? Ten perhaps? Twenty? Give up the blue again, and the attendant Immutables would take the body away to be buried.

"But the last time he was awakened, the machine malfunctioned? Yes. I think so. Something went wrong. Either during the process or right after? Yes. Otherwise his blue would be with the rest. That red light you see upon the device is probably a warning light, something to tell the operator that things are awry within. So Barish was no tech. Or if he was, he had no part or lacked some contrivance. The fact that he did not fix it means that he could not. And whoever or whatever Barish was, it went forth from this place knowing it would do no good to return."

I went back to Thandbar's body, lying on the cold floor of the place. Such is the contrary nature of mankind, or perhaps only of the Peters among mankind, that I now wished most heartily to do what I had fought before against doing. Now that it was impossible, I was determined to do it.

"Since you are so reasonable, Wizard," I said. "Reason us a way out of this dilemma."

"I will wait for Queynt," she said. "Since he may have some knowledge of the device. If he does not, then we will think again."

She went up out of the place. I heard her talking to Yittleby, who had remained behind when Yattleby went away, saying something about patience. I took some confidence from the impatience of the krylobos. It was better than fear. I walked around and around the machine. Surely there was some way it could be understood? Surely some way that a Shifter could understand it.

In Schlaizy Noithn, I had become a film upon a wall in a place where my very presence was a danger. I reached a tentative finger to the machine, flowed across its metal surface like oil, a thin film, an almost invisible tentacle. This filament poured into a crack, down through the interstices of the mechanism. Here were wires and crystals, hard linkages, soft pads, rollers, some kind of screen which scattered light, a device for casting a narrow beam and manipulating it. I went deeper. This is what Dealpas had done to Izia upon the heights of Mavin's place. Here were strangenesses which I entered and surrounded, tasting, smelling, creating temporary likenesses of. Where was the failure? Where the malfunction? No part of it ached, throbbed, was fevered. Should this dark crystal be alight? This cold wire, should it be warm? Who could tell? No network of nerve enlightened me. I flowed deeper yet.

Who were the voices crying to me? Why did Dorn cry so loud? Why did Didir sting me with her voice? Out? Out of where? Of what? The mysteries which lay around me were tantalizing. Why come out?

Was that Jinian? Silkhands? I felt hands upon me, pulling me, some inner person walking my veins and my nerves, hauling upon my bones. I wanted to tell them to let be, but it would take a mouth and lungs to do that. A mouth. Lungs.

Panic. So does one who is more than half drowned struggle to the surface of water, gasping for breath, unable to breathe. Someone helped me from within. Silkhands.

And I lay upon the floor of the place while Silkhands and Queynt hovered over me and screamed and cried on me.

"Fool, fool," said Silkhands. "Even Mavin would not have tried such a thing."

"Fool, fool," wept Jinian. "Oh, Peter, but you are hopeless and I love you."

I was not afraid until I knew what I had done, which was to spend the better part of two days trying to become a machine. Silkhands was worn and exhausted. She had spent the time since her arrival trying to extricate me. If there had been no other reason for her to come to the Wastes of Bleer than to save my life, I was grateful for Windlow's vision and the musician's song. It was she who had come into my inside out body and followed it down into madness, calling it out of its strange preoccupation. When I learned of her effort and my foolishness, I wept tears of weary frustration.

"I don't know what's the matter with it," I confessed.

"And nor do I, my boy," said Queynt. "I had little knowledge of maintenance. We had techs who were specially trained to do that work. It may be that the books are here, somewhere, and even the parts we may need, but I find Jinian's reasoning persuasive. If Barish could have fixed it, he would have done."

"I find it odd," said King Kelver, "that the plans of a thousand years would be allowed to go awry on the failure of one mechanism."

I could not have agreed with him more. However, I had no time for such fine philosophical points because of the news they brought. "The Elator told me last night that Huld is coming," said the King. "I am to betray your location to him when he arrives. He grew impatient and left Hell's Maw last night."

Jinian had my map upon the floor, measuring the distance with her fingers. "Three days," she whispered. "They will be upon us within three days. Four at most!"

In a few moments I built and discarded a hundred notions. I could take Wafnor and make a mountain fall. Buinel would burn the bones as they came toward us. Hafnor would flick me to the Bright Demesne where I would repeat my call for help. Didir would Read Huld's mind. All these wild thoughts tumbled one upon another until Jinian took my hand, and I knew she had followed them almost as though she could have Read them.

"Peter. You can manage two or three of the Gamesmen of Barish at a time. If worst comes to worst, you will do it and we will all pray your success. But oh, how much better it would be if all of them fought at our side."

She was right, of course. I leaned upon her shoulder and gave a great sigh, half weakness and half weariness, thinking the whole time of roast fowl. My weakness was simple hunger, and I said so. She remedied the lack as soon as I expressed it by putting a mug of hot soup into my hand and crumbling hard bread into it. As I ate it with a tired greediness, she went on.

"There is something we are not thinking of," she said. "Something simple and obvious. The song we heard in Xammer was learned at the Minchery in Leamer from a young songsmith who dreamed it. It is the same music we heard when the giant strode across us in the hills behind Three Knob. It came from Thandbar, somehow, and Thandbar's blue is in your pocket. Somehow, Peter, the separation of body and blue is not as complete as we thought, for something sensible of Thandbar escaped, rose up from his body lying here in the cold wastes of Bleer to stride across the world crying for our help. There is a clue there we are not seeing, Peter. Help me think.''

''It probably has something to do with cold,'' I mumbled around a mouthful of bread. ''In the School Houses, we always kept the blues cold. They have not been cold in my pocket. Perhaps that has something to do with it. Perhaps it is natural for them to recombine, and the machine only aids that process. . . .''

''What does the machine do, Peter?''

''Ahh,'' I said, remembering chill wire and hostile casing, the infinite lattices of crystal in which I had lost myself. ''It warms the body, warms the blue, scans the blue and Reads it into the mind of the body. Having seen the innards of the machine, I can do part of what the machine does. I can Read the blue, I think, with Didir's help. And Shattnir can help me warm the place. But I don't know how to Read the thing back into a body. It seems all a puzzle. . . .''

''I can Read the body,'' said Silkhands. ''If you will link with me, as they linked in the Bright Demesne when they searched for you. As Tragamors sometimes link to increase their strength.''

I shuddered, remembering that such a linkage was precisely what Mandor and Huld had demanded of me in Bannerwell—of me, or of Mavin. Still, this was to no evil purpose. It took me a while to work myself up to it, but once we were started it seemed to flow along of its own movement. It was not as simple as that sounds, and yet it was simpler than I would have expected.

First was Shattnir, gathering all the warmth she could from the sun to bring it below and warm the chamber of the Gamesmen. Then was Didir, to set her pattern firmly in my head, telling her what we intended, begging her to stay within and help me, show me the way.

Then I took the blue of Thandbar in my hand and put my arms tight around Silkhands as she laid her hands upon Thandbar's head. He came into my mind and greeted me with such joy that it burst through me in a wave, a wordless, riotous joy, the rapture of a prisoner released, a caged thing set free. ''Only free,'' I heard him murmur in my head. ''Only free.'' I remembered it as one of his names and knew in that instant what innate quality it was had enabled him to escape the cold room and move out across the world. His Shifter's soul could not have been held, had not been held. I had no time to think of it, for with Didir's pattern tight in my mind I began to Read him, spark by spark, shivering lattice by lattice, sending my warmth down the chill circuits of his being, following those circuits as Silkhands Read them from me and impressed them once again into the body before her.

Time went, seeming hours of it, days of it. Pictures fled through my head. I saw Schlaizy Noithn, bright in the noon light, where Thandbar walked with a loved one. I saw far mountains as seen from above by the eyes of a mist giant. I heard music, not only the wind song I had heard before but generations of bell and flute in the high, wild lands of the shadowpeople. I became tree, mountain, road, a whole legion of beasts I had never seen and knew nothing of. In Thandbar's day, they had lived closer to mankind. In the intervening centuries they had fled away.

I saw memories of Barish: Barish lecturing; Barish pounding a table; Barish laughing; Barish cajoling. I felt horror at the things being done by some Gamesmen, revulsion, anger, and felt Barish play upon that horror and revulsion. In Thandbar's mind, I heard Barish's voice. "We will accumulate the best, like seed grain. We will plant them in the ground of today, for a mighty harvest in the future," his voice ringing, passionate. In Thandbar's mind, I Read belief, then doubt (centuries of doubt), then terror at a conviction of eternal imprisonment. Out of that terror he had fled like mist, to walk the wide world calling for help from his kinsmen.

So the pictures fled across my mind as the blue melted away in my hand, becoming a featureless lump, a sliver, a nothing at all. The body before us stirred, stirred again, until at last its eyes opened, its mouth moved. "I dreamed you, Healer," it whispered in a voice whiskery with dust and age. "I dreamed you." The eyes blinked, blinked, tried to focus. I knew they saw only blurs of light, mute shadows. At last they fastened upon me, and the dusty voice said, "Kinsman. Thanks."

And after that was a long, cloudy time in which Silkhands lay upon the floor exhausted and I trembled in my place like a wind gong perpetually struck, and the others had to take us up, we two and Thandbar, to wrap us up warmly and feed us to the wild piping and cheers of the shadowpeople. It was night. "How long?" I whispered to Queynt.

"You were both exhausted when you began," he said. "You must not try any more tonight. Silkhands could not, in any case. On the morrow, raise up Dealpas. She must help you. Then Didir, for she can do what you have done if I understand it aright." So I slept. Bones marched against us from over the edge of the world, and I slept. Horror collected itself and thundered toward us with drums and trumpets, and I slept. If I had been condemned and upon the scaffold ready to be hanged, I would have slept. There was no more strength in me to stay awake, and morning came and moved itself toward noon before I wakened again to find Silkhands sitting beside me, looking a little wan but determined.

"Come," she said. "Let us waken Dealpas."

Which we did, though Barish's Healer did not wish to be wakened. She fought us the whole way, moaning and weeping, carrying on as though she were the only creature in the world ever to have felt pain. Her whining sickened us, and I was ready to give up and let her lie there forever, but Silkhands was not. I felt her do something I had never known of before: she administered a mental spanking—a lashing along the nerves like a snake striking—and we had Dealpas' attention at last. When we had her awake, she began to moan, half-heartedly, and Jinian came forward to shake her into full wakefulness.

"I have no patience with this Broken Leaf nonsense," she cried into Dealpas' pouting face. "I know not why Barish chose you as a worthy one of his Eleven, why he chose you from among all Healers, unless perhaps there were no others in your time. Well, you are not the best, by any rule, not fit to wear Silkhands' smalls, but you will do what you will do or by the Giant of Thandbar I will teach you what pain is!"

Dealpas was stung, furious, her pain forgotten. I linked with her, somewhat reluctantly, to raise Didir, and in that linkage I learned what had set Dealpas upon her course of whines and plaints. Barish had thought her pretty, had babied her, had petted her—the more she whined, the more petting. So it was I began to doubt that Barish was what I had thought him to be. Wizard, perhaps, but not all wise to have spoiled her so.

We did not work together as well as Silkhands and I had done, but Didir was helping from within to raise up her own body, so all went well and expeditiously in the end. She came up off the stone slab in one fluid movement, not at all grandmotherly, but lithe and still young. "Peter," she said to me, looking full into my eyes, "there will be a better time than now for thanks. Be sure that time will not be forgotten." She hugged me then, and kissed me as a mother might (as Mavin never had in my memory) and went off above to gather some power and settle some ancient matter between herself and Dealpas. When they returned, they were ready for work, and I did not hear Dealpas whine again.

The two of them began with Shattnir, who rose as she had slept, straight, all at once, rising as if she had lain down the night before. I saw her keen eye upon me, recognizing me, and was not surprised. There had been much more life in the blues than I had known. They had changed while with me, while within me. They had used me as I had used them, and I prayed as I saw her glance that she would consider the bargain good. Then she gave me a quick, mocking smile—nothing about Shattnir was ever wholly human—and went about her way.

Meantime Silkhands and I awakened Dorn. Having done this once before, I did not need Didir's help again but was able to Read out the blue of Dorn as though I read a familiar book. Oh, there were surprises, particularly in his youthful memories; and there were terrors as he gained his Talent and learned to use it, but still, what I had known of him was the greater part of him, and he rose at last to greet me by name.

"You do know me," I mumbled.

"How should I not, Peter? Have I not walked in your head as a farmer walks his fields? Have we not raised up ghosts together?"

"I wasn't sure you would remember," I said weakly, remembering myself thinking things I had rather he not know of.

"Why shouldn't I remember a friend?" he asked me, drawing me into an embrace. I had never felt for Mertyn or for Himaggery what I felt in that instant for Dorn. I had never known Mertyn or Himaggery as I knew Dorn. Perhaps he had shaped some essential growing in me, as a father might shape it in a pawnish boy or a loving thalan who knew his sister's child from infancy. What he said was true. I remembered him as a friend. He had never had to do me any hurt, not even for my own good, and so there was no taint between us.

Then Dealpas and I awakened Buinel while Silkhands rested and Didir took time to learn all that was happening. I felt her searching mind go forth, seeking Huld, I thought. It was not difficult to raise up Buinel, only boring. In my whole life I was never to meet anyone so relentless in putting down any spontaneous thought or evanescent desire as was Buinel. He wanted rules for everything, and he wanted them graven in bronze or cut into stone so that he could see they were no temporary things. Well, we persevered, Dealpas and I, she with her mouth all twisted up

479

in distaste and some anger still. When we had him fairly roused he became deeply suspicious of us for having wakened him, so we turned him over to Queynt and Dorn. If they could not settle him I cared not whether we got him settled, though I did owe him much for having saved our lives from the Ghoul. Then Silkhands and Didir returned to wake Hafnor, Wafnor, and Tamor, one after another, each time quicker. It was true, with practice the thing became much easier. Wafnor gave me a glad hug, from a distance, his sturdy body creaking as he bent and twisted, trying to free himself in a few short minutes of the stiffness of centuries. Hafnor gave me a teasing wink. If he had had more power, he would have done something silly and boyish, I knew it, but he had to go above to warm himself in the sun. There was no power below except what Shattnir brought down to us from time to time for the work.

Then Silkhands and I were alone once more, only Sorah and Trandilar upon their pedestals. And Barish. I stood there looking down at him, fingering the lone blue in my pocket. Now that I had given up the others, it seemed an evil thing to keep Windlow by me, an evil thing to keep him so imprisoned. He had no body of his own. It had been burned and destroyed in the place of the magicians. Barish had no blue. It had gone into some other body, perhaps, or been destroyed by the machine. Why not put the two together? Then Windlow might at least live again, live long, and be no worse off than he was now. The body would be strange, but surely it was better to visit a strange place than not to live at all. Silkhands and I were alone in the place. The others had all gone above to seek for Huld or plot their strategy or discuss ways in which we might leave the mountaintop without condemning the rest of the world to Huld's fury.

I called her over and showed her Windlow's blue in my hand, letting my eyes rove over the body of Barish.

She did as I had done, looking back and forth from one to the other. "Why not," she said. "Let us do it now before someone comes down and makes some objection."

"He may only live a little while, to be killed in that battle which is coming," I warned her.

"He will at least die in reality then," she said bitterly, "not be lost in some rock crevasse forever, caught in neither living nor death, perhaps in that same terror Thandbar felt."

480

I nodded, took Windlow's blue into my hand and put my arms around her as she laid her hands upon Barish's head.

Then was maelstrom. Nothing which had gone before had prepared me for it. There was Windlow, surging in my mind like a flood, like a mighty stream pouring over a precipice. There was something else, surging to meet it as the tide meets the outflow of a river, battering waves which meet in foam-flecked flood to crash upon one another, flow around one another, mix together in an inextricable rush and tug and wash. Cities toppled in my head; rivers burst mighty barricades; millennia-old trees fell and splintered. Faces passed as in an endless parade. The sun made a single glittering arc across the sky, flickering between darkness and light as day and night sped past. Then the struggle eased, slowly, and I felt things rise in the flood to heave above the waves, to rock and stabilize themselves upon the flow like boats until all within was liquid and quiet above the steady roll of whatever lay below. Windlow's blue was gone. Silkhands leaned back within the circle of my arms, exhausted. I heard someone come into the room behind us, recognized Queynt's step but was too strained to turn to him as he gasped.

The figure before me on the pedestal opened its eyes. Someone behind those eyes smiled into my face and said, "Peter?" Then that same someone—or another—looked across my shoulder and spoke to Queynt. "Vulpas?" I felt myself thrust aside as Vitior Vulpas Queynt moved to his brother's side.

His brother.

My friend.

Windlow.

Barish.

The same.

# 12

# The Bonedancers
# of Huld

"YOU HAD HIM ALL THE TIME!" Queynt advancing as though to strike me.

A voice from the pedestal, laughing weakly, not Windlow's voice. Not entirely Windlow's voice. Pattern and intonation different. Not so peaceful, not so kindly. "Oh, Vulpas. He didn't know he had me. Poor lad. And he didn't have much of me, at that, or all of me, depending upon how you look at it. He didn't know; Windlow didn't know."

So that Queynt turned again to that voice which seemed more familiar to him than it did to me. "Windlow?"

A long silence. I looked at the body on the pedestal, close wrapped in its Wizardly robes. It had not moved yet, seemed uncertain whether it could. One hand made a little abortive gesture; a foot twitched. The eyes were puzzled, then clearing, then puzzled once more. When he spoke it was tentatively, slowly, as though he had to consider each word and was even then not certain of it.

"The body they brought for me, Vulpas. The bodies were always supposed to be brain-burned. Plenty of those around. Every Game always left them littered about, weeping women, mothers crying, pathetic bodies, able to walk, breathe, eat—nothing else. They were supposed to bring one like that. So they did; body of a Seer named Windlow. Only it wasn't brain-dead—maybe half, maybe only stunned, sent deep. . . .

"The machine. It had been acting strangely. Meant to go to the base and get some tech to come back with me and fix it. I didn't go. Why? Forget why. The time before, the last time I was in this body—the machine didn't separate me. Not all of me. Most of me was still here, in the body, cold. I dreamed. . . .

"Dreamed I saw Thandbar go out of this place like a wind, like a mist, singing. Dreamed little people came in here, singing. Wanted to say

'Help,' wanted to ask them to find Vulpas, find Riddle. Imprisoned. No movement. No voice . . .''

"Who was it then, who went out of here?" demanded Queynt. "Who was it Riddle put the blue into? That last time. When you were supposed to meet me?''

The figure on the slab moved, a supine shrug, a testing of long unused muscles. "Windlow, mostly. Partly me. The machine broke that time, once for all, finally. Screamed like a wounded pombi, like a fustigar in heat, screamed and shrieked and grated itself silent. The light went on. I saw it when I departed, and Riddle said something about not bothering to come back, there was nothing anyone could do. . . .''

"But if you knew all that," I said stupidly, "then why didn't you tell me, Windlow? Why all the mystery? The hiding and hunting and not seeming to know everything there was to know about the Gamesmen and the book? Why all that?''

"Ah, lad." Whoever it was began to sit up, struggling more than any of the others had had to do, achingly. I moved forward to help him, and he patted me on the arm in a familiar way. "I didn't remember. *Windlow* didn't remember. It was all so dreamlike, so strange. How would Windlow tell the difference, Vision or reality? And it was then that the moonlet fell, the world shook and tumbled and fell apart. Then it was run and run and try to stay alive, partly Windlow, partly Barish, the memories all mixed and tumbled with the world, all the people and all the landscape. I forgot Vulpas, forgot the Gamesmen almost, forgot the book almost. Then later some memories came back. Were they memories? Visions of a Seer? How would Windlow-Barish know? And then the memories began to tease, began to make mysteries. Then Windlow-Barish began to search for the book, search for the Gamesmen, remember odd things. Did he ever come back here? Why would he? If he did, the way was lost I suppose. . . .''

"What do you mean, did he?" I shrieked at him. "If Windlow is in you at all, he knows whether he did or not! *Think* him. *Ask* him." I was grieving. I had not meant to trade Windlow, whom I loved, for this stranger.

There was long silence from the pedestal, then the rustle of his cloak, the harsh scratch of the embroideries rubbing upon one another. His voice, when it came, was more as I remembered it. "Right, my boy. Of course. I did not come here. I did not remember this place. I did remember the book, the Gamesmen, but did not remember why they were important. Well, why would Windlow remember any such thing?''

I turned to him desperately. ''Are you in there, Windlow? Have I killed you?''

He laughed, almost as Windlow would have done. ''No, Peter. No. See. All of Windlow is here when I reach for him. I remember the garden of Windlow's House, the meadow you chased the fire bugs through. I remember the tower in which Prionde had us imprisoned, the way we escaped by creeping through the sewer. . . .''

''You did not creep,'' I said. ''We carried you.''

''You carried me. Yes. And I came to Himaggery's place, to the Bright Demesne. It's all there, my boy, all the memories of Windlow's life. They may not be exactly as they were in Windlow's head before, but they are there.''

I felt as though someone had told me I was not quite guilty of some grave crime. The face was not Windlow's face, the body not Windlow's body, but in those memories Windlow still lived. Except—he lived alloyed with another. Silver melted with tin is still silver, and yet it appears in a new guise. One cannot call pewter silver with honesty, and yet all the silver one started with is contained therein. Unless, I thought, the mix was rather more like oil and wine, in which case the oil would rise to the top and the wine lie below, seething to be so covered. Was he silver, Windlow, or oil? Or was he wine? Did it matter, so long as he lived? For a time.

For it would be only for a time. Until what he knew and thought became no longer relevant or necessary and was forgotten. But that was the same with all of us. We were only what we were for a time, at that time. Then our own silver began to mix with the tin of our future to change us. I knew this to be so and grieved for Windlow while I grieved for me. In time I would not be this Peter, even as now I was not the Peter of two years ago who had grieved for Tossa on the road to the Bright Demesne. Yet that Peter was not lost. So Windlow was not lost, and yet he was not Windlow, either.

Silkhands took me by the hand and led me away, shaking her head and murmuring to herself and me. She had loved him, too, perhaps more than I had done, and I wondered if she felt as oddly torn as I did. We did not speak of it just then. Instead, we sat beside the fire, drinking tea and looking into the flames as though to see our futures there, my head feeling like a vacant hall, all echoing space and dust in the corners. We heard Queynt and Barish-Windlow come up out of the place, so we went below to raise up Trandilar and Sorah. If what was to come was wreck and ruin upon us all I did not want them lying helpless under the stones.

There was some milling about when they were all raised up, with much talk, before Hafnor flicked himself away to the north, hoptoad, to see what moved against us. Night was coming, the second night since we had raised up Thandbar. I had spent two days and a night below, and the morrow would be the third day since Huld's host had left Hell's Maw. I warmed my hands at the fire while hoping Himaggery and Mavin would reach us before Huld did, even though I feared it unlikely. There was nothing much we could do in the dark. I told Thandbar of my meeting with the Bonedancer outside Three Knob, and he chuckled without humor. "Grole, eh? Well, I've done that, or something like. It'll take time to grow big, though, so I'll go back among those rocks when we have eaten. I relish the taste of these birds more than the flavor of stone." He had been hunting, as I had done a few days before, in the guise of a fustigar.

So we sat eating and warming ourselves, thinking small thoughts of old comforts and joys. I kept remembering the kitchens in Mertyn's House and the warm pools at the Bright Desmesne. In the hot seasons, one does not often remember how delicious it is to be warm, but beside this fire in the high, windswept wastes, I thought of warm things. Jinian sat down beside me to take my cold hand in her own and rub it into liveliness. I used it to stroke her cheek, feeling I had not seen her for days. Across the fire, Kelver did something similar with Silkhands and smiled across the coals at me in shared sympathy. Queynt was talking to the krylobos, freeing them from their harness so that they could leave us. They stalked away over the wasteland, into the darkness, making a harsh, bugling cry. "They do not like those who feed upon the shadowpeople," Queynt said. "They will bring some help for us from among the krylobos and gnarlibars. I do not expect it will amount to much, but they will feel better for its having been tried. I wish there were some of the eesty here, though they would probably refuse to interfere. . . ."

Dorn talked of laying bones down again which another had raised, telling stories of the long past and the far away. Some, I am sure, were not meant to be believed, but only to cheer us. Some were funny enough to laugh at, despite the plight we found ourselves in. Then Trandilar took up the storytelling, stories of glamour and romance and undying love, turning the fullness of her Beguilement on us so that we forgot the bones of Hell's Maw, forgot Huld, forgot the cold and the high wastes to live for a time in such lands and cities as we had never dreamed of. And all this time Sorah and Wafnor passed the food among us, saving nothing for the morrow, thinking, I suppose, that we would be too busy to eat then and glad of anything we had eaten tonight. So it was we were all replete, and so Beguiled by Trandilar that danger had vanished from our minds, and we were calm and still as a day in summer, lying close together in our blankets, to drift into sleep. I think Trandilar probably walked among us all night long, softly speaking words which led us into pleasant dreams, for when we woke in the morning, it was with a sense of happy fulfillment and courage for the day. Now it was Barish passed the cups among us, but I saw him gathering the herbs he put into them from the rock crevasses, and the way he searched them out and bent above them, the way he crushed them and brought them to his nose, all that was Windlow. The brew was hot and bitter, but it brought alertness of an almost supernatural kind. We had just finished it when Hafnor returned to tell us our fears were less than the truth.

"This Demon Huld, whom you have made so effectively your enemy, must have been recruiting Necromantic Talents for a generation or more. He has Sorcerers as well, aplenty, and such a host of bones and liches as the world may collapse under. They stretch from horizon to horizon, across the neck of the wastes from the gorge of the Graywater to the valley of the Reave."

"What of the Gamesmen within that host of bones?" asked Jinian. "Talents which are useless against bones may be used against the Gamesmen."

"If one can get at them through the host of bones," replied Hafnor. "You will have to see it for yourself. The Gamesmen are within the bones as a zeller stands in the midst of a field of grain. You cannot get to them without scything what stands in between."

"I have found chasms full of brush," offered Buinel. He was not quite so odd in person as I had pictured him, still fussy and inclined to procedural questions, but he seemed to have grasped the danger we faced and be trying to make sensible suggestions. "When the bones cross them, they will cross a river of fire."

"And I will seek out Huld among the hosts of bones," said Tamor. "He comes from the north, which means I can come at him from out of the sun. If my hands have not utterly lost their cunning in these long centuries." He bent his bow experimentally, heard the string snap, and bit back a curse. "Well, I have others. Lords, what a time and place to awaken to." A little later I saw him go out with his bow strung.

Didir had spent some time with Barish. I saw her holding his hand, leaning her head against his, face puzzled and remote. She had loved him, I had heard. Now he was no longer the Barish she had known. I pitied her; Windlow was her stranger as Barish was mine. Neither of us quite knew our old companions. She stood up beside him at last, laid her cheek against his, then moved away. "I will do what I can to let you know what is in Huld's mind," she said. "Though it is probable that we know exactly what is in his mind now. He will overrun us in order to demonstrate his strength to those allied with him. He says he seeks Barish, but that is probably only pretense. He seeks to overrun the world, and this will be his first trial." She moved off to some high place, striding with great dignity but, I thought, a little sadness. Barish looked after her, the expression on his face one of remote sorrow. I turned from them both, for it hurt to see them.

Trandilar announced her intention of going down into the cavern, with Sorah and Dealpas, and staying there until needed or wanted by someone. "We will be out of the way," she said. "You need no Beguilement. If Visions will help, we will bring them to you. If a Healer is wanted, call down to Dealpas."

Hafnor had gone back to spying on the host. Wafnor had placed himself near a pile of great boulders. Shattnir was standing in the sun, arms wide, soaking up all the power she could to help us all. This left me, Peter, among the Wizards—Barish, Vulpas, Jinian. King Kelver stayed with them also, but I thought I would emulate Thandbar and become a grole once again.

I had barely time to engrole myself and gain size before I felt the tickle in my head which said Huld was seeking his prey. Long and long I had leaned upon Didir's protection in such cases, and strangely enough it did not forsake me. I remembered the pattern of her cover and dipped beneath it as I went on chewing at the stone. He could not find me. With Didir on watch, I thought it unlikely he could find any of us.

I had set myself in a high notch between the flat plateau he marched across and the tumbled stone we were hidden in. Stone lay above me as well as below and to either side. I made eyes for myself for, though groles were blind, I chose not to be. I needed to watch for Himaggery. I needed to see Huld's approach. It was not far to see, not far at all, for he came upon us like a monstrous wave, a creeping rot, a fungus upon that land, white and rotten gray with the brilliance of banners like blood in the midst of it. I could not see individual skeletons, only the angular mass of it, as though a heap of white straw blew toward me in a mighty wind, all joints and angles, scattered all over with white beads which were the skulls of those which marched. I could not see the Gamesmen. I only knew where they were by the shimmering of the banners, for the bones carried nothing but themselves. Within that mass somewhere were drummers, for we could all hear the brum, brum, brum which set the pace of the bones. Perhaps the Bonedancers marched near the drums, to keep their time from the far west of the great horde to the far east of it, coming in an unwavering line. Brum, brum, brum. It sent shivers through the stone I rested upon, louder and louder as they came nearer.

First into the fray was old Tamor, though he had not been so old as to warrant that name when he laid down to sleep. He was younger than Himaggery by a good bit. I saw him come toward the host out of the sun, saw his arrows darting silver, then a retreating streak as he fled away before the spears which came after him. Huld's Tragamors were alert. I did not see him again for a time, then caught a glimpse of him, glittering and high, just before another flight of spears. This time the spears arched higher, and I thought I saw him lurch and fall, but he did not come to the ground. I felt Demon tickle, then Didir's voice in my head. Evidently she knew me so well she could speak to me easily even now. "We see him, Peter. Kelver and Silkhands are working their way around to the west where he came to the ground. There are birds here who will carry them. . . ."

So. Yittleby and Yattleby had returned, their recruitment done, to help us as best they could. Well, at least Silkhands would be out of the battle. At least she and Kelver would have some time to themselves, to share what had been growing between them all this long way from Reave-bridge. If Tamor were not seriously injured, perhaps all three would survive. For a time. Looking at the army marching toward us, I thought there was little hope for any survival longer than a season or two. Huld would not stop with overrunning us. As Didir said, we were only an excuse to try his strength. If he had truly wanted Barish, he would have come with fewer and cleverer than he had brought. No, this was to be warning to the world, a flexing of his muscle. I hated him in that moment, hated him for all he cared nothing about—for love and honor and truth and a word he had never heard: justice.

The bones had come closer. They were approaching a great chasm now, a canyon brimmed with thorn. The bones leapt across it, light as insects, not even brushing the branches. They came in dozens and hundreds and thousands, then the Gamesmen behind them, Bonedancers lifted over the tearing thorn in Armiger arms.

The chasm went up in flame, all at once, a sheet of fire leagues long and tower high. I was too far away to hear the Bonedancers screaming, but I saw them fall in fiery arcs into that towering pyre. The bones kept coming, piling in and burning, falling as the thorn burned away to make room for more. They never stopped, not even for an instant, but went on scrambling across like spiders. Somewhere inside my great grole shape Peter puzzled at what he had seen. Why had the bones kept coming when the Bonedancers died? Other Bonedancers back in the host? Or simply one of those special cases in which things once raised went on of themselves? If that were so, then whatever we might do against the Gamesmen themselves would not help us.

"Some are gone, Buinel," I whispered to myself. "But there are more coming than all the thorn in the world can burn."

The rock beneath me throbbed; boulders began to heave themselves up from the hillside to launch away in long curves toward the center of the host. They were aimed at Huld, surely, but his Tragamors deflected them. They flew aside, bowled through acres of bones, crushing a hundred skulls or more to leave the fragments dancing, a shower of disconnected white, like a flurry of coarse snow. The first great stone was followed by others, and the center of the host milled about, slowed for a moment. What did Huld intend? Would he merely overrun us, smother us under that weight of bones? Or were some among that host seeking us, seeking

489

Barish, making an excuse for this Game, Great Game, the Greatest this world had ever seen?

Still they came on. We had done nothing to slow them, not with Tamor's arrows or Wafnor's great stones. I had seen no evidence that Dorn had tried to put this host down, and having seen the size of it, I did not blame him. It would have been like calming the sea with a spoonful of oil. Far to my right I saw the first files of bones entering the defile where Thandbar waited. "Good appetite, kinsman," I wished him. He was not far from me. Even as I made my wish for him, the first of the horde poured onto the flat before me, threading between the mighty Wind's Bones, the huge star-shaped skeletons of this world, bones arranged like my own grole bones. I settled myself, scrunching into the rock, mouth open.

Didir called in my head. "Peter! Sorah has Seen . . . Seen . . ."

Gamelords, I said to myself. What matter what she has Seen. They are about to overrun us, bury us, sift us out with bony fingers and take us away to the horrors of Hell's Maw. Far out on the field I saw the rush and flutter of krylobos attacking the fringes where some Gamesmen stood. Run, kick, and run away. A few bones fell, a few liches stumbled, nothing more. Big as they were, the big birds were not large enough to afflict this host.

And now a circlet of banners came toward me, Huld in the midst of his Gamesmen, Prionde at his side, borne on the shoulders of his minions, Ghouls posturing in tattered finery around him. Was that Dazzle among them? Oh, surely not. And yet, given Huld's purposes of terror, why not.

And, as I had done for two years, over and over, I reached for the Gamesmen of Barish, for comfort, for kindness, for safety, for reassurance—and found them. All. All with me in my great grole body with its star-shaped skeleton, all with me in my great this-world shape, looking out at the threatening horde where it poured like water among the Wind's Bones. . . .

Between me and the marching skeletons a leg bone loomed, half buried, stone heavy, not stone, so obviously not stone I gasped to have thought it stone so long. These were not Wind's Bones. These were not carvings done by wind and water. These were old bones, real bones, true bones, this-world bones of some ancient and incredible time. I cried to Dorn and Shattnir in my head, screamed at them to help me raise that bone up, to feed me the power to raise that bone up, screamed to Wafnor to break the soil at its base, to all of them to look, see, join, move, fight. I saw the mighty bone heave, the rock around it cracking and breaking to spatter away in dry particles. It came out of the ground like a tree, growing taller and taller, lunging upward from its hidden root, one great shape, and then another linking to it, then another and another yet, the five link bones and then the arching ribs, the neck, the monstrous skull armed with teeth as long as my legs, the whole standing ten man heights tall at the shoulder, moving toward the skeleton host who came on, unseeing, into fury.

The Wind's Bones went to war, to war, and not alone. Others sprouted from the soil of the place, a harvest so great and horrible no Seer would have believed it. They came out of the rock in their dozens and hundreds, sky tall, huge as towers, flailing, trampling down with feet like hammers of steel, the pitiful human skeletons falling before them like scythed grain to be trampled and winnowed by prodigious feet and by the wind. Particles of bone went flying on that wind, west and north, away and away in an endless, billowing, powdery cloud.

Before me the first monster had overstepped Huld to leave him behind with a few of his Gamesmen, a Bonedancer or two thrown into panic, a Ghoul, and yes—Dazzle. They looked about them wildly. I heard Huld screaming at them, threatening them for having raised up these giants. Were they to retreat? Of course. Away, away from the horrors they thought they had raised, away from the creatures who had owned this world before they came, away from this justice they had not sought, into the defile where they might find a way out, but did not.

You must believe me when I tell you that I shut the grole maw upon them and merely held them there in that rock hard prison of myself while I thought long about justice and goodness and all those things Windlow had often told me of. I did not grind at once. I waited. I waited, and thought, and listened to them within, for they could speak and pound upon my walls and threaten one another still, though they did it in the dark. I tried to remember any good thing Huld might have done. He had played a part in Bannerwell, pretending shock and remorse at his thalan's terrible plans and as terrible deeds, but that had all been pretense. It had been his way of doing what he pleased while pretending not to be responsible for it; thus he could continue for a time in the respect and honor of the world. His true self had been seen in the cavern beneath the mountains of the magicians, and in Hell's Maw, for though I had not seen him there, I had heard enough to make me sure of him. What was he, the real Huld, the true man?

And after a time, I answered my own question.

He was not true man at all. He was only aberration, beast, hate and hunger, without a soul. If the Midwives had delivered him, he would not have lived past his birth. As it was, he did not deserve to live further. So. Then the grole bore down and gained out of him what good there was in him. In return for the terror you brought Silkhands, and the pain you brought me, and the horror you brought the world, I bring you peace, Huld. So I thought.

And after a long time there, watching what it was the great bones of this world did upon the wastes of Bleer, I gave up bulk and went up onto the stones to find my friends. Then we sat there together in wonder until the thing was done. Dorn was not moving them, nor was I, nor Wafnor. They drew no power from us. They warred because the world desired that they do so.

I saw in them giants which could have been pombis, or fustigars; things long and curled which might have been groles of some ancient and mightier time. Things with great scimitar teeth raged among the Gamesmen while the trampling of the bones continued. It went on well into the night. Long, long after the last of Huld's Gamesmen were dead or had fled away, the great beasts of the heights continued their battle. Only toward dawn did they begin to collapse and fall, to lie as we had seen them first upon the high plateau, like wind carved things, dead, gone these hundred thousand years. Among them ranged the shadowpeople, singing lustily, piping upon their flutes and calling my name and Jinian's. When we went down to them, they clustered about us and begged earnestly for something roasted and juicy. Not for them any lasting awe, thus not for me. We fed them, and sang with them, and in the dawn we saw Himaggery and Mavin falling toward us out of the sky.

# 13

# Talent Thirteen

THEY CAME, DRAGON AND DRAGON-BACK, Mavin and Himaggery. Behind them came a small host of Armigers, flown not from the Bright Demesne but from some place north of Schooltown. One of Himaggery's Seers had told him help would be needed long before my message reached them. I began to be a little acid about this until Mavin hushed me.

"The Seer said we would not be needed *during* the conflict, but afterward. Indeed, look around you. Where are any Gamesmen standing against you? There are none. Not against one of *my* tricksy line."

She was right, of course. Somehow the battle had been not merely turned but decisively won. Chance was jogging about saying "Ob*liter*ated" over and over. He had observed the battle through his glass from a safe distance. "Ob*liter*ated." The word, I thought, could be applied to a number of things with equal pertinence. There was no time to consider it. Himaggery had to be introduced to Barish and to the Wizard's Eleven, he so overcome by awe and respect during this process as to lose all his crafty volubility for the space of several hours. When Mertyn arrived, the introductions were repeated, and again at the arrival of Riddle and Quench.

I was very stiff with Riddle. He flushed bright red and almost sank to his knees begging my forgiveness. "My only thought was to learn what I could, Peter. I did not want you to know about it, as it was a matter secret to the Immutables. Quench assured me the cap was perfectly safe, that it could not harm you in any way...." He fell silent beneath my glare.

Jinian, who stood beside me during all this ceremony, saved the situation. "Peter knows that you meant him no harm, Riddle. But a Pursuivant is dead in the forests near Xammer, and whether you meant Peter harm or not, the result was harm to someone."

"My fault," asserted Quench. "You must forgive Riddle, young man. I did not understand the complexity of all this Gaming. I did not realize that death often results. I was too many years in that pest hole beneath the mountains. Nothing was real there. All was ritual and repetitions and hierarchy and concern about relative positions in the order of things. Nothing was real. You must forgive him. Hold me responsible, for I am."

The end result of which was that I offered Riddle my hand, though not smilingly, and accepted his explanation for what it was worth.

"It was a year ago, Peter, that I found some old papers of my grandfather's. They told of an ancient contract, a promise of honor between our people and Barish. I had never heard of it. My father was only a child when his father died. I was only a child when my father died. So if there had been a contract, this sacred and secret indebtedness, the chain of it had been broken at Dindindaroo. The papers spoke of a certain place in the north. You recall traveling with me a year ago. I left you below Betand to go on to Kiquo and over the high bridge into these wastes. It was all futile. There was no guide, no map, nothing.

"Then, not a season gone, came this fellow Vitior Vulpas Queynt to tell me of this same contract. He was full of hints, full of words and winks and nods. And at that same time, some of our people found Quench here wandering among the mountains to the west. Well, Quench and I put our heads together, and it seemed the only way we would know anything surely was to raise up my grandfather. As I said, we meant no harm."

"So that is why you were burrowing about in Dindindaroo," I said. "You had only recently learned of this ancient agreement."

"Learned of it," rumbled Quench, "for all the good it did us. I wanted proof the Gamesman Huld was a villain. I wanted to know where Barish had gone, and what this Council business was all about. Our own history spoke of Barish, mind you, and Vulpas too. I wanted to know everything, real things, but you sent us scurrying off to the south on an idiot's quest. Well. I suppose we deserved being ill led for having led you ill. Let it be past and forgotten."

"When we returned," said Riddle, "with empty hands, we went to Himaggery as we should have done in the first place. I knew him to be honorable. We should have gone there first."

"It would have saved us much thrashing about," said Himaggery, who had come up to us in the midst of all these revelations and confessions. "We were hunting Quench all over the western reaches from Hawsport south, and we were hunting Huld everywhere but Hell's Maw. We knew it for a den of horrors, a Ghoul's nest, but we did not envision Huld as master of the place. He had seemed too proud for such dishonor."

"I believe," said Jinian, "that we will find it necessary soon to revise our notions of dishonor." She squeezed my hand and left me to ruminate upon that while the others continued their explorations into history in a mood of such profound veneration that it almost immobilized them.

Dorn was not among the group. I went off looking for him. He was with Silkhands, Tamor, and King Kelver upon a bit of high ground near Barish's Keep. Tamor had been healed of his wound, though not of the wound to his pride, for he had been the only one of us to be wounded at all. He bowed himself away after a wink at me, as did Kelver and Silkhands, hand in hand, oblivious of much else in the world. I think I sighed. Dorn gave me a sharp look which I well recognized, though I had not seen it with physical eyes before.

"You had plans concerning her?" he asked.

"No. And yes," I confessed. "Yes, some time ago. But no, not since Kelver came along."

"And Jinian came along?"

That was rather more difficult. True, she had said she loved me at some confused point during the last day or two. True, she had told me I was clever and that had proved to be marginally accurate, if the outcome of the battle was any test. True, parts of me stirred at the thought of her, at times. But . . .

"She says she is a Wizard," I said.

"Ah," said Dorn. "That is difficult."

"I think it is hard to love a Wizard," I said. "Though it is very good to make alliances with them."

"Who else knows of this Wizardry?"

"No one. I was not supposed to tell anyone, but you and Didir—well, you are part of me. It is like talking to myself. Oh, Chance knows, for he was there when she told me. But she doesn't trifle with the truth, Necromancer. If she says she is, she is."

"Oh, I have no doubt of it. I wonder if you've thought what else she is?"

"Another Talent than Wizardry! I didn't know such was possible."

He laughed. "Peter, the young are truly amazing. In each of the young, the world is reborn. No, I do not mean that Jinian has any other Talent. What she is, other than a Wizard, is a human person, female, about seventeen years old. In my experience, human persons of that age—and those considerably older also—are much alike. Most of them love, hate, weep, lust, tremble with fear. Most of them fight and forgive and resolve with high courage. May I suggest, if you are resolved upon friendship with Jinian, that it be with the person rather than with the Wizard. Likely the Wizard needs no one—not even Jinian herself. Likely Jinian needs someone during those times that the Wizard is not in residence." And he patted me very kindly as though I had been some half trained fustigar.

This so gained my attention that I wandered off for several hours and did not talk to anyone during that time.

Chance caught me when I returned. He wanted to talk about the battle, about the great bones, the mightiness of them. "And they went on and on, long after you'd all given up raising them. So Dorn and Queynt say."

I was truly puzzled by that, but I told him it was true, so far as I knew. "The forces of the world," he said, "according to Queynt. Oh, there's things here we know nothing of, according to Queynt." He spoke proudly, not at all awed or envious, possibly the only person in all that company save Jinian who accepted Vitior Vulpas Queynt as mere man. I knew Queynt had found a follower, a companion, a true friend. Well, part of me said, I no longer need a child minder. Well, part of me said, you will miss him dreadfully if he goes off with anyone else.

So.

What may I tell you?

Of Mavin and Thandbar? She approached him warily, ready to become a worshipper if he proved to be an idol, holding reverence in readiness. When I passed them an hour later, Mavin was telling him some story about Schlaizy Noithn, and he was bent double with laughter. I sniffed. I had not thought it that amusing when it had happened to me.

Of Barish-Windlow and Himaggery, circling one another in mixed an-

496

tagonism and love, Himaggery full of protest and fury at the fate of the hundred thousand in the ice caverns, Windlow equally distraught, Barish trying to fight them on two fronts, justifying his experiment on the grounds of human progress. Himaggery wondered what it was a hundred thousand master Gamesmen were to do, how they were to live when released from age old bondage; Barish overrode Windlow's concern to shout that he expected people to use their heads about it. I pitied Barish and envied him. He had too much Windlow in him to be what he had once been. But then, what he had once been had needed a lot of Windlow in it.

Later I saw him bend down to pluck the leaves from a tiny gray herb growing in a crack of the stone. He crushed the leaves beneath his nostrils and touched them to his tongue as I had seen Windlow do a thousand times. I went to him then and hugged him, looking up to see the stranger looking at me out of Barish's eyes. But it was Windlow's voice which called me by name and returned my embrace.

Of Quench and the techs, gathered around the machine in Barish's Keep, talking in an impenetrable language while some of their group scavenged among the bookshelves. "Fixable!" Quench crowed at last. "The machine can be fixed! There are spare parts in the case. We can take the thing apart and reassemble it in the caverns. . . ." So he had been set on a proper track by Himaggery and Mavin, and I was glad to have him among the people I liked and trusted. I decided to forgive him for that business with the cap. He had not meant it ill.

Of Mavin and Himaggery and Mertyn when they heard that the machine could be fixed? Of their plans to raise up the hundred thousand from their long sleep and bring them all to the purlieus of Lake Yost and the Bright Demesne? They were determined to raise them all in one place and build a better world from them.

Windlow-Barish, hearing this, was puzzled and torn once more. He started to say, "Now wait just a minute. That's not the way I had planned. . . ." But then he fell silent, and I could sense the intense inner colloquy going on. Then the argument started all over again, and this time Windlow-Barish had things to say which Himaggery listened to with respect.

Later, of Jinian and Himaggery.

"Will you have Rules?" she asked. "In your new world?"

"There will be no irrevocable rules," he said ponderously.

"How will you live?"

"We are going to try to do what Windlow would have wanted," he said. "He told us that nations of men fell into disorder, so nations of law were set up instead. He told us that nations of law then forgot justice and let the law become a Game, a Game in which the moves and the winning were more important than truth. He told us to seek justice rather than the Game. It was the laws, the rules which made Gaming. It was Gaming made injustice. We can only try something new and hope that it is better."

She left it at that. I left it at that, thankful that the thing Windlow had cared most about had a chance to survive.

Of Barish and Didir, standing close together and so engaged in conversation that they did not see me at all.

"Well, my love," he said. "And are you satisfied?"

"How satisfied? You told me to lie down for a few hundred years so that we might wake to build a new world out of time and hope and good intentions. So I wake to find others building that world, others in possession of your seed grain, others planning the harvest, another inhabiting you, my love. Perhaps I should think of something else. Have a child, perhaps. Raise goats. . . ."

"There are no goats on this world, Didir. Zeller. You can raise zeller."

"Zeller, then. I will domesticate some krylobos, become an eccentric, learn weaving."

"Will you stay with me, Didir?"

"I don't know you. This you. Perhaps I will. But then I would like to know what it is that Vulpas knows. How has he lived all this time while we slept?"

"Will you stay with *me,* Didir?"

"Perhaps."

Of Buinel and Shattnir, drinking wine in Barish's Keep.

"And my thought was, Shattnir, that he should have written it down very plainly, not in that personal shorthand of his, and have made at least a hundred copies. They could have been filed in all the temples, and certainly it was a mistake to confide in only one line of the Immutables."

"It doesn't matter now, does it?" Shattnir, cold, impersonal.

"It's not a question of it mattering. It's a question of correct *procedure!* If he'd only asked me, I could have told him. . . ."

Of Trandilar.

To me. "Well, my love, and what does your future hold of great interest and excitement?"

I blushed. "I haven't had a chance to think of it yet, Great Queen."

"Ah, Peter. Peter. Great Queen? Gracious. So formal. Do we not know one another well enough to let this formality go? Do you need to think about it, really? I should have thought your future would have raced to meet you, leapt into your heart all at once like the clutch of fate."

She was laughing at me, with me. She stroked my face, making the blush a shade deeper, and then went on.

"You do not want to be part of Himaggery's experiment, do you? There is scarce room in it for Himaggery and Barish, let alone any others. You would not live under their eyes and Mavin's? No. I thought not." She beckoned over my shoulder to someone, and then rose to hold out a hand to Sorah who sat beside us, laying her mask to one side.

"Sister," said Trandilar, "you see before you one who is quite young and confused. It would help him to know where his future lies."

Solemnly, but with a twinkle, Sorah put on the mask, smoothed it with long, delicate fingers, held out her hand in that hierarchic gesture the Seers sometimes make when they want to impress a multitude.

"I See, I See," she chanted, "jungles and cities, the lands of the eesties, the far shores of the Glistening Sea, and you, Peter, with a Wizard—a girl, yes, Jinian." Her voice was mocking only a little, kindly and laughing, and I readied myself to laugh with her. Then, suddenly, her voice deepened and began to toll like a mighty bell. "Shadowmaster. Holder of the Key. Storm Grower. The Wizard holds the book, the light, the bell. . . ." And she fell silent.

Trandilar shook her head. "Peter, learn from me. Mock Talent at your peril. It is no joke." And she helped Sorah away to find a place to lie down.

Of Peter and Jinian.

"It is probably difficult to live in close association with a Wizard," she said to me. "I believe Mavin found it so, which is why she and Himaggery have this coming and going thing between them. But then, it is not easy to know a Shifter, either."

499

"A Shifter is usually the same inside," I objected.

"Usually, though not always. Do we not learn from our shapes what we are? You have told me of Mandor. Did he not learn from his beauty what he became? Oh, I do not mean that there is goodness in some shapes and evil in others, but simply that we learn from them to our own good or ill. So might you change, Peter?"

"Don't Wizards change?" I wanted to ask her, desperately, what the Talent of Wizards might be, but I was too wary of the answer I might get. "Are they always the same?"

She grinned at me. "Oh, we change. I was quite content, so I thought, to become an alliance for my brother with King Kelver, until I met you, Peter."

"Kelver is better looking," I said.

"True, but then he is older. He has had a chance to grow up to his face. You may do the same, in time."

"You do not think me too young for alliancing?"

She sighed. "I think we are not too young to decide what we will do when we leave this place. Himaggery will expect you back at the Bright Demesne. I could return to Xammer. Neither of us wants to do that. I said a silly thing when I said we would do what Barish would have done. Barish will do it. Himaggery will do it. It is their plan, not mine."

I shifted from foot to foot, bit my lip, wondered what to say next. Then I thought of Sorah's words, not the bell tolling ones, but the earlier, laughing ones.

"Jinian, would you like to see the jungles and cities, the eesties, the shores of the Glistening Sea? Queynt is going there, so he says. He would let us go with him."

"Oh, Peter, I would like that more than anything."

So what is left?

Hell's Maw.

We went there, Dorn, Himaggery, Mertyn, Mavin, and a host. There were bones there wandering free, moving on their own, talking to an old, blind man who wandered among them with a key, trying to find the lock he had lost. Dorn put them to rest, large and small, in such form as they may not ever be raised again. There is nothing left of the place now. Every stone of it has been tumbled and spread by a hundred Tragamors as far away as the Western Sea. There I linked the Gamesmen once again, realizing for the first time that I had what Himaggery called Talent Thirteen. Jinian was right. I do not need anyone but me—and a hundred or so Gamesmen with large Talents.

So you may picture us now as we ride to the very highest point of the road across the Dorbor Range, that place where the road bends down toward the jungles of the north. Queynt and Chance are upon the wagon; Yittleby and Yattleby are pulling them along with that measured, effortless stride. Jinian and I are looking back to the south where all the lands of the True Game are spread, town and demesne, land and stream, tower and field, far and veiled by distance in the light of the westering sun. There is no mist giant now to walk the edges of the world. We may walk it ourselves, in time, in chance, in hope.

Who knows?